# PRAISE FOR *A SUMMER* W9-AMO-864

"*A Summer without Dawn* is a credit to the historical genre. Its accurate depiction of events does not take away from the deep psychological richness of the characters. The characters are true heroes such as one seldom sees: a bit larger than life. In short, a captivating book by authors worth watching."

—Le Devoir

"The publication of this great mosaic is an important event . . . In this book survival is no inconsiderate accomplishment: it is the means by which historic truth instills itself into consciences, by which the characters, despite their weaknesses and perhaps even their baseness—but who dares judge?—attain the statue of heroes . . . The authors have created a great beautiful story, which will provide a great many people with long hours of intermingled pleasure and anxiety."

—La Presse

"*A Summer without Dawn* is in the tradition of thick novels that exercise the same effects as a drug, the reader loses all sense of time and becomes completely immersed in the central couple, Maro and Vartan."

—Le Soleil

"The material which forms the basis of this spectacular novel is a treasure trove of adventure and emotion . . . A novel to discover . . ."

—Le Canada Français

"An electrifying novel. . . "

—Journal de Montréal

"This work is quite without parallel in its richness of detail, despite the fact that its action unfolds during the First World War . . . The spirited writing, the vivid style, and the frequent twists of plot, all play a part in keeping interest at the boiling point. I got swept along by it myself: forced to dip into the novel as background for an interview with the novelist, I found myself unable to put it down until I finished it."

—La Tribune

## from the English press

"*A Summer without Dawn* is a penetrating examination of man's inhumanity to man. This strangely fascinating novel is hard to put down."

—The Ottawa Citizen

"This novel is literature for a humanity that is implicitly aware that fiction is not made for its own sake, but to universalize the deepest and broadest urges of civilized people."

—The Toronto Star

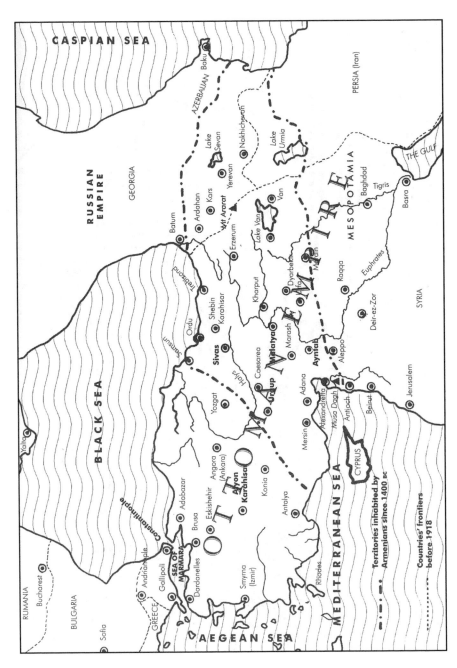

CASPIAN SEA

RUSSIAN EMPIRE

PERSIA (Iran)

AZERBAIJAN

Baku

GEORGIA

Lake Sevan

Nakhichevan

Lake Urmia

THE GULF

MESOPOTAMIA

Yerevan

Batum

Ardahan

Kars

Mt Ararat

Van

Baghdad

Tigris

Basra

Lake Van

Trebizond

Erzerum

Ordu

Shebin Karahisar

Kharput

Diyarbekir

Mardin

Raqqa

Euphrates

Samsun

Deir-ez-Zor

SYRIA

O T T O M A N   E M P I R E

Sivas

Yozgat

Coesarea

Halys

Malatya

Marash

Gurup

Ayntab

Aleppo

BLACK SEA

Yalta

Angora (Ankara)

Afyon Karahisar

Adana

Mersin

Alexandretta

Antioch

Musa Dagh

Jerusalem

Beirut

Eskishehir

Adabazar

Konia

Antalya

Constantinople

Brusa

CYPRUS

RUMANIA

Bucharest

Andrianople

Gallipoli

Dardanelles

SEA OF MARMARA

Smyrna (Izmir)

Rhodes

MEDITERRANEAN SEA

BULGARIA

Sofia

GREECE

AEGEAN SEA

— · — · —  Territories inhabited by Armenians since 1400 BC

- - - - -  Countries' frontiers before 1918

THE OTTOMAN EMPIRE  1914–1918

# A SUMMER WITHOUT DAWN

### AGOP J. HACIKYAN
### JEAN-YVES SOUCY

*translated fom the French by Christina Le Vernoy
and Joyce Bailey*

Interlink Books

An imprint of Interlink Publishing Group, Inc.
Northampton, Massachusetts

First American edition published in 2010 by

INTERLINK BOOKS
An imprint of Interlink Publishing Group, Inc.
46 Crosby Street
Northampton, Massachusetts 01060
www.interlinkbooks.com

First published as *Un été sans aube* by Editions Libre Expression, Montreal, 1991
Copyright © Editions Libre Expression, Montreal, 1991
First published in English, in hardback, by Saqi Books, London, 2000
English translation © Christina Le Vernoy and Joyce Bailey, 2000

Library of Congress Cataloging-in-Publication Data available
ISBN: 978-1-56656-802-9

*This novel is based on true events, but the characters and their lives are fictional. Place names in Turkey and Armenia are given as they were known at the beginning of the century, generally with contemporary spellings that reflect Armenian pronunciation.*

Printed and bound in the United States of America

To request a free copy of our 48-page full-color catalog, please call
1-800-238-LINK, visit our web site at www.interlinkbooks.com, or write to us:
Interlink Publishing, 46 Crosby Street, Northampton, Massachusetts 01060

# CONTENTS

# LIST OF THE PRINCIPAL CHARACTERS

Altan – Riza Bey's son

Aram – the young boy who helps Aroussiag

Araksi Surmelian – Armen's wife and godmother to Tomas

Arif – Riza Bey's son

Armen Surmelian – Araksi's husband and godfather to Tomas

Aroussiag – the woman who saves Vartan near Urgup; her Turkish name is Halidé

Arpiné Mesropian – Vartan's aunt and Mesrop's wife

Ayla – Young Armenian servant in Riza Bey's household; her Armenian name is Vartouhi

Azniv Hanim – Maro's mother

Barkev Mesropian – Vartan's cousin, the oldest son of his uncle, Mesrop, and his aunt, Arpiné

Bedri – Riza Bey's right-hand man

Buyuk Hanim (Grand Lady) – Riza Bey's mother

Diran Mesropian – Vartan's cousin

Emel – Riza Bey's daughter

Eminé – Riza Bey's nurse

Gani Bey – one of the most important government officials in Constantinople

Halit Pasha – general in the Ottoman Army

Ibrahim Alizadé – colonel in the Ottoman Army and Vartan's friend

Kemenché Hakki (Hakki Chelebi) – one of the musicians in the *dervish* troupe and Vartan's friend

Kenan – Riza Bey's son

7

Kerim – a country schoolteacher and Aroussiag's friend

Leyla – Riza Bey's third wife

Lucie Mesropian – Vartan's cousin

Makbulé – Riza Bey's second wife

Maro Balian – Née Artinian, Azniv Hanim's daughter, Vartan's wife, Tomas's mother

Mesrop Mesropian – Vartan's uncle living in Constantinople

Mustapha Rahmi – police commissar (commissioner) in Sivas

Noubar Balian – Vartan's brother

Nourhan – son of Riza Bey and Maro Balian

Oudi Yashar – alias used by Vartan while he was a member of the *dervish* troupe

Riza Bey – governor of Ayntab

Safiyé – Riza Bey's first wife

Shahané – Riza Bey's daughter

Shirag Tevonian – an Armenian revolutionary

Tomas – son of Maro and Vartan

Vartan Balian – Maro's husband and Tomas's father

# PROLOGUE

On 30 June 1915 the German guns started to thunder two hours before dawn. Shells rained down on the French lines near Nouvelle Saint Vaas about 140 kilometres from Paris. The *poilus*[1] in the trenches, who had managed a few hours' sleep in spite of their lack of comfort, awoke. The warming-up of the artillery announced a new German counter-attack. They had been driven back by the Allies only a few kilometres during the last two months on the orders of General Foche. Tens of thousands dead to gain a few miserable square kilometres pock-marked with craters and peppered with human flesh.

At the start of this war the soldiers had marched with a song on their lips and flowers on their rifle barrels as if going on holiday. After a winter spent in the mud of the trenches, their enthusiasm had given way to a kind of stupor. This was a new kind of war . . . more inhuman than ever before. What good was man's courage in the face of the fire and iron that rained down from the sky . . . against the gas that burned their lungs? This was the end of colourful uniforms, of great troop movements, of cavalry charges. Covered by mud and dust and trying to merge with the ground, the men crouched and crept and crawled like moles.

The whole world seemed to be on fire. Almost all of it was. Most of the European countries and their colonies were engaged in the conflict. On one side stood the *Triple Entente*: France, Great Britain, and Russia, later joined by Belgium, Japan, Italy and Serbia. On the other side were the Central European Powers: Germany, Austria-Hungary, the Ottoman Empire and Bulgaria. It seemed inevitable that eventually the still-neutral nations would be forced to take part, willing or not.

---

1.  Name given by the French to their soldiers in the First World War (1914–18).

9

The sun had already risen on the Ottoman Empire at the extreme Eastern edge of the Mediterranean 2,800 kilometres from Nouvelle Saint Vaas. British and French vessels anchored near the entry of the Straits of the Dardanelles were shelling the strongholds of the Turkish Army on the Gallipoli peninsula. The ships were beyond the range of the enemy army guns, but shells exploded on the beach where a beachhead had been established and foam flurries rose around the small boats that were transporting new regiments to the mainland. Already there were more than 100,000 French, British and colonial troops – Canadian, Australian and North African – those under the orders of the British General, Hamilton, and more were arriving continuously. However, since the initial landing in April, the Expeditionary Corps, blocked on a narrow strip of land, had been unable to penetrate to the interior and the Ottoman Army stood firmly entrenched on the heights, fiercely defending its territory and thus cutting off the Allies' route to the capital, Constantinople.[1]

Finally, in February, a Franco-British fleet had vainly tried to force an entry through the Straits of the Dardanelles, which were ringed by fortresses. Mines and large-calibre guns manned by German soldiers had inflicted huge losses on their ships.

Spread out on the hills on both sides of the Bosphorus, one foot in Europe and the other in Asia, the ancient city proudly flaunted its domes and marble minarets. In spite of the war, old Byzantium, renamed Constantinople in honour of Constantine, the first Christian Emperor, was swarming with activity. Neither the passage of the centuries nor her numerous invaders had radically changed the city, which clung to the legacy of the past. The Atmeydan, the Square of Horses, occupied the site of an old Roman hippodrome, thereby perpetuating the plan of the city but, after the Ottoman conquest of 1453, the Christian Church of the Divine Wisdom had become the Mosque of Santa Sophia, having had minarets added to its four corners.

Now Sultan Mohammed V reigned over the vestiges of a once vast empire, which had been dismembered bit by bit during the past century. In the Balkans, Greece, Rumania, Albania, Bulgaria, Montenegro and Serbia had become independent. In Africa, Algeria, Libya, Tunisia and Egypt had become protectorates of European powers. This left the Sultan with only Thrace, Anatolia, Mesopotamia, Palestine and Arabia and, even there, he

---

1.  Present-day Istanbul.

reigned in name only. He still availed himself of the title Commander of the Faithful, but the Muslims of Anatolia considered him to be less and less so. After the Party of the Young Turks toppled Abdul-Hamid II in 1909 to replace him with Mohammed V, the Sultan's absolute power was finished. In principle, the country was ruled by a parliament but in reality there were three men who wielded power: Enver, Talaat and Jemal. In October 1914 this triumvirate had embarked the country in this war on the side of Germany.

At present the Empire was surrounded. Battles were raging in the far eastern part of Anatolia and in eastern Armenia where the Russians had crossed the border and taken the town of Van. Being short of munitions, they were retreating, undoubtedly to gather their forces and strike back later. Further to the south in Mesopotamia, the British had conquered Basra and the Tigris-Euphrates delta. To the west, the Ottoman troops were beating a retreat in the Sinai after having failed to capture the Suez Canal, which was defended by a division of British troops. And then there was the siege at Gallipoli scarcely 350 kilometres from Constantinople in addition to the French and British fleets that controlled the Mediterranean.

None of this tempered the optimism of the Ottoman leaders. The outcome of the battle of the Straits of the Dardanelles filled them with all sorts of hopes. For the first time in history, the arrogant British navy had admitted defeat! And by the Turks! The Ottoman Empire was finally rid of the centuries-old stifling tutelage of France, England, Russia and Italy. With the help of Germany, which had invested massively in Anatolia, especially in the Constantinople-Baghdad railway, Enver Pasha's government could now conduct the affairs of the country as he wished.

His Excellency Henry Morgenthau, the American Ambassador to Constantinople since 1913, was sitting at his desk, still in his bathrobe. He loved the silence of the morning and managed a moment of solitude every day before getting down to his official duties. These had become more numerous and demanding now that he represented the French, Russian and Belgian interests before the Ottoman government. He took advantage of this half hour to scribble a few lines . . . private thoughts, impressions, notes on the latest developments. These not only gave him food for thought but also helped him compile material for the autobiography he was planning to write eventually.

A long face accentuated by a receding hairline and a goatee were balanced by a narrow, prominent nose and ears that were just a little bit too big. Women who met him thought him handsome with his greying hair. A lorgnette and moustache gave him a severe appearance, tempered, however, by the kindness that could be read in his eyes. His usually smooth, relaxed face now had two deep furrows that began between his eyebrows, continued up his broad, high forehead and branched out into horizontal wrinkles. The American Ambassador was worried.

He was increasingly worried about the fate of the minorities in the Empire, particularly that of the Armenians. Nearly two million of these Christians lived in the six provinces of eastern Anatolia, a part of ancient Armenia that had formerly extended into the Caucasus on the other side of the Russian border. Armenians also formed large minority groups in the towns including the capital. The government had a plan to send all of these people to the south of Anatolia into the Syrian desert on the pretext that they had become a security risk since they might give aid to the Russian troops, who were also Christian.

It had become increasingly evident to Henry Morgenthau that the government had another goal in mind: to rid Anatolia of non-Muslim subjects. The headlines of last April 24th, announcing the arrest of more than 200 Armenian intellectuals and notables from the capital spoke for themselves. Now too rumours of the massacre of the Armenians were filtering through to Constantinople, although travel was restricted and couriers subjected to severe censorship. Morgenthau was no longer allowed to use his secret code when communicating with the American consuls in the interior; nevertheless, he sometimes received letters from them by means of the missionaries.

They came ... Americans and Canadians, even Germans ... to tell of the atrocities they had witnessed. According to them, only the United States could exercise pressure on the Ottoman government. To the German missionaries' dismay, the Kaiser had shown no interest in this problem, probably in order not to annoy his ally. Henry Morgenthau could only protest and receive replies from Talaat Pasha, the Foreign Minister, that the internal affairs of the Empire were of no concern to the USA and that Talaat, according to diplomatic regulations, was correct!

The ambassador stopped stroking his goatee, adjusted his pince-nez and picked up his pen to write down a conversation he had had with Talaat. Yesterday, two missionaries had come to see him and brought him gruesome details of what was happening in Konia. After hearing their stories, he had immediately gone to see Talaat and had found the minister in a most terrible temper. For months now Talaat had been trying to get the British in Malta to liberate two of his friends, Ayoub Sabri and Zinnoun. His inability to resolve this affair worried and irritated him. He could talk of nothing else and had asked Morgenthau to use his good offices to speak to the British about the case.

A new effort to get them released had just failed and Talaat was furious. He was forcing himself to appear calm and courteous to the American Ambassador but his scathing remarks and his bulldog-like expression indicated that this was not a propitious moment to move him to mercy. First Henry Morgenthau talked to him of a Canadian Missionary, a Dr McNaughton, who had been unjustly treated.

'That fellow is an enemy agent,' answered Talaat. 'We have proof.'

'Show me!' demanded Morgenthau.

Since Talaat was obviously incapable of doing this, he went into a tirade against the English. It was evident that he would use any British subject who fell into his hands as barter for the liberation of his friends. It boded ill for the fate of the Armenians when the ambassador broached the subject.

Talaat exploded, 'The Armenians are not to be trusted! Besides, whatever we do with them is none of your county's business!'

Morgenthau replied that he considered himself to be a friend of the Armenians and, as such, he was outraged by the ordeals they were being put through. The Pasha shook his head and refused to discuss it. As a show of good will, he did, however, consent to the release of the Canadian missionary. The ambassador felt that there was nothing to be gained by further discussion of the Armenian problem at this time. Fortunately Talaat's temper swung from one extreme to another as unpredictably as a child's. One day he would be violent and inflexible; the next, accommodating and expansively good-natured. Prudence dictated waiting for one of his good moods before bringing up the subject that aroused him to savagery.[1]

Henry Morgenthau put down his pen and lifted his eyes to the window, which gave on to the west. The Russian border lay in that direction more

---

1.  This meeting is related by Ambassador Morgenthau in his autobiography *Secrets of the Bosphorus*, published by Doubleday & Co., New York, 1918.

than 1,300 kilometres away. In that country of arid steppes and barren mountains where the valleys were the only green oases, the Armenians were to be abandoned to their fate.

In the heart of Anatolia lay Sivas, the capital of the province of the same name. The city spread out into the valley where the meanders of the River Halys sparkled under the morning sun. The fields of ripe grain gave a golden colour to the plains. The ochre-coloured mountains that bordered the valley to the north and south seemed to blend into the horizon and gave the illusion that the town occupied the centre of an arena remote from the rest of the world. On the contrary, however, it was a corridor, the ancient route between Constantinople and Persia. Wedged between the Mediterranean and the Black Sea, the Anatolian plateau had always been the bridge between the East and the West, the route used by conquerors, merchants and migrating tribes. Sivas was an important relay station for the caravans that brought silks and spices from Central Asia.

Already settled in this region since the seventh century BC, the Armenian people had suffered the conquests of the Hittites and Persians. Then the armies of Alexander the Great, Caesar's legions, the Byzantines, the pillaging Arabs and the Mongolian hordes filed through. The Seljuk Turks arrived from the Asiatic steppes; the Crusaders traversed the country on their way to Jerusalem. Finally, in the fifteenth century, the Ottomans took over the region before extending their empire into Africa and Europe.

In spite of wars and massacres, the Armenians had survived and prospered. Enterprising and resourceful, they had served as intermediaries between their neighbours. During the twenty-five centuries of their history, they founded five different kingdoms, which had lasted, in total, more than a thousand years; the rest of the time they had borne the yoke of some invader. A century before Christ, Tigran the Great reigned over lands that reached from the Black Sea to the Caspian Sea, from the Caucasus mountains to the border of the Mediterranean. The last Armenian kingdom had been an ally of the Crusaders and had survived in Cilicia until 1375. Then the Turks, the Russians and the Persians had divided among themselves that ancient kingdom dominated by Mount Ararat, where legend had it that Noah's ark had run aground.

The Armenians had a long tradition, possessed their own religion, language and alphabet, and resisted any pressure to assimilate. Drowned in a Muslim sea, they stubbornly conserved their Christian faith, which, according to tradition, had been brought to them by the Apostles Saint Bartholomew and Saint Jude. They were justly proud that, in the year 301 their king, Tiridates III, had proclaimed Christianity to be the official religion, thus creating the first Christian state. As the missionaries from the Catholic and Protestant Churches had been active in the country since the nineteenth century, there had been some conversions but the great majority remained faithful to the Armenian Apostolic Church; a symbol to them of their national identity and a link to their past.

In Sivas, as in other eastern provinces of Anatolia, the Muslims and the Armenians had lived together more or less peacefully for over four centuries. The layout of the town reflected this mutual interdependence and respect although it did not by any means exclude mutual distrust. On the hillside lay the Armenian Quarter with its innumerable chapels, monasteries and schools. On the heights of the city the opulent mansions surrounded by walled-in gardens overlooked a pile of more modest, flat-roofed, whitewashed houses. Through these there wound a veritable labyrinth of narrow streets and paths worn hard by centuries of use.

Farther down, the City Hall, the Market Square and other government buildings formed a border with the Kaval, where the Turks, Circassians and Kurds, who were Muslims, lived. Here stood the glowing, blue-tiled Goek Medressé, the ancient Koranic school, and dozens of minarets rose above the terraced roofs, while stores and houses mingled in happy anarchy.

# ONE

Vartan Balian had not shut his eyes all night. Taking care not to wake his wife, Maro, he got up around five o'clock. He slipped on a pair of underpants and went into his library.

Yesterday the town criers had made public the deportation order for the Armenians living in Sivas. Vartan, who directed a military dispensary on the outskirts of the town, had not heard the proclamation but, on returning home in the late afternoon, had seen the posters plastered on the walls at the street corners. There was no mention of a departure date; it was simply an announcement to all the Armenians to prepare to leave and then to wait. In the meantime, they were forbidden to engage in business or to sell their belongings. As Vartan was serving in the Ottoman army as a reserve medical officer with the rank of Major, he and his family were not affected by what the government called a 'relocation' order. Nevertheless, he did not feel safe. The history of his people teemed with examples of episodes that had taught them to be mistrustful.

Several indications led him to fear the worst. First, the Armenians serving in the army had been disarmed and put to work digging earthworks and transporting equipment. Then all Christians had been ordered to turn in their weapons, even their hunting guns! And now there was this deportation to zones far from the front lines.

The room, its walls covered by maps, bookshelves and a cupboard filled with chemical products, was bathed in the velvety light of dawn. Motes of dust and pollen danced in a thin beam of sunshine that spilt across a desk of inlaid wood. Vartan opened the shutters and blinked. He sensed a slight stench of smoke mixed with the perfume of the climbing roses growing across the front of the house. In Sivas each house had a stable, which

16

sheltered a cow or two, or a goat at least, sometimes even a donkey. The rich also kept horses, so there was always an acrid odour hovering over this town of eighty thousand people, even in the heights where the Balians lived.

A gust of wind moved the leaves of the chestnut tree where turtle-doves were cooing. Vartan leaned out of the window to enjoy the morning breeze. The night had been hot and humid, and his worries had probably aggravated his restlessness.

Vartan looked younger than his thirty-eight years. He had a square face ending in a determined chin marked by a cleft. He had no wrinkles except for a few crow's feet at the corners of his eyes, which were probably due to his habit of squinting slightly when looking at someone. He had a few grey hairs at his temples, but only his wife was aware of this as he artfully hid them when he combed his hair. He was clean-shaven except for a thin moustache that was always well trimmed. Nearly two metres tall, much taller than the average Anatolian, he stood out in a crowd because of his athletic build, accentuated by his European clothes and his gentlemanly bearing.

From the heights of the minarets the light, high voices of the *muezzins*, intermingling and echoing in harmony, chanted the first of the five daily Islamic prayers. The ensuing silence was short as the bells of the Armenian monastery rang for lauds. Sivas was probably one of the last places in Anatolia where Muslims and Christians knelt simultaneously to pray to the one God. In other places the bells were silent or tolled only for the dead.

In the neighbourhood, shutters clattered open. Few Armenians in Sivas and in the countryside had slept that night. Only the old ones remembered the massacres ordered by Sultan Abdul-Hamid II in 1894. It was said that around 300,000 Christians had been killed, hence his nickname 'Red Sultan'. At that time Vartan had been only seventeen years old and the Balian family had not been touched, but the state of siege through which they had lived had made such an impression on him that these events had changed the course of his life.

His father, Tomas, who looked and sometimes acted like a bull, had been a just and generous man, well thought of by his Mohammedan neighbours. He was also a prudent man; although he could not foresee the events that would take place in Afyon Karahisar in the heart of Anatolia, he had turned the family opium farm into a real fortress. He employed a dozen workers, Kurds, to each of whom he had given a piece of land where they erected

17

their tents and lived with their families as they had done while they were still nomads. These men, who were excellent horsemen and fierce warriors, would not hesitate to sacrifice their lives for Tomas Balian, whom they called *Agha*, meaning Master.

Vartan loved these simple, joyful people. Their women did not cover their faces on meeting a Turk and talked freely to strangers. He and his brother, Noubar, had loitered in the Kurd camp as youngsters. There they had played with their children and worked at their sides in the poppy fields. Usually only the men worked in the fields but at harvest time everyone pitched in. This kind of work took patience and precision. The moment the petals started to fall, the prune-sized green capsules were notched. A white liquid latex dripped from the incisions and turned brown as it coagulated. This was opium, which they scraped off with a special spoon the following morning. It gave off the odour of freshly mown grass. Thousands of flowers were needed to obtain a single kilo of opium and the Balians exported tonnes of it to Europe and the USA, where it was refined into morphine for hospital use.

Until the time of the massacres, Vartan had led the carefree existence of the son of a rich family without worrying about the future. He was passionately fond of literature, music, women, and horses. His mother was an accomplished musician and encouraged his liking for the arts; his father preferred more manly occupations for his son and taught him to manage the workers, handle firearms and ride horses. At sixteen, Vartan already had the build of a man and was a superb horseman, the best in the region. His father had even allowed him to participate in the dangerous *jirit* games organized by the Kurds at the end of the working day. Players charged brutally at their adversaries with pointed sticks instead of lances. He also closed his eyes to his son's dalliances with the servants.

The events of 1894 had shocked young Vartan into realizing that fame and fortune were no guarantee of safety and that honesty and generosity were no guarantee against injustice. A higher power ruled over the lives of men and it was not God but politics. Vartan became conscious that his easy and carefree existence was not the lot of all Armenians. On the contrary, iniquitous laws had made them second-class citizens in the Ottoman Empire. They were targeted by special taxes and forbidden access to administrative jobs and military service. With the exception of the large cities where there was still a semblance of law, the Armenians were subjected to the whims and oppressions of government officials and local despots, dispossessed of their land, unable to get fair trials and often reduced to near-serfdom.

Vartan had discovered a new passion – politics – and he plunged into it with total ardour. He decided he would study law and become the defender of his people. He would change things in the Sultan's archaic kingdom! But Tomas Balian had other plans for his son; he wanted him to become a pharmacist, which would be in the interest of the family business.

After bitter discussions, Vartan had bent to his father's will and left for the Armenian School of Getronagan in the capital and then on to Robert College, the American College of Constantinople, which was mostly attended by the sons of minority groups – Armenians, Greeks and Jews. He stayed with his uncle, Mesrop Mesropian, who was a printer by trade. His uncle's older son, Barkev, lived in New York and managed the company that marketed the family opium. The younger son, Diran, was Vartan's age and the two became as close as twins. Diran had also been pushed into political activism by the events of the previous years but, in contrast to Vartan, who favoured constitutional and administrative reforms so often promised to the Armenians, he was for armed action. These differences did not prevent them from joining the same Armenian revolutionary groups and closely associating with the idealists of the Young Turks movement.

Vartan's father died of typhus while his son was at university, and Takouhi, his mother, survived her husband by only three months. The doctor had been unable to determine the cause of her death but her sons knew she had died of a broken heart. Now it was out of the question for Vartan to remain secluded in Afyon Karahisar, turning opium into morphine. His brother, Noubar, was willing to take over the family plantation. Like Vartan, he cared little about morphine and he had his own dreams, which his father had opposed – to bottle and distribute throughout Asia Minor the mineral water which gushed from a spring on their land. Vartan finished his studies and found a post as pharmacist at the Yedikulé, the Armenian hospital in Constantinople, which left him with spare time to write and to participate in political meetings. Some time later he opened his own pharmacy on the main street of Péra, but he continued to write.

His first articles had been published abroad while he was still in his early twenties and had brought him the reward of a letter from Anatole France, with whom he henceforth kept up a correspondence. Now the last letter from the French writer gathered dust on his desk, along with requests from American and English newspapers, asking for more articles on the

Armenian question – articles that Vartan could not write without being accused of collaborating with the enemy.

A donkey brayed in the distance and cocks called to each other from the four corners of the town. Wheels girdled with iron rings screeched on the gravelled streets. Life was slowly starting up in Sivas. The rattling of cooking pots and the murmurs of conversation came up from the kitchen. The steps on the stairs creaked and the ceiling boards cracked. A servant came up and put a jug of hot water in front of the door of the master's bedroom.

Vartan went over to the bookcase on the left side of the window and gently stroked his finger over the spines of three books, which he had had published in Geneva because their publication would have been forbidden in Constantinople. They had all been translated into French and English: *The Fate of the Christians in the Ottoman Empire, The Armenian Question: Fifty Years of Injustice*, and the last one, *One Empire, Several Nations*, which advocated no less than the splitting up of the Empire and its transformation into a modern federation of autonomous states – Palestine, Syria, Arabia, Turkey, Kurdistan and of course Armenia. It had generated a certain stir in political circles, even in the United States and Russia. Mainly because of this book, Vartan had been classified as a dangerous revolutionary by the Sultan's police, although he had already been suspect for having been a member of the Union of Progress Committee of the Young Turks and for having written political articles. He had been forced to go underground and to live at different friends' houses, changing addresses constantly, for more than a year. He was then thirty years old and just married. Maro had shared his lot without complaint and believed as much as he did in the need for social change.

In 1908 the Young Turks' revolution had eliminated the tyranny of the Sultan, Abdul-Hamid II, and Vartan had been able to surface again. As far back as people could remember, there had not been a happier moment in Asia Minor. People danced in the streets of Constantinople – Jews, Turks, Greeks, Armenians and Levantines kissed each other. In the town on the shores of the Bosphorus a clamour arose for a new era of legality, fraternity and tolerance. As Vartan had been a member of the Ittihad, the movement which had revolted against the Sultan to install a parliamentary system, he had been called to participate in the new government. Like many other Armenians who, until then, had been barred from military service, he had joined the army reserves to show his confidence in the new regime.

20

That had been in July 1908. Dissension had broken out almost immediately. A split swiftly led to the organization of two factions: on one side, the Modernists, Westernized and liberal, of which Vartan was the principal leader; on the other side, the Conservatives who now showed their true xenophobic faces. The latter were under the iron fists of Enver, Talaat and Jemal, who preached pan-Turanism – the Turkification of all citizens and the extension of the Empire into the plains of Central Asia to incorporate all the nations related to the Turks.

After several months of internal strife, the ultranationalist party took control and the Young Turks movement became the front for a dictatorship. Vartan had resigned from the government before he could be removed and, to be on the safe side, he had left the capital. In April 1909 the massacres of thousands of Armenians in Cilicia gave a foretaste of the new policies.

Vartan pulled a group photograph of some members of the government out of the first drawer of his oak filing cabinet. He went over to the window to study the faces. Several of the progressive members had already mysteriously disappeared and the moderates like his friend Halit, who in the photograph had his arm around Vartan, had been ousted from power. Halit had joined the army and now held a general's rank. Could it be that he had renounced his ideals of justice?

Looking at Talaat and Enver, who were now the heads of the government, put him into a sudden fury. He remembered the times he had vainly opposed their rise to power. He especially remembered Talaat's innate duplicity and his ability to twist the truth. At the moment he was the strong man of the regime and the deportation of the Armenians was his doing. Vartan tore the photograph into shreds and threw them into an ashtray. He looked around the room and told himself that he would do well to dispose of all his correspondence, especially that with his cousin, Diran, and all the copies of the articles published in foreign newspapers.

Vartan picked up the lukewarm jug of water out in the hall and took it into his room. Maro was still asleep; she lay completely naked, as the sheet had slipped to the floor at the foot of the big brass bed. She was lying on her side, her knees flexed and her back to the door. Her thick dark-brown hair spread out on the pillow and hid her fine, long neck. The morning light modelled the curves of her shoulders and accentuated the volume of her buttocks. A shadow lay across her loins, emphasizing her waist. Her hips were ample, her thighs slender and her calves deliciously rounded. Vartan was moved by the perfection of that figure, unmarred by two pregnancies, the second ending in a miscarriage only a few months before.

She had been just twenty years old when they had married eight years ago. Since then they had lived in perfect bliss and, as time went by, Vartan had grown to love and desire her more and more. His love for Maro had effaced the memory of all those others whom he had loved or thought he loved. He had been called a womanizer and had often had two mistresses simultaneously, yet now he found himself capable of a fidelity he had never thought possible. He could not claim any merit. It was simply that he did not really see other women; he did not even notice when they sometimes flirted with him.

He put the blue earthenware jug next to the matching bowl on the dressing table and leaned over Maro. He lifted her hair and put his lips to her warm neck. His wife moaned sweetly and turned over on her back, still asleep. She was extraordinarily beautiful and all those who knew her thought her the loveliest woman in Sivas. Her pale skin and the purity of her features gave great nobility to her face, although her immense brown eyes and full lips insinuated an intense sensuality. Watching her lost in sleep, Vartan found traces of the same innocence and candour which showed in her face in a photograph taken on her seventh birthday. She looked fragile, and he pulled her towards him. Maro opened her eyes, but her smile could not erase her frightened look. She put her lips to his and they kissed for a long time. Then she put her head on his hairy chest. He put his arms around her, cradling her, as if to keep her from all harm.

'What's to become of us?' she murmured.

He remained silent, pretending not to have heard, but shivered. This question had tortured him all night. He gently disengaged himself and walked over to the dressing table where he started to sharpen his razor on the leather strop.

'What's to become of us?' insisted Maro anxiously.

He turned and answered reassuringly, 'I've already told you. These measures are not applicable to military personnel or their families.'

'But what about our friends? Our neighbours? All the other Armenians in Sivas?'

'Nothing has happened so far, Maro. It won't be the first time a proclamation has been shelved in the Ottoman Empire.'

She would have liked nothing better than to have let herself be convinced, but she had not been fooled by the tone of his voice. His confidence was a front, a pretence. She herself did the same thing in order not to frighten those around her but she was as well informed about the political situation as her husband.

'Is there nothing we can do? Maybe put pressure on the high command of the army or the governor of the province . . . Mumtaz Bey has always been just to the Armenians.'

'The order comes from Constantinople, from the Minister of the Interior personally.'

She lowered her head. It was because of that Talaat and his clique that they had had to leave the capital to take refuge in this provincial town just as the birth of her child was imminent.

'I can't imagine this deportation. How are they going to move so many people?'

Vartan too failed to see how it was to be done in an area without a railroad and with roads scarcely worthy of the name. There were 30,000 Armenians in Sivas alone and maybe two million in all of Anatolia. How could they coordinate the transportation of the people and their belongings when the government was incapable of getting supplies for the army through? In the inevitable chaos a climate favourable to all sorts of crime would be created. Vartan kept his thoughts to himself.

'That's a good question, Maro. I think it's impossible and the government will quickly realize it. The generals will remind the politicians that the country's resources should be devoted to the war effort.'

He worked up a thick lather with his shaving brush and spread it over his chin, cheeks and neck. Maro watched him in silence. Every once in a while their eyes met in the mirror. A mole at the edge of his lower left eyelid added a quirk to Vartan's inscrutable look – inscrutable to others, but a thousand minute signs allowed Maro to read his state of mind. His sinuous, svelte body, his sharp, sparkling eyes and his square chin exuded an impression of calm forcefulness, accentuated by the precise gestures with which he handled his razor. Maro shivered; she longed for him to embrace her to banish her fears.

'We should have left this country in 1909,' she said, neither resentfully nor reproachfully, but rather in a neutral tone reserved for unimportant statements.

He looked at her in the mirror, the razor blade still on his cheek, and said, 'In Europe we would now be in the midst of war.'

She did not remind him that he could have been representing the family business in New York instead of his cousin, Barkev.

Where they would go when they fled Constantinople had provoked the only argument they had had since they had gotten married. Afyon Karahisar had been discarded as being too close to the capital. Since she had been born in the capital, she was not particularly attracted to the provinces of Anatolia and would have gladly opted for anywhere outside the Empire, preferably a big city such as Paris or Marseilles where there were large Armenian colonies already established, or even London or Geneva. She was willing to go anywhere as long as it was not imposed on her. But, in spite of his Western education, Vartan felt a deep attachment to Asia Minor, the land of his people and the cradle of great civilizations.

Maro was nervously biting her thumbnail. 'What will happen to your brother, Noubar? And to our relatives in Constantinople? We have had no news from them for over two months.'

At the beginning of May they had received a letter from Aunt Arpiné, telling them that Diran had managed to escape the police round-ups of April 24th. Hundreds of intellectuals, writers and famous Armenians had been arrested and deported to the interior of the country. Their families still did not know that the majority of them had been tortured and executed.

Vartan answered, 'I don't think our relatives are in danger because of all the diplomats and foreign reporters who live in the city. As far as Noubar is concerned, since he has inherited our father's almost pathological prudence, I wouldn't be at all surprised if he has joined the Mesropians in Constantinople.'

Images of her native city flashed through Maro's mind: her Uncle Mesrop's and Aunt Arpiné's apartment, the main street of Péra, the Golden Horn, the Galata Bridge.

'Couldn't we go back there?'

'Not right now. You know very well I'm in the army and stationed in Sivas.'

'You still have some Turkish friends in high places. Isn't Halit a general? I'm scared, Vartan.'

He was drying his face and stopped short. Maro saw him staring into the distance and she knew he was testing an idea in his mind. He nodded repeatedly and seemed to be talking to himself. 'Unless . . .' He was interrupted by knocking on the door. It was easy to guess who it was. Vartan spoke in a voice loud enough for his son to hear, 'Who's there?'

'May I come in?' asked a fluting voice.

'No, Tomas, your mother and I are dressing.'

'Oh! Then, may I curry Hour-Grag,[1] Papa?'

'Definitely not! He's too nervous. You can help me saddle him in a few minutes.'

'All right,' said the child in a disappointed voice. 'I'll go and draw water with Zeynep.' And Tomas who had come on tiptoe departed, clacking his heels.

'What were you going to say?' asked Maro, ready to cling to the slightest hope.

'It's still too vague. I'll have to think it over. I'll tell you about it this evening.' It was useless to insist. Vartan never spoke unless he was certain of what he was proposing and had thought of all the alternatives.

Maro sighed, 'I had invited Captain Armen and Araksi to celebrate Tomas's birthday, but now . . .'

They looked at each other in silence while they thought about their son, who would celebrate his sixth birthday today, June 30th. Maro's face darkened.

Vartan forced himself to smile and kissed her. 'Don't cancel anything. Let's do things as planned.'

'All right,' she sighed. 'Let him have something nice to remember. Who knows what will happen?'

He pinched her cheek. 'Keep your chin up, my darling.' She nodded but did not feel reassured.

The slate paved hall led on one side to the parlour and the lounge and on the other side to the dining room, kitchen and servants' quarters. Vartan had kept his collection of antique firearms here but the racks were empty now. The flintlocks and muskets had been taken away by a zealous government official when the government had confiscated all arms belonging to Christians.

---

1. Flaming fire (Armenian).

Tomas was standing at the foot of the monumental staircase with its hand-carved curving banister. He wore short pants which reached below his knees, a white shirt and laced-up boots. He was waiting for his father with Sassoun, a small black spaniel, which was his constant playmate.

He was a big, strong child, traits he had inherited from Vartan. Under his very short black hair, his delicate face was all eyes like his mother's, and when he frowned he looked as stubborn as she did. According to Armenian tradition, he was named after his paternal grandfather. He was the pride and joy of his father, who saw himself in his son. But what future was there for this child in this country? Vartan had always hoped to give his son the carefree childhood that he himself had had – full of games and small discoveries. The future did not bode well.

'Jemila and I have given grain and water to the horses and I helped Zeynep milk the cows,' the child announced proudly.

'Wonderful, *hokis*.[1] But you're not to play between the horses' legs. Understand? Remember what happened to your dog, Sassoun.'

'Yes, Papa.' Tomas remembered how Sassoun had limped for weeks after being kicked by a horse.

Vartan kissed the child as he lifted him up on his shoulders.

'Hey! Hey!' cried Tomas as they passed over the door-sill.

Except for Sundays, the Balians never had breakfast together. Vartan had just a cup of black tea. Tomas always waited for his mother to come down so he could join her at the table. As for Azniv Hanim,[2] Maro's mother, she got up at dawn and ate with the two Turkish servants, Zeynep and Jemila. They were not really servants but *evlatlik*s, foster-children. They came from the same village and their parents had placed them with this Armenian family when they were eleven years old to learn good manners, the art of running a household and anything else that was necessary to make them into perfect wives when they got married at the age of fourteen or fifteen. Azniv Hanim had taken them under her wing and, for three years, ruled over them affectionately.

The stable in the back of the garden sheltered three horses. Two were pure Arabian mounts for Vartan and Maro and the other was a trotter for pulling the carriage. Two milk cows were also stabled there.

Tomas never stopped talking and asking questions while he was helping his father saddle Hour-Grag. 'What's the name of this strap? What's it for?

1. My soul (Armenian).
2. Madam (Turkish).

26

How do horses make their babies?' Vartan answered him patiently, explaining.

The father was pleased by his son's insatiable curiosity, thinking it to be a sign of intelligence. Being an only child raised among adults, Tomas was precocious. He understood much more of what was going on around him than he let on, but often found it advantageous to be treated like a little child.

'Tell me, Papa, will I get my pony soon?'

Vartan assumed a mysterious look. 'Very soon.'

'I want to go galloping with you and mama.'

While Vartan was inspecting the shoes of the three horses, the child asked pointedly, 'What day is it today, Papa?'

Vartan pretended he had forgotten it was his son's birthday. Although he felt like smiling, he kept a straight face and answered, 'June the thirtieth. Why?'

'Oh, nothing,' said the child, hiding his disappointment. Seeing that his father was checking the trotter's harness and greasing the axle of the carriage, Tomas asked, 'Are we going for a ride soon?'

Once more Vartan was impressed by his son's insight. 'Not that I know of. But, as your grandfather told me over and over again, a wise man is always prepared.'

To divert Tomas's attention, Vartan seated him on the saddle and gave him the reins. Vartan guided the horse with the bridle and made him trot as far as the entrance where Azniv Hanim stood holding a tray. Her hair was still brown speckled with white, although she was nearly seventy. Since her husband's death two years before Tomas was born, she had always worn black. She was short, bony and gave an impression of frailty which was at odds with her energetic disposition and robust health. Her small, bright eyes, aquiline nose and strident voice were more in accord with her bossy disposition. Her skin was wrinkled but surprisingly white, for Azniv Hanim had always avoided the sun. Only peasants had dark skin, to her way of thinking.

A city dweller to her core, she had left Constantinople reluctantly to follow her daughter and son-in-law to Sivas, but she had had no choice; Maro was all she had left. Her two brothers who had lived in Tehran, Persia had died a long time ago.

Since Vartan had lost his mother, it was the responsibility of his mother-in-law, Azniv Hanim, to manage his household even if Maro did not yield gracefully to this Eastern custom. Obviously this reflected the influence of her education by French nuns – another one of Hagop Artinian's ideas. Nothing had been too good or too expensive for his daughter!

Azniv had to admit that Maro had been a gift from heaven. After twenty-four years of sterile marriage and dozens of vain consultations with famous doctors, Azniv Hanim had found she was pregnant as she was approaching her fortieth birthday. How anxiously she had awaited a boy to perpetuate the family name of the Artinians, but God had decided otherwise! She had hidden her disappointment in order not to lessen Hagop's joy and had vowed to raise the girl according to tradition so that one day she would make someone a perfect wife.

She had failed because Hagop spoiled his daughter. He took her with him on his business trips out of the country and encouraged an independent spirit in her which would have been more appropriate in a boy. She accompanied him even on pheasant hunts. Maro's childhood and adolescence had been an incessant confrontation with her mother over trivialities as well as important things. No small arguments or outbursts – rather, the stubborn, silent strife between authoritarianism and obstinacy. Only after her marriage had Maro become close to her mother. Today Azniv Hanim was proud of her daughter and admired her ability to make decisions. They were much alike; neither let herself be imposed upon. Azniv had spent happy days in her son-in-law's house. Her only fear was to die far from Constantinople; she prayed daily that she could be buried next to her husband in the Armenian cemetery in the Shishli Quarter under the shade of the cypress trees.

Vartan kissed his mother-in-law. '*Parilouys, mayrig*.'[1]

'Look at me, grandmother!' exclaimed a radiant Tomas. 'I'm a real horseman!'

One of the young girls joined them. It was Zeynep. Her eyelids were heavy with kohl, giving her a melancholy look even when she smiled. By Anatolian standards, she was already considered a woman although she was only fifteen. At the end of the year, she would take a husband, a carpenter, chosen by her father, and she sadly awaited the moment when she would have to leave the Balian household where she had known a quiet contentment; but she would have no choice.

Vartan turned the reins of the horse over to her so she could walk Tomas down the road, took the cup of boiling-hot tea which his mother-in-law

---

1.  Good morning, mother (Armenian).

28

offered him and drank it in small sips. In spite of his bad mood, he didn't respond when Azniv Hanim flicked the chaff off the red collar of his tunic with her fingers. Straw fell from his gilded epaulettes.

She scolded, 'You have hay on your beautiful uniform.'

He smiled. She added in a hoarse whisper, which betrayed her anxiety, 'Be careful. It's our passport.' Like most of her countrymen, she still did not fully realize how imminent the danger was.

He nodded his head understandingly and asked, 'Do we have enough provisions for several days?'

She frowned, surprised at her son-in-law's lack of confidence in her foresight.

'I mean staples and smoked meat,' he specified, 'things that keep and are easy to carry.'

Azniv's eyes opened wide in astonishment and she looked around her to see if Jemila was standing near. 'Does that mean that we . . .?'

He interrupted her with a gesture. 'I still don't know. Don't breathe a word to anyone.'

Zeynep was coming back. Vartan put the cup on the tray, thanked his mother-in-law, then lifted Tomas off the horse and kissed him.

'Be good, my dear boy. You'll have a surprise this evening.'

'I knew it! It's my birthday!' cried the happy child, unable to contain himself any longer. 'What's the surprise?'

'If I told you, it wouldn't be a surprise any more.'

Azniv Hanim put her hand on her grandson's shoulder. 'You were born at dinner-time so you won't be six years old until this evening.'

Maro leaned out of the bedroom window with a hairbrush in her hand. She discreetly blew a few kisses to Vartan. The sun made her blink and painted copper highlights in her hair which fell over her shoulders.

Her beauty did not seem quite real and Vartan felt sad. 'Until tonight, my dearest,' he said, trying to make his voice sound cheerful. He was a little uneasy at leaving her without a man in the house.

Jemila came up to the entrance. 'Here's your fez, Major Vartan.'

She had come running down the road barefoot, not seeming to mind the stones, with her multicoloured, flower-printed dress clinging to her legs and a profusion of very small braids swinging around her face. As he put on his red fez and placed the black tassel to the right, Jemila polished his boots with the corner of her apron. She stood back admiringly. She hoped that her father would find her a handsome husband like him, an officer if possible.

Unlike Zeynep, she was in a hurry to marry and run her own house.

'Make Hour-Grag dance, Papa.'

For more than four years Vartan had been training his thoroughbred Arab, using the techniques from the Spanish riding school in Vienna for inspiration. To amuse Tomas, to show off to Maro and to give the impression that everything was normal, Vartan put his horse through a *levade*, a *cabriole* and some of the Spanish paces.

'What a child!' sighed Azniv Hanim reproachfully.

'What have I done now?' asked Tomas, taken aback, not realizing she was talking about his father.

Once he was out on the street, Vartan stopped briefly, trying to engrave the picture in his memory. There was Maro framed by the window on the second floor of the big white house; Tomas, Azniv Hanim, Jemila and Zeynep on the front steps; the dog on the road; the climbing roses around the windows; the shadows of the chestnut tree laced with holes made by the sunlight. On the chimney he could see the nest to which the storks had not returned this spring, a bad omen, according to his mother-in-law. He thought the omens now were more concrete and much more pressing.

Vartan trotted away so as to avoid having to speak to his neighbours and acquaintances. Since he had held political posts, written books and held a commission in the Ottoman army, they would have asked him all sorts of questions – his opinion on the situation, details on the deportation order . . . as if he knew any more than they! Riding at a good pace, he could get away with simply nodding at them.

Zeynep closed the wrought iron gate after Vartan. Tomas held his nose in order not to smell the horsy odour and listened to the fading clip-clop of the horse's hoofs. He could hear mooing from a herd coming up the street: Arshag came every morning to get the neighbourhood cows and take them out to pasture.

Maro drew the curtain in her room and opened the wardrobe. A hanger fell out. As she picked up the garment, she felt a small lump in her throat. Her Paris dress! A folly of Vartan's during their trip to France, a dress designed by Jean Lanvin in white *crêpe-de-chine* with appliqués of red roses and green leaves. It was probably out of fashion as it had been bought in 1912. Was there still a fashion in France now that they were at war?

She could not resist looking at herself in the cheval mirror as she held the dress up in front of her. That trip on the Orient Express, Sofia, Belgrade, the week-long stopover in Vienna, Switzerland, and finally Paris – she had been filled with such wonder as she discovered the 'City of Lights'. Everything had been more beautiful than she had imagined from picture-books and postcards. And Vartan – just as loving then as he had been at the very beginning of their marriage, as he still was today.

Their union had been arranged according to an Armenian custom widely accepted throughout the Near East, which compared the fortunes of both families. The Balians were large landowners and the Artinians prosperous merchants, so they were considered to be of the same class. Maro had been twenty . . . four or five years older than was customary. She had enjoyed a higher education than most girls of her generation, having attended a religious boarding school and then the Lycée Notre-Dame-de-Sion in Constantinople. She had travelled with her father in Russia and all over the Ottoman Empire and had actively taken part in her father's business. She would have liked to study further and to have had a profession, perhaps medicine, but that would have been unthinkable at that time, especially in Asia Minor. Hagop would not have opposed such plans but he had finally given in to Azniv Hanim's incessant pressure, and they had chosen an educated Armenian from the same affluent social class in which they moved. Her father chose the one he found the most attractive; her mother, the one she thought to be the most intelligent – a pharmacist, ten years older than their daughter.

Maro had been afraid when she was taken to a family party to meet her future husband. She considered this imposed choice of a husband to be an indecent custom, which turned her into an object of barter, but had finally consented to go in order not to cross her father. She had, however, the firm intention of defying her parents if she did not like the man. She knew Vartan Balian by reputation, a writer involved in Armenian political movements. Rumour had it that he was quite a ladies' man, but Maro paid no attention to this as she preferred to see for herself.

She had been immediately attracted by his charm and elegance and had been completely conquered when she had realized how intelligent he was. Contrary to most men, he had not only been impressed by her beauty but had treated her as an equal. They had spent all evening talking in the garden and had been pleasantly surprised to find they had so many things in common. She had been afraid of being bored by his talk of politics but instead he had spoken of literature and music. He played the oud[1] brilliantly and had a whole repertoire of Armenian and Ottoman classical music. During their encounters he showed more sensitivity, tenderness, and force of character than she had ever expected.

After their marriage, they had lived in Constantinople where Vartan ran a pharmacy. She loved this busy city with its mysterious atmosphere and its curious mixture of Oriental tradition and Western modernism. There was also the Mesropian family. Maro, who had been an only child, found a brother and a sister – Cousin Diran and Cousin Lucie, who was the same age as she. Uncle Mesrop and his wife, Arpiné, loved Vartan like a son and adopted Maro as one of their own. On the Asiatic side of Constantinople they could get on the Taurus-Express and go on holiday to the Balians' property in Afyon Karahisar. From the European bank, they could take the train for short excursions to Bucharest, the 'Little Paris of the East'.

Vartan's pharmacy was a meeting place for revolutionaries of various kinds – Christians, Jews and Muslims who secretly planned the coming of a liberal state, modern and democratic. Even though she shared Vartan's ideals, Maro had feared for his life. The Sultan's secret police brazenly liquidated their opponents, and Vartan's political writings put him in that category. Maro's fears had been justified because they had tried to assassinate him in his office and only a miracle had saved him. Thereafter, the couple had lived underground for almost a year, moving incessantly. This had been the darkest period of Maro's life – the lack of security and the perpetual feeling of being hunted like an animal. In 1908 the *coup d'état* by the Young Turks put an end to their trials. But within a few months their euphoria had given way to bitter disillusionment. The new regime had no intention of giving equal rights to the Christians and Vartan again became a hunted man. At that time they had fled the capital, although not far enough, in Maro's opinion. The same nightmare had begun again today!

A bit ashamed of having allowed her mind to wander, especially under these circumstances, Maro put her expensive dress in the wardrobe and put on a simple pearl-grey dress. She hurried as Tomas would be waiting for her for breakfast.

Vartan arrived at the gateway of the town. On the other side of the ruined

---

1.   A Turkish string instrument similar to lute (Arabic).

ramparts, heavy traffic had blocked the exit over the bridge which spanned the River Halys – ox-carts, donkeys labouring under heavy loads, sheep and goats being herded to the market, Kurdish mountaineers riding stocky horses with long manes, peasants burdened with baskets, soldiers returning to their barracks. On the other side of the road there was a bottleneck creating quite a commotion.

'Make way! Make way!' cried Vartan, pushing his way into the curious crowd, which moved aside for the beribboned uniform.

He quickly grasped what was happening. Four gendarmes on guard at the bridge had arrested an Armenian family who was attempting to leave the town in an overloaded cart piled high with their most treasured belongings. As the father and mother argued with the soldiers, the peasants and the poor pushed against the vehicle and tried to pilfer from the cart, while the five children tried to protect their property as best they could. The mob grew steadily bolder and more menacing and occasional oaths could be heard above the murmurs.

'Thieves!'

'Sons of bitches!'

'*Giaours!*'[1]

The gendarmes did not know he was only a reserve officer and an Armenian! With people like these who feared the authorities, it was enough to act arrogantly. Vartan drew his pistol and shot into the air. Silence ensued.

'Move on! Move on,' he cried. He pushed people away from the cart with his horse. The soldiers, who had lost control of the situation, were only too grateful for his intervention and finished dispersing the crowd.

Vartan addressed the corporal with authority, 'What's been going on here? Why couldn't you maintain order?'

The guards pointed to the vehicle. 'It's the Armenians' fault. They were trying to get away. We have orders that they're to stay in town.'

'I know that as well as you,' said Vartan. He pointed at the driver with his riding crop. 'But did he know about the order?'

The man, who had recognized Vartan, thought it better not to show that he knew him. Picking up the cue from Vartan, he spun a yarn. 'No, sir, I didn't. My family and I have a little farm about three kilometres from here. We were only going to harvest the hay as we do every year.'

'You can do that next week. Get back in town!' ordered Vartan.

---

1. A non-Muslim, infidel (Turkish).

33

The corporal protested, 'We have orders to arrest them.'

'I give the orders here,' said Vartan curtly. 'I'll refer the matter to the captain who'll decide what's to be done with them.' He took out a notepad and wrote down the name and address of the head of the family and then ordered them to leave. 'Stay home and wait for the authorities to call you.'

'Yes, sir. Thank you, sir.' The man was visibly relieved. He got down, turned the cart around, and leading the horse by the bridle, headed back. into Sivas.

'You did a good job. It will be noted on your records,' Vartan said to the soldiers flatteringly.

He waited until the man's cart reached the old rampart. Then he crossed the bridge, took a left turn and gave full rein to Hour-Grag on the dirt road following the river. Through the poplars on the bank he could see the flour mills where people were repairing the paddles on the wheels to be ready for harvest. On the other bank, there were regular rows of apple, plum and apricot trees. It always gave Vartan real joy to gallop through the countryside. It usually made him forget all his troubles but this morning it did not. The incident on the bridge had rekindled his worries. He was not surprised by the zeal the gendarmes used in imposing the new regulations, but the hostile attitude of the crowd was new in Sivas. If racial hatred surfaced, the worst could be expected.

While he rode away from the town and towards the distant, hazy-blue mountains, he recalled the idea he had refused to discuss with Maro. To leave . . . just as the Armenian family had tried to do, but they had taken too much with them. A flight was not a change of residence! Also, they had been heading south, precisely the same direction the deportation would take them. No! One should try to get away during the night, carrying only what was strictly necessary, and head north. Nothing should be taken for granted. The roads were in bad condition and under army surveillance. The countryside was controlled by bands of cut-throats. His officer's uniform would be useful only a little while, because soon he would be hunted down as a deserter.

He would need money to bribe accomplices, but once at the Black Sea, he could book passage on a ship bound for Constantinople or for any Russian port. How many days would it take to get to the shore? A carriage would be much slower than riding. Even though Tomas could ride behind him, there was still Azniv Hanim to consider and they would have to take provisions and blankets as well as grain for the horses. Maro could stay in

34

the saddle for hours and, if necessary, handle a rifle, but it would be a trying journey for both his mother-in-law and his son. Vartan thought they would have a better chance of success if Armen joined them; he knew the Black Sea and its ports like the palm of his hand. The best deal would be to buy a boat which Armen could pilot. With Araksi, that made six: two on horseback and four in the carriage. Yes, they could still get away without attracting too much attention.

He slowed his horse down to a walk. He could not help feeling ill at ease, even guilty, that he would be abandoning the other Armenians to their lot. Was he being a coward? All his life, he had never retreated except to pounce upon his enemy, but today he was planning to flee! He, who in his youth had dreamed of being a guiding beacon for his people, who had taken an active part in the Armenian insurrection, who had dreamed of leaving his mark on history, was he to sneak away like a thief under the cover of darkness?

On the other hand, of what help could he be to his people? What could one man do against a state machine gone mad? He felt impotent! He was overwhelmed by sadness. He had fought and worked against despotism for so many years, had climbed on podiums, had written pages and pages, had waited, hoped, believed and tried to imbue others with his faith. How was he to deny what he had preached for twenty years? If he were alone, it would be another matter, but he had to think of Tomas and Maro. There had been nothing shameful in fleeing Constantinople in 1909. His life had been in danger and he had ceased to be useful. It had been a wise decision.

He came to a wide clearing where, until recently, the officers had held their equestrian games, especially the hurdle races which Vartan and his friend, Colonel Ibrahim Alizadé, always won. He missed those tournaments as he missed the carefree career officers' boisterous companionship. They had not seemed to mind that he was only an Armenian civilian who had enlisted after the beginning of the war. But things had been changing very fast during the past month. His companions avoided him when possible; only Colonel Ibrahim remained unfailingly friendly.

Now dozens of grey tents were set up in the clearing where a hospital had been improvised because the one in Sivas was overflowing with sick and wounded. Soldiers sent back from the western front were treated here. Vartan had a hard time convincing his commanding officer that he was only a pharmacist and not a doctor. There was such a shortage of medical personnel that he had been put in charge of this clinic.

At least this job took him out of the laboratory in the military hospital where the atmosphere became suffocating during the heat waves. Someone had to alleviate the suffering of these men, most of whom were very young. In spite of his reluctance, he had assumed the role of doctor. He had a good basic knowledge of medicine and, because the surgeon came by very rarely, Vartan had learned how to extract bullets and shrapnel.

As soon as he had left his horse in the paddock under the trees, he quickly made an inspection of the camp and issued orders to the soldiers to burn the old bandages which were stinking out the tents, to empty the slop-buckets and to fetch fresh water.

Then Vartan listened as the young Turkish night orderly, his eyes puffy from lack of sleep, made his report. After reviewing each case, the boy announced in a tired voice with a heavy east Anatolian accent, 'We had some new arrivals this morning – eleven wounded, many in pitiful condition. Half of them are going to croak in less than two days, I'm sure!'

Vartan patted him on the shoulder and walked out with him. 'We'll do our best. Try to get some sleep.' He looked at the still leaves on the poplar trees. It was going to be a long, hot day.

# TWO

On the thirtieth of June, just before noon, a carriage approached Sivas on the road from Samsun. Escorted by twelve horsemen, it carried Gani Bey, one of the most influential government officials in Constantinople. He was only aide to the Minister of the Interior but held more power than most other members of the Ottoman Cabinet.

Gani Bey was a fat man. Although he was sitting in the shade cast by the canopy of the carriage, he was suffering from the heat as the horses' hoofs were stirring up such dust that the air had become suffocating. He was spitting and fanning himself continuously.

'Country of savages,' he muttered between his teeth.

He sat slumped on the cracked, black leather seat, looking like a huge toad. He had enormous glistening jowls, a wide slashed mouth, engorged wattles on his neck and a voluminous belly that made his arms and legs look short. His underlings at the Ministry in Constantinople called him 'The Boar' because of his little round eyes, his snorting breath and, most of all, his odious disposition.

Gani Bey felt reassured by his obesity as he had been hungry all through his childhood. His village, which lay near Konia, had always been short of food during the long winter months. Now he gorged himself with frenzy, as if by doing so he could banish the spectre of famine forever, but his ravenous hunger was never appeased.

As a concession to the heat, he had taken off his fez and put it on the seat next to him. He had also taken off his red tie and opened his collar. Other than that, he remained true to the image of a high government official from the capital. He was dressed all in black – a black, open jacket, a gold watch-chain looped across a black vest – but his clothes looked grey. Everything looked grey because of the dust – his hands, his boots, the carriage, the horses, even the landscape. Sweat oozed from his bald head, dripped on his round cheeks and trickled down his neck. He had taken off his pince-nez to keep them from sliding down off his wet nose and put them in his pocket.

'Country of savages,' he grumbled again, shaking his head.

He pulled out a mother-of-pearl cigarette case, took out a cigarette and inserted it into a holder. The town lay in front of him in a valley where the sun had not as yet yellowed all the vegetation. He could see the horizon looking like the teeth of a saw and he knew that, after his stay in Sivas, he would find himself in the steppes again. Hundreds of bad roads awaited him. How many weeks must pass before he would see the Mediterranean shore and the train which would take him back to Constantinople again? He cursed Talaat, his master, who had sent him off to the heart of Anatolia to solve the problems which had arisen because of the deportation of the Armenians.

Gani Bey sponged himself with a sweat-soaked handkerchief and took a gulp of lukewarm water straight from the mouth of a gourd, but it did not quench his thirst. His head wobbled and his eyes roamed over the landscape without really seeing it. He started to daydream about Constantinople and the shaded garden of his house, which overlooked the shimmering waters of the Bosphorus at Yeniköy. He had travelled by steamboat from the capital to the port of Samsun, which lay on the southern shores of the Black Sea. There the country was still fit for human beings. Its climate was temperate because of its nearness to the sea and the mountains covered by tall trees. But after that . . . nothing but stony hills covered by thorny bushes and scarce, scrawny trees; damned land barely good enough for goats! He had seen nothing but miserable villages where it was impossible to find a decent place to stay. At least Sivas was a real town. He dreamt about the bliss of a real bath in the local *hammam*.

The carriage arrived at the southern entrance to the town where a massive mosque showed off its twin minarets. He could see many beautiful old buildings which had been built over the centuries by Muslims and Christians. There were several monuments dating from the Seljuk era, which had made the town famous, but none of this interested Gani Bey, as he preferred streets bustling with people. The region he had just crossed had made him feel intolerably lonely.

The carriage entered the Grand Bazaar, the only way to reach the government house where Gani Bey was to stay. The driver slowed the horses to a walk. A continuous flow of pedestrians, heavily loaded donkeys and carriages blocked the way already narrowed by the stalls. Above a steady droning, the merchants cried out their wares at the top of their lungs. The aroma of food frying in sesame oil made Gani Bey drool. When he smelled the onions in a mutton fricassee cooking on an open fire, his stomach growled. He smoked a cigarette to calm his hunger. The crowd pushed against both sides of the carriage and the spicy odours gave way to an acrid foul stench – the smell of people who wore their clothes for weeks, even slept in them – the stench of poverty and misery, the stench of his childhood! He shivered in disgust and put a handkerchief soaked in rose-water over his nose. His forty-two years in Constantinople had changed him and he felt a stranger among these little people from whom he sprang.

A carefully buried memory came back to him. He, his mother and his sisters were gathering cow-pats from the fields and roads and they had to work fast to beat their neighbours. Then the women carried them back to their house in their aprons. Once at home they kneaded the dung with hay and plastered it on the outside walls where it dried and turned into *tezek*, a substitute for wood, which was scarce, and coal, which they could not afford. Fat, green flies swarmed around the dwellings and the rain intensified the pervasive foul smell. Gani Bey looked down at his long, carefully manicured fingernails. His childhood filled him with horror.

When he was ten years old, an *effendi*[1] had become besotted with him and Gani Bey, overjoyed, had followed him to Konia . . . fine food, clean clothes and a real bed with snowy sheets! Young Gani had had no scruples in granting his favours to the rich merchant who, in return, had had him educated at the main *dervish*[2] monastery in Konia. Afterwards, the merchant had taken Gani Bey with him to Constantinople where the young boy had pursued lay studies. Since then, he had retained a hatred for Christians, learnt from a fanatic *dervish*, and a predilection for masculine lovers.

Thanks to his protector's connections he had found a position as a government employee. Because of his intelligence and zeal, not to mention the art of wheeling and dealing in which he excelled, he had climbed up, step by step, from his humble beginnings. Greedy and cruel, he had neither pity nor principles and stopped at nothing to further his ambitions. As an officer

---

1. Title for an Ottoman dignitary which has become a polite form of address (Turkish).
2. A member of a Muslim religious order (Turkish).

in Abdul-Hamid II's secret police, he had killed people enthusiastically and tracked down reformers among the Young Turks, but, seeing that the tide was turning, he had teamed up with the same Young Turks and become their informant.

'God-damned place!' he murmured under his breath. However, this country formed part of the Ottoman Empire; was even the core of it. And this Empire, 'The Great Turkey', was the most important thing in the world to him. He believed, as did the other leaders, that history was offering them the opportunity to purify Anatolia of foreigners. All those not of Turkish blood must go or die – first the Armenians, then the Jews, the Greeks, the Arabs, even the Kurds, although the latter would be given the option to leave or become Turks. The founders of the Empire had lacked foresight in letting these people live. The day would come when they would want their freedom again and reach for it. Thus the Empire had lost Greece; the Balkans, Mesopotamia and Arabia would undoubtedly go the same way. There was also the risk that half of Anatolia would become Armenian and the other half Kurdish. There was but one way of preventing this outcome: only Turks must live in this region.

Once past the bazaar, they reached another small square surrounded by modern buildings. As he thought about the mission that had brought him here, Gani Bey forgot his fatigue and, instead of stopping at the governor's residence where a suite had been prepared for him, he ordered the driver to take him directly to the police station. The driver prodded the horses to a trot. Gani Bey reknotted his tie and put on his fez.

The grey weather-beaten boards gave the building a neglected look. It had not been repainted since it had been built at the beginning of the century. The wide façade was pierced by high windows, some of which had broken panes. The police station and the city hall were housed under the same roof. As was customary, the more important dignitaries occupied the third floor. The two lower ones were reserved for the unimportant bureaucrats, the secretaries and the messengers. The dungeons were in the basement.

Three gendarmes were chatting in the shade on the porch. They snapped to attention when they saw the carriage, which could only belong to an important personage.

'You there!' shouted Gani Bey to one of the guards. 'Come, help me get down.'

The man handed his rifle to one of his companions, ran up to the

40

carriage and lowered the step. The springs creaked and the carriage listed as Gani Bey descended. He was so obese he could not move easily, so he leaned on the guard's shoulder with one hand and gave a sigh of relief when he set his feet on solid ground. He dusted the cigarette ash off his clothes and looked up at the empty steps. He was annoyed to see that there was no one to greet him.

'Is this the way that you welcome your visitors?' he snapped. The guard, a typically coarse peasant, didn't know what to say and only blinked rapidly.

Just at that moment, Mustapha Rahmi, the chief commissioner, appeared in the doorway. His complexion was swarthy and his eyebrows were as black and bushy as his beard and moustache. His shirt was wide open over his hairy chest, and his rolled-up sleeves exposed his muscled forearms. He had put on his tunic hastily to greet his visitor.

'Welcome, Gani Bey,' he said, bowing. 'I didn't expect you until after lunch. How was your trip?'

'Vile!' answered the other in a cutting voice. 'Let's go to your office.'

Mustapha Rahmi realized that the high official was in a murderous mood and he became even more worried. He had slept badly and woken up several times from bad nightmares in which Gani Bey was the key player. For years Mustapha Rahmi had known his visitor by reputation; this man's changes in mood could end a career and his displeasure could lead people to prison or worse. The commissioner had always carried out his orders with zeal but he was guilty of certain venial sins – drinking wine, abuse of power, taking bribes and so on. An envious person could have denounced him. Was Gani Bey coming to clean the house, as the messenger who had brought the letter announcing his arrival had said?

They went into the building where the air was thick with dust and tobacco smoke. Gani Bey had nothing but contempt for everything that was not the capital. The sloppy appearance and provincial accent of this grim-looking boor with his pointed goatee confirmed his opinion. What he liked least was the size of the commissioner. Gani Bey had a complex about his height and detested dealing with men who were taller than he and yet here was Mustapha towering over him by a head. Mustapha, however, was a faithful Ittihad partisan and a blindly devoted officer, the type of person he greatly needed now. This entitled the man to a certain respect and so Gani Bey softened and spoke almost cordially, 'I'm happy to make your acquaintance, Commissioner Mustapha.'

41

His words reassured the commissioner, who smiled. 'It is a great honour for me to receive you. I'll have refreshments served.'

'First things first.'

Each step was an effort for Gani Bey. He helped himself to balance with his arms, which gave his walk a rolling gait. His face was purple after climbing two flights of stairs and he was panting like a bellows. Tactfully, Mustapha didn't speak, to give him time to catch his breath.

A clumsy portrait of the Sultan painted on one wall of the room decorated the office of the commissioner. The painter had been more successful with the calligraphy of the *sura*[1] he had painted on the other walls. The branch of a poplar tree that had penetrated through a broken pane formed cottony clusters on the ceiling. There were only a desk, a bottle-green leather armchair, a wooden chair and, to the left of the door, a long bench on which a bamboo cane with a fringed tip was prominently displayed. Gani Bey picked up the cane and whacked it on the bench twice. The first stroke of this instrument caused hardly any pain but, used repeatedly, it could reduce a man's skin to tatters and inflict atrocious suffering. When Gani Bey had been active, he had preferred beating the soles of the feet, a most efficient torture as the prisoner lasted a long time even if he was never able to use his legs again. He put the cane down and turned to hide his feelings.

He moved towards the desk, which was piled so high with official forms that there was only room for an ink-spotted blotter upon which lay an amber *tespih*, a rosary. Gani Bey took this as a sign of religious fervour and was annoyed. He considered Muslim fatalism, the *insha' Allah* (if God wills it), one of the causes of the decline of the Empire and the reason the Armenians, Jews and Greeks were grabbing all the commerce and industry. But perhaps the rosary was only an ostentatious show on the part of the commissioner.

Gani Bey sat down behind the desk while the commissioner, feeling more and more apprehensive, remained standing in front of him. Gani Bey took his pince-nez from the inside pocket of his jacket, wiped them and set them on his nose. Before he could speak, a soldier came into the room, carrying an engraved copper tray with two glasses. Gani Bey gulped down the cold sour cherry juice.

Hoping to soothe him, Mustapha declared assiduously, 'Your orders have been carried out.'

---

1. A chapter of the Quran (Arabic).

Gani Bey stared at him blankly.

'I'm talking about the mayor, Mumtaz Bey,' added the commissioner, needlessly lowering his voice.

'When were the orders carried out?'

'This morning at his country residence. Nobody saw or heard a thing.'

'Is there any danger that the hired killers will talk? Were they your men?'

'I did it myself,' declared the commissioner, proudly showing his hands. 'Mumtaz Bey had no reason to distrust me.' The commissioner raised his glass of cherry juice as if to toast his demonstration of loyalty to Gani Bey.

The latter simply nodded and murmured in a neutral voice, 'Just in time.'

The commissioner was not satisfied and insisted, 'The rosary you see in front of you was his. It will serve as proof to accuse anybody we wish of the crime.' He stood rocking back and forth.

Gani Bey held out his hand and asked, 'My letter?'

The commissioner took the confidential letter containing Gani Bey's orders to eliminate the mayor out of his pocket. It had been delivered the day before by messenger. Gani Bey verified that it was the correct document, folded it and put it away. Mustapha Rahmi felt a shiver run down his spine; now there was no proof that he had been ordered to eliminate Mumtaz Bey.

The assassination, as such, did not faze him at all; it wasn't his first! Life had little value in a country where everyone took the law into his own hands and where the vendetta was a deep-rooted tradition, but there had been neither instigator nor witness to his previous crimes – and a mayor, to boot! He felt sure he could not trust Gani Bey to protect him nor could he think of him as an ally. Gani Bey would have no scruples getting rid of him if necessary.

Gani Bey despised the commissioner's attitude. He reminded him of a big dog begging his master for a bone, but he smiled, pretending to be impressed.

'Good. You've done an excellent job. If I only had more men like you.'

Mustapha beamed.

Gani Bey continued coldly, 'How about the Armenians? How is that coming along?'

'The deportation order has been published. We're only waiting for the escort, but the army hasn't shown us much cooperation . . . the superior officers, I mean.'

'That happens all too often!' raged Gani Bey as he lit a cigarette without offering one to his host. 'But don't worry. All that is going to change. I have *carte blanche* from the government to put matters straight. The deportation of the Armenians is a number-one priority and officers who do not fully and enthusiastically cooperate with the regime will be replaced, even the governors.'

'We have a throng of lukewarm adherents,' agreed the commissioner, who saw an opportunity to get rid of certain rivals. 'You can count on me.'

'How has the Muslim population reacted?'

'Some were surprised! Many others disagreed. They have Christian customers and friends.'

Annoyed, Gani Bey puffed rapidly on his cigarette. 'Let it be known that anyone who helps an Armenian to flee shall be severely punished. The mayor's assassination and some well-staged demonstrations should change their minds.'

'What are your plans for the Armenians who are willing to convert to Islam?'

'That's what I don't want!' shouted Gani Bey, throwing his cigarette butt on the floor and lighting another one. 'Just between us, Commissioner,' he began anew in a calmer voice, 'religion has nothing to do with any of this! Muslim Armenians? Armenians will always be Armenians. On the other hand, if you could find me some Christian Turks to populate Anatolia, I would have no objections. An empire cannot be founded on a religion; on a race, yes!'

Mustapha nodded his head and opened the window as the smoke was bothering him. The cool, clear noise of the little fountain in the courtyard came into the room. Suddenly Gani Bey was overcome with fatigue from his long journey and he remembered the *hammam* that he had passed on the way. How blissful it was going to be to clean off the dust of the road in the steam bath and permit a *tellak*[1] to wash his body with rich lather and perfumed water. He imagined the singular feeling of well-being he would have after the artful massage.

Gani Bey decided to cut the meeting short. 'Did my agents report to you, Commissioner?'

'Yes.'

'Tell them that I want to see them this afternoon.' Saying this, he rose,

---

1. An employee of a public bath-house (Turkish).

never taking his eyes off his listener. 'You shall have lunch with me and we can discuss further arrangements.'

Mustapha was flattered by this show of favour and straightened up as he put his hand on his heart. 'You honour me greatly.'

Encouraged, he rummaged in a pile of papers, pulled out some wrinkled sheets, and followed Gani Bey who had gone up to the window to see if his carriage was still waiting for him. The commissioner smoothed out the sheets of paper and gave them to his superior.

'Here is the list of the important Armenians in town. There are more than two hundred of them. Would you like to take a look?'

A corner of Gani Bey's mouth twitched into an involuntary grimace as he went over the pages of awkward handwriting. The names meant nothing to him. 'There's one name missing,' he said, uncapping his pen. Leaning on the dusty window sill, he added a new name in Arabic letters[1] to the top of the list.

Armen Surmelian was squat and stocky and his neck was so short that his head seemed to be planted on his wide shoulders. According to his wife, Araksi, he was as stubborn as a mule. He found the gate to the Balians' garden locked. This was unusual but he could understand the precautionary measure only too well! 'That damned deportation order!' He swore softly and threw his cigarette butt away as he pulled the bell chain.

To leave Sivas, where they had come seventeen years ago to live out their last days in peace? Where were they going to be sent? What would become of them? The small house and little patch of land on the edge of the Armenian Quarter were all they owned. He was now seventy-two and, after living in Turkish Armenia for seventeen years, he did not believe any of the promises of the government. The Sultan had gone back on his word to the Armenians too many times!

A servant came out of the imposing freshly-painted, white house and walked towards the iron gate. Gold earrings hung from her earlobes and framed her round face.

Armen pinched her chin and addressed her in a deep and slightly guttural voice, 'You always look so pretty, Jemila. I don't understand why you aren't married yet.'

---

1. Up until 1928 Turkish was written with the Arabic alphabet.

She blushed and lowered her eyes. She always felt guilty in his presence. Even though he was very old, she found Captain Armen attractive. Her eyes focused on the grey hairs that sprang out of the collar of his shirt and she blushed even more. She had often observed him surreptitiously while he worked maintaining the flower-beds in the Balians' garden, digging up the vegetable patches and taking care of the animals. The captain's enormous hands and thick fingers were capable of such delicacy and dexterity when they banded grafts on the fruit trees, pruned the rosebushes and nipped the buds of peonies. It was the same tenderness that Armen showed towards children and animals. His hands were like bear paws and would hold one strongly.

Seeing the embarrassment of the young girl, Armen frowned and his half-closed eyes glittered mischievously. 'If I were a Muslim, I would take you for a second wife.'

'Captain Armen!' she protested, embarrassed. 'You're always teasing me!'

'You're wrong! I'm perfectly serious. I'm going to talk to my wife tonight.'

She was used to the old man's teasing, but she never knew if there was a grain of truth in his banter. She giggled and turned away. He limped after her into the garden where phlox and lupins bordered the pebbled walk.

'Shall I tell Azniv Hanim that you're here?'

'That won't be necessary. I'm in a hurry. Just send Tomas out to me.'

As soon as he was alone, his morose thoughts returned. He waited under the shadow of a chestnut tree and rubbed his aching right leg. He found it strange that it should start hurting him after so many years. It was an old wound which dated back to the 1894 massacres when he had saved Araksi and himself from death. His children and grandchildren who had been living in Trebizond had not been so lucky.

Sweat ran down his neck because, to please his godson, he had put on a blue sailor jacket with golden buttons and a black cap adorned with an embroidered anchor above the visor. Armen, who had fished in the Black Sea all his life, had owned a light boat and done some smuggling. Now that he had retired to the interior of the country, he had been nicknamed 'Captain', which he didn't mind at all, quite the contrary.

Absent-mindedly, he looked at the complex mosaic of arabesques made from small stones embedded in the cement of the walk. He went up to a flower-bed and weeded out some withered flowers. The salary he received from the Balians and the money he got from raising chickens allowed him to live decently without dipping into his meagre savings. His respected friend Vartan Balian had chosen him to be the godfather of his son in spite of his modest standing. It was true that Vartan's family lived far away, but any of the important people in Sivas would have been flattered to be chosen as Tomas's godfather. Armen took his role of godfather very seriously especially as he didn't understand what had motivated Vartan, who was such an erudite man, to choose him who hardly knew how to read and write.

'*Parilouys*, Captain Armen.' He looked up. Maro was standing on the steps holding a package wrapped in brown paper. 'Aren't you coming in?'

'Good morning, Maro. We'll be leaving as soon as Tomas is ready. There is a special meeting of the parish council before Mass.'

'He'll be right out.'

She came down the steps towards him. He loved to look at her especially when she was dressed, as today, in the European fashion. The belted waist of her grey dress accentuated her feminine silhouette and she walked with such grace that she seemed to be dancing. Unruly wisps of hair escaped from a thick chignon, which enhanced the slenderness of her neck and gave her head a proud bearing. Armen had never seen a more beautiful woman in his life. An aura of sensuality surrounded her, although her regard was candid and frank. She fascinated the old man and looking at her always thrilled him.

She kissed him on both cheeks and asked him about his wife. He in turn inquired about her health, her mother's health and that of her husband.

'I don't want to be indiscreet but, tell me Armen, are you going to talk to the priest about the deportation order?'

'What else?' he sighed. 'Has Major Vartan found out anything?'

'Nothing for the time being.'

'We're all full of misgivings. That's the worst of it; to wait without knowing what's ahead of us.'

'Do you think it's wise to take Tomas to church?' she asked worriedly.

'Saint Minas is only a few blocks from here, right in the heart of the Armenian Quarter, and everything is calm in town. I was at the market this morning and the Muslim merchants are just as surprised as we are.' He kept to himself the thought that this was only the calm before the storm. Like everyone else, he expected the worst but refused to voice his worries out of a superstitious fear that they might come to pass. 'Don't be afraid. I'll look after Tomas.' He patted his jacket and Maro understood that he was armed, but this only increased her worry. Armen reassured her, 'I always carry it on me. It's a sort of talisman.'

Maro nodded. In this region a man had to be ready to defend himself at all times. Armen was going to add something but didn't as at that moment Tomas came running out of the house with his dog at his heels.

Maro leaned towards the Captain and murmured quietly in his ear, 'Don't forget that you and Araksi are coming to dinner tonight.'

'How could I forget? I'm the one who's bringing his present.'

'Godfather! Godfather!' Sassoun was happily barking and jumping around his young master. The child ran up to his godfather who swept him up in his arms.

'You're getting heavier and heavier, my little good-for-nothing,' said Armen as he kissed him. 'One can almost hear you grow.'

Tomas puffed up. He was very sensitive to Armen's opinion because in his mind Armen occupied the place of the grandfather he had never known. The spaniel kept on jumping and yelping around them. Armen put the child down, leaned over and petted the dog, scratching him behind the ears and pinching up his hide along his spine.

'You're also beautiful.'

'Have you seen my sailor's outfit?' asked Tomas turning around slowly. 'Mama sewed it.'

Armen showed his appreciation by fingering the material of the short, blue pants and jacket with the sailor collar. Lifting his eyes, he met Maro's sombre look. Tomas's carefree joy made the fear which was choking the adults more tangible. Armen took off his captain's cap and set it atop the boy's head, then he ran his fingers through his mop of silver hair.

The boy adjusted the cap. 'Is this for me?' he asked, thrilled.

'I'll lend it to you to wear on the way to church.'

'On the way back, too?' His godfather agreed. 'Look, Mama, I'm a captain.'

Maro kissed Tomas and handed him a package tied with a string. 'Your grandmother prepared some cold meat, olives and halva. You'll give them to the poor.'

She accompanied them to the iron gate. As always, she was uneasy at letting her son go, but she told herself not to be foolish and upset him by forbidding him to go on the outing. She had one last recommendation for them, 'Be careful and you, Tomas, you obey your godfather.' Restraining the dog, which wanted to follow his master, Maro watched the two walk away hand in hand.

They walked slowly down the street on the scorching hot stones, taking advantage of the shade from the wall and the overhanging branches. The imposing houses of the Balians' neighbours gave way to smaller and meaner dwellings the farther away they went. Tomas knew not only all the children in the neighbourhood, as he often played with them, but also their parents and even their grandparents. He waved to those he saw playing in the courtyards and wondered why they weren't chasing each other and screaming in the streets as usual. In fact the street was almost deserted. The few well-established shops – a grocer, a butcher, and a fruit vendor – were all closed. Further down in the commercial district, which was full of small stores and artisans' workshops, everything was strangely still. There were no stalls on the sides of the street nor on the corners. There were no hawkers, no gawkers, no porters carrying merchandise nor apprentices bossing them about. Even the café on the corner lacked its usual turnout of men smoking their *narghilés*,[1] playing *tavla*[2] or doing business. The chairs on the terrace had been turned upside-down on the tables. Vortik had closed the windows of his Kebab House, a famous restaurant, which was always full of businessmen celebrating the conclusion of a deal or of families joyously commemorating some anniversary. The sound of laughter and the smell of grilled meat was missing from the street.

'Is today Sunday?' asked Tomas.

'No,' his godfather replied. He didn't know exactly how much the child had been told about the calamity which had befallen the Armenians but it was not up to him to explain, so he preferred to change the subject and began to tell the boy about his adventures at sea and the storms he had weathered. Of course, he made most of it up but the geographical details were true. Through these fantastic fables he tried to teach his godson lessons about life. As soon as they could see the bell-tower which loomed over the houses, Armen dutifully started to repeat the new prayers which he had been teaching Tomas. As a godfather, it was his duty to give his godson religious instruction.

A grey wall enclosed Saint Minas, the Armenian church of rose-tinted marble built two centuries ago. The walls were decorated with *khachkars*,

---

1. Water pipes (Turkish).
2. Backgammon (Turkish).

49

crosses whose arms were decorated with scrolls carved in bas-relief. The church had an octagonal bell-tower with a pointed roof. It wasn't the largest church in Sivas but was one of the most influential, having many of the important people in the city among its parishioners. A few glossy-needled cypress trees were scattered across the churchyard where the parish beggars, mostly black-clad women, sat on the ground along the long entrance path, waiting for the faithful to walk by. Tomas made sure that the alms his family had given him were meted out justly. He stopped in front of an old hunch-backed woman who was next to last in the line, gave her the package his grandmother had prepared and recited the traditional formula, 'May this be of use to you.'

'May God answer all your prayers,' replied the toothless crone.

'Why did you pick her?' asked Armen as they went through the massive wooden portals.

'It was her turn. I know how to count,' murmured the child.

There were only a few old women kneeling at the front pews in the nave. Armen sat the child down there and told him to be good. 'Say the new prayer you're learning. I won't be long.'

'Where are you going, Godfather?'

'To see our priest, *Der*[1] Khoren.'

'Can't I come with you?'

'No. Sit still, wait and take good care of my cap.'

His godfather left through the little door leading to the sacristy and Tomas knelt down. He loved the calm coolness of this place and the smell of incense and burning candles. He let his eyes wander over the portraits of the saints hung on the side walls. Some looked severe but others like Sourp Hagop and Sourp Stepanos[2] had sweet expressions. The rays of sunshine picked up colours as they filtered through the stained-glass panes and lit up the icon of the Virgin on the altar. The sanctuary lamp sat in front of it – a low flame that slowly consumed the wick set in olive oil in a glass bowl.

Tomas had a strange feeling he couldn't explain. He had been looking forward to his birthday for months and he should have been feeling happy, but something undefined was spoiling his joy. It was like a nagging toothache that caused him to lose all interest in studying or playing. Nothing had changed yet nothing was the same. All those empty streets with the closed shops – the worried looks of the grown-ups even when they

---

1. Title for a married priest (Armenian).
2. St James and St Stephen (Armenian).

were smiling! In vain, he had questioned Jemila and Zeynep, the young servant girls. Downcast, they had turned away. What were they hiding from him? He didn't dare to ask his mother, father or grandmother. Maybe he would try his godfather after Mass.

He told himself that God was probably aware that he was present in the church and it was more than time to begin to pray. He folded his hands and, looking at the Child whom the Virgin held in her arms, he mentally went over the list of the people he would pray for.

In the sacristy, Der Khoren stopped in front of a group photograph of a past parish council. There were at least twenty of these pictures in frames encrusted with mother-of-pearl on two of the walls. The priest could remember each member of his church councils over the years. Several of them now slept under the cypress trees in the cemetery. He absent-mindedly caressed his grey beard, which hung down to his chest. The glass covering the photograph reflected a long oak table around which five still, silent men sat.

Haji Harout, the oldest of the parish elders, was seated at one end. The word *haji*, which had been added to his name, meant he had made the pilgrimage to Jerusalem and bathed in the River Jordan where John the Baptist had baptized Christ. Zaven, a rich landowner known for his integrity and generosity, sat on his right with his head lowered and his eyes closed as if he were napping. Ara, the barber, whose hair lotion perfumed the room, was staring at a lizard on the wall. He was thinking that, at the last meeting, the board had decided to repair the sacristy. Who cared about that today? On the other side of the table Sarkis Zorian, the teacher who also acted as the sacristan and deacon, was scribbling in his notebook. His immediate neighbour, Shirag Tevonian, whom Sarkis had taken the liberty of inviting to this especial meeting, didn't take his eyes off the priest.

Der Khoren ostentatiously turned his back on the table to emphasize his displeasure with Sarkis's initiative. He could not hide his astonishment – Shirag had no business being here.

The name Shirag Tevonian appeared on wanted posters in every police station in the region and here he was, daring to walk around in broad daylight in the city, even if in disguise most of the time! The priest had not expected this famous revolutionary to be so young. He looked more like an outlaw to him. No one knew what ideas and policies he preached or even if he had any! He had led armed actions against Ottoman troops and the authorities believed him to be a Russian agent. Whatever the man had done, Der Khoren believed, like many of his parishioners and especially Vartan, that the actions of the rebels discredited the Armenians in the eyes of the government and gave it an excuse to accuse them of being rebellious and harden their policy. But the priest knew that the teacher believed just the opposite, but now the argument had become pointless. If only Captain Armen would come so they could finish soon.

The priest approached the three pale wooden cabinets that lined the rear wall, opened the first one and took out the vestments he would wear to celebrate Mass. He felt Shirag Tevonian's eyes boring into his neck. The stare was so intense it made him uncomfortable. He felt Shirag was seeing through him and had discovered what he had been hiding from his wife and parishioners – total despair! But Der Khoren would not flinch; on the contrary, he would be an example of courage to his flock. He would preach hope and perseverance, but his words would sound hollow to him. He was obsessed by the words of Christ, 'Father, take this chalice from me.' Today God was offering a chalice not to his Son but to a whole people – to the mothers, the peasants, the merchants, the artisans. Had He turned away from the Armenians who venerated His Name? Was He still in need of martyrs? The priest considered his thoughts blasphemous and pushed them away, repeating to himself, 'Your Will be done. Take me but spare the others.'

Der Khoren had dreamt of studying in the seminary in Jerusalem to become a *vartabed*.[1] His father, who had been a watchmaker in Yozgat, approved the calling of the eldest of his seven children but, as the time of leaving approached, Khoren's resolution weakened. His feelings for his neighbour, Mariam, made him question the future he had planned. Finally he decided to marry her thus reconciling his love of God with his love for a woman, a fact that would keep him from rising in the hierarchy of the Armenian Apostolic Church and condemn him to be a *kahana*, a married parish priest, all of his life.

As he opened the door, Armen Surmelian was surprised to see only a few members of the parish council present. He checked his watch but he was only five minutes late. The meeting had been announced only one hour before which might explain the absences. Armen was an active member of

---

1.   A celibate priest (Armenian).

the council and, although he sometimes reacted impetuously and said things without thinking, his opinion was highly respected.

He walked around the table kissing everyone and shaking hands. He couldn't believe his eyes – Shirag Tevonian! His name was legendary in the region. This young rebel and his men, who called themselves the Brave Ones, had performed great feats in protecting the villages which were near the front line from groups of pillaging Ottoman deserters. Many stories were going around about Shirag's adventures – attacks against army convoys, battles against bands of brigands, rescues of endangered Armenians. Some of these were undoubtedly exaggerated. Each teller of tales was expected to embellish reality, add details and modify a sometimes trite ending, but the stories were based on real events. Armen admired and approved of these young resistance fighters.

Born in Diyarbekir, the black-basalt-walled town that overhung the Tigris just north of the Syrian desert, Shirag had, in the spring of 1910 left the workshop where his father hammered and engraved copper. He was then aged nineteen. He had dreamt of a different future, of an exciting life, of glory if possible. He had wanted to dedicate himself entirely to the cause of his people.

Armen sat down opposite Shirag but near enough to keep him always in sight. Shirag was physically unassuming – tall, thin faced, with slicked-back hair and a long moustache that curled up at the ends. He could have passed for a shepherd because of his tanned skin but his eyes burned with inner fire and his tense, bony body gave the impression of a stretched-out coil, which would snap with the slightest touch at any moment.

Der Khoren sat down at the head of the table facing Haji Harout. There was no point in mentioning the reason for the meeting since only one thing worried them. They looked at one another. Who would be the first to break the ice?

It was usual for the priest to open the meeting with an invocation to the Holy Spirit and for the teacher to read the agenda, but now Der Khoren waited, tight-lipped, putting off telling them what the Reverend Roesler, the Protestant minister, had told him as long as possible. Sarkis Zorian seemed absorbed, staring at the scribbles that covered the page in his notebook, so all eyes turned to Haji Harout, the president of the council. The old man was sitting on the edge of his chair, rocking back and forth, both hands on the knob of his cane. He had a small cross tattooed on his left forearm which identified him as a *haji*. Since he was almost blind, he didn't realize

53

that he had become the centre of attention. Everyone expected Shirag to begin to speak but he remained silent as he preferred for the others to express their opinions first so that he could judge where they stood. The silence became heavier.

Captain Armen found it ridiculous. He cracked his knuckles, leaned forward and looked around. 'Well, since no one seems to have anything to say, let's declare this meeting closed and go directly in to pray,' he said, trying to be funny. Nobody said a word so he continued, 'If it's the word 'deportation' or the word 'relocation' that is frightening you, well, I've said them! What are we going to do about it?' Armen looked at Shirag questioningly but the young man remained impassive.

Zaven put his left elbow on the table and cleared his throat. He had always felt himself to be lord and master of the land on the banks of the River Halys, which his family had held since time immemorial, and he could not conceive that anyone could dislodge him. Money could fix anything. 'We're really worrying about nothing. This deportation order is just a way to intimidate us. They want to scare us so they can levy another tax on Christians, which we'll pay, glad to have got away so easily. I'll pay for those families that aren't able to.'

He endured Armen's and the teacher's disapproving looks but Der Khoren was moved by such wishful thinking . . . this grasping at a thin thread of hope. This had been the reaction of most of the parishioners whom he had encountered this morning and he shuddered at the thought of having to disillusion them.

Ara scratched the kinky, short hair behind his wide, receding hairline. His Adam's apple moved up and down. 'I don't agree with Zaven. We have no proof whatsoever that they'll apply the deportation order in Sivas. Besides, there are thirty thousand of us.'

'And just exactly what makes you think that?' asked Armen sarcastically.

Ara, who was still called the Barber of Kochkiri even though he had left that village more than ten years ago to install himself in Sivas, had a lot of Muslims for customers. 'We have too many Turkish friends. They won't allow it. It would impoverish the town . . . the province, and they know it.'

'That's true,' added Zaven. 'The bigger part of the economy of the province is supported by us. Even if they're lacking in charity, they are intelligent. They will help us out of self-interest.'

Exasperated, Armen slapped the table with the palm of his left hand, 'Do you really think that would stop them? You have a short memory. Do I have to recite the litany of injustices and calamities they have inflicted on us in the last few years?'

Shirag made an almost imperceptible gesture of agreement, which flattered the captain.

Zaven shrugged. 'They have always vexed our people but we're still here.'

'Vexed!' shouted the teacher furiously. 'Thirty thousand dead in Adana in 1909, three hundred thousand victims in '94 and '95. You call that being vexed!'

Zaven bowed his head piously. Waving his hands, the priest tried to calm them down. He felt guilty letting his friends squabble like this instead of telling them the whole truth.

Ara temporized, 'They've assured us the move is only temporary and that . . .'

The teacher cut him short, '. . . and that we shall be installed in new villages? I've studied the maps. Do you want to know where they intend to move us? To the noxious swamps on the banks of the Euphrates River or to the Syrian Desert, a place even the Bedouins avoid, so stop talking about deportation.'

Sarkis Zorian had been informed of the situation just an hour before the meeting. One of his brothers was a member of the Brave Ones and Shirag Tevonian had sent him to ask the teacher for help. Sarkis shared the rebel chief's point of view and supported his plans. He was the father of eleven children ranging in age from four months to fifteen years and he couldn't bear to think of them in one of the death caravans described by Shirag. He did not want any of his pupils to undergo this experience either. Shirag's words still rang in his ears: 'Deportations have already started all over the place. They are nothing but a pretext for killing. The government never had any intention of moving and resettling the Armenians.'

Rubbing the stump of his arm, Zaven again coughed softly and said, 'Haji Harout, you are a personal friend of the governor, Mumtaz Bey. He has always been well-disposed towards the Armenians. Couldn't you go and see him?'

The wrinkles on the old man's face became deeper. The pointed ends of his tobacco-stained moustache rose. He spoke slowly, giving the impression that he was carefully considering his words, 'Times have changed, my poor Zaven. Mumtaz Bey has been pushed aside and is not able to act.'

'And Fakri Pasha?' asked Zaven, almost imploringly. 'He's a good, just man.'

'The pasha has enough to do just commanding the troops in the field. He gets his orders from Constantinople and he'd like to keep his rank of general.' Haji Harout sighed deeply and added, exhausted, 'Friends, let's face it. We are alone . . . all alone.'

Ara made a sign that he wanted to speak. Having thought it over, he had decided to abandon his optimistic stance. 'Unfortunately, Haji Harout is right. My friend Hassan, the barber-circumciser, tells me there are a lot of new faces in town . . . agitators who have arrived from the capital. Everyone's worried. Nobody trusts anybody. According to official orders, Muslims who hide Armenians will be punished.'

Armen observed the others. Ara and Zaven looked sombre and worried. Haji Harout seemed lost in a sad dream, which was understandable; but the attitude of the priest and the teacher perplexed him. Der Khoren's fleeting glances made him look like a child getting ready to confess to misbehaving. As to Sarkis Zorian, who was usually so calm and composed, he was squirming in his chair as if he were expecting something unpleasant to happen.

These two must be hiding something, so Armen spoke directly to them, 'Has anyone anything new to tell us?'

'I do,' answered Shirag Tevonian. 'I have something to say.'

Der Khoren nodded. Shirag pulled himself up to the table, propped himself on his elbows, and, for a quarter of an hour, he described the drama that the Armenians in most of Anatolia were going through – villages destroyed, long columns of deportees marching for days without food or water. He gave a profusion of details. His voice shook with contained rage. Tears spilled down the faces of his shocked listeners. Every once in a while a choked voice uttered an expression of disgust or fury. In spite of his grief, the priest was relieved that he was not the one having to tell them this horrible story. When the young man fell silent, everyone was totally shattered.

'God has abandoned us,' murmured the barber gloomily.

'Ara. Ara.' The priest reprimanded him gently but the same thought had occurred to him.

'It's true,' shouted Ara. 'Why does He allow this? And you, His priest, what do you suggest we do? Pray?'

Haji Harout struck his cane on the corner of the table. 'Ara, that's no way to talk to your priest. If you don't have anything constructive to say, keep quiet.'

'And you, Haji,' asked the barber bitterly, 'what do you suggest?'

The old man didn't respond.

Ara burst into sobs, 'I have six children.'

'Children or grandchildren – we all have them,' said Captain Armen.

The legs of the chair squeaked on the floor-boards as Sarkis Zorian pushed his chair away from the table. There was a strange gleam in his eyes as he declared solemnly, 'We have to resist for the sake of our children, for the old people, for our women.'

The priest, the barber, Haji Harout and Zaven looked at him incredulously.

Armen, happy that someone had come forward with an idea that could lead to concrete action, said, 'Resist? Tell us how.'

'It's Shirag Tevonian's idea. Let's listen to him.'

Shirag began to pace around the table. His thin face and body and his intense expression made him look older than his twenty-five years and imbued him with a kind of authority. He was not going to expose his plans for the liberation of all Armenia to these simple men who understood nothing of politics. They were capable of understanding only what affected them directly. He became impassioned as he spoke. 'Everything is not lost in Sivas. We have to organize a defence for the Armenian Quarter, put up barricades, take up arms. My men and I will help you. They've already begun to infiltrate the town.'

Armen rubbed his chin as he weighed their chances. 'What about arms?'

Zaven interrupted him, 'This is completely crazy!'

Aggressively, the teacher turned to the rich farmer, 'What would you have us do? Buy our way out and convert to Islam to save our skins?'

Zaven's round face turned purple. He shook his fist in Sarkis's face and screamed, 'I forbid you to talk like that. I don't know what's keeping me from . . .'

'My sons! My sons!' said the priest. 'This is no time to squabble.'

The teacher sat down and Zaven took a deep breath to get hold of himself again.

'I understand Zaven's reaction,' said the priest, 'but he's right. He just put it badly. Resisting is foolish.'

Haji Harout and Zaven agreed with the priest. Ara seemed to be in another world and didn't react at all.

'Foolish or not,' said Captain Armen in a voice of authority, 'we have no right to reject this proposal out of hand. We must discuss it.'

'That sounds reasonable,' said the teacher.

'Think,' the priest protested. 'Violence only breeds violence. If we rebel, we shall only confirm that we are enemies of the Empire. We'll play right into their hands and the army will crush us.'

Shirag stopped behind Haji Harout and put his hands on the back of the old man's chair. 'Father,' he said, 'it is the beginning of the Apocalypse. No matter what you do or don't do, you'll be chased from here in a few days. The troops are already on their way to Sivas to escort you to hell.'

'Hell is right,' said the priest, 'and won't it become hell here anyway? A long siege ... many wounded ... many dead ... much famine and disease. Think of the women and children.'

'That would still be better than deportation,' said the teacher in a sombre tone. 'I'd rather see my children die from a bullet in front of my own eyes than know they are lost on the roads, dying of hunger, thirst and exhaustion.'

'You're wrong,' replied the priest energetically. 'The retaliations that would follow a rebellion would be so awful that not one of us would survive. It would mean the total annihilation of the Armenians in Sivas. Even if the conditions of the deportation are inhuman, not all will die. Wouldn't you rather know that some of your children would live to remember you?'

The teacher thought it over. Both he and Armen had been shaken by the priest's argument.

Der Khoren continued in a hoarse voice, this time addressing all those assembled in the room. The words he spoke scorched his throat. 'It's clear to me they want to destroy our people. The only question now is how to survive at any price. Our seed must not disappear if we want another harvest.'

'Der Khoren!' shouted Haji Harout outraged. 'You? Preaching apostasy? The life of our souls means more than that of our bodies. I would rather follow the example of Sourp Hripsimé and Sourp Gayané[1] than deny the Gospels.'

'When heaven is full of Armenian martyrs, who shall preach of God, Jesus Christ, and the Virgin in Anatolia?'

---

1.    Two martyred Armenian saints.

'You're very pessimistic, Der Khoren,' said Haji Harout, turning to Shirag. 'I prefer the proposals of this young man.'

Feeling strengthened by these encouraging words, Shirag began to walk up and down, waving his arms. He smiled faintly as if to reassure himself. 'My friend, Sarkis Zorian, is ready to fight to the last Armenian in Sivas. Der Khoren already sees us being converted *en masse*.' He did not wait for the two men he had mentioned to protest and continued, 'I'm surprised that it hasn't occurred to either of you two that we could win. Armenians have resisted in other places and won.'

'Perhaps,' said Der Khoren in a mournful voice, 'but it must have been by a miracle.'

Captain Armen pounded his fist into the palm of his other hand. 'It wasn't a miracle. God helps those who help themselves. Think of the Zeytounites.[1] Shirag is right. We must not let ourselves be slaughtered like sheep.'

Shirag went on eagerly, 'We can win! In the village of Van the villagers held the Ottoman troops and mercenaries off for a month until the Russians came to their aid. Now they are free! There will be no deportations in Van!'

Haji Harout remained unconvinced and shook his head, 'It's a long way to Russia. How many kilometres would you say, Sarkis?'

'More than six hundred,' said the teacher annoyed at the question.

Zaven shrugged his shoulders, 'Hmph. And from what I hear, they're already retreating from the Ottomans.'

'Then we shall do it alone,' replied Shirag. 'I have many Brave Ones in this region. We shall concentrate here. We have arms and courage, but we need everyone's support. It's up to you, the elders, to convince them.'

'Of what?' exploded the priest. 'Of becoming cannon fodder for the army?'

Armen was trying to get an idea of which course to follow. There were so many things to consider – food, medicine, shelter from mortar shells, which street to block, where to post the men. Every time he thought he had found a solution, new problems came to mind. The Quarter was wide-open. It would be difficult to defend. A doubt he tried to push away nagged him.

'The fact is we have no arms,' he said, as if answering his own misgivings. 'I'm not talking about machine-guns and cannon; we don't even have any rifles.'

Shirag had a ready answer, 'The army has a big munitions depot here.

---

1.  Inhabitants of Zeytoun who resisted the massacres of 1895.

We shall attack the arsenal to get weapons. The factor of surprise should favour us.'

'Major Vartan can help us out. He knows the grounds well.'

Shirag looked annoyed at the mention of Vartan's name. Only a few hours ago, disguised as a *mullah*, he had been to Major Vartan's hospital tent on the outskirts of Sivas to explain the plan to him and to convince the major to help the *fedayis* organize a general uprising of all the Armenians in Anatolia. Despite Shirag's persuasive arguments and exaggeration of Vartan's reputation as a political leader, his words had had no effect on him. Vartan had recognized in Shirag the fiery, enthusiastic young man he had once been himself, and it horrified him. He had tried to convince this young revolutionary that an uprising on the scale that he was proposing would be suicidal and outrageously naive – any ill-conceived action would be like putting a match to a powder-keg. There were strong contingents of the Ottoman army everywhere.

Armen immediately perceived this and it gave him food for thought. He insisted, 'We truly need Major Vartan. Only he can tell us if we have any chance of success.'

'We have no time to go around asking everyone's opinion, major or not. We have to make our plans and take action immediately.'

Shirag's blunt statement made Armen even more suspicious and he kept out of the ensuing uproar.

'Every minute counts,' stated Sarkis Zorian. 'Here is what we shall do.' He pulled a sheet of paper out of his pocket and smoothed it out on the table with the palm of his hand. It was a map of the area surrounding the arsenal, which he had drawn himself. Shirag Tevonian leaned over his shoulder.

'Come here,' said the teacher to the others.

Haji Harout raised his index finger to indicate that they should remain seated. His hands were shaking but his voice had lost its usual quaver. He addressed Sarkis and Shirag, 'First, answer one question. Even if we hold out for two or three months, where will it get us?'

Shirag and Sarkis looked at each other trying to find an answer. The old man went on, ' Nobody is going to come to our aid when we run out of food and ammunition. The Russian army has been stopped; the French and the English are far away; we are forsaken and surrounded.' Haji Harout's words acted like a bucket of cold water on the Council.

Trying to keep the impatience out of his voice, the teacher continued in the tone he used when his students didn't understand something obvious, 'Let's take stock. Do you have any other solution, Haji Harout?'

'None,' admitted the old man, 'I'm not saying you're wrong, but you're rushing things and that worries me.'

The old man had just put Armen's thoughts into words and he added, 'A few hours more or less won't make that much difference. All this needs to be thought over. We have to consult the Grand Council of Sivas.'

'I agree with Captain Armen,' said Zaven.

'I also agree with Zaven and Captain Armen,' said Der Khoren. 'We have to consult with the priests of other parishes and hear what they have to say. They, like Major Vartan, might have more information than we do.'

'More shilly-shallying,' grumbled the teacher, who felt the need for action.

'You really can't expect us seven to take such a decision upon ourselves,' Armen exclaimed, astounded. 'By what right?'

Sarkis had always preached democracy and was disconcerted by Armen's question. He grimaced, shook his head and fell back on his chair.

Finding himself alone, Shirag clenched his fists. 'And now, what?' he asked, searching the faces turned to him.

Haji Harout also looked at the others but he knew them well enough to know that they had reached an agreement even though nothing had been said.

'We shall call the Grand Council of Sivas and the important people in town to a meeting this afternoon. In the meantime, we shall pray to the Lord to enlighten us.' Holding on to the back of his chair and leaning on his cane, he rose with difficulty, thus signalling the end of the session.

Shirag nodded at him. He felt no rancour towards them, only a great pity. 'I know what I have to do,' he said, as he walked towards the door that led to the cemetery. Sarkis moved as if to follow him, but Shirag stopped him. 'Let's not change anything we've agreed on. I'll wait for the Mass to end.'

The teacher approached Der Khoren and helped him put on his chasuble. 'I hope we won't regret this decision,' he murmured. No one had an answer.

While waiting for Armen, Tomas had gone up to the sandbox that held the candles and was amusing himself by snuffing out those that were guttering.

When he saw his godfather come out of the sacristy, he hurried back to the bench, hiding his wax-encrusted fingers. He was the only child sitting in the men's section on the right side of the aisle. All the other children sat in the women's section on the left. Captain Armen knelt down next to him and covered his face to withdraw from the world. Tomas let his mind wander, searching for images of legendary animals in the dark spots on the floor slabs.

Armen felt impotent and could not pray. The carnage that Shirag had talked about had revived long-forgotten memories – the unleashed violence and cruelty of the mob, the gutted bodies of children . . . His life was almost over and he would have voluntarily sacrificed what was left of it to save the young ones, those whom Der Khoren had called the seed of the future. The more he thought about it the more he was convinced that Shirag's and Sarkis's plan was unworkable and nothing new would come out of the meeting of the notables of Sivas. What he found most demoralizing was Der Khoren's discouragement . . . his resignation . . . the every-man-for-himself attitude that could be inferred from his words. It was so unlike him – he who had always shown such faith and force of character that one thought he could withstand anything.

The church was crowded, which was unusual for a weekday Mass. Men who had closed their shops as well as women and children were there. They were hoping for the reassurance of prayer, feeling that by rubbing elbows they could draw the strength they needed from each other.

Eight of Shirag's men sat on the last bench; another one was keeping a look-out in the cemetery, and the tenth one was posted in the bell tower. They had infiltrated Sivas under the cover of darkness and had hidden themselves in safe houses where they had left their rifles and cartridge belts. Now they carried only pistols, which they had secreted under their clothes. The rest of the band would join them at nightfall. Some were praying, others napping.

Shirag came around and entered the church. He sat down in a dark corner in the back where the choir sat on Sunday and looked the congregation over – the men's bare heads, the women's heads covered by scarves, the children's heads in constant motion, the sagging shoulders, the submissive shapes. He realized for the first time just how much he loved these people . . . his people. Up to now he had fought for his ideals, for an abstract cause; the people had been less important to him than his goal. He had lied when he left the sacristy; he wasn't all that sure about what he should do. He had doubts about his resistance plan, which no one had accepted. He was expecting a miracle to happen during this religious office ... an inspiration, even a revelation to take place. Snatches of a prayer from his childhood came back to him and he recited it inwardly.

Der Khoren made his entrance wearing a *saghavart*,[1] followed by Sarkis Zorian, the deacon, and an altar boy wearing albs in the same deep red as the priest's chasuble, which was richly embroidered with flowers and crosses in gold. A long stole, the *ourar*, lay on the teacher's shoulder, symbolizing his status as deacon.

The priest swung the censer, paused at the dais on which the altar was placed and began a monotonous chant; the congregation took it up in unison. At first his voice was shaky but gradually it grew steadier as he recovered his trust in his Creator. He submitted himself unreservedly to His Will. He could not help though thinking that the Eucharist he was about to celebrate was a commemoration of the Last Supper before the Crucifixion. Der Khoren went up the steps to the altar where a dozen candles symbolizing the twelve apostles burned. The altar boy closed the crimson velvet drapes embroidered with large golden crosses that were used to conceal the altar while the priest prepared it. On their own initiative, three cantors went behind the balustrade and took their places a little to the back of the choir. They were going to chant, although they usually sang in the choir only on Sunday since they worked during the week. Someone sat down at the harmonium and the ceremony began to look like High Mass.

Sarkis began to read the day's Gospel at the lectern. By chance, it was a passage from Saint Matthew that told of the beheading of John the Baptist, who was depicted baptizing Christ in a painting that hung next to the altar. Some of the congregation saw the choice of passage as a dire omen.

Shirag, however, drew inspiration from it. It was a fit slaying! And he too was going to become executioner: he would behead the serpent, symbol of the Ottoman administration. The deacon had just finished reading the words 'His head was brought in on a platter' when a cry was heard from the back of the church: 'The *zaptiyés*[2] have surrounded the church!'

Maro was at a loose end. The children to whom she gave free French and

---

1.   A round headpiece worn by an Armenian priest (Armenian).
2.   Gendarmes (Turkish).

piano lessons had not come yesterday as their parents had not dared to let them go out by themselves. It was going to be the same today. It was just as well as she was in no mood to give lessons.

Zeynep and Jemila were polishing the parquet floor in the dining-room, humming a lively air from their village. They had heard the town crier announce the deportation of the Armenians and the comments of the Turkish merchants in the market to their customers. Zeynep and Jemila wondered why anyone would want to harm these people, whom they found to be most hospitable and peace-loving. All they wanted was for the Balian family to stay in Sivas and they preferred not to think about the rest of the Armenians.

Maro found her mother sitting at the kitchen table, which was used to prepare the food. She was skilfully cutting up a whole lamb. There was a small cup half-filled with a blackish liquid next to her. She sipped many cups of coffee during the day and never felt the least discomfort. That and the snuff she sniffed all day long were the only luxuries she indulged in. Otherwise she lived a rather austere life, although she encouraged her family to enjoy all the good things the Lord provided. During the forty days of Lent, which she observed in the strictest manner, she rarely ate meat and was satisfied with bread, cheese, vegetables and yoghurt, but she was always happy to cook elaborate meals for her son-in-law, her daughter and her grandson.

Maro offered to help.

'No, no,' said her mother absent-mindedly. 'You have other things to do. I can get along fine with the two servants.'

Despite the smile and the pleasant tone, Maro felt dismissed. When widowed mothers went to live with one of their children, they considered it their duty to run the household, be it of their son or son-in-law. Azniv Hanim was no exception to the rule and it had led to a latent conflict with her daughter, who had been brought up in the Western way. Maro thought the tradition ridiculous. Perhaps it was all right in a rich Muslim household where someone had to referee rivalries between several wives, treat the brood of half-brothers and half-sisters with fairness and plan the work of a mob of servants.

Maro and Vartan had not wanted a big staff in their house, not for reasons of economy but because they wanted to have a little privacy. Two extra house-maids came for a few days a week and a laundress and her daughter did the laundry on Fridays.

Maro went up to the stoneware water filter by the damp wall, put her glass under the faucet, drank two glassfuls and planted herself in front of her mother. She wanted to stress that she was mistress of the house. 'Don't forget we have guests tonight, Captain Armen and his wife.'

'Everything has already been taken care of.'

'I want the table to look festive – the embroidered linen table cloth, the good silver, the blue porcelain china. We'll open the bottle of Burgundy that I brought back from France.'

Azniv Hanim frowned and raised her voice, 'Don't you think you're overdoing it under the circumstances?'

'On the contrary. One must keep one's head high in adversity.'

'What are you expecting to do? Exorcise bad luck?' Azniv Hanim shrugged ironically.

Maro pulled up a chair and sat down. On any other occasion she would have answered her mother respectfully but firmly that she was no longer a little girl to be told how to behave and Azniv Hanim would have argued with her before giving in. This had become almost a ritual between them since her daughter's adolescence.

Maro sighed and said in a low voice, 'Do you think I feel like celebrating any more than you do? But Tomas is six years old today and I want him to have a happy memory. It's bad enough that we had to cancel the party for all his friends.'

Azniv Hanim nodded. Everything was different when it concerned her only grandson. She, who had raised Maro very strictly, gave in to all of Tomas's whims.

'Have you told him what's happening?' she asked.

'No.'

'You should. The child is so sensitive he surely feels our anxiety. It would be better if he knew the truth.'

'Tomorrow, after his party.'

Sassoun came into the kitchen, attracted by the smell of the meat, and sat down under the table against Maro's legs. She patted him on the head mechanically, her eyes lost in the distance.

'Make us some coffee,' suggested Azniv Hanim.

Maro mixed the ground coffee and water in a *jezvé*[1] and set it on an alcohol burner. When the brew was about to boil over, she filled two small cups with pitch-black coffee. Her eyes wandered over the walls where a

---

1.   A small pot with a long handle used for brewing coffee (Turkish).

battery of copper pots and cast-iron pans were hanging and stopped at the majestic coal-burning stove, which occupied the entire wall under a masonry hood. A sad look came over her face and she murmured, 'We should never have come here, to live in the middle of nowhere.'

'Just remember that a woman has to follow her husband, for better or worse.'

'We should have returned to Constantinople two years ago when Vartan was offered the position of Professor of Political Science at Robert College.'

'He probably had good reasons to refuse.'

Maro's hand shook slightly as she lifted the cup to her lips, and Azniv Hanim added, 'And who can say if we would be any safer in the capital. We don't know what's going on there. Vartan would probably have been arrested along with the others last April.'

Maro grasped her mother's arms, '*Mayrig*, I'm afraid.'

The tense face of the old woman crumpled. She put the knife down and dried her hands on her apron. Her voice cracked, 'I am, too, Maro *jan*.[1] Oh, not for myself. I've lived my life. I'm ready to join your father before God, but for the three of you, I tremble.'

She took her weeping daughter in her arms and let her cry, stroking her hair; Maro would always be her little girl. Gradually she stopped sobbing as she had done when her mother had consoled her in her childish sorrows.

The old woman had collected herself again. 'They call us the weaker sex, but we aren't. A woman possesses an infinite reserve of force and courage and a man often has to draw from it.' Maro nodded; she felt reassured. 'Vartan must be able to count on you and you have to give him confidence. He is clear-sighted and resourceful. Besides, he's thinking of how to get us out of Sivas.'

'Did he tell you that?' Maro was surprised that he hadn't told her of his plans.

'No, he just asked me if we had enough provisions for a trip of several days and I drew my own conclusions.'

'I hope you're right and the sooner, the better. I imagine he'll have to get an authorization for a transfer and that will take several days and several bottles of brandy. You know government employees.'

'You're wrong, *Mayrig*. Vartan is stationed here. He would need permission from the high command. I don't believe he's thinking about leaving openly.'

---

1. My darling or my soul (Armenian).

'You mean . . .?'

'Fleeing, and I'm ready.'

Azniv Hanim was worried; she was slowly realizing the implications and consequences of such a decision.

'If we get away from here, I'll never come back,' answered Maro in a decisive tone.

'We have invested a good part of your inheritance from your father in this house.'

'That's too bad. We'll get by. First, we have to save our skins.'

Her mother thought it over while looking at the dregs of the coffee grounds in her cup. Losing the fortune that this house represented was not the end of the world because Vartan and his brother had Swiss bank accounts and a business in New York, but should they give it up? Such a venture in time of war! Were they acting too hastily?

The church bells started ringing and Maro realized that Tomas and his godfather were late coming back.

'Those are the bells of Saint Minas,' said Azniv Hanim, straining her ears. The quick, urgent ringing of the bells lasted a long time and took on a sinister sound.

'Something is happening,' said Maro, jumping up and running towards the door.

'Maro, wait for me,' cried Azniv Hanim. But her daughter was out and running with all her might.

Sarkis Zorian, the teacher, stopped and stood still for a few seconds with his mouth agape before closing the Holy Book. The Gospel would not be read to the end. The lookout, after having given the alarm, was now ringing the bells to warn the inhabitants of the Quarter. Shirag and his men were standing in the aisle, revolvers in hand. One of them had probably been recognized and followed, or one of their own had denounced the others in hope of getting clemency for himself and his family.

'Shirag,' called the priest. The rebel chief who was giving orders to his men turned. The priest had his arms slightly open and was pointing to his terrified flock. Shirag understood: he was not to endanger the lives of these innocents.

67

'Is there a tunnel or passageway we can use to escape, or a crypt where we can hide?'

The priest stepped down from the altar, shaking his head.

'I shall not surrender!' declared Shirag, brandishing his pistol.

'I certainly didn't expect this,' said Der Khoren, walking down the aisle rapidly. The sobbing women turned their faces towards him, pleading. He tried to reassure his flock and his resolute attitude calmed some of them down. 'I'll go out and talk with them. Don't do anything rash while I'm gone,' he said, walking away.

The gold-glittering robe rippled at each step. He looked impressive and imposing enough to stand up to the gendarmes. Two of the rebels opened one of the panels of the door slightly and the priest stepped out. The other rebels stationed themselves near the high openings in the bell tower and the windows of the sacristy.

Armen took out the pistol he had hidden in his belt. He started to step out into the aisle, but Tomas held him back by his coat-tails. 'I'm frightened, Godfather. Don't leave me.'

The child's terror had nothing to do with the guns; those he was used to. Vartan often took him behind a small hill on Sundays to teach him how to manage arms and shoot a gun, as Vartan himself had been shown before he had learned to read and write. Tomas didn't understand too well what was going on, but he could see that everyone in the church was trembling. Their terror was contagious. Even his godfather looked tense.

'Why are the *zaptiyés* out there?' Armen, who was staring at the back door of the church, didn't answer. 'Are they going to attack us?'

Armen slipped the weapon under his jacket, sat down again, and leaned towards his godson. 'No,' he answered in a low voice. 'Well, maybe yes, but don't be afraid. I'm here. Whatever happens, do exactly what I tell you. If I say lie down, throw yourself flat on your stomach on the ground. If I say run, run without bothering about me. Understood?'

'Yes, Godfather.'

'And if we become separated, go straight home without trying to find me.'

Armen's firm, kind voice partially reassured Tomas who, with frightened eyes, was following the slightest movements of Shirag's men. 'Who are they?'

'Armenian braves!'

The tension was growing in the nave. Sobs could be heard above the hum

68

of voices. Some were talking about going out as they had nothing to hide, thus, nothing to fear from the gendarmes. A woman called out, 'Let the rebels surrender. We have nothing to do with all this.'

This created an uproar. Arguments leaped from pew to pew. For a few moments Sarkis Zorian feared there would be a riot. Something had to be done to keep them busy until Der Khoren returned.

Suddenly he remembered that he was the deacon. 'We shall confess our sins,' he shouted, attempting to master the mob. He had to repeat the phrase until the uproar quieted. One by one the people knelt down for a mass confession and the litany began – 'Forgive me my sins, Oh Lord' – after each phrase as the deacon enumerated all the sins a Christian could commit.

All heads turned to the back as Der Khoren returned. He ordered them to remain kneeling, saying, 'I'm going to give you absolution.'

But the worshippers were so impatient and worried that they rose and some even forgot to cross themselves after the priest's blessing.

Der Khoren turned to Shirag, 'The officer has been kind enough not to take us all prisoners, but he's determined to capture you. You and your men should surrender. You are surrounded.'

'That's out of the question!'

'My poor child.'

'You're all to be pitied as much as we,' replied Shirag.

Der Khoren addressed his flock, 'I've convinced the officer to let us go. March in a single file behind me holding your hands over your heads. Stay calm, don't start running when you get outside, and obey the gendarmes.'

Der Khoren gestured for them to follow him and led them out. The pews emptied in no time. The people jostled each other in the aisles. A bottleneck formed in front of the door as only one of the door panels was open. Shirag slowed them down and lined them up, not letting more than one or two people pass through at a time. The weeping women thanked him and those who were old enough to be his mother looked at him affectionately. Still in his deacon's robe, Sarkis Zorian brought up the end of the procession. Armen was walking just in front of him with Tomas, who, obeying the priest's orders, held his arms above his head.

'Not yet, Tomas. Only after we have passed the portal.' Armen emptied the chamber of his revolver and handed the bullets to Shirag.

Sarkis embraced the rebel chief and said, 'I'll look for your men at the agreed meeting place tonight. If you can hold out until then, we'll take the soldiers by surprise but . . .' He hesitated to mention the other possibility.

Shirag shrugged his shoulders. 'Otherwise, do your best. Try to save your skin.' He pushed them firmly towards the door.

Armen was blinded by the bright sunlight, which was flooding the entrance steps as he came out from the dark interior of the church; he shaded his eyes with his hand.

'Hands up!' screamed a voice in Turkish. 'Move on faster! Faster!'

The door closed behind them and the bolts squeaked. Tomas was walking so fast that his godfather had to lengthen his steps to keep up with him. Dozens of soldiers had taken cover behind the walls that encircled the church. Others clustered on both sides of the iron gate, where a captain carefully scrutinized the faces of each of the faithful before letting them through.

'Move on! Go home! Go! Faster! Move on!'

Everyone started to run except the old ones who were dragging their feet, to the jeers of the laughing gendarmes. Curious onlookers had gathered around the square and in the nearby streets.

When Armen came up to the officer, he saw that there were six soldiers surrounding about sixteen Armenians behind the wall. Except for the priest, they were all of an age to bear arms. Perhaps the gendarmes were afraid the Brave Ones were among them. Armen wanted to protest that they were innocent but Der Khoren waved him on. Thinking of his godson who was pulling him by the hand, the captain kept going, despair in his soul.

'We don't run,' he ordered Tomas. 'March proudly.'

Armen could not keep himself from looking back. The teacher was joining the other prisoners.

'Warn my wife,' shouted Sarkis to Armen as a slap from one of the military brought him to order.

Once they had crossed the square, Armen stopped just before the house on the corner blocked his view. A lieutenant, holding his hands in front of his mouth like a megaphone, was ordering the rebels to give up. Without waiting for an order, the gendarmes opened fire on the church. The stained-glass rosette window shattered and a salvo from the bell tower was the answer.

'Fire!' shouted the officer taking cover behind the wall.

Armen pushed Tomas into a side street as heavy firing burst out. The people who had come out of their houses called by the ringing of the bells quickly went back inside.

'Is this war?' asked Tomas as they hurried away. The streets were deserted except for a squad of soldiers who were climbing up to Saint Minas.

Then they saw a feminine silhouette running in their direction. 'It's mama,' cried Tomas, letting go of his godfather's hand and running to her.

Maro was breathless as she clasped her son to her. 'Thank God!' Sweat was pouring down her face and plastering her hair to her forehead and her chignon had come apart as she ran.

'Mama, there are soldiers shooting at the church and there are Brave Ones inside.'

'I know, I know, my darling. I'll explain it to you later.'

Armen caught up with them. Maro wanted to know what had happened, so he gave her a brief account.

'My God,' she said looking at the bell tower over the roofs. The crisp detonations of the rifles could be heard in the distance. After a few seconds of calm, there was sporadic shooting that sounded like crackling hail.

'Take Tomas home and don't leave the house again.'

Maro gripped Armen's jacket sleeve. 'Don't go back there. It's crazy.'

'I live on the other side of Saint Minas,' he said. 'I'll make a detour to avoid the square.'

She knew he was lying in order to reassure her. He was going to go back to see what was happening in the church.

'Fire only if you're sure you'll hit something. We're going to be short of ammunition,' cried Shirag. He came from the sacristy and ran across the nave to reach the bell tower. He was all over the place, encouraging his men and watching to see that they didn't waste any bullets. They had blocked the door to the sacristy with a table, a cupboard and some of the pews. They had a man posted at the small window which controlled the cemetery. Four others had posted themselves at the side windows of the nave and five of them were in the bell tower, which was the best spot for shooting.

Shirag knew they couldn't hold out for long, certainly not until evening. If only they had their rifles and well-filled cartridge belts. The pistols were short-range weapons and they had only thirty bullets, hardly enough to repel the first assault. Luckily the soldiers didn't know that and were prudently standing in the shelter of the surrounding wall. They were shooting haphazardly into the openings in the bell tower and through the windows of the church, which had lost their panes. Every once in a while they could hear the noise of a machine-gun hidden behind an overturned carriage in the middle of the square. Its chattering was answered by the muffled thuds on the massive wooden door, which was still holding, and by the clear tinkle of the bells as shots shattered against them.

'Shirag,' called someone from the bell tower. He rejoined his men who were plastered against the pillars that held up the roof. The shots, buzzing and ricocheting on the stone, whistled around them. Armenag, Zorian's cousin, was lying on his back, neatly killed by a bullet in the middle of his forehead. He had just turned nineteen. Shirag crawled over to him, closed his eyes and picked up his gun. The first one killed. Needlessly! Without glory! The dozen dead and wounded soldiers made no difference.

'We aren't going to get out of here,' said one of the men who had been grazed on the left shoulder by a bullet.

'You knew this was going to happen sooner or later,' responded Shirag with conviction.

'Yes, but not for nothing. I wanted my death to be worthwhile.' He summed up what everyone was thinking, including his chief.

'We're not dead yet,' exclaimed Shirag.

'Look!' cried a man pointing to the back of the church. 'Something is happening there.'

From the bell tower they could not see the encircling wall on the side of the choir, but the neighbouring street was swarming with more soldiers. Since there were no windows on that side of the church, the enemy could climb over the wall unscathed. They simply would have to reinforce the defence of the sacristy. Shirag slithered down the steps on all fours. As he was crossing the nave, an object hurled from the outside described a semi-circle and crashed on a pew with a metallic thud.

'I almost caught that in my face,' said a man posted at the window. 'What is it?'

When they reached the place where it had hit, Shirag recognized the smell of naphtha. It was a small square can that had a hole punched in its thin metal side and its contents were trickling out on the floor.

'They mean to roast us alive,' exclaimed Shirag. At that very moment another container landed in the aisle. 'Quickly! Up to the bell tower!' he ordered while he ran to fetch the lookout in the sacristy. Returning with him, he saw that more cans had been thrown into the nave. They had a difficult time breathing as the paraffin vapours made them giddy.

They had just reached the stairs to the bell tower when a grenade exploded, setting the gas on fire. A tremendous explosion shook the building. It blew the doors from their hinges and started the bells pealing.

Armen had taken cover at a house on the corner. From there he could see the square and the façade and side of the church. His heart almost stopped beating when he heard the explosion. Tongues of flames spurted out of the windows and doorway and were sucked in again, replaced by clouds of thick black smoke which soon poured out through the bell tower. Fire raged through the centre of the nave almost reached the ceiling.

The soldiers were cheering with joy and firing into the air instead of into the church. An officer ordered them to calm down and shouted, 'Give yourselves up. It's your last chance.'

Only the roaring of the growing fire could be heard. Then three men wrapped in swirls of smoke appeared on the front steps. The overexcited soldiers shot them down even though they had surrendered. Their bodies rolled down the steps.

'Idiots! Fools!' shouted the officer, flushed with fury. 'I'll shoot the next man who fires without my orders.'

A cry came from the church. 'We surrender. Don't shoot.'

'Come out.'

Some forms emerged from the smoky walls, two men supporting a semi-conscious Shirag. He was only slightly burned. His companion's burned body had served as a shield from the force of the explosion. He was in critical shape, unable to walk, and three Brave Ones were carrying him. The soldiers surrounded the rebels and marched them at bayonet point towards the cart where the wounded lay. They also threw in the corpses of the men who had been shot on the entrance steps.

Pillars of smoke continued to pour out of the openings in the church and intertwined above the roof, forming rope-like columns that rose in the warm air.

# THREE

Instead of the usual hustle and bustle, a feverish uncertainty prevailed in the Muslim Quarter of Sivas that afternoon.

'The Armenians did it!'

'First it was the mayor; next, it'll be us!'

'In a church! There were about fifty of them! Armed to the teeth! Ready to slit the throats of our women and children!'

'They say there are thousands of them, hiding in the hills! They'll surround the town!'

With very few variations, the same remarks were heard from groups standing around the merchants' stalls and fountains. On the terraces of cafés, the men argued so heatedly that they forgot to light their *narghilés*. The news of Mayor Mumtaz Bey's assassination had spread like wildfire and the capture of the rebels in the very centre of Sivas had created a climate of insecurity. Even though these two events were not connected, ill-informed people had linked them together; agitators under Gani Bey's orders were exploiting their fears by spreading alarming rumours and exaggerated figures. Some people even insisted that the deportation of the Armenians was a wise measure that had been delayed too long.

After handing his daily report, Vartan came out of the military hospital. In spite of his haste to join his family, he had thought it important not to break the rules. His commanding officer had sounded extremely reserved and cold. When Vartan asked for a surgeon to visit the wounded, the officer had been evasive. Vartan had also noticed the furtive whispers of the nurses, as he went through the wards. He still didn't know anything about what had happened in town.

Once outside, he questioned Izzet, the skinny, bent soldier who took care of his horse. Vartan had often given him drugs for some of his many children, and Izzet's gratitude had created a bond that Vartan sometimes found annoying. Now, he was pleased to tell everything he knew about the mayor's assassination, except that in fact he knew nothing precise. Forgetting that Major Balian was an Armenian, he told him of Shirag Tevonian's capture.

Vartan remained impassive, pretending curiosity, 'Many dead or wounded?'

'Yes, some *zaptiyés* and rebels. They also set fire to the church.'

That must have been the smoke he had seen above the trees! Shirag in the hands of the army . . . poor devil . . . It would have been better for him to die fighting! From Izzet's account, it wasn't hard for him to conclude that the church mentioned was Saint Minas, where Tomas and his godfather were supposed to go today. Vartan shuddered. Without another word, he mounted Hour-Grag and trotted away. Whatever had happened, it meant one thing: social harmony was deteriorating rapidly, as was to be expected.

Vartan rode back through the Kaval Quarter, where he slowed his mount to a walk. The second floor of old frame-houses hung out over the streets, narrowing the strip of the sky that could be seen above the roofs. Wire trellises covered with vines created real tunnels in some places. As usual, the streets were dirty and cluttered with the rubbish that was left after the wild dogs of the neighbourhood had scavenged the rest. The place was swarming with people: men mostly dressed in black with their red fezzes; veiled women in their *ferajés*;[1] girls with their long braids, boys screaming and chasing each other around the stalls; and, among all these city dwellers, awkward-looking peasants, easily recognizable by their short jackets and *shalvars*, their bouffant pants held up with a wide belt.

Vartan made his way slowly through the crowd. A huge crowd was completely blocking one of the streets. A bearded man harangued the crowd, preaching his own *jihad*, the holy war, against the *giaours*, which would assure people eternal salvation. Approving voices and gestures greeted and underlined each one of his remarks. Vartan stopped his horse at the edge of the boisterous assembly, his heart beating fast. Although he felt strong enough to take on any enemy in single combat, the thought of an agitated mob made him panic – perhaps from a long-lost childhood memory.

He took a deep breath to calm himself and rose in his stirrups. He had

---

1.   Dust-coat formerly worn by Turkish woman (Turkish).

to stop this man before he whipped the mob into a frenzy. Only the Sultan had the power to order a *jihad* and it was most improbable that he would risk alienating world opinion. Besides, outside Anatolia, no one would bother to obey him, and this would undermine his pretensions to the title Commander of the Faithful.

Vartan decided to bluff it out. He pointed his forefinger at the speaker and cried, 'You!'

The man shut up and everyone turned to Vartan.

'Yes, you! Who are you to speak in the name of the Sultan? Show us the *ferman* proclaiming the *jihad*.'

Vartan's words stirred doubts in people's minds. They waited for the speaker to answer, but he just looked around for support, confused and visibly nervous. The crowd became restless. A merchant standing in the doorway of his shop on the other side of the street took three steps forward and waved his fist at the troublemaker.

'You're blaspheming! Do you know what we do to those who blaspheme?'

The buzzing rose to a growl. The same people who had been applauding the man's exhortations to kill were now ready to lynch him. Vartan decided not to intervene any more.

More curious people were flocking in. Suddenly a young soldier in green infantry uniform took his place next to the speaker. Vartan recognized the man as a recruit he had worked at the dispensary for a few weeks – a rotten egg.

The soldier pointed at Vartan. 'I know that one. He's an Armenian. We call him '*Giaour* Major'.'

Total silence fell over the crowd. As nimble as a cat landing on all four legs, the troublemaker regained his nerves and took advantage of the incident.

'An Armenian!' he screamed. 'One of those who killed our mayor!'

Vartan found himself confronted with a sea of hate-filled faces. They shook their fists at him and some brandished their knives. With an ostentatious move, Vartan unsnapped his holster and placed his hand on the butt of his pistol. The gesture was enough to stop those who were coming at him.

'Don't let him get away,' shouted the bearded man.

'Let's get him,' added the young soldier.

The demonstrators hesitated; after all, *giaour* or not, this man was wearing the uniform of an Ottoman officer and he was armed! Vartan took advantage of the momentary calm and rode away, keeping his eyes fastened on them, his muscles tense, ready to draw and shoot if necessary. When he was about ten metres away, the frustrated mob began to throw vegetables and rubbish at him, infuriated that he was getting away. He ducked the missiles easily, but not the streams of insults flung in his direction. He pushed his horse to a trot.

'Make way! Make way!' he shouted, so that the pedestrians would scatter and leave him a passageway.

He quickly arrived at another square where a squad of soldiers stood guard. Now that the danger was over, he felt a wave of heat in his belly, spreading down his legs. Police were patrolling the streets of the Armenian commercial quarter; evidently the authorities were expecting trouble. As soon as the way was clear, Vartan galloped home.

Tomas was sitting on the bottom step of the entrance, watching the iron gate. He was impatiently waiting for his father. Since he had returned from the church, the hours had seemed endless. No one was paying any attention to him. Azniv Hanim, Maro, Jemila and Zeynep were busy in the house. None of his friends had come today to play with him. The children from the lower part of town who sometimes jumped the wall to steal fruit from the orchard hadn't showed up either.

Sassoun had no way of knowing that his young master didn't feel like playing. He brought his ball, cocked his head, yelped and then barked insistently. Giving up, he lay down at his master's feet, then rose to chase the blackbirds perching in the chestnut tree, then lay down again in front of the steps.

Tomas was thinking over what had happened in the church, trying to keep the events straight. It was hard for him though, because details assumed large proportions and blocked out the rest. He remembered the crazy look of the woman sitting in the pew on the other side of the aisle: her twisted mouth, her cheeks scratched by her nails. He remembered the frightened eyes of the rebel to whom his godfather had given his bullets. He could still clearly see the yellow teeth of the guard who had spat at Captain Armen's feet. He could still feel the terror lurking inside him, like a beast hiding in the bush, ready to seize him with its claws at the first opportunity.

His mother's explanations hadn't helped Tomas much. By now, he had an approximate idea of what the deportation order meant. That explained the adults' nervousness, his friends' absence and the closed shops, but not the burning of the church. Tomas could not make anything intelligible out of these facts. It was like a jigsaw puzzle to which he lacked an essential piece – the why!

Sassoun picked up his ears. A horse, coming quickly, slowed down as it neared the gate, allowing the child to recognize the singular rhythm of Hour-Grag's hoofs. At last!

He rushed to the doorway and shouted, 'Papa's coming.' Then he ran down to the gate, where Vartan was dismounting. He put his hands through the bars to touch his father's hand. 'Papa! Papa!' he said with relief.

Vartan patted his arm. 'Is everything all right, my soul?'

Words tumbled out of Tomas's mouth, 'They set fire to the church. The zaptiyés. They got us out first. They arrested Der Khoren and the others. They killed the Braves.'

Vartan pulled him towards the gate and kissed him. 'It's all over. I'm here now.'

Vartan was just going to ask him to get the key when he saw Maro bringing it. She was smiling, but he could see her eyes were red. Apart from that, her bearing and her voice showed she was in full control of herself.

'I'm so happy,' she exclaimed, as she turned the wrought-iron key in the lock.

Tomas climbed onto the gate, pushed it with his foot and swung out in a half circle. Maro threw herself into Vartan's arms and kissed him.

'My life,' he murmured, holding her in his arms. He felt her tremble almost imperceptibly.

'Hmph,' said Tomas joining them.

His father tweaked his nose and lifted him on to the saddle.

'Your horse is bathed in sweat,' said Maro.

'I was in a hurry to get home.'

She closed the gate and put her arm around her husband's waist. He wrapped his arm around her shoulders and, guiding the horse, they walked side by side to the stable.

She asked, 'Did you hear about Saint Minas? They haven't released anyone yet. Armen has gone to find out the latest news. The priest and the others are accused of being accomplices to the rebels. The situation is getting worse, Vartan. We have to do something!'

She didn't say what solution she was thinking about. She knew he had already thought of it and she felt it was up to him to speak first. Pointing to Tomas, he made a sign for her to wait until they were alone.

'I've explained it to him as best as I can,' she said. 'Your uniform won't protect us long, Vartan. Do you know what's happening elsewhere?'

He nodded.

'The same thing will happen here very shortly,' she insisted.

He murmured regretfully, 'We can see it coming. It would be wise to leave before it could be too late.'

'Why do you say 'could be'?' She already knew the answer and sensed the conflict, which was tearing her husband apart.

He confirmed her suspicions. 'My duty . . .'

'Your duty is to think of your family first,' she stated emphatically.

'And the others? What about the others?'

'There's nothing you can do for them. You have no right to sacrifice yourself blindly.'

They went into the stable. Vartan put Tomas down, and unsaddled Hour-Grag. Maro took a fistful of hay and began to rub him down roughly. The reasons she had just given Vartan, he had undoubtedly repeated to himself a hundred times, but she still had many others that she would like to tell him.

'Since you're in the army, we shall be the only Armenian family left in Sivas. What help could you be then to our compatriots?'

'I know. I know . . .' he replied.

Feigning innocence, Maro asked, 'What do you think could stop the deportation and restrain these fools in the government?'

'Outside intervention. Pressure from other countries. But first they would have to know what's happening here.' He stopped and stood with his mouth open. Of course, the conclusion was self-evident. Why hadn't he thought of it before? Someone had to cry for help and who could do that better than he? His way of action seemed clear: take up his pen and alert the world to the extermination of the Armenians in the Ottoman Empire. But to do this he would first have to get out of the country; it was the only way he could help his countrymen.

Watching Vartan's relaxed face, Maro realized that his conscience was at peace.

'All right. We shall leave tonight. I'll ask Armen to come with us.'

Maro sighed with relief and dropped the hay in her hand. 'He and Araksi are coming in a few minutes. I'll go and get ready.'

'Would you please have water sent up to the room so I can freshen up?'

She quickly went into the house, feeling a weight lifted from her shoulders. Because of all these unexpected happenings and developments, Vartan had forgotten it was his son's birthday. Tomas was having a hard time, trying to fill the troughs with a pitchfork twice his size. He had not missed a word of his parents' conversation although most of it had gone over his head, except for the part about them leaving.

'Come here,' said Vartan, opening his arms.

Tomas threw down the pitchfork and ran to his father who lifted him high in the air.

'Six years old already! Happy birthday, my son. Forgive us for not feeling like celebrating.'

'It's all right,' said the child. He had not given his birthday a thought since lunch.

'Soon we'll be in another town and then we'll have a party you'll never forget.'

'Are we leaving tonight?'

'Yes, but don't tell a soul.'

'Where are we going?'

'I still don't know, but we'll all go together. It'll be a long and difficult journey. You'll have to be very brave.'

'I didn't cry in the church. Nor in front of the soldiers. I'm not afraid of anything when I'm with you, Papa.'

Vartan tousled his hair, kissed him, and held him tightly before putting him down. 'Let's go and get ready to welcome your godparents.'

Pulling a pony behind him, Armen walked next to the donkey carrying his wife, Araksi. She sat astride, her enormous legs resting against the flanks of the animal. Because she suffered from high blood pressure and albuminuria, she wore black cotton stockings to hide her swollen legs. Vartan had prescribed a diet for her, which she did not follow, as she had no wish to understand the need for it. She never abstained from eating the spicy Armenian dishes she adored. She was stout and big-bosomed; in contrast, her face appeared more delicate than it really was. A forelock of hair had remained stubbornly black while the rest of it was snow white. So she tied a scarf around her head and arranged her lock of black hair in bangs, thinking it made her look younger. She always smiled to show off her magnificent, healthy teeth. She wanted to remain attractive in Armen's eyes. Whenever her illness was mentioned, she would repeat over and over: 'I'm not afraid of death. Not at all, Armen. What makes me sad is getting old.'

He would protest and tell her she would always be a beautiful and desirable woman to him. He would tweak her chin. 'I see you with the eyes of my heart and, to me, you look exactly the same as on our wedding day.'

That never failed to make Araksi smile.

It really was true that Armen's love had not changed; his was a simple, solid, quiet love. When he was a fisherman, they had never become used to being separated, so now they were making up for lost time and were seldom apart.

Armen had not said a word since leaving the house. It was so unlike him that Araksi thought this dinner at the Balians was a chore for him. In her drawling voice, which gave the impression that speaking tired her, she said, 'I'm so happy we're going to this party.'

'It's liable to be more of a wake,' Armen growled. 'I don't understand their stubbornness . . . having a party for Tomas while all this is happening.'

The old woman didn't mind his grumbling, as long as he broke the stifling silence. She insisted gently, 'On the contrary, one shouldn't be alone. I know how they feel. I want to be surrounded by friends. This might be our last meal together.'

'Without a doubt!'

'More the reason to be together. Do calm down.'

'Calm down!' exploded Armen. 'How do you expect me to calm down when we're being . . .' He stopped, realizing he was almost shouting when he should have been reassuring his poor wife. 'Excuse me, my seagull,' he murmured, patting Araksi's hand.

She smiled. It had been a long time since he had used that term of endearment.

He sighed. 'All right, I can control myself for a few hours.' He clenched the hand that was holding the pony's bridle so hard that the nails bit into his palm. He was furious. He was exasperated by his impotence. As they passed the smoking ruins of Saint Minas, he unleashed a litany of oaths. Araksi didn't reproach him; the sight of the blackened walls made her pulse race and she turned her head away so her husband couldn't see her tear-filled eyes. Up until that moment, the deportation had been for her only a storm cloud which God would blow away. She had not grasped what Armen had told her. They were just words . . . terrible words, weightless words, abstract words . . . as unreal as the stories of wars and massacres handed down through the centuries.

The Balians were all on the front steps when Armen and Araksi arrived. Tomas was staggered when he saw the already saddled pony his godfather was bringing. He stood still. He was speechless. His dearest dream had come true! The stomachache that the fright at the church had given him disappeared. The pony was beautifully proportioned. Its hair was copper-toned and its mane and tail were flaxen. It had long, creamy-white eyelashes. The child even thought its eyes had a tender look. The spaniel barked, the pony answered with a long whinny and Tomas giggled nervously. He remained standing on the last step, although he was dying to run to the pony; Azniv Hanim had made him promise to greet his guests first and thank everybody before accepting his present.

Vartan helped Araksi dismount from the donkey. 'How are your legs?'

'Better,' she lied. 'The diet you gave me is doing me a world of good, but tonight I intend to cheat.'

Tomas was impatiently jumping from one foot to the other, while the adults exchanged greetings which he considered to be much too lengthy. When his turn to kiss his godfather and godmother came, Araksi took him by the shoulders, stood him in front of the pony, and turned to the others.

'Our Tomas has been as patient as an angel.'

Vartan pointed to the pony. 'There, Tomas, he's yours. Take good care of him.'

'The saddle is a present from your grandmother and your godfather has been breaking in your pony for the last two months,' Maro explained.

Finally Tomas could go to the pony, which had already made friends with the spaniel. He lightly touched the silky short-haired nose and the pony stretched forward to be caressed.

'You would think he knows me,' Tomas said.

'Of course,' replied Armen. 'Your mother gave me one of your sweaters, so he recognizes your smell.'

Tomas hugged the pony's neck, patted it on the rump, and hoisted himself on to the saddle. His face glowed with joy. He gently touched his heels against his pony's flanks and clucked as he had heard his father do. Maro started to stop him but Armen pulled her back. The pony danced a

82

few steps and rode off at a trot. Zeynep and Jemila ran after them laughing gaily. Tomas turned at the gate, drew up in front of the group of adults and announced in a voice, trembling with excitement:

'I'll call him Gaydzag.'[1]

'The name suits him,' Vartan approved.

'Let's go in and eat,' said Maro. 'You can ride your Gaydzag later.'

Tomas tied his pony to the walnut tree in front of the dining-room window where he could see him from the table. Armen thought the pony might break the branches but that wasn't important anymore. Like all the others he had shared Tomas's joy and forgotten his sadness for a few minutes.

The people of Sivas considered the house built by Adom Shamlian to be one of the most beautiful in the region and the best furnished. The rich importer had regretfully sold Vartan his house with the special pieces of furniture he had collected. All his children had gone to live in Constantinople or the USA and, because of his frail health, he had decided to move to the capital where well-known doctors had their practices.

Araksi never entered these walls without feeling intimidated, which slightly inhibited the familiarity and friendship between her and the Balians. The humble two-room house she and Armen had built together would have fitted into this living room. She was the daughter of a small tobacco farmer, who had gone broke. She had never seen anything as beautiful as this dining-room with its fireplace topped by a marble mantle over which hung an ebony and mother-of-pearl clock, chiming the hour and the half hour. Oil portraits of Vartan's parents and of Maro's father hung on the walls. There were also several marine paintings by Ayvazowski, an Armenian painter by origin, highly regarded by his compatriots as well as the Russians. A cut-crystal chandelier hung over the oak table, which could seat twenty. It served only for decoration since it had been wired for electricity and there was no electricity in Sivas or any other Anatolian town. A glass cabinet, where silver was displayed, a Victor gramophone (His Master's Voice) and two sideboards completed the furnishings.

Maro had brightened the room with bouquets of roses and set the table magnificently but no one except for Zeynep and Jemila was in a party

---

1.   Lightening (Armenian).

mood. As Armen was the eldest, Vartan asked him to say grace. This surprised his mother-in-law, who knew him to be indifferent to religion or worse. The young Turkish girls did the serving, often looking questioningly at Maro. Then they too sat down at the table. Azniv Hanim had prepared her grandson's favourite dishes: fried aubergine, artichoke hearts in olive oil, lamb stuffed with rice and almonds.

After praising the different dishes and congratulating and toasting Tomas, they ate in silence. Like Armen, Araksi was confused by the quantity of cutlery; both of them watched their hostess carefully so as to know which fork to use. The stilted atmosphere and sombre faces made them feel even more ill at ease.

After a few moments, Armen put his knife down noisily. 'I cannot keep on pretending,' he said wearily.

His wife tried to hush him by nudging him discreetly with her elbow, but Armen frowned and insisted, 'It's true! Here we are, having a party, while the others are sharpening their bayonets.'

Everyone except Tomas, who was eating automatically with his eyes riveted on his pony, froze, even Zeynep and Jemila, were feeling guilty.

Maro did not know what to say and looked imploringly at Vartan, who intervened calmly but firmly, 'I understand your feelings, Armen. We all share them. But don't you think we can talk about it after dinner, when we have coffee?'

Armen's shoulders sagged as he lowered his eyes at his plate and protested, 'As if chitchat could make any difference. Words are all we have left. Words and waiting for what's coming.'

'I'm not so sure. There might be a way.'

When Armen heard this, he looked up at Vartan quickly.

'*Sev Dzov*,' murmured Vartan.

The Black Sea! Just exactly what did he mean? Armen seemed perplexed. Vartan made him understand with a turn of his head that he was talking about leaving and, to keep him from asking any more questions, he said, 'That's what I want to discuss after dinner.'

'Yes, of course,' replied Armen, who picked up his knife and fork but didn't start eating; he was lost in thought.

A heavy silence fell. Maro asked Zeynep to put on some music. They owned the only gramophone in town and Tomas was very proud to show it off to his friends, who were fascinated. It was magic to Zeynep and Jemila and they never ceased marvelling at it. During the meal, they competed with each other; running it, winding it up and changing the cylinders.

After dessert, a cake made with lily-bulb flour, Tomas was in a hurry to see Gaydzag again. Maro asked Zeynep and Jemila to accompany him and clear the table later. The adults went into the large living-room dominated by a grand piano, a Pleyel imported from France by Adom Shamlian. The room offered a mixture of different styles: Louis XV armchairs placed next to Chinese lacquered chests; decagonal coffee tables decorated with Arabic motifs; a long divan, a *sedir* covered with an oriental rug and a profusion of pillows; Isfahan rugs; a silver samovar; an imposing *mangal*[1] covered by a conical hood, a magnificent Venetian chandelier – all jumbled together without rhyme or reason.

They gathered in the corner where the *sedir* was. Vartan pulled up a love-seat for Araksi and Armen and an armchair for his mother-in-law. He and his wife sat down on the divan, forming a closed circle. Maro and Azniv Hanim poured the coffee and the cognac. Vartan and Armen lit their cigarettes.

'With your permission,' said Azniv Hanim, taking out her snuff box. Not waiting for an answer, she took a pinch of snuff between her thumb and forefinger, brought it to her nose, inhaled deeply and sneezed into an embroidered handkerchief.

Their faces glum, they drank their coffee-cognacs without proposing any toasts. Armen leaned towards Vartan. 'The Black Sea?'

Vartan gulped down his brandy and breathed deeply. 'This was our farewell dinner. We're leaving Sivas.'

The old man didn't move.

'Tonight!' added Maro.

'That's a good idea,' Armen said, flicking the ashes of his cigarette into a crystal ashtray. 'Everything here is finished.'

'I want you to come with us,' Vartan continued. 'If we travel all night, we can reach the coast. We can rent or buy a boat there.'

'With a little bit of luck, we should be able to do that,' Armen replied, rubbing his chin. He turned to his wife and she patted him on the arm, letting him know that she left the matter in his hands, although she was terrified of such a long trip because of her poor health.

Der Khoren's words – to save the seed – came back to Armen and he sighed. 'We're touched that you should think of us, but we're getting near

---

1.   A brazier with copper engravings (Turkish).

85

the end of our lives. It would be better if you took some of the young ones, the future generation.'

Maro shifted to the edge of the sofa, taking Araksi's hands. 'You're part of our family and we don't want to leave you behind.'

Azniv Hanim gestured at her daughter disapprovingly not to intervene in the men's conversation. This was the second time already!

'Armen, we need you,' insisted Vartan. 'We have to avoid roads as much as possible, so we need a couple of strong arms to drive the carriage across the open fields. You know the countryside well, from here all the way to the coast. Besides, I don't know how to pilot a boat.'

Staring at the bottom of his glass, Armen thought it over. The priest had declared it was everyone's duty to survive. The deportation would be a terrible ordeal for Araksi; now he had a chance to spare her. In addition, he also felt responsible for Tomas and his parents . . . his adopted family! In 1895 he had not been able to save his own as they lived too far away from him in another province, but he had felt guilty all the same. Now he had the opportunity to make amends, even if they were symbolic. He could see the Black Sea so clearly; he could smell the salty air through the aroma of the brandy. How wonderful it would be to navigate once more beyond sight of the shore, guided only by his own instinct. Araksi and he could still expect a few years together. He was in no hurry to die.

He accepted Vartan's invitation and started immediately to lay out his plans in a loud voice. As always, he became completely involved in what he was doing and waved his hands broadly in the air as he spoke. He thought the best way to get out of Sivas was a shepherd's path, which ran alongside his field. A carriage could get through by skirting the obstacles. They could be safe in the hills before dawn and would reach the sea in six or seven days. As their destination, he proposed the small port of Ordu, where he had reliable friends. They would find a suitable boat for them. Then he paused.

'That's all very fine, but where are we headed?'

'Russia,' Vartan replied.

'No,' cried Maro, 'the capital!'

Araksi and Azniv Hanim looked at her disapprovingly; a woman did not contradict her husband in public! Vartan paid no attention to these old conventions and his wife's cry from her heart touched him.

He asked her gently, 'Why?'

'Our relatives are there. Many foreign diplomats take their holidays in the capital, and the situation cannot be as tragic there as here in the interior.'

'We don't really know,' said Vartan. 'Perhaps Uncle Mesrop and his family have left already. My brother, Noubar...'

'We'll see when we get there,' protested Maro.

'Maro!' Azniv Hanim intervened reproachfully.

Vartan stopped his mother-in-law with a wave of his hand. He knew his wife was upset and explained patiently, 'Think! In Constantinople I'll be a wanted man. We'll have to hide, live in fear. Think of Tomas! Think of us!'

She nodded mechanically.

He added, 'What good would I be to the Armenians there as a fugitive? No! We have to leave the Empire. Russia will be a safe haven.'

Maro knew he was right and turned to Armen. 'Could you get us there?'

'It would be easier than to Constantinople. Would Yalta on the northern coast of the Black Sea be all right?'

'I'd prefer Batum. From there we could get to Russian Armenia, to Yerevan. If we want to help the Armenians in Anatolia, we have to join those who are fighting on the Russian side.'

Armen, who knew the region, was pleased with the idea. He had already visited Yerevan and Etchmiadzin, the town where the Catholicos[1] lived. For Maro this took her even farther away from Europe, but they didn't seem to have much choice. Azniv Hanim had the premonition that she would never be buried beside her husband, but she did not protest. Her family came first!

They continued to discuss the practical details – what they needed to take; who would be in charge of what.

'Only the essentials – a few clothes, food for six days and arms.'

'Our entire fortune will fit into a bundle,' said Araksi, who had always had a horror of bothering anyone. 'We can be ready in half an hour.'

The room was getting dark. Maro lit two kerosene lamps which shed a yellowish light. No one had mentioned their compatriots whom they were leaving behind, but they all were thinking sadly about them. The preparations for the trip would take little time, so they still had a few hours to kill. They kept putting off the moment when they would separate, conscious of the fact that they were living through the end of an era, the point of plunging into the unknown.

'Could Maro play a piece for us on the piano?' Asked Araksi, who adored music. 'To remind us of . . .'

---

1. The head of the Armenian Apostolic Church (Armenian).

Maro did not think she could do it so she asked Vartan to take out his *oud*. She didn't have to ask twice. He put the instrument on his lap and started tuning it. He had played this Oriental instrument since he was seven years old. His father had once taken in a wandering musician for the winter. He was a wise old man with a white beard who, in return for their hospitality, had showed Vartan the secrets of his art. Later on, Vartan had had famous teachers, but he still practised many of the old man's teachings:

'First music is born in you; then it passes into the *oud*.'

While he was limbering up his fingers by improvising melodies, Tomas and the young Turkish girls came back and sat down in silence on the floor in front of the *sedir*. Vartan played the old Armenian folk songs filled with sweet sadness. Without even thinking about it, Maro started to accompany the oud with her velvety, vibrant voice. Eyes closed and her hands folded over her stomach, she sang, swaying as though rocking a child. At the base of her throat a tendon swelled when she reached for the high notes. Tomas focused on this spot as he listened to the songs of grieving lovers who had been separated, of flowers and fruits, of distant lands which fired his imagination. He had a hard time making the connection between love and distance and understanding that the name of a fruit could refer to a loved one. He loved the ones which told about birds that had travelled to exotic places and brought back tales of exotic things and people. He shivered. Like the birds, they were going to fly to distant lands. What would they find? Sivas was the only town Tomas knew, except for the ones he had seen in picture-books. Would they see trains? Aeroplanes? He moved over and cuddled up in the lap of his godfather, who stroked him on the head.

That evening Maro's voice expressed troubled undertones and the words of the songs took on new meanings. What she was singing didn't sound like a ballad but like a lament, a wail. Everyone felt his own sorrow and his fear of losing that which was most precious to him. If Maro had not made an effort to control herself, she would have wept; the others, too.

The night, one of the shortest in the year, fell as Armen and Araksi made their way home. The two Turkish girls had been told about the Balians' plans and each of them had reacted differently, according to their personalities. Zeynep, who was sensitive and emotional, threw herself into Azniv Hanim's arms and began to cry. Jemila, who was more circumspect, advised them to take refuge in the village she came from.

'My father and Zeynep's father will welcome you. The whole village will protect you.'

Maro told her that they didn't want to put her parents in danger. 'We know of a safe place. Don't worry,' she said. 'If we're not back in three days, lock up the house and go to your uncle's in Sivas. He'll see that you get home to your families. When we return, we'll come and get you.'

Jemila nodded. She guessed that they weren't coming back. Azniv Hanim took both of them to the kitchen to give them her last orders. Vartan had told Maro to give each one a purse with ten gold coins for their dowries. He lit a storm lantern and went out with Tomas, who refused to go to bed for only two hours. The almost-full moon, which was half-way up its zenith, spread an ashen luminosity on the landscape. There was no breeze and the warm air was heavy with the scent of fading flowers as the garden had not been watered the last two days. Sassoun, overexcited by the changes in the daily activities of the house, was running and jumping all over the place.

Vartan saddled his and Maro's horses and Tomas tried to do the same for his pony, saying, 'Gaydzag is coming with us.'

Vartan had already weighed the question and decided that it was cruel to separate Tomas from his new companion so soon. 'All right, but you're not to ride him; at least, not at first. We'll tie him to the back of the carriage.'

He realized he was only postponing the problem. Once they arrived at Ordu, they would have to leave all the animals behind; but that hadn't occurred to Tomas yet and Vartan didn't want to upset him now. Vartan looked over his son's work and was impressed to see that Gaydzag was properly saddled except for the girth, which needed tightening by one hole. He tied the trotter to the carriage and went back into the house, just as the dining room clock was chiming eleven. Baskets with provisions, blankets and a small suitcase were lined up in the hall.

Looking tense, Maro came up to him. 'We're ready.' Her voice was strained. She was more moved at leaving this house and town than she had thought possible. As for Vartan, a strange feeling of failure pervaded him.

The Muslim Quarter of Kaval was busy in spite of the late hour. Groups of two or three, sometimes even ten men were gathering in the city square. Some were armed with rifles, others with sticks. They all carried either lanterns or torches, which illuminated the square and made it look like a phosphorescent sea. Some soldiers leaned nonchalantly against the walls, looking on indifferently; others were among the jostling throng. When the demonstrators set off towards the Armenian Quarter, the officers ordered the men to shoot into the air.

From his window Vartan had seen a patch of light but had not paid much attention to it. He was too far away to have heard anything that might have alerted him as to the nature of the gathering. He slid the property titles and other important documents into his leather briefcase. For the last half hour, he had been burning papers and letters in the green and white enamelled stove that was used to heat the room in the winter. The fire was roaring and the base of the stove-pipe was glowing red. The stifling heat forced him to open the window. He had just got to the copies of his political essays when he heard the shooting and rushed to the window.

There were more explosions and, for several minutes, the situation was confusing. Then the mass of people split up and luminous serpents of light moved towards the slope of the hill. The demonstrators outnumbered the soldiers who did not appear much bothered. It would have looked like a procession if it hadn't been for the echoes of the shouting, which had now become quite audible. Two words emerged from the howling:

'Armenians! Assassins!'

The noise was getting closer. A cavalry detachment trotted by in a neighbouring street. A platoon of gendarmes was on the move. The Ottoman soldiers were taking up positions in the Armenian Quarter to drive the rioters back.

'What hypocrisy!' raged Vartan.

Those who were sending the army in to maintain order were undoubtedly the same ones who had planned or, at the very least, encouraged this disturbance. He thought that, because of the troops in the streets, it would be better to postpone their departure for another hour, hoping that things would have calmed down before dawn.

Shutters were grating. Awakened by all the commotion, people were sticking their heads out of the windows and shouting from one house to the other. The rioters were gaining ground. The soldiers were ebbing back in a disorderly fashion. Where were the officers? Vartan should go down and, if possible, stop the soldiers' flight, or they might all be killed. He put on his tunic, buckled his belt and made sure his gun was loaded.

On his way out, he ran into Maro who had been awakened by Sassoun's barking. She looked dishevelled and terribly frightened. Her voice shook:

'What's going on?'

90

Vartan summed up the situation and she realized that he was about to go out. 'Don't tell me you're going out there!' she pleaded.

'I have to! We can't leave right now, and if the demonstrators get here . . .'

She clung to him, imploring, 'Stay with us. There isn't anything you can do.'

'Sometimes one determined officer is sufficient to galvanize the troops into action. If the soldiers rally, we are saved. I must go!' He disengaged himself and added, 'I promise I won't take needless risks. If the situation gets worse, I'll come right back. But don't worry; everything is going to be all right. There are hundreds of soldiers on the streets.'

Try as she would, Maro couldn't convince herself that he was right but it was useless to argue. Nothing would make him change his mind. So she stepped aside. Visibly frightened, Azniv Hanim and the two girls waited in the hall. Vartan was worried but he tried to appear calm. He pointed to their belongings which were stacked along the wall.

'Load the carriage while I'm gone, so we can leave the minute I come back.'

Azniv Hanim started to protest, but Maro told her to drop the matter. Vartan took his cavalry sabre and scabbard down from the wall, where they had been hanging with the rest of his collection of weapons. He sheathed the sabre and fastened it to his belt with quick, precise movements.

'Will you please close the gate behind me?' he asked Maro, who was looking at him helplessly. As she went to the sideboard to get the key out of the drawer, he nodded goodbye to his mother-in-law, 'I leave you in charge of the house, *Mayrig*.'

'You can count on me – just you take care!'

When he came out of the stable, Maro was waiting at the gate. The moon shone on her face and lit the tears in her eyes. He took her in his arms, but she could not find the words to express the terrible wrenching feeling in her heart, so simply said, 'I love you, Vartan.'

His only answer was to kiss her before leaping into the saddle.

Vartan galloped. The louder the clamour of the mob became, the faster his fervour changed to rage. The shouts were accompanied by occasional shots. His rash action was obliterating the guilt he felt about leaving town. He was happy to be able to help others. Several buildings in the Armenian commercial quarter were in flames. He glimpsed furtive silhouettes in the dark alleys; some of his compatriots, no doubt, trying to get to a safe place. Then he saw two soldiers rushing towards him.

'Stop!' he shouted.

Looking down sheepishly, they stopped, waiting for him. Vartan rose in his stirrups and asked in an authoritative voice, 'Where are you going? Running away? Do you know the punishment for abandoning your post?'

The older of the two saluted him and tried to excuse himself: 'At your orders, *binbashim*.[1] There are too many rioters for us. We don't know what to do.'

'Who's your CO?'

'A corporal. The lieutenant left.'

The two men seemed distraught.

'You were looking for reinforcements?' suggested Vartan, trying to save their pride.

'Yes, yes, that's it! That's what we were on our way to do . . . look for reinforcements,' the same soldier added hastily.

'Well, you've found me. There are several platoons behind me. Let's go back there.'

Resignedly, the men looked at each other, turned around and began to walk, dragging their feet. Vartan urged them on. They met three other soldiers who had turned their backs on the riot and two more who were hiding in a dead-end alley. Herding the seven reluctant men towards a confrontation with the rioters, Vartan continued down the hill. Now he could hear the rhythmic roar of the mob, reminding him of the noise the surf made at high tide, but it soon became a deafening repetition of rapid staccato syllables:

'Ar-me-ni-ans! As-sas-sins! Ar-me-ni-ans! As-sas-sins!'

The street turned right, just past the school, and, when Vartan reached the corner, he was dazzled by hundreds of blazing torches. He could almost smell the breath pouring out of all those screaming mouths.

The mob! Like lava dashing down a ravine, it was filling the street, grazing the fronts of the buildings on both sides. It was a compact mass, which stretched over several hundred yards, past the next turn in the street and even farther on.

Vartan choked. He could now understand only too well the soldiers'

---

1. Major (Turkish).

impulse to flee, but he was defending his own. He counted eleven soldiers who were falling back step by step before the human tide; now he could count on eighteen men to deploy. He shot twice into the air, the crowd swirled and the flow slowed down. The soldiers regrouped around Vartan. He lined them up to bar the street.

Holding his pistol and horse's reins in his left hand, he flourished the sabre in his right, and ordered, 'Charge with fixed bayonets.'

Some of the soldiers looked at him incredulously. He repeated his order firmly. While they were carrying out his orders, Vartan rode back and forth in the street behind them, haranguing them. 'It's up to us to stop these people from passing and we shall do it. The army's honour is at stake. How can we defeat the enemies of the Empire if we cannot dominate a band of civilians.' Just to be sure that they had understood him, he added, 'We shall not retreat one step. I'll shoot the first man who tries.'

The crowd facing them began to advance again and the soldiers became jumpy.

'Load your guns and aim above their heads. At my command, fire!'

Such a profound silence followed the volley that even the sizzling sound of the torches could be heard. Vartan shouted, 'By order of the Commander of the Faithful, break it up. Go home.'

A hysterical voice interrupted him, 'Let us pass! Let us do justice!'

Like an echo, a mutter arose, then turned into curses and swelled to a roar, splitting up into intelligible cadences:

'Ar-me-ni-ans! As-sa-sins!'

The mob again brandished their torches and sticks. Vartan was watching the contorted faces, twisted mouths and furious madmen's eyes. They were no longer men but ferocious beasts avid for blood. They were one body but, like the hydra, they had a thousand heads . . . a bristling, unpredictable, soulless beast. This was what he had to beat! He felt hatred rise in him and a craving for violence. With his sabre, he would decapitate those monstrous heads. The beast began to creep towards him.

Vartan ordered his men to point their rifles and bayonets at the rioters and advance slowly. They were afraid, but their officer's presence and marching elbow to elbow with their fellows gave them some courage. The rioters hesitated when they saw the troops' determination. The ones in the front tried to stop, but they were pushed forward by the ones in the back. There was jostling and the crowd came to a stop less than a metre from the bayonets. It was the critical moment, the one which would decide the course of events. Vartan again shot into the air and made his way through the soldiers to confront the maddened crowd. Hour-Grag neighed and stamped his feet. Vartan brandished his sabre and shouted, 'Move back! Move back!'

Those who were closest to the bayonets tried to melt into the ranks and, gradually, the mass started to retreat. Vartan signalled his men to advance; they joined him and then passed. The soldiers, emboldened by their success, threatened and drove the people in front of them. Step by step, the rioters retreated to the commercial quarter, where some stores and warehouses were still burning. They stopped at the esplanade. Vartan didn't have enough men to make them evacuate the square; all he could do was block off the entry to the residential area of the upper town. His family now had nothing to fear; he had achieved that at least.

Now that the rioters had stopped in their tracks, they were dispersing. Some were already leaving by a side street leading to the centre of town, breaking shop windows and doors to loot the shops; but that was a lesser evil.

A quarter of an hour later, the cavalry appeared at the extreme end of the square and forced their way through the crowd. Vartan's men cheered and he himself rejoiced when he recognized Colonel Ibrahim Alizadé at the head of the troops. Approaching Vartan, he declared in a subdued tone, 'Major Vartan, you're under arrest.'

Ibrahim lined up his horse up next to Vartan's. Vartan was so flabbergasted he was struck dumb. Ibrahim whispered with a very low voice, 'I beg you, don't make trouble. Just hand over your weapons.'

His tone was so urgent; the cavalrymen who surrounded Vartan watched his slightest move so intensely that Vartan sensed he had better obey. Ibrahim was his friend and was probably doing the best he could for him. Vartan handed over his pistol and sabre and, for the benefit of the onlookers, said in an outraged tone, 'May I ask what's this all about, Colonel?'

'You'll find out at the headquarters.'

Some of the rioters shouted with glee as they watched the man who had stood in their way arrested.

'Rabble! Scum!' muttered Ibrahim. He swept his hand as if brushing away flies. 'Come on! Mop this up! I don't want to see a single civilian on the streets when I return.'

Followed by two cavalrymen, the colonel headed with his prisoner towards the City Hall. Pointing a thumb at the two soldiers who were following them, he said gloomily, 'Don't try anything foolish. I have orders to shoot if you resist. And knowing you, I thought it would be better if I arrested you myself. I was on my way to your house.'

'Tell me exactly what's going on, Ibrahim. Just who gave the order? The pasha?'

'No. An important official from the capital arrived today; he has the power to do anything. I'm sorry.'

'Who is he?'

'I don't know.'

'It must be a misunderstanding,' said Vartan, refusing to give up.

The colonel reached out to touch his arm, but changed his mind when he remembered the men behind them. He only said, 'You can count on my friendship. I'll do everything I can.'

The sombre tone of his voice was enough to dash Vartan's hopes, but he trusted Ibrahim's promise; he was a man of his word. He was so quiet and reserved that this was the first time in three years he had even mentioned the word 'friendship'. They were friends regardless of their different levels of education. They had many things in common: their love of horses and music; their liking for hunting and long cavalcades. They also had similar opinions about the Empire's future. They talked little, but their silences were eloquent.

On his arrival in Sivas, Ibrahim had introduced himself with a recommendation from Halit Pasha, under whose orders he had served in the first Balkan War. His blond hair and blue eyes attested to his Circassian origin. His looks, which were quite rare in Anatolia, not only made him conspicuous, but also made his conquests of women easier. Despite the fact that he was married and had two wives, he was an incorrigible skirt-chaser.

They passed by some half-burnt houses. The neighbourhood shops were being sacked and long lines of men were leisurely carrying their booty away. The moon was almost visible through the smoke hovering over the town and it looked red.

Ibrahim read Vartan's thoughts. 'The rioters are under control. Your family is out of danger.'

'My wife must be worried about me.'

'I'll let her know what happened and take your horse back.'

'Thank you.'

Vartan read a promise of help into Ibrahim's apparently innocuous sentence. The colonel was sorry to have become destiny's tool, which had brought anguish to his best friend. Since he first saw the order for Vartan's arrest, he had been trying desperately to find a way to stop it. At least Vartan would arrive at the jail alive and there was still time for Ibrahim to try to find a way to get him released.

The market place in the vicinity of City Hall was teeming with soldiers mulling about.

'I can't be blamed for anything,' said Vartan, voicing out loud his assessment of the situation.

Ibrahim pointed to groups of arrested people on their way to prison. 'They couldn't be either. Even though . . .'

Vartan realized that they were civilians rounded up by gendarmes.

'Your compatriots,' explained Ibrahim. 'We have a long list of names. I'd like to think that yours got on it by mistake.'

This laconic sentence betrayed Ibrahim's state of mind and was sufficient to alarm Vartan. He remembered what had happened in the capital: first the arrest and then the liquidation of important Armenian people. These were the procedures that preceded deportation.

'The deportation date is almost here. Do you know if the people in the military are still exempt?'

Colonel Ibrahim seemed embarrassed and shrugged. 'Everything changes from hour to hour. I'll inform the general what's happening to you.'

'Please, look out for my family, if you can.'

Ibrahim could not answer without betraying his feelings, so he just nodded.

The high, grey walls of the prison, with narrow barred windows at the top, looked even more sinister under the drab light of the moon. One of the panels of the arched iron gate was half open to let in the numerous guards who were ushering in new inmates. Vartan was surprised that they were taking him to the police station.

'My orders specifically said to take you to Commissioner Mustapha.'

This was another cause for alarm. Mustapha Rahmi detested Vartan, and the feeling was mutual. They stopped their horses at the entrance, guarded by four military policemen.

'I'm bringing Major Vartan Balian in,' Ibrahim said falteringly. The two friends exchanged a meaningful look. 'May Allah protect you,' said Ibrahim softly, as Vartan dismounted.

The two cavalrymen left at a gallop as the gendarmes led Vartan towards the door. He stepped into the smoky hall. Cigarette butts littered the dusty floor, which was flecked with large cigarette burns. The orderly, standing on the left side of the doorway, was practically asleep. At the far end of the room, under the red Ottoman flag with its white crescent and star, sat a sergeant. By the light of a smoking lamp, he was scribbling on a yellow pad. His fez was lying on top of the desk, beside a copper water jug and a dirty glass. He did not even lift his eyes to look at the newcomer who was being brought in.

'Vartan Balian,' muttered one of the guards in a rasping voice.

'Corporal, search him,' the sergeant ordered, consulting the list.

After emptying Vartan's pockets, without any protest on the part of the prisoner, the guards handed the content of his pockets to the sergeant: a tobacco pouch, a handful of bullets, identity papers, two gold coins, four *mejidiyés* and a few *paras*.[1] Vartan knew he would not see any of these again, as this was the normal way for the military guards to supplement their meagre salaries. The sergeant checked Vartan's name on the list with his ink-stained finger.

Feigning self-assurance, Vartan ordered the sergeant, 'Let the commissioner know I'm here. I want to see him right away.'

The man looked at him dumbfounded. Vartan pointed to his stripes. 'I just gave you an order.'

The sergeant guffawed and called the others to listen. 'Did you hear that? He's giving me orders!'

The other three guards burst into gales of laughter. Then a serious look came over the sergeant's face and he pulled a piece of wire from his desk drawer.

'Bind his hands together.'

Vartan knew that if he resisted he would be in for a bad time. They crossed his arms behind his back and tied the wrists tightly. The ones who had brought him in sat him down on a long wooden rustic bench placed against the wall and left immediately. The orderly returned to his usual post by the door.

The hands of the clock showed 2:10. Vartan mulled things over. He would have fooled himself if he claimed he didn't know enough to assess the circumstances correctly. The truth was evident, simple, and brutal: right now he was nothing more than an ordinary Armenian, in other words, one more victim of high-handedness. He had delayed too long to leave Sivas. No!

---

1.   Silver coins and one fortieth of a *kurush* (Turkish).

97

Everything had accelerated. Even as late as last night, he would have been right in thinking that life would continue as before.

He looked at the open door but for the moment it was useless to think about escaping. The sergeant, who was rolling himself a cigarette with Vartan's tobacco, noticed his look he said to the orderly, 'Don't you fall asleep. This one's dangerous.'

As if he had been lashed with a whip, the orderly came to attention, pointing his Mauser at Vartan, and never taking his eyes off him.

Maro was looking out of the window and watching the town slowly calm down. She could still hear the patrols but the yelling and chanting of the rioters had ceased, the torches disappeared and only some reddish gleams marked the places that were still burning. What was Vartan doing? He should have been home by now. It was nearly dawn, and it would soon be impossible to start their trip.

Maro, her mother and the servants had loaded the carriage. Then she had continued burning the rest of Vartan's papers. She kept her gun next to her. She couldn't stop worrying for her husband, whose life was probably at risk at this moment. As time went by, her fear turned into a more diffuse malaise, encompassing everything. Depressed, she decided to go out and walk in the garden. First she checked to see if Tomas was still asleep and then slung her gun across her shoulder.

Azniv Hanim had pulled an easy chair up to the window and was watching the garden. She had a butcher's knife at her side. Zeynep and Jemila were asleep, in a sitting position on the floor and their heads resting against the old lady's legs.

When she saw her daughter's anxious face, she tried to reassure her. 'You're worrying about nothing. I'm sure that Vartan will be back any minute now. I haven't stopped praying.'

Maro mumbled bitterly, 'I think God has turned deaf nowadays.'

'Don't talk like that.'

The bell startled them. Maro was suddenly filled with hope; then seized by doubts when she realized that she had not heard his horse. The two women pressed their foreheads against the pane. The moon was setting and they couldn't distinguish the visitor's face, but the silhouette was not Vartan's.

'I'll go and see,' said Maro, sliding the gun off her shoulder. 'You stay here. Maybe someone is bringing us news.'

'It isn't wise to answer the door.'

'Nonsense! A bandit doesn't ring doorbells to announce his arrival,' said Maro, heading towards the entrance. Barking, Sassoun tumbled down the stairs and followed her out. When she was at the steps, she asked, 'Who's there?'

'Armen.'

The dog recognized the familiar voice and ran to the gate.

'Is everything all right?' Armen asked, as she drew near.

'More or less. We're waiting for Vartan.' Her voice disclosed her worry. As she drew the bolt, she told her visitor that Vartan hadn't come home yet.

Armen was dressed in black so as to be less visible at night and was carrying a small pistol.

'The trouble's over. Vartan will soon be here. If he comes before the hour is up, we'll still have time.'

'What's holding him up?'

Armen wished he could comfort her, but didn't know exactly what to say. He tried his best though. 'Maybe he had to hand in a report or maybe he arrested some looters and had to escort them to the headquarters.'

'It's not like him. He knew how worried I was.'

Disconcerted, Armen tried to hold back the sigh swelling his chest. He couldn't make sense out of any of this. 'I'll wait with you.'

'Araksi?'

'She's frightened like the rest of us.'

As they walked towards the house, they heard hoof-beats from down the street. They listened closely. A horseman was approaching quickly.

'You see!' exclaimed Armen happily, but their joy was short-lived.

There was more than one rider. Armen pulled Maro back behind the spindle trees that bordered the pathway leading to the house. The horses stopped in front of the gate. Sassoun made his presence felt, alternately growling and barking. A man in a military uniform pulled the bell-chain.

'What do you want?' cried Maro from her hiding place.

'Maro Hanim?' It was Ibrahim Alizadé's voice.

She stepped out on the path, while Armen remained behind the trees. She laid her gun down, ran up to him and asked anxiously, 'Colonel Ibrahim, have you seen Vartan?' Then she saw Hour-Grag without a rider; crying out, she covered her face.

'He's alive,' Ibrahim hastened to say.

'Is he hurt?' Maro stammered.

'No.' Ibrahim found it as difficult to tell her about arresting Vartan as doing it had been. He was glad that darkness blurred her face. He blurted, 'He's been arrested. He's at the police station. I've brought his horse back.'

She remained speechless for a few moments. 'He's innocent, Colonel Ibrahim,' she pleaded.

He hesitated. 'I know, Maro Hanim, but innocence doesn't mean anything anymore.'

After the initial shock, fury gripped Maro. 'What do they accuse him of?'

'I haven't the slightest idea.'

Outraged, she opened the gate, took Hour-Grag's reins and put her hand on the pommel, while searching with her foot for the stirrup.

'What are you doing?' asked Ibrahim, astounded.

'I'm going to the police station.'

She hoisted herself onto the saddle, but he wrenched the reins from her hands.

'You can't do that!' he shouted rudely, and then calmed down. 'It's dangerous, Maro Hanim, and your interfering won't change anything. They won't even let you see him.'

'Get out of my way, Colonel Ibrahim!' Instead of obeying her, he guided Hour-Grag inside the courtyard, then stepped outside and closed the gate behind him. Armen came out of the bushes, greeted Ibrahim and told him who he was.

'The colonel is right, Maro. You're being foolish.'

She had to agree. She had been too impulsive. There must be a better way; above all, they must keep their heads. Vartan was alive and that was the main thing. She dismounted the horse, which trotted towards the stable.

'Colonel Ibrahim,' asked Armen, 'is his arrest an error, perhaps? Can we expect him to be freed soon?'

'Alas,' sighed Ibrahim. 'I'm afraid that it's very serious.'

'We should be able to do something.' Maro's voice quivered. 'You're his friend, Colonel Ibrahim. What do you advise us to do?'

'Don't try anything now. I'll know more tomorrow morning. Then we can talk it over and see what to do.' He felt deeply sorry, and he added, 'Believe me, Maro Hanim, I won't let Vartan down. I love him like a brother.'

'Thank you, Colonel.'

'Would you like to come, with your mother and son and stay with us while you're waiting? You'll be safe with us.'

She declined the invitation and, in a way, he felt relieved. As a friend, he had felt obliged to make the offer, but his superiors would have regarded him with distrust if he had sheltered the family of a political prisoner. His efforts to come to Vartan's aid might already have discredited him.

'If anything awful happens, let me know immediately.'

He said goodbye, promising to return as soon as he had some news.

As he was ready to leave, Maro said, 'Try to see him, Colonel Ibrahim. Reassure him. Tell him we're all right.'

The moment she was alone with Armen, Maro burst into sobs. A vision of Vartan behind bars haunted her. She thought about all those intellectuals who had been arrested in Constantinople and about their families who had never heard from them again. She could not live in such uncertainty.

They heard Azniv Hanim calling insistently, 'Come in please, come in.' She had been standing on the front steps since Armen's arrival and had witnessed the entire scene.

Maro rushed into her mother's arms. Holding a lamp in her hand, Jemila appeared in the doorway, looking terrorized. Curtly, Azniv Hanim ordered her to go and prepare some coffee; then, comforting Maro, she helped her up the steps. Armen followed them, cursing quietly.

The milky sky announced the dawn. The fly specks on the window made it almost impossible to see the outside, and the two guards, smoking in the doorway, blocked the view to the square. Stretched out on the bench, Vartan was sleeping fitfully. He woke up suddenly when his chin touched his chest. He looked at the clock on the wall; hardly a few minutes had passed since the last time he had woken up. This had been going for more than three hours. The wire was biting into his wrists so tightly that his hands were numb and the guard refused to let him walk around to restore the circulation in his legs. He even refused to give him anything to drink!

At the beginning, Vartan tried to decide what attitude he would take when confronted with those who had ordered his arrest. Impossible! He felt as if he were in a vacuum. He would have to play it by ear. Now that the rioting had ceased, there was no immediate threat hanging over his family, but how about tomorrow? What if the deportation order did not spare

Maro and Tomas? He became distraught when he thought about them and, right now, he needed all of his energy for himself. He tried to sleep and, during the moments when he was awake, he occupied his mind with trying to remember his brother, Noubar – not the portly forty-year-old but the lanky adolescent who had tirelessly criss-crossed the family lands in Afyon Karahisar. Under the exterior of a pragmatic farmer, Noubar had the soul of a poet of the land. One only had to hear him dreaming aloud of what the plantation would be like when he took charge. He drew up blueprints for fantastic machines equipped with wheels and levers; they looked like mechanical spiders that could nick open the capsules of the poppies and harvest the opium. Sometimes he imagined complex pumping systems, with endless numbers of screws to raise the water of the Akar River into reservoirs and canals to irrigate their fields.

It was a complete waste of time! Vartan could not prolong the image of his adolescent brother for long. The recent history of the Empire, the events of the last ten years and the episodes of his life following his marriage kept unfolding before his eyes. Looking back gave him the impression of a coherent whole, made up of episodes linked by causes and effects, whereas in actual fact the greater part of this past happened simply because of chance and spur-of-the-moment improvised decisions. He could only reproach himself in retrospect for being blind and lacking foresight.

The *muezzin*'s call to first prayer marked the end of the night. The sergeant took off his shoes and unrolled his *sejjadé*[1] and knelt on it, facing Mecca. The guards remained standing to watch the prisoner but their lips moved silently. After a while, the two men were relieved by the day shift. The new orderly was more lenient than his predecessor and gave Vartan something to drink – a glass of lukewarm water that had been left on the table beside the water jug all night.

Vartan could hear the bustling sounds of the awakening town – footsteps, bursts of Turkish or Kurdish conversation, bleating from a flock on its way to the market. At times the wall behind Vartan shook when a heavily loaded cart went by. Had Maro slept? And Tomas, who wouldn't understand why his father wasn't there? This was the hour when Azniv Hanim took her first cup of coffee. He wanted to reconstruct the morning ritual of his household but he could not, because today nothing was as before.

Then there was an endless parade of government officials, messengers and

---

1.    Prayer rug (Turkish).

officers, beginning their daily work. They arrived in twos and threes, joking and laughing. Some glanced absent-mindedly at the prisoner but the majority didn't even notice him. He overheard scraps of conversations and realized that several of them had taken part in last night's disturbances.

All of a sudden, a guard, who was posted outside, stuck his head inside the door. 'He's coming.'

The orderly snapped to attention; the sergeant buttoned the jacket of his uniform and the employees, who were chatting in the hall, instantly rushed to their desks.

Commissioner Mustapha Rahmi looked severely around the room and stopped when he got to Vartan. A broad smile lit up his face and he stroked the point of his beard. He came up to within a metre or so of the bench, and his expression of triumph turned to one of contempt.

'Major Vartan,' he said, feigning surprise, 'finally, we meet.'

'Commissioner.'

Mustapha gestured him to be quiet. 'Save your spit for your interrogation.' His tone expressed open threat. He looked straight in Vartan's eyes as he cracked his knuckles. A flash of cruelty shone in his eyes.

Vartan gave him a disdainful pout. He was wasting his time trying to be polite to the commissioner.

Mustapha's hatred for Vartan dated back, to be exact, to 1910. After the Young Turks movement, the government, under pressure from the European powers, had legislated certain administrative reforms for the Armenian provinces. Mustapha Rahmi, at that time the governor's deputy, was the person responsible for implementing these policies in Sivas and neighbouring provinces, but instead of favouring equal rights for Christians and Muslims in the eyes of the law, he amplified the already existing discriminatory measures against the Armenians. Vartan reacted by submitting a thick file to the French consul in Sivas and by calling on his friends who were still in the government in Constantinople to intervene. In the end, the Armenians of the province gained little, but Mustapha Rahmi served as a scapegoat and was demoted. If it had not been for Vartan's intervention, he would now have been a governor instead of a commissioner.

Mustapha turned on his heels and said to the sergeant, who was about to write something, 'Send the prisoner in to me in half and hour. Now, bring me some coffee.'

The commissioner was sitting behind his desk, sipping his coffee and swinging his leg. He was jubilant. He had not dared put Vartan's name on the list of people to be arrested, because he enjoyed the support of the military commander of the province and he himself was on bad terms with the general. But now, thanks to Gani Bey, he had that damned Vartan in his hands, and he was going to take advantage of it.

Someone knocked at the door. He put his cup down before shouting, 'Come in.'

He picked up the bamboo cane used for beatings; it was lying on the bench. Vartan came in flanked by a couple of robust soldiers and stood facing the commissioner. He knew he could expect nothing from this man and decided to treat him scornfully. The bluff probably would not help him much, but he had little choice.

He declared in a voice full of outrage, 'What's the meaning of this arrest? I demand to be released immediately.'

'Silence!'

Far from obeying, Vartan raised his voice. 'You have no right to detain me. I'm a military man and I'm not liable to civil justice.'

'I told you to shut up!' roared the commissioner.

'Fakri Pasha will hear about this, and you'll pay for it.'

Mustapha hit Vartan across the face with the bamboo cane. Vartan still had his hands wired behind his back and could not fend off the blow, which landed on his left cheek, splitting his lower lip. The cut burnt and blood ran down the side of his mouth.

'I'm a military officer,' he insisted furiously.

'I'll show you what you are,' the commissioner replied, making the cane whistle in front of his face. 'You two, take off his uniform. He's dishonouring the nation.'

The guards asked the commissioner how they were going to do that without untying his hands.

'Cut it into pieces.'

Vartan tried to resist in vain. One of the men opened his pocket knife and reduced the uniform to shreds. They then took his boots off, leaving him in his underpants.

'There,' the commissioner snickered. 'Now you're nothing.'

Vartan trembled with rage and fear of what was coming; nevertheless, he maintained an impassive face and asked defiantly, 'May I at least know what I am accused of ?'

'Of being what you are, a *giaour*.' The commissioner underlined his words with a burst of laughter as he said to his men, 'Hold him tight.'

The guards held Vartan by the arms and stood slightly behind him. The blows rained down. With diabolical skill Mustapha hit the same spot on his chest. Vartan clenched his teeth, resisting the increasing pain, without showing any suffering. Red weals came up on his skin and soon split open under the lash of the cane.

Vartan was dying to curse the commissioner but he held back, afraid of increasing his enemy's fury. He was not going to give that bastard the pleasure of hearing him moan! He fixed his attention on an Arabic pictograph painted on the wall and emptied his mind of everything else. He refused to feel the pain and made himself endure it with stoicism. He hovered in a state of stupor, detaching himself, as if he was not the one suffering the beating. His only concern was not to scream. Yet as he reached the limits of his endurance, he did moan involuntarily, and the commissioner, satisfied, stopped hitting him.

About a dozen red weals striped Vartan's back like a zebra. Mustapha Rahmi threw the cane into the corner of the room and rubbed his tired arm. 'Lock him up in the cellar,' he ordered.

The guards held Vartan up, as they dragged him down the stairs. His legs had given way.

# FOUR

The first of July was a morning of grief for the Armenians in Sivas. The community had been decapitated during the night! More than five hundred people – priests, teachers, doctors, lawyers and tradesmen – were stashed away in dungeons, and the common criminals who had already been in captivity there were freed. Gallows were set up in front of the City Hall.

In a cell originally intended for six prisoners, Der Khoren was urging his sixteen companions to pray and trust in the Lord. The interminable monologue of the priest bothered Ara, the barber, but he sat there listlessly. Before arresting him, the gendarmes had raped his wife in front of his eyes. Her cries still rang in his ears. One floor down, Zaven, the rich landowner, was wailing and lamenting his lot. He was still in his white cotton nightshirt, as he had been pulled out of bed during the night and not given time to dress. Further up in the cellar, in a windowless cell of the police station, Shirag, with absolute serenity, awaited his death. He was hoping it would come soon so he would no longer feel the unbearable pain caused by his oozing burns. He was unaware that Vartan lay unconscious on a straw mattress only three walls away.

Everyone was talking about the riots and arrests of the night before. In the market place business had come almost to a halt. Those who had misgivings about the government's treatment of the Armenians prudently kept quiet. Troops were already in town and the deportation seemed imminent. Many among the local population saw this as an opportunity to become rich. Anyone could profit from the abandoned lands, the furniture, the livestock and the evacuated houses.

Every Armenian household was grieving for a father, a husband, a son, an uncle or a cousin. And the gallows . . . why were they built so hastily?

And why were the soldiers knocking on every door and requiring all the able-bodied men, even boys as young as fifteen, to make up work crews? Suddenly it seemed all the roads and bridges in the province were in need of repair! Nobody was fooled.

During the night, many of the young people, rightly afraid of the worst, had stolen away and headed for the mountains of the south-west of Sivas. There they had joined what was left of Shirag's band, a group of almost one hundred and fifty confused, leaderless rebels. The newcomers had no specific plans, but they wanted revenge and to try to help the families they had left behind. Dozens of them took the solemn oath that made them *fedayis*. They were ready for anything, but they lacked arms.

Tomas woke up from the middle of a nightmare. He had been currying Hour-Grag when the horse seized him with its teeth, tossed him on to its back and took off at a gallop, running over Vartan, Maro and Azniv Hanim who tried to stop him. Tomas screamed but, suddenly paralyzed, could not throw himself off the horse. Hour-Grag neighed, but it was not his usual whinny; he sounded as though he was sniggering. The horse was galloping so far away with Tomas that he would never be able to find his way back again. They came up to a wall of fire and the horse charged into it. Tomas sat up in bed. The smoke still prickled his nose. He shook his head briskly to chase away the bad dream.

It was morning! His father had told him they were going to leave during the night. The child went to the window. Low, wispy clouds floated over the town while everywhere else the skies were blue. The air smelled of wood smoke. The cows, usually out to pasture at this hour, were mooing in the stable. Something was wrong. Noticing that his parents were not in their bedroom, Tomas rushed downstairs. He could hear the murmuring in the kitchen but the conversation stopped when he went in. His mother and grandmother were sitting facing each other across the table. Their faces were drawn and their eyes were red.

Before saying good morning he asked anxiously, 'Where's papa?'

How could they hide it from him? He had to be told the truth sooner or later. Maro wanted to take him in her arms but he stiffened and resisted.

'Where's papa?'

Maro tried to conceal the desolation from her voice. 'He's been arrested, like Der Khoren.'

'Why?' cried Tomas, throwing himself into his mother's arms.

'They're going to release him soon, I'm sure.'

The child's voice trembled. 'Is he in prison?'

'I think so.'

'I hate that.' Tomas burst into sobs.

Maro pressed her head against her son's and cradled him. Azniv Hanim looked away; Tomas's grief broke her heart. She wanted to leave but forced herself to remain seated at the table. She had to stay at her daughter's side, strong and confident, so that Maro wouldn't weaken. While Maro was consoling Tomas, Azniv Hanim heated some milk and spread some butter and honey on a slice of bread.

'You must eat,' she said, as she set the table for him.

Tomas shook his head but his grandmother insisted, 'You have to be strong. When your father returns, he must not find his son weak and sick.'

'*Medzmayrig* is right,' Maro said. 'I'm also going to eat.'

At their insistence, he bit into the slice of bread but he could hardly swallow it. It was hard for him to imagine his father, big and strong, being arrested. Why? He was so good to everybody and everybody respected him. He was an officer. A Major. They had no right to put him in jail. When he got out of prison, he would surely punish those who put him there. That idea comforted him a little.

The cows kept on mooing and the horses neighed. The sounds reminded Tomas of the nightmare that had awakened him, but he thought it best not to tell anyone about it.

'The animals are thirsty,' said Maro. 'Come, Tomas, let's go take care of them.' That would keep the child busy and her from worrying.

Alongside the garden path, Jemila and Zeynep, down on their knees, were silently weeding the flower-beds. Maro told them to draw some water from the well and take it to the stable. Tomas was surprised to see Gaydzak; he had completely forgotten about him since the night before. While he petted the animal, he could see, in his mind's eye, his father as he looked the night before, smiling as he gave Tomas his pony, and as he had looked the morning before when he had made Hour-Grag dance. Then he remembered his nightmare; he looked at Hour-Grag distrustfully and recoiled a little.

After they had watered the animals and stocked the mangers, Maro lingered in the stable. She began to curry her mare and for a moment she even forgot her son was there. Vartan occupied her whole mind.

The sound of hoof-beats, the sweet scent of herbs, the blinding light, the warm red stones – all of it came back to her vividly, as did the excitement she had felt only a week ago when Vartan had galloped after her! He could have caught her easily, but it amused him to control and direct her flight. A female chased by her male! Hot and sweaty, she had taken refuge in a gully, where a brook trickled. Vartan had come to her, eyes sparkling and arms outstretched, and under the chestnut trees bordering the brook, had made love to her twice – first, tempestuously, and then, after a rest, with infinite tenderness. Maro rested her forehead against the flank of her mare.

'Are you crying, mama?' asked Tomas, cuddling up to her.

'It's nothing. I'm just tired.'

'Are you thinking about papa?'

She straightened up and hugged her child. 'Just think of how happy we'll be when he comes back.'

The musty dungeon stank of urine and excrement. A cot covered with rotting straw stood in one corner. Vartan awoke from the sleep of the dead. He moaned as he sat up, for the slightest movement provoked pain in his back. The darkness was total. He explored the floor with his hands, trying to find the water jug that he thought would be there, but found nothing. He pounded on the heavy wooden door and waited, but no one came. It was not until several hours later that the bolts were drawn; he was blinded by the light from the lantern.

'I'm thirsty,' he said to the jailer whom he could hardly see.

'Get dressed. They're waiting for you.'

A bundle of clothes landed at his feet. Vartan slipped on a shapeless grey shirt and put on a pair of trousers, which didn't close at the waist. Although the grimy clothes stank of sweat, he was feeling better than he had on awakening. His mind was alert and his body had worked up some resistance against the pain from his muscles and lacerated skin. He went out into the hall lit by a few storm lanterns hanging from the ceiling.

'Hurry up,' said a second guard.

A stairway led to a corridor. The guards shoved the prisoner in the opposite direction. Further down, a rectangular room could be seen through its half-open door. When they entered it, the rings fixed to the ceiling beams and the three long benches left no doubt as to the use of the room. Vartan shivered as he remembered his morning encounter with the commissioner, but it was not Mustapha Rahmi who was there waiting for him. A fat man, his body almost bursting out of his black suit, sat behind the desk. He was smoking a cigarette. He looked the prisoner over slowly and scornfully. He placed a small, silver-plated revolver within hand's reach and signalled the guards to leave.

'Wait behind the door.'

The voice was familiar to Vartan, but he could not remember the man's face. Guessing that Vartan had not recognized him, the man introduced himself, 'Gani Bey.' He watched the effect his name had on Vartan with amusement, as he exhaled the smoke from his cigarette.

Vartan was so dumbfounded that he did not react. Gani Bey! The Minister of the Interior's right-hand man – his evil *alter ego*! Gani Bey had been Chief of Police under Abdul-Hamid II and Vartan had had a run-in with him. Now he knew the reason for his arrest. And now too he knew that there was no more hope!

Gani Bey confirmed this, saying smugly, 'You're a dead man, Vartan.'

Vartan looked at him contemptuously and remained silent.

'Do you know what brings me here?'

'Would you like a front seat to watch your fanatic, racial theories carried out?'

Instead of being annoyed at these words, Gani Bey was flattered. He nodded and murmured lightly, 'I've waited a long time for this moment.'

Much before the Young Turks revolution, Gani Bey had been a militant in all ultranationalistic organizations; he had actively collaborated with newspapers whose mission was to spread the Gospel of pan-Turkism. Vartan was infuriated; hatred and desperation welled up in him. He was lost, that much was certain. But if he could eliminate this monster, his death would have been worthwhile. His eyes glittered at the sight of the pistol on the desk, but Gani Bey quickly picked it up and pointed it at him.

'I'll be delighted to shoot you if you make the slightest move.'

Vartan thought his last hour had come but shrugged and added sarcastically, 'Now that I've witnessed your triumph, what more do you want from me? You surely don't expect me to congratulate you.'

'Why not?' asked Gani Bey, with a broad smile. 'You're an intelligent man. You haven't tried to argue, nor to proclaim the innocence of your people, nor to attack my philosophy.'

'Philosophy!' snorted Vartan and spat on the floor.

Gani Bey ignored him and went on, 'You know the situation well enough to realize that everything is over for your people. Nothing can stop the tide of history. People come and people go, as do empires, and are replaced by others, who are stronger and better adapted.'

'Spare me your speeches,' Vartan cut in.

His tone surprised Gani Bey. He stiffened and tightened his grip on the pistol. For a fraction of a second he was tempted to fire, but there was time enough for that. He lit a cigarette to calm himself down.

'Before I left Constantinople, the minister especially asked me to see that you were neutralized. He considers you to be a potential embarrassment.'

'Your minister does me great honour,' replied Vartan with heavy irony.

'That's enough,' said Gani Bey, shaking the ash off his cigarette. 'The minister is offering you a chance to save your skin. I myself wouldn't have been so generous.' He paused for a minute to give his words time to sink in.

Vartan watched him distrustfully, and asked in an indifferent tone, 'What are you talking about?'

'You're to write articles for the foreign newspapers and to send letters to well-placed people in the United States and other countries. You're to explain the reasons for deporting the population to places far from the front lines. You're to praise the organization, the humane conditions under which this deportation is taking place and the beauty of the villages where we are resettling the exiles.'

Vartan couldn't help laughing. 'You can't be serious. How can you think for a minute I'd stoop to such a farce?'

'In the past, you've never hesitated to disparage your country to the outside world, to discredit the official policies of the government and to incite the European powers to meddle in the Empire's affairs. Now you have a chance to redeem yourself.'

'Lies! You know very well all I've ever wanted was progress for the Empire.'

'You mean its ruin!' roared Gani Bey, but calmed down immediately. 'We're wasting time. My offer stands. In return for your collaboration, you and your family will be safe – and that's not to mention the material advantages you'll enjoy. After the war is over, you can restart your life outside the Empire under another name or even occupy a high position in the administration of a Greater Turkey. Of course, we expect you to convert to Islam to show us your good will.'

Vartan stared at Gani Bey incredulously. Did he really expect him to accept such a deal? To betray his people and condone the murder of a whole nation?

'No!' he said. More words seemed superfluous.

'Other prominent Armenians wouldn't hesitate.'

'Then let them bring dishonour on themselves. I pity them.'

Gani Bey lit another cigarette from the glowing butt of the old one. He called the guards. They came in and stood next to the prisoner.

Still smiling, Gani Bey said unctuously, 'I'll play fair. I'll give you a little time to think it over. I'm told you have a very beautiful wife and a charming little boy. Think about them during the next three days. They'll be leaving Sivas then and, with a little bit of luck, your wife will become the property of a soldier or a brigand and your son will become a handyboy on a farm where they won't have enough food to feed him. The road will be long and dangerous. But you, you won't even care; you'll be half dead by then!'

Vartan blanched but restrained himself from responding with insult. He had been given a chance; he should not waste it. He bowed his head. 'I'll think about it,' he murmured.

'I strongly advise you to, but you'd better be quick about it.'

'May I send a word to my wife?'

'No. Work for us and you'll see her again.' Leaning heavily on the table, Gani Bey rose and ordered the guards, 'Take him back to his cell and give him something to eat.'

Maro's waiting had now turned into an unbearable ordeal. The hours dragged with desperate slowness. She jumped to the window at the slightest sound and was disappointed each time. Why was it taking so long for Colonel Ibrahim to bring her news? She decided to go to the police station to see the police commissioner. It had taken all of Azniv Hanim's authority and a promise from Armen that he would go and look for Ibrahim Alizadé himself to dissuade her.

At precisely the same moment, Colonel Ibrahim was having a meeting with Commissioner Mustapha, who informed him that Vartan was condemned to death. When he inquired what the Major was accused of, the commissioner became annoyed.

'High treason!' he finally said triumphantly.

'I suppose you have proof?' said Ibrahim, who was quite familiar with the speaker's duplicity.

'Of course!' The question irritated Mustapha Rahmi. 'What business is it of yours?'

'This Balian is a Major in the Ottoman Army. A court martial should . . .'

Mustapha cut him off, 'This matter has already been judged in the capital.'

'In that case, according to the constitution, a condemned soldier has the right to appeal to the Sultan for grace.'

'We're talking about an Armenian, not a soldier!' Mustapha was exasperated. He looked Ibrahim scornfully in the eye and asked artfully, 'Tell me, Colonel Ibrahim, what do you think about the deportation of the *giaours*?'

The Colonel at once spotted a trap. 'I'm sure the government must know what it's doing.'

Following this evasive reply, Ibrahim took leave of the commissioner. He didn't believe the story of treason at all. Mustapha had given away the real reason for Vartan's sentence without meaning to – Vartan was an Armenian! The Colonel realized his chances for saving his friend were slim. It all depended on Fakri Pasha's good will. He would not let Gani Bey belittle him by acting as a law unto himself. If only Ibrahim could persuade the Pasha to support Vartan's cause; then perhaps . . . While crossing the square, Ibrahim noticed the gallows and fifteen dangling corpses. They had been left there since morning for people to see. He knew that the Armenians who were supposedly taken to repair roads would not be returning. Most of them had already been dumped in the bottom of a ravine, killed by a bullet in the neck, or by a bayonet.

The Colonel grieved not only for his country but also for these poor people. Instead of fighting the enemy who were pushing against its borders, they were waging war on innocent civilians. This government, which decided to get rid of the Christians, was the same administration that had provoked the war in the Balkans. That was where Ibrahim had almost lost his life. It had been a senseless war . . . a defeat for which the government held the Ottoman forces responsible. Today these same ministers were on the German side. Ibrahim was convinced that they were backing the wrong horse. He would have liked to know how many other officers shared his point of view.

What was he going to tell Maro? She was undoubtedly expecting her husband to be set free quickly and Ibrahim did not have the heart to tell her the truth. After thinking it over thoroughly, he decided to tell her a compassionate lie: Vartan was holding up well and Fakri Pasha was taking a personal interest in his case. The truth was that the commissioner had refused to permit Ibrahim to see Vartan and, as for the support of Fakri Pasha, the Colonel was making that up because he would not even see the General until that evening.

Vartan was spending his second day in prison. He stood leaning against the wall, eating sticky rice seasoned with a trace of green pepper. Worse than the stench and dampness was the perpetual darkness, which he found unbearable. He had the impression of living through an endless, sleepless night. The lack of any indication of the passing of time confused him and, like an insomniac, he ceaselessly juggled in his mind the same unanswered questions. After the encounter with Gani Bey the night before, Vartan was expecting a final ultimatum: collaborate or die!

The door of the dungeon opened before he had finished his bowl of rice. Colonel Ibrahim's blue eyes gleamed in the light of the lantern he was holding out. As he stepped into the cell, he grimaced with disgust and turned to the sergeant standing behind him.

'Leave us alone. Don't come back until I call you.' Once alone, he put the lantern down and embraced Vartan. 'My poor friend! What a stinking hole they've put you in! And those rags!'

He was not really surprised at the conditions of the cell. Some of the Ottoman jails were even worse but Vartan's pitiful appearance shocked him.

'I'm glad to see you, Ibrahim. What about my family? Are they all right?'

'I saw your wife yesterday. She's worried about you, which is understandable.'

Vartan was moved and, contrary to his usual habit, he let his feelings show. He gripped his visitor's arm. 'You're a good friend.'

Ibrahim was embarrassed. On his way to the police station, he had thought that he was bringing his friend good.news. Now, in the stink and dirt of the dungeon, he thought his news was going to sound ridiculous. He offered him a cigarette and lit one himself.

114

'I've been able to get a trial set for you,' he announced with an enthusiasm that rang false.

Vartan guessed that Ibrahim had gone to a lot of trouble and he patted him on the shoulder. 'That's wonderful! They'll have to find a reason to accuse me and submit some proof. I'll have a chance to defend myself.'

Vartan really was happy. A trial would eliminate the arbitrariness of the accusation and would mean that he would not be wholly dependent on Gani Bey's whim.

'How did you manage it?'

'I played up to Fakri Pasha's pride. He unfortunately has to bow to Gani Bey's wishes; which enrages him. As he is forced to cede on other important issues, he was inflexible in your case.'

'And Gani Bey? He made a deal?' Vartan was astounded.

'I imagine that he prefers not to have the General on his back. He needs him for . . .' Ibrahim stopped short. He had been about to say 'the deportation'.

Vartan saved him from further embarrassment. 'I'm touched by your concern.'

Ibrahim smiled awkwardly. He pulled a metal flask from his tunic and held it out to Vartan. As the latter gulped down the brandy, he said mournfully: 'Don't get too excited. It won't be a real court martial. Gani Bey will preside at the trial, which will probably be brief. I'll be there as an official observer, but I won't be able to do much for you.'

Vartan grimaced. For a moment he had been filled with hope, but now it melted away. To soften the demoralizing effect of his last words, Ibrahim added, 'The trial isn't really important. What's important is that we've gained a little time.'

'Time!' Vartan exclaimed, without hiding his disappointment. 'What difference will that make?'

'All the difference. Gani Bey is here only for a short time. When he's gone, Fakri Pasha can have you transferred to a military prison and then set you free. If not, I'll try to organize your escape, but to do that, you have to stay alive.'

'That's what I want, too, but it's not up to me,' Vartan replied aggressively.

By the flickering flame of the lantern, Vartan silently watched their shadows on the wall, which curved up onto the ceiling. There were graffiti in Arabic script engraved on the stones. A rat scurried across the floor, following a runnel that traversed the cells, carrying urine and faeces to a cesspool at the end of the basement. In spite of his good intentions, Ibrahim had not offered him anything concrete. Vartan still had nothing to hang on to except vague and uncertain hopes. He told his friend about Gani Bey's proposition. Instead of being shocked, Ibrahim saw it as a way out for Vartan.

'Take it if the trial goes badly.'

For a moment Vartan was taken aback. 'You? A man of honour? You think I should betray my people?'

'Of course not, but play along with him. That way, you can delay the deadline.'

'Gain time again?' Vartan sounded sarcastic and regretted his outburst immediately. His tone became friendly but his voice betrayed his resignation. 'No, Ibrahim. Even if I were cowardly enough to make a deal with Gani Bey, it would get me nowhere. As soon as I finished writing all the documents he wants, he'd get rid of me, because I could become an embarrassing witness.'

His friend's defeatist attitude saddened Ibrahim. He had always known him to be resolute, dynamic and quick to react. As far as Vartan was concerned, however, the future looked unremittingly black.

As if reading Ibrahim's mind, Vartan asked, 'What's happening to the others who were arrested?'

A shadow passed over Ibrahim's eyes, but his voice remained steady, 'They're being hanged, about thirty a day.'

'And the deportation . . . When is it scheduled for?'

'Day after tomorrow, I think.'

'And my trial?'

'Tomorrow.'

Vartan touched his friend's arm. 'Will you keep an eye on Maro and Tomas if something happens to me?'

'Of course, but that hasn't happened yet.'

They said goodbye, embracing each other for a long time.

Then Ibrahim knocked hard on the door. 'Hey there! Open up.' He picked up the lantern and turned to Vartan. 'I'll leave you the flask and the cigarettes. May Allah watch over you.'

'And over you too, Ibrahim.'

The door closed and Vartan was left in the suffocating darkness. He did not feel as alone and crushed as before Ibrahim's visit, but he was more acutely conscious of the distance that separated him from Maro – a distance measurable not in metres and steps but in hours and days.

When Azniv Hanim saw her daughter standing at the foot of the stairs, dressed like a Turk in an ankle-length brown *feraje*, with her head and face covered by a *yashmak*, she guessed her daughter's intentions and let out a shriek.

Maro stopped her firmly. 'Don't tell me anything.' Azniv Hanim held her back, but Maro defied her. 'And if it were your husband who had been held in jail for three days?'

From her tone and look, Maro's mother knew that any discussion would be in vain, so she offered to go with her.

'I'll feel better if you're taking care of Tomas.'

'Go and get Armen.'

'It's out of the way. It isn't worth it.'

Azniv Hanim followed Maro as she headed towards the stable. She was trembling inwardly for her daughter, but she knew and understood her only too well to try to stop her. She would have done the same, if it had been her husband. She was far from reassured by the prospect of the trial, as the law in this country was not to be trusted, especially in these troubled times!

Maro backed the horse between the shafts of the carriage. 'I'm not going to see him. Colonel Ibrahim mentioned a certain Gani Bey, who's staying at the government house. He's the big boss, it seems.'

'I'll pray to the Son of God for you to find the right words to reach him. But don't hesitate to mention an important sum of money.'

Maro rattled the bag she had hidden under her loose robe.

'You should, at least, take one of the young girls with you. Your disguise will seem more credible. No respectable Muslim woman would go out alone.'

She was right, so Maro asked Zeynep to accompany her. Before she went out the gate, she pulled her *yashmak* over to cover the lower part of her face. The transparent black veil accentuated her mysterious beauty.

'Be careful,' Azniv Hanim said, hugging her hard. 'Be careful!'

Maro climbed up onto the driver's bench and sat next to Zeynep. 'I'm sure I'll find a way to handle this business.'

Once the gate was closed, Azniv Hanim crossed herself three times – first with her thumb, then with her index finger and last with the middle finger of her right hand.

There were gendarmes everywhere but no one stopped Maro's carriage. She arrived at the governor's palace without any trouble. She left her carriage in the courtyard and asked Zeynep to keep an eye on it. After adjusting her veil, she approached the policeman standing at the front entrance.

'I have an appointment with Gani Bey.'

He pointed towards the hall. 'See his secretary, *Hanim*, the second door on the right.'

She entered the anteroom without knocking, and the man sitting at the desk woke up from daydreaming, all surprised. He had three deep wrinkles across his flat forehead, thick eyebrows, drooping eyelids, and a red mark on his left cheek from leaning on his hand. 'What do you want?'

'I want to see Gani Bey.'

'Impossible. He's working and won't be disturbed.'

'Please announce me and we shall see.'

The secretary shook his head firmly.

'In that case, I'll wait until he comes out for lunch.' Maro sat down in a chair by the only window that gave onto the courtyard.

'You can't do that, *Hanim*. You must go.'

She shook her head as he had done. He sighed and continued sorting some papers. He was only shuffling them from one pile to the other, pretending to read them. His jerky movements were signs of his irritation.

Ten minutes later, Maro went up to him and put a gold piece on the ink-stained desk blotter. 'Try to get me an appointment.'

'I'll see what I can do,' he said, pocketing the coin. 'Who shall I say is calling?'

'Major Vartan's wife.'

Gani Bey received her in a drawing room. The shade of the large linden trees in front of the windows made the inside temperature more bearable. Green reflections danced on the white marble walls and the orange rays of sunlight streamed myriad dusty specks onto the Persian carpet on the floor. Gani Bey sat, enthroned, in the centre of a *sedir*, looking like a podgy Buddha. His blue silk dressing-gown gaped open and bared his hairless milk-white chest. He sat completely still as his visitor approached, and studied her with glassy eyes.

A kinky-haired ten-year-old boy, wearing only baggy breeches narrowing at the ankles, stood next to the *sedir*, fanning Gani Bey. Without being asked, he put the fan on the floor and left the room by a door hidden behind a curtain, his bare feet slapping noisily on the slabs.

Waving languidly, Gani Bey directed Maro to an old, faded easy-chair. She smelled the peculiar aroma of hashish. A small pipe was lying on a low table in front of the couch. Next to it was a crystal water carafe, a bowl of fruit and a plate of Turkish delight. She sat down and took off her veil. In an attempt to secure all possible advantages, Maro had applied her make-up with great care. Gani Bey found her very beautiful but in a way he was sorry that she had removed her veil; this put him in a difficult situation. He was not attracted by women, but he always found something in them that reminded him of his mother, whom he had adored, and he felt vulnerable in their presence.

'A *houri* . . .' he murmured. 'You're an absolute *houri*!'

His breath smelt of garlic and Maro thought he looked like a pig. This lump of lard held their fate in his hands. Hatred enveloped her, but she continued to smile timidly. In his euphoric state, Gani Bey thought she was beholding him with motherly tenderness, and he hoped she would remain silent, because the moment she spoke the spell would disappear. Besides, he already knew what she was going to say. Maro was encouraged by Gani Bey's complacent look and began to speak:

'I'm honoured that you deigned to receive me, Gani Bey. It's said that you have the Sultan's ear. I know only you can set the injustice done to my family to rights.'

He found her flattery repugnant. He sighed wearily and squinted. Then he pointed to a hexagonal table on the right of the couch. There Maro saw a cigarette case, a lighter and a crystal ashtray, and she hurriedly gave them to him.

While he was lighting his cigarette, she continued in a sweet but firm voice, 'My husband, Major Vartan, was arrested and is being put on trial unjustly.'

Gani Bey inhaled deeply but the smoke did not soothe him. His features hardened but his voice remained soft, 'If he's innocent, you don't have to worry about the trial.'

Maro looked him straight in the eyes to show him he had not fooled her. 'There might be some people eager to harm him. A prominent man

119

generates envy. You, Gani Bey, who are an eminent person, know that better than anyone else.' She did not know that he was completely immune to flattery.

The fumes of hashish dissipated in the air, and Gani Bey thought that the interview was becoming tedious but concealed his impatience. This woman intrigued him. She had the nerve to put on this ingratiating air, but he could perceive her contempt. He bit into a Turkish delight to get rid of the disagreeable taste in his mouth before offering one to Maro.

'My husband was a member of the Ittihad. He was a member of the Parliament.'

'I know,' Gani Bey retorted, turning his eyes to the curtains to express his lack of interest. He clapped his hands and the boy with the baggy pants came in.

'Serve us some orangeade.'

All of Maro's efforts to steer the conversation had failed. Losing patience, she pressed on. 'My husband is above reproach.'

The boy served the orangeade in tall glasses engraved with delicate motifs.

'To your health, *Hanim.*'

'To your health, Gani Bey.'

This pretence of politeness exasperated Maro. She knew Vartan was in prison because of this man and he realized that she knew it. She put her glass down and asked bluntly, 'What's he accused of?'

Gani Bey shrugged and answered evasively, 'I don't know exactly. Treason, I think.'

'That's absurd!' she exclaimed. 'Vartan has always been a loyal subject of his Highness the Sultan.'

He smirked ironically. 'What about all those articles he wrote in the foreign press, criticizing the government? Do you really think he was acting like a patriot?'

Maro's face blushed but she said, 'Yes! All he ever advocated was for the government to keep its promises and treat all the Ottoman citizens justly. That's not treason!'

Gani Bey hid his amusement at her ardour and argued, 'In time of war, it is!'

'My husband has written nothing since last autumn.'

'Hamazasp, Aris, Hagopovich, Chris, Lusignan: those are the

pseudonyms your husband has been using lately.' He looked at her mockingly.

She showed no sign of embarrassment, even though what Gani Bey had just said was true. She did not restrain from protesting Vartan's innocence, 'That's false, completely false.' She was glad they had burnt all the compromising papers. She continued vehemently, 'Lately, as you know, my husband has been serving in the Ottoman Army. He has no time to write anything. He has devoted all his time and attention to taking care of wounded soldiers . . . Turkish soldiers! And he would still be doing that today, had he not been unjustly arrested.'

Gani Bey lit another cigarette and pretended to be thinking it over. He was wondering just how far this woman would go to save her husband.

'I'll take your testimony into account, *Hanim*, but, alas, it doesn't depend on me.'

'I'm sure you're much too modest, Gani Bey. One word from you can arrange everything.'

'You have to trust in the justice of the court.'

Maro felt her efforts vanish into thin air. She took her purse from under her robe and laid it heavily on the table, its contents clanking. Gani Bey frowned, but Maro could see that he was not the least outraged. *Baksheesh* was a tradition in the Ottoman government and no one found the practice reprehensible.

'Just in case,' she said, 'please, Gani Bey, don't be offended. This is intended for the men who'll judge my husband, so that they will be lenient with him.'

He shook his head, meaning, 'We'll see.'

Maro was not satisfied and she implored, 'I beg you to intervene, Gani Bey. Don't let him be judged on pure lies.' Then she continued less emotionally, 'My husband is an intellectual and he can render invaluable service to the Empire. He speaks several languages and has several important contacts in the outside world.'

'With our enemies!'

'The army needs people to take care of the wounded at the front lines and Vartan is willing to serve there.'

Gani Bey looked at her curiously. 'Do you love him that much?'

She straightened up and exclaimed passionately, 'More than my life!'

These words expressed what had always been incomprehensible to Gani Bey – that one could love another more than one's self. As he looked at her anxious eyes, expecting everything from him, he was reminded of the Christian legend of Salomé, who had danced to have a man beheaded. This woman who was facing him would do anything to get her husband back alive. He was convinced that if he asked her to undress and dance for him, she would agree, in spite of her propriety. Just how low could he push her if he promised to liberate her Vartan? He was glad he was incapable of feeling love, even for the most beautiful of young men. He who has mastery of his own heart can rule the world!

For a moment he thought of using Maro as a hostage to force her husband to collaborate, but then he decided not to bother. If he remembered correctly, the idea of using prominent Armenians to defend governmental policies to the outside world was Talaat Pasha's idea. He was convinced of the importance of foreign opinion, and was wont to say, 'One day those papers will be very important when someone rewrites history.' Gani Bey had had enough. Only the priorities of the Empire counted for him and the end justified the means.

His stomach let him know that the lunch hour had arrived and he cut the discussion short. He politely smiled at Maro, who was anxiously watching him.

'Rest assured, *Hanim*, I'll do everything I can for your husband.'

The statement she had been waiting so desperately to hear! It took her a few seconds to react and then she beamed. She searched for words to express her gratitude. He smiled benevolently and gestured her to say nothing further. 'Words are not necessary, *Hanim*. It's enough for me to see that look on your face. I'll let you know this afternoon by messenger when you'll see your husband.'

Maro could not help herself and a stream of thanks tumbled out of her lips.

Around six o'clock three *zaptiyés* showed up at the Balians' garden gate. Sassoun barked his head off, jumping up and down on the front steps. The family was in the living-room with Armen, who had just arrived but had not yet told them why he had come.

Maro turned to the servant. 'Jemila, let them in, and Zeynep, prepare refreshments for them.'

She had been burning with impatience since her return from the government house. Ignoring her mother's warnings that she was being over-optimistic, Maro waited excitedly for the messenger to arrive. They went and stood on the landing outside while Jemila ran to the gate.

'Papa isn't with them,' Tomas muttered, disappointed.

Holding him by the shoulder, Maro said, 'They're coming to tell us when your father will be set free.'

When the gendarmes came in, Zeynep offered them some cherry juice. The Sergeant was surprised and hesitated before taking the glass, but then gulped down its contents.

'Do you have any message for me?' Maro asked, stepping up to him.

'Is this Vartan Balian's residence?' he asked, taking a paper out of his tunic.

'Yes. Give it to me quickly.' Maro held out her hand.

But instead of giving the paper to her, he carefully unfolded it. The scar at the corner of his mouth made him look as if he were perpetually smiling.

'I'll read it to you,' he said clearing his throat. 'All Armenians, without exception as to age or status, are ordered to leave this town by tomorrow morning. The government has put one cart and one ox at each family's disposal; they may take food, clothing and personal effects only. The deportees will gather outside the city to form a convoy and an escort of guards shall accompany them for their security. The rest of their belongings will be transported at the expense of the government and will be delivered to them upon arrival at their new place of residence.'

'You have the wrong house, Sergeant,' said Azniv Hanim.

'What do you mean?'

'Military families are exempt from this decree, and this is Major Vartan Balian's residence.'

He shrugged. 'I have the same orders for everyone. You have to leave tomorrow morning, before noon. Otherwise, you'll be forced out.'

'There must be a mistake,' Maro insisted in a desperate voice. 'I've just been to see Gani Bey and . . .'

The Sergeant wasn't even listening anymore. She pulled the sheet of paper out of his hands. The deportation order was printed in a greyish ink, which came off on her fingers. She reread it, giving herself time to calm down. She realized that Gani Bey had deceived her cruelly. She crumpled up the paper, threw it on the ground and hurried into the house. Her footsteps resounded on the stairs. Tomas wanted to run after her but his godfather held him back.

Azniv Hanim dismissed the soldiers, then turned to Zeynep. 'Show them to the gate, my child.'

Before leaving, the Sergeant warned them, 'Be ready at dawn, or . . .'

Armen picked up the wrinkled sheet of paper and inspected it as he followed Azniv Hanim to the living room. She took Tomas's hand and advised him to leave his mother alone for a while.

'She'll be back with us in a minute. She probably has a headache.'

'I want my father,' sobbed Tomas.

'Be brave, Tomas. Now you're the only man in the house. You must be reasonable and help us.'

Tomas sniffed and nodded. He picked up the picture-book he had been leafing through before the guards had arrived, but now he just turned the pages, while watching Armen's and his grandmother's slightest gestures and letting Sassoun lick his tears.

Armen showed the deportation order to Azniv Hanim. 'I received one, too. That's why I came over.'

'The hypocrite,' raged Azniv Hanim. 'It was too good to be true. I told Maro but . . . she rejoiced too soon.'

While they were still trying to think of a way out, Azniv Hanim was just setting the table at home when she heard a racket outside. She turned to the window, but the hazelnut bushes were blocking the view.

Tomas ran in shouting, 'Grandmother! Grandmother! The *zaptiyés*! A lot of them!'

She went out. Eight or nine soldiers had forced the gate and were entering the garden. Sassoun was running around them and barking. He ran to the first guard and tried to bite him on the leg. The man booted him away and the spaniel retreated, howling, towards the house. The soldiers guffawed loudly.

'Sassoun,' screamed Tomas. 'They've hurt Sassoun.'

Azniv Hanim ran and grabbed her grandson by the collar. 'Stay here,' she said.

The dog joined them at the entrance and Tomas checked to see if he was hurt. 'Take him into the house and close the door.' Then she turned to the soldiers and, in a voice shaking with anger, she asked, 'What do you want? Just get out of here.'

124

The Lieutenant, who was in command of the detachment, approached her, while his men filed on to the stable. He remained standing at the foot of the steps, hand on hips, legs apart, staring mockingly at the old woman.

His insolence did not faze her. 'Just what is this all about?'

'You have got horses. We need to take them.'

'You have no right!'

'We have all the right. You won't be needing them anymore,' he replied, amused. Pleased with his little triumph, he hurried to the pathway along which his men were returning, pulling two cows and three horses behind them. Hour-Grag didn't like being led by an unfamiliar hand, and accordingly was snorting and pulling back. A soldier hit him repeatedly with the butt of his rifle. Standing behind the glass door, Tomas felt his heart stop – Hour-Grag, his father's beloved horse! Then he saw them taking his pony, Gaydzag. He wanted to run out and stop them, but his grandmother was outside the door, holding the knob and blocking the way. Tomas kicked at the door, yelling at the top of his lungs.

'The bastards!' whispered Azniv Hanim. 'They're even taking the saddles and the carriage.'

Tomas's screams unnerved her completely and she lost her head. She grabbed a rake that was leaning against the wall and ran at the guards.

'*Shan zavakner!*'[1]

The Lieutenant ducked the blow and retaliated by hitting Azniv Hanim in the face with his fist. She staggered and then the officer slapped her. She crumpled on the walk. Tomas wanted to go out and help his grandmother, but he was paralyzed by terror. It was only after the soldiers were out on the street that he ran to her.

Pastor Roesler, the director of the Swiss orphanage, received Maro and Armen warmly but his face fell when Maro asked if they could stay with them until Vartan's trial was over. The Armenian teachers had already been arrested. The women who worked there had returned to their families to get ready for their imminent deportation. This left only the pastor and his wife to care for the children whom the Ottoman authorities would soon take in charge.

'They're closing my orphanage,' complained the Protestant minister.

---

1. Sons of bitches (Armenian).

'Young Christians in a Muslim institution! What a farce!'

'Can't anyone do anything?' asked Armen.

'I asked the American Consul to intervene. They simply told him to go to hell.' Pastor Roesler clasped his hands and raised his eyes to heaven, 'What's to become of these poor children?'

Under the circumstances the director didn't have to say more. Another disappointment. Another defeat. But they mustn't lose heart.

The streets were swarming with gendarmes and soldiers, leading horses and mules by their bridles and herding sheep, goats and cows ahead of them. As these left the Armenian Quarter, others arrived with ox-carts with enormous, high wheels, the kind that had been in use in the Near East since the time of the Hittites.

'They certainly aren't wasting any time,' grumbled Armen, before leaving Maro in front of her house.

Zeynep was waiting near the gate. She was as white as sheet. The door lock was broken and the iron gate wide open. Nervously, she told Maro about what had happened to Azniv Hanim and about the soldiers who had stolen the animals.

'The soldiers forced the door; they took the horses, even the saddles and the carriage, and they hit the *Hanim* in the face. They slapped her . . .'

'Spare me the details,' Maro said impatiently, as they both ran to the house.

'Is she conscious?'

'Yes.'

Maro found her mother sitting in the kitchen, with swollen lips and a compress on her left eye. The old woman was busy scolding Jemila who was walking up and down and wringing her hands.

'Stop walking in circles. You're making me dizzy.'

In spite of her protests, Maro examined her mother's eye, which was already turning black. Azniv Hanim also had a large bruise on her cheek.

'Are you sure they didn't break anything?' Maro asked worriedly.

'No, no.' replied Azniv Hanim gruffly. 'It doesn't even hurt any more. It was all my fault. I acted like a fool. I slapped the Sergeant first.'

'That was foolish, Mother. You ought to lie down.'

'We have too much to do,' she said, putting the compress on her eye again. 'A cup of coffee and I'll be ready for combat.' She went over to the alcohol burner and added hoarsely, 'Let this be a lesson to us all. From now on we have to watch our step. We're just like cattle to them and our lives depend on the whims of coarse brutes.'

Wide-eyed in a corner, half hidden by the iron stove, Tomas sat watching. When his mother came near, he burst into tears. He could barely whimper, 'Gaydzag! They took Gaydzag!'

Maro took him by the hand out of the kitchen. 'Come, my darling. I have to explain what's happening to us.'

After the usual evening meal of *lapa,* a dish of overcooked insipid rice, Vartan was taken handcuffed to the room in the basement, where he had been with Gani Bey two days before. Since he had been shut up in the dark, his eyes hurt from the light of the hall lamps, although they were very dim. He was dirty and had a four-day-old beard. He scratched his chest, as he had been bitten by the many bedbugs infesting his straw mattress. They had kept him from sleeping, but his physical suffering was nothing compared to his mental anguish. He was tormented, worrying about his family who needed him now so badly. What would become of them? About his own fate he had no illusions.

As he entered the room, Vartan overheard the end of a sentence: '. . . your intolerable meddling!'

Gani Bey was sitting at a table flanked by Commissioner Mustapha and Colonel Ibrahim. The latter greeted Vartan with a discreet wink to hearten him, but Vartan could tell from his frown he was worried. Gani Bey had probably been upbraiding him and Mustapha was making no effort to hide his glee. Already bored, Gani Bey kept looking at his watch. This then was to be his trial – a crude mockery of justice!

The two guards sat on a bench at the end of the room, while Vartan stood facing the judges. Gani Bey looked him up and down disgustedly and asked, 'Have you thought over my generous proposition?'

'My answer is no.'

Unperturbed, Gani Bey lit a cigarette. 'Read the charges, Commissioner.'

Mustapha coughed twice and began to recite the text which he knew almost by heart:

'Major Vartan Balian, an Armenian pharmacist, reserve officer in the Army and renowned political journalist, is accused of having organized

127

armed rebel groups in the province of Sivas. His main accomplice is a man called Shirag Tevonian.'

Vartan cried indignantly, 'That's a web of lies!'

'Silence,' ordered the commissioner, 'or back to your cell you go and your trial will continue without you.'

Gani Bey said sarcastically, 'Did Shirag Tevonian come to see you in your tent at the hospital to talk about the weather?'

Vartan had been expecting them to bring up the articles he had written for the foreign press and had prepared to defend himself, even though he knew they would not let him speak. As for Shirag's visit, however, he did not know what to say.

The commissioner went on reading: 'The accused has been in contact with several subversive organizations planning to overthrow the legitimate government of the Empire by encouraging an invasion by enemy powers.'

Vartan could not keep himself from speaking out again. 'Those are nothing but cheap suppositions.'

Instead of getting angry, Gani Bey smiled. 'There's worse yet to come. Please continue, Commissioner.'

'Vartan Balian is also accused of the murder of the mayor, Mumtaz Bey, which took place on the outskirts of Sivas on June the thirtieth 1915.' Mustapha Rahmi put the paper down on the table and crossed his arms.

Colonel Ibrahim turned to Gani Bey, 'Those are very grave accusations and Major Vartan has an impeccable reputation. Do you have any proof?'

'Proof and witnesses,' responded the commissioner. 'May I?' he added turning to Gani Bey.

'Please go ahead.'

'Bring in the witnesses,' said Mustapha to one of the guards.

The guard left and returned with two men: a civilian with a prison-style hair-cut and a corporal who looked drunk. Mustapha addressed the civilian:

'Please state your name and occupation.'

The man, who sported a thick, drooping moustache, said in broken Turkish, 'Arpajioglou Ismael, knife-grinder.'

'Do you recognize this man?'

'Yes.' answered the witness.

'When did you see him?'

'Four days ago. I saw him come out of Mumtaz Bey's house.'

'Alone?'

'No. He was with another man, and they were running.'

'Can you tell us the time?'

'I don't know. I don't know how to tell time.'

'More or less?'

'Dawn. The muezzin had already called the first prayer.'

'All right,' said the commissioner. 'You can go.'

The man seemed to be relieved.

'One moment, please,' said Colonel Ibrahim. 'I'd like to cross-examine the witness.'

Gani Bey was incensed. 'That's out of the question. May I remind you that you're here as an observer and not as a defence lawyer.'

Ibrahim's lips tightened angrily. He shot Vartan a distressed look. He knew his friend could not be guilty of the murder of Mumtaz Bey, nor of anyone else. False witnesses! He was revolted by this parody of justice, but could do no more than inform Fakri Pasha of this matter.

Vartan listened to the second witness, the Corporal, who lied about how he had searched the prisoner after his arrest, and found in Vartan's pocket the amber rosary that Mustapha was now holding up for all to see. Under Gani Bey's approving eyes, the commissioner went through the whole process briskly. He was choosing his words carefully and speaking in a quiet tone, which he thought appropriate for a magistrate.

'We've established beyond the shadow of a doubt that this *tespih* belonged to Mayor Mumtaz Bey. It therefore constitutes irrefutable proof of the involvement of this man called Vartan Balian in the crime.'

'What eloquence!' declared Vartan in mock admiration. 'It is unfortunate that no court clerk is present to record such a beautiful speech.'

His pride pricked, Mustapha banged the table with his fist and got to his feet. He opened his mouth to let out an insult but, controlling himself in the presence of Gani Bey, he held it back. His expression, however, spoke volumes. He was breathing hard, as if he had just stopped exercising violently.

Gani Bey took charge. 'Irony will get you nowhere. Have you nothing better to say in your defence?'

Vartan knew he was lost and would gain nothing further by arguing so he replied wearily, 'I could say, the last witness was not present at the police station when I was taken there. My wife, my mother-in-law, and two servants could testify to the fact that I was at home at the time of the mayor's murder. But I realize all that would not be of any use.'

Gani Bey was amused. He took out a sheet of paper from his briefcase.

He remained patient and kept his voice amiable, probably because of Colonel Ibrahim's presence. 'I have a signed confession here from Shirag Tevonian, your accomplice. He admits having conspired with you and having helped murder Mumtaz Bey.'

Vartan shrugged. 'Well, if that really is his signature, I can imagine how you obtained it. The commissioner has a well-deserved reputation for cruelty.'

Mustapha Rahmi's hand gripped the edge of the table. He was ready to explode. Ibrahim leaned over to look at the confession. The signature was an illegible scribble but a fingerprint of dry blood authenticated the document.

After hesitating for a moment, Ibrahim risked intervening again. 'I imagine, Gani Bey, that you have rechecked the evidence and the truth of the testimony.'

The high official's jowls shook. He was outraged. 'Colonel Ibrahim, how do you dare put in doubt my competence and the integrity of Commissioner Mustapha, the future governor of Sivas?'

'That was the farthest thing from my mind,' Ibrahim hastened to say. 'Please excuse me if my words offended you. I wish only to serve justice.'

'Then keep quiet,' retorted Gani Bey cuttingly. 'Justice can take care of herself without your help.'

Vartan's patience gave way to fury. 'Justice! Don't use a word whose meaning you don't know. This trial is nothing but a grotesque farce.'

'Shut up, you son of a bitch,' shouted Mustapha, rising so fast that he knocked his chair over.

Instead of obeying, Vartan raised his voice, 'Your evidence is contrived. My only crime is to be an Armenian like all the others you've been hanging in the square.'

The commissioner could no longer control himself; he hurried around the table towards the prisoner. Vartan blocked his adversary's blow and then struck him with his fists, which had been tied together. Groggy, Mustapha reeled back, tottered and supported himself against the table. Vartan had reacted instinctively, but he did not regret what he had done. At this stage, no accusation could be reversed.

A guard approached him and struck Vartan between his shoulder-blades with his Mauser. Vartan fell on his knees, gasping for breath. The commissioner took a jack-knife out of his pocket.

130

'You'll pay for that,' he hissed between clenched teeth. The blade snapped out with a dry click.

'Commissioner Mustapha,' ordered Gani Bey, 'I forbid it.'

The commissioner still made a couple of passes at Vartan's throat but returned to his seat. He continued to glare at Vartan with hatred, knowing that his hour for vengeance would come. Ibrahim was afraid for his friend's life. With his eyes he begged him to remain calm.

Gani Bey closed the folder lying on the table. 'Vartan Balian, you have been found guilty of murder and sedition. I sentence you to death.'

Still kneeling, Vartan listened to the sentence unperturbed. He had known all along that the game was up.

As expected, Gani Bey repeated his proposition. 'You still have a chance to escape death. Will you collaborate with us?'

'No.'

'Then your wife and son will be on the road with the others tomorrow morning.'

'And if I consent to write the lies you are going to dictate to me?' Vartan asked.

'Your family will stay in Sivas and you can rejoin them when you have accomplished your mission.'

'You must think I'm an idiot. Do you really expect me to believe your promises? The moment I'm no longer of any use to you, wham!'

Ibrahim wanted to delay the hour of reckoning as long as possible. He still had not given up trying to find a way to save his friend.

He cut in insistently, 'Accept his offer, Major Vartan.'

Vartan shook his head. He had made his decision the evening before. Ibrahim wanted to gain some time, but it would lead nowhere. Vartan would be under strict surveillance in prison and Maro and Tomas would serve as hostages against his escape. The day they decide to eliminate him, his wife and son would suffer the same fate. He preferred to think of them in exile with Azniv Hanim and the other Armenians, where they would, at least, have a chance of surviving.

Gani Bey smiled at Vartan. 'Our minister will be sadly disappointed. He loves so much to read your praises of his policies.'

'May he burn in hell!'

Vartan's furious reply enhanced Gani Bey's good humour. He asked the commissioner to fetch the other condemned prisoner. The guards dragged in another man and dropped him at Vartan's side – Shirag Tevonian! His eyes dull and his face reduced to an open wound, he was barely recognizable. His broken jaw hung open and, each time he exhaled, little red bubbles formed at the corners of his lips. Vartan's heart turned over.

'Recognize your accomplice, Vartan Balian?' asked Gani Bey happily. 'His life is in your hands. Accept my proposal.'

When Shirag heard Vartan's name, he reacted and his lips moved slightly, 'Vartan Balian?'

'I'm here.'

'Forget about me.' Shirag hiccuped painfully.

'For the last time,' said Gani Bey, 'do you accept?'

Shirag answered, making a last effort to raise his voice, 'Let them finish me!'

Vartan touched the young man's arm compassionately and spat in the direction of the table. The commissioner came up and encircled Vartan's neck with his left arm and with his right hand he gripped Vartan by the hair and kept his face turned towards Shirag.

'Look at him. See how he dies,' he roared. 'And your turn is coming.' He called one of his men, 'Aim at his head.'

The guard put the mouth of his rifle barrel against Shirag's temple. Shirag began to recite *Our Father* . . . His voice grew louder as if he were using the last of his strength for this prayer.

'Still not willing to change your mind?' asked the commissioner, tightening his grip on Vartan's neck.

Vartan remained silent. The best thing that could happen to Shirag would be to die quickly. Vartan joined Shirag in his prayer and forced himself to keep his eyes open. When they reached the words *Thy will be done*, a shot tore apart Shirag's head. Tatters of flesh and drops of blood spattered Vartan.

'Now it's your turn,' said the commissioner, releasing him and drawing back.

'No!' said Ibrahim forcefully. His voice was full of authority. 'No, don't kill him here. He should be shot before a firing squad. It would be excellent for the morale of the troops.'

'I agree,' Gani Bey's eyes glittered. 'But he shall not be shot. He shall be hanged in the market square! The people need an example!'

# FIVE

Even though the sun had just risen, pale and diffused in a milky sky, the heavy, humid air made clothes cling to the skin. The roosting birds were caught in a silent torpor. In the distance, the donkeys brayed incessantly.

The rust-coloured ox kept looking at Tomas placidly. The boy could see his own reflection in the beast's moist eyes. It was licking its muzzle, as black as its hoofs, while Sassoun sniffed around its legs. Tomas brought an armful of hay from the stable, put it on the ground and the ox stretched its neck to reach the fodder. It had a wooden yoke fixed to the base of its horns. It was true then. They were leaving!

The child swallowed hard. The miracle he had hoped for had not happened. Before he woke up this morning and saw the ox and the cart, Tomas had been sure that something would happen . . . some unforeseen event that would allow them to stay at home. Perhaps his father would come back! Until the night before, his belief had enabled him to remain calm and reasonably strong. He had cried once only, and then secretly in his bed. Now he had nothing left but his determination to be brave to bolster up his mother and grandmother.

Tomas went upstairs and hesitantly entered Vartan's library. It was the first time he had been there since his father had left. This was his favourite room in the house. The maps and placards of human anatomy made him dream. What joy it was to look at the collections of minerals, fossils and insects. It was a room full of treasures! His father had told him that books harboured all of man's knowledge and there were hundreds of books here on the shelves. The smell of the leather bindings hit him full in the face.

A little bit of daylight filtered through the closed curtains. The clock had stopped and the velvety silence overwhelmed the child. Sheets of paper were strewn over the red flower-and-fern-patterned carpet. He picked one up and studied it carefully. It was his father's handwriting. He tried to decipher it. He really didn't know how to read, but he could recognize some of the slender letters of the Armenian alphabet. The graceful lines made him think of the moments he had spent in this room doing his exercises in calligraphy. While Vartan read, leaning on his elbows at the desk, he would sometimes look up and start talking about the importance of knowledge and learning. More than happy to be distracted from his homework, Tomas would ask questions, and his father would tell him all about the history of the world, about the kings of Armenia, about different people of different races, about stones, about animals, about stars. Vartan knew everything! Sometimes he talked for hours, but Tomas was never tired of listening to his father's warm, enthusiastic voice, teaching him about life and things. Pictures would roll before his eyes and words would take him to faraway lands, so far that, at times, his father would ask a question that caught him unawares.

The little boy went slowly around the room, taking care not to make the floorboards creak. The objects seemed to be looking at him with curiosity, some even with resentment as if reproaching him for being there without permission. Although he was upset, he continued his inspection. The books were piled up so high they made him feel dizzy and afraid of being squashed. He gently ran the tip of his forefinger over the spines of the books that were within reach. His heart ached and the corners of his mouth drooped; now he would never be able to read all these books and become wise like his father.

With a trembling hand, he opened the cupboard with the glass doors, the one that he was forbidden to touch. It contained the mysterious instruments pharmacists used – oddly shaped mugs, test tubes, flasks, cupels, pipettes, a microscope, scales, pestles and mortars. Everything fascinated him, especially the bottles with their yellowing labels and threatening skulls. Tomas lifted the stopper of an ether bottle and breathed in the vapours. They made him giddy.

His father had promised to teach him the secrets of chemistry one day. A tear drop ran down the child's cheek. He closed the cupboard and stood in front of the terrestrial globe floating on its pale wooden pedestal. If he stood on tip toe, his nose reached just a little above the equator. Constantinople lay near the letter A in Asia Minor. To the right, a little distance away, there was a dot, exactly the width of Tomas's thumb. That was Sivas.

Vartan had marked it in Indian ink. The child spun the globe idly.

He sat down behind the huge desk, which dwarfed him. Usually the top of the desk was crowded with piles of papers but today there was only the desk blotter, the inkstand and the stone that served as a paper-weight. Tomas played distractedly with the sharp, black stone; he knew it was obsidian. Even the tiniest object in this room reminded him of his father. He sniffled as he opened the upper drawer, which contained a small silver box holding a silver seal. He took it out and pressed it hard against his forearm. When he let go, there was a hollow oval with three ridges of flesh – Vartan's name in Armenian letters. Since the seal was reversible, there was the same thing on the other side in Arabic letters. That side Tomas did not use. He put the seal back in its box and slid it into his pocket. Someday he would give it back to his father. He left the room, closing the door carefully.

The voices coming up from the kitchen sounded sad even though they were saying ordinary things. 'No, not that pot,' said Azniv Hanim in the same melancholy tone she used when talking about her late husband. Tomas slid his hand into the pocket of his short pants and felt comforted when he touched the silver box. With this talisman he could always conquer his fear.

'There, my darling,' Maro said, kissing him on the cheek. Deep, dark circles lay under her tired eyes.

The child wanted to reassure her by appearing to be calm. 'Are we leaving soon?'

'Eat your breakfast first,' she replied, in a choking voice.

'Do I have to take my school books?'

'It isn't necessary.'

She was incapable of controlling herself any longer and went into the drawing room, leaving him with Azniv Hanim. A sob rose in her throat; it was too late for tears. Maro sat on the edge of the divan and her eyes wandered over the walls but nothing caught her attention – the paintings, the sculptures, the furniture, the antiques, the piano – nothing meant anything to her anymore! She felt she had already left this house where she had spent eight happy years.

After eating, Tomas helped to pack the cart. Azniv Hanim climbed into it to arrange the sacks and packages the servants were bringing.

'There's room for a few toys,' she told her grandson.

He shrugged and shook his head. He was no longer a child and, to prove it, he lifted a heavy basket of food up on the cart.

'Be careful, *shekerim*.[1] You'll strain yourself,' Zeynep said in Turkish. She usually spoke to him in Armenian but, when she wanted to express her feelings, she spontaneously went back to her mother tongue.

A soldier called from the street, asking if they were ready.

Azniv Hanim said 'no' and told Maro not to hurry too much, as they had to wait for Armen. As she got down from the cart, Jemila threw herself on her knees and embraced Azniv Hanim around the waist.

'For the love of Allah, *Hanim*, take me with you. I don't want to stay here.'

'Me too,' added Zeynep.

'I would love to, but it's impossible.'

Azniv Hanim was touched by such loyalty even though she was angry that the young girls were refusing to understand the situation. She made Jemila get up.

Zeynep kissed her hand. 'I beg you, *Hanim*.'

Annoyed, the old woman said brusquely, 'I've told you three times already that it's forbidden for Muslims to accompany the Armenian deportees. I'm going to give you some money to go back to your village.'

'What's to become of us?'

Azniv Hanim put her arms around the two young servants. 'You're pretty. You'll be married soon. You'll be happy and have many children. When we come back, we'll come and visit you in your village.'

'You'll always be welcome, *Hanim*.'

Captain Armen's cart looked like a farmer's going to market. He had cut everything he could in his garden. When his wife remarked that they would not be able to eat all those vegetables before they rotted, he told her that they would share them with the needy. He simply didn't want to leave anything behind; he had even destroyed the unripe fruit and vegetables, mumbling, '*Anassounner*,[2] you won't have them.'

The thousands of vehicles, most of them driven by inexperienced drivers, caused many traffic jams in the narrow streets. The authorities had planned for the Armenians to leave town in successive waves but, faced with contradictory orders from bossy military guards, the families thought it

---

1.　My sugar (Turkish).

2.　Animals (Armenian).

wiser to get on the road as early as possible. The vehicles moved more slowly than the pedestrians. Exasperated, the guards swore at the deportees.

When he was about forty metres from his house, Armen handed the reins to his wife. 'I forgot my tobacco, Araksi. Just let the ox go at his own pace. I'll be back in a few minutes.'

He went back to his house where he had left the door ajar for the cat. When he passed the green board fence, he stopped to take a final look at the house where he had expected to spend his last days and at the distant mountains. The soldiers had trampled the high, thick special wheat in the field, which he had fertilized with his sweat. His almond-tree . . . his apple-trees . . . his pear-trees . . . his vineyard . . . the branches were already bending under the weight of the still-green fruit. It was going to be an exceptional harvest this year. The chickens were cackling in the lower courtyard. Armen could hear chirping; he had forgotten his birds! He unhooked the cage hanging on an outside wall and set the goldfinches free. They flew away awkwardly.

'Hurry up,' cried a young soldier who was passing by.

Armen swore, '*Anasdvadzner!*'[1] He took sticks of firewood, which he had stacked in front of the door the day before, into the house, then soaked them with kerosene until the oily liquid spread out on the earthen floor. Without hesitating, Armen lit a match, dropped it on to the piled-up sticks and ran out to catch up with the cart.

Araksi was waiting, holding a brown paper cone in her hand. 'Your tobacco was in your bag, along with your bottle of *raki* and your cartridges.'

'Not so loud.'

Soon the noise of a roaring fire was heard above the rumbling of the wooden wheels. The soldiers hurried towards the burning house and stood there helplessly, waving their arms angrily. Armen looked straight ahead at the road and sniggered, but tears welled up in his eyes.

'Just what have you done?' asked Araksi, dismayed. 'We had such joy in building it.'

'I don't want them to enjoy it.'

'What if the *zaptiyés* come looking for you?'

'Pooh! They have other fish to fry,' he replied, sounding less worried than he really was.

'You old fool!' Araksi grumbled. The tenderness with which she patted her husband's arm belied her gruffness.

---

1. Literally godless people (Armenian).

'We're not coming back, Araksi. Don't you realize that?'

'As long as we're together . . .'

Maro and her mother were boarding up the windows of the ground floor. It was Azniv Hanim's idea and, even though Maro didn't see much point to it, she had agreed; at least it would keep them busy until Armen arrived.

The stable still smelled of horses and cows. Tomas's heart gave a turn when he saw the corner where Gaydzag had his stall until the guards took his little horse away. Just when his dreams had come true. His chest heaved as he sighed deeply.

Sassoun was sniffing the empty stalls; suddenly he stopped, picked up his ears and, barking, took off like an arrow. Since Tomas didn't feel like playing, he didn't pay any attention to the distant barks that were calling him. Poor Sassoun didn't understand what was happening to the family. He was going to miss the house and the garden. Tomas must not forget to take his bowl.

The dung had not been taken out and the flies were swarming around it. Tomas took the shovel off its hook and started to clean the floor. The shovel, bigger than he, was so heavy he could hardly handle it. His skin became moist and the sweat ran down his face. He worked frantically, stopping only to wipe his brow with the back of his hand. When he finished loading the wheelbarrow, he put the shovel down; placing his hands over his back, he leaned back, moaning as his grandmother did every time she was bent over for a long time kneading the bread.

He spread his legs to keep his balance and took hold of the handles of the wheelbarrow. The muscles of his arms trembled as he lifted it. He almost turned it over twice but managed to get it to the manure pile behind the stable. Once back inside, the child leaned against the wall to rest for a few minutes. He then made another trip with the wheelbarrow, which he found harder than the first. After that, Tomas strew fresh hay on the floor, hung the shovel up and rubbed his hands for a long time. There, this was a job well done. That it was useless made no difference. His father would have been proud of him. After a last look at his work, he closed the door and shot the bolt.

He marched with deliberate steps towards the side of the house. His grandmother had told him that, in his father's absence, he was the man of the house, so he had to behave like one. There was some water left in the oak tub placed under the gutter drains to gather the rainwater. He splashed his face, washed his hands and dried them on his shirt. Then he whistled for Sassoun but the dog didn't respond. As if this was the time to be playing *bahvdouk*![1] Tomas called in a commanding tone, 'I'm not playing, Sassoun.'

Tomas looked everywhere the spaniel usually hid – in the vegetable garden, behind the well, under the spindle bushes. After calling him several times, he became worried. The dog was not with Maro, not with Azniv Hanim, not by the ox. Tomas's voice became plaintive. 'Come here, *shounigs*,[2] come here.'

He walked around the cart and then he saw him near the gate. What a relief! Tomas forgot that he had intended to bawl the dog out.

'Here, Sassoun!'

The dog didn't move, didn't even wag his tail. He was lying on the path, something he never did. Was he sulking? Was he sick? Tomas ran! Suddenly, he was afraid! His heart beat in his throat, hammering as if it would burst. Sassoun was lying on his side in the centre of a dark pool, a red gash in his flank.

'Sassoun !' screamed Tomas, falling on his knees.

The dog lay still, glassy-eyed. Blood was running out of several wounds on his back and chest. It wasn't true! It was a nightmare! Tomas felt a flush of heat and then his head swam. Deathly pale, he caught Sassoun by his hide and shook him, crying hoarsely, '*Shounigs! Shounigs!*'

His friend was dead – deader than dead! The child knew it, but it took several seconds for it to sink in. He burst into sobs, shaking with spasms. He caressed the dog's head. He touched the wounds, not minding the warm blood staining his hands. What was he going to do without his dog? Everybody was abandoning him – his father, Sassoun, Gaydzag, his house – it was like the nightmare he had when Hour-Grag had snatched him and carried him away.

Distraught, he lifted his head. A couple of soldiers standing near the garden wall were observing him and smiling wickedly. Tomas jumped up. With their bayonets, they mimicked an attack on someone on the ground, pretending to run him through repeatedly. The child recoiled in terror. The narrow blades of their bayonets were red. These soldiers had killed Sassoun! Tomas stared at them with hatred in his eyes.

'You want some of the same?' asked one of the guards. He had a long nose but his left nostril was missing, probably a victim of an infection so

---

1.   Hide-and-seek (Armenian).
2.   My little dog (Armenian).

common in Anatolia. Tomas etched the guard's face in his memory. One day when he had grown up he would find this man and avenge Sassoun.

Although he was afraid, he went up to the dog slowly and bent over him. Looking steadily at the guards, he slid his hands under the still-warm body and lifted it up. Sassoun seemed heavier dead than alive. Tomas was no longer crying, even though his eyes were burning. Now that he was a man, he would act like a man! Panting, he walked backwards, carrying the dog. He must not show he was afraid. He laid the body in a flower-bed of white phlox and roses. He would bury him there . . . but where was the spade? A hard tap on his shoulder startled him. The soldier with the eaten-up nose had followed him and barked, 'Go tell your family they're to leave immediately.'

Tomas fled towards the house and joined Maro and Azniv Hanim who were trying to nail shut the door to the entrance hall. They screamed when they saw the blood-smeared child.

'The soldiers killed Sassoun,' he said between clenched teeth. 'They're ordering us to leave.'

Outraged, Maro threw her hammer on the floor and took her son in her arms. 'Weep, my darling, weep. It will help you.'

But Tomas couldn't. He felt more like screaming and hitting but didn't want the soldiers to hear him grieving. He freed himself from his mother's arms and she didn't insist.

'I'll go and find a clean shirt for you.'

To give himself courage, he put his hand into his pocket and fingered the silver box which contained his father's seal.

Azniv Hanim was convinced that the dog's death was a bad omen. Without a word, she picked up a small package from the steps and took Tomas behind the hazelnut bushes. She wanted to distract him and give him something to do. She undid a roll of cloth. It was a money belt. She had sewn pieces of gold into it. Both she and Maro were now wearing belts like it under their clothes. They had also secreted pieces of jewellery in the seams of their dresses. She tied the belt around her grandson's waist.

'It's not too heavy for you?'

Although he was uncomfortable, he shook his head.

'Take good care of it. It's part of our fortune. We might need it some day.'

The trust his grandmother had put in him confirmed Tomas's belief that he had no right to be a child any more.

Captain Armen stopped his cart in front of the gate. He exchanged a few sharp words with the military guards who wanted him to keep moving. Then he went to greet Maro and her mother, while glancing furtively at the load in their cart.

'All right. Let's get going.'

'You seem to be in a hurry.' Azniv Hanim was surprised.

'The sooner we're out of here the better.'

He was afraid he would get arrested for burning down his house and the women couldn't get along without him. Tomas threw himself into his godfather's arms and told him how Sassoun had died. He made a super-human effort not to cry. Armen was angry at himself because he could not find the words to comfort his godson.

'God will punish these men,' he said, as he put the child down.

'We must bury Sassoun,' Tomas said determinedly.

Maro put her hand on his neck and pushed him gently in the direction of the cart. 'We don't have time, darling. Jemila and Zeynep promised to do it.'

The young girls kissed the child who was like a little brother to them and promised to bury the dog with great care. Tomas hoisted himself into the cart with his lips pinched together. Maro found the endless goodbyes of the Turkish girls tiresome. She was in a hurry to leave and couldn't stand the sight of her house any longer.

Mother and daughter sat on the back-board and goaded the ox. Tomas stood behind them perched on a big basket. The cart wobbled and swivelled. The ox plodded forward, its muzzle almost scraping the ground.

'Don't look back,' said Azniv Hanim to her daughter. 'Remember, Lot's wife turned into a pillar of salt.'

Tomas didn't need to be told. He stared at a spot on the road where big green flies were swarming and furtively wiped off a tear with his thumb. The sound of Sassoun's barking still resounded in his ears. He would never have a dog again!

The house with its boarded-up windows and doors was left further and further behind. The abandoned stork's nest on the roof seemed to be ready to come tumbling down and the climbing roses were turning yellow as they had not been watered for several days. The house seemed as if it had been abandoned a long time. Scarcely a week ago, it had still echoed with laughter and songs, with the chords of the piano and children's voices reciting a French lesson; now it stood there in twilight and in silence, only the furniture and ornaments bore witness to a lost happiness.

Zeynep carried a water bucket. Following the Turkish custom, she poured its contents over the ruts left by the wheels of the cart to wish them a good journey.

'May Allah watch over you.'

She walked before them to the gate where Jemila was waiting with all their bundles. Their uncle from Sivas who would be in charge of seeing them back to their village was carrying the gramophone which Maro had given to them. He bowed to Azniv Hanim while Jemila and Zeynep ran alongside the cart, beating their breasts and lamenting.

By now, the thirteen prisoners in the dungeon no longer paid any more attention to the screeching sound of the nail Sarkis used to chisel the stone wall. The teacher had picked it up in the prison courtyard when they were let out for daily exercise. He engraved crosses with ornate arms into the wall, and just below them the same phrase both in Armenian and Turkish: *The just are condemned because of their race, their language and their faith, and here they await their death.* He had patiently incised the names of all the Armenians who had been arrested. He dedicated all his time to this task, from morning to night, working feverishly, as he feared that his hour would come before he was able to finish.

'Sarkis, stop for a minute,' said Vartan, going up to the window.

The teacher obeyed. The four men who were playing cards fell silent. Others who were lying down sat up on their hay mattresses. They could hear a muffled rumbling in the distance.

'Thunder,' said one of the men. 'Somewhere out there the sky's turned dark.'

Sarkis put the nail in his pocket and went to Vartan. 'No, that isn't a storm.'

Vartan pushed him against the wall. 'Squat down so I can climb on your shoulders.'

Sarkis lifted Vartan up to the small opening near the ceiling. He gripped the bars firmly and pulled himself up to take some of the weight off of Sarkis's shoulders. The window opened to the east and he could see the hill where his house stood – that white spot among the foliage . . .

'What is it then?' someone asked impatiently.

142

Turning his head from one side to the other, Vartan tried to work out from which direction the noise was coming. He soon realized that the continuous rumbling came from all over. The deportation! He jumped down. His companions watched him closely, waiting for an explanation.

He said grimly, 'Tonight we'll be the only Armenians left in Sivas!'

They bowed their heads and some covered their faces with their hands; one man burst into tears and another exclaimed, 'Oh, why didn't they hang me this morning?'

Every day at dawn, the guards haphazardly chose thirty to forty men to be taken to the gallows. Vartan suspected that his poor companions' composure was no more than a front, a way of preventing themselves from sinking into total misery. This explained their sudden despair. They had accepted their lot, but none could tolerate the thought that his family might suffer the inhuman conditions of an exile such as Shirag had described. Vartan was just as dejected as they were, but with a difference. Far from being shattered by the picture of Maro, Tomas and Azniv Hanim on the road to Syria, he felt such rage that he rejected the idea of death.

Looking helpless, the teacher stood up and said in a lifeless voice, 'Our poor children . . . our poor wives.' Suddenly he became furious, 'We had the chance to stop this from happening. We should have done what Shirag proposed. We should have defended ourselves like the Armenians in Van.'

While Sarkis continued to bemoan the lack of resistance in Sivas, criticizing his fellow citizens and himself for their cowardice, Vartan recalled his conversation with Shirag in the hospital tent and he told Sarkis to stop.

'We can't change the past. All of us did what we thought best at the time. You must not reproach anyone, not even yourselves.'

The teacher calmed down. Vartan was right. Regrets were vain. He remembered he was a deacon, and to show his faith, he changed his tone.

'God will gather us in His arms, my friends. History will keep . . .'

Furious at his submissiveness, Vartan cut him short. 'History! Who cares about history!'

'Major Vartan,' cried the teacher, 'I would have thought that a man of your stature . . .'

'Do you want us to march to the gallows singing hymns?' Vartan turned to the others, who were following the conversation with interest. 'Is that what you all want?'

143

A man, scratching his lice-infested head, grumbled, 'What else can we do?'

'Try to escape,' replied Vartan.

'We talked about it at first,' added a young boy, completely disillusioned, 'but there's nothing we can do. Look at the stone walls . . . the solid bars . . . the exits are guarded.'

Vartan knew that better than anyone. He had visited this prison a year ago during an outbreak of dysentery. 'I know. For a man alone, escape is practically impossible, but for a group . . . that's another matter.'

The men gathered around him. With their faces unshaven for almost a week, their grime and their rags, they no longer looked like prosperous merchants nor educated men but like a band of cut-throats ready for anything. Their eyes shone.

'What do you mean?' Sarkis was curious.

'When we were in the courtyard this morning, the metal doors were open for several minutes. Has anyone noticed if this happens often?'

'It's only happened once in the four days we've been here,' answered someone.

'Well, the next time it happens, we'll all push at the same time and get out.'

'Bah!' exclaimed disappointedly the one who hadn't stopped scratching his head. 'What about the guards?'

'I counted four outside the gate and nine others on the wall.'

'You forgot the two machine-gunners in the corner of the courtyard.'

'I did see them.' Vartan was irritated. 'All right. That makes fifteen guards and one machine gun. So . . .'

'And some twenty or more guards who play backgammon in the guard post?'

Vartan raised his voice, 'Stop interrupting me!' He calmed down quickly. 'During our walk, I reckon there will be about three hundred of us in the courtyard. When we try to leave, I'm sure they'll open fire, but we outnumber them and surprise will be on our side. Most of us will get away and, before the gendarmes in the guard post have time to react, we'll be on the street. There, we'll split up and then it's every man for himself.'

The men looked at each other undecidedly. Sarkis objected, 'How many of us do you think will survive?'

'I really don't know, but even if it's only ten, it would be worthwhile.

Remember, we're all condemned to death. For my part, I prefer a bullet to a rope.'

This argument made them think. Someone asked, 'Once outside, what do we do? The town is full of soldiers.'

'You know all the streets and alleys in Sivas. You know all the houses, all the stores, all the abandoned warehouses. There are lots of places to hide and, when night falls, you can make it to the hills. And once there . . . by the grace of God . . .'

Sarkis began to pace the floor, rubbing his cheek. 'Really, we have nothing to lose.'

The others discussed among themselves and quickly came to the same conclusion. Then Vartan added, 'Tomorrow, when they let us out to exercise, pass the word around and at the first chance . . . The longer we wait, the fewer of us there will be to try to escape.'

'Do you think the others will agree?'

'It's up to you to convince them.'

'What if they get cold feet at the last minute and only a small group tries to rush to the door?'

'That's always a possibility,' admitted Vartan, 'but there's no way of knowing that beforehand.'

From then on, time seemed to crawl. Each one mentally ran over his own situation and decided that his reasons to survive were better than those of the others. And each one hoped not to be chosen for the scaffold before the escape was attempted. Vartan lay back, closed his eyes and mentally drew a plan of the surroundings of the prison. He tried to remember every detail of the neighbourhood and decide which way to go. He would have to keep separate from the others in order not to be spotted. Planning kept him from thinking too much about his wife and son.

Maro drew her cart up behind Armen's. She had put on her riding boots and her feet were propped up on the back bar of the swingletree. She held the reins firmly but soon realized it was a waste of effort. The ox followed the carts docilely. She turned to speak to Azniv Hanim but the screeching of the axles made conversation impossible. Besides, looks sufficed for what they had to tell each other. After silently nodding, each retreated into private thoughts.

The same silence prevailed in the other vehicles. Even the children, staring wide-eyed, were silent except for the babies who babbled happily. There were practically no men in the carts except for the very old ones and the youths under fifteen. Very few women had thought to wear a veil and Azniv Hanim considered them foolish.

They had first evacuated the lower part of the Armenian Quarter. By the time the deportees from the higher section of the town passed by, they could see peasants, paupers and even guards busily looting the abandoned houses. Maro knew the same thing was happening in her house where the boards on the windows and doors would make no difference.

At the market place, men formed two solid walls through which the deportees had to pass. Street vendors loudly hawked water, juices, fruit and sweetmeats to the bystanders. Many were shaking their fists, shouting insults and threatening any Armenian who might fall into their hands. The escort team of armed guards was the only thing preventing an outbreak of violence. The merchants stood around to keep an eye on their stalls. They looked worried as they recognized customers among the deportees and realized that their businesses were going to suffer because of their leaving.

The Kaval Quarter was altogether different. A heavy silence hovered over the empty streets. From their windows veiled Muslim women watched with compassionate eyes while the sad parade filed by. They could imagine what it must be like to lose not only one's home but, in fact, everything. The half-naked children whose laughing and chasing about usually filled the streets with happy noise, stood silently in front of the doors to their houses.

Every once in a while, Armen waved reassuringly to Azniv Hanim's family. Maro kept her eyes riveted on the ox's knobbly spine. Her mind was completely busy with thoughts of Vartan; she felt as if she were being physically torn apart as the distance between them increased. It was as if a heavy weight were crushing her and making it hard to breathe – as if her entrails were being harrowed by each turn of the wagon wheels. She played with her wedding ring and did not notice when they passed the ruins of the ancient walls of the city nor when they crossed the bridge.

Tomas stood up, teetering on a pile of blankets. The column extended as far as his eyes could see and the cavalry soldiers rode back and forth alongside the carts. The child had never seen so many people together before. There must be thousands rolling and raising dust, which remained suspended in the still air. When he turned to look back he saw a steady stream of carriages, soldiers and people coming from the town.

146

Thick-bellied, dark-blue clouds gathered to the west, forming a gigantic mountain range above the real one, which was now disappearing into a greyish mist. The sky was quickly becoming overcast. In spite of the mooing and the noise of clattering hoofs and wheels, the wind could be heard rising. A sand-and-dust-storm swept across the plain, bending the poplar trees.

'A storm!' grumbled Azniv Hanim. 'That's all we needed!'

She joined Tomas in the back of the cart and helped him cover their belongings with a tarpaulin as best they could. She told him to get under it.

The wind blew on them violently, rough and loaded with stone particles, scratching and bruising their skin. Maro lowered her head and pulled the black *charshaf* over her face, leaving only her eyes uncovered. The air cooled and a heavy, lashing rain began to fall. One could see no more than twenty paces ahead. The oxen refused to move on.

'The trip's starting badly,' Azniv Hanim complained. Maro didn't bother to answer. It was only rain.

Twenty minutes later the storm stopped as suddenly as it had started. The clouds drifted towards the east and the wind dropped completely. The sky turned an immaculate blue and the sun began to draw the wetness out of the earth. Steam rose from the fields. The hoofs of the oxen slipped on the drenched ground where the wheels had marked deep ruts.

Half an hour later there was no trace left of the downpour. Waves of heat swirled up from the earth; the air quivered; the land rippled; and the horizon shimmered. Nothing seemed real – the green and yellow fields where peasants toiled, the endless rows of trees, the isolated houses at the corners of the fields, the town they were leaving behind, the ochre-coloured hills – nothing except the jolting of the carts and the acrid taste of the dust, which coated their mouths and burned their throats!

Six kilometres south of Sivas the caravan came to a halt on the plain. The gendarmes ordered the deportees to set up camp even though it was only the middle of the afternoon. For a while there was total bedlam as everyone looked for relatives or friends. The traffic piled up and the guards shouted and cracked their whips. Gradually, the camp became organized and order reigned. Armen and Maro pulled their carts up at an angle to each other so as to have some privacy. The hobbled oxen grazed around the wheels.

'We have to find something to drink,' said Armen, as he rinsed his mouth with *raki*, which he then swallowed.

'I have a full waterskin,' Azniv Hanim reminded them.

'Save your water. You never know. I think there's a well over there.'

'May I go with you?' asked Tomas, who was missing the company of men.

Armen knew that the child would feel more secure with him. 'Come along. You can give me a hand.' They took two copper buckets with them.

'Let's stretch the canvas between the two carts to have some shade,' suggested Azniv Hanim. 'Maro?'

Maro stood frozen, staring at the town, which looked like a mirage at the foot of Mount Tejir. Her mother touched her shoulder, startling her, and said tenderly, 'Don't worry about him. He's a resourceful man.'

'If you only knew how I've prayed; how I'm praying,' added Araksi, trying to comfort her.

Azniv Hanim hugged Maro and whispered in her ear, 'Be sensible.'

Sensible? Deep down Maro knew that part of her would never be sensible, and that she would refuse to admit that life could separate her from Vartan. How could she be sensible when what was most precious to her had been torn away from her? What sense could her life have far from the man to whom she belonged? Her stomach contracted; her blood was thumping in her temples. She felt like screaming!

'Maro,' insisted her mother.

Maro did not answer. Biting her lips, she helped stretch the cloth which would serve as an awning. The least movement took considerable effort. Araksi threaded a rope through the eyelet of the tarpaulin and willed herself to be cheerful.

'The stork always comes back to his nest.'

Azniv Hanim frowned and so did Maro. The nest on their roof had remained empty this spring. Araksi realized that her proverb had not had the desired effect, but that did not keep her from using another one.

'One has to show a good face to bad fortune.'

'That's easy to say,' answered Maro irritated.

Azniv Hanim picked up the baton from Araksi. 'One has to make the best of a bad lot and live one day at a time.'

'And help one another in adversity,' Armen's wife added.

Maro looked at them affectionately and, in spite of herself, a slight suggestion of a smile covered her face.

'Don't worry. I'm not going to become a millstone around your necks.'

Tomas and his godfather came back, carrying their full buckets. Armen didn't say a word but the tendons in his neck protruded and a swollen vein throbbed in his temple. Araksi immediately recognized the signs of her husband's anger. She took the bucket from him before he started to wave his arms and spill the water.

He threw his fez on the ground, kicked it and swore, 'Those rat-faced sons of bitches! May their Allah kick their arses into hell!'

'Armen! That's no way to talk in front of your godson,' said Araksi.

Tomas defended his godfather. 'The *zaptiyés* are bad!'

Araksi calmed her husband, while he explained the reason for his outburst.

'Those *zaptiyés* guarding the well are selling the water. Those swine are selling the Lord's water. What else do they have in store for us in the days to come?'

'Water them,' said Araksi, pointing to the animals, who were stretching their necks towards the buckets. 'That will keep you from using foul language.'

After their cold meal, when Tomas had fallen asleep under the tarpaulin between the vehicles, they drew aside with their glasses of tea. Now that the heat was gone, the mosquitoes had started to torment them. Fortunately, Azniv Hanim had some citronella oil to ward them off. Armen told the women about the news circulating throughout the camp. The reason they had stopped so near the town was to wait for more deportees from the surrounding villages.

'When they searched the town, they found empty houses and they suspected that their inhabitants were hiding in the homes of their Turkish friends.'

'What's the mood like in the rest of the camp?' inquired Azniv Hanim.

'Dismal! Everyone expects the worst. Many of our guards are not real gendarmes but outlaws put into uniform, and we're just a group of old men, women and children. We'll be easy pickings for them. But they don't know . . .' He pulled the three women closer to him and lowered his voice. 'Tomorrow we shall pass by the Saint Jude Monastery. It's been abandoned since the monks were slaughtered two weeks ago. The *fedayis* and the young people who escaped from Sivas are setting up an ambush there.'

The women were astonished. Azniv Hanim did not believe it. 'Just rumours!'

'Maybe, but it's better than nothing.'

'Do we have a chance?' Maro was very interested.

149

Armen looked dubious. 'I don't know. We'd better not wait until the battle is over to try to get away. It'll be sheer chaos, and we must take advantage of it.'

'It's too risky,' protested Azniv Hanim.

Araksi agreed with her, but Maro thought they should not miss the opportunity.

'Of course it's risky, but just think about what lies ahead of us.'

'The guards will shoot us down like rabbits,' moaned Araksi.

'They'll be too busy fighting off the attackers.' Armen patted her on the thigh to comfort her but she was not reassured. 'We don't have any other choice, wife.'

He knew that it would be an impossible ordeal for Araksi. Her swollen legs and weak heart would prevent her from running but he also knew that he would never abandon her. And neither could Azniv Hanim! Too bad! He must think only about Maro and Tomas; maybe they could make it to the hills.

Maro was exalted. She started to plan and clarify things, saying to herself, 'In this part of the country there are many caves, grottoes and even some shepherd's huts, all in ruins. If we travel by night, we can reach Zeynep's and Jemila's village.'

She could already see herself returning to Sivas as soon as the situation had calmed down. Ibrahim Alizadé would help her look for Vartan, but what if he . . . She refused to consider that possibility. One thing at a time – first, they had to get away from the convoy.

Araksi was scared. Armen came close to her and looked into her eyes. She could notice the love and affection in his intense look and remembered that they had agreed to sacrifice themselves for the younger ones. Had the moment come? So soon?

Armen whispered to her lovingly, 'We shall be together, until the end.' That promise was enough for Araksi.

Azniv Hanim who was sitting beside her understood what had passed between husband and wife. Of course! Araksi had a hard time walking! And she was not sure if she herself would be able to follow her grandson and daughter on these treacherous paths. Not for long, certainly! It was going to take all of Maro's courage to go on without her.

'We'll do whatever you say, Armen,' said Azniv Hanim, 'but if any one falls from fatigue, the others must not stop.'

'You're right,' affirmed Armen. 'Araksi feels the same way.'

Maro was stupefied. Blinded by the possibility of staying in the vicinity of Sivas, she had never given any thought to Azniv Hanim's or Araksi's physical condition. The three of them turned to Maro, waiting for her to agree. She knew she would never be able to abandon her mother but, wanting to avoid all argument, she nodded.

The convoy rattled off a little after dawn and reached the hills within the hour. The escort broke it up into several groups of three or four hundred vehicles, each one due to head off in a different direction. Armen and Maro were assigned to the first group, which took the route to the Saint Jude Monastery.

The rough road ran along a dry river-bed. They arrived at the foothills three hours later. The sun beat down on them and its glare reflected from the rocks. The oxen could no longer low. They suffered as they swished away with their tails the thousands of unrelenting flies swarming on their backs. Just before taking the final turn that would prevent them from seeing the Halys plain, Maro looked back at Sivas for the last time. It lay like a bauble of mother-of-pearl nestling in a wooded bower. Her heart ached! Then she looked ahead at the heights speckled with rare thorny bushes and tufts of faded grass, at the steep and rocky slopes and the barren cliffs, and shivered.

They had been on the move for only half a day, but already time had lost all meaning. Crushed by the heat, the deportees felt as if they had been walking in this desert forever. The guards hustled them, frequently lashing the drivers with their whips. All in vain! The exhausted oxen refused to obey the goad, and kept their heads lowered, choosing where to set their hoofs.

As they struggled up an incline, there was a commotion in the column. All heads turned in the direction of a ravine down below. The drivers stood up to get a better view and immediately sat down again. Maro followed their example and her stifled scream blew the *charshaf* away from her face. Never had she seen anything so awful! Corpses! A pile of cadavers, arms and legs entangled! A mountain of flesh for dogs and jackals to scavenge on!

'Oh, my God!' wailed Azniv Hanim.

'Tomas,' Maro breathed to her mother.

Azniv Hanim, grasping the situation, pulled the boy close to her and distracted his attention by showing him the circling buzzards high in the cloudless sky.

'They're coming from all over. Why are they gathering here?' Tomas asked.

'How should I know? Sometimes birds have funny ideas.'

'These birds stink,' complained the boy, holding his nose.

The smell of carrion nauseated them – all those rotting bodies. It couldn't be the men who had been arrested last night; there were too many of them. The dead must be the men from Sivas who had been formed into workcrews five days before. Women who had reason to believe that their husbands and sons were among them began to wail, and their laments echoed back.

The road went downhill again. Armen signalled to Maro in a conspiratorial way. They could see the monastery now, its stones golden in the sunlight. The rectangular building topped by twin cupolas had been built on a scree-covered slope and dominated the small valley. A few fruit-trees grew at the foot of the high wall surrounding the cloister. The fields had lain fallow for years.

In Araksi's opinion, they were moving much too fast. These were her last moments. She was not afraid, only immensely sorry that she was going to be separated from her husband. She hoped she would be the first to go and would not see him die. She leaned her head against Armen and ran her hand up his chest to touch the revolver hidden in his pocket.

'Promise me, you won't let me suffer.'

He looked grave and, without answering, stroked his wife's cheek. To keep herself from thinking about what was about to happen, Araksi thought of her dear little house in Sivas, the winter evenings when the wind whistled around the roof and the snow beat against the windowpanes, while she and Armen played dominoes by the glow of the lamp and sampled the pear brandy she had made the previous summer. They had spoken rarely but their eyes met constantly; Armen had nodded; this was his way of showing how happy he was. Now their home was nothing but a heap of scorched ruins.

Maro scanned the surroundings, trying to decide in which direction she would lead her family. The scattered rocks would give them some cover, but how was her mother going to manage in this difficult terrain? Yet there was no other choice. Maro showed her mother which way they would run.

'That would be my choice also,' approved Azniv Hanim.

'It's a stiff climb. Do you think you'll be able to?'

'You watch out for Tomas. That's more than enough,' her mother replied brusquely. 'I'll be at the top before you.'

'We'll stay together.' Her mother's bravado did not fool Maro.

'I forbid you to wait for me. Find a hiding place for the two of you. I'll find you and if I don't . . .' Her voice broke.

Maro choked, '*Mayrig*!'

'If you love me, you'll do as I say. We must think of Tomas only. I live on through that child. If he ever dies because of me, all my life will have been in vain.'

Maro lowered her head and Azniv Hanim remained serene. She turned to Tomas and took him by the shoulders. 'We're going to try to get away very soon.'

'And join papa!' He had been waiting for this moment since early that morning, when his mother had brought him up to date.

'You'll see, grandmother, we . . .'

His grandmother shook him. 'Listen to me. Stay with your mother and pull her by the hand so she never stops running. I might get out of breath and go slower. I don't want her to wait for me. Do you understand?'

'But, grandmother, I'll hold you by the hand too.'

She smiled. 'No. I can't run for long. Captain Armen, Araksi and I will find you later.'

Tomas gave in. Azniv Hanim kissed his cheeks several times. 'One day, Tomas, you'll be big and tall and have children. I want you to name your first daughter after me.'

'What? Do you mean Azniv?'

'Yes, because it means 'noble'.' she said, lowering her head.

The nearer they came, the more imposing the monastery looked. The deportees were frightened and twitchy. Were there really Armenian resistance fighters in the monastery? Would any of the deportees be able to escape? They were surrounded by mountains. Everything had seemed so much easier yesterday when they were all discussing it. Now many were questioning their ability to carry out the plan, and a good number of them decided not to try.

The bells sparkled in the belfry. About twenty Brave Ones, dressed in monk's habits, with hoods pulled low over their faces, filed out through the open gate to meet the caravan. The guards, walking along the first carts, on the side opposite the monastery, suddenly opened fire on the monks. Some friars fell and others ebbed back towards the gate. They aimed their guns hidden under their habits, but they didn't dare shoot, afraid of hitting the deportees. Rifles appeared at the top of the wall. From there the resistance fighters could aim better and shot down several guards, who were busy turning over the carts to form barricades. Some of the monks ran back to the portal and swung it shut, leaving behind about a dozen of their brothers lying on the grass. The whole skirmish had lasted less than two minutes.

Armen had climbed up on the seat in order to see over the carts in front of his. Now they were about 400 metres from the monastery. Was this the right time to make a run for it? He glanced at the hill on his right. Soldiers! Hundreds of soldiers had taken up positions on the summit from where they dominated the building and shot at the enemy relentlessly. The defenders used their rifles to fire back without much success, as the soldiers had taken cover behind the rocks. Two heavy machine-guns sprayed bullets at the monastery.

Maro saw that soldiers were occupying the exact spot by which she had planned to escape. Others surrounded the small valley. It was impossible to run. Armen was waving his arms to tell her to get out of the way. A regiment on horseback galloped along the column of vehicles. The officer at its head was using his sabre on the deportees as he rode past. The Armenians were running about in total confusion, trying to get to the bottom of the valley. Whether out of amusement or spite, the two machine gunners started raining bullets on them.

Everyone took refuge under the carts. Araksi had to beg her husband to take cover. Secretly she was relieved as the escape had been postponed. A little more time! If they were to die tomorrow, at least they had gained another day. She concealed her feelings from Armen who was burning with rage. Betrayed! It was obvious that the army had been forewarned about the ambush.

Azniv Hanim and Maro were lying flat on the ground on both sides of Tomas. Occasionally stray bullets whistled over their heads. The child was praying with his grandmother; Maro could not. Her last hope was disappearing. She felt death in her soul! She looked at a bunch of violets trampled under a hoof, but what she really saw there were Vartan's eyes – his tender look as he leaned over her to whisper words of love. She would have given half her life to see his eyes again. She stretched out her hand but her fingers found only emptiness.

154

The siege lasted for over an hour. Of the two hundred and fifty Armenians who were entrenched in the monastery, only thirty could still hold a rifle. Many were only adolescents and did not know how to shoot. At first they did only the reloading but now they had to replace the wounded. Bodies were strewn both in the inner courtyard and in the gallery running along the high wall. A few windows, narrow as loopholes, and the bell tower were the only positions affording scant protection to the defenders.

In spite of all this, the army was finding it costly to take the monastery, so the soldiers were using the women as living shields. They bound them in pairs, tying their hands behind their backs, and pushed the women in front of them as they approached the building. The hostages shouted to their compatriots to fire all the same but they did not. The soldiers threw grenades but this only blew the bodies in the courtyard to pieces. The thick walls protected the survivors.

Seeing that the grenades had no effect, the young captain in charge of the operation ordered a ceasefire. Little by little, a strange silence fell. The beleaguered Armenians also observed the truce. The eighteen women who had been used as shields were ordered to march towards the gate. Weeping, they obeyed. Half way there, the soldiers riddled them with bullets.

The cavalry officer moistened his fingers with saliva to smooth back a lock of hair that had fallen over his eyes, and then shouted through cupped hands, 'Surrender or I'll execute all the deportees in the convoy.'

Machine guns began to stutter again. A little later, a white flag appeared on the bell tower and the bursts of fire ceased.

'Come out.' Satisfied, the captain lit a cigarette.

The doors opened and the Armenians filed out, hands above their heads. Some were wounded. Shirag Tevonian's men were recognizable by their black shirts, riding breeches, the cartridge belts crossed over their chests and the long daggers still in their belts. The rest of the young men from Sivas looked ragged. Among them was Varouj Zorian, the teacher's oldest son, who was going to be fifteen in two weeks.

The soldiers lined them up against a wall, while they searched the cloister, looking for other survivors. Soon the moans of the wounded who were being finished off could be heard. The captain reserved the task of directing the execution for himself. He put on his gloves and inspected the outfits of the firing squad. Then he lifted his sabre.

'Ready. Aim . . .'

'Long live Armenia!' shouted Shirag's second-in-command, who had planned the ambush. His cry was taken up by his companions but the volley of shots muffled their voices.

After the monastery the climb became harder. When they reached the summit, the deportees never got a chance to catch their breath. Using their cudgels, the escorts forced them on. Maro picked up an old woman, Gullu Abayan, whose cart had turned over. She had her two granddaughters, Sossi and Maritsa, twelve-year-old twins, with her. It was impossible to tell them apart. They had pretty little faces, turned-up noses and small, intelligent eyes. Long pigtails hung down over their shoulders. Azniv Hanim and her family shared a gourd of water with the newcomers. The water was warm and did not quench their thirst, but all the same it was a balm to their parched mouths and throats.

The road narrowed to a tortuous path dug up by the hoofs of the herds driven to new pastures. Now the convoy moved on a windswept plateau. The sun seemed closer and was beating down on the rocky ground. Here nothing grew but sparse broom and thorny bushes on which goats nibbled. Amazed, a young shepherd in rags stared at the caravan. He approached to offer them cheese, but the guards pushed him back after snatching one of his goats.

The convoy advanced through a fog of dust, which made breathing difficult. In the back or in the front only three or four carts could be seen, but in between the view stretched to the purple mountains on the horizon. In the distance, Maro noticed groups of horsemen travelling alongside the convoy, probably to prevent any attempt at escape. When Tomas joined his godfather, Maro gave the reins to her mother and sat with the twins in the back.

They travelled all afternoon through a monotonous landscape that made them feel that they were standing still. There was no glimpse to be had of their final destination. Before the sun went down, the camp was set up in the middle of a steppe, where there was not a single tree or water. Armen and Maro manoeuvred their carts to park them in the centre of the camp as the night loomed menacingly. They could not water the animals because they were saving what little water they had for themselves. The vegetables they had brought were wilted, so Maro fed the most withered heads of lettuce and cabbage to the oxen. As they had no more alcohol for the stoves and no wood for a fire, they had a cold supper: a little cheese, *khavourma*[1] and some stale bread.

Night fell and the torrid heat gave way to a cool wind, drying their sweat-soaked bodies. The temperature dropped again suddenly. They were at an altitude and the night was going to be cold.

A lot of rumours circulated, many of them started by the guards: the government had annulled the deportation order and they were all going back to Sivas; military trucks were waiting for the deportees to take them directly to Aleppo the following day. There were people who really believed these. Other stories were more alarming still: the prisons had been emptied and thieves and brigands were roaming the countryside; bands of savage mountaineers armed to the teeth had been brought in from the east and were patrolling the hills. Even though Maro refused to believe all these tales, the glowing campfires in the distance worried her and Armen's nervousness did nothing to reassure her.

He had placed the carts next to each other, leaving a space of about four metres between them, and yoked an ox at either end to form a square, which offered them some protection. While the old women were laying out a canvas on the ground and spreading the blankets, Maro took Armen aside.

'What's going on? What are you worried about?'

'The guards are getting drunk.'

'Oh,' she said, putting her hand over her mouth, 'may God protect us!'

'You'll sleep in the middle with the children.'

And so Araksi and Armen lay on one side and Azniv Hanim and Gullu on the other. The twins stretched out next to Maro and Tomas cuddled up against her breast. The stars seemed so close; Maro, lying on her back, gazed at them, feeling as if they were pinning her down. To entertain the children while they were falling asleep, she showed them the constellations and named them. In her head she could hear Vartan's voice teaching her how to recognize the stars.

'Why can't we see God and the saints and the angels in the sky?' whispered Tomas.

'Because they're invisible,' replied the twins in unison.

Tomas didn't say anything else. He had just seen a constellation which looked like a dog – a spaniel like Sassoun. He closed his eyes but saw an even more atrocious image – the body of a child lying on his side near the

---

1. Roasted, salted lamb (Turkish).

monastery. He bit his knuckles. Maro could feel him shaking and, thinking he was cold, pulled him closer to her.

The guards had set up their tents in the back on the other side of the path. Although there were less than fifty of them to supervise more than fifty thousand deportees, they didn't really have a hard job. A few of them patrolled the camp; others smashed carts to get wood to feed the big bonfire. They skinned the goat they had stolen from the young shepherd and put it on a spit. Liquor was flowing freely and the party was getting lively. They began by singing songs and then dancing, accompanied by happy shouts that rang through the air. In no time such simple acts of pleasure would not be enough for them.

Reeling, they went to the nearest carts in search of women. An older couple tried to protect their three daughters. Other families did the same. The soldiers soon picked up their bayonets, daggers and sabres. A murderous frenzy overcame the guards and they attacked everyone within arm's reach.

Nobody in the camp slept. Armen was standing guard with a revolver in his hand. The blood-curdling screams were followed by crying and wailing. One could hear the thunderous laughter of the drunken men and the pleading voices of young women who were being dragged into the guards' tents. Rape and torture! Maro could not help feeling relieved at having been spared this martyrdom but her compassion was mixed with shame and boundless fear. The victims' screams tore right through her, body and soul. Curled up, she pressed her thighs together and waited for dawn to break. The twins were aware of what was happening and were in a state of panic. One of them cuddled up to her grandmother and the other pressed herself against Maro's back and clasped her around the waist. Tomas stuck his fingers in his ears and ground his teeth; every now and then he dropped off to sleep, only to wake up with a start almost instantly.

When the seemingly endless night was over, they yoked the oxen without a word. Araksi divided the last of the cheese. Everyone received a small ball, which fitted in the hollow of their hand. Azniv Hanim gave out some dried fruit but there was nothing more to drink.

All the rest of the deportees detoured around the place where the escort had set up their camp but Armen, who wanted to take a look in spite of his wife's protests. Someone had to bear witness to these crimes. He had thought, after seeing the massacres of 1896 twenty years before, nothing could surprise him, but he was wrong. They could not compare to the horror he now found. No battleground since the Mongolian invasions had ever offered such a spectacle of cruelty. Numbed, he tripped over outspread bodies. Suddenly he saw her: sitting naked on the ground, she was staring at the horizon with empty eyes. He went up to her but she didn't react. Her white skin was bruised and lacerated and her thighs stained with blood. She could not have been more than seventeen but her haggard face made her look like a hundred.

Armen bent and touched on her shoulder. 'My daughter.'

She didn't move. He put his hands under her armpits and lifted her up. She stood up obediently but kept staring into the distance. He covered her with a strip of cloth he found lying on the ground and put his arms around her shoulder to guide her. She walked mechanically in a state of shock. Armen noticed that she never even blinked.

He shook her gently. 'There's nothing to be afraid of any more.' She gave no sign she had understood.

Armen went back to the cart Araksi was driving. He put the young woman in the back, climbed up himself and wrapped her in a blanket. She remained as he had placed her with her legs dangling over the road. Armen took the seat next to Araksi. He would have given anything for a straight shot of liquor.

Soon thirst became part of their endurance test and, as the hours went by, it turned into obsession. Ravens flew straight as an arrow towards the place where the convoy had left its dead. Buzzards and smaller birds of prey also flew by and, of course, the inevitable vultures with their huge rounded wings. Rocked by the turning of the wheels, Tomas and the twins slept. Gullu held her *charshaf* over them to provide some shade for their faces. Leaning on Maro's shoulder, Azniv Hanim dozed.

Maro prodded the ox constantly because otherwise the beast refused to move. The animals were completely exhausted. Some had collapsed and others refused to budge in spite of the blows. When this happened, the guards forced the deportees to abandon all and continue on foot. The sick and the old found places in other vehicles, but soon many were walking.

When the sun reached its zenith, the leader of the escort team ordered a halt. The deportees remained on the trail. There was no spring, only the ruins of a shepherd's hut, about a hundred and fifty yards from the road. The guards stood in the shade of the half caved-in roof.

Tomas got up, rubbed his eyes, and looked around incredulously. Had

159

he been travelling? The monotonous rocky plateau, the surrounding mountains: the landscape was identical to yesterday's.

'I'm thirsty, mama.'

Maro took him in her arms and kissed him before putting him down. His forehead was burning.

'My poor darling, we have nothing more to drink.'

He started to cry.

'Come over here,' said Armen, who had come up. 'My wife still has two or three juicy cucumbers.' He carried Tomas and the twins to his cart where Azniv Hanim, Araksi, and Gullu had improvised an umbrella with a piece of cloth.

Maro approached the young girl, whom they had forgotten. That dull look! She stroked her cheek.

'What's your name?'

The girl did not seem to hear. She was far away. Maro opened the blanket and discarded the rags covering the girl's bruised body, which glistened with sticky sweat.

'How is she?' asked Azniv Hanim from under the shade of the cloth.

'In a state of shock. I'll take care of her.' Maro took her by the hand and led her to the back of her cart. The girl followed docilely. Maro uncovered her and dressed her in one of her own dresses. She talked to her constantly and tenderly, hoping to bring her back to reason.

'The sun is burning your pretty face. I'll find a straw hat for you.'

Maro was rifling through a basket when a rumbling noise made her lift her head. Horsemen were galloping across the plateau, heading in their direction. Soldiers! The hoof beats thudded like the hide of a drum being beaten. The horses branched out and formed a row parallel to the convoy. Then the riders burst into a rapid ululation. They were charging!

'*Chetés*!' someone cried. 'Kurdish bandits.'

The deportees crawled under their carts, and those who had none fled in the direction of the sheep-pen. What about the guards? Leaning against the walls of the shepherd's hut, their guns at their sides, they were eating leisurely. Maro realized that the soldiers would not help them. She jumped down to join Tomas and the others.

Wearing grey turbans and sheepskin jackets, the bearded horsemen seemed to have sprung out of the beginning of time. Knives and pistols hung on their belts and they brandished antique guns or shiny *yataghans* above their heads. The *chetejis* spread out the length of the convoy, yelling out their war cry.

Lying under the tarpaulin, Armen drew his pistol. A horse stopped very near and a deep, amused voice said, 'You! You're not afraid?'

'The girl!' screamed Maro.

'Stay here,' cried Azniv Hanim but Maro was already gone. All Azniv Hanim could do was to stop her grandson from following his mother. The brigand was lifting his sabre to kill the young girl, who stood still.

'No!' shouted Maro and ran towards them, pulling three pieces of gold from her money belt. In her excitement her *charshaf* fell off. The fierce-looking, flat-nosed man stared at her amazed. She pushed the girl aside and held out the pieces of gold.

'Leave her alone. Take this instead.'

He grabbed Maro by the wrist. 'You're the real treasure, my beauty.'

She fought him off with all her strength as he tried to hoist her up on his saddle. Realizing he couldn't do it single-handed, he threw his sword down and grabbed her by the hair. She tried to pull him off the horse, which shied, but he only laughed at her efforts as her feet were off the ground. A shot rang out! The man jolted, opened his hand and let go. Maro fell to the ground and lay still. The horse left at a gallop and the rider, who had been hanging on to its mane, fell off a bit further up.

'*Yallah! Yallah!*' screamed the *chetejis* running up to the scene.

Tomas escaped from Azniv Hanim and fell on top of his mother who was lying on her stomach. He shook her. '*Mayrig! Mayrig!*'

Maro pulled him down. 'Don't move! Shut your eyes and play dead!' He obeyed.

Revolver in hand, Armen walked away from them as quickly as he could in the direction of the sheep-pen, hoping to divert attention from his family. Perhaps they would not risk killing him under the very noses of the gendarmes. The horsemen were at his heels and gaining on him. Armen turned to face them. Three rifles pointed at him. He aimed but his opponents were quicker. The three detonations could not be told apart. They hit him in the middle of the chest. Armen spread his arms wide, took a step back and fell to the ground.

'Armen!' shrieked Araksi, 'Armen!'

A horseman with the build of a giant stopped near the body, leaned over his horse's neck, grabbed Armen effortlessly by the ankle and lifted him half-way up. He spurred his horse to a trot and made three full circles,

161

dragging the body so that the head bounced on the stones. His companions fired into the air and made their horses rear. The bandit then left the body and went to join in the plundering.

Araksi had fainted in Azniv Hanim's arms, who implored her not to move.

'Wait until the bandits have left. There's nothing you can do for him any more.'

'I want to die! I want to die!'

Hoofs hammered the ground not far from Maro, who whispered to Tomas, 'Not a word! If they touch you, don't move.'

A horse passed over them. One of the hoofs came within a few inches of Tomas's head. The horseman jumped off and picked up the three pieces of gold. He searched Maro, who pretended she was lifeless, while his hands pawed her roughly. He found the money belt crammed with gold coins, cut it off with his dagger and remounted. They took the young girl. Maro could not interfere without endangering their lives. As the *chetejis* rode away, they took several carts, including Maro's, and piled into them their plunder and a number of women and children.

'Can I move now?' asked Tomas petrified.

'Not yet.'

The noise of the wheels and hoofs, the cries of the captives and the victory songs of the bandits faded away.

'Armen,' sobbed Araksi. Held up by Azniv Hanim, she approached her husband's body.

Maro got up and took Tomas in her arms. Now that the danger was over, she was shaking like a leaf. Tomas was crying and repeating incredulously, 'They've killed my godfather! They've killed my godfather!'

Maro kissed him and set him down next to the twins who had buried their heads in their grandmother's skirt. 'Stay here, my darling. I'll go and help Araksi.'

'I want to go to him. He was my godfather! Mine!'

Deaf to Maro's pleading, he ran to his godfather. Armen was lying on his back; his eyes closed as if he were asleep. His face was full of cuts and bruises and a flap of hairy scalp was hanging over his ear. His chest was spattered with blood. Tomas stopped crying – It hurt too much! He fell on his knees and knotted his fingers with his godfather's. He remembered the strength and warmth of that hand when he had held it on the way to church. He closed his eyes, wanting to recite the prayer for the dead. He could hear

Armen's voice teaching him the words, which now had acquired a totally different meaning. He thought about his father. When would he come? How would he find them? Disheartened, the child put his hand in his pocket and clutched the silver box with the seal.

The guards came out of the sheep-pen and started the convoy on its way again. Araksi refused to leave Armen. Her old neighbour, Manuel, who had joined them, offered to carry him. He lifted the body up by the shoulders and Maro took the legs. Tomas picked up the sailor cap from the ground and put it on. They laid Armen in the cart and Araksi climbed up and sat next to him.

'You drive,' said Maro to her mother. '*Diguin*[1] Abayan will sit next to you and I'll walk with the children.'

Azniv Hanim searched through a sack behind the seat and handed Armen's clothes to Maro. She returned to the idea she had had on the first day. 'Make yourself look pregnant.'

Maro protested but her mother was adamant.

'You saw what happened and next time Armen won't be there.'

By the time the convoy set off, Maro looked like a woman in her last weeks of pregnancy. A veil covered the lower part of her face. The dust and dirt disguised her beauty and her eyes had lost their sparkle. Tomas, who didn't understand the reason for the disguise, told his mother she looked like an old woman.

Araksi had laid her husband's head in her lap but could not stand the sight of his bruised face. She covered it with her handkerchief. She waved away the flies attracted by the blood and talked to him so quietly that Maro, who was walking alongside her, couldn't hear anything.

Maro felt guilty about Armen's death and avoided meeting Araksi's eyes. She would have liked the old woman to say something to ease her guilt; one word would have sufficed. When she couldn't stand it any longer, she said, 'I loved him, our Armen.'

Without looking up, Araksi said, 'And he loved you, like a daughter.'

Then she continued her silent monologue. Maro finally looked at her and saw Araksi cradling her dead husband like the Madonna in the *Pietà* and it brought back her own grief. Her fake belly reminded her of the

---

1.   Madam (Armenian).

miscarriage she had suffered a few months back and of Vartan's intense disappointment. Vartan . . . She was filled with profound despair and had the greatest difficulty pushing away the idea that Vartan was dead.

As if he had read her mind, Tomas asked, 'When is papa coming back?'

Maro caught her breath. 'I don't know,' she said almost harshly. 'I'm sure he's still looking for us.'

Tomas held on to her skirt while she caressed his neck. The captain's cap covered his ears and bobbed with each step. Maro could not give up because of him – he was the living proof of their love! She wanted to tell him not to lose hope but she thought words would be empty of all meaning right now.

'I'm sure your godfather is in heaven. Pray to him to protect and watch over your father.'

After a few moments Tomas cried aggressively, 'Why doesn't God punish the bad ones?'

'He will, Tomas, he will!'

A little while later he complained, 'I'm thirsty, Mama. My throat hurts.'

She picked up some pebbles and wiped them off on her dress. 'Put them in your mouth. It'll make your saliva flow, but be careful not to swallow them.'

'Does it really take away the thirst?' asked one of the twins, who were walking hand in hand alongside her.

'Yes. Try it.'

Two hours later, Azniv Hanim turned around and announced, 'We're arriving somewhere.'

Through the dust they could see the bluish slope of a valley. A ramshackle conglomeration of fieldstone houses with tiny stables attached to them, perched at the edge of the plateau, but, in the centre, there was an unexpected treasure – a fountain! Smelling the water from afar, the oxen speeded up. The deportees started to laugh and cry hysterically as if their dehydrated bodies had come to life at the thought of water.

The shepherds' dogs snarled. They wore collars with sharp-pointed steel studs to protect their throats from the fangs of the wolves. A gigantic pine tree with gnarled branches, the only one anywhere to be seen, cast its shadow on the square. The men and children of the town gathered around. Veiled women stuck their heads out of the glassless windows. The villagers' curiosity overcame their fear of the *zaptiyés*.

A thread of limpid water spilled out of the fountain into an overflowing basin, which irrigated the small gardens. Suddenly this water was neither

164

abundant nor free. On the pretense that the villagers wanted to be paid for it, the guards decided to sell the water. Those who had no money had to depend on the charity of others.

Reassured, the village people little by little drew near the dirty, feverish-eyed deportees and offered the few things they had to sell: goat cheese, potatoes and onions. Maro obtained a piece of bread in exchange for a sapphire earring.

A timid woman whispered softly, 'May God watch over you,' before she retreated quickly into her house.

Suddenly the Armenians started to protest. The guards were seizing the young girls and boys and pushing them to the other side of the square. A guard shoved Maro and she almost fell. She pulled Tomas to her but the man was more interested in the twins. Gullu barred his way but he struck her on the head with the butt of his rifle. She rolled to the ground and the guard dragged away the howling twins.

Azniv Hanim implored Maro, 'I beg you, don't interfere.'

They raised Gullu to her feet. 'My little granddaughters!' she moaned. 'What will they do to them?'

The guards cleared the square of the deportees at bayonet point. Maro and her family stayed near one of the last houses. The villagers made a circle around fourteen young Armenians. The Sergeant climbed up on the pedestal of the fountain and proceeded to auction them off.

'Pretty young wives. Strong, young boys to work the fields. Make your bids.'

The bargaining went on a long time right under the eyes of the terrified, incredulous parents, who were incapable to stop the sale of their children. The peasant women whispered advice into their husbands' ears on the choice of the merchandise. These were poor people. They bought eleven children for a few *kouroush* – less than the price of a sheep. Some of the Armenian families tried to console themselves that these children, at least, would be spared the horrors of the road and the cruel destiny awaiting them. That was not Gullu's attitude. When she heard the screams of her granddaughters as they were being dragged towards a house, she ran to save them. She ran into the Sergeant in the square, who tripped her and then kicked her in the ribs and stomach. He then searched her and got up, beaming, with a gold necklace in his hand.

When the Sergeant left, Azniv Hanim went to help Gullu, but her heart had stopped beating. Azniv Hanim closed her eyes; she could do no more.

165

The escort team forced the convoy on and Gullu's body remained behind where it had fallen. Livid, Tomas turned to his mother and she took his hand.

'Don't worry about Sossi and Maritsa. They'll be well treated like our Zeynep and Jemila, and they won't be thirsty as we are.'

Tomas was not convinced. He preferred being thirsty to being separated from his mother and grandmother. How could he live without them? He bowed his head. The child in front of the monastery . . . Armen . . . and now, Gullu. For the first time he realized that he, his mother and Azniv Hanim could be killed. He sank into such despair that he refused to speak. He began to talk to his godfather, who was now in the company of the angels.

The narrow, twisting road wound its way down into the valley. The stones loosened under the hoofs and the wheels and rolled down into a chasm on one side of the road. Azniv Hanim refused to surrender the reins to her daughter, although Maro had more experience of driving. She thought that, in case of an accident, the loss of two old women and a dead man, would be a lesser tragedy, and Maro didn't insist.

'Can you still walk?' she asked Tomas.

He was lost in a pleasant dream and didn't hear her. It was morning and he was waking up in his bed with Sassoun at his feet. He would be joining his parents in their room soon. His father was wearing his uniform and the room smelt of Cologne water. Smiling, Vartan held out his arms to him.

Maro became worried. 'Tomas, are you all right? You're not too tired?'

'No.' He was annoyed at having been awakened from his daydream but did not show it for fear of worrying his mother. His feet and calves hurt but he said, 'It is easy. It's downhill.'

The convoy reached the valley which was already in the shade because of the high cliffs surrounding it. They stopped at a dry river-bed. The guards ordered them to unhitch the oxen and the animals went down into the mud. They pawed the ground, knowing instinctively that water would well up in the holes made by their hoofs. The deportees also dug into the mud to fill their gourds with water.

Araksi couldn't stand any more. All day long she had been holding Armen's head and shoulders in her lap and the weight had slowed down the circulation in her legs. Nevertheless, she took a pick and a shovel and told them in a shaking voice that Armen had brought these tools in case they needed to bury someone on the trip.

'It will have to wait,' said Azniv Hanim, taking the tools from her. 'First we need to eat something to get our strength back.'

They shared the bread and two small potatoes Azniv Hanim had bought. Much to her disgust, Araksi refused to touch the food and took only a sip of water. They ate in silence.

Afterwards Maro said, 'My mother and I are going to dig.'

Araksi pointed to a hillock a short distance from the river bank. 'The grave will be out of reach of the spring floods there.'

Tomas tried to help with the digging but the earth was heavy, compact and crammed with stones. When the hole was a metre deep, Azniv Hanim panted, 'That's enough. It's the best we can do. Armen will understand.'

A few old women dressed in black helped Araksi but, as they had no water, they were not able to wash the body as tradition demanded. Widow Kaloustian gave a sheet to be used as a shroud and anointed him with oil according to the ritual. People gathered around the body to walk in procession up to the hillock. It was the first time they had united in prayer. Up to now, they had only shared fear and suffering, but now they were sharing faith and a belief in resurrection. A blind man led by a young boy climbed up to the grave and with an astonishingly loud and precise voice chanted the *Iverin Yeroussaghem*. All took up the words in unison, 'He shall pass through Jerusalem.' They had become a community again. At first their voices were timid; then they swelled and were enriched by echoes until they filled the narrow valley and rose above the mountains. It was a moment of grace in the midst of a storm. Even the guards stopped to listen, with never a thought of interrupting the ceremony. The burial became a symbol. They were praying for all those left unburied in front of the monastery, for those who had died the previous night, for the dead lying at the bottom of the ravine and for all those who would fall by the wayside along the endless road. Many reminded themselves that soon they too would pass through Jerusalem.

When Armen's body was in the grave, Araksi spread a rug over him and Tomas added a tiny bouquet of wild flowers he had gathered along the bank. Then he put on the captain's cap and said wistfully, 'My godfather told me he would sleep well under the shade of the cypress tree next to the church.'

When Araksi heard this, she fell on her knees at the side of the grave. She shrieked with grief, and tore her blouse. They had to carry her away. The crowd dispersed. Maro wanted to lead Tomas away, but he insisted on finishing burying the dead man.

'He was my godfather, my godfather,' he repeated stubbornly.

He picked up the shovel with a rage that made him strong. He kept thinking about the fat birds that had circled over the dead waiting to devour them. They were not going to touch his godfather! Armen was going to get to heaven in one piece.

Once the grave was filled, they erected a heap of stones above it. Tomas adjusted each stone so it would not fall off during a storm.

Widow Kaloustian, who had stayed behind to pray, went through her bag and called to Tomas, 'Come here, boy.' She put three dark seeds into his hand and said, 'These are cypress seeds.'

Tomas's eyes lit up. 'Thank you very much. Captain Armen will be happy.'

Maro helped him choose the place to plant the seeds, as Tomas wanted the branches to shade the grave in the afternoon. When they were finished, she hugged him. 'Your godfather must be proud of you.'

'When I'm big, I'll come and build a church here, as he wanted.'

When they returned to the river, Maro saw the carts were being driven away by the guards.

Azniv Hanim was outraged, 'Two blankets; that's all I could save. Now we have to walk.'

Widow Kaloustian and Antaram Khatoun, Der Khoren's cousin by marriage, were taking care of Araksi.

'I won't be able to walk,' said the latter.

'We'll help you,' protested Maro.

'No! My legs . . . My heart . . . I won't get very far.'

'Don't say that!'

The widow made a sign to her not to insist. She patted her bag. 'I have some potions in here that will cure Araksi. Why don't you leave us alone?'

Night fell quickly. Since they no longer had the shelter of the carts, the deportees huddled together for warmth in the night.

Azniv Hanim and Tomas were sleeping under the same blanket. Maro shared the other one with Araksi. When she woke up at dawn it was cold and she was shivering. She noticed that the old woman was no longer at her side. She got up. Although her body felt numb, she rushed towards the hillock, and there found Araksi stretched out over Armen's grave. She shook her but the woman's body was ice-cold. A small vial fell from her clenched hands and shattered against the stones. Maro realized that the Widow Kaloustian had given Araksi one of her potions that would allow her to join her husband. She knelt on her knees and cried, not so much for the dead as for those who wanted to survive.

# SIX

Was it the nineteenth or the twentieth of July? Vartan had lost count of the days, and for their part, his two remaining cell-mates didn't give a damn. They lived from day to day – from the evening, when they escaped execution until the following dawn when it might be their turn. Each one squatted in his corner. They did not talk any more. Their silence accentuated Vartan's solitude.

They had not been able to carry out their plan to escape in a group. Someone had given them away and the metal door had never again remained ajar when the prisoners were in the courtyard. The straw mattresses of those who had already been executed still cluttered the dungeon, making it look larger than it really was. The light which came in through the narrow window fell on the crosses and inscriptions Sarkis Zorian had etched into the grey stone wall. After he had died, four days before, Vartan had taken over his job, engraving the names of those who were still alive. It seemed he was destined to be a journalist to the end, only he would not have time to add his byline!

Any moment now, he would be dangling at the end of a rope. A guard had warned him a while ago that his execution would take place today. The City Hall clock struck six . . . then seven . . . and Vartan was still waiting. He had been expecting to die for so many days now that death had lost all meaning and did not frighten him any more.

He heard footsteps in the hall. He stood up. A bilious-looking guard appeared and held out a grey shirt. 'Vartan Balian, here's your outfit for the hanging.'

Without a word Vartan took off his grimy clothes and put on the shirt, which reached down to his knees. His cell-mates said goodbye to him, hardly able to conceal their relief at their own reprieve. Two guards had accompanied the non-commissioned officer. They tied Vartan's hands behind his back and took him to a small room on the ground floor, where a barber was sharpening his razor. They sat him down on a bench. The floor was littered with hair clippings. The barber shaved his head and got rid of his three-week-old beard.

A Lieutenant with slick, greasy, black hair came in; pointing his riding crop to the prisoner, he asked the Sergeant, 'Balian?'

'Yes.'

Legs apart, he stood in front of Vartan. The points of his waxed moustache curved up like kiss-curls and his close-fitting green uniform gave him a certain bearing.

'Governor Mustapha Bey . . .'

'You mean 'Mustapha Rahmi'!'

'*Governor* Mustapha Bey,' insisted the Lieutenant. 'For the last time he's asking you to convert to Islam and to collaborate with the Ittihad.' He pointed to the barber. 'Ali will circumcize you on the spot.'

Vartan shrugged to indicate his indifference.

In a voice devoid of emotion, the officer went on, 'Accept. It's the only chance you have to save yourself and your family. Accept and you'll be a free man again in ten minutes.' Vartan maintained a stubborn silence. 'Think of your wife and son suffering on the road, with the rest of the deportees. If they knew that one word from you would end their misery and yet you refused to say it, what would they think of you?'

The Lieutenant seemed to be reciting a lesson and Vartan imagined he could hear the commissioner's voice – his lies.

'Tell the commissionar to go to hell!'

The officer raised his eyebrows. 'It's your life. Let's go then.'

A huge wagon pulled by two horses was waiting in the centre of the courtyard. There were already about fifteen condemned men standing on the floor of the wagon. Its high slatted sides were topped with several strands of barbed wire. Vartan glanced around with the vague hope of escaping. The Lieutenant, who was used to taking the prisoners to the gallows, could guess their state of mind from the slightest signs on their faces. He noticed the way Vartan was looking around and pressed the barrel of his gun against his neck.

171

'Don't try to pull anything on me. A brand-new greased rope is waiting for you.'

Surrounded by a detachment of soldiers, the vehicle advanced towards the market place, accompanied by the roll of drums. The Lieutenant rode proudly at their head. A passage had been cleared between the stalls but the excited mob pressed against them from both sides. The daily executions never lost their power of attraction. They had become opportunities for carousing. At the other end of the square there was a platform with a row of gibbets – fifteen of them! The soldiers were taking down the bodies of the men hanged the day before and piling them into a wagon that would carry them out of Sivas.

Vartan was indifferent to all of this; he was looking inward. He could see those he had loved and who continued to live inside him. Every smell that came from the stalls evoked a memory, some from as far back as his childhood, especially the smell of peaches which were now in season. He could see his young mother lifting him up to the lower branches of a peach-tree.

A gendarme let down the barbed wire. 'Get down.'

Vartan jumped down and leaped towards a covered passage between the stalls, which gave on to a side street.

The Lieutenant shouted, 'I want that one alive!'

Vartan ran awkwardly because his hands were tied behind his back. Two guards caught up with him and knocked him down before he could reach the passageway.

The Lieutenant came up and hit him across the face with his whip. 'Hold him until they knot the noose around his neck securely.'

The wagon full of corpses passed in front of the condemned men, but none bothered to look at them. The end was near. They no longer tortured themselves with thoughts of their wives and children.

They were forced to climb up on the platform and then up the ladders that were leaning against the gibbets. The nooses swung in front of their faces. Vartan felt the executioner's hand on his shoulder and then the rough noose tightening around his neck.

How many of his compatriots had held on to the same rungs of this ladder? How many of them had died at this very spot where he was going to give up his soul? What had been their last thoughts?

He heard the voice of the Lieutenant behind him. 'I'll personally push the ladder away from under you.'

The roll of the drums quickened – or was it the blood beating in his temples? Vartan fixed his eyes on the summit of Mount Tejir, which was clearly silhouetted against the deep blue sky. Suddenly he felt alone – completely alone! An infinite distance separated him from the mob, the henchmen, even his condemned neighbours, and all the familiar faces inside himself had faded away. He could hardly feel his body; it was as if he had already started on his journey to the world beyond. The only thing remaining was the haunting smell of peaches. He had never imagined that dying could be so very lonely.

Vartan leaned his head back to gaze up at the sun. He simply could not realize that he would never see it again, nor feel its warmth. Would there be another life? How Vartan would have loved to have the blind faith of his childhood, but his reason told him that he would be engulfed in a void. Tomas . . . Maro . . . For how long would he live on in their memories? Images imposed themselves on his mind: Maro, at their bedroom window; Tomas on the front steps with Azniv Hanim and the servants; the dog under the shadow of the chestnut tree; the roses outlined against the white wall . . .

He felt someone touch his leg, started and stiffened as the rung of the ladder gave way under his foot.

The Lieutenant stepped up to him. 'Isn't that your name they're calling? Aren't you Major Vartan Balian?' He had to repeat his question twice before Vartan nodded. 'Over here!' shouted the officer.

The hangman loosened the noose and helped the prisoner down from the ladder. Stunned and incredulous, Vartan let himself be led to the end of the platform. The sun had blinded him and he could hardly see the lieutenant who saluted and said, 'Here he is, Colonel.'

That face? It was Colonel Ibrahim Alizadé! Vartan relaxed. His friend grabbed his arm roughly. 'Follow me.'

Vartan understood that he should not say anything or show any emotion in front of the Lieutenant. He was still in a state of shock and did not fully realize what was happening. He felt as if the blood had started to flow in his veins again. Slowly he became aware of an intense pain in his neck, a sensation of strangling as if his body were really undergoing the torture for which it had prepared itself. Only now did he become afraid of death.

In front of the gallows a long line of guards kept the mob at bay. The turmoil subsided. The nut, fruit, sherbet and *ayran*[1] vendors fell silent. Everyone seemed to be holding his breath.

---

1.   Diluted whipped yoghurt (Turkish).

The Colonel dragged his prisoner down the covered passageway behind the gallows. A closed vehicle was stationed in the alleyway. They climbed in.

'Straight ahead,' the Colonel ordered the coachman, in a strained voice. The horse had barely begun to trot when they heard the crowd's delirious roar. 'We just made it,' the Colonel said quietly.

He hugged Vartan who could only repeat, 'Ibrahim, Ibrahim, my friend. I still can't believe it.'

'You must have given up on me, but I was on a mission far away from Sivas.'

The Colonel gave no further explanations. He pulled the curtain aside and looked out to make sure they were not being followed.

Suddenly Vartan realized that his friend had rescued him on his own. 'You didn't have any orders about me. You've put your life in danger!' Ibrahim grinned like a child who has done something mischievous and got away with it.

Vartan was touched. 'How can I ever repay you? Happy is the man who has a friend like you!'

'You have another one. I'm not the only one involved in this operation.' For the moment he refused to say anymore. Silently he cut Vartan's bonds.

The carriage turned into a wide bustling avenue, which led to the American School for Girls and the coachman accelerated. At last Vartan could ask the question that had been burning on his lips for a long time. 'Do you have any news about Maro, my son and my mother-in-law?'

Ibrahim's face darkened. 'Unfortunately, I wasn't able to prevent their departure. I was away from Sivas and I just returned tonight.'

Vartan's shoulders sagged and he sighed deeply. 'Do you know which route the Armenians from Sivas have taken?'

'Of course, I've made inquiries. There are several convoys. Each has a different itinerary, but eventually all will go through Malatya. I think they're being taken by way of Aleppo.'

Vartan nodded with a sad face. 'A head start of two weeks. But they can't be moving too fast.'

Ibrahim touched him on his arm. 'You mustn't think of joining them. All of Anatolia is criss-crossed with caravans of deported people. It would be impossible to find three people in such a multitude. The army has put up road-blocks. The *chetés* are sacking the countryside. You won't get through.'

Vartan looked his friend straight in the eyes. 'What would you do if it were your family?'

Ibrahim lowered his head and did not answer. He would do exactly what Vartan was thinking of doing.

'A horse and a pistol. That's all I need.'

'You shall have them, of course.'

'Where are you taking me?'

'Be patient,' the Colonel replied with an enigmatic smile.


An ancient palace that served as headquarters for the army was squeezed in between the Mosque of Twin Minarets and the bathhouse. The carriage drove into the courtyard, where Vartan had often attended official receptions. Instead of using the main entrance, the colonel took him through a side door leading directly to the wing reserved for important visitors. They reached an anteroom with a small ornamental fountain in its centre. The walls were decorated with verses from the Quran and a portrait of the Sultan. Vartan could not understand why Ibrahim had brought him here.

Ibrahim took him into a larger room decorated with antique furniture, a rich rug and a gold-framed group photograph of Enver, Jemal and Talaat, the three principal Ittihad leaders.

'Now, will you tell me . . .?'

'Don't spoil his fun. Sit down and wait.'

In spite of his curiosity, Vartan stopped asking questions.

'I'll wait for you in the anteroom,' said Ibrahim

Once alone, Vartan let his eyes wander around the room. A tray of dried fruit and some bottles of liquor sat on a pedestal table. The temptation was too much for him: he bit into a fig and took a swig of cognac straight from the bottle. The alcohol made his stomach contract in a cramp. Exhausted, he leaned against the pedestal table; not daring in his state to sit down and risk dirtying the upholstery. The stink of the dungeon – of the wet straw, the grime and the sweat – clung to his skin so strongly and he felt like heaving.

The door at the end of the room opened and a General, dressed in a green infantry uniform buttoned up to the neck, entered. A roll of flesh hung half over his gilded collar. He was tall but walked slowly, as his considerable portliness hindered his movements. His little black eyes practically disappeared under his puffy eyelids and his chubby face looked kind. He put out his hand and Vartan took it suspiciously.

175

'I don't think you remember me, Major Balian.' Unlike his body, his voice had not changed at all.

'Halit Pasha!' exclaimed Vartan, overwhelmed. 'Forgive me for not recognizing you, but it's been a good ten years.'

'Yes,' said the officer rubbing his belly, 'and the good life . . .'

Vartan still remembered him as a fiery young man and a talented speaker. He was quite skinny in those days and had a bony face. They had met when they were both militant in the Union and Progress Committee. They had sat together in Parliament with members of the Progressive Party and Enver and Talaat. Now here they were – one a powerful general, and the other, a crushed, disappointed convict!

During the ensuing pause, Vartan searched the General's eyes, wondering if Halit was still the same man with the same passion for justice. Had he changed only physically? He could still read kindness in the General's eyes. Vartan thought he could see something else – a deep lassitude or even disenchantment. Halit Pasha opened his arms. Vartan hesitated, pointing at his clothes. The general shrugged and pulled him close.

'Halit Pasha, I'm so happy to see you again.'

'Vartan Balian,' the general replied, slapping him on the back. 'Vartan, my brother.'

They stepped back, looked at each other and smiled. Their friendship had not changed. Each thought back to the years of their youth, which they had devoted to the pursuit of the same ideal.

A shadow passed over Halit Pasha's face. 'What a waste,' he sighed.

Vartan nodded in agreement.

Halit Pasha took a packet of cigarettes from his pocket and pointed to the two easy chairs that stood side by side. Without being asked, Vartan poured two glasses of cognac. They sat down and clinked their glasses.

Exhaling smoke from his cigarette, Halit Pasha pointed to the photograph of the three leaders of government. 'We were really taken in by that band of swindlers, but their end is near. Preparations are being made in secret.'

Vartan observed gloomily. 'It'll be too late. Hundreds of thousands of Armenians will have been exterminated.'

Halit Pasha looked at the cognac swirling in the glass and murmured, 'Poor people! Poor country!' He put out his cigarette in a fury and threw the butt against the photograph of the leaders. 'How I have enjoyed deceiving them by saving you!'

'I'll be grateful forever, Halit Pasha.' Although he already knew the answer, Vartan asked, 'Is there any way of stopping this horror?'

'I don't think so. The moderate faction has been excluded from power. Because I refused to collaborate in the deportation, I've been sent to the Russian front, hoping my old bones will stay there.'

'If the enemy were to invade the country, that would bring the Ittihad down.'

'For the time being we can't count on that. I've just been in Gallipoli. Kemal Pasha[1] is holding off the French and the English. I'm sure he will push them back into the sea; it's only a question of time.'

They emptied their glasses in silence. The Pasha leaned over and put his hand on Vartan's. 'Ibrahim told me about your family. I'm deeply sorry.'

Vartan's features tensed and he bit his lip.

'Do you have a son?'

Vartan's eyes filled with tears. 'Yes. Tomas. He's six.'

'All is not lost,' continued the General who intended to be encouraging. 'You'll find him again someday, I'm sure of it. What's important right now is to get you out of here.'

Vartan knew that Halit Pasha would do all in his power to dissuade him, so he did not speak of his intention to go and look for his family.

'Would you like to come with me to the eastern front as my aide? If you want to, you can cross the lines into Russian Armenia from there.'

'I prefer not to leave the Empire.'

'You're right. It would be better to go to Constantinople. They don't bother the Armenians too much and you have relatives there, too, if I remember correctly. You could join some of our friends who are organizing the overthrow of the three jackals in power. Helping them would be the best way to help your family and your people.'

'It's a long way,' answered Vartan, pretending to be considering it.

'You'll have a uniform, a service record and money. I'll make out an order for a mission that will make it easier for you to move around.'

'If things turn out badly and I'm caught, you're taking an enormous risk, and so is Colonel Ibrahim.'

'And you, Vartan? Did you hesitate one minute before hiding me for weeks in the basement of your pharmacy on Péra Street when the Sultan's secret police were looking for me? And when I was sick with typhus in

---

1.  Mustapha Kemal, the future Atatürk, founder of modern Turkey.

prison, didn't you send me medicine every week? When Ibrahim told me they had arrested you, I made a detour to go to Sivas. It was the only way I could repay my debt.'

'Right now it is I who am indebted to you and I don't know how to thank you.'

'By staying alive, Vartan Balian. The Empire, or what will be left of it, will be in dire need of people like you.'

There was nothing left to say and it was useless under the circumstances to start reminiscing, so the General put an end to their conversation.

'I have to leave immediately. Colonel Ibrahim will lock you up in the military prison and this evening he'll take you out of town.'

They embraced each other warmly.

'Do you remember the little inn in Yeniköy,[1] where we ate so well? We'll go back there together some day.'

'God bless you, Halit Pasha. Be careful of the Russian bullets. May Allah protect you.'

'Don't worry. Death never knocks twice.'

An endless procession of ragged, dazed people struggled through a cornfield. The stalks grew above the grown-ups' shoulders and way over the children's heads and the leaves rustled like wrinkled parchment.

Fifteen military guards watched over five hundred of them. It had been two weeks since they had left Sivas. How many of them had fallen by the wayside and been abandoned to death and the vultures?

Now there was no more crying, no more weeping. The deportees didn't even have the strength to talk. They moved on, resigned, with their eyes riveted to the ground and obsessed with one thought – the next step. They avoided looking ahead, as they had no more goals. Their itinerary depended on the whims of the guards, who amused themselves by choosing the worst possible roads and making them walk in circles.

Azniv Hanim leaned on Tomas's shoulder, while Maro put an arm around her mother's waist to hold her up. She had a fever and her teeth chattered in spite of the stifling heat. Sometimes she would utter incoherent phrases, imagining she was young again. Her forces diminished day by day;

---

1.   A suburb on the Bosphorus.

each morning she was more exhausted. She would often beg Maro to abandon her but Maro refused to answer and pulled her mother on.

Maro walked as if in a dream. She was soaked in sweat and her head was buzzing. She had only one thought: to go on – to survive. She had forgotten why she was doing all this. To stay upright, to go on, to get through another day was enough for her. The weight of her fake belly added to her weariness, but it had protected her from the outrages many of the other women had suffered.

Tomas wore Armen's cap, pulled down over his eyes, to protect himself from the sun. He gnawed at an ear of corn that was still green. The husks of the kernels stuck in his teeth and the slightly sour-tasting paste dried up his mouth, but his stomach still craved this indigestible food. He had holes in the heels of his socks and blisters on his feet where his leather boots had rubbed. Fatigue, hunger, thirst and heat – Tomas had stopped complaining about these long ago. He had erased all memories of his life in Sivas. He thought of nothing – not even of an end to his suffering. He had not said a word for days. He walked on as if he had never known anything but misery – as if he had been walking forever. The nights were the worst. He had such beautiful dreams they frightened him more than his worst nightmares.

A range of steep hills, the extension of the Tahtali Mountains, stretched out to the left of the caravan. A slope covered with thorny bushes and strewn with rocks separated it from a cornfield. To the right of the field, the valley lay fallow and had been left to the goats. There were three small houses, leaning against each other in the middle of this desolate wilderness.

A band of *chetejis* were following them at a distance for the last two hours. What did they expect to steal from people who had absolutely nothing?

'Giaours!' The guards' cries were followed by shots. Four guards fell off their horses. The others turned back and galloped away. Six *fedayis* who had been hiding in the cornfield were shooting at them. The deportees stood rooted to the spot.

'Run, all of you!' screamed a *fedayi*, waving his arms. No one moved! It was all too sudden – too unreal. Further up, the escort team was regrouping to counterattack. 'Run! They're coming back!'

'They're our people!' cried an old man, weeping with joy. 'They're ours!'

Maro was quick to react. She assessed the situation at a single glance – the gendarmes were behind them and in front of them there was the bare naked plain; to one side, the howling *chetejis* were bearing down. That left only the bushy slopes.

She pulled her mother along. 'Come on! Let's run!'

'I can't. You go, both of you.'

'No. I'm not having that. Come on.'

The other prisoners scattered in all directions as if obeying a signal. The gendarmes attacked the *fedayis,* who stood their ground firmly. Tomas pulled his grandmother by the arm and Maro half-carried her. They dashed forward to freedom. Azniv Hanim ran by sheer force of will! Nearly 200 metres to the first bushes! Panting, she collapsed twenty pace before reaching them.

'Rest! I have to rest! I can't go on any more!'

Maro bent over her mother, while the fight raged behind them. 'Get up, *Mayrig,* one more effort.'

Tomas jumped nervously from one foot to the other; he could hardly resist the urge to run and hide in the nearby bushes.

'Hurry up, mama!' He was afraid. He took off the heavy belt stuffed with gold coins and threw it on the grass. Maro half-lifted her mother onto her back. Tomas led them to a goat path and went ahead, pushing aside the sharp, thorny branches. Maro found strength in herself that she hadn't known she had. After a few minutes of winding through the bushes, she collapsed behind a boulder. Azniv Hanim had fainted.

'Grandmother! Grandmother! Wake up! We have to go on!' Tomas was slapping her hands.

'Let her rest a moment,' said Maro, herself completely breathless. She climbed on top of the boulder to see what was happening in the valley. Two members of the Armenian resistance had fallen. Seven military gendarmes were wounded, unable to move; the others would have beaten a retreat if it hadn't been for the fact that a dozen *chetejis* had joined their ranks. The *fedayis* who were still on their feet faced their enemies. Instead of dispersing, they were covering their countrymen's escape. The rest of the brigands were pursuing the deportees who had imprudently chosen to escape to the plain.

Azniv Hanim recovered consciousness. 'You and Tomas must go.'

'We shall stay together, *Mayrig.*'

'Be reasonable,' begged her mother.

'Can you still manage to walk?'

Azniv Hanim got up. She leaned on her daughter's shoulder and they went on. The terrain was difficult and riddled with dead branches and stones. Maro told herself that it would be just as difficult for the horses. They could still hear the shots and cries behind them, as they climbed a slope out of the valley. They had to stop often to let Azniv Hanim catch her breath but gradually they succeeded in putting more distance between the gendarmes and themselves. Maro was exalted and her strength grew. Freedom was an arm's length away! Tomas felt the same. Lively as a squirrel, he darted between the scattered rocks, going ahead to reconnoitre and pick the easiest ways.

'We're going to make it, my darling,' said Maro to encourage him.

He exhorted his grandmother to keep going. 'This way, *Medzmayrig*. Here, there's a nice rock for you to sit on.'

Azniv Hanim felt a sharp pain constricting her chest. Each breath burnt her lungs. She could no longer feel her feet being cut by the stones; her legs were giving way. She took it stoically and at each stretch walked a little further than her strength permitted. She blamed herself for holding Maro and Tomas back and at the same time blamed her daughter for refusing to go on without her.

Sometimes they could hear noises and see shadows in the bushes. They thought there were others also trying to escape. Suddenly Maro froze in dismay. The side of the hill was not as smooth as it had appeared from the valley. A few hundred yards ahead of them was a gully. To the left – to the north – a steep slope ended in a peak. In the other direction, it appeared to drop and turn into a difficult but more manageable slope.

'That way,' said Maro.

The sun was setting fast. If they could only find a hiding place for the night. Maro searched the face of the rocks, looking for a crevice or a shelf wide enough to hold them. She could hear echoing sounds of the horses' hoofs, oaths in Kurdish and Turkish and snatches of voices which drew ever nearer. She put her mother's left arm around her neck and forced her to move faster. Azniv Hanim was no longer fully aware of what was happening.

There was a wide gorge in the hillside and Maro headed for it, hoping to put some distance between them and their pursuers. The bushes became sparser and thinner and they could see many other deportees going the same way. They came to a dead-end where a cave yawned and realized that the horsemen were herding them there to trap them. It was too late to turn around. Maro screamed with rage. Their best bet was to go in first, flatten themselves against the back wall, and let others who came later form a living shield against the guards and the bandits.

Tomas was intrigued. 'Is this a secret tunnel? Where does it lead?'

'Nowhere!' Maro replied sadly.

The child could feel his mother's disappointment and realized they were prisoners again. He glanced over his shoulder worriedly. More deportees were coming, followed by the hoof-beats of the horses.

'Go into the cave, Tomas and find a place where your grandmother can lie down, the further in the better.'

He was afraid of the large, black hole but even more afraid of the bandits. He went in with an old, bald man and a woman. The rays of the setting sun entered the cavern and he could see that part of the ceiling had caved in and blocked it about fifty metres from the entrance. The cool air was nice. Tomas found a place he thought was all right and returned to look for his mother.

The cavern had been used as a shelter for shepherds and their flocks. Maro laid her mother down on a stack of hay and dry dung for protection from the cold rock. Azniv Hanim was shaking and her teeth were chattering. A tiny bit of water oozed from the wall. Tomas joined the other children who were fighting for a chance to lick the rock, and wet a handkerchief, which he gave to Maro who used it to moisten her mother's chapped lips.

'*Mayrig . . . Mayrig . . .*'

After several attempts, Maro heard a murmur that resembled more of a death rattle. 'Sleep.' Maro lay down beside her mother and put her arms around her to keep her warm.

The day had seemed endless to Vartan. He had stretched out but had been unable to sleep. Impatiently, he paced up and down the cell like a bear in a cage. He was in the military prison adjacent to headquarters. He was the only prisoner on the floor. He was desperate to catch up with the deportees; every hour that he lost increased the distance between his family and himself.

'After the last prayer,' Ibrahim had said.

He trembled each time the Judas-window clicked open. The guards thought he was just another prisoner, except he was entitled to ample meals.

But even this was not really unusual, as officers who were waiting for their trial were entitled to order anything they liked, provided they paid the price.

Vartan kept busy, trying to remember the geography of the region between Sivas and Aleppo: where the towns were located, the mountain ranges, the rivers, the roads. Aleppo! On the edge of the Syrian Desert! 500 kilometres as the crow flies and probably twice that distance on the winding roads! That province was more Arabian than Turkish. Vartan should have found his family long before that. The convoys were probably moving at a snail's pace. According to Ibrahim, the ones from Sivas were split into different groups and each followed a different route. All of them, however, converged on Malatya, where there was a control camp. There he would try to intercept them. If he pushed his horse to the limit, he could make it in four days.

After the evening meal, the minutes dragged on interminably and the hours stood still. Vartan sat in the dark, chafing to leave. Finally he heard footsteps and the door opened. A young sergeant in a cavalry uniform came in. The light from the hall shone on his tense face. He passed his tongue over his bushy moustache.

'Major Balian?' he asked quietly.

'Yes.'

Vartan stepped up to him and could see that he was empty-handed. Where was the uniform they had promised him? The papers? The gun?

When the sergeant saw that the prisoner was about to speak, he put his hand over Vartan's mouth. 'Don't say a word. Follow me and do as I tell you.'

The empty corridors smelled of disinfectant. They went down a stairway and headed for the back of the building. The young officer was so nervous he could hardly fit the key into the metal door that gave onto the stable yard. He stepped out to take a look and motioned to Vartan to follow him. A nag hitched to a cart full of hay stood there.

'You're going to hide in there. Two men will drive the cart out of town and leave it there. They know nothing. They're only obeying orders without asking questions. Don't let them see you. Wait until they leave before you get out of your hiding place.'

Vartan had not expected anything like this . . . no identity papers, no horse. Something must have gone wrong. Too bad! He thought it wiser

183

though not to mention Ibrahim's name. The important thing was to get away. Then he would manage somehow.

'Thank you,' he said as he slid under the hay.

The Sergeant covered him up and left without another word. The pollen and dust made Vartan want to sneeze. He made some space in the straw to be able to breathe and see out. A good half-hour went by before the two soldiers came. They were drinking and talking loudly. These two idiots could spoil everything!

The cart started off skirting the prison walls, went up a dark alley and finally came to a street where restaurants and cafés were still open. The passers-by looked curiously at the cart full of hay. It was late at night for such a vehicle to be on the road. Vartan was angry. So much for a discreet exit! He got ready to jump and run at the slightest hitch. Fortunately nothing untoward happened and soon they were approaching the dark bulk of the old city walls.

He heard an authoritive voice. 'Where are you going with that?'

The cart stopped. The soldiers who were on guard at the city gates approached. Vartan sank deeper into the hay. It turned out that one of the guards was the cousin of one of the drivers.

Jokingly he asked, 'Well, Fikret, what are you stealing from the army?'

'Not me. It's one of my superiors.'

'I hope you're getting your cut.'

'Do you think I'd go around like this in the middle of the night because of his pretty eyes?'

The two soldiers driving the cart climbed down and shared half a bottle of *raki* with their buddies. They lit cigarettes and started joking and laughing together. This went on for a long time. Finally the cart moved on and turned right just before the bridge.

Vartan could see they were taking the road going to Tokat and then to Samsun. It was about time! His throat was full of dust and he was suffocating. He stuck his head out. The town was falling behind. The Halys River murmured below the road and, in front of them, the vast plain was drowned in darkness. He felt he was coming back to life.

A quarter of an hour later, the cart stopped again. The two soldiers set off to walk back to town, with their guns slung over their shoulders. After about twenty paces they stopped to roll their cigarettes. Vartan watched them impatiently. The flame of the lighter illuminated their faces.

One of them cried out, alarmed, 'Did you see that?'

'Yes!'

They loaded their Mausers. Had they discovered him? Was it a trap? Vartan sneaked up towards the driver's seat in the front of the cart. He froze at the sound of two shots. Then he heard a third one. The horse reared and took the bit between his teeth. The soldiers did not even try to stop it. They were much more interested in an enormous snake they had just killed.

Vartan couldn't reach the reins, which had fallen to the ground. The cart jarred and jolted. He had just enough time to jump before it turned over into the ditch. The horse pulled free from the broken shafts and trotted towards the town. Vartan stood up and wiped the straw off his collar. He was free!

'Psst. Vartan.'

Vartan turned around to see where the voice was coming from. Further up the road a figure emerged from a walnut orchard. It was Ibrahim. Vartan ran towards him, grabbed the big man by the shoulders and shook him, laughing.

'You saved my life, Ibrahim. Now you're giving me back my freedom.'

'You would have done the same for me.'

The Colonel sounded uncomfortable and it was clear he did not want Vartan to talk any more. He pulled him into the trees. There were two saddled horses tied up there. Ibrahim lit a candle and stuck it into the ground.

'The sooner you get going the better.'

'Is there something wrong?'

'No . . . well, I don't know. I just have a strange premonition.' Then he tried to laugh away the uneasiness he had just provoked. 'Today Melek, my first wife, reminded me that it was Tuesday.'

'And?'

'Allah created the darkness on Tuesday. It's an unlucky day for human undertakings.'

'Is that all?' Vartan was relieved and he said reassuringly, 'Certainly not for an act of charity.'

'That's what I told Melek. The undertaking that failed was your execution.' As he spoke, Ibrahim unhooked a bag from the saddle of one of the horses. He opened it up and handed some clothes to his friend. Vartan put on the officer's uniform and buckled the belt with a pistol holster hanging from it. He pulled on the boots, which looked brand new.

'Here's your military record,' Ibrahim said. 'You're Lieutenant Shakir

Ismael. Halit Pasha himself signed the order for your mission. Here's a purse full of money.'

Every time Vartan accepted something from the Colonel and their hands touched, he found that his friend's hands were clammy.

'This road leads to the Black Sea.'

'That's not the way I'm going,' Vartan replied firmly.

Ibrahim understood. 'I chose this place for that reason. There is a fork on the road a little way up, but . . . you know the orders say you're to go to Constantinople and not south.'

'Well, if necessary, I can always say I'm going to Aleppo to take the Taurus-Express.'

Ibrahim patted the saddlebag. 'Here's everything you need for a long trip: food, tobacco, shells, razor, compass, map and water for two days.'

'But it's your horse!' Vartan objected.

'I'm giving him to you. He'll take you far.'

'I can't take him. Any other horse would do.'

Vartan knew the horse was the apple of Ibrahim's eye. This horse with his shiny black mane had no rival in long-distance travel.

'You cannot refuse my gift without offending me. I'll feel much safer if you're riding Yildiz.[1] I've put the bridle with the brass ornaments on him. That will impress the military guards.'

'Thank you, Ibrahim. I'll take good care of him.'

When they got to the road, they kissed in farewell; they were deeply moved. They knew they would never see each other again and there were no words. Vartan mounted; Yildiz, sensing that the rider was not his master, stamped and reared.

Ibrahim stroked Yildiz's nose. 'Our ways are parting, my friend. Knowing you has given me much happiness and leaving you is giving me equal pain. I'll never forget you. Go and fulfil your destiny.' He was speaking more to Vartan than to the horse.

With a knot in his throat, Vartan simply said goodbye. He turned and slowly rode down the embankment to the river. The horse hesitated a moment before entering the current. Jupiter, shining with a bluish glitter over the southern horizon, seemed to be showing the way.

---

1.   Star (Turkish).

The cave was full. The guards had combed the valley until nightfall to capture the deportees who were still at large. The latecomers, most of them wounded, had to climb over other people to find a place to sit. The domed ceiling amplified the crying and moaning. A woman, losing all hope of survival, had gone mad, and was whimpering and wailing. The dreary, rattling monotone was exasperating. Someone vainly shouted for her to be quiet. An old man recited a prayer in a loud voice, and the commotion slowly died down.

The guards were on watch around a fire in front of the cavern. Tense, they loudly discussed the afternoon's assaults, the possibility of another attack by the *fedayis* and what they were going to do with their dead. The Armenians were afraid – afraid of reprisals that would surely follow. There was a commotion outside the cavern and the deportees heard horses and vehicles approaching. The rumour started with those closest to the entrance of the cave and travelled to the back. High-ranking army officers had just arrived. Everyone began to speculate about the meaning of this. They were hoping the presence of these superior officers would mitigate the guards' inhumane behaviour. Perhaps they would be given something to eat and drink at last. They turned out to be half right. The guards did stop attacking the prisoners, but no water or food was distributed.

Tomas slept, nestled up against his grandmother. Although Maro was exhausted, she roused herself to check on her mother's condition. Azniv Hanim had not regained consciousness since they had arrived. Her fever had subsided, but Maro was worried about her feeble, slow pulse and her constant wheezing. She kept on whispering, '*Mayrig . . . Mayrig . . .*', but Azniv Hanim did not react. Could she hear her? Maro pressed her cheek against her mother's and stroked her hair. 'I'm here, *Mayrig*. I'm taking care of you. Rest. You'll be better in the morning, you'll see. I'll take care of you. You're going to get well.'

At dawn the grey light filtered into the cavern and Maro saw that her mother's hands and feet were swollen and had turned black. Her face was ashen and her lips were blue.

She had no fever; on the contrary, her forehead was cold. No! She could not die! Maro fought against despair. She had to find a way. Perhaps there was a doctor among the officers who had arrived last night; they might have some medicine. She asked an old woman who was sitting next to them to keep an eye on her mother and son. The woman nodded and continued praying out loud. Maro elbowed her way out through the crowd.

The guard at the entrance to the cavern had his back turned. He was watching several of his comrades dig ditches; others were sleeping rolled up in blankets on the ground. One large and one small tent had been set up a few hundred paces away between a loaded wagon and a carriage. Two men in long, ample white robes and turbans were watching the vehicles and the tents. Next to them a boy was busy cooking on an alcohol burner. Maro rushed towards them.

'Halt!' yelled the guard, but she hurried on.

The guards dropped their picks and shovels and ran after her. She zigzagged to escape their grabbing hands and shouted to the men standing in front of the tents.

'I want to see an officer.'

At first no one moved. Then the guards scattered. Some ran ahead to cut her off. They were having fun. They were laughing and shouting obscenities. She dodged around a corporal who grabbed her skirt and ripped it. The clothes with which she had stuffed her false belly fell out, much to the amusement of the guards.

'She's ready for another baby,' cried one of the soldiers closest to her. He grabbed her arm, threw her down and rolled over with her on the ground. She fought furiously and bit his hand. The others came to his aid and threw themselves upon her. She scratched their faces until they pinned her arms down, but she continued to twist and kick off the guards who wanted to take her. Her blouse was torn off and the sight of her bare breasts excited the men even more. Dozens of hands mauled her.

She fought and howled, 'Let me go! Let me go! I want to see an officer!'

The two horsemen had ridden up and were watching the scene from their saddles. The one was still smiling, amused by the ploy of the fake belly and the fiery energy of this woman defending herself. She looked at him and the fury in her eyes became a plea. He stopped smiling.

As the men bared her thighs, she said to him, 'I want to talk to the commanding officer.'

A hand tore her veil away and her thick, luxuriant hair spilled out around her head. When he saw her face, the horseman was shocked. He knew that beautiful face.

'Let her go!' he ordered.

The guards did not hear him. He made a sign to the giant who accompanied him. The other jumped off his horse and kicked the assailants off her as he hit them with his crop. 'Didn't you hear the *mudur*,[1] you sons of whores!'

He hit them hard. A guard turned around to protest and the giant cavalryman knocked him to the ground with a single blow. His erection was visible through his open fly. The others decamped without waiting for their turn.

The horseman dismounted. A man wearing a white cape ran to take hold of the bridle of his horse. The *mudur* came up to Maro, who was trying to cover her breasts and thighs with the tatters of her skirt. He wore an olive-green jacket belted at the waist and beige riding-trousers. He looked at Maro, intrigued. He had silver-grey hair at his temples, thick, ink-black eyebrows, and a thin, smooth face with protruding cheekbones. He held out his hand to help her get up.

'You want to talk to me?' He had the calm assured voice of someone who was accustomed to being obeyed.

Now that she had his attention, Maro knew that she had to arouse his curiosity. 'I shouldn't be in this convoy. It's all a mistake.'

The man's grey-green eyes showed surprise. He interrupted her, 'Come and see me in my tent in five minutes.'

In his tent? But Maro could not afford to be sceptical, so she agreed. She pointed to the bucket of water standing next to the burner.

'May I, *Effendi*?'

'Of course,' he replied, snapping his fingers. 'Abdullah.'

The boy dropped his pots and pans and bowed to Maro. 'Follow me, please, *Hanim*.'

He was thirteen or fourteen years old and when he smiled he exposed very white teeth. His mop of curly black hair was like the fleece of a Persian lamb. Maro plunged her hands into the water and drank avidly. Then she washed her face and straightened her dress as best she could. This was her only chance to talk to someone who seemed to enjoy authority. She must not waste it. Her mother's life was at stake, as well as Tomas's and her own. If she had to use her charms, she would.

Bedri followed his master into the tent. He was husky, had a massive neck and hairy arms and looked like a bull. A thick, drooping moustache made him look even coarser. At fiftyish, he was older than his master. In contrast with the *mudur*'s refinement, he was rough and ready. The two men were worlds apart and yet they were indispensable to each other.

---

1.  Director (Turkish).

In his grating voice Bedri asked, 'Why are you wasting your time on this woman, Riza Bey? We must leave.'

'We'll leave when it suits me!' Riza Bey snapped. But the flare-up was only momentary and when he had calmed down again a sad expression came over his face. 'You see, Bedri, I had a dream last night.'

Bedri turned aside and lifted his eyes to heaven. There was no arguing with Riza Bey. In spite of his wealth and education – he had studied theology in Mecca and even gone to a university in Paris for two years – he was more superstitious than an old woman. Bedri stepped out, mumbling, 'I'll send the woman in.'

'Tell Abdullah to make some coffee.'

Bedri found the young boy by the burner and gave the order. He looked at Maro contemptuously and jerked his thumb in the direction of the tent.

An army cot occupied one side and a metal trunk the other, leaving a wide passage in the middle. Riza Bey stood next to a folding table upon which lay a map. He motioned her to sit down on the trunk. She had to push aside a book, a basket of peaches and some dried dates, the sight of which increased her hunger.

Abdullah brought in a tray with two small, steaming cups sitting on a couple of tiny saucers. He served his master before offering a cup to Maro. Coffee! Sugar! She was in such a hurry that she burnt her lips. She thought of her mother, who adored coffee and had not tasted any for such a long time. Riza Bey could not take his eyes off her. His vague expression gave him a pensive air. Good manners demanded he speak first.

'It's strange,' he said in a deep, melodious voice. 'I had a dream last night, which is still bothering me. I was galloping on a plain when a tornado tore me off my saddle and carried me up into the air. I was flying over some very high mountains when the wind stopped suddenly. I fell for a long time, turning and twisting, and landed in the turbulent waters of the Euphrates River. The current carried me towards a roaring waterfall. I swallowed water and was sinking, but a hand pulled me to the shore. When I reached the river bank, there was a woman kneeling beside me.'

He stopped to sip his coffee. Maro was astounded. What nonsense! While hundreds of people were suffering all around him, this man, on whom their lives depended, was calmly recounting a dream. As she sipped her coffee and listened to his foolishness, Azniv Hanim was dying. But she controlled herself, sensing it was better not to upset him.

He went on, 'What amazes me is that the woman who saved me looked like you.'

'That's only a coincidence,' she said.

'There is no such thing as chance. The tiniest drop of rain falls on the exact spot at the exact moment that Allah has decreed.'

Maro didn't know what to say so she just nodded.

'Dreams are messages. Do you know how to interpret dreams?'

'No,' she answered and immediately regretted her response. She could have interpreted this dream in a way that would have inclined him to be kind to her.

'What was it you wanted to say to me?' His voice was chilling.

Maro thought it would be better not to speak of her mother, so she answered, trying to sound confident, 'I am the wife of an Ottoman Army officer. I should not have been sent in this convoy, nor should my mother and son.'

'And your husband?'

She was careful not to mention Vartan's arrest. 'He's a major, a medical officer. He's serving at the front. I wasn't able to let him know.' She removed an oval silver locket from her neck and opened it before handing it to him. In one side was a photograph of Vartan in uniform. 'Here. Look.'

But what caught Riza Bey's attention was the other photograph in the locket. It was a picture of Maro taken in Paris. His eyes travelled from Maro to the picture, as if he wanted to convince himself that this deportee in rags was the same elegant woman dressed in western clothes.

He closed the locket and returned it to her, saying, 'A most handsome man.'

'The commissioner in Sivas had assured me that we could stay, but the *zaptiyés* forced us to leave.'

He nodded calmly, twirling his moustache.

'And now,' continued Maro pitifully, 'my mother is dying.'

'I'm sorry to hear that.'

'She needs a doctor and some medicine, urgently.'

'We have nothing like that here,' he said sullenly. He poured his coffee grounds into the saucer, swirled them around and held it out to Maro.

'Do you know how to read it?'

Just as she was speaking of her dying mother! Was this man completely heartless? Maro wanted to throw the saucer in his face, but he was waiting for her to answer, looking like a worried child. This time she was not going to waste the opportunity to take advantage of his gullibility.

Without blinking, she said, 'I do it all the time.'

She carefully examined the designs formed by the grounds. An idea, quick! The first thing that came to her mind was the house in Sivas. Yes! The coffee residue that had stuck to the sides of the saucer looked almost like walls and a roof.

'I see a big house . . . at the end of a long road. There are a lot of people. They're happy. It looks as if they're celebrating a happy event. Perhaps a triumphant home-coming! There are trees all around and just to the side a bell . . .' She was going to say a belfry of a church but she stopped just in time and finished by saying, 'a minaret of a mosque.'

Riza Bey beamed. He offered her a coin, which she refused. He looked surprised.

'One must always pay or the prediction doesn't come true. You should know that.'

Cunningly she pointed to the basket beside her. 'Fruit would be more precious to me than gold.'

'Take all you want,' he replied good-humouredly.

Maro stowed away three peaches and a handful of dates in the *charshaf* which lay folded over her lap. As she moved, the book lying on the edge of the trunk fell. She picked it up quickly and apologized. As she touched the leather binding, she shivered. A book! Like a flash of lightening, the image of Vartan's library crossed her mind.

'*Beauty and Love* by Ghalib Dédé, a great poet, dead for more than a century,' Riza Bey explained, picking up the book and putting it on the trunk.

Maro came to the point. 'Please let me return to Sivas. I can find someone there to take care of my mother.'

'That's impossible. You'd need a large escort to get there alive. Besides, isn't your mother too sick for such a trip?'

'I have relatives in Constantinople,' pleaded Maro.

'Stamboul is a long way away,' he said pensively. 'Let me think about it.' This Armenian woman attracted him. She was well-bred and determined. She was cultured, expressed herself easily, and her beauty pleased him even though she was skinny, unkempt and dressed in rags and had dark shadows under her eyes. Riza Bey prized beauty above all else. When he gave the photograph back to her, he felt he had lost something. What would he feel if she left forever? He wanted her, and what he wanted he always took. His

192

dream took on importance. This was the woman who had rescued him from the waters – same eyes, same look, same mouth. This could only mean she was destined to play a role in his life. The big house at the end of the road, the people, the trees, the mosque – she had described the *konak* where he lived in Ayntab.[1] All these omens could not be wrong. How could he interpret the triumphal return? Maybe he would find that out the next time she read his cup.

'You should not be with the ... displaced persons. I shall take you under my protection. We'll be leaving soon.'

Tears welled up in Maro's eyes but she insisted, 'Not without my mother and son.'

Riza Bey was much too happy to refuse her anything. 'We shall go through Darendé. There they can take care of your mother. How old is your son?'

'Six.'

'What's his name?'

'Tomas.'

'And yours?'

'Maro Balian.'

'Maro is enough. Maro! I love the sound of it.'

'And you, *Effendi*, what's your name?'

'Riza Bey.'

Maro stood up and bowed. She tried to give him her mother's money belt, which was full of gold coins. Flustered, he refused.

'Don't thank me. I'm simply doing an act of charity like a true believer.'

Maro took advantage of the opportunity he had unconsciously provided. 'People are dying of hunger and thirst in the cavern.'

Annoyed, Riza frowned. Without knowing it, Maro had touched a sore spot. What he had seen happening in this region during the past week haunted him. All that cruelty! All those needless deaths! And he was partly responsible. Riza had agreed to supervise the deportation in the southern part of the country without weighing the consequences. It was one thing to transmit orders from the capital to the governors and mayors, to decide which towns to evacuate, to trace the routes on paper, to pinpoint on a map where the control had to be set up; it was quite another to see with his own eyes the effect of his measures on human beings!

Riza Bey was repelled by Panturkism. Unlike most of his countrymen,

---

1.   Present-day Gaziantep.

he held the Arabs in esteem, having lived closely with them and employed many of them on his family's cotton plantations. To practise Panturkism was to exclude the Arabs from the Empire and to cut oneself off from the rest of the Muslim world. On the contrary, all the different people should be united under the banner of Islam. It was a mistake to exterminate the Christians. Islam demanded they be converted to the true faith by persuasion or intimidation. This Riza Bey had done with his Armenian stewards and workers, thus assuring eternal salvation for himself, while acquiring a group of competent, honest workers.

Riza Bey was convinced the government of the Young Turks had embarked on the wrong course. The part he was playing went against all his religious convictions but he had come to terms with this dilemma; it was the price he had to pay in order to obtain an important administrative post eventually.

Being the eldest, Riza Bey had been managing and increasing the fortune of his family. His grandfather and his father had already acquired huge cotton plantations in the vicinity of Ayntab. He had also added citrus groves in the region of Antalya. Since he was now forty-six, it was time for him to think about a post in public life. For generations, his family had provided the Sultan with governors, ministers and even a Grand Vizier.

Bedri entered the tent. His implacable look and cruel eyes sent shivers down Maro's back.

'The people are hungry and thirsty,' she repeated to Riza Bey pleadingly.

He smiled benevolently. 'I've already given the pertinent orders, haven't I, Bedri?'

'Yes,' answered the latter who would not have dared contradict his master.

Riza Bey turned to Maro. 'Go to your mother and I'll send for you.'

She put her hand on her breast. 'I thank you from the bottom of my heart, Riza Bey.'

After Maro left, Bedri exclaimed, 'What orders?'

'You heard me. To give food and water to those poor people.'

Bedri was astounded at the compassion in his voice. Riza Bey, whom he had known ever since he was born, always surprised him. He was totally unpredictable: a lamb who could change in a second into a lion.

Their fates had been bound together for a long time. Bedri had been an old friend of Riza's father. While working for Sultan Abdul-Hamid's secret police, he had found out that they were planning to assassinate Riza Bey, who was then a member of the Young Turks Party. Upon Bedri's warning, Riza Bey had been able to flee to Medina and then to Paris. During the Young Turks' revolution, it had been Riza's turn to save Bedri from the gallows by using his influence and ties in the government. Afterwards, he had taken Bedri into his service as his aide and trustworthy servant. He was the one who did the dirty work for him.

'What's going on, Riza Bey?' he asked amiably. 'I don't understand.'

'Since when has it been necessary for you to understand?' asked Riza dryly. 'You have only to obey.'

Faced with the proof submitted to him by the agents of the governor of Sivas, Fakri Pasha, the military commander of the region had no choice but to order the arrest of Colonel Ibrahim Alizadé and to turn him over to the civilian authorities . . . his best officer, and to top it all, an intimate friend! Even though he was a major-general and approved of what Ibrahim had done, he could do nothing for him. Like most high-ranking officers, Fakri Pasha had an Ittihad agent on his staff, a guardian angel checking his loyalty to the government policies.

Colonel Ibrahim was taken directly to the same room in the police headquarters where Vartan had been tried. He was stripped and firmly tied to a narrow bench on which he was forced to lie. The guards withdrew and left him with two henchmen, who leisurely unwrapped and laid out their instruments of torture on a chair. Then they took off their shirts and lit up their cigarettes while they talked about the purchase of an ass one of them was considering.

Ibrahim stared at the light in the ceiling and tried not to think about what lay in store for him. Twenty minutes later Mustapha Rahmi made his entrance. He was thrilled with his job as governor but he was also excited about coming back into police headquarters where he had reigned supreme for so many years, although he would have preferred to have returned there under other circumstances. Gani Bey would be furious when he found out about that damned Balian's escape and would hold Mustapha responsible. He approached the bench and carefully sized up the Colonel's lean, sinewy body. Then he spat in his face.

'Dirty dog!' Mustapha cracked his knuckles, trying to calm down. 'Lieutenant Yilmaz, who is assigned to the military police, reported that you abducted our prisoner, Vartan Balian, who had been condemned to death. Do you deny that?'

Ibrahim knew that there was no escape – either the rope or the firing squad awaited him. All he wanted was not to be tortured. If Mustapha wanted him to talk, then talk he would.

'No. I do not.'

'Why?'

'Because we were friends. He had been condemned unjustly.'

'Was anyone else involved?'

To incriminate Halit Pasha wouldn't change anything.

'I did it on my own.'

'What did you do with this Balian?'

'I gave him a mule and took him out of town.'

'Where did he go?'

'Towards the coast.'

Ibrahim lied very convincingly. He did not care if Mustapha thought him a coward.

'Do you know what his plans were?'

'I think he was heading for Russia.'

'Was he going to join anybody special?'

'I don't know.'

'Was he armed?'

'Yes. He had a pistol.'

'How was he dressed?'

'Like a peasant.'

'Did you give him any papers?'

'Yes, I bought them off a Kurd.'

'What was the name on the papers?'

'Alioglou Izzettin.'

'Is there anything else you should tell me?'

'Nothing. That's all I know.'

'All right,' said Mustapha as he walked away.

Ibrahim thought he had spared himself a lot of suffering, but Mustapha came back brandishing a cane. His squinty eyes glittered alarmingly from under his lids.

He chuckled. 'Something tells me you're confessing too readily.'

He began to whip him on the feet. Ibrahim gritted his teeth in order not to scream but the pain became unbearable. It blazed up his legs directly to his heart, which was skipping beats. Ibrahim could not hold back his screams any longer.

'Wait! I have something more to tell you.'

'Wait until you're asked!' Mustapha barked.

He continued to strike him harder and harder until his feet were reduced to a bloody pulp.

Mustapha wiped off his forehead. 'Now talk.'

Ibrahim no longer had any intention of doing so. His suffering was so great that any more savagery would, he thought, make no difference. He was wrong!

'His fingernails,' Mustapha ordered the henchmen.

One by one they pulled out his nails. Ibrahim gave them new details. Mustapha was accustomed to this kind of interrogation, he was easily able to detect any kind of false answer. He kept up the relentless assault on his victim. By the end of it all, Ibrahim had confessed everything. His face was contorted in agony. He hurt as he had never thought possible. His heart pounded in his chest and could not find its normal rhythm. He was terrified that the torture would start all over again.

Mustapha Rahmi was triumphant. He had the information he wanted: Lieutenant Shakir Ismael was on the road to Aleppo. All that was necessary now was to telegraph Gani Bey and send out wanted posters all over the country. He put his face close to the prisoner. 'I would have thought you would have resisted longer. How wrong can you be?'

He placed his heavy hands around Ibrahim's throat and squeezed hard until the colonel's heart stopped beating.

Maro retched as she entered the cave. The air was foul with the intermingled smells of urine, excrement and unwashed bodies. The slight euphoria she had felt when she had heard she was going to leave the convoy evaporated into thin air when she saw their misery. She felt guilty at abandoning them to their fate.

'Mama,' shouted Tomas, who had been watching for her return near the entrance. 'Grandmother's awake.'

'Praised be the Lord!'

Tomas's appearance shocked her, as she approached him. His emaciated face exaggerated his enormous eyes, from which all liveliness had been

197

extinguished. One more week and he would look like the skeletal children from Erzinjan. It was Maro's duty to save him at any cost, and she did not have to be ashamed of any means she used. It was out of the question to tell Tomas the good news she brought: all the faces turned towards her – expressionless, apathetic faces.

'They're going to give us water,' she announced in a loud voice.

'Water . . .'

'Water ...' The magic word echoed all over the cavern.

'What happened, mama?' asked Tomas, looking at her torn clothes. 'Did the zaptiyés hurt you?'

'No, darling. Everything is all right.'

She hurried to the back of the cave but it was slow going because she had to step across so many bodies. She was afraid of the condition in which she would find her mother.

'Did your grandmother speak? Does she seem better?'

'She's going to die.' The child's voice shook.

'Don't say such silly things.'

'The healers said so.'

She whispered into his ear, 'Don't worry, Tomas. We're going to take her to a doctor.'

Two old women were beside Azniv Hanim. They had sat her up and were chanting prayers. One rubbed her back and the other used a smouldering olive leaf to draw the sign of the cross on the sick woman's forehead and body.

'This will heal you. This leaf was blessed in church on Palm Sunday. The smoke will chase away the evil spirits.'

Widow Kaloustian threw the burnt leaf away. Maro recognized her and took her by the shoulders to pull her away from her mother.

'What have you given to her?' She was thinking about the vial of poison in Araksi's hand.

'Only prayers and salves,' answered the widow. She lowered her voice, 'Your mother doesn't have much time left.'

'Leave us alone,' ordered Maro.

She laid Azniv Hanim, who was panting, back down. Only a thin draught of air passed through her chapped lips.

'Grandmother's going to die.' Tomas was terrified.

'Be quiet,' Maro said impatiently.

She handed him some dates and a peach. He couldn't believe his eyes. He held them tight against his chest, cupping them in his hands, while looking around apprehensively to see if anyone had seen the fruit, but no one had. He crouched facing the wall and devoured them.

Finally, Azniv Hanim responded to Maro's insistent calling by moving her fingers feebly. Maro bit off a piece of peach and rubbed it over her mother's lips but she could not swallow it. She half-opened her mouth and Maro trickled in some of the juice she was squeezing from the fruit.

Azniv Hanim hardly raised her eyelids and sighed, 'Maro.'

'I'm here, *Mayrig*. I'm here.'

'Maro ... I ... I ...'

'I've talked to one of the officers. He's going to take us to Darendé, where there is a doctor.'

'Too late.'

'No. You'll get there.'

'So tired ... Can't move ...'

'Don't talk. Rest.'

Exhausted, Azniv Hanim closed her eyes and slept. Maro watched over her for hours, holding her hand. When were they finally going to leave?

Tomas was distressed, watching his grandmother's agony. He stayed in the corner, stared at his feet and pretended not to hear when Maro asked him to come and pray.

Then, to everyone's surprise, the guards began to distribute food at the entrance of the cave. Tomas hurried there and fought as avidly as the others to get his portion and a bit more. He was acting like a small animal ready to do anything to survive. He took a piece of bread, a tomato, two apricots and a gourd full of water back to his mother.

Azniv Hanim seemed to have revived a little. Maro made her drink a few sips of water. The old woman's eyes were sunken and the skin over her cheek bones was almost translucent. She looked at her grandson kneeling beside her.

'You have to eat, grandmother, to get strong.'

'You can have my share, Tomas.'

He kissed her on both cheeks. 'Don't die, Grandmother! You can't!'

'Take good care of your mother.' Her voice was getting weaker. She looked into Maro's eyes. 'Maro. It's the end.'

'No,' insisted Maro, barely touching her mother's cheek. 'You're getting better. You're even talking.'

'For the love of God, help me.' She tried to lift her hand.

Maro held her up while Azniv Hanim made the sign of the cross on her grandson's forehead with her thumb and then did the same to her daughter.

'God bless you.'

'Grandmother, please don't leave us!' Tomas burst into sobs.

'Take my hand and pray with me.'

He obeyed. Azniv Hanim moved her lips in silence. Tomas's throat was chocking so much that he could hardly get the words past it.

Unconsciously, Maro joined her voice with Tomas's. She couldn't conceive that the one who had carried, fed, loved, and protected her until she had grown up was now dying. Her mother had to stay alive; she had to continue to breathe until they reached the next town, and the next, until they reached safety. She couldn't leave them now, now that everything was getting better. Azniv Hanim's lips stopped moving. She clutched her daughter's hand. Maro kissed her on the mouth and held her tightly to keep her from slipping into another world.

'*Mayrig! Mayrig!*' she pleaded like a little girl.

But Azniv Hanim had stopped breathing. Maro cried softly and rocked her while caressing her face and stroking her hair. Tomas felt very alone. He laid his face on his mother's lap and put his arms around her waist. They didn't even notice when the people gathered round them to start saying the prayers for the dead. Maro and her son were alone in their grief.

'Come,' said a husky voice.

The prayers stopped and Maro lifted her head. Bedri's tall figure loomed over the kneeling crowd.

'My mother's dead!'

'Riza Bey is waiting for you.'

'My mother's dead. I have to bury her.'

'Do as you please. Riza Bey's leaving.'

He turned on his heels and hurried towards the exit.

Like a flash of lightning, Maro grasped that this was her only chance of escape. She must not let it slip through her fingers. She crossed her mother's hands over her breast.

'Come,' she said to Tomas, and, pulling him by the arm, she followed Bedri.

# SEVEN

The moon was shining on the gravelled road. As he came up an incline to the top of a hill, Vartan saw his image reflected in the waters of the Euphrates. His horse seemed to be happy riding through the night and Vartan had to rein him in so he would not tire out. He let him gallop only for short distances. They had been riding long stretches for three days. To get to Malatya faster, Vartan had cut through the mountains. He had not met any convoys but had seen bodies abandoned by the wayside, in the ravines and in the Armenian villages, which had been completely razed to the ground.

He passed by a fork where a secondary road led to Kharput, the ancient Armenian fort previously called Kharpert. He crossed a sleepy village and came to the river; the road had been following its twists and turns for a long time. The muffled rumblings of the waters merged with the rustling of the foliage on the banks. A humid breeze carried a sweet scent, which was reminiscent of the budding poplars in the springtime. He felt elated as he neared his goal, yet he was also plagued by misgivings.

In front of him he saw a light from a campfire beside the road. He slowed his horse down to a walk and advanced cautiously. Horses neighed and Yildiz answered. Now the people in the camp knew that someone was coming. A large fire danced by a brook. Vartan counted about twenty shadows. Several of them blocked his way. He unsnapped the strap which secured his pistol in his holster. They were civilians – Kurds, to judge by their outfits and their long mops of blonde hair and beards. All were armed – some carried antique rifles with damascened barrels; others, brand-new Mausers.

He greeted them, '*Selamaleykum*.'[1]

'*Aleykumselam*,' answered a man, who spoke Turkish with a marked Kurdish accent. 'Where are you going?'

'Wherever the Sultan, the Commander of all the faithful, orders me to go. Let me through.'

The grey-haired, bearded speaker stuck his fingers into his belt, which held two small pistols and a knife. He looked at his companions questioningly and continued unctuously, 'We have no intention of interfering with your mission, which must be of great importance for you to be riding during the night. Your horse is in a lather. Have a drink of lion's milk[2] with us and give your horse a rest.'

Vartan had no choice but to accept their hospitality. If he tried to force his way through the roadblock, it would be like trying to pass through a sieve. They all looked like cut-throats and Vartan resolved to be very diplomatic. He dismounted and tied his horse to a bush. The men formed a circle around him.

'That's a beautiful animal you have there,' said their leader.

'Yes. I've already killed one man who tried to take him away from me.'

This was the kind of answer that these louts liked and they nodded approvingly. The leader put his arm around Vartan's shoulders and led him towards the fire. 'A man who doesn't know how to defend what's his doesn't deserve to keep it.'

At the edge of the fire Vartan could see half a dozen carts piled high with all sorts of things – furniture, sacks of clothing, pots, harnesses and trunks tied with ropes. These were highwaymen from the mountain villages, where this calling was considered a respectable profession, robbers whose ancestors had attacked the rich caravans coming from Persia, Arabia and Asia. Nowadays, they pursued the same line of business but with slight variations.

Vartan pointed to the carts and declared in a tone he hoped sounded admiring, 'You look like the famous *kabadayis*[3] to me.'

They felt flattered and their leader exclaimed, 'By Allah, you're a man of quality. You are among friends now. We'll let you go without harming you.'

'Don't tell me you had other intentions!' said Vartan, smiling mischievously.

---

1. May the peace of God be with you (Arabic).
2. *Raki*. An allusion to the whitish colour it takes when mixed with water.
3. The tough ones (Turkish).

The giant looked sheepish, shook his head and burst into booming laughter. 'My name is Osman *Agha*.'

'I'm called Shakir Ismael.'

They sat in front of the fire where bits of goat meat were grilling on spits stuck vertically in the ground. Everyone drank straight from the bottles of home-brewed *raki* and pitchers of water handed round the party.

'Are you the leader of the tribe, *Agha*?' asked Vartan.

'Yes. Our herds graze in the Dersim Mountains.' This chain of mountains ran south of Erzinjan.

'What brought you here so far from home?'

'The Turk had need of real warriors. He hired us to help the military guards but now we're going home.'

'You don't like the work?'

Osman *Agha* was obviously ill at ease. He looked at his guest mistrustfully and took a slug of *raki* instead of answering.

Vartan leaned towards him and whispered, 'I'm going to tell you a secret. I'm not a Turk. I'm a Circassian. I serve in the Ottoman Army because I have no choice.'

Osman's face relaxed and he grumbled angrily, 'To kill unarmed old men, women and children – that's not work worthy of self-respecting warriors. I know there are Kurds who are willing to do the government's dirty work but shame on them!'

'You mean the way they're massacring the Armenians?'

'What else? They're Christians, I know, but in our village we've always got along with them. The Turk wants the whole country for himself. Today it's the Armenians. Tomorrow it'll be the Kurds.'

His men raised their fists and hurled insults at the Sultan. Osman calmed them down and continued, 'Nobody is going to tell us what to do in our mountains. We shall turn the rifles the Sultan has given us against him when the time comes.' The men cupped their hands around their mouths and ululated.

Osman *Agha* walked Vartan back to his horse. He kissed him and called him brother. Now that they were far from the smoke of the fire, Vartan noticed a sweetish odour, which intrigued him.

'What's that smell?'

'You could say it's the odour of the nectar that flows on the flowering slopes of the Dersim Mountains in the spring, couldn't you?'

203

'I don't know your mountains. Is it flowers I can smell?'

'That smell, my brother, is the smell of death. If you went near the river, it would not be pleasant. You would note only the stench of rot. The Euphrates carries bloated bodies, swollen up like water skins. When they hit the rocks, they burst and spill their guts.'

They parted wishing each other a good journey, and Vartan continued in the dark. The road descended gradually to a plain.

At dawn, Vartan was riding through rich vineyards and orchards and then tobacco, cotton and vegetable fields. At the junction of the road to Sivas by way of Hassan-Chelebi, the military guards had placed a checkpoint. An officer and two men slept beside the still-smouldering embers of a fire; only one man sitting on a stone was on guard. He did not even ask to see Vartan's papers when Vartan stopped to talk to him. The man was almost keeling over from exhaustion and answered Vartan's greeting in a slurred voice.

'Do you know if the convoy from Sivas has passed by?'

'It's been an unending stream for over a month. How do you expect me to keep account of where they came from? They're all supposed to end up together at a camp just south of Malatya. Maybe they can give you some information there.'

As Vartan came into the town, he met about twenty *arabas* driven by veiled women and carrying children, both boys and girls. All were under twelve years of age and looked either terrified or dull-eyed. Vartan stopped the vehicles. The woman who headed the line thought he was checking papers and handed him a wrinkled sheet, a pass, signed by the *kaymakam*[1] of the province. He learnt that they were widows of soldiers who had fallen at the eastern front. Instead of granting them a pension, the authorities had given each of them some Armenian children. Vartan was intrigued. 'What are you going to do with them?'

'Sell them to families whom Allah has not blessed with enough children.'

Sell them! His heart ached. 'Are they . . . *giaours*?'

'We'll convert them. Do you want one? Look at them. They're pretty and already big enough to work the fields. A bit thin, perhaps, but at this age they fatten up quickly. A boy? A girl? I'll give you a good price.'

Vartan shook his head and waved the woman on. If he could have, he would have taken all the children with him. His first reaction was to turn away and spur his horse to a gallop, but he could not. He had to look and

1.  Governor (Turkish).

bear witness. He had another reason, which he did not want to admit even to himself and which forced him to scan each little face. Tomas might be among them! Pain turned into rage. Not only had these children been torn from their families but they would be forced to forget their faith, their language and their culture. Vartan could read the distress in their eyes as they slowly filed by. His heart broke each time one of the little faces was lost to view forever. He could do nothing for them, but he did not have the right to stand idly by. He watched them go and then spurred his horse brutally on.

While Vartan was leaving Malatya, Riza Bey's carriage, driven by Abdullah, was entering the city on the western road from Caesarea. Bedri rode ahead and six Arab horsemen, the *mudur*'s personal guard, rode behind. These men, sons of workers whose families had been in the employment of Riza's family for generations, were devoted to him and considered him their sheikh.

Maro had been travelling with Riza Bey for three days. He had always treated her properly and been very patient with Tomas, who answered all his questions with a brief 'yes' or 'no'. However, Riza Bey's interest in her had become increasingly obvious. He wanted to know everything about her. He questioned her about her life, her family, her childhood. Maro conjured up her youth in Constantinople, talked about her parents, about her trips, about Vartan – especially about Vartan, to remind him that she was another man's wife. Riza Bey's interest became intrusive at times. Maro had to manoeuvre carefully to discourage any familiarity without upsetting him, but she felt that time was working against her.

Surrounded by the escort, the vehicle forced its way through the crowded streets. Standing in the shade of their awnings, shopkeepers called out to the passers-by and each deal became an occasion for passionate bargaining. The street vendors with a cylindrical tank hanging from their shoulders and a basket full of glasses hanging from their waists added their cries to the hubbub as they hawked their lemonade. All this activity did not seem to distract the men drinking and smoking their *narghilés* on the café terraces from their lively discussions. It was the eve of Ramadan, the ninth month of the Muslim calendar, a period during which they were obliged to fast from sunrise to nightfall as well as abstain from smoking and lovemaking.

Maro watched the scenery with blind eyes. Once again she had lost herself in memories of her mother – not the old woman she had left in the cave but a much younger one on the arm of her husband, Hagop Artinian. No traces of the squabbles and quarrels with her mother remained. She was filled with Azniv Hanim's words and gestures, filled with all the love and tenderness she had received for twenty-eight years. Had she thanked her enough?

Azniv Hanim had given her answer already. 'The only way I can repay my mother for the love she gave me is to forget about myself and pass it on to my children.'

Maro no longer felt alone in her grief. The gesture of her hand as she protected her son's face from the rays of the sun linked her with all the women who, since the beginning of time, had given life and wept for the dead.

Tomas looked around with a mixture of curiosity and sadness. It reminded him of the bazaar quarter in Sivas where he had loved to go. He stood up the better to see a spectacle that was new to him. Onlookers surrounded a bear-keeper from the shores of the Black Sea. The hairy brown bear stood erect on its hind legs, dancing to the music of a tambourine and a *zourna*, an oriental clarinet. Every time it danced by, the children squealed excitedly and their mothers hugged them tightly. With much hilarity, the young men pretended to want to mount the beast.

War and the fate of the Armenians seemed to be the least of the preoccupations of the inhabitants of Malatya, where the rhythm of life had remained unchanged for centuries. The appearance of an automobile, its top down, transporting German officers was incongruous.

'Look, mama! An automobile!' exclaimed Tomas, amazed.

'You'll see others, my boy,' said Riza Bey. 'If you like, I'll let you ride in one.'

'Thank you.' answered Tomas, just to be polite. His voice was expressionless and he looked away. In spite of his mother's admonitions, the child could hardly hide his dislike for their host.

A whole wing of the governor's palace had been reserved for Riza Bey, and servants had been put at his disposal. He despised the governor and declined his invitation to lunch, saying he was too tired. In any case, Ali Bey would soon be relieved of his post, as Gani Bey had informed Riza in the same telegram sent to give him an appointment in Malatya.

He and Maro would dine in their apartment. The occasion did not turn out to be as charming as Riza Bey had dreamed. He had ordered some musicians, but Bedri's uncouth presence and the child's cold stares inhibited him. He was in a hurry to be alone with Maro – to court her. To provide an opportunity, he had decided to let Bedri settle some pending problems in Malatya. He himself would not go directly to Ayntab but would make a long detour via Diyarbekir and Urfa under the pretence of making an inspection. After the meal Riza changed his clothes with Abdullah's help. Bedri had followed him to get his orders. The camp at Malatya was a key point in the deportation network, one of the checkpoints through which the columns coming from the north-east of Anatolia had to pass. The situation left much to be desired. There were already fifteen thousand Armenians crammed in here and many others would arrive in the following days.

'You have to clear this for me,' said Riza Bey to Bedri, while Abdullah attached his collar. 'You're to dispatch all these people into the Syrian desert.'

'We lack men to guard the convoys.'

'Go to the local prison and pick out those you need.'

'That pig of a governor won't set them free. You know him. He's always trying to put a spoke in the wheels. He's a Christian sympathizer.'

Riza Bey, who was slipping into his black jacket, burst out laughing. 'Don't worry. By tonight he'll be worth less than a landless farmer.'

'Allah be praised!'

'I'm leaving this afternoon to see what is happening in Diyarbekir. I'm counting on you to put everything in order. There's a person called Gani Bey in the palace. He's an aide to the Minister of Interior. He's my superior officer in a way and, as such, yours also. He can be of help to you should you need it, but be careful. He's very touchy and quick-tempered. When your job in Malatya is finished, you'll find me in Ayntab.'

'All will be done according to your orders,' said Bedri, taking his leave.

A few minutes later Riza Bey went to the wing of the palace where Gani Bey was installed. His way of walking was haughty and supple; his custom-made suit fitted his every movement. His mother had often told him he looked like a prince and sometimes he almost believed her.

He met Maro holding her son by the hand in the hall. As she was in private, she had taken off her veil. Riza Bey thought she looked better already; her skin had lost its muddy colour and her eyes their feverish glint. She was blooming again like a plant reviving under the rain. He had taken her along without considering how long he would keep her or what he would do with her. She had been only a passing fancy for him, a precious object he could live without. But, after only three days, he already felt a deep attachment to this fascinating woman.

With a subtle smile, Maro asked him, 'Am I your prisoner, Riza Bey?'

He was astounded, 'Whatever gave you such a preposterous idea?'

'I wanted to take a walk around the town, but one of your guards stopped me.'

'I gave that order for your own safety. As long as you and your son are with me, you have nothing to fear, but alone . . . Of course, you're free and if you absolutely must go out, Abdullah and two guards will accompany you.'

Maro had planned to go to the American School, which they had passed on their way into town, thinking that the director might be able to send a message to Uncle Mesrop in Constantinople, but she did not want Riza Bey to know.

He continued, 'You can go out but is it worth your while? We'll be leaving in two or three hours after my meeting with Gani Bey.'

Maro shuddered when she heard that name. Gani Bey! The one who had had Vartan arrested and had mocked her. He must not see her and recognize her!

Hiding her feelings, she answered, 'In that case, I'll wait in my room.'

'That's wise of you.' Riza Bey was satisfied. He read Maro's words as a sign she wanted to please him. He went up to her and lifted her chin. 'Is my tie straight?'

Instinctively, Maro stretched out her hand to straighten it, but quickly stopped, hating herself for having reacted without thinking.

'Your tie is straight,' she said almost inaudibly.

'How about my suit? Do I look presentable?'

He was driving her into a corner. What could she do but admit his undeniable elegance? Aware of his good looks, he teased her with his eyes as he waited for her answer.

'You look very well.'

'You're flattering me,' he said, tousling Tomas's hair, who took it without protest.

Maro nodded briefly and left, raging inside and pulling Tomas after her. Stroking his thin moustache, Riza Bey watched her go. How beautiful she was! Those blushing cheeks, that nervous stride of a wild animal. What was her body like beneath those ample robes? Riza Bey felt desire rise in him. He sighed and walked away.

Before entering Gani Bey's apartments, he stopped and looked at himself in a mirror. He thought he looked very dapper in his black suit. He knocked on the door of the antechamber. A beautiful boy, whom Gani Bey had taken into his service in Sivas, opened the door and walked ahead to announce him.

Riza had met Gani Bey twice before in the capital, first at a meeting of the Ittihad and later at a party in the Dolmabahché Palace on the shores of the Bosphorus. That had been before Gani Bey had been given an official mission. Today Gani Bey was the superior officer who had come to check on his subordinate's work.

Gani Bey, as enormous as ever, sat on a low divan in front of an arch, which gave on to a shaded interior courtyard with a warbling fountain. As if to emphasize his authority, he had not even bothered to put on a high collar or a jacket. He made no effort to rise but smiled at his visitor and his flabby cheeks puffed out.

Riza Bey bowed. 'What a joy to see you in our region!'

'It's my pleasure to meet again a man I esteem so much.' Gani Bey invited Riza to sit in front of him and offered him a cigarette from a pack of Circle d'Orient, the finest Turkish brand. The boy served refreshments and withdrew.

'Did you have a good trip?'

'The roads were terrible and the heat was exhausting,' replied Gani Bey, as he flicked his cigarette ash on the floor, 'not to mention the stench in some places.'

Understanding a little of the way in which his superior officer's mind worked, Riza Bey judged it prudent to belittle his own achievements and to emphasize his shortcomings.

He said ruefully, 'I know what you mean. I gave orders that the convoys were to avoid the main roads and the bodies were to be disposed of in out-of-the-way places, but it is easier to ask an ass to recite the Quran. I have to put up with the dregs – brigands and dull-witted brutes – for collaborators.' Things would go better if I had some real soldiers.'

As Riza Bey had expected, his superior protested, 'You don't have to excuse yourself, Riza Bey. You're doing an excellent job with what you have at your disposal. Our minister has been very impressed with your reports, and what I've seen since landing in Samsun confirms his opinion.'

'Thank you, Gani Bey. I don't think it desirable, however, for the mass graves to be out in plain sight of foreigners who travel through Anatolia.'

Gani Bey waved away the objection, 'What's the difference? With the war raging everywhere, what are a few cadavers in Anatolia? What is of utmost importance is to empty the east and the north of all undesirable elements. Once that's done, we'll be able to clean-up.'

'That shouldn't take too much time. According to my estimates, the greater part of the deportations will be finished when winter comes. Then we shall start combing the hills for those few who have escaped us.'

'Good! You're one of the few who have understood the importance of this operation – to eliminate everyone who can perpetuate that race, to convert the children and to force the young women given to Turks to bear little Turks!'

'Adoptions are going well because the government gives needy families a monthly pension of thirty pounds for each Armenian child they take in, but the foreign missionaries are thwarting our programme with their orphanages and many governors prefer to collaborate with them rather than with us.'

'That's why I'm here. I'm doing the same things as I've done in other places. I've replaced Ali Bey with one of our own. I still have to remove the Governor of Ayntab.'

'It's about time!' exclaimed Riza Bey.

'Isn't that where you live? I've decided to make you the governor of that province.'

Riza Bey could not hide his joy. He was really surprised. He had expected this reward but not so soon. 'You do me great honour. May Allah shower you with blessings.'

Gani Bey accepted his show of gratitude with a nod and lit another cigarette. 'There's only one condition. You shall continue to organize the deportations.'

'That shouldn't be too difficult as most of the deportees arrive in this region anyhow.'

'You shall also supervise the governors of the neighbouring provinces.'

'All shall be done as you wish. You will never regret the trust you have put in me.'

'I'm sure of that. One more thing. In addition to the reports in code you have already been sending, you will also send uncoded reports for the benefit of inquisitive eyes. You are to deplore the situation of the deportees, to report the miseries they are suffering and to suggest ways for the government to better their conditions.'

Riza Bey smiled understandingly. 'I shall write about the relocation of the Armenians to zones away from the war. I shall say that the government has been feeding them and building villages to house them.'

'Exactly!' Gani Bey was enchanted that Riza Bey had caught on so quickly.

Riza Bey was immensely happy. His career in the national administration looked more promising than he had ever imagined. He had been right to endorse the policy of the Ittihad although he did not agree with it. As always, he had had a hunch and had been able to judge which way the wind would blow. Governor! Some day maybe Minister of State. He must telegraph the good news to his mother, to the *Buyuk Hanim*, the Grand Lady. She would be so happy and proud of him. What a welcome she would prepare for him. All of a sudden, Riza Bey remembered Maro's predictions – the triumphal return which she had seen in the coffee grounds. It had come true! The Armenian woman really had second sight. Blessed was the day he had saved her!

In southern Malatya, the orange-grey summits of the Anti-Taurus range spread out from east to west on both sides of Bey Mountain. The camp nestled at their feet in a dusty dell. The squat tents and the smoke from the fires could be seen from afar. Before he arrived, Vartan had to go by an immense fire, which stank of the sickening smell of burning flesh. While the guards looked on indifferently, the people were burning the dead.

The khaki-coloured tents belonged to the guards; the deportees slept in the open. Some had improvised sun screens from old rags. The camp covered several acres and Vartan passed through unnoticed by the guards. A strange silence hovered over the crowd, broken only by the crying of babies and the fits of coughing that depressed him deeply. There were no latrines and the breeze could not disperse the foul smell of excrement, urine and filth.

A passageway straight down the centre led to a well guarded at all times by the *zaptiyés*. Small groups of refugees had gathered on both sides of the passageway and the free spaces between them formed a network of narrow, crooked paths. Except for a few old men and boys, there were only emaciated, half-naked women and children. Their faces were hardly human any longer. Ravaged by hunger, thirst and weariness, disfigured by sickness and wounds, furrowed by wind and sun, sunk in complete despair and resignation, they waited for death to deliver them.

The thought that Maro, Tomas and Azniv Hanim were among these human wrecks made Vartan feel faint and filled him with terror. He could not believe this nightmare. Until now the deportation had been a vague concept for him and had had nothing to do with the misery spread out in front of his eyes. He, who had never been able to see a sick person without feeling compelled to take care of him, now faced thousands of suffering human beings without being able to help a single soul.

Vartan ground his teeth and advanced slowly, torn between the hope of finding his family and the fear of the state in which he might find them. At first he rode but then he dismounted and pulled his horse along by the bridle. He searched the camp in all directions stopping in front of every group. For hours, he scanned the faces disfigured by suffering, trying to recognize a familiar one. Sometimes a shape made his heart beat faster, but each time he was disappointed. As time went by, he stopped hoping. It would be nothing short of a miracle if he were to locate his family in the first place he searched for them. If only he could get his hands on a list; that would be a starting point. Those he asked if they knew anyone from Sivas stared at him empty-eyed and shrugged. A newborn baby's cry caught his attention. Five old women were kneeling around a woman lying on the ground. Vartan went up to them. A skeletal woman had just given birth to a completely normal, lively child.

The old women sacrificed a few drops of water to baptize the newborn. One of them pulled out a tiny vial and performed the ritual unctions on the baby's face, hands and feet. 'This is medicated oil for my arthritis,' she said as she tucked the vial away, ' but God has seen stranger things.'

That voice! Vartan had heard it before! He approached the woman and touched her on her shoulder. Startled, she turned and looked at him suspiciously. The other old women stepped back and the mother pressed the baby to her. The old woman's fleshless features were unrecognizable but the intelligent look in her eyes was the same. It was the Widow Kaloustian, the healer who had had a shop of medicinal herbs in Sivas! When he had gone to buy effusions for Azniv Hanim from her, she used to tease him, saying that he had come to steal her secrets.

'What do you want?' she asked crossly in Turkish.

He answered in Armenian, 'It's me. You used to accuse me of trying to discredit your shop so people would use my chemical poisons.'

She studied his face for a few seconds and then pulled his hands to her cheeks. She was weeping. 'Vartan Balian! I'm dreaming!'

'Not so loud,' he said looking around.

'How is it possible . . .?'

'It doesn't matter. Just tell me, have you seen my wife, my son, my mother-in-law? Are they here?'

'If you only knew what we have lived through. There are no words to describe it.'

'My family,' insisted Vartan, shaking her slightly.

'Your mother-in-law died of exhaustion a few days ago.'

Appalled, Vartan nodded. He asked apprehensively, 'My wife? My son?'

'I didn't see them after that. A man took them away.'

'Took them away? How? By force? Along with other deportees?'

'They were alone with him in his *araba*. I think he saved them because you were an officer.'

'What makes you say that?'

'Because if he had wanted your wife as his mistress, he wouldn't have bothered with the child.'

Vartan breathed a sigh of relief. Maro and Tomas were alive and far from the misery of the convoy! Perhaps the man who had taken them was one of his officer friends.

'Do you know the man's name?'

'I'm sorry. I only saw him once.'

'Was he in uniform?'

'No, he was a civilian.'

'Is there anyone here who would know who he was?'

'I don't think so.'

'You're the only one I've found from Sivas. What about Armen? Araksi?'

'Dead! All the men have been killed. There are still a few women and

213

children here from Sivas, but you probably don't know them. The others fell along the way, were sold as slaves or put in other convoys. It's terrible. It's . . .'

She stopped short and gestured with her chin towards a man approaching quickly in spite of his corpulence. His fez was askew.

He frowned and looked Vartan up and down scornfully. Vartan did the same and before the other could speak, Vartan said with great self-possession, 'What do you want?'

'I ask the questions here! Your name?'

'Lieutenant Shakir Ismael.'

'The spy!' exclaimed Bedri, reaching for his revolver. Vartan did not ask any questions but launched himself straight at him. He butted him in the stomach and caught the hand that was drawing the gun from the holster. Bedri encircled the neck of his opponent with his free arm. They struggled. Suddenly Vartan felt a sting in his left thigh and simultaneously was deafened by a shot. Lashed by the pain, he felt a surge of energy and was able to bring his enemy down. He fell on top of him and pushed his knee into Bedri's groin. The hold on Vartan's neck slackened. With one hand he kept the hand holding the gun pinned to the ground and with the other reached for a large rock and hit Bedri on the temple. Blood spurted! He hit again and his opponent passed out.

Vartan looked around. The shot had attracted no attention and none of the guards seemed to have noticed the brief fight. He got up quickly, jumped into his saddle and trotted through the small islands of refugees to get to the main passageway.

How could he get away? His horse was tired after their night's journey. Horsemen sent in pursuit would soon catch up with him. The town! Who would think of looking for him there! There he could melt into the crowd. He passed a group of military guards who were deep in a game of knuckle-bones. He waved to them and spurred his horse to a gallop. The wound was only superficial but it stung. The bullet fired from such close range had ripped the thigh and gunpowder had singed the skin around it. Vartan pressed a handkerchief to it to stem the flow of blood.

The man had said, 'The spy!' What had he meant? Was it Vartan Balian who was wanted or Shakir Ismael, the man whose identity he had borrowed? Ibrahim had said that the papers were false, that Shakir Ismael had never existed, so they must know about his escape. What had happened in Sivas since he had left? Ibrahim? Halit Pasha? He hoped nothing had happened to them because of him.

Instead of asking useless questions about his friends, Vartan took stock of his situation. He now knew that Maro and Tomas were alive and that someone had taken charge of them, but why and under what conditions? Still, nothing could be worse than the deportation.

His most urgent problem was his own safety. He knew they had discovered his assumed identity and it was no longer possible for him to move about freely. Of course, he could always travel on the mountain roads and through the deserted places to avoid being captured, but where would that get him? On the contrary, he needed to go through the towns and villages, mix with the Turks, frequent their houses, open his ears and ask questions. What was he to do?

Just as he arrived at the town, he had an idea – the American School! There they would help him get false identity papers. At the least, he could hide out for a few days while his wound healed and the gendarmes lost interest in him.

When Bedri regained consciousness, he felt as if his head were caught in a vice. The pain seemed to be stronger on the left side. He brought his hand up to his temple and lowered it again, now covered in blood. Still dazed, he sat up and gathered his thoughts. Shakir Ismael, the spy – the one described in the wanted poster, which Bedri had held in his hands a few hours earlier. He got up with great difficulty and screamed for the guards. They came running from every direction. Those who had been on guard on the north side of the camp had noticed a lieutenant leaving in a hurry about half an hour before. Bedri dispatched a dozen men in search of him, promising a reward of fifty pounds for his capture, preferably alive.

There was nothing else he could do other than to wait and hope others would have better luck than he. He was in a rage. To think he had had the spy right there in front of him. To have captured him would have earned Bedri esteem from the authorities and a substantial reward. Suddenly he remembered that the spy had been conversing with an old woman. She was still standing there next to a woman lying on the ground with a baby in her arms.

He beckoned her. 'Who was the man talking to you when I arrived?'

'A soldier,' answered Widow Kaloustian.

'Is his name Shakir Ismael?'

The woman hesitated for a second. 'If you say so.'

'What did he want?'

'My money and my jewellery but I told him they had already been stolen.'

He struck her with the back of his hand and she crumpled to the ground. 'You're lying, you old witch.'

Widow Kaloustian sat up and faced him. A trickle of blood ran from her lower lip.

'You knew him,' Bedri insisted. 'It was obvious. What did he want?'

'I told you. My money.'

Bedri hit her again, but this time she saw it coming so she did not fall down. 'You'll talk eventually. Better to save yourself some trouble.'

She smiled mockingly, 'What have I got to lose? You could kill me. It would be a deliverance for me and you'd learn nothing.'

Bedri was furious. The cut on his forehead began to throb. He knew enough about human beings to realize that this old woman would not talk, even under torture. Deaf to the mother's protests, he grabbed the infant and held it at arm's length by its feet. The newborn cried as Bedri drew a knife and held it close to the little, jerking body. The mother held out her arms, begging to have her child returned.

Kaloustian winced and Bedri laughed triumphantly, 'Well what did he want?'

'News of his family.'

'And?'

'They're all dead.'

'What else do you know?'

'Nothing.'

'Where was he coming from?'

'I don't know. I've told you everything, I swear.'

Bedri let the baby fall on its mother, who barely managed to catch it. He picked up his gun and shot the widow in the breast. She fell without a sound.

'There's your deliverance!' he declared, before walking away.

An hour later the sergeant who had led the search party came to Bedri's tent to make his report. 'Nothing, not even a trace.'

216

'You good-for-nothing,' screamed Bedri. He struck him with his fist and sent him reeling back towards the entrance to the tent.

Bedri jumped on his horse and left for the governor's palace.

Using a map spread out at their feet, Riza Bey was giving a résumé of the current state of operations to his superior officer. All the convoys were converging towards Aleppo and Urfa. 'And from there?' asked Gani Bey.

'Ras el 'Ain, Raqqa, Deir-ez-Zor, and the end of the line – the sands of the desert or the waters of the Euphrates.'

'Excellent! Very good!' said Gani Bey, sitting back on the sofa.

The boy entered and bowed in front of his master. 'Bey Effendi, there is a man called Bedri who is asking to see you. He says it's urgent.'

Gani Bey was intrigued, 'He's my aide,' said Riza.

'Your aide? If I'm not mistaken, this man was very active during the reign of Abdul-Hamid, wasn't he?'

'Yes, but he's vindicated himself by his devotion to the cause of the Ittihad. He never flinches at any order. I have him well in hand. I'll vouch for him.'

'That's good enough for me,' answered Gani Bey with a conspiratorial smile. 'Who hasn't committed some small sins in his youth?'

At that precise moment Bedri entered. He felt intimidated and stood at attention in front of the two seated men, not knowing who to address first.

'Well?' asked Riza impatiently.

'The spy!' Bedri blurted out. 'The one they're searching for. I've seen him!'

Riza did not know what he was talking about but Gani Bey turned livid and exploded, 'What? Here in Malatya? I was sure he was on his way to the capital or to Russia. Are you sure it's really he?'

'He was wearing a lieutenant's uniform and told me his name was Shakir Ismael, the name that was on the wanted poster. I tried to arrest him. Look!' He turned his head to show his wound. Gani Bey questioned him further and Bedri recounted his fight with Vartan and gave a full description of him.

As the details accumulated in Gani Bey's mind, he could see the face of the man whom he had wanted to execute. How he regretted not having allowed Commissioner Mustapha to kill Vartan before his very eyes. Instead he had listened to that traitor, Ibrahim. That Armenian had had accomplices even in the army. Talaat Pasha was right to suspect that high-ranking army officers were planning a *coup d'état*. Balian . . .

He had thought Balian innocent but, like many important Armenians, a potential threat, so it was safer to eliminate him. What a mistake he had made! Vartan was surely in league with the rebels and the subversive element in the army, perhaps even in the pay of the enemy. And such a man was walking about freely.

'Too bad you let him get away!' Gani Bey was furious. 'I would have paid a good price for his head. What was he doing in a deportee camp?'

'He was looking for his family.'

'Naturally,' said Gani Bey thoughtfully. 'Was his family there?'

'No, they're all dead, it seems.'

'Did you alert all the police stations in this region?'

'Yes,' answered Bedri.

Gani Bey helped himself up by leaning against the low table placed in front of him and began to pace back and forth in his rolling gait, rubbing his hands and mumbling to himself. 'The army must surely have a picture of him. I'll have posters printed and distributed throughout the Empire. We must put all the men available on his trail. I want every hill combed, every person on the road questioned, every house of even the smallest village searched.' He stopped in front of Bedri and ordered, 'Go and tell the new governor to come here immediately.'

Riza Bey stood up, intending to take his leave. 'You seem very worried, Gani Bey. Can I be of any help to you?'

Gani Bey had been so upset that he had forgotten Riza was present. For a moment he looked at him in surprise. 'Yes, you can see to it that the search doesn't stop until this man is arrested.'

'Am I to understand that you are talking about a spy?'

'A spy, a rebel – I don't know enough yet. He's an Armenian I had condemned to death in Sivas. Balian! Vartan Balian!'

Maro's husband! Riza's astonishment showed in his face. Gani was intrigued. 'Do you know him?'

'No,' said Riza, once more in control of himself, 'but the name seems to be familiar.'

'That's quite possible. He was a congressman in the first government of the Ittihad in Constantinople. Afterwards, he wrote a lot of slanderous lies about the Empire, which the foreign press published.'

218

Riza pretended to be searching his memory. 'Now I remember. I once had a farmhand with a similar name.'

'That's certainly not him.' Gani Bey was taken in. 'The one we are searching for is an intellectual.'

'Dangerous?'

'I didn't think so, but one must bow to the evidence. If only we had his family to use as bait!'

Riza Bey swallowed hard. 'I'll offer a big reward to whoever captures this man. Rest assured, Gani Bey, it won't take long.'

Parting, they agreed to meet again in Ayntab in about ten days. Riza did not feel safe in Malatya any more; Maro's husband was looking for his wife and son. Had he found a trail that would lead him to Riza? Now it was out of the question to make a detour through Diyarbekir. They had to reach his lands in Ayntab as quickly as possible. He would have to take precautions and be careful that Maro did not find out her husband was still alive and in the vicinity. She had lied to him, telling him that her husband was fighting at the front. It had been clever of her not to introduce herself as the wife of an officer who had been condemned to death. It was one more proof of her intelligence. Riza would not let anyone take her from him.

After getting lost in the labyrinth of small, winding streets, Vartan came to a wide street bordered by plane trees and found the American School. There were two sentinels on guard in front of the iron fence. Inside the garden, more soldiers wearing pointed helmets were drinking in the shade of a pistachio tree. One of the sentinels informed him that the Americans had left for Alexandretta and that an artillery company now occupied the building.

Vartan was disappointed, as he had counted on receiving help from the Americans. He went on his way. Farther up the street he saw a copper shield on an encircling wall which announced: Swiss Protestant Mission. The two-storey rectangular grey stone building with large, tall windows resembled a school. Vartan had nothing to lose by trying his luck with the Swiss missionaries. He dismounted. As he put his weight on the wounded leg, the pain made him clench his jaw. He rang the bell several times.

A woman in a white dress came to the gate. She was a plain, square-faced blonde of about forty, with wide hips and a large bosom. She had small, determined, pale-blue eyes and marched like a well-trained sergeant. She was out of breath and each inhalation raised the gold cross she wore on a chain around her neck. She looked her visitor over.

'What do you want now?' she asked in broken Turkish. 'All our papers are in order.'

'I'm not who you think I am,' said Vartan in French. 'I would like to speak to someone in charge.'

For a moment, she looked surprised and then continued in French, 'I'm in charge. Who are you? What do you want?'

'Could we talk in a more discreet place?'

He had been looking over his shoulder frequently and the missionary felt his nervousness. She also noticed the wound he was trying to hide with his hand. Perplexed, she asked, 'You're not Turkish, are you?'

'Armenian.'

She was suspicious, 'Do you have any identity papers?'

'Yes, but false, of course.'

'Are you wanted?'

He nodded. She looked him over from head to foot and then looked him straight in the eyes; she saw an honest, open face. She did not think it was a trap. The authorities would not have sent a man in uniform. After hesitating for a moment to make sure that no one would see him enter, she opened the gate and let him in.

'Come. Put your horse in the stable. Be quick.'

He followed, pulling Yildiz by the reins. The missionary walked quickly to get the visitor out of the sight of her little ones, who might be frightened by the uniform. Besides, anybody might pass by and see him. Vartan had difficulty keeping up with her, as each step provoked stabs of violent pain in his thigh.

The stable had not been cleaned for several days. There was only one horse, an old knock-kneed nag.

'The army requisitioned all the others,' she explained, pointing to an empty stall. Vartan tied his horse up. She waited for him in the doorway and pointed to his torn trousers. 'What about your wound?'

'It's only a flesh wound. It can wait.'

She held out her hand. 'My name is Deborah Langlet.'

He would have preferred not to give her his name but he had to put her at ease. 'Vartan Balian, from Sivas.'

'What can I do for you?'

'I'm looking for my wife and son who were in one of the deportee caravans.'

Her face became sad and she answered with compassion, 'You have all my sympathy, Mr Balian.'

'Do you have anyone here from Sivas?'

She frowned while she thought it over for a minute. 'It's hard to tell. Our orphans come from all over. Many are too young to know the name of the place they came from.'

Vartan told her his story briefly. Deborah Langlet did not know who had taken Maro and Tomas. 'It could have been anyone,' she said kindly. 'Believe me, it's the best thing that could have happened to them.'

'That's easy for you to say,' he lashed out.

'No,' she said sweetly, 'but anything is better than one of the convoys. We're lucky that some of the Muslim families have taken in some of the children.'

'Taken in!' exclaimed Vartan. 'This morning I saw children who were to be sold like cattle.'

'I know. It's terrible. But keep telling yourself that at least they will survive. The Swiss, German and American missionaries have taken in all those they can, but we can't cope with this enormous task. My house is full of Armenian orphans. Because of the war, money from Europe arrives with great difficulty. We lack even the most essential things. At any moment the gendarmes could come and take our children away. The governor, Ali Bey, has been protecting us but there are persistent rumours that he will be replaced. I'm worried about the future.'

'Does the outside world know about what is happening here?'

'More or less. Less than more, I imagine. A few echoes in the newspapers. Communications are difficult and everyone's attention in Europe is focused on the war.'

'What are the diplomats doing?'

'The Swiss Ambassador and others from other countries have lodged a protest with the government in Constantinople, but the Ottoman officials speak of an organized displacement under humane conditions admitting, at most, a few outbursts of violence that are quickly put down by the military.'

'That's a lie!'

'Of course. If you could only hear some of the horrible tales the deportees tell. I have also heard accounts by eye-witnesses, travellers, mainly

German officers, who were still in shock from what they had seen – and military men are not, by nature, very impressionable.'

'The whole world must be told. We have to appeal to the consciences of people who can force the government to act. We must . . .'

She interrupted him and held out her hands, 'Yes, we must, but how?'

'Perhaps I can do something, but I need your help. Can you get letters and documents out of the country via the missionaries or the consular service?'

Deborah Langlet started to walk up and down, fanning herself with her hand. She could roughly see what he was proposing. She was sure she could get someone to take this man's mail out, although it was risky. If she hesitated, it was only because she was afraid for the little children in her charge. On the other hand, how could she remain inactive faced with the terrible crimes against humanity that were being committed in Asia Minor? She stopped in front of Vartan, put her hands on the small of her back and bent backwards. Her corset made a cracking noise.

'What did you have in mind?'

'I'm a political journalist. With what you tell me and with what I have seen, I can write articles which, if published outside, will cause an impact. I can also send detailed reports to some important people in Europe and America.'

'Then I agree,' she said.

'Could I talk to the children?'

'You'll have to take off your uniform; otherwise you'll frighten them. I'll give you some clothes that belonged to our gardener. Please don't ask too much of them. Many are in a state of shock. Some have either forgotten how to talk or don't want to. All of them still have all the atrocities they've seen in front of their eyes.'

Vartan's stiffened as he stared at a damaged painting. What kind of look did Tomas have in his eyes now?

'How old is your son?'

'He's six.'

'He's with his mother. That's already something. You have to keep your faith in divine providence.'

'I shall find them again,' said Vartan determinedly. Out of pity, the missionary kept her thoughts to herself. Vartan guessed what she was thinking and added, 'Even if I have to search every house in Anatolia.'

'Be realistic, sir,' she said. 'It's going to be hard enough for you to survive. You're wounded and wanted. Unfortunately, I know of no one in Malatya who could get you new identity papers and I can hide you for only a few days without endangering my orphanage.'

'Three days. I don't ask for more. Of course, I'll pay for my board.'

'You'll have to make do with the stable. The children are occupying every corner of the house. I've even moved my office into the hall.'

'That will be fine, Miss Langlet. I'll be as discreet as possible. I'm ever so grateful to you and . . .'

She cut him short, not wanting to listen to his words of gratitude. Deborah Langlet hated for others to feel indebted to her, to praise her charity and dedication; on the contrary, she thought that nothing she did was ever enough and that she was not worthy of her calling, even though for twelve years she had devoted herself to easing suffering and spreading the gospel of Christ. Vartan opened his purse and gave four pieces of gold to the missionary.

'It's far too much,' she protested.

'You said you were lacking essential things. I only wish I could do more. Do you know if Dr Black is still the director of the American School in Caesarea?'

'I think so.'

'The school hasn't been closed?'

'The last I heard, no.'

Dr Black had been one of Vartan's mathematics teachers at Robert College and they had kept up a correspondence until recently. He was a resourceful man who maintained his acquaintances with all kinds of people. He would find a way to get false identity papers so Vartan could travel without difficulty, but Caesarea was more than 300 kilometres away. It would take Vartan far from the region where his wife and son probably were, but he had no other choice.

Deborah brought him clothes, tea and cookies as well as bandages for his wound. 'Come into the house when you're ready and I'll introduce you to the children.'

Vartan took off his uniform. The bullet had left a long gash with gaping black lips. Luckily it had not damaged any major blood vessels. He poured water over the wound to clean it thoroughly and then disinfected it with iodine.

His mind wandered to other things. Whom should he write to? First to his brother, Noubar, and then to his cousin, Diran, to bring them up to date

223

with his situation. They just might have news of Maro. He was sure she would seek refuge with his Uncle Mesrop in Constantinople. He would take a chance and send her a letter too.

He should address the report about the situation of the Armenians in Anatolia to Lord Byrce, a British politician, who was sensitive to all injustice and *au fait* with the Armenian problem. He would also send one to his old friend, Anatole France. These two men commanded a large audience and would know how to arouse international opinion. He would send another copy to his brother, Barkev, who lived in New York. Then he and the other Armenians living in the USA would have to see to it that President Wilson was informed about the facts in the report. Only the American government could successfully exert enough pressure on the Ottoman Empire and its ally, the German Kaiser. What impact would his messages have? News about what was happening in Anatolia was already filtering out through the diplomatic pouches and the missionaries. His voice would be only one more among many and would perhaps also go unheard, but at least he would have done his part.

Yildiz started to stamp his hoofs and neigh. Vartan went to the door and cautiously looked out. Several horsemen were riding by in a hurry. Judging from their dress, they were Arabs. He quickly drew back.

Riza Bey had tied his *araba* to a closed carriage. He seemed cross and impatient to leave town. To dispel his nervousness, he fingered his *tespih* constantly. He looked cold and hard. When Maro had asked how long the trip would take, he had answered her curtly. This was so unlike him that Maro felt insecure. He sat facing her, their knees almost touching, and unless she kept her eyes down, she could not help looking at him. She pushed the curtain aside and looked out at the houses filing by.

A woman in white came out of an austere grey building. Maro could see children playing quietly in the courtyard. She felt a pang in her breast when she saw the gold cross engraved on the copper plate which identified the Swiss Protestant Mission. The vision of that haven disappeared and the carriage carried Maro and her son towards the unknown.

# EIGHT

By the end of July 1915, the situation of the Armenians in Asia Minor was going from bad to worse. Enver Pasha, the Minister of War for the government in Constantinople, had launched an offensive against the Russian positions. Eleven infantry and cavalry divisions advanced into the valley of Alashkert in the direction of Mount Ararat and were threatening Yerevan, the capital of Russian Armenia. To halt this enemy, the Russian Army and volunteer Armenian regiments withdrew from Van and its surrounding regions.

Hundreds of thousands of civilians were left defenceless. Fearing bloody reprisals by the Ottoman troops, the people fled in total panic over the border. Already affected by wartime rationing, Russian Armenia was now overrun by new waves of refugees, who swelled the numbers of those already taken in. Epidemics raged and provisions were in short supply. Shelters would have to be built before the onset of winter, which could be ferocious at these high latitudes. Emissaries of the Catholicos, His Holiness Kevork V, were busy collecting funds from the Armenians living in Europe, America and Cairo. The Supreme Patriarch also redoubled his appeals to the Allied leaders, the king of Italy and the American president in an effort to get them to intervene on behalf of the Armenian victims of the Ottoman government's extermination policy. Foreseeing the eventual fall of the Ottoman Empire, the Catholicos sent a delegation, which was now shuttling between the Quai d'Orsay and the Foreign Office. Its mission was to promote to the French and the British the idea of an independent Armenia, which would include Cilicia.

In Anatolia, the deportations were in full swing. After the inhabitants of the north and east, it was now those living on the shores of Cilicia and the south-east who were being driven out of their homes. The towns in the central region and the west – Konia, Angora, and Brusa – had been left alone, but it would not be long before they would suffer the same fate. At Musa Dagh, in the Amanos Mountains on the edge of the Mediterranean, several thousand Armenians had taken up entrenched positions in the hills overlooking their villages. At great sacrifice, they had been holding the Ottoman Army at bay since July 21$^{st}$ and showed no signs of yielding.

For weeks the Armenians in Ayntab had watched their compatriots pass by in vast convoys heading for Aleppo. Police cordons prevented them from going to the aid of these women and children, many of whom had been walking for a month, even if it were only to offer them a drink of water. Despite official declarations that only the Armenians from the war zones near the Russian border were to be moved, the Ayntabis were not reassured. Had not more than fifty families been expelled from the town already? And the Armenian bishop kept on warning his flock. Some of the well-to-do Armenians who had friends in the administration had been able to obtain passes and had fled to Baghdad, Amman or Jerusalem, where they hoped to find safety. The others had no choice but to go on with their lives while trying to maintain a semblance of normality.

Situated to the south of the Anti-Taurus and the Anatolian steppes, the town of Ayntab lay in a gently rolling countryside, which opened on to the Syrian desert and Mesopotamia. Even though the Mediterranean was less than 200 kilometres away, the Amanus Mountains blocked the maritime winds and the summers in Ayntab remained sultry and dry. Washed by the Injirli River, a tributary of the Euphrates, the city was built around three almost perfectly aligned hills. One of the hills was crowned by a fortress built by the Roman Emperor Justinian and rebuilt in the eleventh century by the Seljuk Turks.

The area's numerous quarries furnished plenty of excellent and cheap building material; hence most of the buildings were of hewn stone. Countless gardens along the banks of the river formed a belt of greenery that ran from north to east. This is where all the cemeteries lay – Muslim, Christian and Jewish. As the town lay at the cross-roads of several assorted civilisations, it had a very diverse population – Turks, Armenians, Kurds, Arabs, Assyrians, Jews and Greeks.

The surrounding plain, planted in vineyards and olive and fig groves, was rich land. The wheat and cotton fields extended as far as the eye could see.

Riza Bey's domain lay near the road to Marash, a few kilometres beyond the bridge over the River Injirli.

Fieldstone and adobe houses of farm-workers lined the winding road through the pistachio groves that had made the fortune of Riza Bey's ancestors. The enormous two-storey *konak* and the dome and the minarets of the mosque could be seen from afar, rising above the plantation. The poor people of the town knew the way to the mosque built by Riza's grandfather very well, as it was there that food was distributed to the needy.

The manor-house built of white limestone blocks was decorated with pilasters, bosses and green marble friezes with interlacing leaves and flowers. Its architecture showed a strong Arabic influence. The two wings running perpendicular to the main building formed an interior courtyard, which sheltered the *selamlik*,[1] the kitchen, the storerooms and the servants' quarters. A high wall pierced by an entrance gate enclosed this paved courtyard. A double staircase led up to the main entrance of the house, sheltered by a portico with cabled columns. In the back, the beauty of the building was complemented by a vast rectangular garden. The mosque and its annexes abutted the high wall that enclosed the garden. At some distance from the *konak*, hidden by a curtain of almond-trees, were the warehouses, stables, sheep-pens, barns and the farmers' small, flat-roofed dwellings.

There was great excitement in the household this afternoon. Buyuk Hanim had received a telegram from her son, announcing his arrival and his appointment as governor of the province. 'The year 1293 will be blessed above all others!' she had told her daughters-in-law when she excitedly announced the good news. Buyuk Hanim was a traditionalist and always used the Muslim calendar, which began with the *Hegira*, Mohammed's flight from Mecca in the year 622 of the Christian era. The honour that had been bestowed upon Riza Bey reflected on the entire family and it was fitting to celebrate it with pomp and splendour. Buyuk Hanim suffered from arthritis and a persistent backache and moved about slowly, but this was such an important event that it gave her wings. She was everywhere and saw to everything, reeling off orders, hounding the servants, bullying her daughters-in-law and scolding their children. It would have been unthinkable for her to share the running of her household with anyone else. As long as she was alive, she would cling jealously to the title of Buyuk

---

1.　That part of the house reserved for men (Turkish).

Hanim, or Grand Lady. Safiyé, Riza Bey's first wife, would just have to wait for her turn!

The telegraph operator had been unable to hold his tongue and all of Ayntab already knew that a new *vali* governed the province. Several leading citizens sent emissaries to Buyuk Hanim to find out when they would be able to pay Riza Bey their respects. The mother had taken it upon herself to invite the most important of them to a reception, which would begin at nightfall. When the boy who was keeping watch warned her that Riza Bey's carriage had just entered the road leading to the *konak*, she sent everyone to go out and wait in the paved courtyard for the great occasion.

The mother installed herself in the front row under a large white parasol held by a young maidservant. Although bony-faced and scrawny from the waist up; she had inordinately wide hips, so when she walked with her bosom thrust forward, her voluminous hindquarters had a difficult time keeping up. Excited and proud, she kept rehearsing to herself the words of welcome she would offer. Riza Bey's three wives and their six children, along with his old wet-nurse, Eminé, stood behind her. The elder sons, Turan and Ramazan, were absent; they were studying at a military academy in Germany. The twenty-three servants lined up on both sides of the long façade of the house.

Buyuk Hanim had a passion that made her feel slightly guilty – she collected family photographs. Of course, Islam forbade human images, but Buyuk Hanim told herself that photographs were not paintings or sculptures. They were more like an image reflected in the mirror and the Prophet had not forbidden the use of mirrors! The old woman's most prized possessions were albums filled with photographs of her loved ones. Many of them were of Riza in the company of distinguished people – diplomats and foreign travellers. She thought it essential to keep a record of the important moments in their lives, so for today's occasion, she had hired Ayntab's resident photographer, a Jew named Naim Sarfati. Small, bald and perpetually beaming, he stood behind his big black camera, which was mounted on a tripod.

'Take our picture while we're waiting,' ordered Buyuk Hanim.

He bowed, adjusted his camera and said, 'Look this way, please. Don't move.'

'Zehra! Be quiet!' Buyuk Hanim snapped at her three-year-old grand-daughter who was jumping up and down. Frightened, the child looked at her mother, Leyla, who quieted her with a motion. Riza Bey had married

228

Leyla four years ago, when she was sixteen. Although she was third in rank, she liked to think she was his favourite wife . . . and the prettiest! She glanced discreetly at her rivals, each wearing her *yashmak* of nearly transparent silk.

Makbulé, the second wife, was a bird-brain and a glutton, whose constant eating had coarsened her beauty. Three consecutive pregnancies had not helped matters either. She looked much older than her twenty-nine years and had nothing left to excite a man's ardour. As for the first wife, Safiyé, she could have been Leyla's mother. She was thirty-nine years old! The skin around her eyes was already wrinkled and, if it had not been for the henna she used, the hair at her temples would have been grey. She had given Riza five children but, as she was now undoubtedly too old to carry another one, it was not surprising that he treated her more like a beloved sister than a lover. Leyla felt sure of herself and closed her eyes. Riza's two-week absence had seemed endless. She yearned to be in his arms again, to abandon herself to his caresses.

Safiyé thought they should have waited for Riza Bey inside. A dry, scorching wind was blowing in from the desert and the temperature had climbed to forty-seven degrees Celsius. It was inhuman to ask them to stand here like this under the sun, especially since, because of the fast, they had had nothing to drink since dawn. Finally they heard the horses and the cheers of the workers and their families who were waiting at the front gate. The carriage entered the courtyard and stopped in front of the staircase.

Riza Bey got out on the side opposite the house and walked around the carriage. He looked very handsome in his white suit. Buyuk Hanim thought that he looked like his father but even more elegant; Safiyé began to worry as she thought he looked tense. Makbulé felt relieved, as she dreaded her mother-in-law's wiles and whims and felt safer when her husband was at home. Leyla shuddered as a hot wave of desire flooded her body.

Riza Bey smiled at his family, then lowered the footboard and opened the carriage doors.

'What is this?' Leyla muttered huskily between her teeth.

Makbulé, not understanding her neighbour's anxiety, naively responded, 'It's a woman, of course. Can't you see?'

Safiyé snickered sardonically. From the attention Riza Bey paid to his passenger, from the way he looked at her and gave her his hand, Safiyé knew that he was not indifferent to this woman. She took it philosophically. Why should her husband deprive himself if he desired this stranger? He was courteous and generous; she was sure that he would not neglect or mistreat his wives because of a mistress. Twice before, Safiyé had seen another woman install herself in the house and she had had no reason to complain. Right now she was amused at Leyla's vexation because she herself had no conception of what it was like to be possessive or jealous.

Leyla squinted to show her hostility to her husband's first wife and then turned to scrutinize the stranger from head to foot. How old could she be? The black veil that masked her features enhanced her enormous, velvety-brown eyes. Leyla interpreted her frightened look as false modesty and reserve; more, it could even have been a sign that the woman was shifty and calculating. She told herself that a man might easily fall for such a look, might even find it bewitching. Even the fullness of the long violet robe the stranger was wearing could not conceal her svelte body, which nevertheless curved in all the right places. At the slightest movement, her breasts and hips were revealed under the soft draped fabric. The slimness of her waist was shown by the fall of the robe. Leyla could see her delicate wrists and ankles, her narrow hands and tapered fingers. It was not necessary to see her face to know this was a woman of quality. The way she carried her head high, with shoulders held slightly back, as well as her slow, graceful gait were signs of a woman aware of her beauty and power over men. Unaware that she was imputing her own attributes and behaviour to the newcomer, Leyla felt threatened by her.

Buyuk Hanim watched coldly as her son approached, followed by Maro and Tomas. How dare Riza bring a woman to the house without first having consulted her mother! He was spoiling her joy. Suddenly, Buyuk Hanim forgot the welcoming words she had prepared.

Riza kissed his mother's hand and brought it up to touch his forehead. 'great is my happiness to be with you again, *annejiim*.'[1]

'I have to talk to you,' she replied curtly.

Since he had expected her to react this way, he did not lose his composure. He turned and paid his respects to Eminé, his old wet-nurse, in the same way he had greeted Buyuk Hanim. She beamed and looked as happy as a mother seeing her son home again.

'I'm so proud of you, Riza Bey.'

He kissed his wives, beginning with Safiyé and ending with Leyla. Then his children came to greet him one by one, kissing his hand before bringing it to their foreheads – first the boys, Altan, Kenan and Arif, who were

---

1. My dear mother (Turkish).

230

respectively thirteen, seven and four years old. Then the girls, Shahané, aged sixteen, Emel, seven, and finally Zehra, the youngest one. He was overjoyed to see them again and murmured a loving word to each one.

Tomas felt a knot in his throat as he watched the scene. How he envied these children. He thought of his father and remembered his joy when his papa returned home at the end of the afternoon. Above all he did not want to cry or show his pain. He put his hand in his pocket and grasped the box containing the seal with the name Vartan Balian. He was astonished to see a boy around his age holding a wooden model of a glider. Tomas had almost forgotten the word *play*. The child saw Tomas looking at it and hid his toy behind his back.

All eyes were turned on Maro and in them she could read feelings ranging from curiosity, to indifference and to open hostility. She found the experience intimidating but waited patiently for the interminable welcoming to end. The presence of the women and children was reassuring, for there had been times when he had doubted Riza Bey's word, fearing he might be taking her to a hideaway, where he could keep her sequestered, or that he would change his mind and abandon her along the way. But everything was happening as her saviour had promised – the *konak*, his mother, his three wives, his children. Perhaps she could even expect to be put on a train to the capital soon. Here, in this home governed by rules, in the bosom of a real family, she did not have to face brute force. Tomas and she could regain their strength for the long, difficult journey to Constantinople.

Riza Bey ushered Maro into the group. 'This is our guest, Maro, and her son, Tomas,' he said, before introducing the members of his family.

Maro bowed to his mother, 'I'm infinitely grateful to you for receiving us under your roof, Buyuk Hanim.'

The old woman answered with a brief nod. Despite the newcomer's unaccented Turkish, the sound of her name betrayed her Armenian origin. Leyla shot a look of contempt and hatred at the stranger. Makbulé simply fluttered her eyelashes and inclined her head. As much to please her husband as to assert herself before her mother-in-law and needle Leyla, the first wife said warmly, 'Welcome to our home.'

To Riza Bey these words proved once again the deep friendship between Safiyé and himself and the understanding that had evolved during their twenty years of marriage. He acknowledged his gratitude with a slight nod of the heard then turned to the servants. They showed their allegiance with a *temenna,* touching the right hand first to the heart, then to their lips and then to the forehead.

Delighted, Riza turned to his mother and said, 'Let lambs be slaughtered and *raki* distributed so that our people can feast tonight.' Then, pointing to Maro, he told Eminé, 'See to the comfort of our guest. Give her a suite on the second floor, the one in the middle with the balcony overlooking the garden.'

Hearing these words Buyuk Hanim stiffened and Leyla turned purple. The second floor contained the harem, the apartments reserved for the women of the household; strangers were not allowed. Riza Bey was the head of the family and Buyuk Hanim could not protest in public but he would soon find out what she thought about all this.

'How about a photograph?' asked Naim Sarfati.

Buyuk Hanim did not react so Riza Bey answered in her place, 'Of course.' He gathered the family together for a group portrait and placed Maro and Tomas among them. This was one photograph Buyuk Hanim would not put in one of her albums. When the photograph had finished, Riza Bey offered his arm to his mother and they went into the house together. The others followed.

The light of the setting sun streamed through the stained glass panel and splashed large blue and violet spots on a wall covered with framed photographs. Buyuk Hanim sat in her green easy-chair next to a cypress lectern shaped like a winged dove. On it lay a thick volume with a silver clasp. Other albums lay on tables around the room. Here in this small sitting-room next to her bedroom, Buyuk Hanim often withdrew for hours. Thanks to her beloved photographs she could again feel close to her brothers and sisters, those living and those dead, to her five children and to her grandchildren at all the different stages of their lives. Through metal daguerreotypes and paper prints, she relived the history of her family.

Riza Bey ignored the *sedir,* which was crowded with cushions, and remained standing in front of his mother. She first asked about his trip and then gave a brief account of what had happened in Ayntab during his absence.

'Tonight, I have, in your name, invited a few prominent people to come and congratulate you.'

'That's fine.'

That digression over, Buyuk Hanim slowly brought the conversation around to what was on her mind.

'Did you bring presents to your wives again to encourage their vices?'

Riza Bey just smiled and his mother answered the question herself, 'A book for Safiyé, the dreamer, rare delicacies to tempt Makbulé, the glutton, finery for Leyla, the flirt, is that it?'

He burst out laughing. 'And a photo album for you!' He pulled out from his case a morocco-bound volume with Buyuk Hanim's initials embossed in pure gold. He had ordered it from one of the local artisans in Ayntab on the day he left.

His mother's wrinkled face softened as she leafed through the black pages with a trembling forefinger, dreaming of the moment she would mount the photographs in their silver paper corners.

'Thank you,' she said, pulling Riza to her to kiss him on the forehead. 'You always know how to please me.' She was about to add that, of all her children, he was her favourite, but restrained herself. She placed the album on her lap and patted it, saying, 'This one should be devoted exclusively to the career of Riza Bey, the governor.'

He knew he hadn't disarmed his mother and, sure enough, the smile quickly faded from her face. 'As far as I can tell, you've also brought along a present for yourself.'

He pretended not to understand. 'What do you mean?'

'A mistress! With a son into the bargain'

Dismissing her comment with a wave of his hand, he protested, 'It's not what you think, *annejiim*.'

'You haven't seen yourself with her. Your wives caught on right away. You're in love, Riza.'

He frowned. Was his interest in Maro that obvious? But that was a far cry from being in love!

'Who is she anyway?' she asked offhandedly.

Although Riza knew that she had realized immediately that Maro was not Turkish, he went along with his mother, 'An Armenian whom I saved from death.'

Outraged, she lifted her arms to heaven and cried, 'A Christian! Have you lost your mind, my son? You, the governor? She must leave at once!'

Riza stood up. His voice admitted no argument, 'When the time is ripe and not a moment sooner.'

Buyuk Hanim sighed. It was useless to argue when her son used that authoritarian tone.

He did not want to offend his mother, so he explained, 'She and her son suffered enormously because of the deportation; they've walked all the way from Sivas. Charity . . .'

His mother seized the opportunity to attack again and said ironically, 'Charity! Don't take me for a fool. I have eyes to see. She's a beautiful woman in spite of everything she's been through. Have you been seduced by her beauty?'

Riza's face remained unperturbed. To avoid causing her anxiety about the future, he preferred not to say anything about the dream in which the Armenian woman had saved him from death. Donning his role as the unquestioned head of the family, he said, 'It's my business.'

'As you wish, but let her stay with the servants, not on the same floor and next door to me and your wives.'

'She is a lady of quality. She shall have a room in the harem.'

The mother had no choice but to submit to his will, but she saved face by remarking, 'This heat has exhausted me. Let me get some rest.'

A mosquito net suspended from the ceiling surrounded the bed placed in the corner of the big, white-walled room. A lacquered commode, a pot-bellied chest and a table inlaid with mother-of-pearl completed the furnishings.

'You'll find this room very comfortable,' said Eminé, as she stepped aside to allow Maro and her son to enter.

Light streamed into the room, partly from a wooden-latticed window, but mostly from a door opening on to a wrought-iron balcony. Eminé placed Maro's tapestry bag on the table. She moved shuffling her feet, her slippers hissing softly on the carpet. Her small waist accentuated her obesity. Her face was round and so fat that she did not have a single wrinkle. Her heart-shaped mouth was always smiling and her eyes sparkled, showing an unfailing joy for living. She was sixty-four years old, only five years younger than Buyuk Hanim. She had come into the family as a slave in 1870 to take care of the newborn baby Riza. Although she had never been freed, she was like a member of the family and Riza loved her like a mother. It was from this woman who had raised him that he had acquired both his superstitions and his generosity, which went beyond the sharing required of all believers.

234

The room led into another small sitting-room, which contained a divan, a green-velvet easy-chair, two low inlaid tables and a prayer rug.

'Your son can sleep here,' said Eminé. 'I'll have another mosquito net installed. The insects are voracious at night.'

Tomas pulled his mother by the hand and complained, 'I'm hungry and thirsty, Mama.'

'Remember it's Ramadan. The people in this house are fasting and we have to do as they do. Be patient, my darling. The day will end soon,' whispered Maro.

'He's hungry, isn't he?' asked Eminé.

She went to Tomas and laid her hand on his shoulder. She had been shocked by his sunken cheeks, thin legs and his grown-up look of disillusionment when she had seen him get out of the carriage. She had restrained herself from going to him and taking him in her arms then, but Tomas's plaintive voice now brought out her compassion and here, in private, she gave rein to her natural impulses, took him in her arms and caressed his face. He made no attempt to resist, as the old woman looked so kind and her gestures were as sweet as her voice.

'Do you understand Armenian?' asked Maro.

'Only a few words. We have some Armenian servants here and most of the tradesmen are Armenian. What did you say to your son?'

'That we have to fast until night.'

'Not the children,' she said, raising her arms. 'Poor little thing. We're going to serve Riza's children dinner. Your son shall have dinner with them.'

Tomas more or less understood what the nurse was saying and shook his head. His mother said, 'Tomas is very shy.'

'Then we'll serve his meal here.'

She went out into the corridor and clapped her hands. A young servant who had been waiting at the top of the stairs came running. She was hardly thirteen years old and seemed very nervous.

'Bring the child something to drink, water and *sherbet*,[1] and ask for his dinner to be brought up. Do you understand?'

'Yes, *Hanim*,' said the girl, bowing.

Eminé explained to Maro, 'She's new here and an Armenian like you.' She closed the door and added, 'You only have to call if you want anything and I'll see to it. There's always a servant on call in the corridor.'

---

1.   A sweet fruit drink (Turkish).

235

The two women joined Tomas on the balcony. The edges of the huge rectangular garden looked a bit like a jungle – fig, arbutus and oleander made dense copses from which slender stems of eucalyptus and a few palms emerged. Some of the palm branches had been yellowed by frost the previous winter. On the other side a low, circular basin shimmered next to a pavilion, which was half covered with climbing roses.

A gravelled path bordered by lawns and flower-beds divided the garden lengthways. Two children were playing there. The boy tossed his glider to his sister who ran around, trying to follow its unpredictable flight. Seeing that Tomas was interested, Eminé leaned forward.

'The boy is called Kenan and his sister Emel. I'm sure they would like to play with you.'

Tomas stood still and said nothing. Thinking he had not understood her, Eminé repeated her words more slowly, spacing them far apart, but he still did not react. These children were Turks like the *zaptiyés* who had arrested his father, driven them out of Sivas and forced them to walk for days and days until Armen, Araksi and Azniv Hanim had died. Faced with children the same age as himself, Tomas thought of the friends he had lost and especially of the little girl who had been killed by the soldiers in front of the monastery. How could he play with these children? Tomas was prepared to be polite to these people but nothing more.

Maro made a sign to the nurse not to insist and the latter said in an understanding voice, 'Yours has been a cruel fate, hasn't it?'

'I prefer not to talk about it.'

'You're right. One must forget. Now that you're here, your troubles are over. You'll see. Riza's house is a peaceful, happy place.'

Maro gazed at the horizon on the western side of the garden. The sun had just set behind the range of the Amanus Mountains. Over there was where the Mediterranean began. The port of Alexandretta was only a few days' sail from Constantinople. Turning her head to the right, she saw some even more imposing mountains – Anatolia, from where she had just come; straight to the north was Sivas. On the other side a minaret and the mosque blocked the view. Maro felt fenced in by the stone walls and the mountains. She had entered a world where her fate depended on the will of one man.

'What kind of a man is Riza Bey?'

'Just and affectionate! Even when he's angry, he's still kind. He has never beaten any of his wives nor raised his hand to his children. How many men can say the same?' She pressed her hands against her heart, which made her look proud of her beloved son. 'There aren't many like him. Have you noticed how handsome he is? The depth of his look? He's tender in spite of his strength.' She lowered her voice to add admiringly, 'On top of that, he's virile.'

'Does he keep his word?'

The question surprised the nurse, who arched her eyebrows. She took a few seconds to answer, 'He does what he says he will do, but a woman should never ask a man to keep his word. That would be insulting! A woman should be happy to obey.' Then Eminé added in a low voice, 'But if she's clever, she often gets what she wants.'

The servants brought in Tomas's dinner and put it on a table in the sitting room. Before withdrawing, the nurse laid her hand on Maro's arm like a mother. 'If you have a problem or want anything, please don't hesitate to tell me. I'll do everything I can for you.' Maro was surprised by so much kindness and thanked her warmly.

Maro found Tomas kneeling in front of the table, eating voraciously. Before she could say anything, he said with his mouth full, 'I washed my hands and said the blessing first.'

Maro smiled and sat down on a cushion. It warmed her heart to see her son eating with good appetite. She wanted him never to know hunger nor thirst nor fear again. That would be the only goal that would rule her conduct from now on.

She drank three glasses of water, one after the other. 'Aren't you fasting?' asked Tomas.

'Not when we're alone. If I pretend, it's out of respect for our host's customs.' She saw from the gleam in her son's eyes that he was teasing her and his attitude made her happy. 'Is it good?'

'Yes! I've already finished the vegetable soup.' Then Tomas ate the aubergine salad and the minced beef. He kept his eyes fixed on his mother the whole time. 'Are we going to stay here long, mama?'

'I don't know, my darling. The only important thing is that we're safe.'

'Do we have to eat with the others?'

'We can't stay locked in this room. It would be impolite to the people who are sheltering us.'

Tomas grimaced, 'Do I have to play with the children?'

'No, not if you don't want to, but you won't be able to avoid them. They look nice.'

'Yes, but they're not Armenians,' grumbled Tomas.

237

His look was eloquent and Maro guessed what he was thinking. She stroked his cheek. 'These children are not responsible for what the soldiers did. You shouldn't bear them a grudge. Try to forget what we've been through.'

Tomas looked shattered, 'I'll try, mama, but I dream about it every night.'

Maro opened her arms and he threw himself against her. He was trembling. She hummed a lullaby she had sung to him when he was a baby. Then Vartan had accompanied her softly on his *oud* while he watched over them lovingly.

Two large bouquets of roses perfumed the living-room where Safiyé had withdrawn to wait for her husband's visit. She had dyed her hair with henna and put rouge on her lips. Her skin, the colour of antique ivory, looked luminous. She had a rather square face with regular features, hazel coloured eyes and a calm, pensive expression. She had a reputation for being serene but it was really only an illusion. She had always vibrated with an inner restlessness, although she herself didn't know the reason for it. Over the years she had learned to control it but never to make it disappear.

Daydreaming, she sat with an open book on her knees, staring at the silk tapestry hanging on the wall. Her reverie was a series of disconnected images. Her mind felt light, floating like a leaf blown by the wind. Her eyes left the tapestry and roamed over the framed lithographs – illustrations of Constantinople, Baghdad, Medina, Cairo and some European towns. A vague nostalgia made her sigh.

Originally from Urfa, about forty-five kilometres east of Ayntab, Safiyé had never left her family's home until she went for her confinement under Riza Bey's roof. Her horizon had always been limited by the dismal hills and stony plains of this region. How she would have loved to see the world! She imagined it began on the other side of the mountains. Her keen curiosity had never been satisfied and Safiyé mourned silently for all she would never know. Her education had had only one goal – to make her the idle wife of a rich man. She knew how to sing, how to embroider, how to converse and how to behave. How to read? How to write? What use were they to a woman?

It was only after she was married that she learned how to read with the help and encouragement of Riza Bey. For that, she felt grateful to him, every day. At last she had access to books! She had read all the ones written in Arabic in her husband's library: poetry, mystical works (these were somewhat beyond her) and old travel tales. The others, written in French, were incomprehensible to her and she could only admire the illustrations, often having to guess what it was they depicted.

When the first flames of newly-wed passion had abated, Riza had found in her a wise and intelligent companion, a friend whose advice he valued. Like everyone else, he had been taken in by the image she projected. She did not wish to disappoint or disillusion him, so Safiyé never dared to open her heart. He would leave on his travels never knowing how badly she wanted to go with him. Her fondest wish was to see Stamboul or Baghdad, if only once!

She recognized her husband's particular way of knocking and jumped up. The open book dropped on the carpet. 'Come in.'

He was wearing a white linen Arabian robe. Safiyé walked up to him slowly in order to admire him at her ease. He kissed her tenderly.

'My dear husband,' she murmured, 'Your absence has seemed so long!'

He held his wife's hands, 'My dove, I have missed you terribly. How many times have I gone to sleep imagining your voice reciting poems to me.'

She ran her lips along Riza's fingers, caressed his cheeks and then brushed his eyelids with her lips. Uneasily she observed, 'You look exhausted and tense. Is there grief in your heart?'

'Only the fatigue of a long journey.'

She drew him towards the divan, 'I can't offer you anything to drink, but at least sit down and stretch out your legs.' She knelt on the floor in front of him, took off his shoes and massaged his feet. 'Tell me, Riza, what did you see during your journey?'

He laughed. 'Stones. Nothing but stones, steppes covered with yellowed grass, ravines, dried-up rivers. What did you imagine?'

'There must be cities out there.'

'Cities like Urfa or Ayntab.'

Safiyé refused to believe him. Riza had lost the ability to marvel; she would have seen differences, in the landscape and the people.

'And you, my sweet, what did you read while I was gone?'

She blushed, lowered her eyes, to confess, 'Fuzuli . . . *Leyla and Mejnoun*.'[1]

---

1. A work dating from 1535, the *Romeo and Juliet* of the Orient.

'Again!' Riza Bey teased her.

She fluttered her eyelids. 'I think they're like us. All lovers are soul mates.'

'You're right,' he said, pulling her to him.

He gave her a book which she took with feigned surprise but her pleasure was genuine. She ran her forefingers over the gilded letters of the title, *Beauty and Love,* and the name of the author, Ghalib Dédé. Pressing the book against her breast, she clasped Riza's hand and thanked him effusively. Suddenly her voice changed, 'Shall we have time to read these poems together?'

'Of course,' Riza replied.

'You were so busy before. Now that you're a governor . . . Besides your new wife will want you.' She said this without jealousy or bitterness. Safiyé was only afraid of having fewer opportunities for intimate conversations with her husband, for those were the only times when reality and dream became one for her.

'How could I live without our conversations, my dear Safiyé? And you're mistaken. Maro is not my new wife; she is a friend. At least, I hope she'll become one.'

Now Safiyé's face darkened. A mistress was one thing, but a friend! Now she did feel herself threatened.

Riza stroked her cheek. 'One can have many friends, just as one may have several wives. Each one is different; each relation is unique. Who could ever bring me the peace I find with you? What other soul could communicate with mine as yours does?'

His words eased Safiyé's fears. She gazed at length at Riza's honey-coloured eyes. She felt herself melt, felt her body open. Perhaps this time her flesh would respond to passion if he took her immediately. She had always offered herself out of duty rather than desire. But he did not stir and Safiyé's senses resumed their usual listlessness. Afterwards she felt relieved. The moments of utter abandonment such as the women talked of secretly in the *hammam* terrified her more than anything, for she was certain that if she ever succumbed in that way she would never recover her self-possession.

She smiled. 'What's she like, this . . . Armenian?' She instantly withdrew the question. 'I don't want to intrude.'

'No. On the contrary, I want to tell you about her, but I don't really know her yet. She is a cultivated woman who has studied and travelled. As well as her own language and ours, she speaks French. And she told me she can play the piano.'

Safiyé's eyes shone and she asked eagerly, 'And her temperament?'

'She's determined and firm. She knows what she wants.'

'Is she gentle? Friendly?'

'I believe so,' said Riza, as he rose to embrace her. 'Excuse me, my soul. I must see the others and prepare to entertain my guests.'

She held him back by his sleeve, her eyes pleading. Riza knew her well enough to know what she was waiting for.

'Maro will be homesick and lonely the first days. Would you be so kind as to try and make her feel at home?'

A broad smile brightened Safiyé's face.

After leaving Safiyé, Riza made his way to Makbulé's room. She was sitting in an armchair by the window, taking advantage of the last hours of daylight to do some embroidery. Her needle kept her hands busy. Otherwise they would have been tempted to do what they usually did – carry food to her mouth. She must fast! To skip a meal was not difficult but going for hours and hours without munching sweetmeats, dried fruit or nuts was.

It was unfair of Leyla to assume that Makbulé was no longer attractive to a man. Her plump body did not diminish her beauty in the least; on the contrary, it accentuated her feminine charms. Her skin, the colour of goat's milk, had a strange luminosity that seemed to originate from deep within. It was perfectly smooth, her eyebrows were almost invisible and her hair was as soft as down.

Her body invited caresses, caresses that were necessary to dissipate Makbulé's almost pathological timidity. Once that shyness had been overcome, she felt no restraints and lovemaking with her turned into a grand production of bursts of laughter and lusty remarks. Using the most vulgar words to designate the parts of the body and sexual act excited her. It was only on these occasions that she abandoned the formal mode of address. When she was not inflamed by desire, she behaved like a shy, frightened girl who longed for protection.

This was the way that she now received Riza Bey. She snuggled up to him, shivering and trembling in his arms. 'Hold me, my husband. Keep me close. Guard me with your strength.'

As always, Riza was touched by this unlimited trust, which was like that of a small animal. Ever since his passion for her had abated after two years

241

of marriage, he had regarded Makbulé more as a child than a wife. There was something paternal about his love for her.

'I wish I were very small so you could take me in your arms and cuddle me.'

This was almost a ritual. He put an arm around her waist and the other under her ample rump and lifted her up. She let out a cry of surprise and clung to his neck, as he walked up and down rocking her. She rested her head on her husband's shoulder and closed her eyes. How good it felt to be carried away, to abandon herself to Riza's strength. When he desired her, he would carry her to the bed where she would lie still and let herself be undressed. Otherwise, he would put her down in the armchair, which was what he did now.

Riza Bey pinched her waist and she squirmed and giggled. 'Are you fasting, Makbulé?'

'Yes, of course.'

'Is it hard?' he asked, half-mocking, half-compassionate.

She sighed deeply. 'It's getting harder every year! I spend the whole day deciding what to eat when night falls and I've changed my mind twenty times.'

Riza stopped laughing. For a glutton like Makbulé, fasting must be a terrible ordeal. 'Try to think about something else. Forget about food.'

'I cannot. Images of food dance before my eyes like the mirages that fool a traveller in the desert.'

He patted her hand encouragingly. 'The merit you earn in the eyes of Allah will be all the greater.'

She looked as if this was small consolation to her. Riza Bey held out a box from which enticing aroma escaped. She quickly unwrapped it and looked at it, surprised. She had never seen this kind of confectionery before.

'What is it?'

'Nougat.'

She ran her nose along the box and had a hard time resisting the impulse to taste the sweets with the tip of her tongue.

'Will you be able to hold out until nightfall?'

She glanced at the already darkening sky. 'Yes!' she replied with confidence and closed the box. 'Thank you, my dear husband. I'm so excited that I'll be tasting something new.' She then looked at him with the same mischievous look she wore when she made love, and rose on her toes to whisper in his ear the latest wanton story she had heard in the kitchens.

242

When he left, Riza Bey was roaring with laughter.

When Riza Bey entered Leyla's drawing room he was dazzled by the light of the countless candles burning on a table. The scent of incense hung heavy in the air. The young woman was skulking in a dark corner. She reproached him sulkily, 'I'm the last, as always!'

'Come here, my little capricious one. Come, let me look at you.'

'Sit down first, master.'

Wondering what she had dreamed up this time, Riza Bey sat on the *sedir*. Catlike, Leyla drew near. The tiny bells at her ankles and the many bracelets on her wrists tinkled. As she stepped into the light, he could see her body through the transparent veils she wore. Thick strokes of kohl emphasized her eyelids and lengthened her thin lashes. Her hands and feet were tinted with henna. She wore a diadem studded with diamonds, big earrings and several necklaces. Her bare feet slapped on the tiled floor and her jewellery clinked rhythmically. She threw back her head, setting off her narrow, slightly turned-up nose, her prominent and pointed chin. Her mouth seemed disproportionately wide in her slender face. Her slim body undulated and her hips swayed. Leyla's frailty was only an illusion; she was all muscle and nerves and as tough and strong as she was stubborn.

She turned lovemaking into a kind of contest. After tantalizing her man, she would feign reluctance. Riza would pursue her but nimble and clever, she would slip through his fingers. The game would last until Riza, mad with desire, would use force to pin her down on the bed. She would struggle for a moment longer and then abandon herself, roaring and howling, to his embrace. Leyla insisted that the two other wives hear the echoes of her lovemaking.

For Riza Bey it had been love at first sight when he had first caught a glimpse of her. She had been sixteen years old. Her father, a Shiite Muslim, had opposed the marriage, swearing he would rather give his daughter to a Christian than to a Sunni. He was not a rich man, however, and an alliance with Riza Bey was an unexpected opportunity for his daughter. However, all of Riza Bey's efforts to sway the father had been in vain. As the months went by, Riza Bey, unable to sleep or eat, became consumed by his passion. Finally, he found a way. He bought a piece of land situated above Leyla's father's land and dammed up a spring to keep the overflow from irrigating the good man's fields. Threatened with imminent ruin, her father gave in.

Leyla beat on her tambourine and swayed her hips in front of her husband. 'Now it's your turn to suffer, my cruel master. You made me languish for lack of love for two whole weeks. I shall remove my veils one by one. Your hunger will turn to pain and you shall beg me on your knees to put out the fire in your loins.'

Normally Riza adored it when she danced for him. She had such style and was so supple that many a professional dancer would have envied her, but today he was not in the mood.

'Another time,' he said. 'I'm in a hurry now.'

She tossed away the tambourine, crouched in front of him and groped between his thighs. 'In this case, take me quickly! Here on the floor!'

He grasped her by the wrists. 'This is Ramadan. We can't make love in the daytime.'

She moaned, disappointed. He lifted her chin and kissed her to console her.

'What did you bring me?' she asked. 'A jewel? Silk?'

He gave her a pair of gold lamé slippers. Each one was ornamented with petals of flowers embroidered in pearls. She was excited like a child. She was trying on the slippers when a cannon from Ayntab sounded, marking the end of the fast and the beginning of the evening.

'The cannon!' she cried, throwing herself on her back, 'Take me!'

She tore off her veils, exposing her breasts with their greenish-black nipples, her belly and her crotch, from which she had recently shaved the pubic hair.

'Leyla!' exclaimed Riza, hardly able to contain his exasperation. 'I told you, I don't have time. Buyuk Hanim is waiting for us in the garden.'

She was stunned! Never before in four years had he refused her advances. It took a few seconds for her to react. She jumped to her feet. 'Don't I please you anymore?' she asked accusingly.

'Of course you do.'

'You don't want me, is that it?'

'Not right now, that's all.'

It was inconceivable, but he was refusing her! She exploded, 'You fucked your Armenian and you're sated, aren't you?'

'Enough!' he snapped.

At any other time she would have obeyed, but rage and frustration blinded her. Fists on her hips, she said sarcastically, 'Everyone knows Christians don't keep Ramadan! Was she as good as I am? Did you enjoy it at least?'

Riza Bey understood his wife's state of mind well enough, but yet he was losing patience. He repeated in a firm voice, 'I told you to hold your tongue, Leyla.'

'If you think I'm going to let myself be shoved aside by a *giaour* . . .'

'That's enough,' he roared.

She gave in tearfully but began to whimper. He searched for words to make her understand. Her voice full of tears, Leyla reproached him, 'You ruined my father to get me, you almost starved my mother and brothers and sisters to death, and now you're rejecting me! All right. Refuse me if you will! But you won't see me turning into a wizened old mule like Safiyé or a fat goose like Makbulé!'

Livid, Riza Bey grabbed her arm. 'Take those words back.'

Leyla clenched her teeth and kept silent. Her husband's grip tightened. She endured the pain for a few moments longer before muttering reluctantly, 'I . . . I wasn't thinking about what I was saying.'

He released her but his voice was still shaking with rage. 'I forbid you even to think such things about Safiyé and Makbulé. Don't ever be disrespectful to them again. You have a lot to learn from them. As far as my guest is concerned, you shall smile at her and make her feel welcome in our house. Is that understood?'

Leyla wept as she rubbed her arm, but the blow to her pride hurt even more. In spite of that, she kissed Riza's hand and implored his forgiveness. He softened and wiped away the tears that were making streaks of kohl run down her face.

'Silly little fool . . . I may not always be able to restrain myself as I did just now. Don't push me too far.'

She asked pitifully, 'Do you still love me?'

'Of course,' he said, kissing her.

Leyla waited until Riza Bey's footsteps were no longer audible in the corridor; then she picked up the golden slippers and hurled them at the door.

Tomas had placed his godfather's sailor cap on a stool next to the divan where he was lying. This was his way of taking possession of the room. Maro sat next to him as she waited for someone to come and fetch her. A little earlier, Eminé had informed her that she was to dine with the rest of the family under the *asma alti*[1] in the garden. Remembering Buyuk Hanim's glacial welcome, Maro was not looking forward to this meal but there was no way of evading the obligation without committing a blunder. She would have to smile, sham and pretend to be interested in the conversation. Pretend again!

She had almost finished reciting bedtime prayers with Tomas when someone knocked on the door. She opened it. It was Riza.

He kissed her hand and said, 'You look lovely.'

'Thank you,' she said, lowering her eyes.

She was wearing a thin silk robe that had been sent up by the nurse. The tunic, edged with embroidered gold, was caught at the waist by a green belt and fell all the way to Maro's ankles. She had made up her eyes and pulled her hair into a chignon that emphasized the perfect oval of her face. This vision of grace and harmony enchanted Riza and he thought again of his mother's words. Was he in love? Perhaps! He had not yet asked himself the question in this light.

By the light of the gas lamp, Riza Bey's thin lips looked moist. The shadows emphasized his prominent cheekbones and made his eyes look even greener. Proud and self-assured, he examined Maro so intensely that she felt uncomfortable. She could not ignore what was obvious; Riza Bey's face plainly betrayed his feelings: desire, or even worse, love or something close to it.

'Do you find your room comfortable?'

'Yes, of course.'

He gestured broadly. 'Make yourself at home here. We are all happy to have you and your son among us.'

'All of you? Really? It seemed to me that . . .'

He waved his hand as if he were chasing a persistent fly. 'Don't go on first impressions. They were just very surprised. Remember, my mother didn't know you were coming.'

'Did you tell her that my stay would be brief?'

Instead of answering her, he strolled to the balcony door. Maro followed him trying to sound casual, 'Oh, let me give you my Uncle Mesrop's address in Constantinople so you can send him a telegram. That way I can leave and not unduly abuse your and your mother's hospitality.'

The prospect of her disappearing from his life saddened Riza. The pleasant sense of well-being he had felt before now vanished. There he had

---

1. A bower, literally under the climbing vines (Turkish).

his answer – yes, he was in love! Staring into the night, his mind played with the word *love* for a few moments. This would explain the surge of youthful energy he had been feeling the past few days. A new passion at forty-six! The suggestion of a smile on his lips disappeared. How could he persuade Maro to stay here long enough to conquer her without holding her prisoner? Tell her her husband had been hanged? Tell her her uncle no longer lived in Constantinople? No! That would be too easy. He would forever doubt if she had stayed out of need. He wanted her to choose him above all others. He wanted her to love him and abandon everything for him.

Looking thoughtful, he turned to face her. 'Things aren't as simple as that,' he said, with a helpless shrug. 'The telegraph is used for matters of national importance and the army controls it strictly. The same with the trains. On top of that, you would have to travel with the troops – uncouth, rough men. You would have to make a long stretch of the journey on foot as the line is interrupted at the Taurus Mountains where the tunnel is still under construction.'

'I've known worse,' murmured Maro.

'It's going to be hard to organize, even for me, the governor.'

Maro was not really surprised by Riza's answer as she had guessed his feelings for her. However, she was disappointed and let it show, even exaggerating it a little.

This had the desired effect. Riza Bey added hastily, 'Please try to understand. I didn't say it was impossible, only very difficult. Leave it with me and be patient. I repeat, this is your home. Rest now and enjoy the peace of this house.' He took her hands in his and she dared not withdraw them.

'You trust me, don't you?'

Always these loaded questions! She got hold of herself and nodded.

He drew a little closer and declared solemnly, 'We're at war. The country around us is topsy-turvy because of the terrible events you have just gone through. Your poor mother . . .'

Maro gave a start and pulled her hands from his grip. Her cheeks flushed and she barely managed to contain the fury that welled up inside her.

Riza Bey's voice became even more vibrant, 'Contrary to what you may think, I have nothing to do with those who want your people to disappear. This is a decision of the government and, like everyone else, I have no choice but to obey, even though I love your people and I respect their faith.'

His arguments calmed Maro a little and he continued more confidently,

'I've taken in seven or eight Armenians as servants. Entire families live safely on my properties. I've done all I can for my Armenian friends. Now that I am governor, I'll be able to help them even more. But you must understand that my means are limited. If I do too much, I will be relieved of my post and my successor might well be a cruel and faithless man.'

His words disturbed Maro. She no longer knew what to think.

Riza took her hands in his again and almost pleaded, 'Please, Maro, don't confuse me with your enemies. Rather see me as a friend who protects you, as a relative who has taken you in. See the walls of my house as ramparts that prevent the storm which is raging outside from touching you.'

There was sincerity in his face and the warmth of his gaze made him look even more handsome, but Maro also saw in his eyes such hunger that she felt threatened.

She fended it off by asking a question that showed her distrust. 'Why such concern for me?'

He pretended not to have understood and she repeated the question. Riza Bey let go of her hands and shrugged. He smiled like a worried child and started to pace, marking his words with wide sweeps of his hands, 'Why do you always want to pin a name to everything? Does the brook ask itself why it runs towards the plain? Does the cloud worry about the way the wind is blowing? I obey the leanings of my soul without asking myself about divine intentions. You must learn to abandon yourself to the designs of God.'

'We have a saying – God helps those who help themselves.'

He smiled impishly. 'But one still has to know when to stop struggling and leave matters to God.'

Riza's steps had taken him to the door of the sitting-room where a second lamp was burning. Seeing that Tomas was not asleep, he walked over to the divan.

'Is my talking keeping you awake?' he asked gently.

'No.'

Riza Bey spoke slowly so the child, who barely knew Turkish, would understand him. 'Did you eat well?'

'Yes.'

The man sat on the edge of the divan, lifted the mosquito netting, and stroked Tomas lightly on the cheek with the backs of his fingers. 'I've been telling your mother, you are among friends here. No one can hurt you anymore.'

'Yes,' replied Tomas, still on his guard.

'I've noticed that you like horses.'

Tomas said nothing but his eyes betrayed his sudden interest.

'Do you know how to ride?'

'Yes.'

His eagerness amused Riza Bey. 'I have a big stable. If you want to, you can accompany my sons on horseback.'

Tomas nodded spontaneously. Riza tousled his hair, murmuring affectionately, 'Good night, my boy.'

'Good night.'

Satisfied that the child no longer showed his dislike, Riza returned to the other room. Maro went to kiss her son while Riza waited for her in the corridor, which was lit by gas sconces. When she came out to join him, he held out an emerald necklace.

'Something for you.'

Maro stepped back involuntarily. 'Oh, no.'

'It's a gift for you.'

'I can't accept it.'

He insisted, 'Just to please me?'

'Thank you very much, Riza Bey, but I must say no.'

'To refuse a gift is not done.'

She stood firm. He looked her straight in the eyes and his smile took on a sardonic twist. 'Are you afraid that I might expect something in return?'

She was at a loss for words. He seemed upset and his voice filled with emotion, 'If I want to adorn you in jewels, it's only to erase the first image I have of you – sprawled out on the ground, filthy and miserable, and surrounded by a bunch of men preparing to rape you.'

Maro grimaced involuntarily when she remembered.

Riza Bey continued, 'I'm revolted by that memory too. There was such a look of despair in your eyes that it still distresses me. Please erase that scene from my memory. Be beautiful.' He put the necklace around Maro's neck and fastened the clasp.

She permitted him to do it but said it firmly, 'Of course, you understand that I shall return it when I leave.'

Ignoring her comment, Riza invited her to follow him. At the end of the corridor, beside Buyuk Hanim's apartments, a spiral staircase descended to the garden. The women used it to go outside without putting on their veils, as they would have had to if they had gone through the ground floor.

Riza Bey appeared, silks rustled and jewellery jingled as all the women except Buyuk Hanim rose. They were bedecked with sparkling rings, bracelets and necklaces. The vanilla-like scent of the heliotrope perfumed the arbour. Buyuk Hanim smiled as Maro kissed her hand.

'My respects, Buyuk Hanim. And a thousand blessings on you for your hospitality.'

'Your presence honours our table, my daughter,' replied the old woman with stilted politeness.

Maro was surprised at her change in attitude and her nervousness subsided. The welcome of the wives, the nurse and especially Shahané was warmer. Even Leyla was charming, although she was secretly appraising Maro's beauty because she regarded her as a rival. After her husband's tongue-lashing, she had decided to change tactics. She would not let her jealousy show, but instead deploy all her charm to reconquer Riza's heart.

'Come and sit down next to me,' she said to Maro, pointing to an empty chair she had reserved for her on her left. That way, Riza would not be able to admire the Armenian without looking at Leyla too, and she was convinced that her youth gave her the advantage.

A musician was waiting in the back, holding a *saz*[1] in her arms. At Riza's signal she began to play folk airs. From the kitchen a servant brought the *hors-d'œuvres*: dried meats with garlic, pickled vegetables, dried mackerel in olive oil, stuffed vine leaves and aubergine. The moment a dish was emptied, it was replaced by another. They ate slowly, trying a bit of this and a bit of that, being careful not to overindulge, as the meal would last for hours. The pleasures of being together and partaking in conversation were as important as the food to everyone except Makbulé, who had starved all day. Riza Bey sat among the women of his household like a lord surrounded by his court. Witty and charming, he spoke at length, his tone lofty and his gestures broad.

Although they all, each in turn, tried to draw her into the conversation, Maro felt out of place. Riza Bey, who already knew a great deal about her, asked a lot of questions to give her an opportunity to shine. Maro, however, was weary of joining in this game but her brief responses fooled neither Riza nor Safiyé. The first wife watched each of Maro's gestures intently, drinking in her every word with an attentiveness and curiosity that Maro found perplexing. Safiyé took advantage of a rare moment of silence and leaned towards Maro and said, 'Tell me, you who have travelled so much, when

---

1.   A string instrument (Turkish).

you go great distances, is it possible to see that the earth is round?'

The other two wives and Shahané sniggered. Irritated, Safiyé confided to Maro, 'Riza Bey had the same reaction when I asked him.'

'You have the curiosity of a child,' rebuked Buyuk Hanim.

Safiyé waited for Maro to speak.

'No matter how far one travels, the earth always looks like a flat disk surmounted by a dome.' The first wife's disappointed look saddened Maro. She remembered one of the geography lessons a nun had taught her and added, 'Except at the seaside. When a ship sails towards the shore, you first see the smoke, then the smokestacks and the masts and finally the hull. That is proof that the earth is round.' She picked up a peach and a dried date, and used them to illustrate the phenomenon, one representing the earth and the other the ship.

Safiyé beamed. 'Ah,' she said, looking at her companions triumphantly, 'I'm not as naive as you think.'

Buyuk Hanim shrugged her shoulders and said, 'You've taken a giant step forward. One more item of useless information to stuff in your head.'

Safiyé was so happy that she laughed at her mother-in-law's acerbic remark and winked at Maro conspiratorially.

The conversation moved on to other subjects and Maro lost interest. Soon the voices seemed so distant. What was she doing under this vine-covered roof with these people with whom she had absolutely nothing in common? She felt overwhelmed and everything seemed unreal. She closed her eyes and saw once more the agonized face of her mother. She shut out the image, but others began speeding past in her mind – Vartan, their house in Sivas, her father walking down a street in Constantinople, Araksi lying dead on Armen's grave and the cavern resounding with death rattles. She felt faint and opened her eyes again to find Riza watching her anxiously. She smiled to show she was all right.

The moon had risen and the nearby minaret stood out against the star-studded sky. One could now discern the encircling garden wall between the branches. Were they really protecting walls, as Riza Bey had assured her? To Maro they were the walls only of a prison. Bits of the conversation she had had with Riza Bey came back to her. He had avoided committing himself to organizing her departure for the capital and she was in no position to demand anything. One thing was certain – for the moment, she and Tomas were safe from the deportation and she had better not jeopardize their safety. Riza's attraction to her was another thing in her favour. He probably had no desire to see her depart but, on the other hand, he would not want to disappoint her. She thought of Eminé words: 'A clever woman gets what she wants.' The idea of using Riza's feelings towards her repelled Maro. Besides, it was a risky game.

A servant advised the master of the house that his guests had arrived. He left the table to go join the men in the *selamlik* with whom he would celebrate part of the night.

An hour before dawn a distant rumble like thunder at the edge of the horizon sounded in Ayntab. It was answered immediately by a drum roll in the courtyard of Riza Bey's house. Everywhere people were being awakened so they could eat and drink before another day of fasting began. Maro tried to fall back to sleep but a few minutes later a servant knocked on the door. The girl had black braids and big, dark eyes.

'Good morning, *Hanim*. Do you want to go down to the dining room or be served up here?'

She was searching her words and pronounced them awkwardly. She must be the Armenian girl Eminé mentioned, Maro thought.

'What's your name?'

'Ayla.'

'Your real name?' asked Maro in Armenian.

The girl's little, pointed face turned red and she looked anxiously over her shoulder. Maro took her arm and led her inside. 'Don't be afraid. I'm an Armenian like you.'

'I know,' replied the young girl quietly, 'but . . .' Her fear was obvious; guiltily she murmured, 'Vartouhi.'

Maro felt sorry for her and stopped questioning. 'Bring me something to eat.'

A quarter of an hour later the servant returned carrying a tray, which she set on a low table by the window.

'Sit down, Vartouhi,' said Maro, squatting on a cushion. She spoke softly in Armenian but the servant girl seemed terrified.

'I can't, *Diguin*.'

'No one will know.' Maro insisted and Vartouhi reluctantly obeyed. Maro invited her to help herself from the dishes but she did so only after much urging.

'Why are you afraid?'

'I don't want to be sent away. Here I have food to eat and a corner to sleep in.'

'Where are you from?'

'Balou.'

'Where's that?'

'Very far away, east of Kharput. I lost my whole family.'

She did not have to go on. Maro could well imagine the ordeals this girl had suffered. They exchanged a long look, which eventually became charged with more and more emotion. Trembling, Vartouhi bit her lips. She resisted when Maro tried to take her in her arms even though she was dying to be a little girl again, consoled by her mother. Those days were gone forever; behind her there was only death and desolation.

'May I leave now? They'll be worrying about me in the kitchen.'

'Yes. Thank you . . . Ayla.'

The young girl was relieved to hear the woman use her Turkish name.

Life moved on in an apparently unchanging rhythm in Governor Riza's large mansion on the outskirts of Ayntab. The days flowed slowly, each alike. The other children won Tomas over and he made friends with Kenan and Emel, who were more or less his age. Riza Bey gave him a horse so that he could accompany his two friends on their rounds of Riza's lands, guided by Abdullah. In Tomas's mind this little piebald horse was a link to his pony, Gaydzag, and blotted out the period in between. Tomas had had another dream about Vartan and in it his father had repeated that Tomas should wait for him. The dream had given Tomas an unshakeable faith in the future. Strengthened by that faith, he played through the days with that heedlessness that only children are capable of.

Maro encouraged him in this, even though it made her feel more alone. She only wished to get to the capital as quickly as possible, but the necessary arrangements depended completely on Riza. As she shared the status of his wives, she could not leave the house any more than they could. Except during the month of Ramadan, they visited the *hammam* every week, and would spend all day in the company of the other women of Ayntab; otherwise, theirs was a life of seclusion. Musicians, jugglers, bear-trainers and a master of the *karagoez* (shadow theatre) were brought to the *konak* and the women enjoyed these entertainments as much as the children. However, these pastimes were not enough to fill the endless hours of the day.

Riza Bey was so absorbed in his functions as governor he had neglected to send a telegram to Uncle Mesrop. When she brought up the subject, he would reply, 'Trust me. I'm waiting for the right moment. Be like Tomas, Maro, and enjoy the hospitality of my house. Who knows what tomorrow will bring?'

Except when he was away from Ayntab, Riza Bey did not let a day pass without spending several hours with Maro. He multiplied the number of his gifts and she could not refuse them. He was always polite and more and more attentive. One evening he invited her to go for a walk with him, something she had tried at all costs to avoid.

'I want to show you the place where I used to go to dream when I was young,' he told her.

It was the first time that Maro had left the mansion since she had arrived. After they went through the portal guarded by two armed men, they turned right and passed in front of the mosque. The wind from the desert had dropped and become less stifling. The full moon gave the olive leaves a silvery sheen and painted bluish shadows at their feet. Riza Bey led Maro on to a path that cut through a pistachio plantation. He explained that his family had cultivated these trees for more than two centuries and had exported pistachios all over Asia Minor.

The ground became rockier and Riza Bey offered Maro his arm. She pretended not to notice and quickened her steps. After walking for a quarter of an hour, they reached the crest of the hill where a twisted pine tree stood against a rock as tall as a man. There was a crevice in the rock: a place to sit.

'I used to pretend this was a throne which had belonged to an ancient king. Look, it's all there: the high back, the armrests and a footstool.'

He struck the trunk of the pine with the flat of his hand. 'I planted this tree more than forty years ago. You know, I've never shown this place to anyone else. It's my secret corner.'

Riza Bey seemed to attach such importance to this place that Maro did not want to disappoint him and explored the rock with her fingertips.

'Sit on the throne and see how fine the view is.'

She sat on the still-warm stone. The turpentine smell of the tree flooded over her. Below her stretched out a shadowy plain, crossed by the Injirli River, its twists and turns glittering in the moonlight. On the left were the three hills of Ayntab. Lights shone in the houses where people were still celebrating the lifting of the fast. In the distance, dogs called to each other.

Riza Bey's white clothing formed a pale splash against the dark mass of the pine. He murmured confidentially, 'When I was a child, I used to think I'd become a king the day the throne became a perfect fit for me and that all the land down there would belong to me.'

He swept his arm to include the horizon and then laughed. 'To make my dream come true, I had to buy it all. Everything you see from here to the river is mine.'

'It must be wonderful to have your dreams come true,' said Maro, as she got to her feet.

He put up a hand to stop her. 'Please, stay there. Put your arms on the armrests and rest your head. The throne suits you marvellously. Don't move.'

Riza Bey came near and removed her veil. He took out a diadem from his robes, set it on Maro's head and stepped back to admire her. She played his game reluctantly. With pinched lips she stared at the horizon. The cold light of the moon made her young face look like marble and set the stones of the diadem aglow.

'A queen!' Riza Bey was ecstatic. 'A real queen!'

He went down on one knee before her, brought one of her feet to his lips, kissed the instep and said, 'My queen!' Maro pulled her foot away quickly. Riza stood up and declared, 'I love you, Maro. I've loved you from the first day I saw you.'

'No!' she protested, trying to break away.

He gently pushed her back on to the seat. 'Listen to me, Maro.'

'I don't want to listen to anything!'

'Let me speak,' he insisted firmly.

She raised her voice, 'Riza Bey! You know that I belong to another man.'

'That doesn't change the fact that I love you and want you to be happy.'

'I can be happy only with Vartan.'

'You can't stop me from loving you.' He spread his arms in a gesture of helplessness and complained, 'I'm crazy about you and nothing can change it.'

'There is a way. Let me leave as soon as possible.'

Riza Bey stepped back a few steps to contemplate the valley. His tall silhouette blocked part of the view. His elegant profile stood out against the lights in Ayntab like a figure in a shadow play. It shook Maro up. She had been dreading this moment for several days and had been preparing herself for it. Still, it wasn't easy to reject this man to whom she and her son owed their lives. Above all, it was important to save his self-respect.

'Please try to understand, Riza Bey. It has nothing to do with you. My heart already belongs to another.'

He turned to her and said in a voice resonant with emotion, 'I know all that and I'm not asking for your love. Just let me love you, Maro, knowing that my feelings will never be returned. Let me cherish you and spoil you with gifts.'

'Riza Bey,' she answered sweetly, 'you're putting me in an impossible situation. I know that I am causing pain to the generous man who saved me from certain death.'

He pressed his hand to his heart and leaned towards her. He had his back to the moon and it was hard for Maro to distinguish his features. Suddenly she felt his breath on her face.

'How could I suffer if I expect nothing from you? Only a little tenderness, a little friendship, a little affection. A few days, a few weeks; it's so little if you consider all the years of your life, and it means so much to me – to me, who will love you to the end of my days. You wouldn't be so cruel as to refuse me a few crumbs of happiness.'

Maro didn't know how to respond to his beseeching voice.

Riza Bey continued with typical oriental lyricism, 'Don't say anything. It would shatter my dreams; I can feel it! Don't let your gentle voice, my divine *houri*, destroy the joy that swells my heart. Let my eyes drink in your silent beauty so that it may ravish my soul.'

Panic-stricken, she lowered her eyes. 'Let's go back,' she suggested.

'Not yet,' he answered, when she tried to return the diadem. Satisfied that she had stopped protesting, he offered his hand and helped her up.

'Very well, let's go back, if that's what you want – in silence to savour the magic of this night.'

Holding her hand, he guided her on to the road home. It was far from silent. Anyone who had ears to hear could not fail to be deafened by the buzzing and humming of a million insects and the rustling of the dried grasses. A rabbit bolted, an owl hooted, a branch cracked; flushed by the passing strollers, a partridge clucked.

Riza Bey was exultant. He had finally opened his heart to Maro and from now on he would be able to give free rein to his feelings. Perhaps because of the place, so laden with memories for him, and the way he felt about this woman – love tinged with admiration – Riza felt like the romantic adolescent he had once been. The years seemed to have melted away and he was living a new beginning. With her, he wouldn't hesitate to be his true self and in their intimacy, he would be able to put aside the mask of the hard, intransigent man he wore as a leader of men.

As Maro walked ahead of him down the narrowing path, Riza Bey was seized by overwhelming desire. He became a male animal tracking a female. He put his hands on Maro's waist. She tried to free herself but he put an arm around her and pulled her body against his. It was a silent, unequal fight. Every movement she made, in her attempts to break away, incited the man to tighten his grip, to clasp her more tightly to him.

'Riza Bey . . .' she begged.

Deaf to her pleading, he lifted her hair and kissed her nape and nibbled on her neck. He panted as his feverish hands ran over her body. Still she fought, but she was no match for his strength. He turned her head and his mouth searched for hers. Her resistance only increased his passion. He lifted her up and laid her on the rough ground, immobilizing her under his weight. In his haste to remove her clothes, he tore one of the panels of her dress. Realizing that fighting was useless, she let him have his way. When he penetrated her, she let out a long sigh which sounded more like a groan. Once he was in her, he covered her with his body and remained still for a long while. He held her wrists and kissed her, feverishly whispering words of love. Maro relaxed little by little and only then did Riza's loins begin to move slowly.

'Let yourself go. You know you want me. Your body doesn't lie.'

She turned her head aside, her nose in a tuft of bruised thyme. Heady from its haunting aroma, she wept very quietly.

# NINE

The massive silhouette of a volcano with its eroded peak appeared before Vartan's eyes. A frayed crown of snow made the crater look as if streams of white lava were flowing down its sides. Mount Argaeus![1] He had made it! To the north of this mountain lay Caesarea, barely forty kilometres away. That was nothing compared to the three hundred he had already travelled.

According to the angle of the sun, it must be the middle of the afternoon, Vartan thought. He sat down under the shade of a boulder. Although he was soaked in sweat, his teeth were chattering. He had been suffering from regular bouts of fever, which lasted from one to two hours and left him weak and thirsty. The wound on his thigh wasn't healing well and the infection was spreading throughout his body. He would have to wait for Anthony Black, the head of the American School in Caesarea, to give him some medicine, always supposing that Anthony had not been forced to leave town.

Vartan was disheartened. His horse, Yildiz, had broken a leg on the fourth day of his journey. He had had to shoot him and then had been forced to continue on foot – almost three weeks of walking, walking away from the region where undoubtedly Maro and Tomas were.

After spending three days in the Swiss orphanage, he had left Malatya during the night, trusting Miss Langlet to send off the letters and articles he had written. The surveillance in the town and its immediate surroundings had slackened, but the army and the guards controlled all the roads. Vartan had taken to the high plateau, which stretched out towards the northern part of the Taurus Mountains.

Punctuated with easily scaled summits, incised with valleys, the steppe

---

1.   The highest mountain in the Middle East; present-day Erciyas.

unfolded its majestic landscapes, where solitary eagles flew. Small brooks ran towards the Mediterranean. In some places, flocks of sheep grazed on a rocky slope. To the south-east the mountains piled up endlessly on each other like gigantic steps. Their blurred reddish-bronze and green colours changed from rose to lavender, until they melted into the blue of the sky.

Vartan leaned against the boulder and scanned the gently undulating plain spread out in front of him. Vineyards on a hillside, apple orchards on a slope, rows of Lombardy poplars and the small golden rectangle of a barley field showed that the region was inhabited. He searched for a roof, a farmhouse where he could ask for shelter. As he was dirty, unshaven and dressed in a torn uniform, he could arouse suspicion in Caesarea and be questioned. It would be better for him to make himself a bit more presentable. There was no house in sight, but a slight movement caught his eye: a peasant at work.

The wound in his thigh caused him a stabbing pain with each step. Limping, he began to walk again. Half an hour later he came to the edge of a ploughed field, where a man was holding on to the shaft of a wooden cart pulled by a couple of lazy oxen. He wore the usual Anatolian peasant's outfit – a pink shirt, faded baggy cotton trousers and leather sandals called *chariks*. A twelve-year-old boy walked alongside the animals, hitting them occasionally with a long switch. The child spotted the visitor and told the man, who stopped the team.

'*Eyvallah hemsheri*,' he shouted.

'Greetings to you too, my friend,' responded Vartan.

The sturdy, stocky peasant dried his hairy hands on his trousers. A groove of an old scar ran down his left cheek. The stubble of his bushy beard gave his chin a bluish tint and a thick moustache hid half of his mouth. Vartan's dishevelled appearance made the man look at him distrustfully.

'Are you hurt?'

'Yes, and I've been walking for days.'

The peasant's eyes under his black, bushy eyebrows looked shifty. 'What are you doing around here?'

'My company was attacked by infidels in the mountains. I'm the only one who got away.'

The peasant was still suspicious. He rubbed his stomach, which brought his hand closer to the holster on his belt.

To reassure him, Vartan touched his stripes. 'Don't worry! I'm not a deserter. I'm Lieutenant Akdar on my way to Caesarea to report to my Colonel.'

'Do you have anything to show who you are?'

Vartan handed over his orders. The farmer unfolded the paper and examined it, holding it upside-down. 'I don't know how to read.'

This was just what Vartan had counted on, because the name on the orders was Shakir Ismael. He pointed to a line written in Arabic script and to the seal of Halit Pasha.

'Look here. This is the name of the Sultan.'

'What's his name?'

'You mean you don't know?' Vartan acted surprised.

Thinking that the Lieutenant was reproaching him for his ignorance about the Sultan, the peasant burst out laughing. 'I don't have a very good memory. I even forget the names of my own children.'

'Do you have many?'

The man swelled with pride and held up nine fingers.

'How many wives?'

That number he knew. 'Two,' he answered, 'and you?'

'Four! As the Prophet allows.'

The peasant was impressed. One had to be rich to keep that many women. 'My name is Suleiman Karabiyik.[1] Come home with me and get some rest.'

'Gladly! God bless you, Suleiman.'

The farmer's son had gone to look for a jug under a thorny bush. Instead of drinking from it, the peasant poured the contents over his head and splashed his face. Vartan found this very strange.

'Is the water pure? Can I drink it?' he asked, when Suleiman handed him the jug.

The latter frowned, startled, and looked at Vartan suspiciously again. 'What do you mean, drink? It's Ramadan.'

Vartan corrected his blunder hastily. 'I thought it was over. I must have lost count of the days.'

This answer satisfied the peasant. In spite of his parched throat, Vartan had to content himself with refreshing his neck and forehead only. The farmer left his son in charge of the oxen and led his visitor to the farm. On the way, he noticed that Vartan was shaking.

'You're trembling.'

---

1. Black moustache (Turkish).

'It's only a little fever.'

'Maybe you have malaria.'

'No. It's because of a wound in my thigh.'

'You're wrong. It's malaria. I've had it, and one of my sons too. My second wife is the only person in the region who knows how to cure malaria. You couldn't have fallen into better hands. Allah must have sent you to me.'

Vartan thought it wiser not to insist on the cause of his illness. It was much better if the man was convinced that they had met by divine guidance. The whole attitude of the farmer had changed; he put his arm around Vartan's shoulder and his voice became friendly. 'You should have drunk some of the water. The sick don't have to fast. The moment we get home, you can eat and drink all you want.'

'Could I wash and shave, too? And if you have a needle and some thread, I could mend my uniform. Just look at me! Me! A lieutenant in the Ottoman Army! I would be ashamed to present myself like this to my superiors. I have some money to pay you.'

'Money!' the peasant was outraged. 'Suleiman Karabiyik's hospitality cannot be paid for with money. It's given freely as the Prophet teaches!'

'Forgive me. I didn't mean to offend you.'

Suleiman smiled broadly and made a sign that all was forgotten. They passed by a field where women and children were harvesting the wheat with sickles.

'Those are mine,' said Suleiman, indicating the field and the workers with a sweep of his hand.

Boastfully, he pointed to another stony green field, an olive grove, a cornfield and an irrigated vegetable garden. He beat his chest. 'And I don't rent that land from an *agha* either. It all belongs to me and my brother, Nazim.'

He went on telling Vartan about the animals they owned: two oxen, one heifer, a she-ass and her little one and several sheep, goats and chickens. Suleiman was a rich man by Anatolian standards. The farm consisted of a large stable, behind which there were three high haystacks and two adobe houses standing side by side. Suleiman pointed to the one on the left, which had tiny latticed windows.

'That's the harem, where my wives and my brother's wives live.'

Two children, less than three years old, were playing in front of the door to the harem, next to some sleepy hens that were sitting in nests they had dug out of the dusty soil. In the shadow of the stable, the she-ass, with her little one between her legs, panted, staring at the fields. The appetizing aroma of baking bread mixed with the stench of dung.

Suleiman pushed Vartan into the house on the right, which had only one room. Two-thirds of the earthen floor was covered by hay mattresses and saddle blankets. The thick walls kept the room relatively cool. Still standing in the doorway, the peasant called to the other house.

'Aysha! Aysha!'

He seated his guest and served him some *raki* in a little tin cup. He would have given anything to have one himself, followed by two cigarettes, but he resisted the temptation; he would wait for sundown.

'May you live long and sire many children,' Vartan said by way of a toast.

'Thank you.'

A woman came in. She wore a short, pale-green dress over a pink *shalvar* and sheep-skin slippers. Her head and face were covered by a white *yashmak*, but her almond-shaped eyes, thick eyebrows and long eyelashes revealed her Circassian traits. She examined Vartan curiously.

'Bring something to eat and drink for my guest.'

She hesitated. Had she misunderstood? 'What about Ramadan?'

'This officer is ill,' explained Suleiman. 'He's not obliged to fast. Come and look at him. You need to take care of him. I'm sure he has malaria.'

She went and bent over him, laid her cinnamon-tinted hand on Vartan's forehead and paused a moment. He could feel her moist palm tremble slightly. Then she lifted his eyelid with her forefinger and thumb but, instead of examining his eyeballs as she was pretending to do, she looked directly and without shame into his face.

'It's malaria!' she said to her husband. 'I'll give him the treatment.'

She left and Suleiman beamed. 'People come from all over for her to heal them.'

'Do you think she could do anything for my wound?' asked Vartan, touching his aching leg.

'No. Aysha has the gift only for malaria. You'll see. In three days, you'll have recovered all your strength.'

'But I must leave tonight.'

Suleiman was taken aback. 'That's out of the question. You'll rest in my house for a while. Never let it be said that I let one of our brave officers take to the road while he was still sick.'

His small, crafty eyes searched his guest's. Suleiman was smarter than he looked. Vartan could not refuse his hospitality and the useless treatment without offending him and awakening his suspicions.

'I'm deeply touched by your generosity,' Vartan said, taking some gold coins out of his pocket. 'Since you don't want my money, would you please make an offering in the mosque in my name?'

The peasant grinned, showing his tobacco-stained teeth, and pocketed the coins. This officer was truly a man of quality.

Aysha brought in a copper tray, with some still-warm bread, some apricots and *ayran* in an earthenware pot. She and her husband retired, while Vartan ate heartily. Suleiman returned shortly after with a razor, a small piece of grey soap and a jug of water. He carried a pair of folded trousers and a shirt over his arm.

'Take off your uniform. The women will clean and mend it. Sewing is not a man's job.'

Vartan undressed and Suleiman winced when he saw the blackish bruise on Vartan's right thigh.

'It looks worse than it really is,' Vartan said in a detached tone.

He was really worried about his wound. The lips of the purple cut gaped open. The scab was cracked and filled with pus. The whole leg was so swollen that his boot felt tight. The wound needed cleaning and disinfecting, before it was bandaged.

'Do you have any alcohol?' Suleiman pointed at the bottle of *raki* left on the ground.

'I mean the kind of alcohol that is used in the burners.'

'No. Do you want me to get the village fortune-teller? He'll make an amulet for you.'

'That won't be necessary. The army surgeon will fix it up in no time when I get to Caesarea.'

'You know more about that than I do. I'm going back to the fields. Try to get some sleep until the evening prayers. I've invited some friends to break the fast and I'd like you to join us.'

'I'd be flattered.'

Suleiman left. Vartan shaved, washed and lay down in his underwear on one of the straw mattresses at the end of the room. He closed his eyes briefly but opened them almost immediately when he heard light steps approaching. It was Aysha. Vartan reached for his trousers lying next to him.

'Don't worry,' said Aysha. 'I won't stay long.'

263

She came up quickly and knelt by Vartan's side. The veil that was covering her head slid down on her shoulders, leaving her face uncovered. Her fleshy lips pouted. She shrugged her shoulders, as if answering an inner reproach, but she didn't cover herself again.

Aysha was just twenty. She was very much aware of her beauty and hated having to conceal it after her marriage four years before. She missed the covetous looks she used to inspire in men and was bored on this isolated farm, which she rarely left. How she missed the feasts, the hustle and bustle of the mountain village where she was born, where friends met and talked to each other at the wells. Aysha felt old already. Suleiman didn't look at her anymore. She was only another possession to him, neither more nor less than any other animal in his herd. If he ever found out that she had taken off her veil in front of a stranger, he would beat her until she spat blood. Too bad! She was going to take the risk anyhow. She needed so much to feel beautiful in a man's eyes.

'Here's the medicine for your malaria,' she said, showing him a fresh egg. She broke the shell with her fingernail and removed the small fragments. So great was her dexterity that she removed the shell without breaking the membrane that contained the white and the yolk. Then she pierced a hole and let the contents flow on to a plate. She dipped the empty pouch for a moment in lemon juice. Since Vartan was a pharmacist, he was curious about folk remedies and watched the operation with amusement.

'Give me your left hand,' she said.

She touched his palm lightly and was astounded. She had never known a man whose hand was not calloused, and this lieutenant's hand was smooth, almost soft, a sign that he had never worked with his hands. A rich man's hand! What did he think of her? Did he notice her beauty? Aysha could read nothing in his inscrutable face. She rolled the membrane of the egg around his little finger.

'There,' she said, holding his hand.

'Is that all?'

'Yes. Let it dry in place. It will hurt, but you will get well.'

'Thank you, *Hanim*,' said Vartan, withdrawing his hand putting it on his thigh.

'Do you need anything else, Lieutenant?'

He shook his head. The young woman refused to leave until he told her that he would like to sleep. Then she put on her veil and left the house. He fell asleep at once.

The pain woke him an hour later. The membrane had hardened and was strangling his finger like a noose. His hand was swollen and the pain was spreading all over his body. He tried to tear off the dry membrane.

'No!' Aysha cried out.

He was startled, as he had not realized she was there. She caught Vartan's hand, but it was too late. He had already torn the membrane with his nails.

She reproached him, 'You shouldn't have done that. You have to wait for it to crack and fall off by itself, if you want to get well.'

She crouched next to Vartan, her face still uncovered. Her enigmatic smile made her beautiful young face look arrogant. Uneasy, Vartan glanced at the door furtively.

'Everyone's out in the fields,' said Aysha reassuringly.

'Have you been here long?'

'I've been watching you sleep. You sleep very deeply.'

She pretended to be taking his temperature by putting her palm on his forehead. It felt like a caress and he shook off her hand and sat up.

'I'm much better,' he said coolly, 'thank you.'

'You're still sick. We must repeat the treatment tomorrow.'

He certainly didn't feel like repeating the painful treatment. 'That won't be necessary, *Hanim*.'

'Suleiman will be angry if I don't cure your malaria.'

He could hear the fear in the young woman's voice, but he also detected a nuance of irony. Vartan suspected that she knew he did not have malaria. She looked at him intently, with a strange expression on her face he could not define, but her familiar attitude displeased him. Suleiman was probably very touchy about his wife's honour. Vartan started to put on the trousers his host had lent him, but stopped when he noticed a brown pack on his thigh.

'What's that?'

'It's mud and goat's dung. It heals wounds,' Aysha replied.

He winced, thinking about the danger of tetanus. He stood up to allow the mixture of earth and excrement to fall off. Then he rinsed the wound with the water that was left in the jug. He must have been really deeply asleep not to have felt anything when she put the pack on. One of the buttons on his drawers was open. Could it be that . . .? He looked sharply at Aysha, who had covered her face with her veil, so all he could see were her almond-shaped eyes with their half-closed lids. She bowed and left.

265

The sun was touching the horizon when Suleiman returned with a man and introduced him as his brother, Nazim. They were both exactly the same size. Nazim regarded Vartan suspiciously and remained reserved. A little later three boys, aged fourteen to sixteen, arrived. Night fell, and the barely audible cry of the muezzin from a neighbouring village modulated through the still of the evening: 'Allahu Akbar, God is great. Allahu Akbar. Allahu Akbar. There is no other God but Allah. Come and pray. Come and pray. Come and pray. Allahu Akbar. Allahu Akbar. Allahu Akbar.' Even to the ears of a Christian, these noble words evoked the presence of God. This powerful call asked all souls to share in the mysterious spring of life, and Vartan gave no impression of acting or pretence when he turned towards Mecca with the others and imitated their gestures, while he prayed privately.

When night fell, they spread straw mattresses out in an irregular circle in the gravelled yard and lit a bonfire in the middle. As the guests arrived, Suleiman and Nazim greeted them warmly with hugs, kisses and good wishes. Suleiman introduced Vartan to them very formally: Burhanettin, the coppersmith; *Tek-Geoz* Sedat, the baker, whose first name meant that he had only one eye; Osman, the muleteer, who transported charcoal from village to village; Nazim's brother-in-law, and two farmers from the surrounding lands, *Sarilik* Sitki and *Beli Kirik* Rahmi.[1] Their raven-black mustaches, their sunbaked faces, their lopsided fezzes perched on their shaven heads and their white shirts, belted in with wide wool sashes, made them all look alike. The last guest, the cantor of the Quran, *Hafiz* Shevfik, was bald and nearly blind. Around his lips his white beard was stained yellow from the smoke of the cigarettes he rolled with remarkable speed, without losing one shred of tobacco.

They stretched out while the women brought in bottles of *raki*, jugs of water and platters of food. Suleiman and his brother were doing things in style. There was grilled lamb, fried aubergine, rice pilaf, stuffed peppers and tomatoes and garlic-flavoured yoghurt.

At Suleiman's insistence, Vartan gave a detailed account of the rebel attack on his company and how he, the only survivor, had played dead to escape. For days, as he travelled across the steppe, he had eaten only roots and bulbs, digging them up with his hands. The men listened to the tale with childlike absorption and were wide-eyed with wonder. A few put in some acid comments about the Sultan's war. They did not really understand what it was all about but they did know that on account of the war the

---

1. Literally jaundiced Sitki and split-back Rahmi (Turkish).

army regularly requisitioned rations from them. Then the conversation turned to the usual topics, the prices of produce and lewd stories. Vartan listened to the conversation absent-mindedly. The party became livelier as the guests ate and drank. These illiterate men knew nothing of life outside their province and lived in such a state of blissful ignorance that Vartan envied them.

In the middle of the night, three young men left the banquet and came back wearing cartridge belts across their chests and a rifle hanging from their shoulders. They said goodbye to the guests and disappeared into the night.

In answer to Vartan's question, Suleiman explained, 'They'll guard the farm until dawn and will shoot any prowler on sight. Lately we've been attacked several times.'

'Attacked?'

'Yes, by infidels or deserters, wanting to steal our cattle.'

'It happened on my place too,' added one of the other farmers.

Nazim cut him short by raising his glass, 'Let's drink and leave serious things for tomorrow.'

The others followed his lead and the party livened up again. Vartan had thought about getting away during the night, while his hosts were asleep, but the presence of armed boys in the fields made him change his mind.

Suleiman looked around at his friends, who were having such a good time and was filled with pride – so much drink and food. He thought of the rich harvest his fields produced, his women in the harem, his children growing strong, the new tunic and robe he had just bought, the pilgrimage to Mecca he would make after the war.

Rejoicing in his good fortune, he exclaimed, 'Allah, we live in a paradise filled with blessings! Sing for us, *Hafiz*. Sing a long song for us.'

The old man gulped down some water, wiped his mouth on his sleeve and took several deep breaths. His deep, pure voice rang out. The men stopped eating and stared into the fire. Every time the melody moved their hearts, they murmured the word *'aman, aman'*, an exclamation of joy. Vartan was filled with longing. The old man seemed to be in a trance. He sang reverently, first in Arabic and then in Turkish. Nazim brought Hafiz Shevfik an *oud* but he put the instrument on the ground and excused himself.

'My fingers are stiff from working in my garden all day.'

'Pass it to me. I'll try,' Vartan said.

Surprised, Nazim handed him the *oud*. Vartan laid it on his knees, tested the strings and strummed a few chords. Then he began to play a long *taksim*.[1] He quickly forgot the time and the place and his recent misfortunes and the uncertain future. The notes flew over the fields and out to the mountains, carrying him along with them.

None of the guests had ever heard the *oud* played so masterfully. At last silence fell and Hafiz Shevfik began to sing again. Later, when he stopped to catch his breath, he signalled to Vartan to take over. For a while music and song alternated, as if the two musicians were getting acquainted. Then, without consulting each other, they joined their talents together. Softly the *oud* accompanied the balladeer, and the music filled the night with sweetness. The men held their breaths, their souls touched by grace. Behind the latticed windows of the harem, the women's eyes reflected the glow of the fire. When the feast was over, Hafiz Shevfik congratulated Vartan.

'Where did you learn to play so well, Lieutenant?'

'Oudi Tartar taught me.'

'Now I understand. He's the greatest.'

'You sing divinely, Hafiz.'

'Thank you, but your *oud* did all the work.'

After everyone had left, Nazim thanked Vartan for having delighted his guests. 'You may stay with us as long as you wish,' said Suleiman, hugging him. 'I'd like to keep you for the ceremonies that mark the end of Ramadan.'

The two brothers disappeared into the harem. Vartan stayed outside watching the embers die. The short August night was already paling. He was exhausted and feverish, but he had no desire to sleep; he had just lived through an experience that he wanted to prolong. This farm lost in the hills seemed like a haven to him. A distant detonation brought him back to reality. A fugitive could not let himself be lulled by such illusions. He went in to lie down, stepping over the children lying haphazardly on the floor. He found a place on a blanket next to a little boy. As the child cuddled up to him, Vartan saw his son's face!

'Get up, you lazy-bones,' laughed Suleiman loudly. 'The sun is almost at its zenith already.'

---

1.   An improvisation on an instrument (Turkish).

Vartan opened his eyes. Suleiman was not addressing him, however, but the three youths who had been guarding the farm all night. They got up, yawning and stretching. Suleiman's own eyelids were swollen with sleep. It was customary to sleep as late as possible during the day to make the fast seem shorter; nevertheless, there were chores that could not be put off. Vartan stood up but he was weak and the fever made his head spin.

'Lie down,' Suleiman suggested. 'Aysha told me you ripped off the egg membrane too soon, so she's going to repeat the treatment.'

'I need some fresh air.'

Vartan's bad leg was so stiff, it made walking very painful. The muscles around the wound were cramping and, after taking the few steps to the door, he was exhausted. He sat down in the shade of the doorway. Suleiman bent down and examined him worriedly.

'Do you want me to notify the army to send a vehicle to fetch you?'

'Don't trouble yourself,' Vartan hastened to say. 'It's only a little fever. Malaria, maybe. Last night's party tired me out. I'll be much better after your wife's treatment.'

Suleiman nodded, 'Of course. What a party that was! My friends are going to be talking about it for a long time to come.'

The children drew near, hoping that Vartan would tell them some new tales, but Suleiman chased them away.

'Let our guest rest. Besides, we have to go to work.'

Disappointed, they joined the four women, who were waiting for them in front of the other house, and everyone went up a stony path. Nazim and the three youths came out of the stable, carrying a heavy wooden sled. They set it in the centre of the yard. One of the boys, a shotgun over his shoulder and a sickle in his hand, followed the women. Nazim and the two others led the oxen, hitched to a cart, in the opposite direction.

Suleiman and his brother had nineteen children in all, counting the eldest who was serving in the army. With these and their five wives, they had enough workers, so it was not necessary to hire outside help for the harvest. Everyone worked in the fields, except Aysha, as she was still nursing a three-month-old baby.

Aysha arrived and, under her husband's admiring eyes, she peeled the egg and rolled the membrane around the sick man's little finger. In her husband's presence, she appeared coldly distant. Vartan was inwardly furious that he could not find a way to avoid this useless, painful treatment, especially as, at that moment, the young woman, her back turned to her husband, winked at him as though they were accomplices in some plot.

'Are you sure it's malaria?' asked Suleiman.

'Of course,' she replied, without batting an eyelid.

Reassured, he laughed, shaking his index finger at Vartan, 'We shall see just how brave our officers are.'

Vartan's lips were chapped and his throat was parched. Aysha brought him some water and returned to the harem. Suleiman was preparing the sled, which they would use to thresh the wheat. It was a long wooden rectangle, curved at one end, to which a steering wheel had been fixed. They would yoke the oxen to the vehicle. The animals would pull it over the grain strewn on the ground. Stone wedges set into the underside separated the grain from the chaff. Suleiman hammered in the loose stones with a mallet and replaced the ones that were missing. Every once in a while, he paused to look at Vartan and cited some proverb or other, whose moral summed up his philosophy of life.

'The earth gives to those who love her.'

'You do the best you can and Allah takes care of the rest.'

Vartan held his finger out in the sun to hasten the drying out of the membrane. It shrank rapidly until he could feel the strangling. The pain became worse and worse. He broke out in a cold sweat and gritted his teeth to keep from crying out.

'We're still holding out,' Suleiman teased.

'Holding out,' replied Vartan, clenching his teeth.

When the other was not looking, he bent his little finger trying to make the membrane crack. Fissures appeared on the surface, but it took forever for them to go through the thickness. Finally the grip relaxed and Vartan groaned so loudly that Suleiman heard him.

'Bravo,' Suleiman said, on his way to the well. 'I've seen people faint.' He brought up a bucket full of water and poured it over his head to cool off before going out into the fields. Dripping wet, he approached Vartan.

'Try to sleep now to give the treatment a chance to act.'

He helped him up and led him inside.

'You're a good man, Suleiman.'

The peasant patted him on the shoulder. 'It's an honour to have you in my home.'

In spite of the stifling heat Vartan fell asleep. A while later, a touch on his cheek made him start. Aysha was bent over him, stroking his face. Seeing

Vartan's severe look, the young woman's unveiled face darkened briefly.

'I've prepared a linden tea for you.'

Vartan sat up, took the glass and thanked her politely, but remained on guard. Without a word she took out a piece of sugar, put it to his lips and pushed it into his mouth. This was a rare delicacy that Suleiman reserved for grand occasions only. While Vartan sipped the steaming liquid, Aysha devoured him with her eyes. Her nostrils quivered and she breathed heavily.

She rasped, 'How handsome you are.'

He choked and almost spat the liquid out on the floor.

She continued to speak to him, using the familiar form of address, *sen*.[1] 'And how do I look to you, if I may ask, Lieutenant?'

Vartan told her, 'You should leave, *Hanim*.'

She turned her head and lifted her hair. 'Look at my neck. Have you ever seen a finer one?' With a theatrical gesture she opened her bodice to show her full, round breasts with their swollen nipples. 'Look! Look at what I'm offering you!'

Vartan tried to rise but she threw herself on him with all her weight and spilled the linden tea. With her face inches away from his, she begged, 'Tell me I'm beautiful.'

'You're beautiful!' he replied impatiently. 'Now leave me alone.' He tried to push her off but she clung to him.

'Take me, my handsome lieutenant. We have all the time in the world. The little ones are asleep and the others won't be back until evening.'

'No! Your husband has been generous to me. He received me under his roof.'

'Suleiman is an oaf, who neglects me!' Her voice was full of disdain. 'I expected a different kind of life.'

Vartan realized from the sound of her voice and her look that she was unhappy. He took her by the wrists and gently pushed her away. 'Please, Aysha. Don't insist. I can't.'

She squinted and her smile was ironic. 'Don't be afraid that I'll find out you're not a Muslim. That I already know.'

Her words caught Vartan so much off-guard that he let his surprise show. Aysha burst out laughing and blushed. 'While you were asleep yesterday, I saw that you have not been circumcized.'

'It's not what you think,' Vartan retorted, looking for a plausible explanation.

---

1.   You, second person singular (Turkish).

She looked triumphant and murmured, 'I won't tell anyone that you're an infidel. It'll be our secret.'

The threat implied was quite clear, and Vartan wondered if it wouldn't be more prudent to accept her advances, but then he realized she would not hesitate to blackmail him. Trying to pretend he was not afraid, he said with a sardonic smile, 'And just how are you going to explain to Suleiman that you've seen my penis?'

For a few seconds she seemed perplexed, but then she shrugged. 'Oh, I'll find a way. He's such a simpleton that he'll believe anything I say.'

She threw a leg over Vartan and sat on his stomach. She cast modesty to the winds! She shook her shoulders to make her breasts quiver and laughed wildly. She would have never believed that she could desire a man like this. The fact that he was a *giaour* and that there was danger involved only increased her excitement.

'You have no choice,' she said assertively.

'I'm sick and wounded.'

'You don't have malaria. You have a fever because you haven't had a woman for a long time. I saw the desire in your eyes when you looked at me.'

'You're imagining things,' cried Vartan. 'It's not true!'

She turned pale with anger. 'Are you saying I'm not desirable, that I'm not good enough for you?' She bit her lip and her slanting eyes flamed.

Vartan suddenly realized that he must avoid antagonizing her. On the contrary, he must flatter her. He took her hand. 'I didn't say that, Aysha. You're very beautiful and desirable. You are everything a man could wish for.'

Soothed, she brought her lips to Vartan's, who kissed her for a long time, biting her tongue.

She lifted her head, her eyes glassy, 'No one ever did that to me before.'

He caressed her cheeks, her neck, her shoulders and her breasts. Her mouth was half-opened and she was panting.

'My beautiful Aysha. I would like to make love to you but I'm in no condition to do so. My body can't respond to my desires.'

She touched his genitals through his trousers to make sure he was telling her the truth. Disappointed, she sighed. 'Kiss me again.' After the kiss, she got up, closed her bodice and declared with assurance, 'We'll make up for it. There'll be other opportunities in the coming days.'

Vartan sat up on the straw mattress. He didn't want to disillusion her.

'I'll be yours whenever you want,' she said languorously and threw him a kiss with the tips of her fingers.

The moment he was alone, Vartan removed the shirt and trousers Suleiman had lent him. He took the uniform that was hanging on the hook on the wall. The tears were not visible any longer; the women had mended them properly. He had to get away from this farm as quickly as possible, even though he might not be able to walk for long and might even have to spend the night only a few kilometres away.

Warned by intuition, Aysha went to the window and stood on tip-toe to look in the room. With his back to the door, Vartan was putting on his trousers. He was leaving her! He was abandoning her! He had been toying with her! Her cheeks trembled with rage. She felt like screaming, but remained frozen for a few minutes, struggling with her feelings. Her body ached at the thought of never seeing this man again, of losing him before he had made love to her.

The simple act of dressing had left Vartan out of breath. Dizzy, he leaned for a long moment against the wall. It was no easier to get his boots on, since his right foot was swollen. When he put his bag over his shoulder, it felt too light. The gourd was there, along with his pistol, his dagger and his papers, but his holster was empty. Perhaps Suleiman had put his pistol away to keep it out of reach of the children. Too bad! He slid his purse and papers into the pocket of his jacket and left the house. Aysha was nowhere in sight. She must be taking care of the young ones or cooking the evening meal. The sun was midway down between its zenith and the horizon. It must be around five o'clock.

Without making any noise, Vartan went to the well, drew up a bucket of water and drank to his heart's content before filling his gourd. Just as he was putting in the stopper, a shot rang out. A bullet whistled by his head. Suleiman ran up, pointing a pistol at him.

'Don't move,' he shouted.

There was no escape! The peasant stopped at the stable. He was panting and his face was red.

He said sarcastically, 'So, you're sneaking away, Lieutenant, like a thief . . . without even saying goodbye.'

'I was just going to tell you that . . .'

'Silence, you son of a bitch!' Suleiman screamed. His face was purple, and the tendons in his neck stood out. 'Throw your bag down on the ground and come over here, you infidel dog!'

Vartan obeyed. 'Listen. Things are not like you think they are,' he protested as he drew near.

'Shut your mouth!' He ordered Vartan to stop about fifteen paces away from him and sit on the ground, out in the full sun. He looked at his prisoner with bloodshot eyes and spat at him. 'Dirty pig! You've dishonoured my house! You shall pay for that.'

Suleiman was playing with his gun and Vartan thought he would shoot him at any moment.

'I should kill you like you killed the officer you stole the uniform from.'

'That's not true,' Vartan contradicted him.

'I told you to shut up. Save your spit for the interrogation. You're a rebel, so I'm going to hand you over to the army. They'll make you talk. You'll tell them the names of your friends.'

These words told Vartan what to expect. The sun beat down on him but it was useless to ask for permission to sit in the shade. Out of the corner of his eye Vartan saw Aysha's silhouette go in the house. The slut!

They sat facing each other in silence for a long time. Vartan was trying to find a believable explanation why he was not circumcized, but he could not.

'My oldest son is risking his life fighting *giaours* like you.' Suleiman's voice indicated that his fury was giving way to dejection. He was angry at himself for having wasted his friendship on such a man but, above all, for not having been able to distinguish him from a believer. Even Hafiz Shevfik had been fooled.

'When I think that I received you like a brother!' Suleiman bemoaned.

His tone gave Vartan the feeling that perhaps all was not lost. He stretched out his hand towards Suleiman. 'I can explain. Listen to me and then you can judge.'

'Too late,' exclaimed Suleiman, as he got up.

His brother, Nazim, arrived with two gendarmes, a sergeant and a corporal, and two of his sons, both carrying shotguns. Vartan rose with difficulty. Nazim spat in his face and turned to the gendarmes. 'See, I wasn't lying to you. Here he is.'

Suleiman stepped back from the circle that had formed around the prisoner. He knew he was the victim in this affair but, curiously enough, he did not feel the thirst for vengeance he should have felt. Instead he felt sorry for this man, who had nearly become his friend. He should have killed him near the well, while his anger was still undiminished. Now he observed the

274

proceedings with detachment. The Sergeant, a man in his forties who had lost his left eye in a brawl, looked at the prisoner; he was perplexed.

Vartan saluted him and declared with authority, 'There's a misunderstanding, Sergeant.'

'Liar!' screamed Nazim, pointing his gun at Vartan.

Unperturbed, Vartan drew out his military record and showed it to the Sergeant, without actually turning it over to him. 'I'm a Lieutenant in the Ottoman Army. Please take me to your superior officer.'

'That's what we intend to do, Lieutenant,' said the Sergeant, impressed by Vartan's self-assurance.

'What? You're calling him Lieutenant?' Nazim exploded, as he caught the guard by the shoulder and spun him around. 'He's an impostor! An infidel!'

The Sergeant shrugged off his hand. 'Don't touch me. I'm the one in command here and I said we're taking him to see the Captain. He shall decide what's to be done.'

'To hell with your Captain!' Nazim shouted. 'I don't need anyone to prove he's an infidel.'

As quick as lightning, he grabbed the prisoner and threw him to the ground. Vartan fought desperately but Nazim was big and strong and his sons helped to hold their captive down. Nazim unsheathed his dagger, cut the military belt, pulled down Vartan's trousers and pointed to his penis. 'Just look at that and try to tell me he's not a Christian.'

The Sergeant and the Corporal could see that Vartan was not circumcized.

'Now, are you convinced? He's either a rebel or a saboteur.'

'More reason for him to be questioned by the Captain himself,' said the other. 'Let's go.'

The two boys still held the prisoner by his shoulders, pinning him to the ground with all their weight, while Nazim brandished his dagger.

'I want him alive,' the Sergeant shouted.

Before he could intervene, Nazim bent down, grabbed Vartan's penis, pulled the foreskin with his left hand and with two precise movements cut it off. Vartan screamed, blood spurted and the three torturers burst out laughing. Nazim stood waving his trophy triumphantly in the face of the Sergeant, who blinked his one eye rapidly.

'Eat it if you're still not convinced.'

The two soldiers, enraged by his arrogance, pointed their rifles at Nazim.

275

The two boys let go of Vartan, who was trying to cover his genitals with his hands.

'That's enough,' the Sergeant ordered.

He had picked up the military record, which had fallen on the ground, and was trying to decipher it with great difficulty. Shakir Ismael! He knew that name from somewhere. Of course! The poster at the post office! This man was wanted and there was a big reward on his head. These peasants must not find out, otherwise they would claim a large part of the reward. He slid the booklet into his pocket and kicked the prisoner in the ribs.

'Get up!'

'Just a minute, please,' Vartan was still in a state of shock from the savage circumcision. He tore a piece off his shirt, made a bandage for his penis and put it gently inside his trousers. He stood up. Nazim and his sons jeered at him. The sergeant shoved him towards a rutted path that snaked west, through the cornfields. Nazim shot jubilantly into the air and the two youngsters followed suit. Suleiman watched his guest limp away. In a bid to rid himself of his bitterness, he went to the harem, looking for Aysha to beat her up.

Vartan tottered; each step wrenched a muffled moan out of him. His mutilated organ burnt and the bandage barely protected him from the chafing of the trousers.

'Faster! Faster!' barked the Corporal. He was a young fellow with a thin moustache; he emphasized his words by striking Vartan on the back with the butt of his rifle. Vartan rolled to the ground and the Sergeant realized that he was truly sick.

'Help him up,' he ordered the Corporal, who obeyed, grumbling.

Vartan could not walk any more, so they had to hold him up. They advanced so slowly that it took them half an hour to reach the place where the ruts turned into a bad road. The gendarmes were tired and dropped their prisoner to the ground. The older one, the tall one with greying hair, exclaimed, 'We're not really going to take him all the way back to the village, are we?'

The Sergeant took him aside and told him about the big reward offered for the capture of their prisoner. His face lit up, but then he glumly said to the Sergeant, 'We won't even see the colour of that money. The Captain will get the reward and the glory. We'll get a nice pat on the back.'

'That's true,' added the Sergeant. 'We've seen that happen already. Remember?' He rubbed his bad eye, which itched every time he was upset. The same thought had crossed his mind only a few minutes ago. He took off his fez to wipe his shaved head.

Vartan had been listening to their conversation. Ignoring his suffering, he decided to risk everything. Taking out his purse, he jiggled it until it tinkled. The guards rushed up to him.

'These are gold coins. Leave me here and they're yours.'

Gold! Their eyes glittered greedily. The Sergeant had the last laugh. 'All we have to do is take them, and then take you to headquarters anyhow.'

'I'll tell the Captain. He'll confiscate the money and keep it for himself.'

They looked confused. 'Let's do what he said,' the Corporal suggested.

As the Sergeant still said nothing, Vartan added, 'What's more, I'm not that wanted man at all. I stole this uniform. You'll get no reward anyway.'

The Corporal convinced the chief that the prisoner would probably die from his wounds.

'All right,' said the Sergeant, taking the purse and emptying it into his palm. He gasped as he saw the golden coins glittering in the sun. He counted six, three for each of them. Once they had pocketed the money, the Sergeant began to reconsider. He pointed at Vartan with his chin. 'What if someone finds him and he tells on us?'

Vartan protested vehemently but he was out-shouted by the Corporal. 'Let's kill him.'

He cocked his Mauser but the Sergeant stopped him. 'No shooting! There could be people on the road.'

The two soldiers began to beat Vartan with the butts of their rifles. He tried to protect himself with his arms, but a blow to his temple knocked him out. They continued to beat him on the head and chest.

'He's had enough,' the Sergeant said.

Vartan lay inert, covered in blood. They took his boots and uniform, intending to dispose of them farther on. If the body was found, no one would know who he was.

'Do you think we should hide the body under some stones?'

'The wild dogs and vultures will take care of it,' the Sergeant said, waving the men on.

'Are you going to see the widow, sir?' Memo, a nine-year-old boy, who was never at a loss for words, asked Kerim teasingly, and the children surrounding him burst into giggles.

The teacher, a thirty-year-old bachelor, could not help but smile. He was used to this banter. All of Urgup suspected that he was having an affair with Halidé, nicknamed 'The Widow' because she had refused all proposals of marriage since her husband's death three years before.

Kerim turned and clapped his hands. 'Scram! Buzz off! Little monsters!'

The children, who adored him, were not fooled by his frown and grumpy voice; they knew how sweet, patient and generous he was. They were sons and daughters of poor peasants, and they attended his classes entirely free of charge. The little lay school was run in the back of the café, and was supported by Greek merchants, who were numerous in the region, and Armenian craftsmen, with the tuition they paid for their children. That was, of course, before the authorities brutally chased these people away.

Kerim perceived this national calamity as a personal insult. For years he had set an example of mutual tolerance and respect by putting Muslims and Christians, rich and poor, together in the same class. Now it seemed to have been all in vain. The ostracism and persecutions that he and his parents had suffered were back again. At that time, just before the turn of the century, the Tatar Muslims had fled from their native Crimea, invaded by the Russian Tsar, and found refuge in Anatolia.

The children left him on the outskirts of the village, after respectfully saying goodbye. Shouting, they ran off in the direction of the volcano, which was riddled with troglodyte dwellings.

The flat-roofed houses of the tiny town of Urgup were crowded at the foot of the mountain. Kerim took the road to the neighbouring village of Sinanos. His frail figure stooped forwards, as if fighting the wind. He advanced rapidly with long, pliant steps, waving his arms.

The air was still on this late summer day. He wore European-style black trousers and white shirt and his shirt-sleeves were rolled up to his elbows. His face was angular, his nose straight and his eyes sad. He looked annoyed. Now he knew who the man was whom he and Halidé had found half-dead on the road. They had deduced immediately that he was a Christian, because of his freshly circumcized penis. In vain, Kerim had insisted they must not hide him at Halidé's, but it was no use arguing with her when she had her mind set on something.

Halidé's small fieldstone house stood back from the road on the sunny side of a small knoll; a cave dug in the volcanic rock served as a stable and storage place. Originally it had been a forge, where the young woman's late husband had plied his trade as blacksmith. There, Halidé had built an oven to fire the pottery which she made and sold for a living. She added to her income by weaving silk rugs for Caesarea's rich families.

She had climbed up on the roof to pick up two baskets full of apricots that had been left there to dry in the sun. Worried about an imminent storm, she looked up frequently to check the overcast sky. The first autumn rains were nearly due. Kourt,[1] her huge, shaggy-haired sheepdog, was barking at the road. Halidé recognized Kerim by his walk. She turned and waved at him. She was dressed all in black, as was customary for a widow. She put her hands on her wide hips and her eyes proudly roved over her land: the neat, walled vegetable garden; the well, shaded by a tropical elm tree; four apricot-trees; two apple-trees; long rows of grapevines; the haystack; the little shelter where the ass, turkeys, chickens, a few sheep and two goats all lived.

'Come down. I have to speak to you,' Kerim said, as he arrived at the foot of the stepladder.

'Better come up and help me get the apricots in before it rains.'

He climbed up and she noticed he was nervous.

'Is anything wrong?'

'Let's get this in under the roof first.'

He went down the steps, holding a basket on his shoulder, and took it to the stable. By the time he returned, Halidé had finished filling the second basket.

'How is he doing?' Kerim asked.

'He hasn't opened his eyes yet, but his wounds are healing nicely.'

The certainty in her melodious voice was typical of the twenty-four-year-old's innate optimism. Nothing seemed impossible to her. When she reached the ground, she put the ladder against the wall. She threw her shawl back over her shoulders. Her shiny black hair, which frizzed over her forehead, was pulled back tight and covered her head in tight waves; it ended in a braid reaching down her neck. Her skin was tanned. She had a narrow face with hollow cheeks and a thin neck that made her look deceptively frail. Her shoulders were square and her figure solid. Halidé was not one to shun hard work.

'What's the matter?'

She joined Kerim in front of the stable. He kissed her on both cheeks. He was a good head taller than she was. A mat of thick black hair showed through his shirt unbuttoned at the neck. He took out a piece of paper, which he had folded eight times. It was a poster. Halidé could not read

---

1.   Wolf (Turkish).

279

Arabic, but the photograph of an officer caught her attention. She looked at it more closely to check if the mole on the edge of his eyelid was not an inkspot caused by a fault in printing. Their patient had a similar mark on his eyelid. The shape of the head . . . the ears . . . the lips . . . the dimple in the chin . . .

'It's him!' she exclaimed.

'Yes.'

Halidé thought the man in the picture handsome, an attribute that was not apparent in his thin, swollen face now. 'What does it say?'

'He's an Armenian, who's been condemned to death. He's wanted as a rebel and traitor. He's carrying false identification papers in the name of Lieutenant Shakir Ismael. His real name is Vartan Balian, and he's a major in the Ottoman Army.'

'A major?' Halidé could not quite believe it. She smiled. The fact that he was a hunted man made their saving his life even more important.

'I don't see what you're so happy about,' complained Kerim, as he nervously folded the poster. 'See! I was right when I didn't want to bring him here.'

She was indignant. 'Would you have left him in the ditch?'

'Of course not, but we should have hidden him in the underground church near Goremé, as we did with the others.'

'Who would have looked after him? He would have died!'

Kerim had to admit that she was right. 'That's true, we couldn't have known, but now . . . we have to move him.'

'It's out of the question,' she said in a tone that admitted no contradiction. 'He hasn't come to yet, and he still has a high fever.'

Kerim insisted, 'Charity has its limits, Halidé. Please understand. It's too dangerous.'

The young woman's expression became obstinate. 'It's my business. After all, he's at my house.'

'If they find him, they'll suspect me too, and everything we have been trying to do will be in jeopardy. You're being rash now, Halidé!'

She chuckled and patted him on the shoulder. 'And you? You're getting jumpy, my dear Kerim. No one has to know that he's here. The people from the village don't mix with me much and you know why. Who would think of looking for him here?'

'Who? The gendarmes, that's who.'

'If they come, I'll tell them he's my husband and I'll show them his papers. No one would recognize the Major with his two-week growth of beard.'

Kerim shrugged and sighed. It was useless to insist. With her usual quick wit, she would have an answer for everything. Kerim thought it was a shame that such an intelligent woman had not been able to study, but would that have made her any happier? He doubted it. She accepted her lot philosophically and seemed to find happiness and contentment in her daily existence. Learned as he was, Kerim could not say the same. He felt constantly dissatisfied without knowing the reason. As though he were waiting for something, but again without knowing what.

Halidé looked at Kerim. He had that absent look again. What was he thinking about? After two years of seeing each other twice a week, she still did not know him. She knew that a big part of this shy individual would always be an absolute enigma to her. For instance, his feelings: he was tender towards her, warm and intimate, but he treated her like a sister, never made any advances. He was the only one she would have considered marrying . . . but he had never proposed.

Halidé took him by the hand. 'Stay for dinner.'

He followed her into the house. There was only one perfectly square room pierced by two windows on the south. A vertical loom leaned against one wall. On the right, there was a raised, clay platform, which served as a bed and there a man lay under a thick goatskin. Pottery jars were lined up along the foot of the walls, under the wooden shelves, which held the cooking utensils and clothing. Braids of onions and net bags holding dried fruit hung from the thick ceiling beams. The furniture consisted of a small coffee table, which held some dishes and stoneware pots, and a hand-crafted wooden trunk with iron corners.

'It's hot in here, like a *hammam*,' Kerim remarked.

'Not so loud,' Halidé whispered, looking in the direction of the bed. 'He needs to sweat the illness out.'

There was a glowing fire in a pit scooped out in the centre of the earthen floor. Unlike the peasants, who burnt dried dung, Halidé burnt charcoal, which she bought to fire her pottery. A kettle was boiling on one side of the pit. A pungent smell of herbs came from a large copper pot hanging from an iron trivet over the pit.

'I'm boiling a hen. All he can eat is broth.'

Kerim tore up the poster and threw it into the fire. A flame leaped up and blackened the bottom of the copper cauldron.

Halidé sat at the edge of the platform and moistened the sick man's chapped lips. Kerim leaned over to inspect the thin face shiny with sweat. It really would be difficult to associate this bed-ridden invalid with the Major shown on the poster.

'Has he said anything yet?'

'Just senseless mutterings. He's delirious most of the time.'

'Do you think he can hear us?'

'I don't think so.'

When Halidé stood up, Kerim leaned over the sick man and put his mouth to his ear. 'You're with friends,' he whispered. 'You've nothing to fear. Just rest.' Kerim's gesture touched Halidé, but he was embarrassed and sought to cover it up. 'Well, you never know.'

Halidé pulled down the goatskin and then a thick felt blanket. A sheet still covered the sick man.

'He's going to suffocate under all that!' said Kerim.

'It's to make him sweat,' she said, taking off the damp sheet which she handed to him. 'Go hang it over the garden wall.'

When Kerim returned, Halidé was delicately sponging Vartan's perspiration away with a cloth. His pale body looked enormous in the dim light.

'He has the body of an athlete,' murmured the teacher admiringly. He rolled a cigarette as he watched Halidé happily taking care of her patient like a mother. 'Would you have liked to have children?'

'Oh, yes! I lost one and then Yashar died.' She looked him straight in the eyes and added, 'I would have to marry again to have a child now.'

Kerim understood what she was insinuating but did not let on.

Halidé finished washing the sick man from head to foot and took off the bandage from his thigh. The skin had lost its nasty blackness but the wound was still swollen and purple. Pus oozed out and Halidé pressed his thigh to make it flow freely. She wiped it with the corner of a cloth and threw it towards the hearth. Then she washed the wound with alcohol.

'Are you sure you're doing the right thing?' Kerim asked.

Annoyed that he should question her competence, she replied dryly. 'I'm following doctor's orders.'

They had called in Dr Leonidas, a Greek physician, whom they thought they could trust. As he lived far away in Caesarea and they wished to avoid arousing the suspicions of the people of Urgup, he had been able to come only twice.

'Get the cobwebs. They're on the little table beside the cups.'

Kerim brought her a package wrapped in brown paper. She took out an opalescent substance and skilfully put it over the wound. Then she bandaged it again. Everyone knew spider webs were an excellent antiseptic and they were difficult to come by. Kerim and his students had been put in charge of that task and it had turned into a game for them.

'I'm going to need some more,' Halidé told him.

Kerim laughed. All the spiders in Urgup hardly sufficed for the job.

Most people regarded spiders with great respect. According to legend, they had saved the life of the Prophet Mohammed by spinning their webs over the entrance to the cave, where he had hidden from his pursuers. She used the webs to dress the cut of the circumcision as well.

She lifted him easily, pried his lips open and trickled a little broth into his mouth, then rubbed his throat with her thumb to make him swallow. She repeated this procedure until he had drunk two cups. She laid him back with infinite care, dried his mouth and beard and ran her fingertips through his hair. 'He's sleeping like an angel.' She got up, happy and completely satisfied with herself. 'Look, Kerim. He looks like a fragile child.'

The teacher thought Vartan's big, sinuous body made him look remarkably virile.

A dozen gendarmes surrounded Vartan threatening him with their bayonets. He was tied and vainly trying to avoid their blades as they stabbed him. He fell to the ground, blood dripping from his wounds, but he was not dying.

Vartan awoke from the nightmare with a start. He was sweating, although he was cold. He was tied down. He opened his eyes and the light blinded him. His head buzzed. Looking through a fog, he could barely make out a room and a woman dressed in black. He thought he was in the farmer's house and being watched by Aysha. He plunged back into unconsciousness, a sleep full of horrible visions, atrocious scenes. He had had these brief awakenings for a week now, like a drowning man surfacing temporarily for a moment, and afterwards had sunk back into sleep, where swirling dreams again carried him away.

Finally, one morning, he woke up with a clear head. He had vague memories of faces bending over him, sometimes Maro, sometimes his mother humming a lullaby. His body ached. Suddenly everything came back to him: the trip to Caesarea, the circumcision, the three guards who tried to kill him. He wanted to bring his hand to his head but found his right arm tied down. However, the left one was free, so he used it to touch his face. He had a thick beard. He turned his head and saw the back of a woman dressed in black, who was weaving. He meant to speak forcefully, but he could only manage a rattling whisper. The woman got up and stepped lightly towards him. Two big black eyes shone in a tanned face.

'Blessed be the Lord!' she exclaimed, as she picked up a jug and a cup.

Vartan tried to sit up but could not.

'Don't move. You're still too weak.'

'Where am I?'

'Near Urgup.'

'Urgup?'

'It's near Caesarea. Don't talk any more. You'll tire yourself.'

She sat on the bed, slid her hand under Vartan's shoulders and helped him sit up, holding his head against her shoulder. He felt dazed.

'Here. Drink some of this.'

She offered him some goat's milk, which he drank. She pressed her hand against his forehead and said happily, 'Almost no fever.'

He was surprised at the familiarity with which she treated him. 'How long have I been here?'

'Three weeks.'

Three weeks! It must be September. A thousand questions burned on his lips but a sharp pain in his temples kept him from talking, even from thinking. He stretched out and rested silently for a long while. When he opened his eyes again, the young woman was still at his side, looking at him tenderly. He did not feel completely at ease and looked around the room suspiciously.

Halidé guessed what he was thinking. 'You have nothing to be afraid of. I know who you are, Major.'

Stupefied, he kept his composure. 'And who are you?'

'A woman who hates violence and injustice,' she said evasively. 'You're talking too much. Don't waste your strength.'

Wise words, but Vartan was tortured by curiosity. He touched his head and found a lot of scabs. 'Why have you tied my arm?'

'Doctor's orders. You have broken your collar bone.'

'A doctor?' Vartan sounded worried.

284

'He's a friend, a Greek.'

'How many people know I'm here?'

'Besides the doctor, only Kerim and me. He was with me when I found you.'

Vartan was out of breath from talking. He breathed in with his mouth wide open for several minutes before saying:

'Who is Kerim? Is he Greek too?'

'No. He's a Tatar from the Crimea. He's the village teacher. It was he who saw the poster. He's a true friend.'

She explained to Vartan that there were posters with a picture of him on the walls of the police stations, market places and the coffee houses, offering a reward for his capture. She finished by saying, 'You'd better keep your beard.'

'What about the neighbours?'

'Nobody knows you're here. The village is far away.'

He sighed deeply but had no other choice than to surrender himself to the care of this woman, whose name he did not know. His eyelids burnt and felt heavy.

'You should go back to sleep,' the woman said, picking up the jug and walking away.

Vartan wanted to say something but fell asleep. The usual nightmares did not assail him and he slept peacefully.

The smell of frying onions awoke him and his mouth watered. He was hungry! The young woman was cooking in front of the hearth. Rays of sunlight penetrated the room diagonally through the two windows. The afternoon was ending. When she saw that her patient was awake, Halidé brought him something to drink.

'I still haven't thanked you for what you did.' She put her finger on his lips to stop him from talking, but he continued, 'Right now, I don't have the means to repay you.'

'God will return it to me a hundredfold,' she said, with deep conviction.

'If I get out of this and survive the war, you won't have to wait long for your reward.'

She laughed outright. 'Don't be foolish. You've thanked me and that's enough. We won't talk about it any more.' Humming softly, she turned to her pots.

Vartan explored his body with his left hand and found himself to be shockingly thin. His penis still hurt when he touched it, but that was all. The wound in his thigh had healed. He shut his eyes and relaxed. Why was this Turkish woman running the risk of sheltering him? And Kerim? Their behaviour did not make sense and he did not like things that he could not explain.

September! What had happened to Maro and Tomas? They probably thought him dead and he wouldn't be able to look for them for a long time. Look for them? How and where? Sunk deep in gloomy thoughts, he jumped when Halidé said:

'Kerim will be glad you are conscious. We thought you would die from your wounds. Even the doctor was pessimistic. You must be a very strong man.' She tasted the food she had prepared before going on, 'Kerim is coming for dinner this evening. We're having lamb but you'd better have some soup with rice. Your stomach has been empty for too long.'

Everything seemed so simple to her; so normal. She behaved as if she had known him intimately for a long time, while, to him, she was a perfect stranger.

'I don't even know your name,' said Vartan.

'Halidé.'

He pushed aside the goatskin and the felt blanket, and she came to help him.

'Are you too hot? You have to be careful not to catch a cold.'

'I have to go out.'

'You're too weak,' she said and bent to pick up a chamberpot. 'Do you need any help?'

The question astonished him but then he remembered he had been as helpless as an infant in the arms of this woman for the past several weeks. This state of total dependency bothered him. 'I can do it myself,' he declared, taking the pot. He turned on his left side with his back to the young woman and relieved his bladder. He would have preferred for her to leave but she stood at the side of the bed. She had become familiar with his body, and its functions were not shameful to a peasant like her, but it was terribly embarrassing for Vartan who would have liked a cloth to cover the pot before giving it back to her.

He was exhausted and gasped, 'Why?'

'What?'

'Why all this kindness and care for a total stranger? Why?'

Halidé perceived the distrust in his voice and was hurt that he could doubt her generosity.

'Kourt! Kourt!' she called towards the open door. A few seconds later the big dog came in and sat at her feet and sniffed at the bed. She patted the animal on the head, 'I found him two years ago, lost in the snow. He had been almost torn to pieces by wolves. I nursed him and healed him. He's never asked me why.'

Vartan could not help smiling. 'I didn't mean to hurt your feelings, Halidé. I think your generosity knows no bounds but. . . .'

'But?'

'If they were to find me in your house . . .'

She shrugged, to show that the idea did not bother her. Vartan wondered if this woman was completely heedless. On the other hand, she did know that he was wanted, and they were looking for him.

'Doesn't anyone ever come here? Villagers like to visit each other a lot.'

'The nearest neighbour is at least a couple of kilometres away and I keep to myself.'

'Is your husband at war?'

'No, I'm a widow.'

'What about your relatives?'

'I don't have a family any more.'

The curtness of her answers gave Vartan to understand that she did not want to talk about herself. Her eyes had clouded over. It must hurt her to talk about her past, so he did not insist.

'I'm going out in the garden,' she said and left, accompanied by the dog.

Kerim arrived shortly before nightfall and was delighted to hear that the sick man was conscious. His sagging shoulders, receding hairline and stooped back made him look older than he was, but his frank, clear eyes were young and naive. He was certainly not handsome but immediately likeable. Vartan shook his hand and thanked him warmly.

'Halidé did it all,' Kerim said modestly.

'Why?'

Halidé who had kneeled by the hearth, raised her eyes to heaven and shook her head. That question again! She had changed her black dress for an orange peasant robe, embroidered with green flowers. Kerim clasped his hand behind his back, as he did when teaching.

'Why?' he asked heatedly. 'Why? Because you are an Armenian! Hateful crimes are being committed in our country now and I want no part in it. I want to cut myself off from the government and all those that bend their backs and obey. I would rather be considered a traitor.'

'One day, it's the others who will be judged as traitors and you will be considered a hero.'

'I don't expect that much,' laughed Kerim, embarrassed. 'For me, it's enough to be at peace with my conscience.' He sighed deeply to dissipate the blush he could feel on his cheeks. He clapped his hands, 'Ignorance!' he exclaimed. 'Ignorance is the cause of it all. This country will never progress until . . .'

Halidé interrupted to admonish him gently, 'Kerim! You're not going to give us a long speech. Not tonight. The Major just woke up.'

The teacher smiled sheepishly. 'As always Halidé is right. Please excuse me.'

Vartan came to the teacher's defence. 'I'm interested in your ideas, Kerim. I would love to hear more when my mind is less foggy.'

'It will be my pleasure,' replied Kerim, beaming. 'We'll have many occasions to talk.'

They propped Vartan up on the bed against the folded goatskins for his meal. Halidé wanted to feed him but he insisted on doing it himself with his left hand. She and Kerim pulled up the low table and sat down on the rug. Two smelly oil lamps barely lit the room, leaving the corners in darkness. The conversation turned to banal subjects: the poor harvests that worried them, the shortness of food during the winter and the village gossip.

Vartan asked Kerim, 'Do you know a Dr Black who is in charge of the American School in Caesarea?'

'Only by reputation. The government closed the school and he's gone.'

A groan escaped Vartan. There went the hope he was hanging on to.

'Did you have any deportations?'

'Unfortunately, yes,' the teacher said, lowering his eyes.

Halidé bit her lips and Vartan could see the shame in her eyes when she said flatly, 'It will be a hard winter. The onions are growing extra layers.'

They both understood she wanted to change the subject and respected her wishes.

After dinner, Halidé served tea and Kerim rolled a cigarette and offered it to Vartan. Halidé lit it with the flame from one of the lamps. Vartan had not smoked in a long time. The first draught made him cough and the second made his head spin, but then he was filled with an immense feeling of wellbeing. He looked around at the white walls, where reflections from the lamps fluttered, and at his host and hostess who were smiling at him. Against all reason, he knew he could trust these two people implicitly.

Instead of making him forget, the environment revived all sorts of memories in Vartan. He told his story without their asking and without mentioning any names. Halidé and Kerim listened to him silently. His voice was dull, but he continued to speak, in spite of his sudden exhaustion, in spite of the pain which his words evoked. He felt the need to share the heavy burden that was crushing his heart.

When he finished only the plaintive bleating of a kid calling to its mother could be heard.

Tears streamed down Halidé's face. 'I'm putting myself in your wife's and son's place,' she said, staring at the wall, as if she were seeing something that made her suffer.

Kerim was appalled; he gripped Vartan's hand. If he had not been so shy, he would have kissed him on both cheeks. He waved goodbye to Halidé and left without a word.

Halidé helped Vartan to lie down again. Her face was now more composed but her eyes were still red. 'You're right to keep on hoping. I'm sure you'll find them!'

She stretched out by the hearth and rolled herself in a felt blanket. She could not fall asleep and later her sobs awoke Vartan. He could not understand why his story had moved her so much.

Riza Bey was in his sumptuously furnished office in the principal government building in Ayntab. He was fuming. He had just finished deciphering a long telegram from Gani Bey from the capital. Reproaches! Unjustified reproaches!

It was true that quite a number of Armenians were still living in Ayntab: those who had converted to Protestantism and were protected by American or German missionaries; or the specialized craftsmen, in other words, the ones working in the munitions factory. The real reason for not deporting these people, whom Riza had cited to Maro as an example of his leniency, was their undeniable importance to the country, and he was ready to defend his actions. But, the rest of the reproaches . . .!

Was he to blame that a French cruiser had taken aboard four thousand

Armenians who had been resisting since July at Musa Dagh and had carried them to Port Said in Egypt? How could he have kept this information from leaking abroad? Gani Bey was doing him a great injustice.

Riza reread one of the passages in the telegram:

'The German News Agency has reported to the Minister of Interior certain actions, which he judges to be inadmissible. On October the fourth, an organization called the American Inquiry Committee published a detailed report about the fate of the Armenians in Anatolia. In London, two days later, a certain Lord Bryce gave a well-documented speech in the House of Lords on the same subject. It seems evident that they have some contact with people living in Anatolia, in your region, to be exact. You need to watch and to limit, as much as possible, any movements of foreigners, missionaries or diplomats, and take all necessary measures to stop the dissemination of eye-witness accounts that could be detrimental to our government.'

Measures! Measures! Gani Bey had many good ones. 'If he's not satisfied, let him relieve me of my post,' Riza Bey grumbled. 'I have my lands to look after. I shall certainly tell him so.'

The ringing of the telephone stopped him: two long rings and then two short ones. Someone was calling the General. Telephone service had just been installed in Ayntab and there were only about twenty subscribers in the town.

Riza picked up the telegram again. There was another part that worried him:

'The foreign press has published certain articles, which I have reason to believe are the work of Vartan Balian, who is apparently still at large. To be exact, there was a description of the camp in Malatya, where your right-hand man surprised the man in question. It is imperative to put him out of commission. Intensify your search. Since the Minister of the Interior has not been informed about this matter, avoid mentioning his name or making any reference to him in your official correspondence.'

Furious, Riza crumpled the telegram, put it in an ashtray and set fire to it. He took a cigar from a box given to him by a German officer. Maro's husband! He had forgotten about him. He was nothing for Riza to worry about. Balian could not harm him in any way. Besides, he did not know where his wife and son were. The only thing Riza feared was that Maro would find out that her husband was alive. She seemed to be slowly getting used to the idea of staying in Anatolia, and her son had quickly become accustomed to his new life.

Shutting his eyes, he could picture Maro's face, her eyes sparkling with intelligence. He could imagine her voluptuous lips, saying to him for the first time, 'I love you.' His joy was brief, as her husband's face came to mind, not the blurred face on the wanted poster, which Riza had prudently forbidden to be posted in Ayntab, but the smiling face in the photograph Maro kept in her locket. Jealousy gnawed at him. Whatever future awaited Maro and him, there would always be that shadow from the past between them.

He stood up abruptly and the green leather chair squeaked on the marble floor. He stood in front of the large mural map of Anatolia, drawn up by German topographers. The different shadings brought out the mountainous zones. Riza's eyes followed the courses of the rivers, paused at the names of the towns and villages, scrutinized the valleys and scanned the plateaux, as if he could chance to find the fleeing man. 'Where could he be hiding?'

He put the moist end of his cigar against the paper and traced a route from western Malatya to the Russian border. Another one to Persia. A third one in the direction of Baghdad, and the part of Mesopotamia that was in the hands of the British. Any reasonable man in Vartan's situation would have chosen any of these routes. There was, however, still another possibility that he might be heading towards Aleppo, where thousands of Armenians lived in harmony with the Arabs. Aleppo! Hardly 200 kilometres from Ayntab.

While he was toying with the last idea, there were three knocks on the door; it opened before he had time to answer. Thinking it was his secretary or some other government employee, he shouted without turning around, 'I asked not to be disturbed.'

'Excuse me, Riza Bey. It's important.'

Bedri walked up to his employer, who looked up and asked impatiently, 'What is it now?'

Bedri ran his forefinger inside his tight, detachable collar. His face was red and puffy. Since Riza Bey's appointment as governor, Bedri's authority and prestige had also grown. The important people of the town treated him with deference and respect. Today, he was dressed in a black suit, white shirt and a tie, although he found these clothes uncomfortable; besides, the ill-fitting suit made him look like a simpleton.

'We've found the tracks of the spy,' he said, happily brandishing a telegram.

The governor jumped, 'Where?'

'In Caesarea.'

Riza turned to the map. Caesarea did not correspond to his calculations. What the devil was Balian doing there?

'Did they arrest him?'

'No. Shakir Ismael's identification papers have shown up at the police headquarters in Caesarea. They were brought in by a soldier, who obtained them from a merchant. And the merchant found them on the side of a secondary road.' Bedri glanced at the telegram to make sure that he had not omitted any details. 'That's all we know.'

He watched his master's reaction through half-open eyes. Relieved that Balian was not in the immediate surroundings any longer, Riza stared at Caesarea on the map. He chewed on his cigar nervously. This news! Just as he had been thinking about the man. The coincidence was highly worrisome. He would never have any peace of mind as long as this man was alive. He turned to Bedri, who was surprised to see how worried his master looked.

'What do you think about this?'

Bedri rubbed his neck, which was red from the tight collar. He already knew what he was going to answer but pretended to think it over. 'He's got rid of the identification papers, so by now he must have assumed another identity.'

'But why Caesarea?'

'Why not?' As Bedri shrugged, his ill-fitting sleeves crumpled up.

Thoughtfully, Riza Bey walked to his desk, relit his cigar and then walked over to the window, which opened on to a paved courtyard, where several soldiers stood chatting. He turned to his aide and asked, 'Are they searching the region?'

'I should think so.'

'You think so!' shouted Riza Bey furiously, flicking the cigar ashes on the floor. 'I want no stone left unturned. Each and every inhabitant must be questioned.'

'I imagine he's no longer anywhere near there,' Bedri replied, unable to understand his master's interest in the affair. 'In my opinion, he's probably on his way to the capital.'

'Your opinion is not good enough for me. You're to go there and direct the search personally.'

Bedri's cheeks trembled. He hated the idea of such a long trip. He hated to leave Ayntab and be deprived of the new prestige he was enjoying. 'The army and the guards can do the job. What difference would my presence make?'

Furious at having his orders questioned by his aide, Riza Bey said with a knowing smile, 'You were a member of Abdul-Hamid's secret police. Your experience will be useful to them.'

The mention of this episode in his past, which was a flaw in the eyes of the present administration, made Bedri blanch. He hastened to agree. Riza pointed to the ashtray full of charred paper.

'Gani Bey wants this man out of the way by any means. You'll have all the help you need. When you get to Caesarea, the authorities will have received orders about this matter from Constantinople. Organize the search but, in the meantime, you will start your own investigation. Get ready to leave today.'

Bedri bowed and hid his irritation. 'At your orders, Riza Bey.' He salaamed; his shoulders sagged as he turned to go. Before closing the door, he paused and asked:

'And if I find him?'

Riza ran his forefinger across his throat and clacked his tongue.

'It'll be a pleasure,' Bedri guffawed.

The end of October was drawing near. The days were becoming shorter and the nights longer and colder. The autumn rains, which, at first, generously irrigated the soil parched by months and months of drought, were now running off the fields in rivulets and digging furrows in the banks of the roads. The torrential rains were followed by intervals of drizzle, and the skies remained grey and overcast.

Sitting on the edge of the platform that served as a bed, Vartan was trimming his beard. His hand shook so much that he had to put down the scissors. He could scarcely recognize the face reflected in the little, round mirror, not because of his thick beard but because of his hollow cheeks and sunken eyes. His features had hardened and the crow's feet at the corners of his eyelids had deepened; two wrinkles lined his brow. There was more grey

293

at his temples and little flecks of white on both sides of his beard. He had aged and looked more and more like his father.

He walked to the window, holding on to the wall. He still limped, but at least he had the use of his right arm and did not need the sling. His fever was gone but he was very weak and tired very quickly. He suffered from violent headaches. They made him feel as though a drum was beating inside his head, tightening the noose around his skull.

The window faced south-east. The fields were neglected in this season; they were red or brown rectangles, depending on whether they had been left with stubble or had been plowed. Vartan stayed a long time at the window, his look lost in the distance. In his mind he was covering the hundreds of kilometres of mountains separating him from the towns where Maro and Tomas might have been taken. Aleppo, Alexandretta, Ayntab, Adana, the names assumed a mythical resonance in his ears. Where were they? How were they surviving? He couldn't imagine what was happening to them or how they might be living, and not being able to picture them drove him crazy.

He must return to Malatya and begin his patient search for them from there. Perhaps Miss Langlet had already received some news of Maro through the other missionaries. It was even possible that a message from his cousin Diran was waiting for him at the orphanage in Malatya. How much longer before he would be in a condition to take such a trip? Above all, how was he going to go? Now that Dr Black had left, he knew of no one who could provide him with new identity papers. Go to Constantinople? There he had relatives and friends, but the idea of going further from the region where he had lost track of Maro was repugnant to him, because he believed, irrationally, that by doing so he would lose them forever.

Halidé stood on the door-sill and observed Vartan, who had not seen her coming. He was still at the window, probably thinking about his wife and child. He never mentioned them but Halidé could tell from his melancholy look that he thought about them constantly. Sometimes he remained locked in deep silence for hours, and she did not dare disturb him.

'Take it easy,' she said, as she entered the room.

He turned slowly. 'Quite the contrary. I have to exercise my muscles.'

She shook out her wet shawl and hung it on a wall near the door. 'You're trying too hard. Let time, the healer, do its work.'

'Time is my enemy,' he said sadly, attempting to move towards the bed.

'Wait! I'll help you.'

He obeyed. Had he refused, it would have only provoked a heated argument. Halidé did not like her charitable impulses to be thwarted. She put an arm around his waist. 'Lean on my shoulder.'

The rain had gone through her shawl and her dress was soaking wet. 'Don't walk so fast,' she said affectionately.

What she really wanted was to prolong the physical contact; she loved the heavy hand on her shoulder and the feel of Vartan's back muscles against her arm. Above all, she loved the feeling that this formerly strong, powerful man depended on her. Halidé was sorry that she did not have to wash and dress him any more. Now she could touch him only with her eyes. It seemed to her that they were becoming estranged after having been very intimate, but maybe that was only her imagination.

Sitting down on the bed, Vartan thanked her again for all she had done for him and added, 'I'll leave as soon as I'm able to.'

Halidé turned without a word and went to shut the door. 'It's very humid in here.' She took a package from her cape. 'I bought some coffee. I'll prepare it.'

Vartan watched her light the charcoal in the *tandir*. Coffee! Where did she get the money to buy such a luxury during wartime? The sale of pottery and rugs could not bring in that much. It was one more thing to add to the list of things that intrigued him about Halidé's household. These last weeks she had bought provisions that were far more than one person, even two, needed for the winter. Not just wheat, which was the basis of the diet of the Anatolian peasant, but also pieces of dried mutton, which she had hung from the rafters, olive oil, nuts from the Black Sea, pistachios and almonds, sugar, salt and tea. That was without counting what she had brought from the market and stored in the stable. There were also her frequent absences, which Vartan could not explain. At least once a week, Kerim came to fetch Halidé just before nightfall and did not bring her back until the following morning, sometimes not until the following evening. At first, Vartan had thought they were having an affair and that his presence in the house forced them to find their privacy elsewhere, but this explanation did not stand up. Why did they always lead the donkey with them, loaded with big baskets? The border was too far away for smuggling. Then what? Vartan had not been able to come up with any explanation that seemed remotely plausible. If his friends were engaged in illegal activities, as their silence on the subject led him to believe, they were risking eventually attracting the attention of the guards, and this made Vartan feel more insecure.

The water was boiling. Halidé mixed in the coffee and poured it into small cups. Her black eyes, so lustrous that they seemed to be lacquered; shone when they rested on Vartan, and her thin face looked like a young girl's. They drank their coffee in silence and then Halidé returned to her loom.

A piece of cardboard with a design for weaving lay on the upper bar of her loom. That would keep her busy for at least a few months. Strands of silk in all colours hung from the wall, near at hand. Each time she changed her thread, Halidé would turn her head to look at Vartan, who sat on the bed, watching her weave, but she was convinced that he was not really seeing her. She would have loved for him to talk to her while she worked. Such a learned man would know so many things, but he probably thought that a peasant woman like her would not understand him. It did not matter! His presence was enough to make her happy. She had almost forgotten just how empty a house without a man could be. She started to sing very softly, swaying gently to mark the rhythm. Without realizing it, Vartan began to hum the ancient air he knew so well.

Kourt barked several times and then fell silent. Halidé hurried to the window. 'It's Kerim,' she said, relieved.

He was out of breath and agitated. 'Soldiers! They're searching every house in the village.' He turned to Vartan, 'They're looking for you.'

Vartan got up from the bed. 'Do they know I'm in Urgup?'

'No, because they're searching in Caesarea also and all over the province.'

'Then they'll come here eventually!'

Vartan could hardly hide his nervousness. Halidé remained surprisingly calm. She took off her shawl and went up to Vartan. 'They're not going to find you. Come.'

'I'll help him,' Kerim added.

'You'd better carry the blanket and the goatskins.'

Vartan put his arm around the shoulders of the young woman and she covered their heads with her shawl. Kerim went out first to check if the way was clear and walked ahead of them to the stable. The air was cool and it was raining heavily. Vartan's slippers slipped on the wet earth but he held on firmly to Halidé. He wanted to leave. The soldiers would search the stable and he would be caught like a rat in a trap.

'I don't want to cause any trouble for you.'

Halidé chuckled.

296

Vartan continued, 'You'd better take me out to the hills. If they find me there, you and Kerim won't be in any trouble.'

'Let me do it my way. They won't find you,' she said with assurance. The cavern, dug more than a century ago, served her as a stable. The crumbly stone of the walls, originally white, had acquired a dark grey patina. The smoke from the forge, which now held a pottery kiln, had blackened the ceiling. The smell from the animals, especially the ammonia from the chicken dung, impregnated the air and overpowered them as they crossed the threshold. Way in the back, the donkey turned his head to look at them and brayed. The goats and sheep went on chewing their cud in their stalls. The beehive-shaped kiln stood to the right of the entrance. Piles of charcoal lay next to mounds of dried clay. Near the left wall, thick flagstones covered the pits dug into the ground to store grain.

Kerim untied the donkey and took him out of his stall. Then he took down the manger, which hid a hole in the back wall. Halidé lit a lantern and slipped through the space, which was less than one metre high. Kerim handed the blanket and goatskin to her.

'If you don't need me anymore, I'll go back to Urgup.'

Halidé's voice came back muffled, 'All right. Keep me abreast of what is happening.'

The teacher touched Vartan's arm. 'Everything will be all right.'

'Thank you, Kerim. Don't worry. If they catch me, I'll never mention your name.'

Vartan crawled in to join Halidé. The short, narrow passageway led to a small room about four by five metres and just high enough to stand upright. In one corner, jars and baskets of provisions were piled up and in the other, a bunch of hay made a bed.

'You'll be comfortable here. It'll only be for a few days, no more.'

'It's a thousand times better than being caught, but tell me . . .'

She interrupted, 'Wait. I'll be back.'

She hurried out and disappeared. Vartan looked the place over. The stone was still white and the marks left by the pick were still visible. It was evident that this chamber had been added recently. The packed-down bed of straw suggested that someone else had stayed here before. A box of matches lay next to an olive-oil lamp. Halidé came in from the house, carrying a chamber-pot, a jug of water, bread, nuts and dates. She slipped a package behind the jars.

'I'll bring you more to eat when the danger is past. During the night you can risk going out. Don't be afraid of suffocating. Fresh air comes in below the manger.'

She was leaving but Vartan held her back by the arm.

'Tell me,' he said, pointing at the place where they were.

'A hiding place is always useful,' she said evasively.

Vartan refused to release her. 'This hiding place, your expeditions at night, what does it all mean?'

She hesitated for a moment and then said, 'I help my people, that's all.'

This answer only increased Vartan's curiosity. He looked straight into her eyes, trying to understand her. 'Who are you?'

She knew he was going to continue questioning her until he got an answer, so she regretfully took out the package she had hidden behind the jars and unrolled the cloth to reveal an icon of the Virgin and the Child, an Armenian silver-plated cross and a family portrait.

'You're an Armenian!'

'Before I married a Muslim, my name was Aroussiag.'

# Ten

'*Je, tu, il . . . nous, vous, ils*'

A boudoir on the ground floor had been converted into a classroom. Maro's six pupils were repeating the personal pronouns in unison, pointing to the subjects mentioned as they did so. At Riza Bey's request, Maro had been teaching French to his children and Tomas since the beginning of October. Only his thirteen-year-old son, Altan, was not present. He was already studying German with a private tutor, and had managed to be excused from studying another foreign language. Maro was glad about this, as Altan openly showed hostility and scorn towards her and Tomas.

She stood next to an old, faded globe, looking down at the children seated on cushions on the floor. Tomas sat between his two friends, Emel and Kenan, to whom he sometimes whispered the correct answers. He was proud of his mother, who was considered to be so erudite, and was happy to mix with other pupils as he had done in Sivas. He smiled. Safiyé, her daughter Shahané, and Eminé sat on ornate ottomans behind the children. Eminé knitted as she rocked Zehra, Leyla's little girl, who was asleep in her lap. Shahané was not listening; she was worried about her fiancé fighting in Mesopotamia, from whom she had not heard for several weeks.

Safiyé sat on the edge of her seat and followed the class with great interest, her voice mingling frequently with those of the children. She was avid for knowledge and never missed a class, whether it was French, arithmetic or geography. Buyuk Hanim was naturally opposed to these classes; she thought studying was a complete waste of time for the girls. However, at Safiyé's urging, Riza Bey brushed aside his mother's objections and gave his approval for the classes.

'*Je suis, tu es, il est, nous sommes, vous êtes, ils sont.*'

Teaching helped Maro fill the empty days, which otherwise seemed so very long. On the other hand, she regretted having accepted the job when she realized that this gave her a crucial role in Riza's household, and that consequently she had lost her status as a guest. The lesson came to an end and the children instantly dispersed.

Safiyé gestured meaningfully to the wet-nurse, who was carrying the sleeping child, and said, 'We still have three hours before dinner.'

Maro knew what Safiyé had in mind. She smiled in understanding and took her by the arm. Safiyé noticed that she looked troubled. 'What's the matter? You seem weary, sister.'

In the garden two gardeners were raking the paths. Pulling her veil over her face, Safiyé ordered them to leave. When they had disappeared, she let the veil fall to her breast.

'You can confide in me,' she murmured, putting her arm around Maro's waist.

Maro gazed at her imploringly. 'I want to leave and join my family in Constantinople.'

Safiyé flushed, turned her head aside and walked on in silence. She looked at the rosebushes without really seeing how profusely they were blooming after the recent rains. Her reaction underlined what Maro already knew. She could not expect Safiyé to intercede for her; on the contrary, Safiyé's friendship was one more link that chained her to this house. It was impossible, however, to be angry with her.

They arrived at the pond, where some leaves floated on the surface and others had sunk to the bottom, carpeting the floor. The air was mild, charged with the pungent smell of decomposing undergrowth. Safiyé checked to make sure that there was no one in the pavilion who could overhear them.

'Has Riza been unkind to you?'

'No.'

'Has he been less tender or affectionate?'

Now it was Maro's turn to blush. She shook her head in lieu of answering.

Safiyé seemed relieved. 'I'd be very surprised if that was the case, as he loves you dearly.'

'But I don't love him.'

Intrigued, Safiyé studied Maro for a few seconds and said, 'You will.'

Maro grasped her arm firmly. 'But I don't want to. I'm already married.'

Safiyé patted her hand to calm her. She could not understand Maro's attitude, as all the indications were that Maro's husband was dead. Neither could she understand her stubborn resistance to Riza, who certainly deserved to be loved. Maro was on the verge of losing her temper, but remained silent until she regained her self-control. They entered the pavilion, flicked the dead leaves off the bench and sat down. Maro was trying to work out how to get Safiyé to help her leave.

'Tell me, Safiyé, do you love Riza?'

'Yes! From the bottom of my soul!'

'Then how can you accept sharing him with two other women, even three?'

Safiyé smiled. 'That's the kind of question Leyla would ask. She's so possessive and jealous.'

'I'm like her. I could not accept the man I love belonging to others.'

Safiyé became thoughtful. She pushed back a strand of hair from her forehead. She really did not know how to explain her views on the relationship between a wife and a husband. She shrugged. 'I've never seen things that way. One woman cannot presume to satisfy all the needs of a man.'

'Do you think that one man can satisfy all the needs of a woman?'

'Of course! A woman is made differently from a man!' Safiyé was feeling more and more uncomfortable with the turn the conversation had taken. She was afraid Maro would think less of her.

Maro noticed Safiyé's embarrassment and tried to reassure her. 'I'm not judging you, Safiyé. I know that tradition and the law force the wife to submit to the husband's will, and it is impossible to rebel. However, in my religion, it is unlawful to have more than one wife. I'd like to know how you really feel about this.'

Her friendly tone soothed Safiyé's apprehensions. 'Riza's having two other wives has taken nothing away from me, nor made him love me any less.'

'You can say that today, but how did you feel when Makbulé arrived . . . and then Leyla?'

'I knew from the beginning that such a day would come. Each time I rejoiced, hoping to find a new sister and a friend in his new wife. Unfortunately, that was not the case either with Makbulé or Leyla, but when you came . . .'

Maro did not even have time to protest that she was not the fourth wife

301

when Eminé came running up to them, waving her arms.

Safiyé rose, pressing her hand against her breast. 'Has something bad happened?' she called to Eminé. 'Is it the children? Riza Bey?'

Eminé was so out of breath that she couldn't answer but shook her head as she slowed down.

Maro put her arm around Safiyé. 'Don't worry. You know how she dramatizes things.'

Gasping for breath, Eminé flopped down on a bench in the pavilion and began fanning herself with her hand.

Safiyé was uneasy. 'What happened?'

'The book!' Eminé panted.

Annoyed that it was such a trivial matter, Safiyé added sternly, 'All right. What about the book?'

'It's disappeared!'

'Impossible! It was in my room. Did you look everywhere?'

'Yes. I even went to look in Riza Bey's library.'

The book in question was one which had fascinated Safiyé for years: Dante's *The Divine Comedy*, with illustrations by Gustave Doré, published in Paris in 1868 by L. Hachette and Co. For weeks Maro had been reading the long poem to Safiyé and Eminé, translating it slowly into Turkish as she went along and explaining each illustration in detail.

'No one could have stolen it,' Maro exclaimed. 'Don't worry, Eminé. We'll find it.'

Safiyé thought it was important. 'I was leafing through it only this morning and I remember putting it on the night table next to my bed. Who could have gone into my room?'

Maro tried to make light of the incident. 'Maybe Leyla or Makbulé borrowed it, or maybe one of the servants put it somewhere else when she cleaned.'

They heard the slap of bare feet on the gravelled path. A young servant girl ran towards them, her black braids bouncing around her head. Maro recognized Ayla, the young Armenian. When she arrived at the pavilion, she curtsied before Safiyé and Eminé and then turned to Maro:

'The mistress wants to speak to you in her apartment.'

'Who? Buyuk Hanim?'

'Yes.'

Safiyé looked puzzled.

'It's a bad sign,' Eminé added.

Maro remained unperturbed. She had been expecting a confrontation with her for some time. 'It's all right. I'm glad to have the opportunity to tell her a few things.

'She's very . . .' began Eminé, then caught herself and waved the servant away. 'I wanted to warn you; Buyuk Hanim is very touchy. Save her pride. Be polite and defer to her.'

'The book!' exclaimed Safiyé. 'I'll bet she has it.'

'We shall see,' Maro replied, as she walked away.

Ayla was waiting in front of Buyuk Hanim's drawing-room and announced Maro. The old woman sat enthroned in a green armchair with her feet resting on a cushion. Maro kissed her hand as tradition demanded. Riza's mother ordered the servant to bring tea and invited Maro to sit down opposite her in a low chair covered in a floral needlepoint. She took a pinch of snuff out of a gold snuffbox, sniffed and sneezed into a lace handkerchief. Maro was touched, as it reminded her of her own mother, who dipped snuff all day long.

'May you live long,' she said in response to the sneeze.

'Thank you. And how are you?'

'Very well, Buyuk Hanim.'

'You've been here for four months now, haven't you?'

'Yes, and I'd like to take advantage of this opportunity to thank you for your having taken me and my son under your roof.'

Buyuk Hanim nodded and kept her hands folded in her lap. Other polite formulas followed, which gave both of them time to study and assess each other. The game continued until Ayla returned with a silver tray and served the tea.

Bringing the glass to her lips, Buyuk Hanim looked straight at Maro. 'You really are a great beauty,' she said flatly.

'You make me blush.'

The old woman's eyes were hooded behind her half-closed lids, like a wildcat looking at its prey. There were many things Buyuk Hanim did not understand about this Armenian woman, beginning with her self-assurance and poise that shone through the modesty and reserve she affected. Buyuk Hanim could not imagine Maro's previous life, but she thought that it must have been very liberated. She was like a mare that had run loose for a long time, and was now having problems adjusting to the harness.

Good manners demanded that Buyuk Hanim speak first. Maro met her stare without blinking. Riza's love protected her and made her feel safe. She knew she displeased Buyuk Hanim by her behaviour and manners and disturbed the established order of the *konak*. Sometimes she did it inadvertently, sometimes on purpose, not in a spirit of rebellion but to emphasize that she was different. And she could stand up to Riza Bey, who thought he owned her.

Maro's composure and her unapologetic way of looking directly at Buyuk Hanim, instead of keeping her eyes respectfully lowered, annoyed the old woman and reminded her of what it was that was bothering her. She did not know just where to begin. Something tangible! She picked up Dante's book, which she had hidden under an album on the lectern.

'I've learned you've been reading this book to Safiyé and Eminé.'

'Yes,' said Maro, unperturbed. 'Would you like me to read it to you, too?'

Buyuk Hanim was not fooled by her deferential manner. This woman was defying her! She slapped her palm down on the cover of the book.

'It's a heathen book!'

'We got it from Riza Bey's library,' Maro reminded her.

'That doesn't matter. My son is not always discerning. You're preaching your religion to Riza's wife and his nanny.'

'With all respect, I must say you're mistaken, Buyuk Hanim.'

'Hah!' Buyuk Hanim was incensed. She opened the book to a page where she had turned a corner down.

'This is a Christian picture, isn't it?'

She showed Maro a crucifix surrounded by a multitude of angels, an etching that illustrated the fourteenth canto of Dante's Paradise.

'Yes,' Maro admitted, 'but it's not a religious book, nor a prayer book. It's a poem, a story book, if you wish, an imaginary voyage into another world, written by a poet . . .'

'Enough! I don't wish to hear any more!' Buyuk Hanim interrupted.

Maro lowered her eyes as a sign of submission.

'We shall burn this book, this work of Satan.'

'No! It's a rare work of art, which is hard to come by nowadays,' cried Maro impulsively. Immediately she regretted her outburst.

Buyuk Hanim gazed at her furiously. She was beside herself, breathing so hard she inhaled the snuff stuck to the sides of her nostrils, and sneezed.

That settled her nerves to some extent. Then she put the book on the floor.

'I'll take this matter up with Riza, who shall decide what's to be done with the book, but it's out of the question for you to continue to read it to Safiyé. You're not to mention it to her. Do you understand?'

'Yes, *Hanim*. I shall do whatever Riza Bey decides.'

'I hope you're not teaching your religion to the children during your lessons.'

'Never!' protested Maro vehemently. 'Safiyé can vouch for that. She's always present.'

'Safiyé, humph!' Buyuk Hanim showed her distrust. 'She's crazy about anything new.'

'I give you my word, *Hanim*. I teach only Arabic writing and French conversation.'

'You forgot arithmetic and geography! And to the girls! It would be better if they learnt how to sew and embroider.'

'Whatever they learn will be useful to them. If they know how to add and subtract, they can manage their husbands' households better.'

Realizing she would never gain the better of this woman, Buyuk Hanim gestured that the discussion was finished and held out her glass.

'Serve me some tea.'

The way the old lady reacted reminded Maro of her mother's behaviour every time she realized that she was losing an argument. The two women resembled each other in certain ways and, in spite of herself, Maro felt inclined to be indulgent towards Buyuk Hanim. She poured her tea and took some for herself. They drank in silence. Maro looked around the room stealthily, intrigued by the large number of photograph albums.

'Oh, and that awful piano!' snapped Buyuk Hanim, putting her glass down.

'I don't understand.'

'It's bad enough that you play for Riza Bey and for his wives in the evening. But your practising right after lunch, just when I'm taking my nap!'

'Your nap?'

Maro was astonished. She didn't excuse herself by telling Buyuk Hanim that she had been giving lessons to Leyla at Leyla's specific request.

'Yes, I sleep very little and even then quite badly. I need a nap in the afternoon. Everybody in this house knows that.'

'No one ever told me.'

Maro now understood why Leyla had been so insistent on taking piano lessons at that time. Her friendliness was sheer hypocrisy. She must have taken *The Divine Comedy* to her mother-in-law. From now on Maro was going to be wary towards her.

'I'm terribly sorry to have disturbed your nap. It won't happen again.'

'Very well,' the old lady said, delighted with Maro's show of good will. 'I was sure that you were not being nasty, but only ignorant of the house rules. It's the same with your lack of restraint.'

'Lack of restraint?' asked Maro, pretending to be surprised.

'Yes. You frequently forget to wear a veil on the ground floor. You're too familiar with the servants. Twice you've spoken to Herr Mueller, the children's German tutor. Whatever did you have to say to that man?'

'I only greeted him politely, as good manners require.'

What she had tried to do was to tell him about her situation, but the German had not been willing to listen.

'It's simply not done. You're in a Muslim household and the women of this house do not speak to strangers and certainly not with their faces uncovered.'

Maro took a deep breath, as if getting ready to dive into water. She thought carefully about what she was about to say and weighed the consequences. She dropped the conciliatory tone she had assumed since the beginning of the tête-à-tête, and declared evenly but firmly:

'Buyuk Hanim, I'm not a woman of this household. I respect your traditions, but I have another religion and I belong to another world, to which I long to return.'

The old lady was flabbergasted by Maro's words and could only stammer, 'B . . . b . . . but . . . b . . . b . . . but . . .'

'It was good of your son to save our lives and to take us into his family. It was an act of great charity, and Allah must be greatly pleased. Nevertheless, I should like to join my relatives in the capital, but Riza Bey has done nothing to make it possible for me to leave. What you've just said shows that you, the mistress of this house, feel that I am not part of this household, nor shall I ever be. So I beg you, Buyuk Hanim, to convince your son to send me to the capital.'

As she pleaded, her voice became more heated. She clasped her hands together to keep them from shaking, while looking at Buyuk Hanim expectantly all the while. The wait for a response seemed interminable. The old woman took out her snuff-box to give herself time to think. At last she pointed to an album on the low table.

'Give it to me.'

When she had it in her hand, she took out a large photograph, which had been slipped between the cover and the first page. Maro recognized the picture taken by Naim Sarfati on the day of her arrival in Ayntab.

'Look to the right. You can see yourself and your son.'

'Yes?' She did not know exactly what the woman had in mind.

'This photograph,' Buyuk Hanim said, 'is a picture of Riza Bey's family, and you and your son are part of it.'

'No!' Maro exclaimed, agonized. 'I'm married. I belong to another man!'

Still holding the photograph, which she had just decided to insert into the album, Buyuk Hanim decreed, 'Any woman who conquers Riza Bey's heart is part of his household.'

Tears in her eyes, Maro lowered her head. 'With your permission, I should like to leave.'

Buyuk Hanim's voice softened. 'I still have things to tell you . . . My daughter, it would be better if you converted to the true faith and sent Tomas to the Koranic school with Riza's sons.'

Maro lifted her head quickly and said defiantly, 'That's out of the question!'

'We have all the time in the world,' Buyuk Hanim reminded her, unperturbed. 'For the time being, I'd like you to watch your words and not fill the other wives' heads with dangerous pagan ideas.'

Maro rose without saying a word, nodded briefly and walked quickly towards the door.

'You may leave!' Buyuk Hanim shot out sharply.

When Maro received Riza's invitation to have coffee in his apartments, she knew that Buyuk Hanim had told him of their conversation. Just as well! Now he knew how she felt. Every time she opened up the subject of her departure, he deftly avoided answering by pretending not to understand. Perhaps she should have insisted before now; she had shown far too much patience and Riza undoubtedly interpreted her patience as tacit acceptance.

Riza's apartments, which Maro knew well, were at the end of the hall and covered the entire north wing of the second floor. The entrance was through an antechamber, furnished very simply, with a rosewood desk with gilded handles on the drawers and a glassed-in bookcase, containing

Morocco-bound volumes, rolled documents, plans and maps.

Riza Bey welcomed her with a charming smile. If he was angry, he concealed it completely. His prominent Adam's apple was visible through the V-neck of his white shirt; his sleeves were rolled up to the elbows, exposing his strong arms. When he saw how forlorn Maro looked, he refrained from kissing her on the mouth and instead he kissed her hand.

'My soul,' he murmured.

She tipped her head politely. 'Good evening, Riza Bey.'

Still holding her by the hand, he led her into the next room. Although he was annoyed that she was not appropriately dressed, he made an effort not to reveal it by concentrating on her health.

'You're not feeling well?'

'No!'

'Is something bothering you?'

'Yes!'

Riza Bey had not expected such frankness and was lost for words. She contravened all the rules of good behaviour for Ottoman women. He stepped aside to let Maro precede him into the drawing room. It was a fairly large rectangular room with a miscellaneous collection of costly furniture in various styles. A profusion of rich rugs and potted ferns created a muffled ambiance. A superb silver brazier with a conical cover sat next to a gramophone, which was playing a Chopin nocturne. The sound had become somewhat distorted, however, because the wax cylinder was so badly worn.

Riza sat down on a divan draped in red velvet. There was a table inlaid in mother-of-pearl in front of him and on it lay a plate of sweetmeats. Maro knew what was expected of her. She added water to the ground coffee and put it on to heat, then poured the thick liquid into two demitasses. When she served Riza Bey, he moved over, expecting her to sit down beside him, but she chose to sit on a chair. Although he smiled, she could tell by the slight contraction of his jaws and the hint of a frown that he was angry.

Once more Maro defied convention and spoke first. 'I had a discussion with your mother this afternoon.'

'I know.'

'It seems she's displeased with me in many ways and for many reasons.'

'That's not the way she put it to me. My mother's very old-fashioned, I don't want her feelings hurt.'

'If I did so, I didn't mean to.'

'I believe you.'

308

'It is impossible to change so drastically.'

'No one is asking you to,' he said, mollified. 'It would be enough to temper the way you react sometimes and keep certain thoughts to yourself. They may seem harmless to you, but they make my mother worry that you may be a bad influence on the other women in the household.'

'With Dante's poetry and geography lessons?' asked Maro sarcastically.

'That's not what I'm talking about,' said Riza Bey impatiently. 'I'm the master in this house and I, and only I, decide what is permitted under my roof! I authorized those lessons and they shall continue.' Riza Bey interrupted himself to sip some coffee. Then he went on more kindly, 'With a little bit of tact, Buyuk Hanim can be led to accept new things. My mother's very conscious of appearances. Pay attention to details, such as wearing a veil, keeping the proper distance from the servants and not talking to strangers.'

He wanted to minimize the whole business because he was in a quandary. He wanted to take Maro's part, yet he agreed with his mother that her attitude perturbed the *konak* and put the rules of conduct in doubt. Her spirit of independence, her straightforwardness and her tendency to stand up for her ideas were mainly due to her western upbringing, but they could easily be mistaken for a scorn of tradition. These traits sometimes upset Riza Bey too, but at the same time they were part of Maro's charm.

Maro, having no wish to rake over the everyday squabbles and quibbles, asked point-blank, 'Did your mother tell you that I want to leave?'

Riza's face hardened and he answered curtly, 'Yes, but I rather wish you'd spoken to me first.'

She exploded! 'I have spoken to you, Riza Bey! Twenty times, if not more, I've tried to tell you, but you never listen to me!'

He looked at her severely but gave no answer. Instead, he merely handed her his empty cup. 'You see,' she said, 'it's always the same.'

He sighed and looked sad. 'Haven't I done everything to make your stay pleasant?'

'Yes,' she admitted.

'Don't I treat your son like my own?'

'Yes.'

He raised his arms and looked confused. 'Then, what? You live in a palace. I love you as no man has ever loved you. What else can I do?'

'Give me my freedom! My freedom, Riza Bey! Your palace is a gilded cage.'

309

'I'm surprised. You enjoy the same freedom as my other wives.'

She jumped to her feet and clenched her hands. She was infuriated at his hypocrisy. 'Freedom for you means never to leave these walls, except to go to the *hammam* in a well-guarded closed carriage! Let's face it, Riza Bey. I'm your prisoner!'

She expected a violent reaction; instead he looked downcast. 'Your words hurt me – me, the person who loves you more than anybody in this world!'

She stiffened and answered sharply, 'If you loved me as much as you pretend you do, you'd have contacted my family in Constantinople a long time ago.'

'I can't!'

Maro softened. 'But you promised! You promised to send me to the capital!'

He cut in categorically, 'Oh, no, I didn't! I said I would see what I could do, but it's impossible for you to leave right now.'

'Why?'

'Typhus is ravaging the country, we're at war and travel is restricted. Everything is under control and, at the same time, everything is in total anarchy. To have written to your relatives would have jeopardized my own safety.'

'I don't believe you. You're very powerful, Riza Bey. I know you have authority over the governors of the neighbouring provinces.' Maro had learnt about this from listening to some of the women talk in the *hammam*.

Disconcerted, Riza turned red. He smashed his fist into his palm. 'I forbid you to question my word!'

Although intimidated, Maro still muttered, 'What else can I do? Everything leads me to believe that you . . .' Seeing that the rational approach would not move him, she changed tactics and instead begged, 'Let me go, Riza Bey.'

'And lose you? Never!'

She let herself fall back into the chair. 'Now we have the truth!' She stared absently at her hands clasped in her lap.

Riza went around the table to stand beside her and said gently, 'How can a woman as intelligent as you are think that a man who is passionately in love with her would let his love go?'

She remained silent and still, as he laid his hand on her shoulder. 'I love you, Maro. You're everything to me!'

'And what if I don't love you?' she asked, looking up.

'You're interested in everything I do. Isn't that love?'

'That's only politeness.'

'And the affection for me that I feel in you?'

'Gratitude and friendship.'

'Now it's you who are lying. There are some things which cannot be misread.'

She shrugged. 'What do you know about women? Their bodies!'

He tightened his grip on Maro's shoulder. 'That isn't fair! You're being cruel to me, but I won't hold it against you. You will learn to love me as I deserve.'

She sniffed. Riza lifted her chin, forcing her to look at him. She was crying. 'I want to make you my wife and Tomas my son. I can give you security, wealth and comfort.'

'No! I shall not marry you and my son shall not be yours! I shall be the mistress of Governor Riza Bey because I have no other choice, but don't expect anything else from me!'

He lifted her out of the chair, stood her up and held her tight. 'For now that's enough,' he murmured. 'The rest will come in good time.' He put his strong arm around her waist and drew her towards the curtain which hid the door to the bedroom.

'Not tonight, I beg you!'

Riza held her more insistently. 'We shall sleep together like brother and sister, but I want you with me, my little dove!'

The rain trickled down Bedri's back and he shivered. To warm up, he went to get the bottle of brandy that he kept in the sidecar of his black German motorcycle. Empty! In a rage he threw the bottle against a rock, where it splintered. He had had enough! He was tempted to return to Ayntab and report that Vartan was dead and buried. But no! If, against all probabilities, he should turn up one day, Riza Bey would never forgive Bedri for having cheated him. He did not understand why this man's capture was so important to his master.

Bedri listened to Suleiman and Nazim as they related in detail the story of a wounded officer who called himself Lieutenant Akdar: how they had sheltered him; how they had tried to cure his malaria and, especially, how they had brutally circumcised him. It all served to convince Bedri that

Vartan must have been hiding in the vicinity of Caeserea. He stopped the motorcycle, took a military map from his coat's pocket and bent over it to protect it from the rain. He ran his finger about ninety kilometres up the road. He would have to do this in every direction and to be careful not to miss any side roads or trails. He would have to stop at each farm, search the houses, stables and sheep-pens again, even though they had already been searched twice. Balian could not have evaporated. Somewhere someone knew something!

Vartan was using a wooden pitchfork to feed hay to the sheep and goats, while Halidé, or rather Aroussiag, as she preferred to be called, strewed grain in the chicken coop. In spite of her insistence that he spare himself from unnecessary work, he never missed an occasion to exercise his muscles, flaccid from illness and inactivity.

After the gendarmes' first visit, Vartan had come out of his hide-out in the stable and returned to the house but a week later there had been another search and they had almost caught him. After that, he never left the hiding place except at night and he was always back in before dawn. He had the disturbing sensation that the noose was tightening about his neck. Aroussiag, by contrast, was optimistic and thought it highly improbable that he would be caught.

'You're too suspicious,' she said, gripping his arm. 'You don't trust in Divine Providence.'

'That's the only reason I'm still alive.'

'How about your friends who saved you from the scaffold? The missionary who sheltered you? Kerim and I who picked you up out of a ditch? Did all of that happen because you were suspicious?'

She was right up to a point, so Vartan conceded, smiling.

Aroussiag had the same attitude towards the winter. People here were terrified by the onset of winter. They were often snowbound for days, fearful of not being able to hold out until spring, because food was scarce and the cold intense. She did not share this fear. She talked about the solitude and the hardships of winter with a hint of joy in her voice. Vartan knew that this was partly due to his company. Her attachment to him was plain and she showed her affection and tenderness more and more openly, even though he did not encourage her in any way. He kept his distance, but he could not always prevent her warmth and familiarity from setting the tone of their relationship, nor indeed conceal his affection for her.

Suddenly Vartan laid down the pitchfork, dashed to the stable door and signalled Aroussiag to stop raking the hay from the loft.

'Listen!'

There were sounds of distant backfiring. Aroussiag joined him, cupped her ear for a moment and exclaimed: 'An automobile? Around here?' The sound of the engine became louder and got closer.

'Let's not take any chances,' Vartan said, walking into the hiding place.

Aroussiag replaced the manger in front of the opening and tied the donkey in its stall. She went back to the doorway, pulled her veil over her face and called Kourt, who came running and sat at her feet.

A motorcycle approached, skidding on the muddy road. It slowed down and came up the path leading to the house. Aroussiag, holding the dog by his collar, looked out and waved to the motorcycle rider. He came up to the stable, stopped the engine and got off. His leather helmet wrapped his head and hid his ears, the tight chinstrap emphasized the flabbiness of the cheeks and the thick, round goggles seemed to be sitting on his heavy moustache. He looked quite funny, but Aroussiag was too frightened to be amused by these details.

'I'm conducting an investigation for the government,' he said authoritatively. 'I have some questions to ask you.'

Her voice betraying no fear, she replied with slightly affected politeness. 'Don't stand out in the rain, Bey Effendi. Bring your vehicle in.'

She stepped back so that he could bring his motorcycle into the stable. The smell of burnt oil was enough to overpower the familiar odour of dung. Kourt growled softly and bared his fangs as he watched man's movements.

'That's very kind of you,' the visitor said hoarsely, and he took off his misted goggles. He slowly removed his oilskin coat and examined the stable carefully. Then he brought out a poster, unfolded it and showed it to her. 'Have you ever seen this man?'

Aroussiag looked at it briefly and said indifferently, 'No, I haven't. I've already told the guards that twice. They searched the house, the stable, even the haystacks.'

'Are you very sure?'

'Absolutely.'

'Do many people come by here?'

'Very few. Peasants . . . travelling salesmen . . . sometimes a *hodja* wanders by as he goes from village to village preaching.'

313

'Do you remember seeing a different kind of traveller about three months ago?'

'That was a long time ago.' Aroussiag pretending to be thinking back, trying to recall. 'I don't know exactly what you mean.'

Bedri became impatient. 'You know, a Christian missionary or a European!'

'No, Effendi. That I would have noticed and remembered.'

'A vehicle carrying a wounded man?'

'No.'

Bedri sighed deeply and stared absently at the rain while he rolled a cigarette. 'Do you know everyone in Urgup?'

'Yes, I do.'

'Do you know if anyone is hiding a stranger? In a small village, everybody usually knows everything.'

'Some of the families have taken in some Armenian children as servants. Other than that, I've seen no new faces.'

Bedri flicked away his cigarette.

Aroussiag drew near and, feigning innocent curiosity, asked. 'Could this man be in Urgup?'

He shrugged desperately. 'Here! There! Anywhere! The last time he was seen was about twenty kilometres from here.'

'He must be a very important person for the guards to want to catch him so badly.'

'But he isn't! I've been wondering if . . .' He stopped suddenly, realizing that he was about to confide his doubts and resentment to a peasant. He pulled himself together and again became the interrogator.

'Where's your husband?'

'He's in the army.'

'You mean you live here alone? So isolated? Aren't you afraid?'

She pointed to her dog, who was still showing his fangs. 'And I have a loaded rifle in the house.'

Her determination amused him and he smiled. He placed his hand on the handlebar of the motorcycle.

'You're soaking wet,' Aroussiag sounded concerned. 'Don't you want something hot to drink? I can make some linden tea for you.'

He grimaced. 'No, thank you, but I could really use a glass of liquor.'

'Come over to the house. My husband left a bottle of *raki*.'

Crouching at the opening of the hiding place, Vartan was following the conversation, trying to see the face of the motorcyclist through the slats of the manger, but the donkey had blocked his view and he had been able to see only the muddy boots. He knew that rasping voice from somewhere but he couldn't remember where. It was probably a coincidence. He admired Aroussiag's guts! She had acted so naturally that she had disarmed all suspicion.

Ten minutes later they returned. Bedri thanked her and pushed his vehicle out. The motor had to be coaxed to start and the constant backfiring was loud enough to drown out his oaths. Then at last there was a deafening roar, as the motorcycle took off in the direction of Urgup. Aroussiag let Vartan out of his hiding place.

'Bravo!' he said. 'You were perfect!'

Flattered, she smiled. 'I found out something. The guards have stopped combing the region and the police have ended their investigation. This policeman thinks you're probably dead and he's sure that, if you're not, you're no longer in this region.'

'Did you find out anything about him?'

'He comes from Ayntab. He's going back there in a few days.'

'Ayntab! Then he's the man who wounded me in Malatya!'

Aroussiag pressed his arm. Her voice sounded happy. 'You've nothing to fear as long as you stay here, especially as we'll be snowbound soon.'

Maro had opened the curtain of the carriage which was bringing her back from the *hammam* and was leaning against the glass window of the door, watching the houses of Ayntab file by. Her companions – Shahané, Safiyé and Eminé – were quiet, exhausted from the long day at the public bath-house, exhilarated from having been with their friends and almost drunk from so much chatter. It was the same every time they returned from their weekly excursion.

These outings, which at first had seemed like an escape for Maro, had become a real ordeal – a whole day of listening to droning, insipid conversations and screaming children who ran around among the half-naked women! All the customers were aware that Maro was the mistress of the governor of the province, so they avoided her as much out of contempt and distrust as out of envy. Maro would have gladly stayed at home if it had not been for the fact that the outing involved a crossing of the town where she could see what she thought of as real life. The carriage passed the Balikli market and Maro caught a glimpse of the YMCA building.

After Riza had laid his cards on the table, Maro had no more illusions about her future and was filled with a profound despair. She tried to hide her sadness from Tomas, but sometimes she could not keep it from showing. Nothing could cheer her up. She forgot only when she was teaching the children, playing the piano or translating *Madame Bovary* into Turkish for Safiyé. Reading reminded Maro that there was another world outside the cloistered *konak*. Weak echoes of it filtered through from the gossip of the women in the *hammam* and the little news that Vartouhi, who had become her devoted servant, brought back from the market. No newspaper ever entered the house and the numerous foreigners – German military men, missionaries and diplomats – who called on the governor had absolutely no contact with his wives. The year 1916 had just begun and nothing led Maro to believe that it would be any different from the one before. She could see no end to her seclusion and the future looked like an infinite repetition of today.

The boulevard turned and led straight out of town. After the Latin monastery came the Ak Yol Mosque. In front of it there was a large crowd gathered around a newspaper seller who was shouting out the headlines. Maro ordered the driver to stop.

Safiyé drew near the window. She was as curious as Maro. She half-opened the door to listen to the news:

'The battle of the Dardanelles is over!' the newspaper vendor was shouting at the top of his voice. 'Our brave soldiers have pushed the enemy into retreat. The English and the French have taken heavy losses and are re-embarking. Constantinople is no longer threatened! The Ottoman Empire has been victorious again!'

Hoorays and shouts arose. Safiyé ordered the driver to go on as the other carriage carrying Buyuk Hanim along with the other wives and the younger children was waiting for them some way away. Maro wondered out loud if what she had heard was only propaganda.

'Of course not!' answered Safiyé proudly, as the carriage set off. 'One of the wives of Ahmed Jemal Pasha, who commands the Third Army, told me the same thing confidentially at the *hammam*.'

Maro stared out into the street again, lost in thought. The Allies were leaving! She simply could not believe that the Ottoman Army had successfully resisted the might of France and Great Britain. Official sources said that the Russians were blocked off at their borders and the British were immobilized in the south of Mesopotamia. If that was true, then the collapse of the Ottoman Empire, which was what all Armenians were secretly hoping for, would not come soon and the deportations and massacres would continue.

Compared with the rest of the Armenians who were suffering on the road to exile and dying in the camps in the desert, compared even with those who were precariously surviving by hiding under false identities or pretending to have converted to Islam, she had been lucky. Suddenly she was ashamed of her black silk dress and her massive gold necklace. But what about all those other Armenian women locked up in harems whose children were being raised as Muslims? Should she and they be thankful to God for sparing them?

After they had crossed the bridge, the driver called out, 'Safiyé Hanim! Safiyé Hanim!'

She lifted her veil before sticking her head out to see what it was all about, then opened the door wide, turned to the other passengers and said, laughing, 'Look who's coming!'

Five horsemen were galloping through a vineyard towards them. Kenan and Tomas rode in front of Riza Bey and his servant, Abdullah, who were reining in their horses. Altan trotted far behind them. Maro was worried her son was riding too fast but was reassured when she saw he had his horse completely under control. How he had grown in these six months! As he drew near, he reminded her more and more of Vartan – the same piercing look, the same pronounced cheekbones, the same self-assurance in his bearing.

The vehicles stopped and Riza Bey went up to the first one to pay his respects to Buyuk Hanim. Tomas and Kenan stopped at the second one. Both of them were drenched in sweat, as were their mounts.

'Did you see how I was galloping, mother?' Tomas was elated.

'Yes, darling,' said Maro smiling.

'We two are the fastest,' added Kenan proudly. The two boys exchanged conspiratorial looks and burst out laughing.

'Look, Mother,' he said, making his horse take two side steps. 'Just like father with Hour Grag.'

Maro felt a pang in her heart but nodded approvingly. Right now, Tomas was the picture of happiness and Maro told herself that she had no right to

317

jeopardize his carefree existence. Riza Bey came up and looked at both boys proudly.

'They're already accomplished horsemen!' he exclaimed. 'I'll make them strong, brave men – real leaders!'

The boys were flattered by his words, beamed and sat up straight in their saddles. Altan joined them; he was sulking and his mother noticed it immediately.

'I shall be a general,' declared Kenan.

'And I shall be a major like my father,' said Tomas.

Looking pointedly at Riza Bey, Safiyé asked her son, 'And you, Altan, what will you become?'

The boy, who had taken a fall while racing the two younger ones, lowered his head and shrugged.

Understanding his wife's plea, Riza announced, 'Altan shall be a manager of men. He shall manage the land with an iron fist.'

Altan could not believe his ears. His eyes lit up and he declared, 'You will see, father. You will be proud of me.'

He turned his horse around, spurred him and took off down the road, ululating loudly. Imitating his cry, Kenan and Tomas followed him and the coachmen barely held their horses in check as the uproar had upset them.

'Go with them,' Riza Bey ordered the young Arab standing a bit to the back of him.

Safiyé bowed her head and said, 'I thank you in Altan's name.'

'I love all my sons, and Altan does everything he can to learn and to please me. I always know how to acknowledge goodwill.' Saying this, Riza Bey looked hard at Maro, who understood that his last words were intended for her.

Maro was leaning against the balustrade of the balcony and gazing at the glittering garden. The sun had lit a thousand fires in the raindrops left on the leaves by last night's storm. The winter had been mild and rainy in Ayntab. Sometimes a south-west breeze from the Mediterranean brought a bit of cool air and Maro liked to imagine she could smell the sea, but this only amplified her desire to leave.

Someone knocked at the door. Vartouhi walked in lightly and rapidly and joined her mistress on the balcony.

'What is it, Vartouhi . . . I mean, Ayla?' Maro often forgot and used her Armenian name, which made the girl nervous.

'I'm supposed to go with Eminé and Buyuk Hanim to the market. I'll be back this afternoon.'

Maro pulled her into the room. 'I would like you to run an errand for me.'

Ayla smiled, 'Of course, *Hanim*.'

'Do they ever leave you alone sometimes, when you go into town?'

The young girl did not understand. Maro spoke more clearly. 'Could you go to the American School or the YMCA without anyone noticing?'

This time Ayla realized what Maro was driving at, and her eyes widened with fear. 'No, *Hanim*. I'm either with Buyuk Hanim or with the other servants.'

'Are there any Armenians or Jews among the tradesmen you see?'

The young girl hesitated for a moment and then said, 'Yes.'

Maro opened one of the drawers in the dresser and took out a letter and a gold bracelet.

'I would like you to pass these on to a merchant discreetly and ask him to send the letter to Constantinople. The bracelet is to pay him for his trouble.'

Ayla hid her hands behind her back; her voice trembled. 'I can't, *Hanim*! I can't!'

Maro caught her by the shoulders and insisted sweetly, 'Nobody will notice, if you choose the right moment.'

'I cannot!'

'I know it's dangerous, but you're the only one I can ask, Vartouhi.'

'Mistress . . .' the girl moaned beseechingly.

'I promise nothing bad will happen to you. You know I have a lot of influence over Riza Bey. I'll protect you if you are caught. I'll say I ordered you to do it and, if anyone is punished, it'll be me.'

Ayla shook her head again but, faced with Maro's imploring look, she agreed. She slipped the letter and bracelet into her bodice.

Maro kissed her on the cheek. 'When I leave here, I'll take you with me, Vartouhi.'

Once out in the hall, the girl patted the letter in her bosom and her eyes filled with tears. She went down to the ground floor and slipped into the *selamlik*, where Riza Bey had his office. Bedri, absorbed in checking the account ledgers of the province, sat at a table at the end of the room, to the left of the door leading into the governor's office.

'What do you want?' he asked Ayla rudely.

'I want to see the master,' she said haltingly.

'What for?'

She blushed. 'It's . . . confidential.'

'Confidential!' Bedri exploded. 'Just imagine! Confidential!'

She insisted, 'The master told me to come and see him quickly.' Bedri was puzzled for a moment but then got up, grumbling, 'What's your name?'

'Ayla.'

He went into the office, came out and waved her in. Shyly, she entered the room with verses from the Quran painted on the wall. Riza Bey sat behind an imposing desk littered with papers.

He looked up and smiled engagingly. 'Come in. Don't be frightened.'

She entered trembling, with tears in her eyes.

'You don't have to feel guilty. You're only following my orders.'

She nodded, plunged her hand into her bodice and handed the letter and the bracelet to Riza Bey, who said, 'Good! I knew I could count on you.'

She was upset for having betrayed Maro, she clasped her hands together and begged through her sobs, 'Please, Bey Effendi, don't punish my mistress.'

He chuckled. 'My brave little one, don't be afraid for your mistress.'

He examined the envelope which was addressed in Arabic script to Mesrop Mesropian, 3888 Shahin Bey Street, Harbiyé, Stamboul. He tore it open. As he had expected, the letter was written in Armenian. He held it out to the servant. 'Do you know how to read your language?'

'Yes, Bey Effendi.'

'All right. Read it.'

She took the letter reluctantly and began to decipher Maro's fine handwriting, while translating simultaneously.

'The fifth of January 1916.

Dear Uncle Mesrop and Aunt Arpiné,

I pray for this letter to reach you and find you alive and in good health. We were deported from Sivas at the beginning of July. Vartan was arrested and condemned to be hanged. Since then I have had no news of him, but I cannot make myself believe that he is dead. My whole being tells me he is still alive. Unfortunately, my mother, Azniv, died during the deportation. Tomas and I are in good heath and safe. The Governor of Ayntab, Riza Bey, has taken us under his protection, but I don't know when we shall be able to make the trip to Constantinople.

What has become of you, my cousin Lucie, and my cousins, Diran and Barkev? I have been told that, in Constantinople, the situation for the Armenians is all right. I hope this is true. If, by some miracle, Vartan contacts you, please reassure him about us and tell him where we are. I don't know when we shall be able to join you. Tomas and I kiss you and pray to the Lord to reunite all of us soon.

Maro.'

Ayla put the letter down on the corner of the desk. Riza Bey picked it up and burnt it in an ashtray. 'Maro Hanim must not know that you gave me this letter. What were you supposed to do with it?'

'Hand it over to a merchant.'

'Tell her you did that, understood?'

'Yes, Bey Effendi.' The girl was desolate.

'You've acted in the best interests of your mistress. That letter could have fallen into the hands of the police or the army and caused great trouble for her relatives, not to mention what could have happened here. Probably even I could not have stopped them from arresting her. Maro Hanim still does not understand what is best for her and her son. You must help me to keep her from doing anything foolish.'

Ayla wanted to be convinced that Riza Bey spoke the truth and that she had acted correctly, but she could not, even though she had really no choice.

Dismissing her, Riza Bey added, 'You won't be a servant all your life. I'll find you a good husband when you are old enough to get married; in the meantime, keep me informed.'

She bowed deeply and went out to join Buyuk Hanim, whose carriage had just entered the courtyard.

Tomas was crossing the dining room that afternoon when Maro came in from the garden. He was all excited.

'Can I go to the Koranic School with Kenan, mother?'

The classes in religion were given by Piri Hodja in the mosque, next to the *konak*. This seventy-three-year-old man was the *muezzin* and led the Friday prayers. As Eminé and Makbulé were close by, Maro hid her surprise and annoyance.

She took her son by the hand. 'Come with me. We'll talk about it.'

321

They went to her room where they found Ayla arranging Maro's cosmetics and jewels on the dresser.

Maro immediately asked her, 'Did you find the merchant you were looking for at the market?'

She lowered her eyes, as she did most of the times. 'Yes, *Hanim.*'

'Did everything go all right?'

Ayla nodded and Maro was relieved.

'Thank you, my dear.' Then she asked her to bring them tea and a snack from the kitchen, specifying, 'Bring enough pastries for the three of us.'

When she and Tomas were alone, she sat on the bed and talked to him in Armenian. 'What was it you just asked me?'

'I'd like to go to Piri Hodja's school.'

Maro grimaced. 'Did Riza put that idea in your head?'

'No, but I want to do what Kenan does.'

'You can't,' Maro said gently.

The child looked upset. 'Why not?'

His mother pulled him to her and stroked his hair. 'In the mosque Kenan is studying the Quran, the book of his religion. You . . . you have another religion, that of Jesus.'

'But, Mother, I could learn the Quran and still love Jesus.'

'No,' Maro said firmly. 'You'd only get mixed up. It's good to be friends with Riza's children and to learn to speak Turkish, but you must not forget you are Armenian. Now we are forced to live like they do, but some day we'll be with our family again; we'll live according to our traditions and faith and speak our own language again.'

Tomas looked serious and nodded at each of his mother's statements.

She went on, 'Your religion is part of your heritage. It was your father's, your grandmother's, your godfather's and your grandfather's, whose name you bear. Each time you pray, you say the same words they said thousands of times before. It's as if they were continuing to pray with your voice. Do you remember the prayers your godfather, Armen, taught you?'

At the mention of those names, Tomas swallowed loudly and tried to hold back his tears. 'Of course, I remember!'

He tried never to think of his grandmother, Armen and Araksi, the deportation convoy, the dead child in front of the monastery, the cave. He had succeeded in burying these memories deeply in his mind, so that when he looked straight ahead, he could see only blurred images out of the corner of his eye. Moved deeply, he started to recite:

322

'*Hayr mer vor hergines . . .*'

Maro joined him, and together they said the Lord's Prayer. They were just finishing when Ayla came back with another servant, a fat, curly-haired woman in her thirties. She was also carrying a tray. They put the food down near the window and the other servant withdrew.

'You'll join us, Vartouhi,' Maro spoke in Armenian. 'Today is a holiday. It is January the fifth.'

Vartouhi who had seen this same date on Maro's letter, was ashamed. She felt guilty and swore to herself never again to betray this lady who was treating her like a daughter. They sat down on the floor around the table.

Tomas was intrigued, 'What holiday is it, *mayrig?*'

'It's the eve of *Dznount*, Armenian Christmas.'

'Christmas?' Tomas repeated incredulously. The word had magical connotations for him.

'Do you remember Christmas last year?'

Tomas remembered the presents he had received the thirty-first, but Christmas was vaguer in his mind because it had become mixed up with other religious festivities. His uncertainty showed.

'And you, Vartouhi, do you remember?'

'Yes,' Vartouhi choked.

She could see her parents, her brothers and sisters, her uncles, their wives and children, all gathered together to celebrate Christmas at her parent's home.

Maro began to reminisce. 'When I was a little girl, I found the day before Christmas Eve very long. We had to fast all day to be able to take Communion at the end of the High Mass, which seemed to last forever. You, Tomas, fell asleep during the Mass last year.'

'I'm older this year. I would have stayed awake.'

'Of course. You would have fasted like a grown-up. It would have made your father very proud.' She held in a sigh and continued to talk of her childhood. 'After Mass, we gathered at my grandfather's, where there was always a banquet prepared. He was a small man and squinted, which gave the impression that he was always laughing. My cousins and I carried candles and went to sing in front of the neighbours' houses.'

'I did that, too!' Vartouhi exclaimed joyfully, glancing at the door as she sang, '*Chrisdos dznav yev haydnetsav / Tsez yev mez medz avedis*[1] . . . After that we knocked on their doors and they gave us gifts.'

---

1. Christ is born and revealed today / good tidings for thee and us (Armenian).

'That's right,' added Maro.

'That must have been fun,' said Tomas, who had done none of these.

'At home, we ate *anoush abour* at Christmas,' recalled Vartouhi dreamily.

'Sweet soup?' Tomas was astounded. 'What's that?'

'A kind of wheat pudding with dried fruit. Your grandmother prepared it every year and you liked it very much.'

Tomas looked cross at having forgotten it. The young people sat spellbound as Maro started to relate the legend surrounding the birth of Christ in a stable. They leaned across the table like conspirators. Then she taught them a hymn, which she sang in a deep voice, her hands crossed over her chest, while she moved her head in time to the music.

*Khorhourt medz yev zkancheli*
*Vor haïsn avour haydnetsav*
*Hovivkn yerken ent hreshdages*
*Dan avedis ashkharhi*
*Dznav nor arkah*
*I Betlehem kaghaki.*[1]

Tomas and Vartouhi were so completely absorbed in Maro's words that they forgot the cakes and tea – which had long since become cold.

---

1.  Oh, great and marvellous mystery / Revealed to us today / Shepherds and angels sing ·/Announcing good tidings / Onto us is born a King / In Bethlehem (Armenian).

# ELEVEN

The first snowstorm of the winter was blowing hard on Cappadocia and Aroussiag's house creaked under the onslaught of the wind. The oiled paper, used instead of glass to seal the windows, was vibrating like the hide of a tambourine beaten by the fingers of a spirited dancer. At times one could hear what sounded like the long howl of a wounded animal, but it was only the wind whipping over the ridge of the rocky peaks that dominated the village of Urgup. Since noon, the snow had been swirling and piling up on the ground, forming drifts around any barrier it encountered. No one noticed that night had fallen earlier than usual.

Occasionally a fleeting, elfish flame spurted from a bed of burning coals in the fire pit, dug in the middle of the floor of packed earth. Vartan and Aroussiag were sitting on a carpet in a cocoon of warmth and light and reverently eating their *anoush abour*. She had made up her eyes with kohl and put up her blue-black hair in a chignon. Vartan's long beard stood out against the beige sweater she had knitted for him. To try to make it a cheerful Christmas, she had prepared all the traditional dishes of lamb, rice and chicken, but the occasion had brought back nostalgic memories, so they ate in silence.

She had put the photograph of her family on a chest between the icon of the Virgin and the cross and kept glancing at it. It vividly reminded Aroussiag of her native village on the mountainside from where she could see the grey-blue expanse of the Black Sea. She could hear her father's deep voice, her mother's lilting speech and the high, sharp laughter of her brothers and sisters in the moaning wind.

Vartan noticed the young woman's sad expression when she looked at the photograph on the chest and knew what was on her mind. 'Why do you

325

always imagine the worst? Perhaps they fled by boat or they're hiding out in the mountains.'

She looked heartbroken. 'No, they didn't. I heard the village was razed.'

She had had no news from her family for the last five years. Her parents had opposed her marriage to Yashar, an eighteen-year-old Muslim who worked as an apprentice to a blacksmith. Cursed by her father, she had eloped with her lover and settled in Urgup where they had married. It had been easy for her to take a Turkish name and pass as a Muslim but, with Yashar's permission, she had kept on secretly practising her own religion.

'You shouldn't feel guilty. You couldn't have done anything to stop it.'

'But if I were with them, I could have helped take care of them.'

'You're torturing yourself needlessly. Nothing would have changed if you had been there.'

She picked up the photograph and murmured wistfully, 'My father was a quiet, hard-working man, who was always worried, but my mother had great faith in God's Mercy. She sheltered and spoiled us. Look at these children, Vartan. Their lives still lay ahead of all of them.'

'They might still be alive.'

She shook her head emphatically and her voice became hard, 'I prefer to think they're dead. At least, they would be with the Lord and not suffering anymore.' She looked into Vartan's eyes. 'It's better to accept it.'

He knew she was implying that his plan to look for his family was crazy. He could have argued that he was almost sure his wife and son were still alive, but under the circumstances, he thought it out of place.

She continued tearfully, 'You can't imagine what I went through when the authorities drove the Armenians from Urgup. I felt like a Judas – a coward and a traitor. I was even afraid that someone in the village would remember that I wasn't a Muslim and denounce me. I think I would have denied it.' Full of shame, she covered her face with her hands.

Vartan tried to stop her from blaming herself. 'It would have been absurd for you to have gone with the others when you could avoid it – absurd and even suicidal in God's eyes.'

'Do you really think so?'

'Of course. If you had gone, I would have been dead now, like the others.'

She had never looked at it that way. Now a little calmer, she lowered her hands, uncovering her face.

'How many of your compatriots have you helped?'

She shrugged as if it were of no importance. 'That's nothing!'

The truth was that, all through the summer and autumn, she had hidden hundreds of Armenians in the ancient underground churches in the valley of Goremé. She had consoled them, fed them and cared for them with Kerim's help and turned them over to either Greek families or the American missionaries. From the latter she received funds sent by the American Near East Relief Committee; she also received help from Armenian communities throughout the world, but now that winter had closed the roads, Aroussiag had temporarily put a stop to her charitable activities.

A sudden gust of wind pushed a swirl of snow through the opening that served as a vent for the smoke in the upper part of the front wall. The embers flared up, the flame of the oil lamp flickered and a cold draft blew past Aroussiag's neck, making her shiver. She threw a fistful of charcoal into the *tandir*.

'Shall I make some tea?'

'Not for me, thank you.'

She would have liked to sit closer to him but did not dare. She would have liked him to describe Constantinople to her once again, or to have him tell her about his life as a pharmacist in Sivas – about his spacious white mansion, with its dining room and library, even a piano and horses! It was a world unknown to her and it fired her imagination, but Vartan was not in the mood to dig up the past. The only thing that mattered to him was the future – to find Maro and Tomas again.

Vartan reached for the old *oud* Kerim had given him. He had found it in a junk shop and his friend had patiently restored it. He searched for a suitable Armenian folk song to brighten their mood a little, but could only think of nostalgic airs. One melody haunted him.

'Do you know what a crane is?' he asked, as he tuned his *oud*.

'Some kind of bird.' The question surprised Aroussiag.

'A beautiful, long-necked water bird. When they migrate, they fly very high in undulating rows. Their raucous croak makes the heart break when it announces the coming of winter but the same sound makes the heart leap with joy when they return in the spring.'

Vartan strummed the strings and sang the words he had known since childhood, but never fully understood until today: *Groung ousdi goukas, dzara yem tsaïnit*[1] . . . The throbbing melody picked up the same theme as the melancholic verses, the subject of which was the news the migrating

---

1.   O crane, where are you coming from? / I am a vassal to your call . . . (Armenian).

birds were bringing from home. Tears came to Aroussiag's eyes; it was her mother's favourite song! She looked at Vartan and knew that his thoughts were straying southward towards the Syrian desert – to that faraway land where he thought he might find his family. Aroussiag felt abandoned and hurt; the house seemed cold to her. The howling wind drowned the singer's dreamy voice momentarily. When was Vartan going to realize she was hopelessly in love with him? Was it possible that he still did not know? For a moment she was tempted to cry out that Sivas and Constantinople were finished for him – that he was no longer a major, nor a pharmacist, nor a writer, but a hunted man, who should consider himself lucky to be alive in this little hut; that he must forget who he had been and not nurse any illusions about the future.

She immediately felt guilty for having such thoughts. The tenderness she felt for this wonderful man, so hurt by destiny, the need she felt to surround him with loving care welled up in her as strongly as did the desire to belong to him. Her face was full of despair. She felt like a little girl and, at the same time, like a woman, and she was confused and did not know how to act.

When Vartan put the *oud* down, she gave in to a sudden impulse. She slid over to him, snuggled against his chest and remained very still. Caught unawares, he did not react for a moment; then put his arm around her shoulders. She shivered even though the fire was going full blast. Undoubtedly, the song had inspired the same feelings of loneliness and isolation in him as it had in Aroussiag, and their feelings were heightened by the storm raging outside.

He threw prudence to the wind and held her to comfort her. He, too, needed to touch, needed a woman's warmth and affection. Aroussiag breathed hard. She lifted her tense face to Vartan; her eyes begged. He understood why she had come into his arms, perceived the depth of her naked desire, and his head spun. They rolled to the floor, carried away by passion.

Aroussiag awoke at dawn. The house was glacially cold and clammy. She stayed in bed for a long time, pressed closely against Vartan's warm body, but finally got up reluctantly. She could no longer ignore the pitiful bleating from the stable. Careful not to disturb his sleep, she pulled the goatskin over him and dressed by the light of the fire. An inexplicable happiness permeated her entire being and made her feel lighter, yet her body felt heavier.

Dazzled, she stood still on the door sill. It was no longer snowing and everything was pristine white. The world looked new, brand new! Aroussiag had a vision of a new life beginning for her. A raven perched on the highest branch of the apple tree flew away and its croak echoed the cry of joy that was trapped in Aroussiag's throat.

When Vartan tried to speak with Aroussiag about what happened on Christmas night, she stopped him. She thought that he was going to tell her he was sorry – that he was going to belittle the importance of their love-making – that he was going to tell her he was married and still cherished his wife – that, as he was going to leave eventually, she should not get her hopes up. If she refused to listen to him, he couldn't revert to the reserve he had shown towards her before that night. Anything but that! Illusions? They sufficed for Aroussiag. Every day brought its moments of joy; each night its frantic embraces. She would not ask for more. She did not want to think about what lay ahead.

'Don't say anything,' she would murmur, laying her hand on Vartan's lips. 'When the time comes, you'll do what you have to, and I'll try not to hold you back. I don't expect anything from you.'

That was a lie. Aroussiag was sure it would never happen. Each day that passed linked them closer together and, little by little, Vartan would forget his plans to return to Malatya. By tacit agreement, they remained silent about their feelings after that. This left room for Aroussiag's beautiful dreams to grow. She never said 'I love you' for fear of putting Vartan on the defensive, but every look and every gesture was a declaration of love. She took Vartan's least kindness, his tiniest attention as a demonstration of his devotion and love for her.

The icy days of January forced them to stay inside, and the hours passed peacefully and sweetly. Her legs crossed under her, Aroussiag worked on the vertical loom that stood against the wall. Vartan improvised on his *oud*, watching her dancing fingers cross over each other in swirling rhythm, as they untangled and knotted the silk threads. He had all his strength back and idleness weighed heavily on him. He waited impatiently for the snow to melt, so that the roads would be passable again. He suffered thinking of the pain he would cause this woman, who had had the misfortune to fall in love with him, a stranger, who was only passing through. He had to admit that he, too, had become attached to her and would be sorry to leave.

He played music and she wove; the soup simmered on the hearth while the wind whistled outside. For Aroussiag it was the picture of perfect love and, as the weeks went by, she became convinced that her dream had come true.

Kerim now regarded them as a couple. Since Christmas Day, the teacher had noticed a radical change in Aroussiag and had immediately grasped the reason for it. He was very happy for them, for he held Vartan in high esteem. Since they never spoke of their love, Kerim never brought the subject up.

Snow or hail, stinging cold or thaw – whatever the weather, the teacher came every day to hear his friend play the *oud*, to chat and to pore over an occasional newspaper from the capital. Weaving her rugs or preparing a meal, Aroussiag followed their conversations in wonder, proud of her lover's knowledge and eloquence.

One afternoon, in the middle of February, Vartan was out in the garden, wearing a felt overcoat over his shoulders. He smoked as he watched the sheep grazing by the hay stack. Kourt barked repeatedly to welcome Kerim as he rushed in. He was wearing a Persian-lamb *kalpak*, which pressed down on his ears and made them stand out. He looked like a bear in his stifling-hot, dark cardigan, which bulged out over the numerous sweaters he wore underneath. The glare of the powdery snow made him squint, and he seemed extremely excited.

He cried out cheerfully from the road, 'Are you pretending to be a shepherd?'

Hugging him, Vartan teased, 'How do you manage to walk with so many clothes on?'

'I'm cold by nature.' Kerim rubbed his red nose. He pulled some printed sheets out of the pocket of his cardigan and said excitedly, 'I've just come from Caesarea and I got some newspapers. There is news about the Armenians in them.'

'Let's go inside. Kourt, watch the sheep.' The dog ran towards the haystack and Vartan took Kerim into the house.

While Aroussiag prepared coffee, the two men sat down on the rug and Kerim spread out a daily newspaper, which he began to scan.

'There are several articles about the Empire's victory over the Allies at

Gallipoli,' he noted, as he turned the first page. 'It also says that the situation is stable on the Russian front.'

'That's nothing new. With all that snow over there, it would be hard to mobilize troops. Anything on the Armenians?'

'That comes later.' Kerim scrutinized each page carefully. 'In Europe the Germans are shelling the French and English lines incessantly and everyone is expecting a new offensive.'

Kerim loved to read aloud and Vartan restrained himself with difficulty from pulling the newspaper out of his hands. Aroussiag noticed Vartan's exasperation, and handing him a cup of coffee, smiled understandingly.

Finally the teacher came to the article he had mentioned and cleared his throat to read, 'The foreign press is making a big fuss now about the ploys the Armenians are using to discredit the government of the Ottoman Empire. The necessary measures taken to relocate civilians away from the war zones are made to appear like harassment of these people, despite the assurances of the representatives of neutral nations. Many missionaries who have travelled in Anatolia can testify to the humane treatment given to the population by the Turkish government during the relocation.'

'Humane treatment!' Vartan roared. 'They have a gall!'

'It's propaganda,' Kerim agreed sadly and sipped his coffee.

'Lies!' exclaimed Aroussiag, embarrassed because she was not too sure what the word 'propaganda' meant. 'What else does it say?'

Kerim continued reading, 'At the instigation of Russia, the Armenians are using all their tricks in Paris and London, even in Washington, to promote their scheme for an independent Armenia to be created at the expense of the Empire. They demand nothing less than the six eastern provinces of Anatolia – Sivas, Erzerum, Kharput, Dyarbekir, Bitlis and Van – even though the majority of the population there are Turkish-speaking Muslims.'

Aroussiag interrupted Kerim and turned to Vartan, 'Is it true that the Turks are a majority in the east?'

'Of course not! Since the dawn of history that region has been Armenian, but if the massacres continue at the present rate, the Armenians will not only be a minority; they will cease to exist!' He waved a hand to invite Kerim to continue reading.

'This senseless plan would also include part of the rich agricultural lands of Cilicia, so that they could have access to the Mediterranean. To achieve their goals, these Armenians, who are Russian citizens, have formed subversive organizations, encouraging uprisings of their coreligionists in the Ottoman Empire, spreading lies and calumnies and inventing all sorts of stories about the so-called massacres of Christians. Russia's desire to annex new territories is evident to everybody.'

Kerim put down the newspaper and emptied his cup in quick little sips. Vartan stroked his long beard, pondering what he could read between lines.

'What are you so happy about?' Aroussiag asked, surprised he was enjoying this.

'For a newspaper in the capital to react in this way means that a lot of information about the massacres has seeped out to foreign countries. Right now, the only way to force the Ittihad to stop the atrocities is to appeal to international public opinion or bring the war to a quick end by defeating the Sublime Porte.'

Kerim looked annoyed. Even though he detested the Ittihad and was extremely critical of the government, he did not go so far as to wish for an Allied victory over his adopted country. 'We have to hope for a quick armistice before the collapse of one side or the other.'

'Don't count on it too much,' answered Vartan. 'This war might drag on forever.'

Kerim sighed deeply and passed his tobacco pouch to Vartan. He picked up a small piece of glowing charcoal with some tongs and lit the cigarette he had just rolled. 'I simply cannot imagine the Empire dismembered,' he said gravely.

'It's inevitable. The empire has been losing territory for the last thirty years and the trend will continue no matter what the outcome of the war is.'

Kerim nodded. Vartan continued, 'Perhaps, it's all for the best. Think about it, Kerim. Unless there's a revolution, your noble projects for modernizing Anatolia can't be realized.'

'The Sultan could get rid of the Ittihad and put a new government in its place – more moderate and less bigoted.'

'Mohammed V is only a figurehead. The Young Turks put him on the throne and control him. We need a cataclysm, a total defeat, in order to change the country.'

Kerim stared at his hands and cracked his knuckles. He remembered his discussions with Vartan, his diatribes against the government and its local representatives, his oaths against the employees who fanned violence instead of preaching tolerance, his eager impatience for these structures from the

332

dark ages to fall. 'The country will never progress, as long as the peasants are being exploited,' he used to say. 'They have no chance to improve their lot, as long as they're kept ignorant in order to manipulate and fleece them better. All the land belongs to the *effendis* who have nothing but their own profit in mind.'

Kerim believed in the notion that only education could break this infernal cycle of poverty. Checking the teacher's expression out of the corner of his eye, Vartan knew what Kerim was thinking.

'It's not education that will get the land redistributed.'

Wondering whether he had missed something, Kerim was shocked. He did not feel like embarking on an argument about his favourite subject right now, because he felt there must be a flaw in his reasoning. He would have to think all this over again calmly. 'A revolution . . .' he murmured, disgusted.

Aroussiag could see that Kerim was nervous and his mind in a state of confusion. She gestured to Vartan not to insist.

Kerim asked hesitantly, 'Vartan, do you think it would be possible to have an independent Armenia?'

Aroussiag waited anxiously for Vartan to reply. He sighed deeply. 'The way things are now, it's difficult.'

Kerim declined Aroussiag's invitation to share their lentil soup and left to get back to the village before dark. Vartan walked with him for a short distance. The road showed ruts left by an *araba* pulled by a team of oxen. The setting sun gave a rosy hue to the harsh, snowy landscape and cast purple shadows in the hollows.

Vartan laid a hand on Kerim's shoulder. 'I'm afraid I expressed myself badly and you may have misinterpreted my words.'

'I don't know what you mean.'

'When I said that it would take a real revolution to change the order of things, I did not mean to minimize your efforts with the children. It's important that you teach them to read and write, add and subtract. Although you won't change the country, you will allow some people to live better.'

Kerim smiled mockingly, 'I don't overestimate the value of my mission. In fact, I doubt its importance. Considering everything, your revolution has to start some place and no one can tell whether it will be by politics or by weapons.'

'That's right. Your teaching may be the beginning of a revolution. Every act counts. If I only could do as much for my people!'

'What do you mean?'

'I'd like to travel through Anatolia and send out articles, describing the situation of the Armenians to the outside world. Of course, it would not stop the deportations but at least I would have done my bit, like you with your classes.'

'That's right,' said Kerim.

'I feel so useless.'

By way of answer, the teacher gave him a great hug and went his way.

Before going in, Vartan finished clearing the path to the well and drew a bucket of water. Aroussiag was warming the soup on the hearth; she got up quickly when he came in and confronted him.

'You don't believe in an independent Armenia.'

Her strange attitude and her blazing black eyes took him aback and he defended himself: 'I never said that.' Then he hung his coat on the hook on the wall.

'But just now . . .'

'I yearn for such a country, but most of the territory you're talking about is now a battlefield. We have to wait for the war to end to see if our dream may come true.'

His words gave her some comfort. 'We shall have our own country!' She returned to her cauldron and continued, 'And there shall be no Russian Armenians – no Ottoman Armenians – only free Armenians, who shall govern themselves.'

He looked at her surprised, as he had not had the slightest notion about her interest in politics.

'I speak little, but I listen a lot,' she added, with a smile.

He took two bowls and two spoons from the shelf and placed them on the table.

'Would you go and live in that faraway land that you know nothing about?'

'I left the Black Sea to come to live here.' A shadow passed over her face. 'What about you, Vartan, would you hesitate?'

Vartan smiled sadly. 'Let's be realistic, Aroussiag. We may have to wait many years before Armenia becomes an autonomous state.'

Aroussiag thought his answer evasive and persisted, 'You saw what it said in the newspaper.' She continued, 'The Armenian National Committee, along with the envoys of the Catholicos, are negotiating with the French and English. The European powers will give us our independence.'

Vartan was puzzled. The newspaper had mentioned Armenians without being more specific. How did Aroussiag know that they were part of a national committee and under the command of the head of the Armenian Church, the Catholicos?

He prompted her by remarking, 'The Ottomans would have to withdraw first.'

'The Russians will drive them from the Armenian provinces.'

'And what if the Tsar won't give them back to us later?'

She countered, 'France and England will force him to and besides . . . who knows how long the Tsar will remain in power in Russia?'

That idea! He had heard it before, voiced by Shirag Tevonian, the rebel, in almost identical words. Without taking his eyes off Aroussiag, who was serving the lentil soup, he sat down to eat.

'The things you know!' he said finally, looking impressed.

Aroussiag was so embarrassed she almost dropped the soup kettle she was putting down by the hearth. She blushed but soon pulled herself together and went to sit next to Vartan.

'Your soup is delicious.' He tore off a piece of bread and crumbled it into his bowl.

She thought the subject closed and thanked him for the compliment. Then she announced that she was going to Urgup the next day.

Vartan asked her point-blank, 'Do you collaborate with the freedom fighters?'

'No!' she shot back.

'You don't trust me.' Vartan stopped eating and the silence became heavy.

After a while, Aroussiag looked straight into his eyes. 'If you really want to know, yes, I've known some of the resistance fighters.'

'Could you put me into contact with them?'

'It would be difficult now. I used to meet with them often until last spring. Sometimes they would stay here and I relayed their messages but, after the deportations began, many were executed and others fled to Russia to fight there.'

'Haven't you seen any of them again?'

She hesitated. 'Well . . . I've hidden two or three who were wanted.'

Vartan had the feeling that she knew much more than she was

pretending. 'I won't ask any more questions. You're right. With these things, the fewer people who know, the less risk that something may leak out.'

Aroussiag was worried that she had hurt his feelings and retreated a little. 'It's not that I don't trust you.' She realized at the same time that Vartan's curiosity was motivated by his hope of finding a way of getting on the road again, and she wanted to disillusion him quickly. 'Our network has been totally destroyed by the massacres. There are still some sympathizers like me, here and there. They've not been sent away, because they've pretended to convert or the government needed them because of their special skills, but we no longer have any means of getting in touch with each other.'

'None? Really?' asked Vartan, trying to hide his disappointment.

'Before fleeing to the mountains last September, a *fedayi* gave me a message, but I could never relay it.'

'What about the American missionary to whom you entrusted your orphans?'

'Reverend Matthews has helped in many ways, but he has refused to become involved with the resistance; he is afraid that the government will expel him from the country.'

Vartan frowned, and started to eat again automatically. He was deep in thought, trying to find a way of returning to Malatya. Aroussiag reached out and gripped his thigh firmly, just above the knee, to remind him he was no longer alone.

Vartan sat on the bed, with a board resting on his crossed legs. He had been writing for over half an hour. It was an article in English, in which he was trying to expose the economic necessity that a future independent Armenia include part of Cilicia, the Armenia Minor of the Crusades. It was only a mental exercise, since he had no means of dispatching it to any newspaper or journal outside the Empire. Reverend Matthews could perhaps have taken care of it, but he would not be back before spring. At least Vartan could translate it for Aroussiag to test the effect of his thoughts on a reader.

The sun was streaming in through the windows and the door, which had been left open on this early March morning. Drops of water plopping from the icicles on the edge of the roof could be heard distinctly, and a southerly breeze forecast an early thaw.

Aroussiag often glanced at Vartan surreptitiously, never changing the rhythm of her weaving. This man was not in the least like her late husband. When Yashar wasn't busy forging a ploughshare, shoeing a horse or tilling the soil, he would sit with a cup of coffee and smoke and daydream for hours. Aroussiag had never felt alone, as she had known intuitively that her husband's thoughts could never distance him from her, from their hut, their fields or their village.

It was altogether different with Vartan. Reading or writing carried him away and when he dreamed it was of a world Aroussiag did not know. He was different from her, different from all the men she had known, and this was probably why he fascinated her so much. His erudition, his vast culture were not a barrier between them. He shared his knowledge with her willingly and she, being quick-witted, learnt quite fast. No! What separated them were his memories and affections, which he kept alive and to which Aroussiag would never have access. They were very private. When he sank into one of his long silences, he became a total stranger to her.

The steel nib of Vartan's pen grating on the paper got on her nerves and, to block it out, she started humming a lament. The song praised the beauty and ruggedness, the storms and gales of the country; it spoke of the wolves prowling around the flocks, of roaring torrents in May, when the flowers lay like carpets on the slopes; it also spoke of the storks when they came back to nest, of the warm spells, of the gurgling springs hidden away under the poplars and of the rich earth humid with the sweat of men, spilling its bounties like a female's belly yielding up its young.

Vartan had stopped writing under the spell of her melodious voice, but it was not Aroussiag he was hearing. The song carried him back eight months to his house in Sivas, when Maro had sung it just before they were to flee to the Black Sea.

Kerim arrived accompanied by Kourt, who had run up the road to greet him. He stopped at the door and looked in, embarrassed at having surprised his friends in a moment of intimacy. Aroussiag's song ended like a declaration of love and Kerim mistook Vartan's stillness for rapture. The moment seemed fragile, and he held his breath as he looked at them. Happiness had made Aroussiag bloom. Now she had a man to lean on and help with the daily chores. Everything in her bearing showed her exuberance; her movements were less abrupt, more fluid. Kerim wondered if he should keep his news to himself. Vartan suddenly sensed another presence and turned to the door quickly.

After exchanging the conventional greetings and a few words about the weather, the three of them sat down to have tea. Overcoming his last scruple, Kerim went straight to the point. 'Vartan, perhaps, there's a way for you to travel safely.'

Although eager to know what Kerim had to say, Vartan noticed that Aroussiag had gone pale, and he motioned him not to say any more.

'Pashazadé Shahir[1] Mithad, the *dervish* who's a renowned singer and composer, is gathering a troupe to leave on tour to the south-east of Turkey – Urfa, Aleppo, perhaps, even to Hama and Beirut.'

Aroussiag lost her temper. 'You don't really mean for him to join an order of religious fanatics, do you?'

'You're right.' Vartan was disappointed. 'There's nothing of the mystic about me and I can't see myself twirling round and round for hours.'

His words reassured Aroussiag and she recovered her composure.

Kerim smiled. 'You won't have to. There are plenty of whirling dervishes in the monasteries. What he's looking for is musicians – the best! He hires laymen and I'm sure that when he hears you play the *oud* he'll take you on.'

'Did you say the south-east?' asked Vartan, sunk in thought. He was afraid of rejoicing too quickly, for fear of another disappointment.

Aroussiag protested, 'It's crazy! It's suicidal! Vartan is a wanted man and would be discovered immediately!'

'I don't think so,' Kerim said, upset at Aroussiag's reaction. 'The authorities are all for Mithad's project. They think a group of musicians will distract the people from the miseries and shortages of the war, and they're going to give them travel permits.'

'A perfect cover!' said Vartan approvingly. 'Who would suspect a pious *dervish*?'

'They'll find you out even before they hire you!' grumbled Aroussiag.

'Not if I take Vartan to the audition and he identifies himself with your late husband's papers. Pashazadé Shahir Mithad knows me well and has no reason to mistrust me. Once Vartan is accepted, he'll be given another name and other identity papers.'

'Why another name?' asked Vartan.

---

1. Poet (Turkish).

338

'It's the custom. You'll be named for the instrument you play, *Oudi*. You'll become Oudi Yashar.'

'When is the audition?'

'Tomorrow. Mithad is in Caesarea now and leaves two days from now for the main monastery in Konia.'

'Could you get me a book about the dervishes and their founder, Mevlana? I'd like to impress him, so that he'll hire me.'

'Don't try too hard. In his eyes you're no more than a simple peasant, a wounded soldier, who has been demobilized. Your talent as a musician will be more than sufficient to impress him.'

Aroussiag bowed her head. The decision had been taken, without her having been able to interfere; she had no sound arguments. From an objective point of view, it seemed an ideal solution for Vartan, but it did not change the fact that, for the second time in her young life, she was losing her man. After these months of happiness, she did not see how she could go back to living without love – alone in resigned detachment!

'The tour will last only seven or eight months,' Kerim added. 'Then the troupe will return to Konia and the musicians will be free to go back to their families.'

Aroussiag's spirits lifted. Vartan took her hand and reassured her tenderly, 'I'll be back by winter.'

Vartan's obvious excitement belied his words; he was already gone. If he found his family, he would never return to Cappadocia. For her that would be even worse than being a widow, as she would know he was still alive and with another woman.

She bit her lips, got to her feet and said calmly, 'I'm going to the stable. An ewe is about to give birth.' Grabbing her shawl, she threw it over her shoulders and walked up the narrow path through the snow, taking no notice of Kourt, who was jumping around her joyfully. The two men exchanged worried looks.

'It isn't your fault, Kerim. Let me take care of it.'

Kerim nodded and got ready to leave. 'I shall borrow two horses and come back for you at dawn.'

They parted in front of the door. Vartan waited for him to go down the road before he went to join Aroussiag in the stable. Blinded by the sun, he did not see her at first in the dark cavern; then he heard sobs. He turned and saw her leaning against the kiln. He tried to take her in his arms but she pushed him away.

339

'Aroussiag,' he murmured tenderly.

'There's nothing more to say. You have what you wanted.'

'I shall come back!'

She continued to cry as if she had not heard him.

'Just think. I shall be able to help the cause of our people. I shall be in a position to write articles for the outside world about what is happening in Anatolia. Among other things, I'll be travelling from village to village and will be able to serve as a messenger for the resistance. You said that you didn't have any means of communicating with each other. This way, I shall also do my bit.'

Her cheeks were shiny with tears. She stared at him and shot back, 'Don't try to deny that you're leaving to find your wife!'

'That's true,' he admitted unperturbed. 'I have never hidden my intentions from you.'

She argued, 'How are you going to find one woman and one child in a country that is upside-down. It's impossible and will only bring you sorrow – if you don't get killed first, that is. It would be much more reasonable to wait for the war . . .'

'Reasonable!' exploded Vartan. 'Reason doesn't count when the heart speaks. You should know that better than anyone. Was it reasonable to leave your family and marry a Muslim? But that didn't stop you from being happy. And didn't that same unreasonable marriage keep you from being deported?'

She was hurt by his sarcasm. She turned and walked away towards the sheep-pen. 'What about me in all this?' her voice quivered.

Vartan approached her from behind and put his arms around her. He did not know what to answer.

'What am I to you?' she asked.

In view of his imminent departure, he became aware of just how much this woman meant to him and held her even closer. 'This isn't easy for me either,' he whispered in her ear. 'I have become used to living with you. You're a wonderful woman and I'm going to miss you terribly.'

'But that's not keeping you back!' she sobbed.

'Please understand, Aroussiag, I cannot do otherwise.'

She understood only too well! To accept it was another matter. 'You will forget me.'

'Never! And not just because I shall be indebted to you forever, but because of that something special in you, which I will never find in anyone else.'

She turned and kissed him passionately, gripping him by the shoulders. 'I pray to God for you to find your wife and child, but if you don't, will you come back to me?'

He looked deeply into her tearful eyes and said without the slightest hesitation, 'Yes, I shall!'

The audition went well. The dervish was astonished that a peasant should play with such virtuosity until Vartan explained to him how he had had this gift since early childhood, how he was able to remember a melody after having heard it only once and how his fingers found the notes instinctively on the *oud*. Pashazadé Shahir Mithad thought that Allah must have sent him this man of great talent – a talent he would use to raise men's souls – and, asking no further questions, engaged him on the spot. He would ask the administration in Caesarea to give Vartan new papers under the name of Oudi Yashar, and told him to meet him at the monastery in Konia the following week.

Vartan spent his last days in Urgup memorizing the names on Aroussiag's list; about a dozen people in towns and villages who could refer him to other safe contacts. Kerim found some merchants who would take Vartan as far as Aksaray, but from there he would have to find a way to get to Konia, where the troupe of musicians were supposed to catch the train east.

One would have thought from Aroussiag's radiant face that she had accepted the situation but inwardly she was consumed by sorrow and maintaining her calm demeanour cost her tremendous effort. She lived only for the moments when Vartan made love to her, when she had the illusion that they united and became one, but this momentary magic quickly vanished. Then Aroussiag would cling to Vartan with desperate passion. She was going to lose him! His arrival had brightened her life like the sun when it briefly pierces an overcast sky.

The day before Vartan left, Aroussiag killed a small turkey and prepared a feast to which she also invited Kerim. They drank two bottles of white wine produced by a Greek wine-grower who was the teacher's neighbour and friend. Despite the lavish table and the drinks, it was not a happy occasion. The mood was heavy and stilted. They all had a lot to say but words refused to come. They were too upset. Their silences were eloquent and their looks even more so.

When Kerim hugged him at the door, Vartan said simply, 'Take care of Aroussiag.'

'If you can, let us know how you are, my friend.'

In bed that night, Aroussiag begged him, 'Tell me you love me, even if it's not so. Tell me you love me and make love to me all night.'

'I would not say it if it weren't true. I love you, Aroussiag!'

'I'll wait for you forever!'

Dawn found them drunk and exhausted from love, as they had not closed an eye all night. Their leave-taking was heart-rending. Aroussiag remained standing at the door in spite of the bitter cold and watched him leave under the leaden light of the snowy sky. A pouch hanging over his shoulder and his whitish coat flapping at his sides, he turned to wave at her, but then did so less often as he moved farther away. He was taking her heart with him! From now on, she would be like a robot and spend her life waiting for him. When he turned the bend and disappeared, Aroussiag was gripped by the premonition that she would never see him again.

Pashazadé Shahir Mithad was perched on the seat next to the driver of the carriage. The wide, white *dervish* robe camouflaged his skeletal body. His fingers were mechanically telling the olivewood beads of his rosary, while he gazed out over the rich plain before him – the western corner of the so-called 'Fertile Crescent' of antiquity. He was thinking complacently of the exceptional talent of the six musicians he had gathered this year. The concerts they had just finished giving in the small coastal towns between Silifké and Mersin had been most successful. Now that they were used to playing together, the troupe was ready to face the more critical audiences in larger towns and cities.

It was now May. They were travelling in a long wagon pulled by two horses, as the distance between towns was shorter. The conversation was lively in the wagon. Kanouni Zeki, who played the *kanoun*[1] with such dexterity that he seemed able to make the instrument sing, had been talking for the last fifteen minutes, giving them some news about the war that he

---

1.  A kind of oriental zither with seventy-two strings (Turkish).

had picked up in Mersin. His habit of peddling gossip had earned him the unflattering nickname of 'The Poor Man's Gazette.'

'Bird of ill-omen!' laughed Zournaji[1] Osman, an old bear-trainer who had abandoned his trade after his trained beast had bitten off half of his left cheek. 'When will you finally give us some good news? Why don't you try to forget what's happening elsewhere and enjoy the blessings that Allah has showered upon us?'

'That's right,' agreed Kemenché[2] Hakki. 'We'd do better to talk about music, women and love. Oudi Yashar, my brother, tell them how much we drank last night. Tell them about the beautiful Moorish dancer we saw. What breasts! What a waist! I could have put my two hands around it!'

Vartan, who was sitting at the edge of the wagon bed, dangling his legs over the road, turned to him, 'Better you tell them, brother. I can't tell it as well as you do.'

Hafiz Ismael, the singer, and Tambour Vasfi, the tambour player, who was also in charge of taking care of the horses, joined the others in asking Kemenché Hakki to tell them all about the Moorish dancer. The violin player gave a very graphic account of her dance on a copper plate and described how she had taken off her veils one by one until she was completely naked.

Vartan was not listening; he was watching the port of Mersin and the turquoise waters of the Mediterranean fade into the distance – the sweet air, the luminous sky, the banana and palm trees, the cactuses, the cliffs covered by pine and oak trees, the small, idle fishing boats, the villages with their red-tiled roofs. It was such a contrast to Cappadocia that Vartan was still wondering if he wasn't dreaming. He was treading upon a land where great civilizations had flourished and legendary conquerors had passed through. The ruins of splendid monuments strewn throughout the land bore witness to this past. He was heading towards Tarsus, the home of Saint Paul and the town where Cleopatra had met Marc Anthony! One last rise in the road blocked their view of the sea.

Not to be a hunted man any longer, to be able to move about in a crowd, to sit at a table in a café without being afraid of the police filled Vartan with a euphoria that sometimes made him lose sight of the real purpose of his trip. The music also made him forget and his companions' joviality and happy-go-lucky attitude were infectious.

---

1.   Player of *zourna*, a primitive clarinet (Turkish).

2.   A small three-string violin, played like a cello (Turkish).

343

Kemenché Hakki proposed they walk; so they jumped off the vehicle and followed a few paces behind the wagon. Hakki was a giant, and to see him coming, rolling his shoulders, made one think he must be in the habit of handling a sabre or a plough and not of playing the violin. He was, however, a sensitive musician and had earned a living with his *Kemenché* ever since he had run away from home when he was fifteen. Now, at thirty-three, his amorous adventures were his only subject of conversation. He was handsome, square-chinned and virile looking, and his green eyes had the look of a perpetually astonished child. Vartan could not explain why Kemenché, who was artless and humble, admired him so much so that his admiration at times became an intrusion. He touched Vartan on the arm and spoke with an accent that betrayed his Laz[1] origin.

'Oudi Yashar, my *aghabey*,[2] I will never understand you. You're so secretive. Even when you are playing in front of a crowd, one would think you were alone with your *oud*. Just now too, I could see you were far away; looking into a vast void. Tell me, what were you thinking about?'

Vartan couldn't tell him that he was touched at finding himself on Cilician soil – that he was thinking that long ago this had been the kingdoms of the Rubenids and the Lusignans, the Little Armenia where his ancestors had died defending their liberty – that this had brought to mind the ordeals currently affecting his people. So he lied.

'I was thinking about a woman.'

'A broken heart, is it? I can tell by your glum look. Believe me, my experience in matters such as these has been vast. There's only one cure – to make love to seven women in one day.'

Vartan burst out laughing.

'Seven,' said Hakki, convincingly. 'That's the sacred number. That remedy healed me once and I have not suffered from heart-break ever since.'

Vartan was amused. 'Where did you find seven women in such a short time?'

'I paid. In those days I was selling opium to a French trader from Syria and I was rich.'

'Aren't you rich any longer?'

'I spent it all on making love, because I'm a good believer.'

'What's that got to do with it?'

'To sleep with a woman is an act of charity. Our religion says that a

---

1.   Lazes are people from the shores of the Black Sea.
2.   Literally older brother, a respectful greeting for someone not related (Turkish).

charitable man should share his precious possessions, and what is more precious than this?' He patted his penis through his trousers.

Vartan exploded in laughter and Hakki was thrilled.

'You see how powerful love is? Just talking about it has made you happy again.'

Pashazadé Shahir Mithad was a pious mystic and could recite by heart the twenty-five thousand, six hundred and eighteen couplets of the *Mesnevi*, the masterpiece of their founder, Mevlana Jalaleddin Rumî. This did not keep him, however, from valuing money or selling rosaries to the people who gathered along the way. He was a fanatic and observed the rules of his order to the letter, but with his musicians he was indulgent. He closed his eyes to their faults and pretended not to hear their impious conversations as long as they did not try to slip away.

They had a rehearsal every afternoon. Pashazadé Shahir Mithad joined them with his reed flute used by members of his sect. The music attracted the peasants and bystanders; as soon as he saw that there were enough people in the audience, he would get up and start to spin. This was the *sama*, the sacred dance, which was usually done in a group. His skirt would flare out as he spun faster; he would turn his right hand towards the ground and his left hand towards the sky, his face would become transfigured and his eyes empty, as he went into a trance and achieved supreme union with God. Even though he seemed to be absent, afterwards he was able to tell exactly when a musician had played a false note!

The spectators observed the show with superstitious awe, feeling they were in the presence of a saintly man. At the end of the *sama*, the dervish was neither dizzy nor out of breath, while the audience was panting. Hakki would take up the collection and the poor people, who probably did not have enough to eat, emptied their pockets into the small wooden bowl. Such exploitation of the common people's gullibility revolted Vartan. If Pashazadé Shahir Mithad wanted to enrich his monastery, he had only to demand a higher fee from the rich merchants and magistrates at whose receptions the troupe played regularly.

When they were only an hour from Adana, Vartan saw a young girl not more than eight or nine years old standing on the edge of the road. She was begging, holding out her hand and blindly staring at the few people who were passing by. No one took any notice of her. She was dishevelled and her hair hung to her shoulders and framed her dirty face with its black eyes. Feeling sorry for her, Vartan took a coin out of his pocket and went over to her.

'Thank you,' she whispered, and her hand closed over the money.

'Where do you live?'

She shrugged. From her accent Vartan gathered that she was Armenian, but he continued to question her in Turkish.

'Nowhere! The peasants I worked for put me out. They didn't have enough food for themselves. That was two or three weeks ago, I don't remember exactly when.'

Vartan was upset. Barely surviving from day to day, this orphan in rags, without a roof over her head, was the symbol of his people. The cart had stopped not far away and his companions were calling him. He ran up to Pashazadé Shahir Mithad, who was looking impatient.

'Can't we take her with us, just into town?'

The old man raised his black eyebrows and answered dryly, 'We're beggars ourselves. What are we to do with another beggar?'

'You're right, but she's a young Christian. I'll hand her over to the authorities and they'll take charge of her.'

The *dervish* twirled the ends of his long beard. 'It might be more charitable to leave her where she is.'

Vartan, trying to play the zealot, said severely, 'The government is relocating the Christians. It's our duty to support their policies.'

The *dervish*, suddenly afraid he might be talking to a member or a sympathizer of the Ittihad, thought it wiser to agree. 'Do what you think is your duty.' He then turned and told the driver to get going.

Vartan went back to the girl and held out his hand. She followed him without question and showed no surprise as he lifted her into the cart.

'Are you thirsty?'

She nodded and Hakki, who was watching Vartan with interest, passed his gourd to the girl. She drank quickly and the water dripped down her grimy face to her chin.

'I'll bet she's as hungry as a bear,' declared Zournaji Osman.

His mutilated face made him look fierce, but he was as docile as a child. He gave her a piece of bread, which she wolfed down. The musicians laughed, but they were not making fun of her. They were only trying to

346

cover up their feelings, since all of them at one time or another in their lives had been hungry. After she had eaten the bread, cheese and dried fruit, she sat still again and her face became impassive.

In Adana, at the inn, where they were to stay for the next five days, Vartan found a way to get rid of Hakki, who insisted on accompanying him. He took him aside and explained, 'After I take the girl to the police station, I want to visit one of my relatives in town. I'll meet you back here in two or three hours.'

'Couldn't your relatives use a little servant girl?' Hakki asked, pointing his chin in the direction of the little girl.

Vartan pretended not to mind one way or the other; he took the girl by the hand and walked away.

They crossed the old Roman bridge over the River Jeyhan and arrived in a noisy, crowded commercial quarter. Dromedaries, donkeys and carts were struggling to get through. Children clustered around the street vendors and added to the confusion. Vartan had the impression he had been in this town before, but this feeling of familiarity was only due to the fact that all the markets in large Anatolian towns were more or less alike. He bought a glass of lemonade for the young girl, who was looking less frightened, and asked her what her name was.

She hesitated for a moment and then murmured, 'Nayiri'.

He wanted to talk to her in Armenian, to hug and comfort her, but for obvious safety reasons, she had to go on thinking he was a Turk. They went down the main street lined by shops and vast *khans*. At the end of the street, two narrow minarets rose above a mosque of black and white marble blocks. It was newly built and, as it was Friday, the men were gathering for prayer. When they passed by the gate, Vartan saw some of the faithful washing their feet in the ablution fountain in the courtyard, while others were throwing grain to the pigeons as the Prophet had ordered.

Next to the *medressé*, the Koranic school, there was a narrow, dead-end alley. It was the jewellers' street. Most of the shops were empty and closed as there were no qualified craftsmen to replace the Armenians who had been deported. Many of these skilled artisans also owned their businesses and their names were still on the shop signs. Joseph Varon's shop was the next to last. He was a Sephardic Jew. When Vartan and Nayiri entered, he was talking to a German officer, who looked at them suspiciously through his monocle. While Vartan waited for them to finish their business, he tried to overhear what Varon was saying. 'Don't worry. This shop was founded at

347

least a hundred years ago, and we are known as the best lapidaries in the region.'

Satisfied, the German put the ring in his pocket and left. Vartan approached the cross-eyed shop-owner, who was in his fifties, with a moustache and white hair.

'Mr Joseph Varon?'

He smiled at his visitor. 'That's me. This is the first time I have the honour to serve you as a customer.'

'A friend of yours sent me.'

The jeweller frowned and he looked the visitor over from head to foot distrustfully. 'You're sturdy for a musician. What instrument do you play?'

'The *oud*,' said Vartan, surprised that the jeweller should know his trade.

'Who's she?' The merchant pointed at the girl standing near the two workers.

'She's an orphan.'

Joseph raised his eyes to heaven, sighed and told her, 'Wait for us here and don't touch anything.' Then turning to his son, 'Moriko, take care of the customers.'

He took Vartan by the arm and guided him to the back of the store into a dark room full of boxes and cases, then up a rickety staircase to the second floor. They entered a dim parlour, barely lit. Daylight filtered through a couple of latticed windows facing the street.

The jeweller turned to Vartan, 'You still haven't told me your name.'

'Oudi Yashar.'

'Don't you have another name?'

'Vartan. Vartan Balian.'

Varon's wide smile made the points of his moustache rise. 'I'm glad to meet you, Mr Balian. One cannot be too careful.'

'That's normal nowadays. We're living in troubled times.'

Varon asked him to make himself comfortable on a shabby divan covered with a rug. While he was serving the vermouth, he said, 'I loved your books back in better days.'

Vartan could see that the other was still suspicious and to test him he asked, 'which one?'

'All, but especially the one in which you refer to the rebirth of Israel.'

'Oh, *Several Nations: One Empire*.'

'That's rights,' answered Varon, nodding.

Vartan took the glass his host was offering him. 'To your health, Mr Varon.'

'To yours, Mr Balian.'

They drank looking at each other, and Vartan said, 'You were expecting me, I think.'

'You're right. Pastor Matthews came to see me a few days ago, straight from Cappadocia and told me about you. Do you know him?'

'To tell you the truth, I haven't had the honour of meeting him.'

'You must. He's a remarkable human being, dedicated to bettering the lives of the minorities living in the Empire.' Joseph Varon glanced into the bottom of his glass, swirled the vermouth around and nodded repeatedly. 'It's been terrible. All my colleagues and friends, lifelong friends, Mr Balian, have been sent away. Did you see the street? Three-quarters of the stores are closed.'

'Tell me, Mr Varon, do you have any idea of the situation of the Armenians in the south-east?'

'Besides the children in the missionary orphanages, and those working as servants in Turkish households, and the very young ones who have been adopted, and the women married to Muslims or taken as mistresses, there are no Armenians left north of Syria.'

'What about in Syria?'

'How many are still alive in the camps in the desert and in the swamps on the banks of the Euphrates River, Ras el 'Ain, Raqqa and Deir ez-Zor, I don't know. Luckily, several thousands are safe in a military camp in Aleppo and others have found refuge further south in Hama, Beirut, even as far away as Jerusalem.'

None of this was news to Vartan; it only confirmed what he already suspected. He looked so forlorn that Joseph Varon spoke to him in a kind voice, 'I know you're looking for your family. I've made inquiries and I don't think they are in the vicinity of Adana. You might have a better chance of finding them in Aleppo.'

'I thought that would be a likely place, but I don't know when I'll be able to get there. As you know, I'm travelling with a group of musicians and cannot go where I like or as I like. I have to trust in chance.'

'Don't give up, Mr Balian. We have heard such incredible stories, no human mind could have invented them. For instance, a mother and daughter, separated for months, met on a street corner a thousand kilometres away from their native village. Luck, would you say? Perhaps that, or the Will of God.'

'I haven't given up. I fret and burn with impatience, but that's different!'

The jeweller's face lit up with a gratifying smile. Vartan wanted to change the subject. He pulled the envelope Aroussiag had given him from the pocket of his peasant shirt. Joseph Varon slipped it quickly under the divan, cocked his ear towards the staircase and gestured Vartan to be quiet. Someone had come into the shop. When he was sure it was a customer, the jeweller lowered his voice and asked, 'What's your next stop?'

'Marash. Then Urfa and Malatya, but nothing is certain.'

'I have a few messages for you to take to friends there.'

'That's one of the reasons I came to see you. Our friend also told me that, perhaps, you could get a few articles out to some of the French and English newspapers.'

'It might take time, but I can assure you they will get there.'

Vartan was pleased that his pen would once more serve the cause. 'Thank you very much, Mr Varon, for that and everything else you've done for my countrymen.'

He stroked his moustache and studied Vartan in the same way he scrutinized each jewel. 'You know, Mr Balian, the decisions the Allies will take at the end of this war will be crucial for many.'

Vartan refused to get into a political discussion. He nodded, glanced towards the staircase again, and stepped closer to his visitor. 'I have it from a reliable source that the English are encouraging an Arab revolt by promising them their independence. It's got to the point where the Sultan's army is having difficulty maintaining discipline, even among its Arab officers! You and I must help the Allies in every way we can.'

'What exactly do you want me to do?'

'Gather information.'

Vartan could not help laughing. 'Am I to play the spy?'

The jeweller laughed too. 'The spy? Let's not exaggerate! It's enough to watch and listen. Since you're going to travel a lot and play at receptions, where influential people meet, you can gather thousands of tiny bits of useful information. Our English friends are very interested in the movements and deployment of troops, the assignments of the superior officers and the positions of the artillery batteries on the coasts.'

There was no doubt that Joseph Varon was striking a bargain, but Vartan found the terms agreeable. The two men continued to discuss the practical details and Vartan turned over the two articles he had secretly written while sharing a room with Kemenché Hakki in the inn at Mersin. For the first time in years, Vartan had not used one of his pseudonyms but had signed his own name, thus telling those who knew him that he was still alive.

Without hesitation, the jeweller agreed to keep the little girl until he could hand her over to a missionary, but when she saw that Vartan was leaving, she tried to follow him. Vartan bent down and whispered in her ear in Armenian, 'I can't take you with me, Nayiri. Mr Varon is a friend and he'll help you. Don't worry. You won't be alone any more.'

She was so surprised to hear him speak in her language that she stood still with her mouth agape. Vartan kissed her on the forehead and pushed her gently in the direction of Joseph Varon. Her eyes were filled with immeasurable sadness as she waved goodbye to Vartan, and she started to cry.

He walked away quickly and never looked back, but kept on repeating her name, so that he would never forget the child that fate had put in his way. Fate! Like Nayiri, Vartan had only fate to count on.

# TWELVE

Playing at being soldiers, Tomas, Kenan, Emel, Arif and Zehra were parading about in the big steam room at the *hammam*. The clacking of their wooden clogs on the marble floor covered with soapy water added to the hum of the conversations and the gurgling of the wall fountains. The women were lying on the *goebek tashi*[1] while the *tellaks*, the bath attendants, rubbed them down with horsehair mittens. After trying unsuccessfully to hush the children, they glared at them but did not dare scold them because they were the governor's children. Safiyé, who was lying stretched out on her stomach while a servant washed her back, rose up on her elbows and ordered the children to stop the racket. They stood at attention and saluted her. She could not help smiling. Because of the way she was lying, her breasts spread out on the towel covering the marble slab.

'They look like figs,' murmured Kenan.

'Figs as big as melons,' added Tomas.

The two younger children did not understand what they were talking about, but Emel laughed and whispered to the boys, 'Mine will look like my sister's.'

'Bah!' said Kenan, 'Shahané's are only lemons.'

'At least they don't look like half-empty water skins,' Emel said, disgusted. Even though she had joined the two boys in harshly judging the women whose flesh was flaccid, who had big bellies, bulging behinds or sausage-like thighs, it made her uneasy. She was afraid of having an ungainly figure too as she got older. Wasn't her own mother, Makbulé, too fat?

'Well, I shall stay beautiful like Maro,' she said to Tomas, who blushed. When the other nude women were being massaged he always watched

---

1.  Literally umbilical stone, the central stone platform heated from below (Turkish).

them with great interest. On the other hand, he avoided looking at his mother if by chance he saw her naked, except for the *peshtemal*, the large, thin bath-towel, tied around her waist to cover her private parts. Seeing her like that made him feel guilty, perhaps because he was not used to accompanying the women to the *hammam* from early childhood like the others.

'Let's go see my mother,' piped up Zehra.

The others hurriedly agreed. Leyla made no pretence of modesty and had no objections to being found naked by the children. On the contrary, she took a perverse pleasure in observing the feelings her body produced in Kenan and Tomas and was flattered by Emel's envy.

Still in Indian file but now headed by Zehra, the children went around the central platform. Light filtered in only through the stained glass dome of the building. The warm, damp air of the room, permeated by the acrid smell of the *zirnik*[1] that the women used as a depilatory for their pubic areas, armpits and legs, had become suffocating. Sounds were muffled and shapes distorted by frosted glass.

Women stood in front of the *kournas,* marble water basins, washing and splashing themselves with water from small copper or silver bowls. There were gales of laughter as they talked among themselves about men or sex, thinking that the children who were playing around their feet did not understand the meaning of their words.

For Tomas the *hammam* was a magical place. The presence of so many naked women made him heady and, like his friend Kenan, he felt they all belonged to him . . . except for his mother, of course. He knew he was on the verge of uncovering one of life's biggest mysteries and, from week to week, expected to break through and finally understand it all. He and Kenan had long talks after each visit but were never able to come to any satisfactory conclusions. Emel would join them in a hidden corner of the garden, where they examined their genitals without getting any closer to an answer. She had promised to ask her mother, but kept putting it off.

Riza's wives did not wash in front of the others. Like all the other well-to-do women, they each rented one of the alcoves around the room for the day. Even before Zehra pushed aside the towel that her mother had hung over the entrance to serve as a curtain to the cubicle, the smell of the *zirnik* stung their noses. Leyla's whole body was daubed with the bluish-green sulphur paste mixed with lime which stank so much the women avoided

---

1.    Yellow sulphur mixed with lime (Turkish).

using it at home. She waved the children into an alcove designed to hold two people at the most.

'Rinse me off,' she said.

They fought over the silver bowl but finally Zehra won and Emel, Kenan and Tomas had to make do with their cupped hands. With her arms crossed over her head, she turned over slowly, squealing and shrieking as the sprays of water splashed her. 'It's too cold! Not on my face!'

Little by little, the nauseating product trickled to the floor, carrying little black, curly hairs along with it. While Tomas was splashing Leyla's armpits and arms, he was taking a good look at her breasts with their dark-pointed nipples and mentally comparing them to grapefruits. Emel noticed Kenan winking at Tomas to tell him to look a little lower down. As Leyla spread her legs to turn, her vulva gaped open slightly and the fleshy pink petals of its small inner lips became visible. She saw through the boys' little game and smiled with amusement, displaying her white teeth. Water dripped from her wet hair and formed beads on her smooth brown skin. Her flesh was as firm as the marble statues in Riza Bey's garden, over whose rounded forms Tomas sometimes ran his hands. The two boys would have loved Leyla to ask them to rub her all over with the horsehair mitten or, at least, to soap her back.

'Come to the *soghouklouk*.[1] Buyuk Hanim is waiting for you to have a snack,' announced Eminé, sticking her head into the alcove.

'We're coming,' answered Leyla.

The nurse glanced furtively at the boys to see if they had erections. This would have been noticeable through the wet trousers clinging to their skin. If so, the manager of the establishment would have to forbid them to accompany their mothers to the *hammam*; they would have to come with their father in the evening instead.

'I'll join you later,' Maro's voice rang out from the next compartment. When she was sure that the nurse and the children were gone, she examined her body meticulously. There was no doubt about it; her breasts were getting heavier and her hips wider and, although it did not show yet, her stomach was definitely swollen. The worst had happened! It explained the nausea she had occasionally felt in the mornings these last weeks. Ever since the deportation her menstrual periods had been irregular and she had not given much importance to the fact that they had stopped. It was now at least . . . three or four months. Pregnant! She was so shocked and surprised

---

1. The anteroom to the *hammam*, which serves to cool off (Turkish).

354

she could not fully realize the catastrophic consequences. She raged against it! No! Impossible! She did not want it! The words went around and around in her mind like an incantation to ward off evil, but naturally to no avail. She had to bow to the inevitable.

Maro suddenly realized that Leyla had opened the curtain and was staring at her curiously. Leyla had not really accepted the situation; however, in order not to displease Riza Bey who had begun to make love to her again assiduously, she hid her dislike behind a friendly mask. Maro was not fooled, however. Afraid that Leyla might suspect her condition, Maro pretended she was being cynically self-critical.

'I was just taking stock of the ravages of time.'

Those words puzzled Leyla greatly. No self-respecting woman, she thought, would ever say such a thing to a rival. Feigning sympathy, she said, 'I imagine I will have to do the same some day . . . in the far future.'

Maro wrapped herself in the blue-and-white-striped bath-towel and accompanied Leyla to the *soghouklouk*. It was furnished with leather divans covered with thick towels to let people rest before returning to the steam room or before leaving. In a corner reserved especially for her, Buyuk Hanim was supervising the two servants who were unpacking the lunch basket containing fried lamb and meat balls, stuffed vine-leaves, goat's cheese and sweetmeats. One of the servants served tea. The governor's mother was wearing only a bathrobe, as were her daughters-in-law, the nurse and all the other customers, but this did not lessen her aura of authority.

'There you are! Finally! You certainly took your time!' she chided Maro and Leyla. They were not really late but Buyuk Hanim was trying to impress her neighbours.

The two women understood this, bowed and said respectfully in unison, 'Please forgive us, Buyuk Hanim.'

Maro ate without appetite. Even though she tried to take part in the conversation, she could not help brooding over the disastrous discovery she had just made. She looked strained and absent-minded. Frowning, Leyla did not take her eyes off her; the others thought they had had a spat and ignored them. Wanting to lighten the mood, Eminé told anecdotes about Nasrettin Hodja, a popular legendary personage, who looked at the world from the back of his donkey and made fun of men's shortcomings.

For several days Maro tried to convince herself that she was wrong, but everything confirmed she was pregnant. Sometimes she could physically feel the presence of a strange body within her, but it had to be her imagination because she could only be in her fourth month . . . her fifth at the most.

She did not want this child! It was not hers. She hated it and she hated Riza Bey for having forged a new bond to keep her captive. She was ashamed of this pregnancy, torn between rage and despair with no one to turn to and no way out.

Maro carried her secret for a week and it weighed on her more and more heavily. When she could stand it no longer, she decided to confide in Eminé and sent Ayla to look for her. Eminé came in a few minutes later, carrying two cups of coffee on a tray. When Maro dismissed Ayla, Eminé was delighted. She put the tray on a small octagonal table.

'Would you like for me to tell your fortune?'

'Save that for Riza.'

When Eminé heard Maro's scathing tone, she realized that something was wrong. 'Come and sit by me,' she said amiably, easing herself onto a cushion.

Maro sat down and took the cup that the nurse was offering her. Since she could not bring herself to speak, the nurse said quietly, 'I don't have to look at the coffee grounds to know. I can see the signs; you can't fool an old midwife.'

Maro was taken aback, burst into sobs and covered her face with her hands. When Eminé tried to hug her, she stiffened.

'You surprise me,' murmured Eminé, patting her arm affectionately. 'This is good news . . . a blessing from heaven!'

'It's a calamity! A disaster!'

The old woman could not understand Maro's reaction. She had thought Maro was used to the idea of living the rest of her life in this mansion, basking in the governor's love. 'Riza Bey will be delighted.'

'Riza Bey!' shot back Maro bitterly. 'If you only knew how little I care how he feels.'

'But . . . once he knows you are carrying his child, he will make you his wife immediately.'

'I shall never accept it!' shouted Maro furiously, 'Never!'

This cry from the heart disconcerted Eminé. 'You'll never find another man like Riza. He is handsome, rich, powerful and in love with you.'

Maro groaned and spat out, 'You don't understand, Eminé. I hate him!

He took me by force. He keeps my son and me prisoners. How do you expect me to love him?'

'He did save you.'

'He saved me from the massacres he directs!'

'No!' Maro's words outraged Eminé. 'On the contrary, Riza Bey protects your people.'

'That's a lie! He's the big boss in this region. Why do you think he's away so often? To organize the massacres in the neighbouring provinces!'

'Hush! You mustn't say that!' The nurse was pale and petrified. 'It's impossible. I've known Riza since he was born. He's severe but he's just and charitable. You have no right to say such lies. I forbid you even to think them.' Eminé was deeply hurt.

Maro was sorry that she had lost control and antagonized her when she needed her the most. After a moment of silence she touched the old woman's arm and murmured contritely, 'I didn't mean what I said. I'm not thinking straight.'

'Because of the child you're carrying?' Eminé was appeased.

'Yes. You see, I don't want it.'

'Why? A child is life. It's the future.'

'Not for me. I still hope Riza Bey will let me go one day as he's promised to. If I give him a child, he'll keep me forever.'

Eminé believed a woman changed her family when she took a husband; thus Maro's only family now was Riza Bey's. She also believed in fate. 'There is nothing you can do. The child's here.'

'No,' said Maro decidedly, 'It's not here yet and I want to keep it from coming! There are ways to do that.'

The nurse recoiled, blinked, picked up the coffee cup with shaking hands and took a sip without answering.

'You must know how,' insisted Maro.

'But I don't!' Eminé warded her off and started to rise.

Maro held her back. 'Liar. You're a midwife.'

'Don't ask this of me!'

Maro went up to her, kissed her on the cheek as the children did when they wanted her to do them a favour and begged her, 'I need your help, Eminé. I implore you.'

'No. I cannot kill Riza Bey's child.'

'He already has eight children and Leyla and Makbulé will give him more.'

'No!'

'You said you were my friend,' said Maro reproachfully.

'So you are! You are dear to my heart, but what you're asking . . . No, I cannot! Riza Bey is my master.'

Maro continued to argue trying to sway her, but ran up against a stone wall. Suddenly she became completely disheartened. She hit her stomach with her fist and screamed, 'I shall not have it! I shall not have it! I would rather die!'

Eminé bit her knuckle. She had lived long enough to know when women were truly desperate – women she had saved from shame and suicide by giving them potions to induce abortions. Maro's determination would only increase and she might take drastic measures; then Eminé would feel guilty for not having helped her.

'You are in an advanced stage of pregnancy. It could be very risky. I would never forgive myself if something happened to you.'

'If you don't do anything, there will surely be a tragedy.'

Maro's threat confirmed Eminé's apprehensions and she decided to intervene. 'I shouldn't!' she said resignedly. 'You're forcing my hand!'

Relieved, Maro hugged her. 'You're more than a friend to me. You're my sister.'


The following day Eminé went to Ayntab to a herbalist she knew and got a potion, a secret mixture of plants and other things, which would provoke a miscarriage. Later, when she handed Maro the porcelain jar, she asked, 'Are you sure you want to do this? It will make you sick for a whole day.'

Maro was relieved because she had been worried that Eminé would change her mind.

'Take half when you wake up in the morning and the rest at noon. You must not eat anything. Don't even drink water. The potion will take effect the next night.'

Maro hurriedly hid the jar in a drawer under a pile of clothes. Now that she had the means to put an end to her condition, the wretchedness of the last seven days disappeared, leaving her feeling very weak.

She had decided to wait for Riza Bey to leave before she did anything. Next day, he was going to inspect a piece of land he had just acquired near Osmaniyé about sixty kilometres west of Ayntab. He planned to take Tomas and his two sons with him as he frequently did and would be away two or three days, which should give her ample time to recover.

She slept very badly that night, haunted by the thought of what she was about to do . . . something which was considered a sin . . . but God, who could see into men's souls, would not hold it against her on Judgement Day. She was worried of course but, above all, she was eager for it to be over.

She was still awake at dawn when Piri Hodja, the *muezzin*, called to prayer. She shook the bottle and swallowed half its contents. As the bitter, brown liquid numbed her mouth and rasped her throat, she grimaced. Her stomach cramped violently and she felt like vomiting. She would have given anything for a sip of water to alleviate the burning sensation.

Riza Bey and the children left around noon, much later than the scheduled time. An unexpected visit by the chief of police of Ayntab had delayed their departure. As soon as they left, Maro drank the rest of the potion. She retched as she had done in the morning. Her discomfort increased steadily. After nightfall Maro tried to drink a little water because she was unbearably thirsty but immediately brought it up again. Her belly was hard as a rock and bluish veins showed through the stretched skin. She felt as if a knife had been thrust into her, which twisted and tore at her entrails before piercing her spine. She gritted her teeth and stoically endured the last stages of labour. The contractions came closer and closer, harder and harder each time. She could not help thinking that she was expelling a little person from her body and she was overcome by the same sorrow she had felt when she had lost her second child. How Vartan had wanted that baby.

A little before dinner time, when Eminé came to Maro's bedside, she found her unconscious. Her features were drawn, her skin damp and deathly white, her forehead burning hot, her lips blue and cracked. She did not respond when Eminé shook her. The old woman squatted on the floor, rocking her upper body and slapping her knees, wailing, 'Oh, what have I done! What have I done! What a calamity.'

Three days later, as soon as Riza Bey and the children returned from their trip, Tomas ran straight to his mother's room and opened the door, shouting cheerfully, 'Mama, I'm back. I have . . .' He stopped when he saw his mother in bed and Ayla making signs for him to be quiet. His happy face became worried.

'Not so loud! She's sleeping.'

He went near the bed and began to tremble when he saw her pale face, the dark shadows under her eyes and her bluish lips. 'What's wrong with her?' he choked.

'She's been sick, but she's much better now.' Ayla tried to take him in her arms but he pushed her away, knelt at the side of the bed and took his mother's hand. It was ice-cold. He watched the regular rise and fall of her chest to make sure she was not dead.

'Mama,' he called very quietly, 'mama.'

His mother continued to sleep as if she were never going to wake up again. At one moment Eminé and Buyuk Hanim had thought they would lose her before Riza Bey's arrival, but fortunately Maro had shown occasional signs of improvement during the last twenty-four hours. Tomas found her face thinner and her eyes sunken. He stared at her cracked lips and could see his grandmother as she lay dying.

'Please don't die, mama! Please don't die!' he cried.

'Don't be afraid. She's only resting,' whispered Ayla in his ear.

Tomas swept her aside roughly. The more he looked at his mother, the more afraid he became that she would die and abandon him. What would he do without her? It was all his father's fault. Why had he never come to join them. Why? They had waited for him for so long. A thought occurred to Tomas, which he pushed away with all his strength. He wanted to scream! He was never going to see his father again . . . and his mother was going to die . . . and he would be all alone!

Maro moaned.

'Mama,' he shook her cold hand, 'mama!' She did not react. Tomas jumped off the bed and ran towards Riza's room shouting, 'My mother's dying! My mother's dying!'

'What's going on?' asked a voice behind him.

Tomas stopped and spun around. Riza Bey was coming out of Buyuk Hanim's apartments.

'Mama's dying! Mama's dying!' Tomas grabbed him by the wrist and dragged him along saying, 'Mama's very sick! You have to save her! Please! I don't want her to die!'

Riza, who was already worried because Buyuk Hanim had mentioned the word typhus, among other illnesses, became scared and ran, pulling the boy along by his arm.

Ayla bowed to Riza Bey and said reassuringly, 'Maro Hanim has been ill but she's better now.'

Without glancing at the girl, he went straight to the bed. What he saw confirmed his fears and distorted his judgement. He could hardly recognize her! Only a terrible illness could have changed her so radically in two days. He pushed Tomas towards the door.

'Go and find Abdullah and tell him to saddle his horse immediately.'

Tomas disappeared like a gust of wind.

'Have you called a healer?'

'No, Bey Effendi, Eminé has been taking care of Maro.'

He returned to the bed and touched Maro's hot, sticky forehead and then her ice-cold hands and feet, abnormal in this heat.

'Where does she hurt?'

'In her stomach, Effendi.'

He ran his hands over Maro's abdomen, at first very lightly and then, more strongly. He could feel a hard mass, which made him more afraid. He could hear Tomas's words in his head – 'My mother's going to die'. No! He would not allow it. He would not lose her like this. He caressed the pale cheeks of his beloved and, realizing his powerlessness, felt an uncontrollable wave of anger. He could not ask Allah for anything, as everything had already been decided for all eternity. He could not bargain with Him as did the infidels with their god, but his despair was so deep that he promised, 'I'll build a new mosque in Ayntab.' He did not give voice to the implied condition.

Buyuk Hanim was silently ranting against her son for having allowed a stranger into the harem. Never in the forty-nine years she had lived in the *konak* nor in all the years since Riza's grandfather had built it had such a thing happened! She had ordered her daughters-in-law to keep to their rooms. She and Eminé, wearing veils, followed each step and watched the Austrian doctor's every move to make sure that even the way he looked at Maro was professional.

Doctor Ernst was assigned to the staff officers posted in Ayntab. He thought it strange that he had been called to the house of the Ottoman governor, especially as it was to treat a woman. It was most unusual for a Muslim family. When he went back to the camp, his fellow officers were not going to believe it, so he tried to memorize every detail. He was a bit disappointed as the word 'harem' had conjured up in his mind a legendary palace, but all he had seen so far was an ordinary hall with rooms on either side. He would have to embellish the truth a bit so his friends would believe his story. He was already used to doing this for his patients to raise their morale and thus speed up their recovery.

'You'll have to take that thing off,' he said in German, pointing to the veil Buyuk Hanim had put over Maro's face.

Riza Bey did not bother to translate but took the veil off himself. His mother grumbled.

'Your wife is very beautiful,' the doctor nodded admiringly.

'She's ill!' Riza cut him short.

Ernst realized he had blundered and said, 'Leave it to me.'

He would have liked all of them to step back because they made him feel as if he were back in medical school undergoing an examination. When Maro came to, she was shocked to see a stranger bending over her. She could see a rectangular face, a cleft chin, a curled-up reddish moustache and grey-blue eyes under puffy eyelids.

Then she heard Riza's voice, 'Allah be praised. She's come to.'

She turned her head and saw him smiling at her. Buyuk Hanim was at his side, evidently deploring the situation. Poor Eminé was probably afraid that this scientist was a sorcerer and would discover the attempt at abortion.

'I must examine you, Madam.' His voice was friendly and a little guttural.

Maro, who didn't know German, asked Riza, 'What did he say?'

'You are not to speak to him,' ordered Buyuk Hanim.

Standing between his mother and Maro, Riza stepped forward and said kindly, 'Don't worry, my dove. He's a doctor. He's going to take care of you.'

Herr Ernst, who had already been told of her symptoms, took her temperature, examined her eyes carefully and felt her glands. He knew how touchy the men of this country were about their wives' honour and proceeded very prudently, displaying such great detachment that his gestures were hesitant.

Buyuk Hanim made no attempt to hide her impatience, and the doctor protested, 'I have to do my job.'

'Take your time,' said Riza Bey. 'The only thing that matters is for her to get well.'

'To examine her abdomen, it will be necessary to lower the sheet.'

Without batting an eyelid, Riza pulled the sheet down to Maro's navel. His outraged mother shook her head.

The doctor's facial expression changed slightly as he palpated her belly and Maro knew he had discovered she was pregnant. He had also probably guessed that she had tried to abort because when he lifted his head and their eyes met, there was complicity in his look. Buyuk Hanim quickly pulled the sheet up to Maro's nose.

'It's poisoning,' declared the doctor, putting away his stethoscope.

'Poisoning!' exclaimed Riza, immediately suspecting Leyla.

Happy with the effect of his words, the doctor precised, 'Food-poisoning.'

'Impossible! The food we serve here is first-rate and no one else has been sick.'

'Well . . . you know, with this heat it doesn't take long for food to ferment and the flies ... but she'll improve quickly. Give her lots of water sweetened with honey, milk and yogurt, and then gradually back to a more nourishing diet.'

'You've taken a weight off my mind, Herr Ernst.' Riza Bey patted him on the shoulder.

'She must eat for two.' The doctor smiled knowingly. 'I'm happy to inform you, sir, that your wife is pregnant.'

Riza looked stupefied. He did not react at first, then burst into nervous laughter and turned to Maro with glowing eyes.

'You are going to have a child . . . my child!'

She forced herself to smile; only she knew what it cost her! Eminé breathed easier, knowing that Maro had accepted to carry the child to term and no one would know about that damned potion.

Moved, Riza took Maro's hands and kissed them. 'My sweet dove! You have made me the happiest of men.' Then he turned and took his mother into his arms. 'Blessed is this day. I shall build a small mosque to commemorate it.'

Buyuk Hanim pushed her son away to reason with him, 'A mosque? Don't you think that's crazy? Just because your grandfather . . .'

He lifted his hand to keep her from further objection, 'As I have decided, so shall it be.'

The old woman bowed ungraciously, furious at having been rebuffed in front of a stranger, and left. The doctor and Riza Bey followed her.

Maro closed her eyes and was trying to rest when Tomas knocked at the door. Even though she felt extremely weak, she sat up in bed with Eminé's help.

'Let him in and leave us.'

The child threw himself on his mother and snuggled up in her arms. He was shaking all over as he put his face against his mother's shoulder and sobbed. She ran her fingertips through his hair.

He hiccuped, 'I thought you were going to die like grandmother.'

'I'm all right now, my darling.'

'You will never leave me, will you, mama?'

'Never!' she said lifting up his face and kissing him. She forced herself to smile to reassure him.

'Your hands were cold.'

'I had a fever but it's nothing to worry about.'

'Did the doctor cure you?'

'Completely.'

Tomas lay his cheek against his mother's shoulder and stayed there quietly for a long time. He had something else to say but did not know how to express it. He kept putting it off because he knew intuitively that once said, nothing would ever be the same again. He wanted to enjoy this moment when only he was important to his mother . . . Maro suspected that the news of her pregnancy had made the rounds of the house and that her son knew about it. She did not want to force the matter and waited for the words to come by themselves.

Tomas took a deep breath, then another, still hesitated and finally mumbled without looking at her, 'Is it true you are going to have a baby?'

She caressed his neck and said, 'Yes, Tomas.'

'Why?'

'God decided that.'

'A boy?'

'That's also for God to decide.'

He fell silent and Maro could sense how insecure he felt. Even though she was exhausted, she explained gently, 'Whether or not I have another child, boy or girl, has nothing to do with you, Tomas. You will always be my darling. A mother's heart is made in such a way that she can love ten children without dividing her love into ten; on the contrary, her love multiplies. It's the same for you. You love your father and mother, not half-way but both of them completely. And, besides that, you loved your grandmother, your godfather, Araksi, your dog . . . Do you understand?'

'Yes, mama.' No longer afraid, Tomas sat up and asked, 'When is the baby coming?'

'It's July now. In November, when the winter begins.'

He frowned as if he were solving a very big problem. 'If papa isn't here by then, who will be the baby's father?'

She realized that Tomas did not have the slightest idea how children were conceived and, all things considered, it was better this way. Fortunately, she had been very careful not to let him suspect the nature of her relationship with Riza Bey. He repeated his question and Maro looked for an answer he would understand.

'His father . . . well . . . he won't have one.'

'He must have a father.'

'Then we'll ask Riza Bey to be his father.'

Tomas thought that was the best solution. He would remain Vartan's only son and this child would be neither his brother nor his sister. At the thought of his father, he turned gloomy. He felt guilty about his earlier thoughts when he had feared Maro was dying. No! Vartan had not abandoned them! If he had not come, it was not his fault. They were keeping him away! Above all, he was not dead! No! He could not die!

Tomas had wanted to be reassured. He did not believe his father was going to come soon anymore. For a long time he had been certain that it would be tomorrow or the next day . . . at the most, next week . . . and this had allowed him to be happy one day at a time. Now, Tomas suddenly realized what an enormously long time had gone by since he had left Sivas . . . more than a year, so many days that they blended into each other! So as not to tire his mother, Tomas kept his thoughts to himself. 'Can we write to father?'

Maro swallowed hard as she tried to control her feelings, 'No. I don't know where he is. All we can do, my darling, is to pray very hard.'

At the end of September 1916, Riza Bey returned home after a meeting with Murat Pasha, commandant of the region, and some of the German staff officers. He was alarmed about the situation. In April the Russian fleet had landed a brigade of Cossacks who captured the town of Trebizond; Erzerum was already in Russian hands. In July an offensive launched by two hundred and eighty-two Ottoman infantry battalions had failed after the initial breakthrough. The Russians had counter-attacked and captured Erzinjan. Mustapha Kemal, the hero of Gallipoli, had reorganized the Second Army, withdrawing divisions from Dyarbekir and Malatya. However, in spite of having achieved some small local gains, he had been unable to breech the Russian lines and had been forced to fall back. In these battles the Empire had lost sixty thousand men!

On top of all this, the winter, which swept down unmercifully in these mountainous regions, had forced the army to dig in. They had to take advantage of this breather, which would last only a few months, because according to the German Intelligence Service, the Russians were planning a two-pronged spring offensive against Sivas and Kharput. This was to be co-ordinated with a British offensive in Mesopotamia. Worst of all, the Russian fleet in the Black Sea would try to take the Straits of Bosphorus and Constantinople. All this would mean the end of the Ottoman Empire! Well aware of this, Riza Bey asked himself if he had made a mistake in collaborating so closely with the Ittihad. If the Empire lost the war, he did not doubt that the victors would call him to account for his part in the extermination of the Armenians.

Riza Bey prudently decided that he must cover his back. He had to be ready to defend himself if he were accused. He already had a list of many Christians who would testify that he had protected them and another one of foreign missionaries who would confirm how he had helped them, but this was not enough. He would have to prove that, although he had personally disagreed with the official policies of the government, he had had to follow orders owing to his position as governor. That was the way! Gani Bey himself had suggested it. His official dispatches spoke of leniency, while the real reports had been transmitted in code.

The moment he arrived home, Riza Bey shut himself up in his office to dash off a message to the Minister of the Interior: 'Hundreds and thousands of miserable, perplexed women, children and old men are wandering about on the roads and mountains of Anatolia. In the spirit of charity, I expect the government to take these people back to their homes or wherever it is convenient to take them before winter comes.' He put down his pen and reread the text. There! That would do! Naturally he would keep a copy of this letter and others like it, to be able to show them if it should be necessary.

As he stood up, he noticed a telegram on top of a pile of unanswered letters, which must have arrived while he was visiting Murat Pasha. It was from the capital and Riza began to decode the sender's name: Talaat Pasha, the Minister of the Interior.

'Not again,' he grumbled when he saw the number 854 in the upper right-hand corner. Didn't this man have better things to do than send telegrams?

The message read as follows: 'At this moment when thousands of Muslim immigrants and the widows of our martyrs are in need of food and protection, it is inadmissible to feed certain people's children who will be of no use to us in the future and dangerous as well. Get them out of the police stations and send them back the deportee caravans.'[1]

According to instructions, he burnt the telegram. He would receive another one, not in code, tomorrow, which would say exactly the opposite. This one he was to ignore but he must put it on file. Even the Minister of the Interior was covering his back.

Riza suddenly felt nauseated at all this duplicity and wondered if he had been right when he had agreed to participate in the deportations two years ago. He longed for those times when he had only been a rich, respected man and not a politician. Then, he had all the time in the world to devote to his family and land, but it was too late to go back. He would have to go on playing a double game – giving with one hand and taking away with the other. He must make the Sublime Porte believe that he was zealously carrying out their orders by sending thousands of children to their death while, at the same time, giving in to pressure from the foreign missionaries, consuls and his own compassion and allowing American and European orphanages to stay open and supply food to the Armenian orphans. He sighed, lit a cigarette and left his office.

Bedri rose and made a *temenna*, 'Riza Bey, we have to . . .'

'Later,' said Riza impatiently and kept on walking. He had enough of paperwork and reports, enough of complaints from the local members of the Ittihad who wanted more and more favours, enough of overseeing the rationing, enough of trying to contain the typhus epidemic with his own money, enough of war! He was going to be a father for the ninth time and he was sick of all the death for which he was partly responsible. He would have liked to still feel proud of himself, to be again the just man, the proud man who, although unscrupulous in business and greedy for gain, had been respectful of the principles set out in the Quran. Yet he could not erase what he had done.

He saw a servant polishing the dining-room table with lemon oil and told her to tell Eminé to meet him in the dining room and bring some coffee.

---

1. Quoted from an official document of that time.

His old nursemaid would surely find something cheerful in the coffee grounds.

Safiyé was reading under the shade of a eucalyptus tree while Maro knitted clothes for the child who would be born in two months. Having failed to get rid of the little one, she had passively accepted it and even started to love it as the weeks rolled by. When it moved, she talked to it silently so it would feel wanted and not suspect she had tried to destroy it. This child had not asked to be born and there was no reason for it to suffer because of the way it had been conceived. Azniv Hanim had always said that a baby inside the mother's body heard all her thoughts. Maro did not really believe this but she surrendered to superstition. So that the child would not be confused about who its father was, she tried not to think about Vartan or have negative thoughts about Riza. She wanted this child to be born with all the luck in the world on its side, so she forced herself to remain serene. There would be time to worry about her future and Tomas's later . . . the coming of a second child would complicate it even more.

Tomas was crouching in the corner of the arbour watching his mother from afar. He was unhappy and felt neglected, relegated to second place, even though Maro showed him even more love and patience than before her pregnancy. There was that other one nestled inside Maro's belly and it talked to her constantly. Tomas could tell, just by looking at her, that his mother heard it and answered it. It was a conversation that he and others could not hear – a secret in which he took no part.

Riza paused at the entrance and noted the worry and frustration on Tomas's face. It made him unhappy as he loved this intelligent, wilful child. He walked towards him. 'Would you like to go and see some aeroplanes?'

Tomas had not noticed that someone was watching him and turned around, instinctively on the defensive. Riza repeated his offer and the child accepted readily.

'Go tell your brothers and have the horses saddled. I'll join you at the stables.'

'How many planes are there?'

'Three. They arrived at noon.'

Tomas ran off and Riza Bey went towards the bench where Safiyé and Maro were sitting. It warmed the cockles of his heart to see the friendship between his two favourite women and he forgot his worries. He kissed each in turn on the forehead, first Safiyé, whose eyes sparkled each time her husband came near her, and then Maro, whose relaxed face led Riza to believe that she had accepted her new life without reservations. He put his hand on her swollen belly, which bulged under her pink dress.

'Has he moved lately?'

'This morning.'

'Why *he*?' teased Safiyé. 'It could be a girl.'

'Eminé has seen that I shall have another son. I shall call him Nour.'

'Why not Nourhan?' suggested Maro. 'That sounds better.' She liked that name because it was almost the same as the Armenian name Nouran.

'Nourhan Bey. Nourhan Pasha,' said Riza Bey dreamily. 'Yes, that will do splendidly.'

Riza Bey's horse was already saddled. Tomas, Altan and Kenan were waiting behind the stables, thrilled at the thought of getting on a real twin-engine plane, an Albatross – a rare treat. They might even have a chance to fly. They had dreamed of this moment ever since they had begun to play with their model planes. The stable boys were preparing three other horses for the boys, laughing loudly as they watched a bay stallion mount a white mare in the paddock.

'What's happening?' Kenan asked his older brother.

Altan had lost his forlorn look and was enjoying the spectacle. 'He's making a foal. Look!'

'Bah!' Tomas did not believe him.

Angry that Tomas should doubt him, Altan hit him in the ribs with his fist. 'You know nothing, you little twerp!'

Tomas gritted his teeth as the other added sarcastically, 'Do you see that black thing he's putting into her hole? When you become a man like me, you'll have one just like it and you can stick it into a woman's hole and make a baby.'

His younger brother and Tomas were not convinced. Altan asked one of the men who was standing around to confirm what he had said. The stable hand, a strong thirty-year-old who had lost his front teeth through a horse's kick, laughed and showed how it was done with his fingers. Kenan and Tomas looked at each other aghast. This then was the answer to all the questions they had had after their visits to the *hammam*. It made sense.

Altan, who was jealous of Tomas, took advantage of the occasion to hurt him. He snickered nastily, 'Take a good look, why don't you? That's the way my father mounts your mother and she loves it! Just like the mare does.'

'No!' screamed Tomas, kicking out at Altan who jumped aside.

'Oh, yes, he does! And he gave her a baby too!'

'That's a lie!' screamed Tomas, running away. He refused to believe what Altan had said but he could not disprove it. It did explain what had been bothering him – where that baby had come from. Riza Bey was its father and he had mounted Tomas's mother as the mare had been mounted. Tomas could see the penis of the stallion entering the mare's vulva and was nauseated. Once out of sight of the stable, he leaned against the wall with both hands. His mother and Riza Bey ! He vomited.

# THIRTEEN

Cupolas, minarets, and an ancient Arab citadel on top of a knoll stood outlined in black against an orange sky. Thousands of trees rose above the flat roofs, making Aleppo look like an oasis in the centre of the desert plateau. Crowds of workers were packing salt, which had been extracted from ancient briny river beds, into sacks, piling them up in neat pyramids along the road and loading them on to camels.

A train whistled. Its tall, wide chimney belched out a black cloud, as it entered the station, to the din of screeching wheels and pumping pistons and rods. It came to a standstill, the engineer let off the steam, and the locomotive let out a deep sigh. In the coal car, a man was shovelling lignite. The engine was followed by seven enormous closed wagons and a flat car full of soldiers, crouching behind sandbags from which the barrel of a machine-gun peeked out.

'It's a military convoy,' Kemenché Hakki said, stating the obvious. 'It must be going to Jerusalem.' When Vartan failed to reply, Kemenché Hakki nudged him. 'Oudi, my dear brother, what's bothering you?'

'Nothing. I was just thinking.'

'I also think, but it doesn't make me look as if I was going to a funeral.' Vartan shrugged and Hakki put his sturdy arm around his friend's shoulders. 'Sometimes I can't figure you out, Oudi. You're different from the others. I don't understand you but I love you dearly.'

'Your friendship warms my heart, Hakki.'

Two hefty horses pulled the wagon carrying Pashazadé Shahir Mithad and his musicians. It rolled slowly because of the crowd of curious onlookers that had come to the station to meet the train. It was a soulless building. It had lavender- and pistachio-coloured walls crenellated at the top.

371

Stray cats and beggars were everywhere and idle porters just shoved them aside. Everyone was waiting for the arrival of the passenger train, which had been delayed by the military convoy. Strollers walked around, trying to read the news from the yellowed front pages covering the outside walls of a news stand. Some of the pages were at least a week old, but they all predicted victory for the Empire and its allies before the end of the year.

Hakki and Vartan were walking behind the wagon. It had been over four hours since their last stop and their clothes were covered with dust. Vartan felt neither tired nor thirsty. Ever since they started out for Aleppo, two days earlier, he had been filled with excitement and fresh expectations. And now that they were so close, he was having an attack of nerves.

Finally! Aleppo! At last! Nearly all the deportees had passed through this city. Many Armenians lived there among the Arabs. The man who had picked up Maro and Tomas at the cave where Azniv Hanim had died might have brought them here. From the day Vartan began his search, he had had the idea that he might find his family here and by now he had convinced himself that they must be living somewhere in one of the deportee camps.

It was his way of compensating himself for the disappointments he had had over the past nine months. They had gone through so many towns and villages, had been invited to so many mansions, played in so many public squares, without ever being able to find the slightest trace of Maro and Tomas.

When they reached the square of Bab el-Faraj, Vartan asked Hakki, 'Do you know where we'll be staying?'

'At the Nahiyé Khan. We're almost there.'

'I'll meet you there in a couple of hours.'

Ignoring Hakki who wanted to accompany him, he entered the labyrinth of the old market district and mingled with the crowd. He soon came to a small square. When the sun sank in a red sky, the shopkeepers started lowering the metal shutters of their shops. Men sat around in a dilapidated café and a young boy was lighting the oil lamps. People loitered around on the side walk, in front of a kiosk, eating grilled meat patties, lamb liver or kidneys.

The Ottoman government had had little success in its efforts to Turkify Aleppo. It was a lively town, sophisticated and cosmopolitan, as were many other Anatolian towns. One heard more Arabic on the street than Turkish, along with the occasional Kurdish, Syriac, Chaldean, Circassian and Druze.

There were also large colonies of Armenians, Jews and Greeks. The mixture of such diverse nationalities, the large European colonies and the precarious situation of the Ottoman government in Syria, were the major reasons why the deportation of the Armenians in Aleppo had not been enforced.

Distractedly, Vartan hurried through the crowd. The sudden honk of a motor-car startled him. He stepped aside to avoid being hit by an army vehicle carrying an Ottoman and two German officers. In the middle of the square, an old lemonade vendor, wearing a white turban and carrying a copper vessel on his back, sang out in a whining tone, 'Come drink, and be cleansed.' A couple of young boys stood at his side, offering glasses full of the pink liquid.

Vartan gulped down a glass and handed the old man a coin. 'Thank you. Could you tell me the way to the Armenian Quarter?'

Annoyed, the old man turned to his helpers. While one of them translated, the other one quickly reminded Vartan, 'He doesn't speak Turkish but if you're generous to me, I can tell you.'

Vartan gave him a small coin; but the boy, unsatisfied, just gazed at him blankly. Another coin loosened his tongue. 'It isn't too far, the time it takes to smoke three cigarettes. See that man riding the donkey? Follow him. He's going there.' He spat in a large arc and then guffawed.

Vartan hurried not to lose sight of the peasant, who was whipping his mule with a twig. The smell of frying food from the houses summoned the children who had been playing in the street all day. The peasant stopped when he came to a deserted intersection. Vartan went up to him and offered a greeting.

'*Selamaleykum.* Do you know where . . .'

The man, who had a dark, tanned face, interrupted him. '*Aleykumselam.* I'm from out of town, Effendi, and I'm lost.'

Vartan realized that he had been duped. It was almost dark and there was no one around to show him the way. He left the peasant, who couldn't decide which of the three streets to take, and headed east. Vartan finally saw a red building, took a chance and went down that street. He came to a poor quarter of winding alleys where the full moon lit up the decrepit warehouses and sheds.

He kept walking, seeing nobody, until he noticed a figure crouching in a doorway. A beggar got up and approached him, holding out his right hand, while the left one scratched an oozing wound covering his forehead and half of his face. Vartan searched his pockets for some coins and asked if

373

this was the Armenian Quarter. The man simply stood there, shaking his empty hand and grinning toothlessly. Vartan repeated his question in vain, gave him a few more coins and walked on. The desolation around him depressed him and suddenly he felt very tired. He could not help thinking that he had made a mistake by pinning all his hopes on Aleppo. He should have been more patient and waited for the next day to begin his search.

He came to a place that he thought to be a park, but it turned out to be the Muslim cemetery. The narrow gravestones were crowned by marble turbans. He went around to the other side of it, where he could see a sector lit by a few gas lamps.

The dirty streets were lined with one-storeyed, lopsided, windowless shacks. He could see into the lighted rooms through the wide doorless entrances. A few half-naked women in satin underwear were squatting on the ground or leaning against the outside walls of the shacks. Signs in Arabic, English, French and German advertised: FOR HIRE: BY THE DAY OR THE HOUR. Men, strolling carefree in groups of two or three, were looking the merchandise over and inquiring about the price. Vartan kept on walking, ignoring the offers, but stopped when he heard someone speaking Armenian.

'That one isn't ugly in spite of his beard.'

'He could be a *hodja*.'

Two girls were chatting and fanning a brazier placed on the dirt floor in one of the shacks. A veiled woman sat napping on a wooden chair behind them. One of the Armenians was wearing a western-style lace-trimmed blouse; the other only a pink *shalvar*, which exposed her small, firm breasts. Neither could have been more than seventeen.

Vartan drew near and spoke in Armenian, 'Good evening. May I have a word with you?'

The one whose breasts were exposed lowered her head. The other blushed but looked him squarely in the face.

She asked suspiciously, 'Are you a priest?'

The woman woke and looked up. 'What did he say?' she asked in Turkish.

'We're discussing the price.' She turned to Vartan. 'What do you want?'

He did not know what to say and realized that it was a silly idea to speak to them. They would think he was condemning them. He had no right to put their safety in jeopardy; they were only trying to survive. He was sorry he had stopped, but now he had to say something.

'What's your name?'

'Gulizar.'

'Your real name?'

'That's none of your business.'

'What's going on?' The woman was getting impatient. She peeped sideways at the client. 'Talk so that I can understand. Let him get out of here, if he doesn't have the money.'

Vartan felt sorry for them. 'Are you being held here against your will?'

Gulizar shrugged, and the other one, who till then hadn't said a word, raised her glance to Vartan and said, 'We have to live.'

Vartan could read resignation on her heavily made-up face.

'Do you know if there are any Armenians from Sivas in Aleppo?'

'I don't know. My name is Nektar and I come from Moush.'

Gulizar elbowed her to shut her up and said harshly, 'Do you want to fuck? If not, get out. You can make a lot of trouble for us. Leave us alone!'

As the veiled woman rose and shuffled over, Vartan wished them luck and walked away quickly.

He came to a paved street with two-storeyed stucco houses. Laughing voices called him, 'Oudi Yashar! You rascal, you!'

'Oudi! Brother! Wait for us!'

Hakki, who had been about to enter a whorehouse with Hafiz Ismael and Tambour Vasfi, grabbed Vartan by the shoulder. 'So this is where you were going! There's nothing like the body of a woman to get rid of sadness, although, my dear *aghabey*, it doesn't seem to have done much for you.'

'I'm tired from the trip.'

Hakki did not insist. Since they had been travelling together he had come to know Vartan and respected his need for quiet and withdrawal.

'Which way is the inn?'

Hakki turned to the other two. 'I'll join you later.' He took Vartan by the arm and walked along with him a few steps. 'Do you want me to go with you to a restaurant? Ismael and Vasfi can get along very well without me.'

'No, go back and have fun, Hakki. I'm going to bed.'

'There's fruit, bread and yogurt in the room. I thought you might be hungry if you came in late.'

Such thoughtfulness in such a rough man never ceased to amaze Vartan.

The tour was coming to an end and, unless a miracle happened in Aleppo, Vartan would have no other choice but to go back to Aroussiag in Urgup. If, by any chance, he did find Maro and Tomas, where would they go? South? Those towns were still under the control of the Ottoman Empire. Seek asylum in a foreign country would probably be the best. But how?

The innkeeper had given Vartan the address of the Protestant mission and, the moment the morning rehearsal was over, he hurried there. The guard, a strong, swarthy, twenty-year-old youth, with black eyes as round as marbles, fixed his gaze on the bearded Turk distrustfully and told him that Reverend Matthews was away for a few days.

'I wanted . . .' Vartan hesitated to confide in him because, although he spoke with a Syriac accent, he could very well be a government informer. 'In that case, could I see whoever is in charge?'

'Mrs Matthews?'

'Yes. Please tell her that I'm a friend of the Reverend.'

In a few minutes the guard returned and opened the locked door with a large key hanging from his belt. A narrow garden full of oleanders separated the house from the street. Tall windows were set into the grey stone façade and wide marble steps led to the main entrance. These houses were assigned to foreigners by the government. The war had evidently not lessened the privileges enjoyed by the Americans, thanks to a number of treaties signed with the Sublime Porte.

Vartan removed his fez when he greeted Mrs Matthews, an elegant woman in her early fifties. She received him in a small green room next to the entrance hall. Her face was still smooth and free of wrinkles and she must have been a great beauty once. She wore a white dress with a golden cross pinned on its high-necked collar.

She asked politely but stiffly in Turkish, 'What can I do for you, sir?'

As the guard was still standing at the door, Vartan answered in English, 'Thank you for receiving me. Could we speak in private?'

She was astonished and dismissed the guard. 'Who are you?'

'Vartan Balian, Madam. I don't think . . .'

'But, of course, I've heard about you. I even read some of your articles, before Mr Matthews took them to the consul.' Smiling now, she shook his hand, invited him to be seated in a chair covered with faded needle-point and rang for tea.

'My husband has been expecting you for months. How unfortunate that he should be away right now.'

376

'It certainly is, and I must leave in a couple of days.'

'You shall not leave empty-handed, Mr Balian.'

He jumped up looking radiant. 'You mean you have news of my wife and son?'

Mrs Matthews bit her lip nervously and sadly. 'Unfortunately, that's not what I was referring to.'

Vartan fell back on his chair just as someone knocked on the door. A servant put a tray on a table and left. Mrs Matthews served the tea.

'I'm terribly sorry I raised your hopes. I'm really distressed.' She offered Vartan a cup of tea. 'Do you take sugar?'

'No, thank you.' He was shattered and kept shaking his head. 'It's not your fault. It's only that I . . .' He could not finish.

Mrs Matthews sat quietly for a few moments. She was sorry she did not have her husband's gift of finding the right words at the right moment. She was trying to imagine how she would feel if she had been separated from her husband without knowing what had happened to him. When she thought Vartan had recovered himself, she said, 'Please believe me. If my husband knows nothing about the fate of your family, it's not for lack of inquiries in all the missions. He has also questioned all the deportees he has come in contact with.'

'I know, Mrs Matthews. I don't doubt it for a minute.' His voice was steady but inside he was seething. Only a small flame still flickered in his heart and that coiled spring that had driven him for months was unwinding.

Mrs Matthews realized he was waging an internal battle. 'Don't give up hope, Mr Balian. God watches over all of us.'

Vartan refused to give up. 'I'll never stop looking.'

'There! That sounds more like a Christian!' Mrs Matthews was relieved. 'Your wife and son . . . How old is he?'

'Six . . . No! Seven and a half.'

'The age of reason. Perhaps the kind man who took them out of the convoy is caring for them. Or they could even be safe in Beirut or Baghdad or Persia.' She paused, took a sip of tea and set the cup down on the saucer. 'I'm sorry you misunderstood what I was trying to tell you. I have news about your brother. He and his family made it to Jerusalem before the deportations started.'

'Thank God! At last, some good news.' Vartan rejoiced quietly for a moment. Noubar, like his father, had always been able to look ahead. 'Would it be possible for you to get a letter to him?'

'Of course, only I don't know how long it will take.'

As she poured herself some more tea, she noticed that Vartan had not touched his. She smiled. She had more good news to cheer him up. 'I have more to tell you, Mr Balian. My husband was in Cappadocia last month and he tells me that your friends are well and waiting for you. They received a message from one of your cousins in Constantinople.'

'It must have been from Diran. I wrote to him. What did he say?'

'That your relatives in Constantinople are well but he knows nothing about your wife. The letter is waiting for you in Urgup.' She hesitated, wondering if she were being indiscreet and then asked anyway. 'You are going back there, aren't you?'

'I would prefer to remain in the vicinity of Aleppo or perhaps go on to Jerusalem, but I really don't seem to have much choice. I'm still a wanted man. If I didn't have this cover of a musician in a *dervish* group, I would risk being arrested. I don't have the necessary papers to move around freely, so I'll go back to Urgup. Anyhow, I've already agreed to go on another tour with Pashazadé Shahir Mithad next spring.'

'That's fine. The information you've given us has helped us to locate many Armenian children, take them to our orphanages, schools and hospitals, and thus keep them from becoming Muslims.'

'That's what is important . . . for them to keep their language and religion so that they remain Armenian. We've lost so many adults that we'll need every single child to populate the independent Armenia we'll create after the end of the war.'

Mrs Matthews did not feel like talking about this subject. 'My husband is in a better position to discuss politics with you. I don't understand anything about it. All I care about is for the Ottoman government to let the food and money, sent to help the Armenians, reach us.'

Before he left, Vartan wrote a long letter to Noubar, telling him briefly what had happened during the past year and a half and asking him, if possible, to have someone search for Maro and Tomas in Baghdad, Beirut and Damascus. He thanked Reverend Matthews's wife and took his leave.

'You should go see Der Kevork; he's a priest who has been working hard to help your compatriots. I'm sure he would like to meet you. His church is at the edge of the Barak el-Araman, the Armenian shacks, north-east of town.'

She thought the priest would know how to encourage Vartan, for she could feel his despair behind his calm façade.

She thought the priest would know how to encourage Vartan, for she could feel his despair behind his calm façade.

'Did you say his name was Der Kevork? I'll pay him a visit.'

He was feigning ignorance; Der Kevork was a crucial link in the Armenian network and Vartan had several messages for him.

He hurried to rejoin the musicians, who were attending a reception given by the Chief of Police. Never had music created such a refuge for him. Only music could express the inexpressible, so he let himself be carried away and emptied his heart through the strings of his *oud*. His companions, familiar with his virtuosity, were astonished at the feeling with which he played that evening; they were stunned listening to his mellifluous notes and to the emotional strain which vibrated through his music. Even the guests were inspired by this player and sat very still. When the evening was over, the master of the house congratulated Vartan and slipped a piece of gold into his hand.

Instead of joining the musicians, who walked towards the inn, Vartan stayed with the guests who were heading towards the centre of town. He left them at the next corner and their spurts of laughter faded quickly. Vartan came to a wide, tree-lined street, where the moon was shining on the cobblestones. He walked slowly, being careful not to disturb the silence of the sleeping town. He felt completely empty inside and had no thoughts or feelings, only a strange peace, which he wanted to enjoy as long as possible. He stopped in front of Hotel Baron, the smartest hotel in the region, a modern building built in 1911. He leaned against a plane tree and let the minutes advance. He contemplated the moon going down behind the roofs, but without really seeing it. When he started to walk back, it was nearly dawn.

He stopped in the garden of the inn to roll himself a cigarette. He heard some weak panting coming from the direction of the well. He went to investigate. There was a woman lying on her back, her hands firmly gripping hard a man lying on top of her. She sensed someone was there, let out a gasp, pushed her partner off and ran away, pulling her skirts down. Hakki remained sitting on the ground.

'Oudi, my *aghabey*, you frightened her away,' he said, in an amused voice. 'She's the innkeeper's daughter.'

'I'm so sorry.'

'That's all right. I'd already fucked her twice.'

379

'I saw your face. What's so strange about that?' Hakki realized immediately that he had blundered. He had told Vartan that the army had refused
to take him because he was near-sighted and that he could not see in the
dark.

'You seem to have the eyes of an owl.'

'Well . . .' Hakki was looking for a plausible explanation. 'My *aghabey*,
I beg you to let this be a secret between us.'

'Of course.'

Relieved, Hakki put his arm around Vartan and pulled him gently
towards the inn. In their room, he took out his viola. Vartan protested.

'You're going to wake every one up with your *kemenché*.'

'I'll play it very softly. Listen. It's a piece I composed especially for you.'

He lay the instrument on his thigh and stroked the small bow gently
over the strings. 'I've written this song about our friendship. The melody
came to me easily, but I have been trying for days to find the right words for
it. You'll have to help me.'

'What do you want to say?'

'The joy I feel knowing you; the pleasure it gives me to talk to you, how
different you are from the others, how mysterious you are and how much
I love you.'

Vartan smiled while Hakki played. 'It's a lovely melody, Hakki, my
friend. I'll help you write the words, but let's go to sleep now.'

Hakki began to snore the minute he stretched out, but Vartan, still upset
by the conversation he had at the American mission, could not go to sleep.
He had run up against a wall. All his actions and efforts of the past months
had been in vain. He had to admit that he had subconsciously known all
along that he would not find his family in Aleppo. He remembered all those
encouraging words he had heard from different people. Their voices, with
all the nuances in them, still echoed in his ears. At the time, he had had
grave doubts about what they said, but he still wished to hear them. The
only one who had dared to tell him the truth was Aroussiag, but she had
had her own reasons to want to dissuade him.

To go back to her . . . Back to her hut . . . That would mean abandoning
all hope of finding his family. To join his brother in Jerusalem?
Tempting . . . but then he would miss the opportunity of travelling around
Anatolia with the musicians and the end result would be the same – to give
up his search for good.

Aroussiag's little hut . . . How many times had he thought about it as a haven since last spring. His mind had gone back to it whenever he had been sickened by the sight of heaps of bones all along the roads, deserted Armenian quarters, burnt villages now occupied by poor *mouhajirs*, who were using the churches for stables, cutting down the orchards for firewood and letting the fields that had been lovingly cultivated by generations of Armenians lie fallow. He was sick of listening to the same old horror stories so he could tell the world about them in his articles. These stories preyed so heavily on his mind that he sometimes felt he was living through the deportations again and again. As long as he lived he would never forget, but he had had enough of ruins . . . of loss . . . of death. He would have liked to put an end to his reporting and turn over a new leaf. More and more he felt like rebuilding his life, but he could not – not until he had either found his family or discovered for certain that he had lost them forever.

Depressed at the thought of his impending meeting with Der Kevork, Vartan arose at daybreak. The priest would preach about faith and divine providence and give him a detailed account of all the horrors he had witnessed. How would he restrain himself from telling Der Kevork that he had had enough of deluding himself, that he knew enough about horror, that he was weary, that he wanted to dream about peaceful times? That would sound blasphemous!

Since he wanted to get over the ordeal quickly, he arrived far too early at the tiny church on the eastern edge of the city, near the *souks* and ancient caravanserais. A new section was under construction further up, its ugliness accentuated by the violent contrast of hard light and shadows. The wind raised clouds of dust from the dirt-roads that wound between the board-and-canvas shacks. Here and there a few fieldstone houses were already replacing the temporary constructions, but the overriding image was still one of poverty!

A few things tempered Vartan's first impression – small vegetable plots growing in empty lots, chickens pecking in front of the doors, dogs barking, plumes of smoke rising over the tiled roofs. This was Barak el-Arman! Instead of visiting the priest, Vartan would have preferred to walk among his fellow countrymen, to see how they lived, perhaps to help someone build a stone wall for his house. Instead he headed towards the church.

381

Because of the recent rains, grass was growing between the cobblestones in the walled rectangular courtyard. An old man in a faded black cassock sat on a stone bench, reading a newspaper. He looked up when he heard Vartan's sandals swiping on the cobblestones. His left eye was sunken and the eyelid seemed to have been sewn to his cheek, but his other eye was piercing, as if all life had been concentrated there. A narrow white beard fell to the middle of his chest and made his bony face look longer. His skin was tanned and wrinkled like a dried apricot. He addressed his visitor in Turkish.

'What wind has blown you here this morning, young man?'

'A friendly one,' replied Vartan in Armenian, taking off his fez.

Der Kevork attempted to rise.

'Better let me sit down, Father.'

'As you like.'

Vartan sat down beside him and Der Kevork sniffed, wondering if he were imagining the rare aroma that was making him drool.

'It's what you think it is,' Vartan confirmed, handing him a small brown sack, stained by grease marks.

'Coffee!' exclaimed the priest. He opened the bag, took a small pinch between his gnarled fingers and smelled.

'Coffee. Good coffee. I haven't had any for ages.'

An Armenian blacksmith in Urfa, who had escaped the deportation because of his trade, had given Vartan some messages for the priest and told him about the priest's passion for coffee.

'Loussaper! Loussaper!'

The priest's wife, a woman in her early seventies, ran out from the sacristy. It was obvious from the loose skin on her neck and her flabby cheeks and arms that she had once been obese and had recently lost a lot of weight. She pressed her hand against her breast and reproached her husband for having frightened her needlessly.

'Look! Our friend here has brought us some coffee,' he said excitedly.

She was glad to see her husband so happy and nodded to Vartan. 'Thank you, sir, and welcome.'

'Could you make us some?'

'How would you like it, sir, medium or sweet?'

'Just a little sugar, if you can spare it.'

'Make it very sweet,' Der Kevork exclaimed, and then said to Vartan, 'We'll drink it together. It could be a sign of better times.'

382

Vartan did not understand what the priest meant. He introduced himself.

'I know who you are,' the priest said, patting him on the shoulder warmly. He was much stronger than his frail frame would suggest. 'You write excellent articles that serve our cause. It's a great pleasure to meet you at last, my son.'

'I feel the same way, Father.' Vartan shook his hand, cut the formalities short and came straight to the point. 'I bring you messages from Urfa.'

'Later,' said the priest, who was looking forward to the coffee.

'I'm sure you must have been told that I'm looking for my family.'

'More than once. Twice. First by the people in the network, and then by Pastor Matthews. You have moved heaven and earth, haven't you?'

'All in vain. Have you heard anything?'

'Nothing, my son. I'm sorry. I have even checked the local orphanages and the foreign missions. Your people are not here in Aleppo, nor in the vicinity.' His good eye scanned Vartan's face and his voice became gentle. 'You must be calm, my son.'

'And bow to God's Will?' Vartan could hardly contain his impatience.

Der Kevork kept his voice steady. 'Among other things.' When Vartan did not answer, the priest continued, 'You must start to live again, my son.'

'That's easy for you to say.'

The priest kept looking at the door. What was taking her so long? The water must have boiled by now.

'You need to have another goal, from what I've heard about you.'

'Ah! Write more articles about the deportation? Now you're going to tell me what you've seen. Is that what you mean by starting to live again?'

Unperturbed by Vartan's sarcasm, the old man again looked impatiently at the door. 'You're right, my son. The time for tears is over.'

Vartan, who had expected him to object, glanced at him perplexed. 'What do you mean?'

Der Kevork laid his hand on Vartan's shoulder and continued mysteriously, 'You and I have a lot to talk about . . . unless you're in a hurry.'

Vartan felt a sudden urge to leave immediately. He wanted to spare himself another sermon that would only add to his frustration. 'I don't have much time, Father. I'll have to be back shortly for a rehearsal.'

'I understand.'

The priest's wife walked hesitantly out of the sacristy, afraid of spilling the precious liquid. She advanced slowly, and her large body made her pelvis sway at each careful step. She gave each man a small cup filled to the brim. The cups were chipped. Like all the other people in his parish, the priest lived on the brink of poverty.

'Praise be to God for all His blessings.' The priest inhaled the aroma, closed his eye, tasted the coffee with reverence and murmured, 'One really doesn't appreciate things until they're gone.'

Loussaper watched them as they sipped their coffee. Her husband barely touched the brim of the cup with his lips as he sucked the boiling liquid up slowly to allow it to cool before it entered his mouth.

'If you don't mind, I'd like to take you on a quick tour around my parish, my son; it won't take long,' said the priest, handing the empty cup to his wife.

'Are there many people from Sivas here?' asked Vartan, instead of assenting.

'Very few and they know nothing. I've already asked.'

Vartan followed the couple into the sacristy. The room was crowded, with a rolled-up straw mattress resting against one wall. Loussaper had arranged it for living quarters as best she could. There were also a table and two chairs, some pots and pans hanging on the wall and a charcoal grill. A single chasuble was hanging in the priest's closet, which was also used to store food. Vartan ripped open a seam in the lining of his jacket and took out papers folded up into tiny booklets and covered with minuscule writings. They were messages for Der Kevork. He read them quickly before handing them to his wife to put away.

They went out and Vartan asked the priest, Der Kevork, what he advised him to do about his wife and son.

'Frankly, my son, you can't do anything about them – at least, not until the war is over. Either they were among those unfortunates sent to die in the *jebel*[1] south of the Euphrates or, with luck, they escaped to Mesopotamia, Palestine, Persia . . .' The priest hesitated. What he omitted to say was that Maro, like a large number of other Armenian women, might have become the concubine of a Bey. 'There are so many possibilities. You know that as well as I do. You can worry and fret but it won't change anything.' He watched for a reaction, but Vartan remained unperturbed. 'But, of course you already know this.'

---

1. Mountain (Arabic).

'Of course,' Vartan muttered distractedly.

They went past the wells, walking along a dusty dirt-road that snaked its way among the higgledy-piggledy assortment of shacks. Der Kevork held on to Vartan's arm, not that he needed to – he had things to say, things that only an educated man could understand.

'At the beginning, for almost a year, the deportees arrived here by the hundreds of thousands – countless columns of full wagons. The Armenians from Aleppo were not deported and took in everyone they could . . .'

'That I already know, Der Kevork.' Vartan was barely polite. He did not want to talk about this.

'You don't understand, my son.'

Der Kevork's repeated use of the words 'my son' intensified Vartan's irritation. The priest continued, 'I have no intention of telling you horror stories. What I want you to see is that, until a few months ago, all we did was bury the dead.' He stopped and, with satisfaction, swept his arm in a circle. 'Take a look around you. This is a new quarter. We are living again.'

The shacks looked miserable but they had a roof. Old women were tilling the earth. Children were running around and screaming.

'When you sow, you think of tomorrow. These people are alive. True, they are still dependent on the charity of the rich families in Aleppo – the Altounians, the Mazloumians, the Arevians, and on the aid of the American Consul, Mr Jackson, and the foreign missionaries, but many have small jobs in town, and some are beginning to work in their trades again. The women are beginning to weave.'

The priest was, in fact, voicing the thoughts that struck Vartan when he first saw the settlement. The feeling he had had then was not of a reporter looking for something to write about, but of a wanderer returning to his village.

'Come, my son' Der Kevork said. 'I'll show you something that will make you happy.'

Old women, men and children came out of their houses to greet the priest. Their faces were gaunt but there was a spark in their eyes. As he greeted everyone with the customary 'God bless you,' the priest had some extra words for every one. He knew the name of each person he greeted. Vartan only nodded, content to be amongst his own again.

'You don't have to prove anything to me, Father. I have complete confidence in our people's ability to build on top of ruins. History is eloquent on the subject.'

'I'm not trying to prove anything,' said the priest in a low voice. 'On the contrary, I expect you to . . .'

He took Vartan by the arm. They crossed a checkerboard of small yards and vacant lots separating the shacks and reached the outskirts of the settlement. From there they could see the ruins of a *khan* not far from the Muslim cemetery. Der Kevork sat down on top of a large stone fallen from the top of a wall. Vartan remained standing in front of him, waiting for the priest to catch his breath.

'Many of our people cry out for vengeance, my son, and I can feel this in some of your writings.'

There was a shade of regret in the priest's voice, almost a reproach, but out of respect for his calling and age, Vartan answered mildly:

'Father, I'd like for you to understand that denouncing the criminals in power and demanding justice for the Armenians is not crying for vengeance.'

'You're coming to that again,' said Der Kevork sententiously, 'and it's a mistake. I have no time for vengeance. Don't forget, it's against our religion. I have all these people to take care of, to feed them, and to restore their desire to live. We have to consider tomorrow only.'

'I agree with you, Father. Tomorrow, a new Armenia! This shall be our dream we shall prepare for the day when it becomes reality.'

'That's what has been worrying me.' Der Kevork looked like an embarrassed child. 'You were a member of the parliament and you are a well-known writer. I trust your judgement. Tell me, what's this Armenia you're talking about?'

'If you have read my articles, you already know.'

'I've read and reread them, but I want you to tell me.'

Vartan was in no mood to get into a debate with the priest. Der Kevork took Vartan's silence for lack of confidence and he said, 'I have my doubts. If you're uncertain about the future, others must be wondering, too. I think you should write about this in your articles to make people start to think about their future.'

'Never!' said Vartan categorically. 'It would only demoralize the Armenians who are hoping for a home, confuse our Allies, and provide new arguments for our enemies.'

'Armenia, the Greater Armenia, the eternal Armenia will only come alive again in each of our children,' the priest said. 'Last month I had a vision. A new Moses was guiding our people to the Promised Land and that land didn't look like Anatolia. Perhaps our destiny is to scatter throughout the world.'

'I cannot resign myself to that. Abandon everything without fighting? No, Father. I respect your views but I don't share them. I cannot and I will not spread them.'

The priest was confounded. Vartan looked at the sun to see what time it was.

'I have to join Pashazadé Shahir Mithad's musicians at noon.'

'It was clever of you to join those *dervishes*,' said Der Kevork, hoping to regain Vartan's regard for him. He could have risen by himself, but he held out his hand. It was his way of closing the rift between them. He held on to Vartan's arm. 'You still have time, my son. I'd like to walk back with you and stop at the orphanage to show you the children.'

They could see from far the German school which had now become an orphanage – a dismal greystone building behind a wrought-iron fence.

Vartan thought that Der Kevork wanted them to part on a cheerful note but accepting his invitation would only be another disappointment for him – he would unconsciously examine each face, looking for Tomas. He no longer felt like talking to the children or speaking with the missionaries.

An embarrassed silence fell between them. The priest gripped Vartan by the arm. Vartan felt sorry, realizing that the priest was distraught. 'I'm sorry, Father, I wish I had more time,' Vartan replied. 'What's important is what you are doing for our people. Let's wait and see what happens.'

'You're right, my son,' said the priest thankfully. 'Enough of theories. We must roll up our sleeves and deal with more urgent matters.'

'May God keep you, Father.'

The priest felt uncomfortable for having disappointed his visitor. 'Thank you for listening to my original ideas. Blame them on my old age, my son.'

Vartan embraced the old man and then walked quickly away.

Kourt's frenetic barking alerted Aroussiag and she threw a shawl around her shoulders before going out. It was bitter cold on that last evening of 1917. The frost had silvered the grass and the naked earth. Like the dog, she had immediately recognized the approaching silhouette on the road and her heart leaped.

'Vartan!' She ran to meet him. The black dog ran ahead of her. 'Vartan!'

For almost a year, she had been sure she had lost him and now here he was! A dream come true! She was living a dream! A phrase written about her in his short letter to Kerim, a few month ago, came back to her.

'Give my regards to our friend. Tell her I remember her with affection and that I thank her again for her hospitality.'

According to Kerim, Vartan's discretion was due to his fear of censorship and one had to read between the lines. How many different ways had she interpreted that sentence: *I remember her affectionately.*

He had returned! Here was proof that he loved her. Would they be able to recover the intimacy of the winter before? So many months had gone by, so many lonely nights! Shyly, she stopped short ten paces before reaching him. He had laid down his canvas bag and was petting Kourt who pressed himself against him. He looked even more handsome than she remembered – taller – stronger. Desire rose in her, mixed with emotions she had forgotten about.

He kept on petting the dog absently, saying nothing so that he could look at Aroussiag who was coming towards him. Then he pushed the dog away, opened his arms, and took her in. 'Aroussiag! Aroussiag!' His voice was vibrant as he held her close. He held her close, raised her face and kissed her passionately.

She trembled. 'You're going to catch cold.'

He picked up his bag, which lay at his feet. 'Let's go in quickly.'

'Give me the *oud*.' She carried the covered instrument affectionately, as if it were an infant. Words stuck in her throat. There was no way she could express her happiness.

'I couldn't let you know.'

'You're here. That's all that matters.'

When they arrived at the house, Vartan stopped staring at her and let his eyes roam around the fields, pausing at the haystacks, the fruit trees, the stables, as if making sure that everything was still the same. Aroussiag rejoiced, thinking he was looking around as if it all belonged to him.

'Did you pass by Kerim's school?'

'No, I came straight here.' His answer gave Aroussiag another reason to rejoice, especially when he added, as he opened the door, 'I feel I'm coming home.'

He laid his bundle down on the floor and hung his cape on a wooden post.

'Sit down,' she said, pointing to the bed, 'I'll make you some tea.'

While she was raking up the embers in the fire pit, her eyes never left him and his never left her. They had so much to say to each other that words seemed superfluous; their eyes were doing the talking. As she tried to fill the copper kettle, Vartan went and lifted her off her feet. Carried her to the bed, laid her down and covered her with kisses as he undressed her, fumbling feverishly. Aroussiag's laughter gave way to panting, as she took off her long skirt and offered herself to him. Their coupling was brief and their pleasure violent!

They lay silent, face to face, so close that all they could see were each other's eyes, as the night enveloped them. Slowly, but just as passionately, they made love again. Words gushed forth spontaneously – 'I love you' – 'my love' – 'you're my life'. They fell asleep without having supper and when they opened their eyes, still in each other's arms, it was dawn; and again they became one.

Finally the muffled bleating and braying from the stables made them get out of bed and face the damp, ice-cold room. Vartan went through his bundle and took out something, holding it behind his back.

'*Shnhoravor nor dari*.'[1] He opened his hand. On his palm lay a silver pendant set with a rose onyx.

She couldn't believe it. 'For me?'

He put the chain around her neck and she shivered at the touch of the cold metal on her breast.

'It's beautiful, but . . . I . . . I have nothing to give you.'

'You've given me everything,' He ran his hands over her bare shoulders and breasts.

She closed her eyes, raised herself gently on her toes and reached his mouth. 'I'll never take it off.' It was as if he had given her a wedding ring. With this gift, Vartan was telling her that she was his! Her voice was husky. 'Happy New Year, my love. I swear that . . .' She did not finish but smiled, examining her present closely.

Vartan pulled himself free, picked up his clothes and began dressing. 'I'll feed the animals while you prepare breakfast.'

It was comforting for Aroussiag to watch Vartan take up last year's routine, as if he had never been absent. Vartan had the same feeling when he entered the warm, familiar-smelling stable. The past months seemed unreal. To handle the pitchfork, to draw water from the well, to fill the mangers, to carry away the dung – this work was real, compared to his

---

1.   Happy New Year (Armenian).

389

wanderings and his chasing after chimeras. He remembered the pear-tree in front of one of the shacks in Aleppo . . . 'to live again', Der Kevork had said. To be Oudi Yashar, an anonymous peasant . . . to love a woman who loves you . . . to watch the seasons pass . . . to worry only about droughts and early frost . . . would he be able to forget that once he had been Vartan Balian, writer and pharmacist? To forget he once had a wife and a child . . . to forget about his people's fate? He already knew the answer to that. Bitterly, he left the stable.

'Vartan!'

Kerim's call announced his surprise and joy. He came, running clumsily because of all the layers of heavy clothing he was wearing, and they held each other tightly. His brown eyes shone out from under his fur cap.

After declaring his undying friendship, Kerim asked, 'Why didn't you let me know you were coming?'

'I only arrived late last night,' Vartan excused himself. He could hear anger, perhaps even jealousy, in the teacher's voice. 'It's New Year and you'll eat with us, of course. How are your classes coming?'

Kerim looked crestfallen and his disappointment was patent. 'Oh, times are hard. Many of my pupils have no shoes and can't go out because of the cold. Anyhow, they can't learn anything when their stomachs are empty! Death is rampant! Aroussiag has probably already told you.'

Vartan did not comment.

The three of them sat down to a meal of chickpeas and meat and Kerim inquired about Vartan's travels. He was especially interested in certain towns and regions Vartan had gone through. Vartan described everything willingly, omitting all details about the deportation. Aroussiag was afraid Kerim would ask Vartan about his wife and son. She had deduced from his unexpected return to Urgup that his search had been in vain, as she had known it would be, and she preferred to avoid the subject. She herself refused to think about the fact that his failure had made her happiness possible. She was torn between two opposing feelings: regret at building her life on another woman's grief and sheer joy at having her man back. She felt compassion for Vartan. She was sure that he was deliberately being reticent; he must have been torn by conflicting feelings. Kerim sensed there were subjects his friends preferred not to talk about.

As usual, he rolled himself a cigarette after the meal. 'I don't want to be indiscreet, but what about your cousin's letter?'

Vartan had completely forgotten that Diran's letter was waiting for him.

390

He blamed it on exhaustion and the excitement of having returned from his journey. In any case, Mrs Matthews had already told him most of the news in the letter.

Trying to conceal his forgetfulness, he took the tobacco pouch his friend was offering him, and said casually, 'He must have been afraid the mail would be censored, because he doesn't say very much.'

Kerim would have liked to discuss the political situation but decided to leave it for later.

'We're happy you're back. Aroussiag probably has told you that we had a lot to do this winter. Many peasants are practically starving, and those who had taken Armenian children in are now putting them out. The poor little things are begging in the villages, wandering on the roads and sleeping wherever they can.'

'I haven't told him yet. He was tired from the trip and needed to rest.'

Kerim nodded. He also mentioned that government requisitions for the troops had tripled recently, and got up to leave. Aroussiag knew that he was dying to talk to Vartan much longer and she invited him to come back for dinner.

When they were alone, she handed Vartan the letter, which had been waiting for him for more than four months. The torn envelope was addressed to Kerim and there was no return address on it. Vartan went up to the window to decipher Diran's uneven handwriting:

'Dear cousin,

'We were happy to hear that you're still alive, but terribly sorry to hear of your misfortunes. We have had no news of Tomas or Maro. We have had a relatively easy life here but the tragedy of our countrymen has affected all of Stamboul.

'I shouldn't complain about our troubles, as they are trivial compared to yours. Father had a heart attack from which he has miraculously recovered. My mother and Lucie are well. Your brother, Noubar, and his family have taken refuge in Jerusalem. Barkev is still in New York, busily raising funds for the relief of the Armenians. I . . . I'm doing the best I can, but I have to hide from the police (you know what that is like), so my field of operation is rather limited.'

The rest of the page was devoted to Diran's preaching the need for an autonomous Armenia, raising objections and answering them at the same time. He limited himself mostly to generalities, never mentioning names, nor giving details that could have been useful to the government. There were, however, some veiled references that were quite clear to Vartan. He knew Diran so well that he could visualize his cousin's rage, ardour and enthusiasm through his carefully formulated sentences. At the end of the letter there was an invitation to join them in the capital. Vartan crumpled up the letter and threw it into the fire. He could see Constantinople . . . his uncle Mesrop's apartment . . . the places he had frequented . . . his pharmacy on la Grand-rue de Péra . . . his relatives and friends . . . Maro, just married. Constantinople!

He saw Aroussiag's silhouette through a tear in the oil paper covering the window. She had gone out while he was reading and was leaning against the fence, her forlorn face turned towards the house.

It started to snow heavily on the third day of January and did not stop for forty-eight hours. Aroussiag opened the door often to cast a worried look at the sky. After a brief lull, the wind rose and swept in flurries of snow, which blocked the view. Aroussiag became more and more nervous.

'Are you worried because of the storm?' asked Vartan. 'You should be used to it by now.'

'The children . . .'

'How many are there?'

'Nine. They're in an old church in Goremé. Pastor Matthews was supposed to come and get them, but I'm afraid he won't be able to.'

'Is there anything we can do?'

'Not at the moment. They still have food for two more days. We must wait to hear from the pastor.'

As there were no orphanages in the region, Aroussiag gathered all the abandoned children in the vicinity and Pastor Matthews or one of his helpers came to take them and place them in different charitable institutions. Kerim or Aroussiag had found the majority of these little children in neighbouring towns and villages where they had been begging or abandoned in the streets. Others were sent to them by Greek friends who had been sheltering children; and, sometimes, Kerim and Aroussiag had gone so far as to buy these children from unscrupulous peasants to save them from mistreatment and exploitation.

At dawn the following day, Kerim received a telegram from the pastor, who was snowbound in Aksaray, informing them that, as soon as he could find a truck or any kind of vehicle, he would go to Nevshehir. Even if he did, he might not be able to get any closer because of the roads, so they would have to bring the children to him.

'Nevshehir!' Aroussiag was angry. 'It's ten kilometres from Goremé! They all have to walk in this snow!'

Kerim looked helpless. 'We have no choice.'

'Most of them are weak from malnutrition and some are sick.' Aroussiag looked worried.

'How old are they?' asked Vartan.

'Three to eleven.' Aroussiag sounded tense.

Kerim wanted to reassure her. 'They've been through so much, they're much tougher than they were.'

'If need be, we can carry the younger ones. Let's take the donkey.'

They decided they would stay in Nevshehir until the pastor arrived. That might take several days. Kerim could not be away for so long without arousing suspicion in Urgup. He was sorry, but there was nothing he could do about it. Aroussiag assured him that she and Vartan could manage.

'I'll come and take care of the animals every morning,' he promised.

Aroussiag took out some warm clothes from her chest. 'If we hurry, we can be in Goremé at noon and in Nevshehir before dark. Go and saddle the donkey. I'll join you at the stable.'

Vartan put on his felt overcoat and his astrakhan *kalpak*. He and Kerim stepped out. 'How far is it to Goremé?'

'A three-hour hike . . . maybe even four with this foul weather.'

'And then ten more kilometres with the children?'

'That's right.'

They had just finished harnessing the donkey when Aroussiag arrived. She had wrapped a scarf around her neck and head; her black wool dress showed from under her overcoat, as did her trousers. They had stuffed two big sacks with woollen clothing and blankets, along with provisions as well as a bundle of hay for the donkey. Aroussiag attached the sacks to the pack-saddle and passed one of its loops through the handle of a lantern. The moment the donkey stepped on the snow, it balked and had to be whipped before it would move on.

Aroussiag locked the dog in the house and brought out the shotgun with some ammunition and handed them to Vartan. They separated on the road.

Kerim took the road to Urgup and the other two plunged into the white countryside, which at times became lost to sight in the snow flurries. Aroussiag led the donkey by its bridle and Vartan walked behind, the rifle slung over his shoulder. An icy wind whistled through the branches, whipped their faces, cut off their breath and knifed through their clothes. In spite of the poor visibility, Aroussiag steered a steady course through the maze of irregular fields separated by stone dykes. On the hilltops the ground was bare but the snow had filled up the ravines with deep drifts. They stopped at the edge of a cliff, which sheltered them from the wind.

The hair on the donkey's muzzle was covered with frost. Aroussiag patted it between the ears and talked to it. 'Come on. Tonight you can rest and eat your fill.'

Ignoring her, the donkey began to lick the snow to quench his thirst.

'Are you cold?' Vartan asked Aroussiag, who was huddled against him. She could hardly open her eyes; tears had frozen on her eyelashes. He took off his gloves and, holding her face in his hands, blew gently to warm her red cheeks and nose.

She tried to smile through her frown. 'I was thinking about the children. They hardly have any clothes at all.'

'We have woollens and blankets. We'll make do. The youngest ones can ride the donkey and I'll carry the bundles. The older ones can help the younger ones.'

Comforted by Vartan's voice, she smiled. 'And then there's Aram.'

'Aram?'

'He's fourteen. Kerim picked him up last summer. He refused to go into an orphanage.'

'He's almost a man,' said Vartan approvingly. 'Now there will be the three of us.'

They continued on and shortly after, they entered a strange region. White tuff chimneys, columns of black basalt, writhing cones, enormous needles crowned by flat stones, labyrinths of narrow gorges, volcanic deposits sculpted by erosion into a mineral world – an unreal landscape where the doleful wind seemed to issue from the rocks – Cappadocia! The Christians of the first centuries had taken advantage of the forces of nature and bored into the hills to build churches, monasteries, even entire villages.

The valley of Goremé opened before them. It was a corridor through which the whistling wind scurried. Openings pierced the golden cliffs on both sides. In spite of their situation, Vartan's innate curiosity came to the fore. In this mythical area . . . one of the sacred places of Anatolia . . . his people had dug into the earth to escape from Arab raids and after each storm had emerged to rebuild their villages and make their lands flower again. Even today, these caves served to shelter the persecuted.

'It's there,' said Aroussiag, pointing to three openings in the sheer wall. The outline of a figure appeared in the one on the right. '*Kouyrig.*'[1]

'Aram.'

The boy jumped out and hurtled down to them. He had mistaken Vartan for Kerim. He glared suspiciously at the stranger. His hair was long and tangled, his nose slightly arched and his lips were thin. His bright eyes darted from Aroussiag to Vartan, as though demanding an explanation. Aroussiag introduced Vartan and Aram examined him briefly before holding out his hand. Then he said in a ceremonious tone:

'It's a great pleasure to meet you, Baron[2] Vartan.'

'The pleasure is mine,' answered Vartan in the same tone.

The large black sweater the boy was wearing made him look very fragile, but his grip was strong and firm. A scabbard holding a dagger, a keepsake from his father, hung from his belt. Aroussiag explained to him why they were there and how they planned to hike all the way to Nevshehir.

'I've been through worse.' The boy was secretly jealous and was trying to impress Aroussiag who, he knew, was in love with Vartan.

'How are the children?'

His face darkened. 'Little Anoush is very sick. She refuses to eat and she's burning with fever.'

'I'll take a look at her,' said Vartan, tying the donkey to a thorny bush.

Aram preceded them into what had been a church. Its vaulted hall had at one time probably been decorated with impressive frescoes, which time had half erased. Footprints in the thin layer of snow on the floor led to an opening at the back. It opened on to what must have once been the choir – a dark room, smelling like a chicken coop. Aram lit the stub of a candle and they saw the shining eyes of nine children, sitting very close together on a straw bed near the embers of a fire. A little three- or four-year-old girl threw herself upon the newcomers. Her bare feet resounded on the stone. Sobbing, she buried her face in Aroussiag's skirts. She took the girl into her arms.

'Anoush, don't cry anymore. I'm here now.'

The child put her head on Aroussiag's shoulder and stared at Vartan so

1.   Sister (Armenian).
2.   Mister (Armenian).

hard that her brown irises looked like pin-points in her jaundiced eyeballs. He noticed her gaunt face, her protruding cheekbones, her bluish lips and her skinny legs. She coughed deeply and her chest rattled. He smiled at her, but she turned her head away quickly. The other children stood around them. Those who already knew Aroussiag showed their joy by giggling nervously or talking to get her attention. The three girls who had arrived only the week before stood back warily. They watched Aram, whom they regarded as their big brother, to see how they should act. Vartan shuddered. These boys and girls had been robbed of their childhood and the look in their eyes showed their need to be loved.

Leaving it to Aroussiag to explain to the children that they were going to be moved, Vartan and Aram went to unload the donkey. As Aram hoisted a sack on to his shoulder, he said scornfully, 'I've been told you're a wandering musician.'

Vartan had to smile. The boy must think that this was not a very manly occupation. 'Yes, but I'm also a major in the army.'

Aram gave an admiring whistle, and put his hand on his dagger. 'This was my father's. When I grow up, I'll be a *fedayi* and avenge my family. Could you teach me to shoot?'

'What you and Aroussiag are doing is much more important than taking revenge. To kill more people will not bring your family back.'

Aram chose not to answer and went back towards the church. Aroussiag stuffed the cauldron, a few utensils and what little food remained in the cavern into a sack. They wrapped the feet of the children who had no shoes with strips of woollen cloth and tied them to their calves with bits of string. Their clothes were in tatters and offered no protection against the cold; so they wrapped them in grey blankets, which the children had to hold shut. The wind was still blowing hard and the clouds were getting thicker.

'It's going to snow again,' Aroussiag said, carrying Anoush in her arms.

The little sick girl refused to let Vartan put her on the donkey.

'Don't insist,' Aroussiag said, 'I'll carry her and, when I'm tired, I'll give her to you.'

He put the two youngest ones on the donkey. The caravan was ready. They started off. Aram led the donkey, beating a path through the snow, followed by Aroussiag who pointed out the way. Vartan brought up the rear, carrying the sacks on his back.

Ahead of him walked tiny grey figures, half-bent to fight the north wind; they looked like old shivering women, wrapped in shawls. Their short legs showed through the gaps in the blankets, as they hurried to keep up with Aram. Once the valley of Goremé was behind them, the wind subsided a little; it was less violent as it was no longer funnelled through the cliffs. They walked at a good pace for the first hour and then stopped behind the wall of an old roofless sheep-pen and huddled together to keep warm. Vartan gave out dried apricots.

'We'll make a fire when we get there,' said Aroussiag, standing in the middle of the children. She rubbed their little hands and ears to keep them from freezing. 'Can everybody keep up? Is everybody all right?'

There was a choir of *yes*. Vartan was amazed at the doggedness of these children whose teeth were chattering. They set out on the road again, but this time Vartan carried Anoush. He half-opened his coat collar so that she could bury her face and her hands in it and hummed a lullaby into her ear. Finally, Anoush stopped shivering.

Time went by slowly. There was only this great white immensity, which even their footsteps couldn't spoil. The children were exhausted and their feet were dragging. Although no one had complained, they had to stop to let them rest again. In a short while, it began to snow again – very light crystals blown horizontally by the wind. They grated against the skin like thorns. It became ever more painful to keep on going.

A child dropped to the ground; Vartan bent over to encourage him to get up, but the six-year-old refused to move. He murmured he was all right; he just wanted to sleep. Vartan handed Anoush to Aroussiag and lifted the boy. His new burden was heavier and Vartan began to tire. His sweat-soaked clothes were stiff with frost and the wind made it difficult for him to breathe. Nevertheless, the little fellow in his arms weighed almost the same as Tomas, and Vartan would have walked to the end of the world if necessary.

The light was fading, lending a grey-blue tinge to the overcast sky. Aroussiag called out enthusiastically, 'We're almost there. I can see the entrance.'

Erosion and rock falls had widened the entrance of the first room and the strong wind whirled in. The children sat down on the ground. Aroussiag lit the lantern and said, 'Get up. It's too cold to stay here.'

'Just where are we?' asked Vartan.

'It's an ancient monastery that we use sometimes. The road to Aksaray lies just on the other side of the hill facing us.' Her voice drawled as if she were having difficulty finding the words but she smiled at Vartan and gripped his arms.

'We made it! We made it!'

Aram, who was familiar with the place, had stalled the donkey in a small room next to the one they were in. Aroussiag led the group down a stairway hewn in the rock. On the lower floor they came into a cross-shaped vaulted cave. The dim light of the lantern disclosed frescoes, with scenes from the life of Christ and effigies of saints. Except for a grey strip along the ceiling, the colours had remained vivid and looked almost new – not nine or ten centuries old. An opening pierced the wall at either end of the transept, showing the first part of a corridor which led into the womb of the rocky mountain.

'This is a real subterranean city,' explained Aroussiag. 'Be careful and don't get lost.'

The children were quiet, numbed from the cold, and looked quite disoriented. Vartan thought they should be aroused from their stupor and given a few basic comforts; after that he could look after little Anoush. To get them started, he pointed to the apse at the end of the choir. 'We shall sleep there. Let's build a big fire and make some soup.'

'A fire?' Aroussiag was worried. 'Do you think it's safe? We're very close to the road.'

'The smoke can't be seen at night.'

'We'll choke,' objected Aram gloomily.

Vartan pointed out a sooty circle on the ceiling of the apse and a blackish depression in the floor. 'Someone else has already built a fire here. Look at the slope of the vault. The smoke will go up the staircase.'

Aram was secretly astonished that he had never noticed these details during his previous visits. He was impressed that Vartan had been able to see all that at a single glance. Not to be outdone, he added, 'We just passed by a poplar the wind had blown down.'

Vartan put his arm around Aram's shoulders. 'Let's go and cut some branches.'

'Can I go, too?' asked a ten-year-old boy. Aram looked questioningly at Vartan.

He nodded. 'You look like a strong boy. Come on. What's your name?'

'Arto.'

Aroussiag watched them tenderly as they walked away. Then she clapped her hands to get the children's attention. 'One more small effort. Let's make up our beds.'

Night had fallen and the cold had become more biting. Vartan and the two boys followed the tracks which the snow was slowly effacing. In less than five minutes they found the tree. Aram's dagger turned out to be redundant since the frozen branches snapped easily. They made four trips back and forth to the cavern, gathering enough wood for several days. On the last trip, Vartan showed the boys how to erase the trail they had packed down in the snow with a branch. The wind would finish the job.

The children had spread out the blankets in the apse and several of them were already lying down. Aroussiag had pumped water from the cistern two floors down and was checking their provisions lined up against the wall. Vartan showed the children how to build a fire, while he peeled off the humid bark and split the dry wood into firewood. They threw a fistful of hay on the fire and it flared up, then flickered and threatened to go out because of the melting ice dripping from the thick branches as they thawed out. Soon, though, the flames triumphed and the crackling fire filled the room with light and heat. Aroussiag blew out the lantern to save kerosene. They improvised a tripod with poles to hang the cauldron filled with water.

They woke up the ones who had gone to sleep and they all huddled around the fire, the boys instinctively gathering near Vartan and the girls near Aroussiag. As warmth gradually returned to their bodies, they relaxed and their eyes lit up. Gulina, who was eight years old, cuddled her sister, Anoush, in her arms. Anoush followed Aroussiag's movements with feverish eyes, and coughing constantly. Vartan also watched Aroussiag through the thick smoke as she chopped onions and peeled potatoes. They exchanged a long, loving look.

'Is it all right to build a fire in a church?' asked a boy, pointing to the frescoes half hidden behind the dancing shadows.

'Of course,' answered Vartan, 'because it hasn't been a church for a long time.'

'Doesn't God live here anymore?'

'God lives everywhere – even inside us,' a little girl said seriously.

'Funny, I don't feel a thing.'

The older children laughed and the younger ones, who really didn't know what was so funny, followed suit.

Aroussiag cut up the mutton and dropped it into the cauldron where the *bulghur*[1] was already simmering in the water. She knew the children needed to hear an adult's voice after weeks of living alone, so she asked Vartan a question to which she already knew the answer.

'Why did people in the old days bore into the rocks to make their churches?'

'To protect themselves from their enemies. In those days, bandits roamed this region and people took refuge in these underground cities and blocked the entrances with boulders, and lived in peace. They had underground churches, storerooms and probably even schools.'

Vartan recounted at length how the first Christians lived in Cappadocia, the techniques they used for painting the frescoes; he even told them about the stones spewed out by the volcanoes in prehistory. They listened in silence, fascinated by his words, which evoked events far removed from the daily struggle they had been experiencing for so many months. Vartan could see the thirst for knowledge in their eyes and it warmed his heart. When he fell silent, Aroussiag began to sing a familiar lament, which even the youngest children knew, having heard some of the words before.

A boy, who was reminded of his mother, asked shyly, 'What's an orphanage?'

Without mincing words, Aroussiag explained, 'A place for children who have lost their parents.'

Tears welled up in the boy's eyes. His oval face and straight-cut hair made his head look like an acorn.

'An orphanage,' corrected Vartan, 'is a house where children are loved and respected. They sleep in a bed and eat their meals. They study and prepare for their future.' He described the orphanages he had visited and answered all the questions which poured from all directions. A place where they would no longer be hungry, cold, or scared. It sounded like paradise to these children.

Gulina, rocking her little sister, asked, 'Are your parents dead, too?'

'Yes, a long time ago, but I have a son who's your age. I haven't had any news about him for more than two years. I would be happy if I knew he were in an orphanage and being taken care of.' Vartan could see that the children were upset and a heavy silence fell.

To lighten the mood, Aroussiag called joyfully, 'Soup's ready.' She unhooked the pot. The strong smell made their mouths water. There were only two ladles and four bowls, so they fed the youngest ones first. They

---

1. Boiled and pounded wheat (Armenian-Turkish).

dipped into the thick liquid in which tiny pieces of mutton floated and Aroussiag saw to it that each got his or her fair share. The older ones and the two adults shared what was left. Everyone was cheerful and, when one of them burped, all of them giggled. Aroussiag held Anoush in her lap and fed her with a spoon. She had trouble swallowing and choked every time she was seized by a coughing fit. Aroussiag looked at Vartan questioningly.

He answered, 'We'll see.'

Aroussiag told each of them where to lie down to sleep. This started a lot of arguments, as some of them wanted to sleep next to their friends, while others wanted to be closer to the fire and further away from the dark nave.

In a corner, Vartan was examining Anoush, who still nestled in Aroussiag's arms. He pushed up her shirt and laid his ear against her protruding ribs to listen to her laboured breathing. Rattles – dry, short and superficial – which boded ill. Deep breathings. Gurglings, as if her lungs were full of liquid. She was burning with fever. Pleurisy? Pneumonia? He did not know exactly. When he asked her where it hurt, she showed her head, her throat, her chest. He stroked her cheek, smiled at her and told her she would get better soon. Aroussiag was not fooled by his optimistic tone but decided to wait until they were alone to find out what he really thought. She handed the child to her older sister.

The temperature was pleasant in the apse and the vaulted ceiling reflected the heat from the fire. Rolled up in blankets, often two of them sharing one, the children were falling asleep. Aram had reserved the places at the entrance to the small room for himself and the two adults, thinking they would form a barrier against the dark and the cold.

'Let's pray,' announced Aroussiag loudly. 'Let's pray for those who aren't here. Let's thank God for our food and ask Him to protect us.' She started to recite the Lord's Prayer and was joined by the children's high, clear voices and Vartan's tenor. 'Vartan and I have something to discuss,' she told Aram. 'We shan't be long.'

'Goodnight.' The boy was already falling asleep.

They left the lantern and took the corridor to the right of the transept. Soon the glow of the fire disappeared and they groped through the total darkness by touching the wall.

Aroussiag walked ahead of Vartan. 'I know this place well. We'll come to another room soon.'

Suddenly the wall disappeared from under her fingers. Vartan lit his lighter and saw Aroussiag's bright eyes and, behind hers, the tender eyes of a saint painted on the wall. Then the darkness deepened.

Aroussiag put her hand on Vartan's shoulder. 'Now, tell me the truth about Anoush.'

'She needs a doctor. I know it's impossible and it probably wouldn't do any good anyway.'

Aroussiag sighed. 'What's wrong with her?'

'Pneumonia, I think. And in her wretched condition, she doesn't stand a chance.' He put his arms around Aroussiag and touched her tearful face. 'All we can do is pray.'

'What if I took her home with me?'

'It's too late.'

She wept in Vartan's arms, while he stroked her hair. It took a long time to calm her but finally she murmured, 'It's not just Anoush. It's everything! It's awful! And it gets worse each time I have to leave them. Even when I only see them occasionally, I get attached to them. Can you feel their need to be loved? I cannot reconcile myself to letting them go. I would like to keep them all, love them, make them happy again.'

'I understand, but tell yourself that there are dozens of children to whom you have given a chance for a new life.'

Not for the first time she felt the desire to have a child, Vartan's child, but she was not able to tell him this now, any more than she had been before – a little boy, who would look just like him, or a little girl who looked like her. She searched for his lips in the dark and kissed him wildly.

Aram was the first to wake up. He poked the embers in the ashes to life, put more wood on the fire and left silently. He pumped water to give to the donkey. With the caution acquired from two years of covert work, he stepped out and scanned the narrow valley and the hills. Day had broken, the sun was shining on the snow-covered countryside and a raven flew across the sky. Nothing else moved and he went back down into the cavern.

Vartan had put water on to boil. 'Good morning, Aram. Did you sleep well?'

'Like a dead donkey. It's nice out. The sun is shining. Reverend Matthews might come today.'

As soon as she woke up, Aroussiag hurried to check on Anoush. She took her from her sleeping sister's arms and carried her to the fire to have Vartan look at her.

'Look at her red cheeks. It must be a good sign.'

He touched Anoush. Her fever was high and the rattle in her spasmodic breathing was more pronounced. He sounded distressed when he pointed at the thick, rust-coloured spots of phlegm on her collar and blouse. 'Unfortunately those confirm it's pneumonia.'

Afraid, Aroussiag clenched her jaw. Vartan ran his hand down Anoush's back and felt the spasms in her spine and neck; symptoms that could mean meningitis. Anoush opened her eyes.

'Does your head hurt?'

She nodded.

'More than yesterday?'

Again she nodded. She coughed feebly and had a fixed, glassy look. He realized she had given in to the illness and that her life force was waning.

Vartan tried to tell her with his look how much he loved her and she must have understood, for she stretched out her hands to touch his beard. He kissed her bony, little fingers and noticed that, in spite of the deep circles under her eyes and her scrawniness, she was beautiful. Her red cheeks gave her a false appearance of vitality. Vartan raged inside at his impotence to help her.

To hide his feelings, he turned to Aram who was sitting on the other side of the fire. 'Is the water boiling yet?'

Aroussiag had witnessed the silent dialogue between Anoush and Vartan and understood the child she was holding against her breast was dying. She began to pray silently. Vartan made a linden tea and Aroussiag tried to get the little girl to drink some but she choked and began to vomit.

'She's shivering,' said Aroussiag. Worse; she was convulsing.

'Lie her flat and stay with her. I'll take care of the others.'

He prepared some *bulghur* and gave the children breakfast. Then he took them to the room that opened to the outside to let them get some fresh air. Gulina refused to go with them. She didn't want to leave her sister.

'We have to keep them busy,' said Vartan to Aram, who immediately organized a game of blindman's buff, which he also enjoyed greatly. Vartan joined in and, when they were all tired, he told them riddles and taught them how to play charades.

In the afternoon, Anoush became paralyzed. Her illness was progressing faster than Vartan had expected. Aroussiag and a tearful Gulina remained at her side.

That evening when everyone had gone to sleep, Vartan shook Aram. 'Don't say a word and follow me.' The boy obeyed in silence.

Once at the staircase, Vartan lit a lantern and they descended the steps to the deepest part of the subterranean city.

'What's wrong, Baron Vartan?'

'The little one is dying. We must dig a grave.'

The gloomy sound of his voice shocked Aram. The boy did not understand how a man such as Vartan could be so affected by the death of a child he hardly knew.

Vartan put his arm around Aram's shoulder. 'A real man, Aram, is capable of many feelings – compassion, pity, friendship, love . . . He who is touched by nothing becomes a monster – a beast like the ones you consider your enemies. Don't ever forget that.'

Then Vartan searched the rooms for a suitable place. Aram, who was mulling over what he had just heard, felt the shell of indifference he had built around himself begin to crack and was afraid he could be hurt again.

Vartan chose a small grotto at the end of a long corridor. He drew a rectangle slightly larger than Anoush in the ground with the tip of his knife and began to use the blade as a pick. Aram stood still.

'Aren't you going to help?'

'With what?'

'Your dagger, of course.'

The boy looked horrified. His father's weapon!

'The stone is soft and crumbles like stale bread. I'll sharpen the blade again later. You must realize that using it to bury someone you love is much better than using it to kill an enemy.'

'Have you ever killed anyone, Baron?'

'Thank God, no. I've never had to do that.'

'Me! I wouldn't hesitate. I'd kill all those murderers.'

'And become a murderer yourself!'

'I wouldn't be a murderer! I'd be a judge! That isn't the same thing.'

'The *zaptiyés* who have massacred so many of us also think they're dealing out justice.'

Aram refused to comment and attacked the rock furiously. The activity warmed him up and he took off his sweater.

'Where do you come from?' asked Vartan.

'Near Gemerek.' And without further ado, his story stumbled out in bits and pieces.

The gendarmes had arrested him, along with all the other men in the village. He, his father, his brothers and his uncles were all taken into the mountains, lined up at the brink of a gorge and shot without any explanation. When they fired, his father had pushed him down to the ground and fallen on top of him. Splashed with his father's and brothers' blood, he had been the sole survivor. He had waited until nightfall to escape and returned to his village the following morning to find the women and children had been taken away. Peasants who lived nearby were picking up the few things the guards had not been able to cart away. Others were already moving into the abandoned houses with their families.

Aram had then fled to the hills and lived on berries and whatever he could pilfer from the neighbouring farms. When winter came, he had begged in the villages. By that time, a younger boy and his sister had also joined him. Finally, the three of them had ended up in Cappadocia, where they worked in the fields for a Greek couple, who hid them for some time. There Aram had met Kerim and Aroussiag. And ever since he had helped them unearth orphans and hand them over to the missionaries.

Vartan tapped Aram on the back. 'Your father would have been very proud of you.'

Aram turned aside to hide the tears brimming in his eyes.

They dug a hole a metre and more deep. The heap of rubble would serve to cover the body. When Vartan returned to the apse, he went to where Aroussiag was lying down. She was awake. Turned on her side, with her head on her bent arm, she was watching Anoush sleep against her. Vartan took Anoush's pulse, which was very weak. Her breathing was hardly perceptible. She had probably sunk into a coma.

He whispered into Aroussiag's ear, 'You should try to get some rest. I'll watch over her.'

'I can't. You try to sleep.'

He sat for a while with his hand on Aroussiag's head but was finally overcome by sleep and stretched out. A few hours later Aroussiag awoke him. When he saw her wretched face, he immediately knew Anoush had died. They carried the small body into the nave so Aroussiag could undress and wash her. She rubbed Anoush's skin with the tenderness she would have given to her own child. She had no more tears.

'She looks like an angel.'

A sudden cry startled them. 'Anoush! Anoush!' Gulina had just woken up from a nightmare and was looking for her sister.

'Please bring her here,' Aroussiag asked Vartan.

Gulina sobbed, threw herself on her little sister's body and covered her with kisses. She had just lost the last link with her past and was now all alone in the world. Aroussiag and Vartan let her cry for a long time. Then Aroussiag pulled her close and tried to comfort her.

'Don't cry for Anoush, Gulina; your sister is now in paradise and will watch over you. Remember how she was suffering. Now she's happy. Come. Help me to dress her.'

Aroussiag pulled Gulina away gently; the little girl swallowed her tears and helped fold her sister's hands. She could hear her mother's words as the guards dragged her away, 'Gulina, I love you. Watch out for your sister.'

Vartan lifted her body, wrapped her in a clean blanket, leaving only her face uncovered. To share their grief, Vartan and Aroussiag held hands behind Gulina's back and they knelt side by side to pray.

'She's beautiful,' said Gulina. 'She looks like she's sleeping.' Then she said dreamily, 'Anoush never complained. Before she got sick, she was always laughing. When we lived with the farmers, she helped me in the kitchen to take care of the chickens . . . to water the garden.' For a long time she continued to evoke memories of her sister, more for herself than for the two adults. They stayed there until dawn.

The children all reacted differently when they heard about their playmate. Many of them cried but some remained impassive. Perhaps they were secretly relieved that death had spared them.

Holding the lantern at arm's length, Aram preceded Vartan, who was carrying the body to the room where he had dug the grave. The others followed. Since they had no oil they used water to perform the ritual ablutions. They traced the sign of the cross on her forehead, her hands and her feet, while Aroussiag recited the prayers. As they lowered the body into the grave, Gulina began to scream and Aroussiag led her back to the apse. The others stayed with their hands clasped, staring at the little grey form that was about to disappear.

Someone had to say something to give meaning to her death. Vartan improvised. 'Almighty God, we are gathered here in Your eyes to entrust our sister, Anoush, to You. Take her so she may live forever amongst Your angels. And you, Anoush, be happy with your parents in heaven. Never again will you know suffering, nor hunger, nor thirst, nor cold, but only unending happiness. Intercede for us with Christ so we shall find peace, joy and love. Amen.'

He threw a fistful of rubble into the grave and the children followed suit. He said, 'We have all lost people we love and we must never let their memory fade from our lives, no matter how long we live, because the dead live on through us. Never forget little Anoush! When you feel overcome by discouragement, think of her who was not as lucky as you and is no longer able to see the sun.'

When the hole was full, he took his dagger and carved an inscription on the wall. The epitaph read:

*Anoush Magarian*
*An Angel of God*
*1913–1917*

Vartan had chosen the dates arbitrarily to correspond more or less to the supposed age of the child. Before starting back up the steps, several of the children ran their fingers over the letters chiselled in the stone, as if trying to memorize them.

Vartan found Aroussiag in the church with a man who was talking to Gulina.

'Reverend Matthews,' said Aram.

Around sixty, the missionary was a tall, thin man, whose coat seemed to float around him. The flaps of his fur hat framed his red face with its blonde eyelashes. His finely drawn lips seemed to smile and his pale grey eyes expressed great kindness. Aroussiag introduced him to the children and then left him with Vartan, while she went to organize their departure.

Vartan and he shook hands. The missionary took Vartan by the arm and took him to the back of the church.

'You have no idea, Mr Balian, how happy I am finally to have the honour of meeting you.'

'I'm honoured, too.'

'What a pity we missed each other in Aleppo.'

'I too was disappointed. Can I brew you some tea?'

'Don't bother. I have a thermos in the carriage and I must leave as quickly as possible. Unfortunately, we won't have a chance to get to know each other better.'

Vartan was sorry as he had immediately felt a spark of sympathy between them. It was not really surprising. Hadn't Aroussiag said they resembled each other?

'I hope there'll be another occasion, Reverend.'

407

'Of course, perhaps, in Aleppo. My wife told me you intend to continue your tours with the *dervishes*.'

'I would like to be even more useful.'

The missionary felt Vartan's doubts and protested, 'You couldn't do more than you're already doing. Your articles have made the people abroad aware of the situation. And more important still, the information you gather has allowed us to locate orphans. By the way, I have news of Nayiri, the little girl you found in Adana. She's in Beirut now.'

In spite of the months that had lapsed, Vartan could still see the little beggar girl standing by the wayside; he would write a story about her. They turned at the staircase and walked slowly back to the church, where Aroussiag was helping the children get dressed.

'What news do you have of the war, Reverend Matthews?'

'Nothing new for the last two months. It's been a catastrophe for humanity. But nothing is ever a total loss. We'll rebuild the world. Or rather, they will!' he said, pointing to the children.

'Bless you a thousand times for what you're doing for my people.'

'I'm only doing my duty as a servant of Our Lord, Mr Balian.'

'We're ready.' Aroussiag approached, leading the children.

'What a magnificent woman!' murmured the missionary.

'Yes indeed!' agreed Vartan.


Pulled by two horses, a huge cart with slatted sides was waiting for them at the entrance to the cave. Aram was standing next to the donkey with a loaded pack-saddle. After tearful goodbyes, the children climbed up on the platform and covered themselves with goatskins and rugs. They were afraid of going into the unknown – to leave the only people who had shown them any kindness lately.

'You're not alone,' said Vartan. 'In the future you'll be each other's brothers and sisters.' He was thinking about Der Kevork's words, 'We are the shepherd's dogs.'

His work had been laid out for him. His life until the end of the war would be exactly the same as the year before – the life of a wandering musician. He would write, of course, but essentially he would help children like Tomas and Nayiri.

The carriage turned around and headed west. Reverend Matthews waved at them for the last time.

Aroussiag cried out to the children, 'Be happy.'

Vartan put his arm around her. 'They'll be happy, thanks to you and Aram. He's a brave man!'

Aram beamed with pride and touched the sheath of his dagger. The children continued to wave until the pastor's cart disappeared behind a hill.

With a heavy heart, Aroussiag sighed, 'Let's go home.'

Aram led the donkey and Aroussiag and Vartan followed, their arms around each other.

# FOURTEEN

In March 1917, the British Expeditionary Corps led by General Maude went up the Tigris, pushed back the Ottoman troops, captured Baghdad and joined forces with the Russian Army of the Caspian Sea, which had occupied northern Persia. Their plan was for the British to push into southern Anatolia while the Russians would advance towards Sivas. At the same time the Tsar's Navy in the Black Sea would head towards the Bosphorus and try to capture Constantinople. Suddenly everything changed. The Russian Revolution broke out and Nicholas II abdicated. The Russian Army fell apart as the troops mutinied against their officers. Soldiers deserted *en masse* and headed back home. Western Armenia, which had just been liberated, was left alone again.

Riza Bey had been following the developments with apprehension. Every day he telephoned the High Command to get the latest news. Although he was happy about the deployment of Russian forces in the Caucasus, the presence of the British in Baghdad worried him greatly. Since the Arab revolt, the morale of the troops in Syria and Palestine had been deteriorating and he feared a thrust by the English. It was also possible that the Allies would land in the Gulf of Alexandretta, which was barely a day away from Ayntab. When the United States declared war on the Central European and Ottoman Empires in April, Riza Bey knew it was only a question of time – a few months, a year at the most – and his country would be defeated.

Orders from Constantinople insisted he put a stop to the work of the missionaries and close their orphanages but, knowing that the reign of the Young Turks was coming to an end, Riza Bey decided to do nothing. It was up to him to treat the foreigners tactfully, while letting his superiors in Constantinople think his zeal had not weakened, since he wanted to keep his position until the end of the war. Once the Allies had won, they would need highly placed Turks to help them govern the region.

Maro was sitting in the shade of the thick vines in the arbour, rocking Nourhan, who as usual, had fallen asleep after his feed. She wiped away the sweat beaded on his forehead with the tips of her fingers. Her six-month-old son with his thick brown hair and pink chubby cheeks looked like a cherub. To think he might not have been born because of a potion! Maro suppressed a shiver. She kissed him and he opened his eyes and babbled happily. Everyone in the house, including Buyuk Hanim who had been bewitched by her new grandson, agreed that Nourhan was the happiest, friendliest, most joyful baby ever. He never cried but howled insistently when he was hungry. He was bright and overflowing with vitality.

Nourhan turned when he heard the children crossing the garden on their way to the mosque for their lessons with Piri Hodja. Tomas left the group and joined his mother in the arbour and Nourhan started to wriggle and coo when he saw him.

Maro noticed. 'Look how happy your brother is to see you.'

Tomas's smile was forced as he held out his forefinger which Nourhan clasped. He hated it when his mother called this child *your brother*.

'Do you want to hold him?' She ran her fingers through Tomas's hair.

He shook his head and stepped away to take some pistachios from the table. Maro had not realized he had been suffering from a tragedy for months as he carefully concealed it. She attributed his rare moments of brooding to jealousy of his younger brother and thought it natural for him to fear losing his place in his mother's heart. She did everything in her power to assure him he still came first, both with words and behaviour.

But Tomas was not jealous as his mother thought. A much stronger feeling had pushed jealousy aside. Nourhan's presence was a constant reminder that his mother had betrayed Vartan. She had stopped waiting for him – had abandoned him as she might abandon Tomas one day. She had become Riza Bey's woman. Sometimes he hated her; he was angry with her but his heart ached because he still loved her. He could not sort out his contradictory feelings – could not get out of his misery. He was ashamed – ashamed of his wicked thoughts about his mother!

Riza Bey and Safiyé came towards the arbour as Tomas went out the other side and walked to the pool behind the spindle trees.

'See how Nourhan follows us with his eyes,' said Riza proudly to Safiyé as they entered the arbour. 'That's a sign of great intelligence.'

Safiyé took the baby's hand and he tried to pull himself up. She was enchanted. 'See how strong he is! He'll be a truly virile man.'

Maro smiled, 'Don't make him grow up too fast. Babies are only babies for a little while.'

Safiyé nodded. It had been a long time since her children had been infants and it seemed to her that she had not enjoyed them enough. Sometimes she was secretly envious of the sight of Maro and her baby and wanted to have another one. Was she too old? Her body was still bursting with enough life to share with another small being.

Riza Bey picked up Nourhan, held him at arm's length, turned him upside-down, then tickled him on his neck with his moustache, which made him laugh. 'My son,' he whispered to Nourhan loud enough for the two women to hear, 'have you convinced your mother to marry me yet?' He looked at Maro insistently, but she stopped smiling and shook her head.

Tomas, who was hiding behind the bushes, closed his hand over the silver box that held his father's seal. Raging, he went into the house and walked through the courtyard to the stable. He kept his jaw clenched tightly to keep from crying in front of the stable hands as he saddled his horse. His movements were so abrupt the horse became nervous. Once outside, he mounted and galloped away through the pistachio-trees. He slowed down when he came to the olive grove that dominated the Injirli River plain. He went down the embankment, over the fields and around the landing strip by the river at the end of Riza's estate. Afraid of what he was going to do, he let the tears run down his face. For a second he considered turning back. But his mother deserved to be punished! She would be beside herself with worry. She would come looking for him and he would tell her he had wanted to join his father. She would be sorry and might even understand what he could not tell her. He forded the river where the water was shallow. There were gardens on the opposite bank but soon rocky hills arose and beyond them – the desert!

Thinking Tomas to be with Riza Bey's children, Maro did not notice his absence until dinner. They searched the house and surroundings and finally found out from a stable boy that Tomas had ridden away. It was the first time he had gone anywhere without asking for permission and Maro became very worried.

Riza Bey reassured her, 'Don't worry. Tomas is a good rider and knows every inch of the estate. He'll be home before nightfall.'

They were standing on the front steps and Maro looked at the sky where the clouds were turning red. Soon it would be night!

'It's not like him,' she fretted. 'What could have possessed him?' She sounded anxious and Riza Bey put his hand on her shoulder.

'We'll find him and I'll box his ears.'

'I want to go with you.'

'There would be no point to it.' Riza Bey was firm. 'You stay home and take care of Nourhan.'

Altan and Kenan, who had been questioning the workers, came through the door. Altan waved to indicate that they had not found out anything new.

Deeply affected by his friend's unexplained absence, Kenan asked his father, 'Can I go with you?'

Riza refused, 'It'll soon be dark and you might get lost. I have enough to do looking for Tomas. Did he tell you anything about his plans?'

'No, Father.'

'You two are very close. Don't you have any idea where he might have been headed for?'

Kenan thought of all the places they loved to play in but they were all too near to need a horse to get to, and shook his head.

Riza saw Altan going into the house and called to him, 'Have the horses saddled and tell my men to get ready. You're coming with me.'

Altan, upset at missing dinner, muttered all the way to the stables. 'That little squirt! He's always messing things up!'

Riza led Maro inside. 'Don't worry. We'll find him soon.'

She was trembling. 'I have a premonition that something bad has happened to him.'

He reprimanded her gently. 'You're talking nonsense! You'll bring bad luck down on us.'

She hung to his arm, 'Bring him back to me, Riza Bey! Please, bring him back!'

Riza sent his men to search separately in different directions. He asked Altan to search the ground near the airstrip. As Altan approached, the gendarmes guarding the field greeted him respectfully. No, they had not seen a horseman – not even a boy on foot. More out of fear of his father than out of conscience, Altan rode along the river. The cold light of the evening revealed hoof-prints in the gravel path that led to the river. Altan crossed over and found tracks on the other side. He followed them up towards the hills; as his horse trampled over them, the tracks disappeared in the loose pebbles. Altan climbed to the top where the path glowed red in the light of the setting sun. The expanse of desert at his feet was in twilight and the horizon had turned deep blue. Tomas had got himself lost in the mountains, he thought.

Handing Nourhan to Eminé, Maro paced up and down the hall. She could not sit still. Safiyé had tried everything to calm her down, but had finally run out of arguments and now watched her in silence. Piri Hodja called to evening prayer. It was some time after that when the riders came back. Their efforts had been in vain. Altan was afraid of revealing his discovery since he had carelessly let his horse trample over the tracks.

Maro burst into sobs. What had possessed Tomas? There had been no warning. Maro went over the preceding days and past few weeks in her mind, but found nothing that might give her a clue. Safiyé took her into her arms and cried with her.

'Come, now, my wives,' said Riza jovially. 'Don't be so dramatic!' He, too, was worried but listed all the reasons not to lose hope. 'If Tomas had been thrown, his horse would have returned to the stable, so he must have got lost. One night under the stars is nothing for a strong boy, even if he's only eight-years-old. Some peasants will probably find him and return him in the morning for a good reward.'

'Do you really think so?' asked Safiyé.

Maro sniffled, 'Will you start looking again at dawn, Riza Bey?'

'Yes, my love. The farmers will comb the countryside on foot. My horsemen will search further afield and I'll ask the gendarmes to help. They'll soon find the governor's son.'

Riza's assurances calmed Maro somewhat and she asked to be allowed to retire to her rooms.

When they were alone Safiyé asked, 'You seem more worried than you appear. Am I right?'

'You know me too well, my sweet Safiyé. His flight bodes no good. But keep this between you and me. Send Eminé to me. I want her to read the coffee grounds.'

With dawn hope returned but there was no news the first day. The search intensified during the following days in all the villages and towns of the region, but no one had seen the child. The large reward offered by the governor had brought in only a flood of useless information. Using his influence, Riza Bey made inquiries in the neighbouring provinces, including the settlements to the north of Syria and on the coast, but there were so many abandoned children in the towns and countryside, so many in the orphanages, that the chances of finding one particular child were slim. What everyone found hard to understand was why Tomas had not shown up at one of the police stations or military posts using Riza Bey's name. It was almost as if he did not want to be found.

As time went by Maro's anguish turned into deep depression and it was only caring for Nourhan that kept her from sinking into total despair. To think of Tomas, only eight years old and all by himself – lost in a world at war, in a country ravaged by disease, hatred and want – tormented her. As the weeks went by, her hope vanished and prayer was her only comfort – the only way to ease her cruel feelings of guilt. She had found only one reason for Tomas to have fled – her relationship with Riza Bey. In his childish mind, he might have thought she loved Riza more than she loved Vartan – that she had remade her life with another man. Maro reproached herself for not having foreseen such a reaction, for not having thought it necessary to explain the situation to him. It was all her fault!

Riza Bey's hands shook as he reread the long article. It was published in the USA, translated by the German information services, titled 'Nayiri' and signed Vartan Balian – some place in Anatolia:

'An eight-year-old Armenian girl is begging by the roadside – emaciated, in rags and dirty, Nayiri looks at the world through eyes drained of all life-force. She does not understand what has been happening to her since the guards killed her family. All she knows is she must not speak her language any more, must hide the fact she is an Armenian, must not use her name.

'She does not understand her family has been sacrificed on the altar of pan-Turanism. In like circumstances, who would understand? What civilized human being could conceive that a racist philosophy . . . This child has no notion of political issues; all she cares about is to survive one day at a time . . .'

Riza Bey didn't want to read it again. He folded up the sheets and called for Bedri. Abdullah came in and bowed.

'I called for Bedri!' Riza Bey was annoyed.

'He's in town, Effendi.'

'I want to see him as soon as he returns. Pour me a glass of cognac.'

The bottle and glasses were sitting on a sideboard and the servant spilled a little of the liquor. Riza Bey, who was sitting in a chair facing the window did not see Abdullah's clumsiness so he quickly wiped off the copper tray with his finger and licked it. He presented the tray to his master.

'May I go now, Riza Bey?'

Riza Bey waved him off, lit a cigarette, took two puffs and ground it out in an ashtray. That Balian again! Him again! Although the article, which had appeared in the United States, had caused ripples in certain circles in the capital, it did not matter to him. The main thing was that no blame should be attached to him; yet the contents of the article bothered him because they made him think of Tomas, whom he truly loved. It had been six months since they had heard from him and Maro was desperate. The whole household was in an endless state of mourning. All he needed now was to hear about that damn Balian. Who knew if he had not found out where his wife was? Perhaps he had seen Tomas, organized his flight and would return to get Maro. He must be living under a false name. He could be among the beggars who gathered daily in front of the *konak*. He could be a porter or even a worker hired for the harvest.

Riza finished his drink and told himself his mind was wandering, but he could not help worrying. The Bolsheviks, who had taken over in Russia, were negotiating a peace with the Ottoman Empire, which might bring the war to a quick end. Then it would be easier for Balian to find out where his wife was and come to get her. True, the chances of this were slim but he did not want to run the risk. The loss of Tomas had brought Maro closer to him, as she needed consolation and tenderness, but there was no way of knowing how she would react if her former husband showed up. Riza had to get rid of Balian before the Armistice.

When Bedri showed up half an hour later, Riza translated the whole article into Turkish for him. 'As you can see, he isn't dead no matter what you thought.'

Bedri took it in stride. 'Who'll believe all those lies? Is Gani Bey still asking for his hide?'

'That isn't the point.'

'Then what are you worrying about?'

Riza Bey looked him up and down, wondering if he should confide in him. Finally he pointed to the chair across from him and asked Bedri to sit down. Riza's voice was unusually friendly, so Bedri guessed the matter must be important.

'You know I am totally devoted to you, Riza Bey.'

Riza pointed to the cigarette box lying on the table between them. 'Help yourself.'

Bedri took one, lit it and politely exhaled the smoke to one side.

At last Riza began to speak confidentially. 'The man's presence exasperates me because he's Maro's husband. I want to finish him off once and for all.'

Bedri's face lit up. 'In that case we can use Maro as bait.'

Riza Bey gave him a killing look and Bedri turned red. Obviously his master did not think much of his idea. Perhaps he was afraid his mistress's life would be endangered.

Reading Bedri's mind, Riza Bey said, 'She must never know her husband is still alive.'

'Oh! Then what do you suggest we do?'

Riza Bey was angry with Bedri for not being more subtle. 'Those articles! He cannot have carried them to the outside himself, so he must have accomplices – maybe missionaries – maybe diplomats . . . who knows? He must be in contact with some Armenians who were not deported.'

'You're right!'

Riza clapped his hands. 'Go and look for him. Drop everything else you're doing but find him!'

'Any way I can?'

'I don't care as long as you are circumspect. Get rid of him for me, Bedri, and your fortune is made.'

Delighted by his last words, Bedri rose and bowed deeply.

After crossing the steppe, Vartan began to see scattered pines and knew he was getting closer to Afyon Karahisar, the town where he had been born and had grown up. To one side down from the railway tracks was the Akar River, where he used to fish as a boy. He lowered the compartment window and leaned out, trying to recognize something familiar in the countryside and smell the odour of recently turned earth, which brought back memories of autumn in his native land.

He could see his father on his thoroughbred Arab, supervising the workers who were ploughing with mule teams. He was telling his young sons, Noubar and Vartan, about organizing the work and the secrets of making the land yield a greater crop of ruffled-petal poppies. Vartan had been twelve years old then, but he had already known he was not going to spend the rest of his life on the wind-blown plateau. After visiting his cousins in Constantinople, he had dreamed only of the capital with its harbours full of ships that would carry him away to discover the world.

The wind blew through the compartment and woke up Hakki, who had been rocked to sleep by the monotonous clacking of the bogies on the rails. The other musicians were stretching their legs in the corridor.

When Hakki was sure they were alone, he asked for the umpteenth time since he had found out Vartan had been born in Afyon Karahisar, 'Do you think you can get me some opium? You won't forget, will you? It's for me to sell.'

'I'll try, Hakki, but I can't promise anything. It's been so long. I probably don't know anyone anymore.'

'I could make a fortune with all those European soldiers who are invading us.'

'Doesn't the fact that your country is losing the war bother you?'

'It isn't my war. Some people have made a lot of money out of it. Now it's my turn! We could work together and become rich if you wanted to and you wouldn't have to hide any longer.'

Vartan was startled but pretended not to understand. 'What do you mean?'

Hakki smiled, looked mysterious, winked and made sure there was no one in the corridor. 'I guessed a long time ago you are not what you are pretending to be.'

'Who am I then?'

Hakki shrugged. 'To me you are my *aghabey*, my brother, and that's enough as far as I am concerned.'

Pashazadé Shahir Mithad's return cut the conversation short. As there had not been even a hint of menace in Hakki's voice but only friendly conspiracy, Vartan felt safe. He turned to the *dervish* and asked, 'Where are we to play, master?'

'At a circumcision party, Oudi Yashar, at the governor's mansion. I was informed there will be many high-ranking officers present, even a general. We have to outdo ourselves as they must be feeling very gloomy.'

'Why?' Vartan acted innocent.

'A German engineer has just confirmed that Talaat has resigned as Minister and Grand Vizier. Izzet Pasha has been named to head the committee to negotiate the peace treaty. It's a sad moment for the Empire.'

Vartan was not surprised so he just nodded. Everyone had been expecting the defeat of the Ottoman Army since the middle of 1918. Of course, the resignation of the heads of the government in Constantinople gladdened him but the appointment of Izzet Pasha, a member of the old guard, meant that nothing had really changed as yet.

It was impossible to predict what this peace would mean for the Armenians. Would the Allies live up to their unofficial promises to recognize an autonomous Armenia? Everything was too uncertain and it had been complicated even more by the proclamation of an independent Armenia on 28 May 1918. This event, which could be construed as the first step towards the creation of the greater Armenia desired by all, made Vartan rejoice but he was also worried, as were most of his fellow countrymen.

The fledgling country was in what had originally been old Russian Armenia but had been reduced, on one side by the Ottomans and on the other by the Azeris, to a small expanse of territory hemmed in and cut off from the outside world by the Ottoman Empire, Persia, Azerbaijan and Georgia.

Vartan could not imagine what else his countrymen could have done after the Bolsheviks had ordered the retreat of the Russian troops except proclaim the independence of that bit of Armenia, which had been amputated from its ancestral land, Anatolia. Abandoned by the Russians, volunteers had valiantly defended western Armenia but had had to retreat from Erzinjan, Erzerum, Trebizond and Van as they were outnumbered by an enemy better equipped than they. The Ottoman advance had meant new massacres but the Armenians, who had been pushed back, made a last-ditch stand at Sardarabat and Gharakilissé, inflicting great losses and finally defeating the enemy. These victories had raised the morale of the Armenians, but they were only a respite. Their arch-enemy, the Turk, was at the gates of the newly independent country which lacked everything, but had to shelter and feed floods of refugees who had nowhere else to go.

The train whistled to announce its arrival as it passed through the walls of the city. Under the lowering sky, the mosque and the buildings looked grey. On the hillock that rose above the flat roofs stood the imposing silhouette of the old fortress that had probably given the town its name.[1] Vartan's heart beat fast as he scanned the crowd on the platform, looking for a familiar face, but puffs of steam from the locomotive masked his view.

At the Anadolou Inn where the troupe was staying, Pashazadé Shahir Mithad told his men they had a free afternoon after lunch. In the room they were sharing, Hakki watched Vartan get ready to leave.

'As this is your home town, I imagine you need more than ever to go alone.'

Vartan had no one to contact and did not expect to meet anyone he would dare approach and, besides, he did not like the idea of walking around alone in this town inhabited by so many ghosts.

'Not at all Hakki. I would be happy to have your company but on one condition – that you be quiet and not bombard me with questions. Is that too much to ask?'

Hakki glowed. 'Of course not, my *aghabey*. You may ask anything of me except not to fuck women. I'll be as silent as a carp. If you meet anyone of your race or religion, I'll step aside so you can talk in peace.'

So Hakki knew! He wanted to protest but Hakki stopped him.

'I've known for a long time! You're my brother, Oudi, and your secrets are sacred for me. I'd let myself be chopped up into pieces rather than betray you.'

Moved, Vartan embraced him. 'Blessed be the day I met you!'

'How do you say friend in Armenian?'

'*Enguer*. And you are one of mine, Hakki!'

They reached the commercial quarter of the town where the craftsmen and tradesmen were grouped together, each according to his speciality. They crossed the sector of the charcoal vendors, the sector of the coppersmiths, those of the tailors, silk and rug merchants, shoemakers and finally the confectioners. As in all the *souks* in Asia Minor, eager-eyed salesmen stood

---

1. Karahisar – black fortress; and Afyon – opium (Turkish).

in front of their stalls, scanning the passers-by and inviting them in, always ready to reduce the price for a pair of pretty eyes, for a friend or just because it was a *siftah*, the first sale of the day.

They came to the greengrocers' section, where sacks of rice, sugar and salt and baskets of almonds, chickpeas and dried fruit were piled up to the streets. Vartan stopped in front of an old shop where a ten-year-old boy was sitting on a tin of olive oil.

'Hello, is Hamid Effendi in?'

'No, he died several months ago.'

'Oh!' Vartan was distressed.

'My father bought the store from his widow.'

A man with a grey moustache and almost invisible eyebrows came out. His beady eyes darted suspiciously from one man to the other.

'What's your business with Hamid Effendi? Did he owe you any money?'

'Don't worry. He was an old friend from the Koranic School, may he rest in peace.'

'We shouldn't have bothered you,' added Hakki. 'How much are your dried figs?'

In the main square shaded by the chestnut-trees, the men were playing *tavla* and smoking their *narghilés*. Hakki looked longingly at the bottles of alcohol but did not dare ask Vartan to stop at the café. After passing the mosque, they continued through the narrow streets of what had been the Armenian Quarter. At first sight everything looked the same as on Vartan's last visit nine years ago. The wooden houses were painted white but the paint was chipping off and the flower boxes were invaded by weeds, but the carob trees still shaded the fountain and the neighbourhood bakery still exhaled the aroma of freshly baked bread. Each door made Vartan remember someone but now these houses were occupied by strangers. Here in front of the church of St Stephen, Aghavni Hanim used to sit with her grandson, Souren. Now her place had been taken by an old, veiled woman who was keeping an eye on a group of children playing in the square.

Vartan pushed the heavy wooden door open and the odour of fermenting dung attacked him. The walls echoed with cackling and bleating. Stepping in the droppings that littered the floor, he walked towards the choir through the chickens and sheep munching straw. The altar, the icons and the pews were gone. The frescoes on the wall had been whitewashed and the stained glass windows had been smashed to let in air. A chicken coop! A sheep-pen! That is what the church where he had first received the sacraments had become!

Suddenly he was transported back thirty years. It had been just before the Saturday Mass of Easter. He had stood reciting the canticles he knew by heart in front of the altar draped in black. He had known his parents were proudly listening – his mother in the women's section on the left and his father on the right with all the men. All the lamps had been lit and the gold ornaments and icons glittered. In the upper gallery, the choir had intoned the *Chrisdos haryav i merelots*, 'Christ is resurrected'. Vartan had taken a coloured Easter egg from his pocket, cracked it against the baptismal font and gobbled it up voraciously, thus breaking the endless fast of Lent. His gesture was premature as he should have kept the fast until after receiving Communion. Vartan vividly remembered the dilemma he had faced then. How could Christ die every year and then be alive again two days later? Today he knew human beings could die a thousand deaths and still live on.

He found Hakki waiting on the front steps. At that moment a man went by and turned his head so as not to have to look at the church. Vartan had time enough to recognize him – Parounag Avakian, the watchmaker! Two veiled women followed him. They were walking towards the next street where the houses were bigger and more comfortable, with larger gardens.

Vartan asked a small boy who the man was.

'He's Oral Effendi, the watchmaker. His second wife is my sister. Do you want me to show you the way to his house? He's a very good watchmaker. He'll give you a good price.'

'Thank you, but no. Some other time perhaps. I'm in a hurry now.'

At the urging of his fellows, Avakian had recanted, renounced his language and changed his name to survive. Vartan felt that he was in no position to judge him and decided not to trouble his peace of mind, which was obviously very fragile considering his reaction as he passed the church.

Each street, each square, each tree brought back memories. He felt as if he were moving in a dream – walking on a road he had never left. With each step echoes of the past resounded. There was the school – now deserted – where he had received his first lessons. The house where he had been born was scarcely half a mile away. He began to recite the thirty-six letters of the Armenian alphabet to himself – *ayp, pen, kim, ta, yetch, za* . . . He remembered his father teaching them to him when he was barely three.

422

They left town and walked towards a mineral spring, which was famous in the region.

Hakki commented, 'You must have had a happy childhood to have been so moved. Me, I have no desire ever to go back to my village.'

'That just shows you're wiser than I am.'

Hakki rolled two cigarettes and gave one to his friend. They walked in silence for about fifteen minutes. The houses became sparser and soon they gave way to fields. Vartan took a short-cut leading to a narrow path that hurtled down a hill and suddenly they were overlooking his family's land. The fields stretched as far as the eye could see and were separated by a wind-break of poplars with dead leaves swirling around their feet. Most of the opium fields were lying fallow and those that had been planted looked neglected. He could see only three ploughs where forty or fifty had worked before.

Vartan remembered well how the plough handles shook in his hands, giving the impression they were alive – the feeling of power when he cleaved the earth – the pride he had felt on seeing his straight furrows. In step with the seasons Noubar and Vartan would prune the fruit-trees and vineyards, sow, irrigate, mow and learn the art of notching the capsule of the opium poppies to harvest the juice. While he was studying at the university in Constantinople, he had sometimes dreamed he was mowing, swinging the scythe in a semi-circle from right to left. If he closed his eyes, he could hear the soft, gentle hiss of the blade cutting the grass, smell the sap and feel the pain in his shoulders and waist. Vartan began to walk again.

'You were a long way away, brother,' complained Hakki, trying to catch up with him.

They walked through a muddy field by the river. Here Vartan had played *jirit* with the Kurds after a day's work. The two teams had mimicked cavalry charges using sticks instead of lances. Even though he had been strong and solidly built, Noubar did not like sports and preferred to spend his time running the plantation and dreaming of big projects for its expansion, but he always cheered Vartan on and was proud of his brother's equestrian feats.

A fieldstone house appeared behind some plane-trees. It was an imposing four-storey building with balconies. Vartan gasped as he sat down on the side of the sandy road to look at the pale, rose-coloured walls of the house. Instead of wooden lattices, the new owner had found it simpler to paint the window panes green, the colour of Islam. Vartan could remember how the furniture was arranged in each of the rooms and the view from each window. He could hear long-gone voices and images superimposed themselves in his mind – his father – his mother – cousins who had come to visit in the summer – Maro, who had loved this house – the parties they had given there. This was the one place on earth he considered home and yet he felt a stranger here.

An old man on a donkey came out of the house. As he drew near, Vartan thought he must be Osman, the cook, who had already been working for the Balians when Vartan was born. He looked sad; his back was bent; he was dressed in dirty, old clothes. He squinted at the strangers. Certain that the old man had not recognized him, Vartan greeted him. 'May Allah bless you.'

'May He bless you, too.' The old man reined in the donkey.

'Whose fields are these?'

'Ekrem Effendi's.'

'The *mouhtar*?'[1]

'He isn't the *mouhtar* any more. He's the chief of police. It's his house.'

Vartan needed to speak about the past but did not want to reveal his identity.

'When I came through here a long time ago, a man who had stolen a pig had been caught. People wanted to give him a beating but the *Agha* of this house wouldn't let them.'

'I remember,' said Osman, staring at the ground. 'The master was a good, just man, very generous and charitable. Allah showered blessings on him. I was the cook then and it was a good job. Now I keep the goats – at my age!'

'What happened to them?'

'The Bey died a long time ago and his wife followed him. Then his eldest son ran the estate. He was as good as his father but when the war started, he left.'

'Did he sell the property to Ekrem Effendi?'

'What do you think? He was in too much of a hurry to save his skin.'

'That was wise of him.'

The old man stopped talking and looked nervously towards the house as he goaded his donkey.

Vartan let him go and a sudden strange feeling urged him to turn his back and return to town.

Hakki caught Vartan by the shoulder. 'You! You lived in that palace!

---

1. The elder of the village or neighbourhood (Turkish).

424

Me, I often didn't have enough to eat. I can't even imagine what your childhood must have been like! It must be terrible for you to wander on the road with only your *oud*.'

'It's worse not to be able to use your own name.'

'It's Balian, isn't it?'

Vartan nodded.

'Will you tell me about it some day?'

'About what?' asked Vartan.

'Why, about everything; what you ate, what you did, what your parents were like.'

Vartan laughed softly. 'As a child, I was probably very much like you. Had we been neighbours, we would have most probably become friends.'

Anxious to be charitable, as prescribed in the Quran and confirmed by custom, Metin Bey, the governor of the province, had gathered the children of the poor to have them circumcised at the same time as his own son. Sitting in the middle at the head table, he presided over several dignitaries, who were mostly Ottoman officers in dress uniforms. At smaller tables, laid out as lavishly as the long one, sat men of lower ranks or lesser distinction, including those who did not have the means for such a grand party to celebrate their sons' circumcision. In front of the tables a dozen bronze bedsteads were placed. In them a dozen ten-year-old boys, wearing blue satin hats and long, white nightshirts, lay anxiously awaiting the barber-circumciser who would turn them into men and real Muslims.

The *dervishes* took their places on the dais at the end of the reception room and began to tune their instruments. Vartan looked at the guests and was astounded to see Hâlit Pasha's round face to the governor's right. Except for his hair, which was greyer, the General had not changed since they had last met in Sivas when he had saved Vartan from the gallows. Because he had been staring so intently at his friend, Vartan missed his cue from Pashazadé Shahir Mithad, and everyone looked at him. For a few moments his eyes met those of the General, but Halit did not recognize him because of his *dervish* habit and his beard.

To make the ceremony more solemn, Pashazadé performed a *sema*, something he did not usually do when his troupe played at a private house. Impressed by the ecstatic look on the face of the holy man, who seemed to

425

be in direct communion with Allah, both children and adults alike watched the performance open-mouthed. The governor handed him a pouch of money when he had finished to acknowledge the honour shown.

The troupe started to play secular music – at first light and merry but turning more solemn when the barber began to cut off the foreskins of the boys' little penises. The boys clenched their jaws and remained stoically quiet while their fathers glowed with pride. Then three belly-dancers entered and began to wiggle as if putting the boys' virility to test. The men were amused because, in spite of their pain, the newly circumcised boys could not take their eyes off the half-naked bodies. The barber finished and the guests presented money and gifts to the boys, wishing them long life, good health and unwavering faith and urging them to humility, charity and modesty. An interminable banquet followed and the musicians enlivened the gathering; a swarm of young servants went back and forth to the kitchens. While the fathers of the poor boys were feasting and enjoying themselves, the atmosphere was more sombre at the table of honour, where the men were visibly tense. The officers and their host were speaking softly and Halit Pasha's opinion was often consulted. He would nod authoritatively and underline the points he was making with barely controlled vehemence. Vartan could read the same passion in his face that he had shown as a young congressman when he had wanted to convince his listeners. They were probably talking about the military situation and the future of the Ottoman Empire. Vartan would have loved to be able to eavesdrop.

After the meal, the guests went out into the garden while the musicians fell upon the food and drink the servants brought them. Vartan did not feel like eating and went out into the garden, hoping to be able to see Halit Pasha in private but he, the other officers, and the governor were standing together in the shade of the arbour, still in the middle of a heated discussion, so Vartan returned to the house to wait for a more propitious occasion.

The *dervish*, Pashazadé Shahir Mithad, greeted him reproachfully, 'We have come to expect better of you, Oudi Yashar. Where were you today? I cannot even count the times you were off-key.'

Vartan looked helpless and Zournaji Osman, who was slightly tipsy from the *raki*, exclaimed, 'And you got worse when the dancing girls came in.'

They all burst into laughter, even Pashazadé Shahir Mithad. The sun was setting and they asked the musicians to go to a vast tent pitched at the end of the garden. The guests were seated on rugs and cushions covering the

426

ground. There was a low table in the centre with a large copper tray on it. Servants were passing out bottles, ewers of water and *narghilés*. The troupe was so used to these occasions that Pashazadé Shahir Mithad did not even have to tell them which piece to start playing. The first bars were the cue and three dancers came in wiggling, to the men's shouts of approval. One jumped up on the copper tray while the other two moved around among the men. Their feet barely moved, their anklets and bracelets tinkled and their *zils*, small bronze castanets hidden in the palms of their hands, clinked.

The men were sitting cross-legged as if rooted in the ground. Entranced by the story the dancers were telling with their intricate movements of hands, eyes, bellies and whole bodies, they joined in the sensual celebration by swinging their head in time with the swaying hips of the women. Each undulation, each posture had a meaning and the rhythm carried a sensual message. The alcohol made the men more demanding and they called for the women to undress. Their veils dropped, one by one, and the sexual invitation became more and more explicit. Each in turn dropped their bouffant harem pants and the tiny bolero that covered their breasts and finally stood naked, allowing the spectators to splash their bellies with *raki* and lick it off as it dribbled down their thighs.

As Halit Pasha looked on absent-mindedly, he observed the *oud* player, whose stare was beginning to intrigue him. What could he want? After a while, the general recognized something familiar in that look. Vartan was satisfied to have caught Halit's attention and turned aside before the others noticed anything out of the ordinary. A meal was served in the tent and the party lasted until dawn. It had been a real test of endurance for the musicians and the dancers.

When the party was over, Halit Pasha took advantage of the fact that the governor was occupied with a colonel, approached Vartan, handed him a coin and asked quietly, 'Have we met before?'

Vartan refused to take the money. 'You already gave me more than enough gold in Sivas.'

The General's eyes widened. 'Well . . .' he stuttered, 'well . . .' He was stupefied. He looked around quickly and found the governor waiting for him at the entrance of the tent so he said loudly, 'Here! Take this, my good man, and drink to my health with your friends.' Then he whispered, 'Nine o'clock at City Hall.'

Vartan bowed. 'Allah bless you for your generosity. May your days be long and happy.'

427

The musicians formed a circle around Vartan. 'Let's see it,' said Hafiz Ismael. 'Look! It's gold!'

'Let's do what the Pasha said and go and drink it up,' said Hakki, who had been titillated by the dancers. 'We should be able to find a whorehouse in this town!'

At exactly nine o'clock Halit Pasha was waiting for Vartan in the City Hall. He immediately took him to a small, seldom-used reception room where his *aide-de-camp* served them coffee. The high French doors on the first floor gave on to a public garden shaded by pine trees and the breeze moved the tapestries hanging on the walls and carried in the smell of pine resin. When the aide had left, Halit and Vartan embraced each other.

'You have no idea how it shocked me to hear your voice. What joy to know you were alive!'

'Thanks to you, Halit Pasha, and I thank you again. I'm so glad you didn't leave your bones on the Russian front as you feared three years ago.'

'My time hadn't come.' The General still had his hands on Vartan's shoulders and was smiling. The big bags under his eyes and his drooping eyelids made his brown eyes look like those of a nice dog and exhaustion gave him an air of resignation.

'Did you find your family?'

'Unfortunately not yet.'

Halit Pasha was distressed, but he thought it better not to tell Vartan that Colonel Ibrahim had paid for Vartan's liberty with his life. He asked Vartan to sit down. 'Tell me what happened after Sivas.'

While they drank their coffee, Vartan recounted his life after 1915, not even skipping the articles about the fate of Armenians which had been published in the outside world.

'What a mess our government has made of things! Fortunately the war is almost over. I heard Aleppo was taken yesterday. The English have all of Syria in their hands and are making a push for Anatolia. Their armies are also advancing in Thrace and they may have already occupied Constantinople. It's the end of the Ottoman Empire.'

'You sound almost happy about it!'

'The Empire as such cannot go on as it is much longer. We must replace

428

it and create a new Turkey out of whatever is left, which might be only Constantinople and Anatolia, probably nothing else.'

'Turkey for the Turks,' murmured Vartan cynically.

'Not at all,' protested Halit Pasha. 'A modern state where every race will be able to live in harmony.'

'That's easy for you to say now that the Armenian minority has practically been annihilated.'

Halit Pasha's shoulders sagged. 'I want to tell you that I *am* bitterly sorry for those monstrous crimes! Those responsible shall pay for them.' He looked towards the door before continuing in a low voice, 'The officers now gathered here in Afyon are preparing for what must be done. Kemal Pasha and we are planning to depose the Sultan and install a secular republic. I'm going to Constantinople to continue the battle we fought together in 1909, but this time we shall succeed!'

'I do not share your optimism, Halit Pasha. Frankly, I'll never feel at home in a country soaked in the blood of my people.'

'But it's your country. You were born in Afyon and you've lived in Constantinople!'

'Now I'm just an Armenian.' His dream of a Grand Armenia and Halit Pasha's idea of a Turkish Anatolia could not be reconciled. Both states would covet the territories west of the Caucasus – Western Armenia and Cilicia. Halit knew this also.

'Do you intend to emigrate to the Republic of Armenia? The situation there is disastrous and the economy is in ruins – hundreds of thousands of penniless refugees, epidemics, famine – not to mention that its borders are still not set. New conflicts could erupt at any moment. Believe me, Vartan, the future of that Armenia is much in doubt.'

'You're right. Anything can still happen but we *are* coming to a cross-roads in history. For the first time in centuries, the Armenians can hope for a homeland. I will do everything in my power to achieve that even though my contribution is small.'

Halit Pasha rubbed his chin and nodded. 'I'm speaking to you as an old friend . . .'

Suddenly one of the panels of the French door slammed against the wall. A man stood in the doorway brandishing a pistol. 'What a touching reunion!'

At first Vartan did not realize what was happening but then he recognized him – the man who had wounded him in the camp in Malatya, the one who had come to Aroussiag's. He jumped up from his chair.

'Don't move,' ordered the man pushing the door shut and closing the latch.

'What do you mean by coming in here?' cried Halit Pasha, his face purple. 'I'll have you whipped and put in prison.'

'Silence, traitor! You, an Ottoman officer, dealing with an enemy spy! It's because of people like you that we're losing the war!' Bedri stepped forward and grinned as he looked at Vartan, 'I've finally got you!'

'What do you want from me?' Vartan was trying to gain time. 'I haven't committed any crime.'

Bedri was standing with his back to the window and laughed coarsely. Halit Pasha tried to draw his revolver but Bedri was faster and shot him twice in the chest. At that very moment a slim figure jumped from behind one of the drapes. There was a glint of a blade as it was thrust into Bedri's back. He screamed and dropped his pistol. His assailant struck again and this time Bedri crumpled, hitting the floor with a thud. The entire operation had taken only a few seconds.

'Baron Vartan!'

'Aram!'

Sneering, the boy stood over Bedri who was moaning and whining as he held out his hands trying to ward off the blows.

'Die!' Aram screamed and stabbed him again.

People were knocking on the door and screaming for them to open up. Vartan touched Halit to see if he were still alive and then gently closed his eyes. He caught Aram by the sleeve to get him off Bedri. 'Quickly! We must leave!'

The windows were at least a few yards off the ground but a cushion of pine needles broke their fall and the low branches of the pine trees hid them. Inside, Bedri was calling for help while the door shook from the blows of the rifle butts and the hobnailed boots.

'Why did you keep me from killing that pig?' Aram was furious as they ran through the garden towards the street.

'We have to save our skins. Throw away your dagger.'

They fled down the narrow street mixing with the carefree crowd and then turned into one of the side streets, which was hardly wide enough for a donkey to pass. Vartan knew the town like the palm of his hand and in a few minutes they reached the banks of the Akar River, where they found shelter in an empty warehouse.

Vartan was still in a state of shock and asked Aram brusquely, 'What are you doing here?'

'That guy came to Urgup. He had tortured an Armenian in Adana to find out about our network. He wanted to know where you were so he and his men beat us up – Aroussiag and me – but we didn't talk. Then . . .' He unrolled the bandage around his hand and, horrified, Vartan saw that three of his fingers had been chopped off at their roots. Pus oozed from under the scabs. 'They cut them off, one by one, to make Aroussiag talk. I fainted after the second one. When I woke up, Aroussiag was lying there soaked in blood. They had . . .' He choked and Vartan took him into his arms while the boy cried. Then he continued, 'When they left, I heard them say they would get you in Afyon Karahisar. Kerim gave me some money to come and warn you.' He hiccuped.

'You can tell me the rest later.'

Vartan kept his feelings under control while he planned what he should do next, but he was too shattered to think. Poor sweet Aroussiag, who had been so full of life! The vision of her mutilated body erased the memories of her radiant face, her smiling mouth, her black, loving eyes. She had died because of him! Vartan tried to shake off the thought. He could hear the sound of her voice in his head – hear her singing while her hands juggled with the threads as she wove on her loom.

After a while Aram pulled him out of his grief. He had lost his childish look and seemed older and hardened by his ordeals. He reproached Vartan bitterly, 'You shouldn't have stopped me from finishing him off. I'd sworn to kill that fat pig!'

'He probably won't survive your stabs. You avenged Aroussiag and you saved my life! You're a brave man, Aram!'

It was just what the boy wanted to hear. Very seriously, he put his hand on Vartan's shoulder and for the first time he used the familiar *thou* in Armenian.

'I know where your wife is. The fat pig bragged about it, "I want the spy and I shall have him. In any case, we're holding his wife in Ayntab."'

Vartan straightened as if lashed by a whip. 'That's what he said? Ayntab?'

'Yes. He's called Bedri and he works for the governor of Ayntab.'

Maro! Tomas! Vartan was speechless. He kissed Aram on both cheeks. 'Aram! My son! My friend! You've given me the best news and the worst news. My sadness and my joy cannot cancel each other, but I don't know what to think any longer.'

The boy remained cool. This past week as he had travelled towards Afyon, he had asked himself many times if he should tell Vartan about his wife. Aram had adored Aroussiag and resented the thought that Vartan would forget her so soon for another woman. However, he had decided that Aroussiag would not have wanted him to keep it secret.

'Maybe we should start thinking about how to get you out of this mess,' said Aram cynically.

'We're both in the same boat.'

'Me? I'm a *fedayi*! I've already offered my life and consider myself dead.'

Vartan grabbed him by the hair, shook him, and reprimanded him harshly, 'You still have your life before you and you shall live! Armenia needs your seed and your balls, your courage and your work, not a useless sacrifice! There are already too many dead!'

Aram's pride was ruffled. He shook Vartan off and ran his fingers through his hair. 'I'm not a child anymore.'

'That's true. You've done the work of three men for the past years. I'd be happy if you would become my partner.'

Aram agreed immediately. Underneath the bravado he felt lonely.

Vartan stroked his beard. 'We have to get out of town as soon as possible. Since they're not looking for you, you can go to the Anadolou Inn and ask for Kemenché Hakki.'

'A Turk?' Aram protested. 'They're not to be trusted!'

'You shouldn't generalize like that. He's my best friend and he'll help us. Tell him his *aghabey* needs him. Tell him to bring me a razor. Be very careful and make sure you're not followed.'

More than two hours went by before Aram returned with Hakki. He had had to wait until the military guards had left the inn to reach him.

'They questioned all the musicians about you but especially me because I had been your friend. Of course, I didn't tell them you were an Armenian and a spy.'

'I'm not a spy!' Vartan protested.

'I really don't care. They said you killed Halit Pasha and tried to kill someone else.'

'That's a lie!'

432

'I don't care about that either. If you killed him, you must have had a good reason. You're still my *enguer*.'

Vartan hugged him. 'I knew I could count on you. Can you find me a way out?'

Smiling, Hakki handed him a package of used, mended clothing. 'This will make you look like a peasant and they're looking for a bearded musician.'

Among the clothes and the razor and soap, Vartan found a small, round mirror with a broken edge. Aram brought a little water up from the river in a chipped jug and Vartan shaved off his long beard.

'At long last, I'll see what you really look like,' said Hakki, holding up the mirror.

Vartan was just as curious. As the blade uncovered his cheeks and chin, he could see that time had marked him. The skin was sagging a little at his jaws which coarsened his expression, while the rest of his face looked thinner. His white cheeks stood out in contrast to his tanned cheekbones and forehead. Deep wrinkles formed crow's feet around his eyes. Even his hair looked greyer.

'You look different,' said Hakki simply.

Feeling the cool air, Vartan rubbed his newly shaven skin. Hakki handed him a sheet of wrinkled, yellowed paper folded in four.

'You can use this. It has no photograph and just says that your name is Hakki Chelebi, born in Bodrum.'

'Thank you, but what will you do without papers?'

'I'll manage somehow. Pashazadé Shahir Mithad will vouch for me.'

'If you ever get to Constantinople, ask for me at the Central Pharmacy on the main street of Péra. I'll never forget you, Hakki, my brother. Take good care of my *oud*.'

Hakki kissed him and looked into his eyes. Then he walked away briskly without looking back.

Vartan waited until evening to leave his hiding place. He had smeared dirt on the pale parts of his face. They had no trouble getting out of town in spite of the many police patrols. That same evening what seemed to be a farmer and his son caught the train for Constantinople after having bribed the chief engineer with a gold coin. They got into a wagon full of bleating sheep and strewed hay on top of themselves for protection from the wind, which came in through the cracks in the sides.

Vartan stared at a tuft of wool which hung from a knot in the planks like a tattered flag. He remained withdrawn into himself for many hours incapable of speaking, plunged into his grief for Aroussiag. There was no one to see him cry, for Aram slept, shivering.

# FIFTEEN

The train crawled along for two days and nights, through plains, mountains and valleys and along the shore of the Sea of Marmara, until it came to Haydar Pasha, the Asiatic terminal of Constantinople. Vartan and Aram, exhausted but exultant, crept out of the cattle car and breathed the freer air of the capital. They made their way hurriedly through the crowd of passengers, soldiers, pedlars and porters to the wharf. The slate-grey sea looked mysterious under the fog of this humid autumn day.

Constantinople! How many times had Vartan dreamed of it! He was filled with mixed feelings – excitement and regret – joy and apprehension. Things had been happening so fast lately that he had not as yet had time to sort them out – the slaughter of Aroussiag, the news that Maro and Tomas were still alive; Halit Pasha's murder – all of these, plus the anxiety that he might not find his relatives – Aunt Arpiné, Uncle Mesrop and his cousins, Lucie and Diran. The war was over but he could not yet rejoice. The future was too uncertain. According to Bedri, Maro and Tomas were still captives of the governor of Ayntab and he would feel that a new life had begun only when they were all together again.

'Where are we going?' asked Aram, grabbing Vartan by the arm and bringing him back to earth.

The boy was completely lost and worried about his future, unable to imagine what lay in store for him. He felt distraught and very vulnerable in this crowded city.

Vartan went to the wharf, where the boatmen in their caïques were waiting for customers. Depending on the traffic, they would ply between the European and Asiatic sides of Constantinople several times a day. Vartan overheard them discussing the Armistice, which had been signed in

Mudhros only recently. The terms of surrender did not interest them as much as the presence of the foreign soldiers, which meant an increase in revenue for them.

Because of his peasant-like appearance, Vartan was able to bargain a good price for the crossing to Galata, but the boatman insisted on seeing the money first. They took their places in the caïque, a small boat that tapered to a point at both ends and was painted with green and yellow dragons at bow and stern. The boatman's face was weather-beaten. He was a strong man who handled the oars smoothly; in spite of his sagging shoulders. Battleships were moored very close to the entrance to the Bosphorus, the strategic strait connecting the Mediterranean to the Black Sea. Aram was impressed by the gigantic ships with their bristling cannons.

'Ships of iron?'

'They're warships. Don't you see their flags? That one's British, that one's French and the one over there is Italian.'

The caïque threaded its way through the freighters, warships and boats. Aram put his hand in the water and tasted it to see if it was really salty as Vartan had told him. Everything amazed him and his eyes were hardly big enough to take it all in, but his enthusiasm was catching.

Constantinople spread out over its seven hills, raising its forest of minarets towards the grey sky. On top of the highest hill, the Topkapi Palace dominated the older section of the city. A fresh wind blew in from the Golden Horn and dispersed the veil of fog. One could now see the white marble facade of the Dolmabahché, the Sultan's other palace along the strait. The houses built upon the hills seemed to pile up, one on top of the other.

'What's that?' asked Aram, pointing to the Topkapi nestled in the middle of its park.

'The Sultan's palace. Hagia Sophia is on the left behind that hill and the Sirkeci train station, the terminal of the Orient Express, is on the right.'

Aram shivered! The Sultan, whose name the people in the village had never pronounced without a tremor in their voices. The Sultan, who had the power of life and death over them all. Then he really did exist! Aram suddenly realized that he was even further away from his native land than he had thought. Not only was he in another world but in a completely different reality, totally unknown to him. Vartan could tell from the tone of his voice how confused the boy was.

'Don't you worry. I'll show you around the city little by little and, one day, you'll get to know it as the plain around your village. You'll see. This is the city of a thousand and one dreams, where anything is possible. Look over there.' He pointed to a small twin-engined plane flying over the waters of the strait.

Aram, who had never seen a plane before, kept staring at it until it disappeared in the direction of the Princess Islands in the Sea of Marmara. But this only made him more apprehensive.

'What am I going to do? In Cappadocia I could always get work on one of the farms but here . . .'

Vartan put his arm around Aram's shoulder and said, 'You're not alone. My family and I will take care of you.'

The caïque headed towards the Golden Horn and passed under the Galata Bridge. There were soldiers in foreign uniforms among the crowd of curious onlookers leaning on the railing and the sight of them warmed Vartan's heart. Despite the war, the city still had a sensual appeal. They disembarked and walked towards the tower of Galata. Trams, taxis, horse-drawn wagons, donkeys and pedestrians crowded the street. In the middle of the circus, a policeman on a little platform tried to direct the endless flow of traffic; he waved his arms in all directions and blew his whistle persistently. In spite of the bedlam, the steam sirens of the ships could still be heard.

Constantinople looked the same as when Vartan had last been there in 1913. Neither the attitude of the people nor the atmosphere of the city suggested that a long and cruel war had been fought, and even less that massacres had taken place in Anatolia. In spite of the recent surrender, it was business as usual. Byzantium 'The Impure', as it had been called for centuries, had always adapted itself to its conquerors, even assimilating them. Although the inhabitants sometimes directed angry looks at the French and English soldiers, most of them welcomed the westerners with open arms; after all, they contributed to everyone's prosperity.

The capital was still a marvellous and mysterious city full of intrigues and passions – the meeting place of east and west – a melting pot where races and languages mixed but never melded – a place where anything could happen and often did. Words like these, which he had used to describe the magical power of the city to Aram only fifteen minutes before, came back to Vartan and a wave of carefree joy swept over him.

They climbed up Yuksek Kaldirim, a steep, cobbled stairway with shops on either side, and soon arrived at la Grand-rue de Péra, the nerve centre of the capital and playground of the wealthy Armenians, Greeks, Jews and

Europeans. The street was lined with fashionable clubs, restaurants, pastry shops and stores with signs in various languages. Elegant women dressed in the latest Paris fashions, women draped in *charshafs* and men wearing bowlers, soft felt hats, fezzes or turbans mingled together happily.

Aram sighed, 'It's so confusing. I don't think I'll ever get used to it.'

'You'll fit in quickly,' replied Vartan absent-mindedly. This was the section where he had lived before and he kept thinking of Maro – how they had walked down these same pavements every day to go to Chez Marquise for tea and delicious pastries. He felt the weight of her hand on his arm, the rhythm of her steps matching his. He heard the ring of her soft voice as she commented on the people they met. He could remember the dreams they had had about their future. Vartan hurried, trying to outrun his thoughts.

A little after the Galatasaray Lycée, Vartan turned into a small sidestreet and stopped in front of the building where his cousin Diran lived. Aram preferred to wait downstairs while Vartan went up the stairs, four at a time. When he arrived at the door, he rang the bell – one long and two short rings, their special code. A Turk opened the door and explained that he had been living there for several months and did not know where the previous tenant had moved to. Disappointed but hoping Diran had not been arrested because of his political activities, Vartan descended the stairs and found Aram looking exhausted, sitting on the first step. The trip in the cattle car had been long and tiring and they had been walking for more than an hour.

'Would you like to rest for a while?' asked Vartan, who was also tired.

'I can manage,' replied Aram, who didn't want to become a burden to his friend.

They boarded a horse-drawn tram, which took them back over the Galata Bridge, and they got off in front of the imposing Yeni Jami (New Mosque). Mesrop Mesropian's printing shop was on a narrow street between a tailor's shop and a rug and silk merchant. The sight of the sign in the window – 'Mesropian & Sons', written in red letters – moved Vartan. There were samples of some of their printing work in the window; the sun had faded the ink and yellowed the paper. He could not see into the shop. What was he going to find? His heart beat faster and faster as he pushed the door open and the little bell announced his entrance. The same shrill ring as always! His cousin, Lucie, sat behind the desk, checking the ledgers. She looked up and her jaw dropped. She was a little heavier and her face, which had been angular, was now rounder. She was thirty but her tightly curled hairdo made her look younger than when she used to wear the chignon.

'Vartan!' The pen fell from her hand and spotted the ledger. She shoved her chair back, ran to him and threw herself into his arms. 'Vartan!' She was laughing and crying at the same time. 'How wonderful! I'm so happy! So very happy!'

Chuckling, he held her lovingly. 'I'm very happy, too! I had doubted this moment would ever come! You're prettier than ever, Lucie. How's your father? Your mother? Diran?'

'Well.'

'I've just come from Diran's apartment but he wasn't there.'

'He had to move because of the police.' She frowned and hesitated before asking, 'What about Maro? Tomas?'

'Maro and Tomas are alive, thank God, and I think I know where they are now. They'll be with us soon.'

Lucie sighed with relief even though Vartan's sombre tone made her wonder. She stepped back, glancing at the curtain that separated the office from the work room. 'I'll tell my father the good news. He has to be spared any kind of shock.'

'What's wrong with him?'

'He's already had two heart attacks since the beginning of the war. He's much better but he shouldn't be upset. Wait here.'

She disappeared into the workshop and Vartan winked at Aram who was discreetly standing by the door. Two minutes later, crossly berating his daughter, Uncle Mesrop pushed aside the curtain and came in.

'Spare me! Spare me! These kinds of shocks are good for me. It's the silence that gnaws at my heart.'

Uncle Mesrop, who was at least seventy-two or seventy-three, had lost a lot of weight, including his bulging belly. He used to joke about it, insisting that a respectable tummy was a sign of prosperity. He had become almost bald. He opened his arms to Vartan without worrying about his dirty apron and his ink-stained hands.

'My boy. My beloved nephew. God be praised a thousand times. Lucie says Maro and Tomas will join us soon. My prayers have been answered.'

Vartan thought it better not to disillusion him as to the speedy return of Maro and Tomas. Uncle Mesrop stepped back and took off his gold-rimmed glasses to wipe away his tears. Vartan could see he had big circles under his eyes and his skin was ashen.

'Stop looking at me like a doctor,' laughed Uncle Mesrop. 'I'm healthier than ever.'

'I'm only staring at you to convince myself that I'm not dreaming. I'm really in Constantinople, with you.'

Tears running down his cheeks, Mesrop hugged his nephew again. 'God has performed a miracle,' he sniffled as he took out his handkerchief and excused himself. 'I'm turning into a weeping old woman.' Then he chuckled as he looked Vartan up and down. 'You haven't changed, son. A little thinner, that's all. Don't you think the grey at his temples is becoming, Lucie?'

She nodded. 'Cousin Vartan has always been the handsomest man on earth.' Feeling left out, Aram stepped a little further into the room and pushed aside the curtain to get a better look at the workshop. He could distinctly hear the clatter of the printing press.

Finally Mesrop noticed him and said firmly, 'Hey, you boy! No loitering here!'

'He's with me! He's my friend!' Vartan caught him by the shoulder. 'Uncle Mesrop, I want to introduce Aram who's like my son. He's a hero. He has saved many orphans like himself! And I owe my life to him!'

Uncle Mesrop took Aram in his arms. 'Welcome, Aram. Would you do us the honour of considering us your family from now on?'

Embarrassed, Aram nodded and when Lucie called him 'Cousin Aram' he turned bright red.

'I'm closing up for the day,' announced Uncle Mesrop. 'We're going to feast and drink. Go and look for your brother, Lucie, and join us at the house.'

They took a taxi with no fenders, a Citroën, which dated back to pre-war years, to get to the Harbiyé Quarter. The steep street was lined with newly-built houses sitting next to two-century-old grey frame structures. The windows were half-hidden by lattices, which allowed the Muslim women to look out without being seen. Old Turkish families still lived in their ancestral homes, even though the neighbourhood had become predominantly Armenian.

Short-legged and plumper than before, her white hair tinted blue as usual, Aunt Arpiné gave Vartan an ecstatic welcome – full of joyous praises to the Lord and to all His saints. Laughing and crying, she asked one question after another, without waiting for an answer. She, who was usually so calm and resourceful in accommodating unexpected guests, was totally disorientated today. She tried to do everything at once: serve drinks, prepare dinner, look for suitable clothes for Vartan and his young friend. She moved here and there, making incomplete gestures; she rushed to the kitchen and rushed back again just to say something she had forgotten. Finally, Mesrop forced her to sit down on the sofa and went to get a bottle of cognac and some glasses. The old lady ran her finger through her nephew's hair and kissed him over and over again on his cheeks. Beaming, she held his hands and looked at him quietly.

Vartan's eyes wandered around the room. The two velvet divans, the chairs, the bookcases, the low tables covered with magazines, the large Persian rug and the potted plants in front of the windows – everything in the living room was exactly the same as he had always remembered, but he still felt strange. He had the impression that he had lived through this moment before. Was it perhaps that he had been anticipating it for so long?

To break the silence, he asked, 'Is Barkev still in New York?'

'He joined the Foreign Legion and is in Syria, fighting with the French.'

'Any news from Noubar?'

'Your brother and his wife are still in Jerusalem. They say they'll return after Christmas.'

'I can't wait to see them,' sighed Vartan.

'Are Maro and Tomas with you?'

Uncle Mesrop walked in with Aram, who was carrying a silver tray with four glasses. Vartan took advantage of the interruption to avoid explaining. His aunt looked at him anxiously, waiting for an answer which was not forthcoming. Mesrop served the drinks.

'I drink to the return of Maro and Tomas,' said Arpiné, trying to get Vartan to speak.

'To the day when we shall all be together again,' said Mesrop who had heard his wife's question as he entered the room.

Vartan drank in silence; then, looking from one to the other, he spoke, trying to seem casual, 'To tell the truth, all I know is that Maro and Tomas are living at the home of the governor of Ayntab. I have no idea exactly how or why, or since when.'

'They're prisoners,' blurted out Aram. Cognac had loosened his tongue. The belligerent tone of his voice surprised them and they all turned to look at the boy, who was standing by the window. He understood from their worried expressions and Vartan's severe look that he would have done better to keep his big mouth shut. The name Ayntab had brought back memories of Aroussiag bathed in blood! He turned to stare at the street.

'Aram's telling the truth,' admitted Vartan. 'I have every reason to believe they're being held against their will.'

Mesrop pounded his fist on the arm of the chair. 'That man will have to let them go. Now that the war is over, they'll force him to.'

'I'll see that it's done as quickly as possible,' said Vartan decisively.

A long silence fell. Everyone was trying to picture the situation of Maro and Tomas in the Ottoman governor's residence. To break the silence, Aunt Arpiné added sweetly, 'The important thing is they escaped the massacres and they're both alive. How is not important!' She looked at Vartan insistently, and her look spoke volumes. He nodded in agreement.

'You're right, Aunt Arpiné.'

Uncle Mesrop emptied his glass. 'God has been good and has protected us in these trying times. It's a real miracle our family has been spared, except, of course, for your dear mother-in-law.'

The passing of time had not affected Diran's youthful light-heartedness, which was part of his charm. The few wrinkles on his forehead gave him a pensive look and, as he walked with his head down, he looked lost in thought. But as soon as he spoke, his brown eyes would sparkle with life, and his hands drew arabesques around him. And when he was listening, he would frown, and stroke the tip of his slightly hooked nose with his forefinger.

The two cousins were the same age. People thought they were brothers. Since early childhood they had shared everything – children's games during vacations, gallant adventures when they had been at the university and then their political activities. When they saw each other, they were so moved they couldn't find words to express themselves. They first looked at each other tenderly for a long moment, then they hugged, pounding each other on the back and laughing excitedly.

'You rascal, you!' Diran finally choked out, 'I knew they'd never get you! Your letter two years ago! And then your articles! But will you tell me why you put your signature to them?' Once he had started, the questions tumbled out, one after the other. He was dying to know what Vartan had lived through. 'Why not one of your usual pen names?'

'I wanted everyone to know I was still alive.'

'This is me you're talking to, Vartan. Own up to it! It was your way of heckling the government.'

'I wasn't in any condition to do that but . . . Oh, maybe just a little desire to provoke them . . .'

'I knew it!' Diran was triumphant.

While Aunt Arpiné and Lucie prepared the meal, the men in the living room slowly emptied the bottle of cognac. Vartan had to explain again what had happened to Maro and Tomas. Diran swore and his father gave him a scathing look.

'I'll help you bring them back to Stamboul. I can call on my friends if necessary.'

Diran had read most of Vartan's articles as well as his numerous reports and eye-witness accounts of the deportation, but he wanted to hear it first-hand.

Vartan didn't really feel like talking about the subject. 'This isn't the time, don't you agree, Uncle Mesrop?'

'You're incorrigible, Diran,' Uncle Mesrop chastised his son. 'You never know what's appropriate. Today we're celebrating our luck! We'll deal with wickedness another time.'

Diran did not bat an eyelid. He was used to reproaches from his father, but since his illness, he had stopped arguing with him. 'You're right. It can wait until tomorrow.' But he could not control himself and when Mesrop went to the kitchen he said, 'We have fish to fry. The Turks must pay for what they've done.'

'You mean the Sultan's government,' corrected Vartan. 'I owe my presence here today to several Turks.'

'Of course, I meant Talaat and his bunch.' Diran hated to be corrected. 'And speaking of the people who helped you, what ever happened to that woman in Urgup?'

'She's dead!'

'How awful!'

Aram stiffened; he found it hard to accept that Vartan was taking it so philosophically, and flared up, 'They tortured her! That's how she died!'

Vartan motioned him to be quiet but Aram was staring at Diran, who was listening intently.

'I avenged her with my dagger!' He mimicked a stabbing.

'Tell me about it.'

Diran asked Aram to sit beside him, while Vartan went to wash up for dinner. He was fascinated by the boy's story and bombarded him with questions about his family and his activities in Cappadocia. A hint of envy in his voice disclosed his longing to have been able to participate personally in the action. When Mesrop came back, Aram was talking and waving his arms about. Mesrop noticed that Aram's left hand, which he had been hiding in his pocket, was bandaged.

'Are you hurt?'

'Oh, it's nothing!'

Diran insisted on seeing his hand and Aram showed them with reluctance. Uncle Mesrop and his son were shocked. The boy's amputated fingers brought home to them all the horror stories they had heard.

'You need to go to hospital. They're infected. Didn't Vartan notice?'

'Yes, but it was more urgent to save our lives.' He rolled his fist up in the bandage again and bragged, 'It doesn't hurt that much. It can wait another day. Besides, I'm starving!'

His reply made Uncle Mesrop, who was wiping a tear away with his thumb, laugh. He patted Aram on the back. 'You're the kind of man I love. You'll soon be able to eat your fill. My wife's a very good cook.'

The table in the dining-room had been beautifully laid. They crossed themselves and Mesrop said a prayer for the ones who were absent. Lucie brought in the swordfish kebab, arranged on skewers alternately with tomatoes, peppers, bay leaves and pearl onions. Aram forgot his manners and gobbled down the food like an ogre, but no one said a word. On the contrary, Mesrop kept passing him the platter and urging him to take more. Arpiné stared at him affectionately with the motherly love she usually reserved for her own children and her nephew.

This dinner reminded Vartan that nothing had really changed. He nodded occasionally to conceal that he was listening with only half an ear. Just at that moment, Maro's absence became physically tangible to him; almost three years ago they had dined here. She had sat where Aram was sitting now. Although he was delighted to be sharing a meal with the Mesropians, he could not help being elsewhere, back in another time – the dining-room in Sivas, Tomas's birthday dinner, the music from the gramophone, Maro's marvellous voice, Tomas's radiant face as he thought about his pony hitched outside the house, Armen's, Araksi's and Azniv Hanim's worried eyes.

Lucie tenderly touched his hand. 'What are you thinking about, cousin?'

Vartan started and excused himself for his moment of absence.

'You're dead tired and we're keeping you here talking,' scolded Arpiné. 'Wouldn't you like to lie down for a while?'

'And miss talking to you, my dear aunt? Not to mention missing your fabulous dishes!' Vartan forced himself to laugh. 'Never!'

Diran told everyone Aram's story; how, armed with nothing more than a dagger, he had attacked a man armed with a pistol in order to save Vartan.

Arpiné was stunned. 'But he's so young!'

'I'm sixteen. I'm a *fedayi*!' protested Aram.

Uncle Mesrop went pale and the fork shook in his hand.

Diran whistled in admiration. 'Our future is safe in the hands of children like Aram. I propose a toast to Armenia.'

'Diran!' protested his mother. 'This isn't the proper moment.'

'*Fedayi! Fedayi!*' grumbled Mesrop. 'Violence never solved things.' He took a deep breath to settle his nerves and then lifted his glass. The others followed suit. 'I'll drink to Armenia but I want you to know that arms and violence are not the way to go. In the end, the winner will be the country that has the largest complement of competent, educated people, not the one with the largest army.'

Diran did not agree. 'How about our recent victories against the Ottoman Army on the Russian front? There, we were one against one hundred.'

His father grunted, 'Can you tell me how this handful of soldiers stopped a huge army? Was it because they were armed with better weapons? No! It was because they were inspired! The victories you're talking about only confirm what I am saying. Don't you agree, Vartan?'

Vartan shrugged. His aunt looked at him, imploring him with her eyes to intervene. He had been an umpire between his uncle and his cousin in the past and he hated it. 'I really don't understand what you two are arguing about.'

Diran pushed his plate away and drew a map on the tablecloth. 'I say we must fight for the Greater Armenia we dream of. We must not give up the Armenian provinces in Anatolia to people who have no right to them. My father thinks we should be content with the Armenia we have now – the one that used to be Russian Armenia – because he thinks that enough blood has already been spilled.'

Uncle Mesrop tapped on the table nervously. 'For the first time in five centuries we finally have a country to call our own. It doesn't matter how small it is. It's ours!'

Vartan refused to take sides. He found both arguments valid and lacked the information to be able to see clearly how events would turn out in the following months and years.

'Let's talk about something else,' pleaded Aunt Arpiné. 'Vartan and his friend have just got here.'

Mesrop and Diran agreed wryly and the conversation turned to less controversial subjects.

After dinner they decided that Aram would stay with the Mesropians in what had been Diran's room, while Vartan would stay with Diran.

No sooner had the sounds of the nightlife on la Grand-rue de Péra died down than Constantinople awoke – the needy, the craftsmen, the porters, the shopkeepers – their day would not be long enough to earn more than a pittance. The traffic noise awoke Vartan: the grinding of the cart wheels, automobiles backfiring and sounding their horns, the neighing of the horses. It took him some time to remember that he was in his cousin's new apartment.

In the semidarkness of the room a dozen pairs of eyes stared at Vartan: the photographs of prominent Armenians – officers, writers and philosophers – which his cousin had hung on the walls of the living-room. In the half-light, all those eyes seemed to stare at him. They were the only decorations in the sparsely furnished room. There was a divan where Vartan had spent the night, a mahogany table piled up with newspapers and three unmatching chairs.

Although Diran had kept him up late listening to his adventures and experiences after his arrest in Sivas, Vartan had woken up early. He was in a hurry to start working on the case of Maro and Tomas.

'*Held.*' Just exactly what did that mean? Had they arrested them in order to get him at the end? Hard to say! The most logical explanation was Maro's great beauty. Vartan shook off that thought and concentrated on the means at his disposal to liberate his family.

Diran had set the table in the dining-room next to the kitchen and Vartan joined him there. While Diran ate a large breakfast of bread, white cheese, jam and black olives, Vartan had only his usual tea. He told Diran how worried he was about his wife and son.

'Unfortunately, none of my friends can help you,' said Diran thoughtfully. 'Most of them are still in hiding from the Sultan's police. You should go see the Dean of Science at Robert College. He's the head of the Committee for Foreign Aid to the Middle East in Constantinople and can either help you or at least give you some advice.'

'I'll go there today.'

'And after that?'

'I'll take Aram to the hospital.'

'I didn't mean today. I meant in the weeks to come.'

'I don't know yet . . . until Maro and Tomas are back.'

'We need you. You're an important person, Vartan. The articles you wrote during the war have enhanced your reputation in the eyes of the Armenians.'

'And undoubtedly they have also made Vartan Balian more undesirable in the eyes of the government. Oudi Yashar, the *dervish*, is wanted for murder and I don't know if the police know that he's hiding under that name. I'm walking around with the identity papers of a Turkish friend. For the moment, I think I'd better maintain a low profile.'

'There are other ways you can help our cause.'

'We'll talk about it some other time. I'm not up to it this morning. The only thing that interests me now is to find my wife and son.'

Vartan hired a cab to take Aram to the Armenian General Hospital of Yedikoulé on the shore of the Sea of Marmara. During the long trip the boy was thrilled and astounded by the amalgam of old and new – the many different races, the automobiles and especially the women dressed in European-style clothing that showed their legs up to their calves. After they had waited for two hours in the hall crowded with sick people, a surgeon cleaned and cauterized Aram's left hand. Before leaving the hospital building, Vartan ran into Shant Takvorian, a friend from the university who was now a physician.

'We're short of personnel,' Shant told him. 'We could really use a good pharmacist. Are you free?'

Vartan was surprised and hesitated before saying, 'I'll see.'

Being overburdened with work, Shant did not have any more time to talk about it. They agreed to meet for dinner the following day.

Before getting into the cab, Vartan told his young friend, 'That jacket looks good on you.'

Aram preened like a peacock. 'So you noticed. Your aunt cut my hair, too. She's really nice to me and so is Baron Mesrop.'

'What about Cousin Lucie?' asked Vartan, just to tease him.

Aram blushed and babbled, 'Well . . . she's a . . . real lady!'

Vartan and Aram returned to Constantinople early in the afternoon and took a small steamer to Bebek, another suburb on the Bosphorus. They landed at the wharf, in front of a little public square, and continued on foot. Vartan became more impatient as they approached Robert College. He and Diran had travelled this road so many times together on their way to classes. Scraps of their heated discussions came to mind.

'It's beautiful,' said Aram, to pull Vartan out of his reverie. He was feeling ill at ease in these new surroundings and needed to hear a familiar voice. On this clear day, they had a limitless view and Vartan pointed out the hills beyond the old ramparts on the Anatolian side of the straits.

'Afyon and Urgup lie there.'

Aram swallowed and said, 'So far away!'

Vartan tapped him lightly on the shoulder. 'Don't worry. You'll be happy here.'

'Uncle Mesrop has offered me work as an apprentice in his printing shop, even though I only have one hand.'

'Is that what you want to do?'

'I don't know, but I have to earn a living.'

After passing through the gate of the American College, they left the shoreline and climbed the twisting road up to the campus. They soon arrived at a soccer field surrounded by stone buildings covered with thick ivy.

'This is my college,' gasped Vartan, out of breath. 'Would you like to study here?'

'I learned how to read and write in our village school and that's more than enough.'

'It's not enough! You're very intelligent. If you studied, you could be a professional, an important man, marry a 'real lady', as you call them.'

Aram looked proud. 'I'm already a man and I don't feel like spending years shut up in a school room.'

Vartan did not insist but promised himself to bring the subject up again some other time. While they waited in the vestibule to Washburn Hall, with its highly polished wood panelling, Aram watched the young boys who were playing soccer in front of the gymnasium. The secretary took Vartan, who had identified himself as Hakki, to Dean McGill's office. This room had remained untouched by the years – the same glassed-in oak bookcases, the same leather armchairs, the same stuffy smell. The Dean was in his fifties, silver-haired and chubby-faced. He greeted Vartan ceremoniously in Turkish, thinking his visitor in the three-piece charcoal-grey suit to be a member of the secret police or a highly-placed government official.

Vartan replied in English. 'I attended your college some years ago during the time of Dr Blake – in 1886, to be exact. Hakki Chelebi is an alias. I'm an Armenian.'

Intrigued, Professor McGill said politely, 'I'm happy to welcome an alumnus. What can I do for you, Mr . . .?'

'Balian. Vartan Balian.' McGill's slight frown showed he was familiar with the name, so Vartan continued, 'You're the head of the Near East Aid Committee, which is especially dedicated to helping our orphans. We greatly appreciate its help.'

'Our means are limited while your needs are infinite,' sighed the dean. 'Let's hope that things will get better now that the war is over!'

'Yes, finally we can hope again.' Vartan pointed to the pile of documents on the desk. 'I know your time is precious, so I'll come right to the point. I have a personal favour to ask of you. My wife and son are being held prisoners by Riza Bey, the Governor of Ayntab.'

'Prisoners?' asked the Dean, raising his eyebrows. 'Perhaps he took them in to save them from the deportation. If that's the case, he would send them to Constantinople immediately if you wrote to him. Are you sure they're prisoners?'

'Yes, I am.'

Dean McGill settled back in his chair, looked at the ceiling and rubbed his chin. 'What a deplorable situation! There are thousands of cases such as yours. It'll be a long, arduous job to reunite the families the storm has dispersed. At least your family is alive. You should thank God for that.'

'I have!' With difficulty, Vartan maintained his self-control. 'Is it asking too much to want to see them again?'

'Of course not, but I want to be frank, Mr Balian. There isn't much our committee can do. The situation in the interior is complex and unstable. We don't know exactly who's in power and who decides what.'

449

'Does this mean you can't do anything?'

'No, not exactly. One of our missionaries will pay a visit to the Vali, Riza Bey, but don't bank on the results too much. If they are being held prisoner, he'll send our envoy packing.'

'I would be eternally grateful if you give it a try.'

Dean McGill took down the pertinent names and the address of the Mesropian printing shop. 'I'll be in touch with you but please be patient. Communications are slow.' He showed Vartan to the door and shook his hand. 'If I were you, I would go to the British. They control the Ayntab region. Ask to speak to Mr David Putnam, the secretary of the embassy.'

'Thank you for your help, Dean McGill.' Only slightly disappointed and fully aware that it was not going to be easy to free his family, Vartan bade the Dean goodbye.

He found Aram staring at some oil portraits of founders of the college. 'Who are these men?'

'The one on the left is Mr Robert and the one on the right is Mr Hamlin. They founded this college so that young people like you would be able to get an education and become leaders.'

Aram made a face. 'Me? I'd rather be a revolutionary like your cousin.'

'Has he been putting ideas in your head?'

'No.'

The boy was a poor liar and Vartan resolved to read the riot act to his cousin. As they passed the terrace, which overlooked a Muslim cemetery and the old Rumelian Ramparts dominating the straits, the huge bell in front of Hamlin Hall rang to mark the end of classes.

The following morning Vartan went to the British Embassy, not far from the Galatasaray Lycée. The English had just returned to Constantinople and were still in the process of moving in. Armed soldiers guarded the trucks parked in the back garden. There was a long queue of people, most of them speaking Armenian, trying to get visas.

Vartan spoke to one of the ushers, who told him very rudely that he needed an appointment. Vartan lied and said he had been sent by Dean McGill on a most pressing matter. The usher was perplexed and decided to refer the case to a secretary. He returned a few moments later, smiling broadly, and led him to a blue-curtained waiting room where a picture of George V hung on the wall.

'The Secretary will see you as soon as he's free. May I help you in any way in the meantime? Tea? Coffee? A drink?'

Vartan declined the offer only to regret it later as he had to wait for almost an hour.

At last David Putnam arrived. He had very short greying hair and sported a red moustache. He had the walk and dry manner of a military man, but his voice was captivating and his tone courteous. He had tea served while he listened to Vartan's story attentively.

At the end he nodded and showed his sympathy with a simple, 'By Jove!' Then he pulled a silver cigarette case from his pocket. 'Cigarette?' He put his lighter away. 'So far, you have not asked for anything, but I imagine you are counting on us to get your wife and son released. Right?'

'Released?' Vartan was astounded. 'They're not criminals in jail. They've simply been kidnapped.'

'That isn't what I meant.' Putnam was embarrassed. 'Please, believe me, Mr Balian. I share your distress, as I do that of all your people.'

Vartan smiled at him to excuse his over-hasty reaction. 'Thank you, Mr Putnam. You understand my situation. I was hoping His Majesty's servants could intercede for me with the governor.'

'Of course we will. But it isn't as simple as all that. He's the governor, you know.'

Putnam's reticence surprised Vartan. 'Doesn't your army control that region?'

'Control is easy to say. We're just beginning to occupy Cilicia and our people there are walking on eggshells. The Sultan's army has not demobilized yet and the Ottoman officials are still in their posts. It's a total mess! This governor, Riza, is a powerful man and we need him.'

'Are you telling me you're going to be considerate with him?'

'Yes, I am.' Putnam smiled wanly.

Vartan grasped the arms of his chair to keep his nerves under control, but couldn't help showing his outrage. 'That man was in charge of organizing the deportation and massacres in that region and you're still going to cut a deal with him!'

Putnam motioned him to calm down. 'We have no other choice for the moment. The war criminals shall be punished, of course, as the Allies have warned the Sublime Porte from the beginning. It's up to the judges, however, to decide if Riza Bey is one of these criminals. In any case, according to our informants he protected many Armenians, among them, your wife and son.'

Vartan was seething inside but had to be diplomatic as Putnam was the only one who could help him free his family. 'I'm not interested in being Riza Bey's judge, nor am I really reproaching you for dealing with him. All I'm interested in is having my family back.'

'That's understandable, Mr Balian.' Putnam was grateful that his visitor was not going to make a scene. 'I shall personally see to it. I find it inadmissible that the governor should keep your wife captive in his harem.'

Vartan listened impassively, even though the inference hurt his self-esteem.

The Secretary continued, 'I must treat him with consideration; thus, it is out of the question to send a detachment of soldiers to free your family. We have to avoid embarrassing him in front of his own people.'

Vartan nodded. He understood Putnam's position even though it made him angry.

Putnam, understanding Vartan's dilemma, said kindly, 'The heart cannot rule where matters of state are at hand, but please bear with me, Mr Balian. After three years of waiting, a few more weeks is not the end of the world.'

Putnam stood as if at attention and held out his hand to Vartan to end the interview. 'Trust us, sir; we'll get your family back. Tell my secretary when and where we can get in touch with you.'

'Give the English a chance to show what they can do,' Diran said.

'I feel like going and taking care of it myself,' Vartan replied.

'Don't be crazy! My word! And you used to call me reckless and rash?'

Vartan didn't bother to reply. But as the weeks went by, Vartan became more and more impatient. Riza Bey had told the Committee for Aid to the Near East that he had never sheltered any Armenian woman except for a few servants who were free to leave if they so desired. The local missionary, however, had heard a rumour that the governor had a beautiful Armenian mistress for years. Vartan knew that this woman could only be Maro. The governor's mistress? He was furious but told himself that people always jumped to conclusions too quickly. As for Mr Putnam, to whom Vartan spoke every two or three days on the telephone, he swore on a stack of

Bibles he was doing everything in his power to speed things up. He explained the cause of the delay was the precarious situation in Cilicia and the difficulty in communicating.

To fill up his days, Vartan threw himself into his work, keeping busy from morning till night. At dawn, he sat down at the table he had set before the window in Diran's living-room. The only thing on the table, besides his wedding picture and a potted begonia Aunt Arpiné had given him, was a mountain of papers. He sat at his desk long before the town came to life. The cries from the street inspired and reminded him that he was writing for a vast group of readers and not for a few specialists.

The rest of the day he worked as a pharmacist in the Armenian General Hospital. There was a shortage of qualified personnel to handle the steady stream of sick and undernourished orphans, who poured in everyday from the interior of the country. Thanks to charities and the generosity of the Armenians from Constantinople, many orphanages had been established in the town and its suburbs. As a contribution to the cause, Vartan had accepted only a token salary. He had no money worries at the moment, as Uncle Mesrop had paid him a nice sum for his part in Barkev's last opium sale just before the outbreak of war.

Almost every evening Vartan joined Diran in attending meetings of several different Armenian committees. Backed up by pressure from the Allies, they had managed to make the Ottoman government officially recognize the guilt of the Ittihad in the deporting of the Armenians. As a result, the committees had more freedom to try to locate those women and children who had been forced to convert and get them back to their homes, as well as restoring a few of the properties that had been appropriated in 1915.

A committee of different nationalities, including Turks, Armenians, Greeks and Englishmen, was formed to prepare a proposal that would govern the restoration of the confiscated property. They also formed a board of inquiry to investigate the charges against those suspected of committing crimes against the Armenians. To make sure that none escaped, Diran and his associates were preparing thick dossiers on those involved to give to the judges. In addition, an Armenian delegation was preparing to go to Paris where the peace conference would be held. Their principal reason for going was to set forth the Armenians' territorial claims and ask for guarantees of protection from the Allies.

Unofficially, Vartan was deeply involved in all these projects. Since the government held him suspect because of the articles that continued to appear in the foreign press, he would have been a handicap for his countrymen's cause had he occupied an official post.

He often dreamed of Aroussiag, who would never see the Armenia she had wanted to live in. He remembered the dream she had confided to him just after they had made love. She had seen herself living in a house near the lake at Van or at the foot of Mount Ararat, two places she had seen in etchings. It was a huge house full of children and laughter – their children! Vartan's pharmacy was on the ground floor and she was keeping house and cultivating a big garden just for the fun of it. She had seen the two of them growing old together, happily surrounded by a large family and respected by one and all.

Poor Aroussiag, who had sacrificed herself for others to the end – Aroussiag, so overflowing with vitality and passion, who had spent her love on people and things like a poplar strewing its seed to the four winds – Aroussiag, cut down by an absurd fate, who would never know the joy of being a mother! Her voice silenced! Her hands stilled forever! And all because one day she had bent over a man half-dead in a ditch. Had he loved her enough? No! Not as much as she had wanted and deserved! He felt guilty for having remained silent that night in Urgup when she had told him of her dream, of their house in Armenia.

One evening, as he usually did when he had a few free moments, Vartan went to the Tokatalian Hotel close to the embassies on the main street. This hotel and the Péra Palace attracted all sorts of strange birds and was home to most of the foreigners. The doorman greeted Vartan cordially, a privilege he reserved for habitual customers only.

The hotel with its marble statues, its polished wainscotting, its chandeliers and its potted plants, had kept its old-fashioned elegance that had made it famous before the war. A few people sat in the lobby reading newspapers while waiting for someone or watching someone. Small groups had hurried whispered conversations. The bar adjacent to the lobby was even livelier – employees from the embassies, officers of all nationalities, secret agents, who were not so secret because of the way they were dressed, foreign correspondents, financiers, businessmen, arms dealers, local newspapermen and expensive prostitutes. More business was done here in one evening than in one week at the stock market. Information was bought and sold so frantically that nothing remained secret for long. Here, Vartan often gathered a great deal of information useful to the Armenian cause or for his articles.

A small orchestra was playing Viennese waltzes in the dining room and the music filtered into the bar. Vartan went in to look for William Dawson. The American journalist was easy to spot. Not only was he very tall but his clothes were loud and his style was sloppy. Vitiated by drink, he looked older than forty-six. With his elbows propped up on the bar, he was bantering with a Nordic blonde wearing a dress with a plunging neckline.

When he saw Vartan he called out, 'Don Quixote!'

Coming from this cynic, it sounded like a compliment. Vartan smiled as Dawson kissed the blonde's bare shoulder and then came over to him, carrying a bottle of champagne. They sat down at a table in the back.

Vartan handed Dawson two envelopes. 'Here are the articles.'

'We haven't even drunk a toast yet and here you are talking business already.'

Vartan lifted his glass. 'To the health of the King of the Lazy.'

'To the health of the King of the Idealists.'

Dawson examined the envelopes: one was addressed to Paris and the other to New York. He slid them into the inside pocket of his jacket.

'You lead me into temptation, as the Protestant pastors are fond of saying. Sometimes, I'm tempted to put my byline in place of yours. Don't you do anything but write, Vartan?'

'I get up with the chickens when you're getting ready to go to bed.'

'A monk!' sighed Dawson. 'I have a monk for a friend.'

In spite of his constant teasing, he admired Vartan and considered him to be one of those few sincere men who survived in a rotten world.

He held out a piece of paper. 'This is a postal order from my newspaper – to cover your expenses.'

'No! I've already told you this is my modest way of helping the Armenians. Buy me a drink and we'll be even.'

Vartan ordered a brandy for himself and a double bourbon for his friend.

'Your last article caused a lot of comments. The office was flooded with letters from the readers, asking for more details. My editor would like thirty or forty pages more from you – a history of the Armenian Question, which he'll publish in four or five instalments.'

'Wonderful. You'll have them in a few days.'

'A few days?' Dawson was flabbergasted. 'You're a shame to our profession. You'll discredit all of us. It would take me weeks to do.'

'For my family and me, it's an urgent matter.' Vartan was no longer teasing.

Dawson also became serious. 'I hope you don't nurse much hope of success.'

'I know it's going to be difficult.'

'Just look around this room at these people. What do they remind you of?'

Vartan didn't hesitate for a moment before replying, 'A reunion of greedy heirs in a lawyer's office, waiting for the will to be read!'

'Exactly! Greedy guys have come from all over the world to share in the spoils of the Ottoman Empire. Look at them! English, French, Italians, Americans, Germans, Belgians, Greeks, Jews, Arabs, Levantines, even Armenians! They're all here because they can smell a good deal.'

He pointed to two men with shaved heads. They were drinking champagne with two Turkish officials. 'Even the Bolsheviks are living it up with the people's money and you can be sure they consider each glass they buy an investment and are out for a profit. When the time comes to make important decisions, nobody will have any principles. All those beautiful promises and ideals will be forgotten. In my country we say 'money talks'.'

'I've been writing, trying to convince the politicians to keep the promises they made to the minorities in the Empire.'

'Believe me, Vartan, in the end it's the moneymen who always end up getting the politicians' attention in the name of national interests. It's something you intellectuals will never understand.'

'Life has made me plant my feet firmly on the ground a long time ago, Bill. I know the wave of sympathy we're enjoying right now will eventually subside. Time is not on our side but we haven't lost yet.'

'I certainly hope with all my heart that you're right, Vartan.' Dawson emptied his glass and looked around disdainfully. 'But just look at this scum! They would sell their own mothers for a piece of silver.'

'It doesn't bode well for the future of my country, but I'm not so sure that these people will win in the long run. One of these days I must take you to a nightclub in my neighbourhood. They're preparing a different future for Turkey there.'

'Nationalists?'

'Yes. I'd be willing to wager a bottle of bourbon there'll be a civil war here.'

After ordering another round, Dawson cleared his throat and asked as if it were of no importance to him, 'Are your friends working hard for the peace conference?'

'Yes.' Vartan was leery of Dawson's curiosity.

'How are they doing?'

Vartan was evasive. 'I don't really know.'

Dawson smiled at Vartan's prudence but wasn't in the least offended. He realized that Armenians had every right to be distrustful. 'Do you want to know what I really think, Vartan?' He opened a pack of cigarettes. 'Your people have only one unfailing ally – President Wilson.'

'He's a remarkable man.'

'Remarkable! He's more than that! He's an idealist like you, my dear Vartan!' Dawson took a sip of bourbon, puffed on his cigarette and shook his left finger at Vartan. 'And he's an idealist with power!' His tongue had become thick but he was as lucid as ever. 'Believe me, Vartan, if you really want to help your countrymen, you should go to Washington. It's there, not in Paris, that everything will be decided. Go and show your articles to the President. Meet his advisers. Testify before the senators. That's what you should do!'

This was not the first time that Dawson had voiced this opinion but such a trip seemed inconceivable to Vartan, given the circumstances.

'What's stopping you?' asked Dawson, and then answered himself contritely, 'Oh, yes, your wife!'

Vartan could see Ayntab, the town of three hills. He had been there the year before, with Pashazadé Shahir Mithad's musicians, never realizing he had been so close to Maro and Tomas!

457

# SIXTEEN

David Putnam stood in front of the window, watching something very unusual for Constantinople – a heavy snowfall that melted as soon as it hit the ground. He tapped his silver cigarette holder and the ashes fell on the rug. He was edgy, annoyed at being the bearer of bad news.

An attendant ushered in an excited Vartan Balian, who came straight to the point, 'I got your message, Mr Putnam. What news do you have?'

'Good morning, Mr Balian.' Putnam pointed to an easy-chair and took his time stubbing out his cigarette. Clasping his hands behind his back, he stood straight, gazing fixedly at the portrait of the King for a few minutes while he searched for words. 'I won't beat around the bush. Governor Riza Bey states that he has legally married your wife and she wishes to remain with him in Ayntab.'

'That's absurd! Impossible!' cried Vartan.

'Perhaps,' Putnam shrugged. 'You know your wife better than I.'

'Yes, I do and that's not like her.'

'Well . . . it *has* been three and a half years!'

Vartan leaped up suddenly with a fierce jerk. 'Mr Putnam, I will not tolerate such an insinuation!'

'I'm not insinuating anything, Mr Balian. I'm simply trying to understand. Except for you, I'm not acquainted with any of the people involved.'

Vartan waved his hand to let him know the incident had been forgotten. 'I'm also trying to understand. Did your man speak to my wife personally?'

'I really don't know. I'll ask him.'

Vartan felt somewhat reassured. 'At least now I know where I stand. Maro knows nothing about what's going on. This is proof that she's being held prisoner.'

'I suppose you're right,' said Putnam, sitting down in a chair facing

Vartan. 'Riza Bey seems to be very friendly but he's also very smart. He gives us the impression he's sitting on the fence but for the time being we need him.' He looked Vartan straight in the eyes and added, 'I'm in an awkward position, Mr Balian. You know how politics work. I cannot risk my government's interests for . . . a private matter.'

Vartan understood only too well. He sat lost in thought, stroking his moustache while he mulled things over.

Putnam could guess what was going through his mind. 'You can't, Mr Balian! If you stir up any trouble there, you can count us out! Please think about your countrymen who are returning from exile and hope to make a new life for themselves in Cilicia. That region is a powder keg. Any overt action on your part, whether it succeeds or not, could set it off.'

His words gave Vartan pause. Putnam insisted, 'In your position it's better to stay here in the city unnoticed.'

'Just what do you mean?' Vartan was astounded.

'You should know that I would not deal with anyone without checking him out first. Your articles in the western newspapers . . . Your death sentence in Sivas . . . You're still listed as a dangerous rebel with the Minister of Interior. Gani Bey . . .'

Vartan cut Putnam short, 'That bastard! He's guilty of every sort of crime against the Armenians. If it were up to us, we would bring him to justice.'

'I know, but in the meantime he *is* still powerful and he knows you are here in Constantinople and in touch with us. He's afraid to move against you here but if you go into the interior . . .'

Vartan felt trapped; once more to have to bow to the wishes of the British, who had achieved nothing in two months.

He scoffed, 'Wait some more! Is that what you're about to tell me, Mr Putnam?' In spite of Vartan's sarcasm, Putnam smiled engagingly.

'There have been new developments. Governor Riza Bey is coming here in less than two weeks – on January the twenty-seventh, to be exact. I'm going to meet him myself at the Haydar Pasha Station. Trust me. I'll find a way to convince him to free your wife and son.'

Vartan remained impassive although this news interested him highly. As he said goodbye, he said he was hopeful Putnam's personal intercession would be successful. Privately he was convinced that the mission was doomed from the start.

During the afternoon as he prepared prescriptions in the hospital, he played with the idea of kidnapping Riza Bey and exchanging him for Maro and Tomas. It would be risky, maybe impossible, and it might get the entire Constantinople police force on his back, but he could not see any other way. What had seemed too difficult at first soon became easy – every time an objection occured to him, he found an answer to it. The factor of surprise would be on his side and he would only need a few trusted helpers and a safe place to hide Riza. Vartan stayed home that evening and, with a map spread out before him, made a rough draft of his plan.

Diran came home slightly tipsy a little after midnight. 'The trials will start soon. Too bad you weren't with us tonight to celebrate.' Then he saw Vartan's downcast face and stopped smiling. 'What's wrong?'

'The English can't free Maro and Tomas. You promised to help me.'

'That's right.' He sobered up immediately and sat down astride the chair, leaning his elbows on the back. 'I'm listening.' But before Vartan could speak, he touched him on the shoulder and asked diffidently, 'Tell me, Vartan, have you ever considered that Maro really might not want to return?'

Vartan shook off Diran's hand violently, 'You're drunk!'

'I'm not drunk. I'm speaking as your brother. You've told me a thousand times that one has to consider a matter from all angles, so do that now. Has the idea ever occurred to you?'

'I refuse to even consider it. You know that isn't like Maro!'

'You're right, but . . .'

'Finish what you started to say.'

'I'm just looking at all the possibilities.' Diran spoke hesitantly. 'Riza Bey saved her and Tomas from certain death. He's a powerful man . . . He's protected her . . . She's convinced you were hanged . . . She and Tomas had to survive . . . After three years of thinking she's a widow . . . What's this man like?'

'I don't know and I don't care!' Vartan snapped.

He got up to get his tobacco pouch and the cigarette papers that were on the divan, while Diran went into the kitchen to get a bottle of mineral water. His cousin's words went round and round in his head. Put like that, it might be possible . . . even probable . . . for any woman . . . except Maro! But why should she be the exception? Simply because he could not imagine her in another man's arms?

He absent-mindedly rolled a cigarette, which was too thick at one end.

460

Aroussiag! Wasn't he still mourning for her? Hadn't he loved her, without forgetting Maro? If death had not torn her so brutally from him, he would have had to choose between his two loves. No! He could not reproach Maro for anything!

When Diran returned he found Vartan calmly smoking, looking at a map spread out on the table. He put down a glass of cognac in front of Vartan.

'I thought this more appropriate than mineral water. And now what?'

'What?'

'If Maro ever . . .'

'That's up to her to decide.' Vartan's voice was noncommittal.

His attitude satisfied Diran, who took a sip of his drink.

'But she has to be free when she makes her choice,' Vartan went on. 'And whatever happens, I want Tomas back. He's my son.'

'That's understandable.'

'I want to kidnap that bastard,' Vartan suddenly lost his calm.

Diran whistled through his teeth. 'To kidnap a governor! You don't do things in a small way, do you! Do you have a plan?'

'Yes, but you have to get me the people and the wherewithal.' He put his finger on a dot to the east of the Sea of Marmara. 'This is Adabazar. It's forty kilometres from here. The train makes a water-stop for half an hour there. At the previous stop, in Eskishehir, Riza will get a telegram informing him that the Minister of Agriculture would like to have a brief meeting with him when the train stops at Adabazar. You're going to be the Minister, Diran. You'll bring Riza Bey to the car and we'll take him with us.'

Diran looked at the map and shook his head. 'It's a bit far-fetched.'

'Why? We have every chance to succeed. Why should he suspect anything?'

Diran scratched his head. If one thought about it, Vartan was right. The governor would fall for it. The only thing that worried him was that neither of them had any experience of this sort of thing.

Vartan continued confidently, 'We'll need two cars and one of them has to be posh and shiny.'

'Have you realized how hard it is going to be just to get there? The road is practically impassable.'

'It's the last train stop before the capital. We'll need three more men and a hiding place. Can you do all of that for me?'

'Of course!' Diran never hesitated. He was becoming more and more delighted with the idea. At last, he was actually going to do something. 'I'll take care of the vehicles. I have a close friend who has two cars, which he rents out on a regular basis. I'm sure he'll want to join the party. I also know two strong guys who have plenty of pluck.'

'I'll pay them well.'

'They won't take a penny when they find out why we're doing this. They'll do it as much for the fun as to help you. They can get us some weapons.'

Wrapped up in the project, Diran was beginning to enjoy himself when Vartan warned him, 'Tell your friends we're not going to blow up a train or attack a police station. I don't want any heroics – just complete discretion. Remember, the lives of Maro and Tomas are at stake. Please find me some disciplined men with nerves of steel – no hotheads!'

'Yes, yes, I promise. What about Scutari as a place to keep him? That's a suburb of Constantinople on the Asiatic shore. Mostly Armenians live there as well as several of our supporters. A lot of them are wanted men who've been hiding there during the last few years. The police will probably comb the region around Adabazar.'

'Excellent! I knew I could count on you,' said Vartan, folding up the map. 'If all goes as planned, what will you do then? Will you call in the English once the governor is in our hands?'

'I'd prefer not to involve them. We have to arrange matters privately. Someone from the governor's residence will have to bring Maro and Tomas to Constantinople. The exchange should take place as quietly as possible.' Smiling, Vartan picked up his still-untouched glass of cognac and looked straight at his cousin.

Diran burst out laughing, 'Vartan Balian – gang leader! Who would have thought it? It's so unlike you.'

'I still don't advocate violence, but here I've been forced to take matters into my own hands.'

'Still, it's a far cry from writing newspaper articles, isn't it?'

'I've searched in vain for Maro and Tomas for over three years. Now that I know where they are, nothing is going to stop me!'

'Riza Bey is going to try to get even. Kidnapping is a criminal offence and the Western Allies have no reason to protect you from the punishment the Sultan will deal out. That means the three of you will probably have to live undercover.'

Vartan was unmoved. 'I have an idea of how to keep the police out of this. If it doesn't work, then we'll leave the country. Do you want me to count you out? I'd understand.'

'I'd rather be hung, drawn and quartered. This is Tomas and Maro we're talking about!'

Vartan hugged him. 'I hope I won't regret having embroiled you in this affair.'

'I wouldn't miss it for all the world. It's a joy to be working together again.'

Diran saw the kidnapping as another prank such as they had pulled off as students and this worried Vartan slightly. He thought he would have to keep Diran on a tight rein and direct matters with a firm hand.

That night he could not sleep because he was going over the different phases of the plan to see if he could find any loopholes, making checklists for later use. Nevertheless, he was feeling happy that, for the first time in a long time, he held his destiny in his own hands.

Papazian's car was a brand-new Renault, which could well pass for the official car of the Minister of Agriculture. It stopped at the entrance to Scutari where they had agreed to meet. At this very moment the other car was being ferried across the Bosphorus by a *mavouna*, a fishing boat with a motor. During the night Papazian's brother, who was a fisherman in Koum Kapou, a suburb on the shore of the Sea of Marmara, had brought the Renault across the same way.

Vartan stepped out to stretch his legs and so did Diran's friend, Hagop, who had been chosen to play the part of a security officer. A cold wind whistled through the bare branches of the trees alongside the road and the Sea of Marmara roared in the darkness. Papazian stayed in the car, leaning against the steering wheel as he rolled a cigarette. He opened the window to let the smoke out and looked approvingly at his friends who were crossing in front of the headlights.

'You look just like a minister with his bodyguard. Even the Sultan would be taken in.'

Hagop wore a black suit and a soft felt hat while Vartan looked very distinguished in a grey pin-stripe suit. Vartan stared at the phosphorescent crowns of the white caps in the sea and took several deep breaths to calm down before the big event. Everything had been ready for a week and each one knew exactly what they were to do. Diran had chosen his men well – Papazian, a fifty-year-old giant with a thick, drooping moustache, who was an excellent driver and so cool-headed that nothing fazed him; Hagop and Avedis, both in their thirties, who had been on the run for three years and were willing to take any risk. Vartan thought they looked like policemen, so he had decided to impersonate the minister himself. Diran would be his secretary and meet the train to escort Riza Bey to the car.

Vartan had thought of everything. A few days before he had hired a horse to get to know the road to Adabazar and the approach to the train station. He had also gone to check the place where they would keep the prisoner. Nevertheless, nerves had prevented him from getting a wink of sleep for two nights. Had the police spotted any of his men, he would have to abandon his plan. The governor might be on his guard or he might have simply taken another train. Vartan knew that failure would mean never seeing Maro and Tomas again.

Hagop interrupted his train of thought. 'What are you thinking about so hard?'

'The road's in awful condition. It would be terrible to have a breakdown.'

'Don't worry, my friend. Everything is going to be all right.'

'I'm not used to this and, besides, the lives of the two I love the most are at stake.'

By the light of Hagop's cigarette lighter Vartan could see his gaunt face, which betrayed no emotion whatsoever.

'Well, I've already taken part in several operations like this and, let me tell you, you never get used to it. The tension keeps you on your toes. You're having an attack of stage fright.'

Vartan remembered that before Hagop had joined the underground forces, he had been an actor with a great deal of stage experience.

'Do you miss the theatre?'

Hagop laughed. 'My good fellow, the world's a stage and life an endless play. We're all actors but there's no audience.'

Before Vartan could answer, an approaching car slowed down. It also belonged to Papazian, who usually rented it out complete with chauffeur to tourists who were on holiday in the city. Vartan was surprised to see Aram among the three men in the car. He was wearing a hat too big for him so it came down to his ears.

Diran got out of the driver's seat and happily declared, 'We're ready. Let's go!'

Vartan cocked his thumb at Aram. 'What's the meaning of this? Nothing was ever said about bringing him along.'

'Well, I thought he might be useful. He's quick, strong and bright. I often use him to carry a message or to shadow someone.'

Vartan was seething but kept himself under control. They couldn't very well take the boy back or leave him on the road. He opened the car door and pointed at Aram who was sitting on the front seat.

'You! You sit in the back and you stay there until we're back in Constantinople. Do you understand?'

Aram cowered and shrank even more deeply into his black overcoat.

'Do you have a gun?' asked Vartan, holding out his hand. Reluctantly, the boy produced a shiny, black Luger. 'All right, give it to Avedis.'

Aram protested, 'But it's mine!'

'Do as I tell you!'

'But I might need it,' begged Aram.

'I'll take care of you,' said Avedis, climbing into the driver's seat. He slipped the boy's gun under the seat and gave Vartan an amused smile. 'Aram's going to be a good boy, I guarantee.'

Avedis was very calm. His green eyes sparkled and he had trimmed his sideburns and waxed his moustache as if he were going to a ball. These trivial details made Vartan relax.

'I'm no child,' complained Aram sullenly as he got into the back seat.

Vartan replied gently, 'You're right. Now is the time to show it.' Vartan shook everyone's hands and returned to the Renault to join Diran.

Papazian had attached a small flag to the bonnet of the car. 'Adabazar, Your Excellency,' he teased.

Vartan was in no mood to joke but Diran humoured Papazian. 'Let's be off, my good man, and try not to get His Excellency's car too dirty.'

The muddy road was full of deep ruts because of the recent rains and the shock-absorbers screeched and whined as Papazian zigzagged, trying to avoid the worst potholes.

'It's a well-built car,' said Papazian confidently, at the same time praying silently that nothing would go wrong. Worried, he frequently looked in the rear mirror because the old car following him was being driven by a less experienced driver; however, Avedis was doing all right. Soon Papazian began to whistle but Vartan kept looking at his pocket watch.

'We have seven hours before the train is due,' said Diran understandingly.

Papazian glanced around, 'We'll be there in less than five.'

The day was wan and, on their right, the Sea of Marmara reflected the leaden sky. The countryside strewn with dilapidated cottages looked gloomy. They had to stop to change a flat tyre on Avedis's car. Papazian took advantage of the stop to fill the tanks from one of the cans of fuel they were carrying and checked the oil in the sumps. This caused a delay of more than half an hour and made him even more jumpy.

When a herd of goats further up blocked the road, Papazian exploded. Honking impatiently, he stuck his head out of the window to swear at the goat-herd who was looking open-mouthed at the horseless carriages. Vartan patted Papazian on the shoulder to calm him down as the last of the goats crossed the road. Purple-faced, the taxi driver grumbled as he gripped the steering wheel. When the road was finally clear, he let out the clutch with a jerk.

As they neared their destination, they all became more and more tense except for Vartan whose fears had dwindled. The die had been cast and, faced with the inevitable, he felt astonishingly calm, totally under control, although he still had knots in his stomach.

Papazian parked next to a fountain surrounded by almond-trees and a group of chattering, veiled women. They dispersed when they saw the official car. There was still an hour and a half to spare before the train was due – that is, if there had been no delay, which was unlikely. While Papazian and Aram were cleaning the mud-spattered Renault, Vartan went over each person's part and talked to them to keep their spirits up.

Adabazar was a small, dreary little town surrounded by rocky fields. It owed its prosperity to the railway and potatoes. As today was not a market-day, the streets were empty this cold, humid morning. The men had gathered inside the cafés where there were stoves. A huge mountain of coal hid part of the station, which was a simple rectangle made from pistachio-green boards and roofed in corrugated tin. About twenty unarmed soldiers who had probably been demobilized milled around, trying to warm themselves at a fire fed with coal destined for the locomotives. At the end of the platform where the rear of the train would be when it stopped, workers were unloading merchandise from ox-carts. Lounging against the facade of the station, two railroad employees were smoking.

The two automobiles moved closer to the platform and turned around

466

ready to leave. Papazian turned off the ignition. As they were a good distance from the road, there was little risk of being inspected by passengers and villagers. Their arrival had aroused the curiosity of the soldiers and ox-cart drivers but they kept their distance when they saw the small flag on the bonnet of the car.

Vartan rolled down the window. The wires on the telegraph poles alongside the tracks were humming in the wind. Diran took out a flask of cognac, took a swig and passed it around. They waited in silence.

After a while a carriage arrived and some passengers with suitcases got out. A mounted military guard on his way out of town saluted as he passed the Renault. Vartan took out the revolver his cousin had got for him, flipped off the safety catch and put it on the seat. He did not look at his watch but Diran had noticed his almost imperceptible movement. 'We still have a quarter of an hour.'

Farmers and young boys strolled past; others trotted by on donkeys. The seconds crept by. The train was late – fifteen minutes – half an hour – more than an hour! Would they be able to make it back to the city before midnight? Then they heard the train tooting in the distance and a black plume of smoke appeared on the horizon. Now it was only a question of waiting to see if Riza Bey was on the train. Had he received the telegram at the previous station?

Diran sighed. His face was tense as he turned to Vartan.

'Think about Maro and Tomas,' said Vartan evenly. 'It's up to us to set them free.'

Diran swallowed hard and slapped himself on the thigh. 'It's over. I'm all right.'

Now they could hear the thumping of the pistons and rods. Hagop got out of Avedis's car and stood next to the station door, ready to put anyone who might interfere out of action. Diran followed him closely and waited on the platform among the passengers.

The engine slowed down, the iron wheels screeched on the rails and the locomotive hissed steam. Vartan kept from turning around so that the governor would not see his face when he walked towards the car. Meanwhile, Papazian was monitoring the situation through the rear view mirror.

Diran asked the station-master a question and then walked over to one of the passenger cars. His palms were sweating and his heart was beating as if it would burst. He went straight to the compartment the employee had pointed out. A young, curly-haired Arab boy stuck his head out of the window, looking for someone.

'Is this Riza Bey's compartment?' asked Diran.

The boy nodded and drew his head back. The door opened and a large man in a black suit looked Diran over authoritatively. Diran bowed.

'My respects, Your Excellency.'

'*Aleykumselam.*'

'I'm His Excellency's secretary. He's waiting for you in his car.'

'Take me to him.'

The governor jumped down on the platform before Diran could lower the steps. The young Arab started to follow them but Riza Bey told him to stay with the luggage. Diran waved the curious villagers and passengers aside to clear a path for the governor. From the corner of his eye he could see that Hagop was right behind them. Every second counted! The least false move could ruin everything! Should he try to chat with the governor? Vartan had forgotten to tell him.

Finally, it was Riza Bey who spoke first, 'Do you know what the minister wants with me?'

Diran had an answer ready. 'He wanted to see you in Stamboul but he had to make an inspection tour of this region. I suppose he wants to know something about the agricultural production in your province. We're always faced with shortages.'

'I know that only too well,' said Riza Bey distractedly, looking at the car. He had never seen the model before. 'What kind of car is that?'

'A Renault, Your Excellency, made in France.'

In the car Papazian murmured, 'Get ready. They're coming.'

Vartan gripped the butt of his pistol tightly. Diran opened the door and Riza Bey started to step in.

'Your Excellency . . .'

He fell silent when he saw the barrel of the gun pointing at him and tried to step back, but Diran stopped him.

'Don't move! Not a word!' ordered Vartan.

Diran pushed the governor in, climbed in behind him, and closed the door.

Riza Bey did not realize what was happening and protested, 'You're making a mistake.'

'Silence,' ordered Diran.

The governor was looking hard at Vartan, who had proceeded to search him to make sure he wasn't armed. Suddenly the governor's eyes widened in recognition! Now he knew who his abductor was! He remained impassive, staring at Papazian's neck, but the expression that had flitted across his face had not escaped Vartan's notice.

Standing in front of the Renault, Avedis cranked the motor and Papazian took off like a bolt of lightning. The other car would follow as soon as Avedis had informed the governor's servant that his master had decided to make the last stage of his journey by car. He would have him and the luggage picked up at the Haydar Pasha Station.

Diran tied the prisoner's hands together and Riza Bey made no protest. Everything had gone according to plan; still, Vartan was on his guard and kept looking back to check. The other car was not yet in sight but, once they were out of Adabazar, Papazian slowed down so that their friends could catch up.

Riza Bey looked his kidnapper over out of the corner of his eye. Mentally, he was comparing himself with Vartan; Vartan was also observing Riza Bey with Maro in mind. He had to admit the other was good-looking and, undoubtedly, he knew how to seduce a woman with his voice and manner. Perhaps he had taken Maro by force at first but afterwards . . .? After a few months? A few years? The body gets accustomed to anything and then the heart follows. Had she fallen in love with her jailer?

Their eyes met; both being jealous, they disliked each other on sight. For convention's sake, Riza Bey started to protest, pretending he did not know Vartan's identity. 'You have no right to do this. I'm a governor. You'll rue the day! The police and the army will be on your heels. Let me go! Leave me by the roadside, and I give you my word I shall not make a formal complaint. Your crazy *coup* will come to nothing!'

'In that case, we shall die together,' answered Vartan firmly. It was exactly the same answer Riza Bey would have given had he been in Vartan's shoes. He had imagined Vartan as being slight of build and timid, since he was a pharmacist and an intellectual, but here was a bold athlete ready for anything. Then he remembered that Vartan had escaped from Bedri twice and for three years had wandered through a region where he had been a wanted man. In spite of himself, Riza Bey had to admire his daring. It was useless to try to frighten him; Riza would have to use other means. He would pose as Maro's saviour and promise to consider Vartan's demands but he would use Vartan's precarious situation to try to get the better of him.

'We're wasting time, Governor. I can see from your expression that you know exactly who I am.'

Riza smiled, 'You surprise me, Mr Balian. We had thought you dead on the scaffold in Sivas.'

Vartan did not believe a word he said and the 'we', which evidently included Maro, hurt him, but his voice stayed steady 'You must know why I've kidnapped you. I'll set you free when my wife and son are also free.'

'Free?' Riza Bey pretended to be hurt. 'They've always been free. When I rescued them, they were half dead on the road to exile. I gave them shelter, treated them like my own family. They thought they were alone in the world. Where did you expect them to go in a war-torn country?'

Vartan was not taken in by the governor's sincerity, yet he knew that Maro and Tomas had survived the deportation and all those years of war only because of this man. Could he blame Riza for not having answered the inquiries from the English? Vartan was anxious to know about Maro and Tomas but balked at the idea of asking questions that might weaken his position. Riza Bey realized this and took advantage of it to show his goodwill.

He said soberly, 'Maro is well but Tomas . . .' Here his voice broke.

Vartan cried out, 'Tomas! What's happened to him?'

'He got lost two years ago while out riding his horse. We looked for him but never found him. I'm terribly sorry.'

Vartan was stunned. He searched Riza's face to see if he was lying. Perhaps he wanted to use Tomas to blackmail Vartan, but his expression convinced Vartan that he was telling the truth. The pain was so intense he felt he was being torn apart and he had to grit his teeth to keep from moaning. Vartan's reaction frightened Riza, who added compassionately, 'I loved Tomas like a son. He was happy at my home. As Allah is my witness, I did everything in my power to find him. I had the army search for him. I offered a reward.'

Diran had been observing the countryside flow by while Papazian kept his eyes on the road, but they hadn't missed a word.

'If he were as happy as you say, why did he run away?' Vartan's tone was icy.

'He didn't run away. He went riding alone at the edge of the desert. I think nomads probably took him.'

Vartan lowered his head and fell silent. Tomas! He had thought he would see him again shortly! Tomas! So young! So small! Lost in the dessert! In whose hands? Vartan could see the faces of the orphans in the cave in Cappadocia and the small grave he had heaped stones on. His son . . . Dead? No! He would not admit it! It was inconceivable! But two years? Where was he now? What had become of him? Was he the servant of a brutal peasant? A shepherd in the Kurdistan Mountains? The slave of a camel driver? These thoughts tortured him and he trembled with impotent rage. He had found Maro, only to live with her in endless mourning.

'He can't be dead,' he whispered, not realizing he had spoken aloud.

'That is what I think too.' Riza's voice startled Vartan. 'I have the feeling Tomas is probably in an orphanage run by the missionaries. I've contacted all the ones in Malatya and Syria but have not received any word yet.'

Vartan felt Riza Bey had no right to intrude on his grief and turned on him violently. 'Just why should the missionaries hand over an Armenian boy to someone who is responsible for the suffering and death of so many Armenians?'

Riza had feared from the start that Vartan would bring this up and had his answer ready. 'That's not true, I can assure you.'

'Are you trying to make me believe you had nothing to do with the deportations?'

Knowing that some of the members of the Ittihad in Constantinople were about to be charged in courts of law, Riza thought that in comparison, his kidnapping was the easier way out. Vartan probably had connections with attorneys, so Riza's first priority was to plead his cause convincingly.

'I was a high-ranking civil servant in the government and only obeyed orders. I had nothing to do with the outrages that followed. On the contrary, I often pleaded with the Sublime Porte to put an end to it. I still have the copies of my letters. I did everything in my power to make the displacement of the population as humane as possible. Have you any idea how many Armenians I hid and protected – how many missionaries I provided with money and food to help the deportees? They all bear witness – even the bishop.'

Vartan cut him short, 'Enough! You'll have us all in tears hearing how charitable you were. How about the young woman in Urgup your man, Bedri, murdered a few months ago?'

Surprised, Riza exclaimed, 'I swear by Allah I have never heard anything about this! My aide often acts on his own and sometimes even goes against my orders. I swear on my mother's head I know nothing about it!'

Diran could feel Vartan's rage well up and motioned to Riza Bey to be quiet.

'Blindfold him,' said Papazian.

Diran pulled a big handkerchief out of his pocket and did so. He was impressed by Riza Bey's calm demeanour and speech. This man did not seem to be the violent, coarse brute everyone had been talking about; on the contrary, he seemed cultured and well-mannered. Diran preferred his enemies to be less respectable and he guessed that Riza's gentlemanly manners had been equally disconcerting for Vartan.

Night was falling. Everyone was tired from the long hours spent on the road. They had to stop to fill the tanks of the cars and then continued more slowly as the headlights were low and did not show the pot holes far enough ahead. Vartan did not say another word until they arrived at Scutari.

The cars stopped in front of the gate to the American School for Girls and turned off their headlights. The watchman, one of Diran's friends, opened the gate and guided them to the small stone house where he lived at the end of the park that surrounded the school. A stone storeroom in the cellar, which had served as a hiding place for resistance fighters wanted by the Sultan's police, was to be the governor's prison.

To make doubly sure, they chained him by the ankle to the stone wall. Only then did they remove his blindfold and bonds. He could see Vartan holding up a candle as Diran secured the chain. He glanced around quickly but saw nothing more than a straw mattress and a chamber-pot.

Unperturbed, he said, 'I'm thirsty.'

'We'll send you some water.' They closed the door and barred it.

In the dining-room Raffi was serving an ordinary white wine. Although he was hardly forty-nine, Raffi was already bald and fat. Being single, he lived happily in the house the school authorities had provided for him. He had prepared a cauldron of lentil soup and insisted they all stay for dinner.

Diran and Avedis were in a hurry to return to Constantinople. Papazian said his brother was waiting for him to drive the cars over to the European side during the night, so Vartan and Hagop, who were going to stay to watch the prisoner, drove their friends back to the gate and thanked them for their help.

'If we didn't help each other, we Armenians would never get anywhere.'

'I hope I can repay you somehow some day.'

472

Aram had had a lot of fun today. 'Do you want me to stay with you?' he asked. 'You saw how I can behave like a man.'

Vartan patted him on the back. 'I know, but go and get some rest. You've earned it.'

Diran glowed as he locked the gate. 'It's in the bag. Soon Maro will be with us again.'

When Vartan and Hagop returned to the house, Raffi had closed the curtains and was finishing his second bowl of soup.

'I didn't wait for you. I'm about to collapse,' he yawned, eyeing the divan in the lounge. 'I swear I didn't close an eye all night, I was so excited and anxious.'

Vartan admitted he had felt the same but when he said he was going to take water and food to the prisoner, Raffi was insistent that he should have something to eat first. Vartan refused.

Vartan prepared a tray and took it down to the prisoner. Riza Bey had been lying down but got up quickly when he heard the bar on the door being taken away. Vartan set the candlestick on the warped wooden table while Riza Bey took the tray, sat down on the straw mattress and set it on his knees. The food on the tray was to his taste, but he was especially touched by the addition of the glass of cognac. Vartan leaned against the wall, which had saltpetre. He rolled a cigarette and lit it from the flame of the candle. Riza lifted his glass of cognac in a silent toast and then proceeded to eat heartily while Vartan looked on.

Vartan had buried his grief about Tomas deep inside him. He must finish what he had started and arrange for Maro's release. He forced himself to ignore all the feelings his prisoner stirred up. He refused to think about this man being his wife's lover. When Riza put the tray on the floor, Vartan said aggressively, 'Your life for Maro's freedom.'

Riza was not used to ultimatums and Vartan's manner annoyed him. As much out of pride as out of self-interest, he asked, 'What makes you so sure she wants to leave my house and join you? With me, she has the kind of life you cannot offer her.'

Vartan, stung to the quick, replied, 'Do you call seclusion in a golden cage a life?'

'Security, ease, idleness, servants . . . what more could a woman ask for?'

'Freedom! Autonomy! I know Maro well enough to know she must be suffocating under her *charshaf*, bored to death in your harem.' Vartan spoke derisively on purpose.

Riza Bey stiffened but kept cool. Each one was trying to rattle the other.

'She has changed in these four years. She's no longer the woman you knew.'

'I don't believe you!'

'Don't forget she has got used to living without you like a widow who has remarried.'

'That's not like her. Maro's upbringing is totally different from yours. How could you possibly understand her?'

Riza answered indignantly, 'I was educated in Europe!'

Satisfied with having riled him and surer of himself now, Vartan smiled. 'It's up to her to decide. I will bow out if she decides to stay in Ayntab.'

Riza's face darkened and Vartan could see he already knew what the answer would be. Riza had already decided to admit defeat but he would keep on trying to thwart Vartan's plans. In any case, he must accept losing Maro if that would keep him from going into exile as had other former leaders of the Ittihad. To avoid that, he was ready to concede anything. Above all, he had to convince Vartan of his good intentions.

'All right. How will we go about making the exchange?'

'Is there someone at your home who could set Maro free if you sent a telegram? Someone who'll know the order came from you. You may use a code or something that will be known only to the two of you.'

'My mother.'

'The order must specify that the police not be informed.'

Riza winced. 'What about the censorship? The authorities will know something has happened from the contents of the telegram.'

'Yes, I know but, for some reason, the British seem to hold you in high esteem. I'm sure that in order to save your life, they'll be willing to send a coded message to Ayntab and have a decoded copy delivered to your mother.'

'I'm sure they will but I don't want to be indebted to the English. I prefer to arrange this affair just between the two of us.'

'So do I, but how?' Vartan pretended to be thinking it over and then said, 'Someone you trust could accompany my wife and hand her over in exchange for you.'

Riza Bey agreed.

Vartan added, 'I know the police will be on the alert, so I shall take all the necessary precautions. You'd better not try anything.'

'Mr Balian,' Riza declared solemnly with his hand on his heart, 'I would never do anything which would put Maro's life in danger. I love her with all my heart. I thought she was a widow and wished to marry her but, as she refused, I accepted her decision.'

Convinced he was telling the truth, Vartan stopped him with a gesture. 'What message shall I put in the telegram to let your mother know it's from you?'

'Sign it, 'Riza, your lamb of the dawn'. It's what she used to call me as a child.' Riza had been exhausted by the day's harassing events, but he felt calm. He had no doubts as to Vartan's intentions and if he manoeuvred carefully he might get out of this affair unscathed. 'Mr Balian, I would like to make a deal with you.'

'A deal! My, my!' said Vartan, getting up.

'Aren't you worried about the police hunting you down after you let me go? You and your wife will have no peace in Stamboul.'

'That's my problem!'

Riza was not discouraged by the curt answer. 'I don't want to be called to testify before the war crimes commission. I've done nothing wrong but it's never agreeable to be sitting on the bench as one of the accused. They would of course acquit me, but my reputation would always be tarnished.'

'In other words, you want me to see that your file is never to be handed over to the commission and to promise I'll never lodge a formal complaint against you. Is that what you're proposing?'

Riza smiled, 'You are quick to understand, Mr Balian. May I have a cigarette?' Vartan handed him the pouch of tobacco and the cigarette papers.

'How do you know I have any influence over those who might judge you?'

'If you, a famous Armenian journalist, take up my defence and tell them you have proof of my innocence, who would dare accuse me?'

Vartan took a minute to think it over before answering, 'What proof?'

'I can give it to you. It does exist. I'm not bluffing.'

It was a tempting proposition, especially as he was sure the governor would be acquitted by the commission if there were the slightest doubt.

'You must demonstrate your goodwill – give me a letter to the British Embassy, asking them to collaborate with me and request them, not the Ottoman government, to take care of your liberation.'

'Get me a pen and some paper and it's done.'

Vartan took the tray up to the ground floor and unearthed some paper and a pen in a dresser drawer. Riza Bey stubbed out his cigarette on the damp floor and started to write.

'Does life mean so much to you?' scoffed Vartan.

'Of course it does and I'm not ashamed of it,' said Riza without raising his eyes. 'I have three wives and ten children, including a two-year-old and a one-year-old. I have a large fortune, good health and every reason to hope for a long, happy life.' He handed the letter to Vartan. 'We're not enemies, Mr Vartan. I'm as interested as you in getting this affair straightened out quickly without snags.'

# SEVENTEEN

The next day the kidnapping of the governor of Ayntab was in the headlines of all the newspapers in the capital. Vartan, who was crossing over to Constantinople on the ferry, read the details over the shoulder of the man standing next to him, but there was nothing of note. The reporter only speculated about the motive behind the abduction. He presented two possibilities: either it was political or the kidnappers were out for the ransom money.

Diran was out, but had left a message for Vartan. The secretary of the British Embassy wanted to speak to him urgently. After shaving and changing clothes, Vartan went to the embassy, where David Putnam received him immediately. A middle-aged man holding a pipe and dressed in tweeds was already there, trying to look inconspicuous by standing back. David Putnam was obviously nervous as he introduced them, 'Mr Vartan Balian, Mr Gregory Milton.'

Milton gave Vartan a slight nod as Vartan said, 'How do you do, Mr Milton. Secret Service, I presume?'

Again Milton nodded. Without even asking Vartan to be seated, the secretary pointed an accusing finger at him. 'You're behind the kidnapping of Riza Bey!'

Vartan was amused at the secretary's outrage. 'And just what makes you think that, Mr Putnam?'

'Because you're the only one who stands to gain. Own up, confess that it's you!'

'Perhaps . . .'

Putnam raised his eyes to heaven and wrung his hands. 'Why didn't you wait for us to hand your wife over to you?'

Vartan looked slightly amused. 'Remember, Mr Putnam, you told me this was a private matter and that you could not compromise your diplomatic position, so I decided to arrange the matter privately.'

The secretary squirmed and looked furtively at Milton who was tamping down the tobacco in his pipe. He sighed, 'You're in hot water, Mr Balian, and you've made us your unwilling accomplices. Duty compels me to reveal everything to the Ottoman government.'

'But, of course. Please go ahead.' Vartan sounded very confident. 'It would be in your interests. Fair play and all that sort of thing.'

'Our interests!' exclaimed Putnam sarcastically. 'Where do our interests come into this?'

Milton sat down and asked the other two to do the same. Vartan chose an easy-chair in front of a small oval table across from Milton and Putnam.

'Could you pour us a Scotch, Mr Putnam?' asked Milton. He spoke slowly in a rasping voice.

The Secretary stiffened. His colleague's request sounded more like an order. For weeks these two men had been having a silent contest of power . . . naturally with the utmost politeness.

While Putnam filled the glasses, Milton looked Vartan straight in the eyes. 'My colleague asked you a question and I'm very interested in your answer. What do we stand to gain from your action?'

'Your intervention will earn you the good will of the Sublime Porte and, above all, Riza Bey's gratitude, who will then collaborate completely with you. He has agreed to free my wife and is counting on His Majesty's representatives to facilitate the formalities.' Vartan took the letter from Riza out of his pocket and handed it to Putnam, who had just put three glasses of whiskey and a pitcher of water on the table.

'It's in the governor's own hand,' he said, handing it to Milton.

Milton took the missive and squinted, trying to decipher the Arabic characters, before giving it back to the secretary. 'It's true. Riza Bey is asking us to help Mr Balian.'

Milton's attitude ruffled Putnam's feathers and he bit his lower lip as he read the letter.

Milton asked Vartan, 'Just what do you expect us to do?'

'Very little, Mr Milton. The governor and I have agreed to arrange matters between us amiably and without the authorities' interference. Here is a telegram for Riza Bey's mother. All I need is for you to send it to your people in Ayntab and have them deliver it to the lady. But it needs to be in code so the Ottomans do not get wind of the matter.'

'Is that all?' asked Putnam, who wanted to recover the initiative his colleague had usurped.

'Almost. You also need to inform the Ottoman government that the kidnappers, who are ordinary brigands out for the ransom money, have got in touch with you.'

The secretary shook his finger at Vartan. 'The Minister of the Interior will want to take matters into his own hands and rightly so.'

'Not if you tell him that England is prepared to pay the ransom. He's very fond of Riza Bey but, since the war has proved to be so costly, he will give you *carte blanche*. The main thing is for everyone to believe that this is a simple abduction – nothing more!'

The two Englishmen looked at each other and then Milton said, 'Once he is freed, the governor will reveal the truth.'

'Absolutely not! You have my word on it.'

'You're not going to eliminate him, are you?'

'Of course not, but Riza Bey will hold his tongue. His future depends on it. Once my wife is with me, I'll bring him to you. Then you can call a press conference and gain a nice political advantage over the French.'

From the expressions on their faces, Vartan could see they found his offer tempting but neither of them dared to take the responsibility.

'If you would like to talk this over with your other colleagues, I can wait outside.'

Putnam was relieved. 'Just give us a few minutes, Mr Balian. In the meantime, please pour yourself another Scotch.'

They were gone for at least twenty minutes but Vartan was not worried. The English had too much at stake to refuse to help.

'We've agreed to help you,' Putnam said as he came back in. 'Isn't that right, Mr Milton?'

The latter nodded and proposed a toast to the King's health. Then he finally lit the pipe he had been turning in his hands. 'We'll work with you but, if anything goes wrong, we'll deny knowing anything about it.'

Vartan had been expecting them to take this stand so he simply nodded. Then he took a piece of paper folded in four from his pocket. 'Here is what you put in the telegram.'

~❂~

Riza's abduction had caused great consternation in Ayntab. His three wives and Eminé had all reacted alike – despair, wails and tears. Even Maro was genuinely sad. At first the children cried and then began to ask questions as they could not understand how anyone would want to harm their father, but when they asked the grown-ups, they got no answers. The only one who had received the news stoically was Buyuk Hanim, who continued to run the household and would not let herself give in to her pain. She suffered in silence but put on a cheerful face for her daughters-in-law and her grandchildren. Worry kept her from sleeping at night and all day long she tried to keep calm by repeating, 'It's nothing. All they want is the ransom and, the moment we pay, they'll let Riza go' or 'The police will find him soon and then those responsible will swing from the end of a rope. After all, he is the governor!'

Whenever one of her daughters-in-law or her grandchildren wept in front of her, she became angry and told them to go and cry in their room. Not wanting to see the gloomy faces of the other members of the family, Buyuk Hanim shut herself up in Riza's office where she felt closer to him and could let her guard down. There was also a window there from which she could see the courtyard, where she expected to see a messenger arrive at any minute.

Bedri, who was still recovering from the wounds Aram had inflicted, awaited her orders in the anteroom. Three months ago Riza had put him in charge of guarding Maro to keep her from communicating with the outside world. He felt this duty was demeaning. He was convinced that, had he gone with Riza to Constantinople, nothing like this would ever have happened.

'Bedri!' Buyuk Hanim called in a commanding tone. He entered the office, which was overheated by the glowing, red-hot coals in the *mangal*. He was sure she wanted him to call the police station or the chief of police's house again. She had been doing this every hour and, as usual, she pointed at the black Bakelite telephone sitting on a corner of Riza's desk.

'See if there is any news.' For the first time the fragile old lady was showing signs of edginess. Then she pointed to a British cavalry officer who was entering the courtyard. 'Who's that?'

Bedri recognized Lieutenant Thompson, who visited Riza frequently. 'He's the liaison officer for the British in Ayntab, *Hanim*.'

'See what he wants.'

Bedri ran to the entrance door. Except for a pain in his back when he

480

moved his left arm, his wounds had had no after-effects. Thompson handed his horse to one of the servants, joined Bedri on the front steps and, in impeccable Turkish, asked to be taken to Buyuk Hanim.

'Are you bringing good news or bad?'

'Rather good,' said the Lieutenant evasively.

Buyuk Hanim pulled her veil over her face to receive her visitor. She sat impassively behind her son's desk and only her trembling voice, which had risen to a higher pitch than normal, betrayed her anxiety. Bedri went to leave but she ordered him to stay. Touched by her confidence, he moved a little back to her right.

The lieutenant bowed his head and said, 'My respects, *Hanim*.' The stifling heat was obviously bothering him for beads of perspiration appeared on his forehead.

Buyuk Hanim cut the amenities short. 'Please be brief, sir. Tell me the news.'

'Apparently your son, the governor, is well.' He pulled an envelope from the pocket of his tunic. 'I'm to give you this message.'

Bedri took the envelope and handed it to Buyuk Hanim who opened it with a mother-of-pearl letter-opener.

'Why are you bringing this to me?'

'The kidnappers contacted our embassy in Constantinople.'

She looked for the signature but there was none. The handwriting was not her son's but the final words, 'your lamb of the dawn', could have been dictated only by Riza. Lieutenant Thompson noticed that she had to move the paper back and forth to find the correct reading distance. As she read, her eyes narrowed and he guessed she was livid behind her veil.

'That woman!' she shrieked, slapping her hand down on the ink-blotter. 'The moment I saw her, I knew she spelt trouble!'

Although he was anxious to know what was happening, Bedri did not dare ask for an explanation. He looked at Thompson, who remained impassive. Buyuk Hanim's eyes darted from the letter to Thompson's face. She was breathing hard and fast, trying to hold her anger in check. There was really nothing for her to decide, as Riza's orders were perfectly clear, but she wanted to find a way to save her pride. To gain time she handed the letter to Bedri.

'Here! Read it!'

At last he was going to find out what was going on. As he scanned the message, his face turned purple. He read it again and laid it on the desk. He ground his teeth in rage. That Balian! It had to be him! Again!

'Send me, Buyuk Hanim. I'll bring Riza Bey back to you.'

She did not bother to answer him but continued to stare at the English officer. 'When does the next train leave for Stamboul?'

'In two days, *Hanim*.'

She nodded.

'Does this mean you are accepting the conditions, *Hanim*? I need to send your answer to Constantinople.'

'I have no choice. Bedri will accompany the woman.'

Unable to hide his satisfaction, Bedri asked Thompson, 'What is this Tokatalian mentioned in the message?'

'It's the name of a hotel in the capital where you are to stay until the kidnappers tell you where the exchange will take place.'

'I know how to read!'

Buyuk Hanim asked, 'Lieutenant, who else knows about this message?'

'Only our British diplomats, serving as intermediaries. We hold Riza Bey in high esteem and wish him to recover his freedom quickly.'

'Thank you,' She said in forced politeness. 'We appreciate your help. My son has ordered that neither the police nor the authorities be informed, so that is the way we will handle this matter.'

'Discretion is the basis of our profession, *Hanim*.'

'I don't want it known that all this has happened because of an infidel,' she grumbled.

The lieutenant checked an impulse to smile. 'The official version will state that it was an abduction for ransom.'

He was in a hurry to leave as he was sweating profusely, so he pretended he had another appointment and could not stay to have the cup of coffee that Buyuk Hanim, in accordance with etiquette, had offered him.

When she and Bedri were alone, she said, 'Not a word to anyone. I will reassure Riza's wives and children without revealing the truth but I don't want Maro to know anything until the last moment.'

'It shall be done as you wish, Buyuk Hanim.'

'Bedri,' – she had never sounded so friendly before – 'you've been in Riza Bey's service for many years. You're like a friend to him and will follow his instructions to the letter. I know I can count on you.'

Putting his hand over his heart and bowing deeply, he said, 'Your wish is my command, Buyuk Hanim.'

She propped herself back in the chair, closed her eyes and sighed deeply as Bedri slipped out silently.

'*Anné*, look!' Nourhan ran up to his mother to show her an Arab letter he had just drawn. She was shocked because, for a moment, she had thought he was Tomas. Memories of her past life returned sharply and the present seemed unreal. They were in the room where Maro used to teach the children.

'*Anné*!' The toddler shook the sheet of paper in front of her eyes.

Startled, Maro smiled as she looked at Nourhan's drawing. He was only two and a half but he had this astonishing ability to copy exactly the letters of the inscriptions from the Quran painted on the walls. He could even copy the intricate motifs of the Persian carpets.

'It's very pretty, my love,' said Maro, leaning down to kiss him. He went back to his crayons on the floor. To her, his resemblance to Tomas was uncanny, but perhaps Maro's eyes were playing tricks on her, as everyone said he was the spitting image of Riza Bey.

The pain of losing Tomas overwhelmed her again. Against all reason, Maro still had hope. Eminé encouraged her, as she had read in her coffee cups that Tomas was all right. Maro had hoped that with the end of the war it would be easier to find him. She would have liked to comb the region for him herself, or at least contact the missionaries or the victorious armies to make inquiries, but Riza had forbidden her to do such things. He was taking care of all the necessary steps himself, insisting that his post as governor made it easier for him.

A bolt of lightning struck near by and Nourhan flew into his mother's arms, burying his face in her skirt. She picked him up and lovingly caressed his cheeks. 'Don't be afraid my love,' she whispered in his ear. 'I'll protect you.'

As soon as he felt his mother's arms around him, he stopped trembling. At that moment, Zehra, the young servant girl, opened the door and announced, 'Maro Hanim, Buyuk Hanim is asking for you.'

Maro got up.

'Where are you going, *Anné*?'

'To see your grandmother,' she said, ruffling his hair as she left. 'I won't be long. You stay here with Zehra. Isn't she beautiful? She'll play with you until I return.'

She walked to Riza Bey's office and noticed that Buyuk Hanim was talking to Bedri in the hall. The man was wearing a mackintosh.

'You called me, Buyuk Hanim?'

The old lady screwed up her eyes as she spat out, 'You're leaving!'

'I beg your pardon?' Maro did not understand.

'You're leaving this house! This minute!'

Dumb struck, Maro said, 'But . . .'

'No buts! That's it!' Her tone was caustic. 'You're going to Constantinople to join your husband. It was he, that son of a bitch, who kidnapped Riza.'

Maro was stunned. She simply could not comprehend what was happening. Buyuk Hanim signalled Ayla, who was standing near the dining-room door. The young Armenian girl, who had served Maro for over three years and loved her like a mother, was in tears. She was carrying a coat folded over her left arm and in her right hand a suitcase holding Maro's personal effects. When she saw the suitcase, Maro's reaction was swift and sharp.

'What about Nourhan?' she said, pointing to the door which led to the classroom.

'He stays! He's Riza's son!'

'He is also my son! Mine!'

'That's enough!'

'I won't leave without him!' said Maro vehemently.

She tried to return to get Nourhan but Bedri barred the way, menacing her with his fist and roaring, 'Get ready! We're leaving now!'

Falling on her knees, Maro begged Buyuk Hanim, 'You can't do this to me, Buyuk Hanim. You're a mother, too. You must understand how I feel. You can't take Nourhan away from me when I've already lost Tomas.'

She tried to catch Buyuk Hanim's hands but the old woman stepped back in disgust and turned to Bedri, saying, 'Take her away!'

Bedri caught her around the waist. She fought him and, terrified, screamed for Nourhan. Bedri picked her up and carried her away still screaming. Buyuk Hanim went to the room where her daughters-in-law were, to make sure they did not interfere.

'Bring her things,' Bedri ordered the young servant, as he went out the door, struggling to hold on to her. She continued to scream. In the pouring rain, he threw her into a waiting carriage and climbed in after her. As she tried to open the door on the other side, he grabbed her and forced her to sit down. She continued to yell and howl for Nourhan. Bedri slapped her across the face, stunning her. Shaking with rage and pain, Ayla threw the coat and suitcase on the floor of the carriage and fled into the house. The coachman cracked the whip and the team of horses hurtled forward with the carriage. All around them lightning flashed and thunder crashed.

For days the train carried Maro away from Nourhan – from the place where she was sure Tomas must also be. Her pain grew with each turn of the wheels. She had no more tears and had withdrawn behind a wall of silence to escape Bedri's mocking look.

The baleful whistle of the train-call pierced the air. What had she done for God to condemn her to lose those she loved so much? She felt as if her life had been one tragedy after another. How was she going to get the strength to go on living? How was she going to begin again as they would expect her to? She sat huddled at the far end of the seat, looking tiny in the bulky black dress that covered her from head to foot. The brown *charshaf* covering her head and face made her look like any other veiled woman – all eyes and hands. Worn out, she closed her eyes, wanting never to awaken.

Bedri had reserved a compartment so he could guard her more closely. He despised her and rejoiced to see her suffer. He could not have said exactly why, but he had hated her ever since she first entered his master's tent after he had stopped the gendarmes from raping her. She was nothing more than an Armenian whore who had opened her legs to save herself and her son. She had used her wiles to win Riza's heart and become the mistress of a governor.

The train jolted, Maro's head moved and her *charshaf* fell down, uncovering her head. Even though she was deathly pale and wore no make-up or jewellery, she was still extraordinarily beautiful. Bedri looked her over at his leisure as he had rarely been able to do before – her long, curved eyelashes . . . her velvety, rounded cheeks . . . her narrow, slightly up-turned nose . . . that mouth with lips that tempted one to bite them. He suddenly knew he hated her because she was so beautiful and she could never be his! To get her, he would have had to rape her with the others in front of Riza's tent. Her presence in Ayntab had been a constant reminder that he would

485

never be the respectable, rich master but always the servant who bowed to the master and wielded just a trace more power than other servants. For Riza, the honours and the beautiful women – for him, the dirty work and the farm girls! It was all a matter of birthright . . .!

The tears and shadows under her eyes only added to Maro's insolent splendour. Her pouting mouth looked disdainful to Bedri and his resentment grew. He felt like throwing her on the floor between the seats and taking her by force to humiliate her – to make her feel like a deportee again, only good enough to satisfy the lust of brutal soldiers. The idea excited him and he toyed with it for a few minutes. However, the fear that Riza Bey might find out and punish him stopped him. Once more he had to abase himself, and his rancour towards Maro grew.

The train stopped for lunch at the station in Afyon Karahisar. Maro leaned out of the window to look at the town where she had been married almost twelve years earlier. She searched for a familiar face among those gathered on the platform. Assailed by memories, she sank back against the black leather seat.

The street vendors rushed to the train with their baskets full of food and went from window to window, offering their merchandise. Bedri bought bread, cheese, fruit and mineral water. He was furious. The town reminded him not only of that fellow who had wounded him but also of the chance he had missed to get rid of Maro's husband.

'We're not getting off the train,' he stated.

'But I need to relieve myself,' begged Maro.

Bedri opened his jacket to show her the revolver he carried in a holster. 'If you try to escape, I'll gladly shoot you down,' he said sullenly and escorted her to the ladies' toilet. While he waited outside the door, he smoked one of the cigars he had filched from his master's desk. As they walked back, he bought some tobacco and a newspaper to read in the compartment.

Maro could not eat but took a few sips of mineral water. That taste! It tasted like the water on the Balians' land.

Since she had arrived at Riza Bey's, she had been dreaming of taking Tomas to her relatives' home in Constantinople, but now she felt as if she were being deported all over again. She was leaving everything that was important to her – one son, the memory of another and the man who loved her. As the train pulled away, she trembled to think that they were half way

486

there. She was toppling into another life – not returning to a past peopled with those she loved. That past was gone forever in the turmoil of exile and war. She was entering an uncertain future and the unknown stretched before her.

Vartan could not be the same after all these years. He would have changed. What had he become? And what about herself? She was still his wife, but the long separation . . . Maro could not see how they were going to be able to take up where they had left off. She could not help imagining that Vartan would judge her. She was going to him, empty-handed, without their son and desolate because her son by another man had been torn from her . . . with her body soiled from the smell and caresses of this other man . . . guilty but at the same time innocent. Was she really innocent? For the first time Maro wondered if she had loved Riza and found no answer.

Weighed down by worries, she huddled in a corner opposite the window. Nothing was clear. Perhaps it would have been simpler if she had stayed in the mansion in Ayntab until the end of her days, where she would have always felt like a victim but where she would have had Nourhan to love. There she would also have been able to love Tomas as she waited for him to return. Although the two boys were very different, they seemed to have somehow fused together in her heart. She wept silently.

Bedri, who was gulping *raki* from a bottle, asked, 'Why are you crying – because you've found your husband again or because you're losing Riza Bey?'

Maro remained impassive, while Bedri burst into vulgar laughter. 'The two husbands meeting! Ah! That will be something! I'm glad I won't miss it. The tender wife who has been the mistress of the other and even given him a child. Tell me, did you feel pleasure with Riza Bey?'

He laughed again. Maro pulled her *charshaf* to hide from his gaze.

'If it's any consolation to you, your husband didn't deprive himself either. He had a woman in Urgup, a widow called Halidé who was an Armenian like you. Her real name was Aroussiag. She was younger than you – prettier, too – much prettier! She had a body like a real *houri*.' He chortled as he rolled a cigarette. 'How lovely it's going to be to see the three of you finally reunited!'

From the window of the Tokatalian Hotel, Maro could not believe she was really looking down on la Grand-rue de Péra. She found it hard to recognize, although the buildings were the same as during her last visit in 1913. It must be because of all those European automobiles, those gaudy billboards and the luxurious shops. It was all so modern compared with everyday life inside the *konak*, which went along with the rhythm of the past century and traditions that were even older. Try as she might, Maro could not shake off its dream-like atmosphere. She felt as if she had been transported here by magic, as in the tales that Safiyé had loved to read.

Bedri's voice brought her back to reality. 'If your husband doesn't get in touch with me soon, we shall have to sleep in the same bed, my beautiful one.'

She continued to stare out the window without deigning to answer. Bedri had rented only one room because he did not want her out of his sight. Since he expected some attempt at foul play, he had ordered lunch to be served in their room. His instructions said a car would come to fetch them at the hotel and take them to the place where the exchange would be made. He chain-smoked nervously. He would have preferred to have the police standing by, but Buyuk Hanim had specifically forbidden it. He would have to act on his own and improvise according to the circumstances.

Night fell and Bedri began to think the exchange would not take place until the next day but then a bellboy in red livery knocked on the door and said that they had a visitor downstairs. Bedri checked his gun and put on his raincoat. Maro wound the *charshaf* around her head.

As they went through the door, Bedri warned her, 'If you behave like a lamb, everything will be all right.'

He took her wrist and followed the bellboy down the hall to where Avedis was leaning against a pillar near the entrance. Avedis asked Maro to raise her veil so he could make sure it was her. He compared her appearance with a photograph Vartan had given him and seemed satisfied.

'Follow me.'

'Where are we going?' asked Bedri.

Not bothering to answer him, Avedis walked towards the entrance and Bedri followed close behind, tightening his grip on Maro's wrist. He unbuttoned his coat just in case.

Once they were out on the pavement, Avedis signalled to a car parked nearby. Bedri and Maro got in the back while Avedis sat in the front beside the driver, Papazian, who drove up the street rapidly to Taksim Square and then turned towards the Harbiyé Quarter. Bedri looked out the window with tense concentration, trying to memorize the route they were taking.

Harbiyé! The place where the Mesropians lived. Just the thought of seeing Vartan again made Maro panic. Since she had arrived in Constantinople, all her thoughts had been concentrated on her husband, but her joy was tempered by apprehension. In this town where her love had been born and flourished, where they had known complete intimacy, she now felt as if she were on the way to meet a complete stranger.

Night had fallen and the dew lay heavy under the trees in the Armenian Cemetery of Shishli, which stood near the Bulgarian hospital a few kilometres from the Harbiyé Quarter. Vartan had chosen this lonely site in the middle of deserted fields because it was isolated and safe. Diran knew the watchman who lived in one of the buildings by the gate.

To protect themselves from the wind, Vartan and Riza Bey had taken shelter behind a white marble tomb. Angels with outspread wings knelt on its pediment. Hagop had turned off the headlights and was parked about ten metres away in the central avenue. Diran and Aram had posted themselves behind the tombstones. They were armed in case of trouble. Vartan could hear the wind blowing through the branches of the cypress trees lined up along the surrounding wall. According to a legend from pagan times, this sound held supernatural powers.

'May I smoke?' whispered Riza Bey. He was very superstitious and this theatrical setting made him nervous.

'Feel free.' Vartan had not considered it necessary to tie his prisoner up. Riza Bey took a cigarette from his case and offered Vartan one. Vartan took it, lit it and offered his lighter to Riza.

'Keep it. It's yours. I took it from you in Adabazar.'

'Thank you. It's a keepsake.'

Both times that Vartan had visited his prisoner, their cool politeness had been tempered by mutual respect. Riza did not inspire hate or spite in Vartan, only overwhelming jealousy. For Riza, Vartan's course of action was right and just. He had finally come to terms with his loss, although he still suffered. The waiting seemed endless as both of them thought about the same woman. Riza knew it would be the last time he would see her and Vartan was not sure how she would feel about him.

'Tell me about Tomas.'

Surprised, Riza took a few seconds to answer. 'I have a son called Kenan who is the same age. They were like brothers. Both of them often rode with

489

me. I gave a small thoroughbred to Tomas and he quickly became an accomplished horseman. He is strong, handsome and very intelligent. I'm sure he will . . .' He paused as the sound of a whistle split the night.

The watchman was announcing the arrival of a car. They could hear the squeaking of the gate and the rumble of the motor and then saw the headlights shining on the pale crosses, gravestones and tombs amongst the dark tree trunks.

'Don't try anything,' said Vartan as he gently pushed Riza towards the avenue. The car came to a stop about ten metres from the other car. Papazian turned off the motor but left the headlights on. Bedri got down, holding a gun in one hand and dragging Maro, who was carrying her suitcase.

Someone in front of them shouted, 'Keep walking!'

Maro recognized Vartan's voice and her heart pounded. She could see two men standing in the beam of light. It took her a fraction of a second to tell them apart as they were both the same height and the colour of their hair and dark clothing made them look alike. Seeing them together gave Maro a shock and she felt her knees buckle.

Bedri stood still, gripping Maro's left arm and holding her in front of him as a shield. He put his gun to her head. The scars on his back hurt him but he blamed the damp. Avedis, who had stayed in the car, flipped the safety catch off his pistol, ready to intervene. Aram shook with rage when he recognized the man who had killed Aroussiag! The one he had missed killing! As he aimed his gun at Bedri's head, his finger trembled on the trigger.

Diran, who was standing behind a gravestone on the other side of the path, hissed, 'Come closer, you son of a bitch.' He couldn't see if the veiled figure was Maro or not.

The wind stirred in the cypress trees and the tension rose. One false step, one brusque movement and there would be a shoot-out.

'Keep walking,' ordered Vartan again.

Bedri pushed Maro in front of him. Vartan, blinded by the headlights, could only see only the outlines of two figures but he recognized Maro from the way she moved – the slight sway of her hips. He was even more nervous than he had been when they had kidnapped Riza Bey.

Maro walked slowly over the shiny gravel because Bedri kept pulling her back. She could feel two pairs of eyes fixed on her and they frightened her. It was her life at stake, and yet she didn't have her word to say.

'That's far enough!' exclaimed Vartan in a commanding tone. Bedri stopped, his finger still on the trigger. He tore the veil from Maro and threw it on the ground. Even in the dark, Vartan could see how pale she was. She was even more beautiful than he remembered. She took his breath away.

'Let her go!' he ordered. 'Your master is free!'

Bedri obeyed. As Riza approached, Vartan stood in front of him, blocking Maro's view of the man who had been her protector and lover for more than three years. But then they were face to face. Forgotten for now were the times Riza had been harsh with her – forgotten the times she had felt as if she were his prisoner – forgotten the times he had kept her from getting in touch with her family – nothing counted except for his affection and the tenderness he had shown Tomas. They looked at each other and she saw infinite sadness in his eyes.

When he noticed their hesitation, Vartan's throat tightened. Were they talking? He was too far away to hear, nor could he see them properly in the blinding glare of the headlights, but he thought he had seen Maro bite her lip and his blood ran cold.

Maro stood still and gasped, 'Nourhan!'

'Every time I look at him, I shall remember you,' said Riza, looking into her eyes.

She could not bear the sadness in his look and walked on. One more step and it would all be over. She turned her back on the past and went to Vartan, who was as jittery as she. He put his arm around her, took her suitcase and led her to the car.

Riza Bey was blocking Bedri's view. Bedri shouted for him to get down, raised his gun and aimed.

'No!' shouted Riza and stepped in front of Bedri, but Bedri stepped aside ready to fire. A shot rang out! Maro screamed. Vartan tried to stop her from turning around, but she did so. Aram had shot Bedri in the head and he had fallen at Riza Bey's feet.

'Riza Bey is all right,' said Vartan. 'Come. It's none of our business any more.' He made her get in the back seat and sat next to her. Maro laid her head on his chest and closed her eyes so as not to have to see.

Their car passed Riza and the others standing around Bedri's body. Riza was sorry that Bedri was dead. At the same time he was seething with rage about what Bedri had tried to do. He ordered the others to get rid of the body.

Vartan signalled Hagop to keep moving.

491

# EIGHTEEN

The noisy motor of Hagop's car shattered the silence in the sleeping neighbourhood of Harbiyé. Vartan's simple touch was already more than Maro could bear and her skin burnt under his fingers as she buried her face in the hollow of his neck. The driver's presence gave them a good excuse to keep silent. Neither of them would have been able to find the appropriate words. Both of them realized that their reunion would be even more difficult than they had ever imagined.

Hagop dropped them off at the narrow street where Vartan had rented an apartment after his return to Constantinople. After thanking Hagop and saying goodbye, they found themselves standing on the deserted pavement in the dim circle of light cast by the gas lamp. Only now were they able to get a good look at each other. A lump formed in Maro's throat as she gazed at Vartan. She thought he had aged a little, but the silver at his temples, the crow's feet at the corners of his eyes, his receding hairline and his gaunt face only accentuated his manliness. His grey eyes seemed paler than before but their kind look gave him a gentleness that had been lacking in his youth. Hard to believe that only four years had passed!

'Tomas . . .' she hesitated.

'I know,' He said calmly. He wanted to look at her without the interference of words. He had forgotten how fragile she looked, which was why everybody had always wanted to protect her. Perhaps this was why she had survived the deportation when many stronger men and women had not. Her grave, forlorn look made her even more stunningly attractive. Vartan wanted to hold her close and kiss her but a strange embarrassment stopped him; perhaps he sensed her reticence.

He tried to cover up his confusion. 'I have a list of all the orphanages in the Near East and have already begun making inquiries about Tomas.'

'He's alive! I feel it in my bones! We'll find him.' Her voice trembled.

'Yes, we shall find him!'

They opened a freshly varnished door and Vartan followed her up the narrow steps. The small flame of a gas lamp flickered on the landing, casting shadows. Maro struggled up in her heavy oriental cloak, which made her look even smaller than she was. When they reached the third floor he put his hand on her shoulder, turned her around and searched for her lips in vain for she pressed herself against him and hid her face against his collar.

'I can't believe it's really you!' She had been about to say, but stopped herself, thinking it too forward; then added in the same intimate tone, 'I had almost lost hope.'

'I've never stopped looking for you. I found out from Widow Kaloustian that you and Tomas had been taken away by a government official.'

Vartan felt her stiffen defensively and hastened to reassure her. 'How lucky that you were spared from going with the caravan all the way to Syria.'

Certain now that Vartan would never reproach her for anything, she relaxed.

'You must be dead tired. Let's go in.'

Vartan picked up the kerosene lamp lighting the entrance hall from the console and raised the wick to keep it from smoking. The hall held only the barest minimum of furniture and no pictures hung on the recently whitewashed walls.

'I know it still looks very bare,' apologized Vartan. He carried the lamp into the next room, saying, 'This is the living-room.'

Maro followed him. 'How are the Mesropians?'

'Very well and eager to see you.'

'I tried to send them a letter three times but I'm sure they never got any of them. And your brother?'

'He and Dirouhi fled to Jerusalem. They'll be coming back soon.'

The living-room had a wine-coloured velvet divan, an easy-chair and a pouffe on which lay an *oud*. Next to the window stood a table, which served as a desk and was half covered with books and papers.

Maro dreamily ran her fingers across the strings of the *oud*. 'Do you still play?'

'I was a musician with a troupe of travelling *dervishes* for the last three years. I even went through Ayntab!'

She stepped aside without commenting and Vartan continued to show her around. There was also a kitchen and a bathroom. Vartan opened the door to one of the bedrooms, which held a narrow bed and a night table.

'I got this ready before I knew about Tomas.'

Maro took the suitcase from him, pulled out a crushed captain's cap and shook it to give it shape again.

Surprised, Vartan held out his hand. 'Isn't that Armen's cap?'

'Yes, it is. Tomas always kept it by his bed. It was precious to him.'

Vartan touched the cap reverently. 'Armen . . . How did he die?'

'Trying to stop a brigand from carrying me off.' She stared at the cap, which Vartan was turning around in his hand, and added very quietly, 'Then Araksi died and then my mother, too. It was awful, Vartan.'

He stroked her cheek gently. 'I know. You've been terribly brave.'

She thought of the tragic loss of Tomas, of the pain she was feeling from the loss of Nourhan, and knew she would need still more courage.

Talking about the deportation had clearly saddened her and Vartan decided never to bring the subject up again. He put the cap on Tomas's bed and closed the door.

Their bedroom was the same size as the living room and received the morning sun through the window that opened onto an inner courtyard. A red geranium with only one small flower was crammed into a pot on the window sill. Maro walked to the night table on which stood their wedding picture.

'It was Arpiné's,' explained Vartan.

Maro picked it up and stared at it for a long time. Lord, how young they had been! So innocent! Completely ignorant of what the future held in store for them! What she wouldn't give to turn back the clock!

'We'll go on with our lives where we left off,' Vartan told her. She nodded but wondered how they were going to do that. 'As soon as we find Tomas again, everything will be like it was before,' he insisted.

Did he really believe that or was he trying to convince himself? Maro knew she could never erase what had happened. She could never forget. Must she pretend she had? She put the photograph down and went to the walnut dressing-table upon which lay a straight razor, a shaving-brush and a soap dish. For a split second she saw Vartan shaving as he had done the morning of the day he was arrested. When she looked up, she saw his reflection in the mirror and felt embarrassed to be with him in the same room – it was worse than on their wedding night. In vain she kept on repeating to herself they had been man and wife for eight years. He still seemed a stranger!

Vartan had stood aside discreetly to let her explore the room. 'Are you hungry?'

'No, thank you.'

'Thirsty?'

'Perhaps.'

'A drink, a cup of tea?'

'Tea, please.'

'I'll heat some water for you to wash up.'

She turned away so he would not see her blush. He opened the wardrobe. 'Lucie helped me buy some dresses and shoes for you. You'll find some other things in the drawers.'

His thoughtfulness touched Maro and, for the first time since she had arrived, she smiled. 'That was nice of you!' She pinched the thick material of the oriental cloak she was wearing. 'I'll take this off.'

Vartan thought she wanted to be alone to change and told her he would wait for her in the living room. He stirred up the embers in the cold stove and waited for the water to boil. He went over what they had said since Maro had gotten into the car. Only banal phrases! He had not imagined their reunion this way but perhaps it could not have been otherwise. Just as bewildered as she was, he felt crippled, shy and awkward. Perhaps these trite sentences were necessary to dam the flood of contradictory, overwhelming emotions. It would take a lot of patience and skill to resume their relationship and they would need these ordinary sentences to fill their conversations until they had acquired new ones with the passing of the days . . . and the nights . . . Maro was no longer his wife – only a woman he had once loved – one he still loved and had to court again.

Vartan was sitting on the edge of the chair, playing his *oud* softly when Maro came in dressed in a sky-blue *crêpe-de-Chine* dressing gown. She paused shyly in the doorway. Her wavy hair lay on her shoulders and framed her lovely face. To put her at ease, Vartan did not raise his eyes. She sat on the sofa and took the cup of steaming tea.

'I've been working at the Yedikoulé Armenian General Hospital,' said Vartan, 'and I help out at one of the orphanages.'

Inconsequential words! Good for the occasion! He pointed at the table in front of the window and, sounding slightly guilty, added, 'Of course, I've also been writing articles for the foreign press.'

'Could they use me in the orphanage? I don't want to be idle while we wait.'

'Of course. There's a lot to do. Waiting? For what?'

'Tomas's return, of course. Have you written everywhere? To Syria? To Palestine? To Persia?'

'And to Cyprus! And to Egypt! But the list is long and I still haven't reached the end.'

'I can help. I'll start tomorrow.'

'Tomorrow Aunt Arpiné and Uncle Mesrop are expecting us for dinner.'

She nodded and then asked in a tone that showed how much she needed to be reassured, 'Our son will come back to us, Vartan, won't he?'

'Yes, Maro, our son will come back!' Knowing she felt guilty, he added, 'It's not your fault. You could not possibly have kept him in sight all the time.'

She lowered her eyes and did not answer. He played a little louder – an Armenian air from his repertoire – a melody she had loved and always asked him to play. They looked at each other in a silent dialogue that drew them closer without moving. Very slowly Maro became used to Vartan's tender, loving look, which, at first, had made her feel panic, but her eyes still remained those of a terrified animal. Vartan laid the *oud* on the floor and went to sit next to Maro; then he impulsively drew her into his arms and kissed her passionately on the mouth. Surprised, she let him kiss her but did not respond. Vartan was seized with the desire to take her there and then and thus to efface the memory of the other man. But Maro began to tremble and perceiving her terror, Vartan restrained himself.

He broke their contact and murmured, 'I love you, Maro.'

'I love you too, Vartan,' she whispered.

When he joined her in their bedroom, she was already in bed, holding the eiderdown up to her chin. As he lifted the sheet to slide in beside her, he noticed that, instead of the silk night gown with the lace *décolleté* he had bought for her with this night in mind, Maro had put on the comfortable fluffy flannel one. Her eyes were red from crying and the message was clear. Vartan looked at her sideways and noticed she was wearing a silver medallion – the one he had bought for her in a small jewellery shop on the main street of Péra soon after their marriage. Vartan touched it, marvelling that such a sentimental trinket had survived all these years.

'That's all that's left from Sivas.'

'No, it isn't. There are the two of us – and Tomas! We are beginning all over again and it will be even better than before.'

She tried to look convinced and nodded. He bent over and kissed her lightly on the lips. 'Let's go to sleep. It's been a long, hard day.' He blew out the lamp and turned over on his back.

Maro, relieved he had not insisted, interlaced her fingers with his. 'Good night, Vartan.'

'Good night, my darling.'

She could feel the warmth of his sinewy body through the thick blankets. Lying there in the dark, she was filled with the inner peace of being safe but did not dare abandon herself to it for fear that it might vanish. She knew no harm would ever come to her from him but fear and distrust had become so firmly rooted in her that she could not let her guard down yet.

Images of Riza came to mind. Not the confident, proud face of the governor, nor the arrogant lover who forced her to submit to him, but the beaten man she had glimpsed as she passed by him in the cemetery. She did not feel sorry for him, although she had thought she loved him. She simply felt indifferent towards him. Her complicated feelings for him had been swept away the very moment she had ceased to be in his power. Love? No! Only a passion, which he had nurtured by creating ties, which had kept her completely dependent and which had been reinforced by setting the rules of the game: restraint and reward, harshness and tenderness. He had enclosed her in a dream-like bubble, a bubble which had just burst! Maro could not deny what had happened but she now knew there was nothing between her and Riza. From the moment he had seduced her in the olive grove, she had lived one day at a time, all of them blurring together. Only through Tomas, Nourhan, Safiyé and his other wives, Eminé, and even Buyuk Hanim did her stay in Ayntab have any anchors in time. Her relationship with Riza was on another plane – in another time. It might have lasted twenty days or twenty years. Relieved, she realized she would never miss him, but Nourhan . . .

As Vartan had foreseen, the newspapers in Constantinople had nothing but praise for the way the British had handled the release of the governor of Ayntab. Riza Bey seemed to be keeping his word too. There were many rumours about bandits and ransom but no mention of Bedri's death. Vartan supposed that the incident was closed unless, of course, Riza had informed the police in which case there would be trouble, but he could take care of that quickly.

When Vartan came home from the hospital, he gazed admiringly at Maro, who was dressed in an apple-green dress that revealed her ankles and part of her calves. The post-war fashion with its high waist and straight lines suited her.

'You look wonderful!'

A hint of a smile barely concealed her anxiety. In spite of her reserve and distant attitude, Maro seemed to be happy that he had come home and that was enough for Vartan for the first day. He would draw on his reserves of patience. He kissed her on the cheek and asked what was new. She pointed to the pile of envelopes on the corner of his work table.

'I've finished the list but did not dare go out to post them.' She hesitated for a moment and then added, 'It's stupid but the town scares me.'

He regarded her tenderly, 'We'll conquer Constantinople together. I'm free tomorrow. If you feel like it, we'll go to several of the embassies and to the Committee for Aid to the Armenians to see if there is any news about Tomas.'

'I'd like that.'

Maro held on to Vartan's arm firmly. She felt insecure in this neighbourhood that had once been so familiar to her. She had lost the habit of being free and found it hard to believe she could now do anything and go as she pleased.

'We're early. Let's take a detour.'

Vartan obliged. The setting sun flashed orange on the upper-storey windows; a flock of pigeons fluttered over the street. They took the boulevard that led to Taksim Square and stood in front of the military school, which was surrounded by riding fields. A squadron of cavalry was returning to the stables. People had gathered around the public fountain of the neighbourhood and coachmen were waiting in line to water their horses.

'St Hagop's church is near by,' ventured Maro. This meant another detour but Vartan thought she had probably not set foot in a church for years. They walked along the boulevard crowded with carriages and

498

speeding phaetons. Little by little Maro relaxed; her walk became more supple, her steps more assured and she loosened her grip on Vartan's arm. He took it as a sign of improvement and knew she would quickly adapt to her new life in Constantinople and to him again.

'When you feel up to it, we'll take a walk down la Grand-rue de Péra and go to Chez Marquise for tea as we used to do. Do you remember?'

'Of course,' she said dreamily.

Maro had always had a special attachment for Sourp Hagop's church. Saint James was her father's patron saint and she was very moved when she entered. The rays from the setting sun illuminated the stained-glass windows and cast coloured reflections on the walls. The smell of incense and melting wax awoke cherished memories in Maro. She knelt down to implore God for her two sons. She remained kneeling for a long time. Vartan sat on a bench watching her out of the corner of his eye, wishing he still had her faith. He no longer believed with all his heart, yet he had to admit that the only word applicable to his reunion with Maro was 'miracle'. Aroussiag's image came to mind; although he loved Maro, the young woman from Urgup would always have a place in his memory. He silently recited the prayer for the dead. Before leaving the church, they each lit two candles and set them in the box in front of the Virgin – Maro for Tomas and Nourhan, Vartan for Tomas and Aroussiag. They dared not tell each other for whom they were asking grace.

When they left the church, Maro had been feeling more serene but as they approached Shahin Bey Street where the Mesropians lived she became increasingly nervous. Out of breath, she stopped a few steps away from their door.

Vartan could see that this dinner invitation was upsetting her, so he patted her hand and said, 'They will be so glad to see you.'

'So will I but . . .'

They had always treated her like a daughter, but she was afraid they might be critical of her now.

Vartan wanted to boost her confidence. 'Everything is going to be all right. I'll be there for you.' Maro was touched.

Aunt Arpiné threw up her arms, unable to express her happiness. Weeping with joy and raining kisses on Maro's cheeks and forehead, she hugged her, while repeating, 'The Lord heard us! The Lord heard our prayers!' Breathless, she abandoned herself to tears. The warmth of her welcome reassured Maro that she was not being judged and she kissed her back.

'I'm so happy, *morak*.'[1]

Still holding Maro by the shoulders, Arpiné stepped back to gaze at her lovingly. 'You haven't changed. You're even prettier than before.' Her face clouded over. 'Poor little thing.'

Vartan hastened to clarify the ambiguity of these last words. 'Don't worry. Aunt Arpiné. We shall find Tomas! Maro has already written all the letters for the orphanages and missionaries who have taken in Armenian children.'

Arpiné understood her nephew did not want her to ask about Maro's experiences while she was a captive in Ayntab.

Moist-eyed, Uncle Mesrop, who had been standing behind his wife, held out his arms. 'Come, my daughter, and let me embrace you.'

Maro went to him but she thought she saw an expression of curiosity and suspicion on his face, as if he were imagining her with a man other than her husband. Perhaps she was only projecting on to him the guilty feelings that had overcome her upon entering this house; nevertheless, there was an almost imperceptible hesitation before he pulled her close. That lent an unexpected coolness to his welcome, although he looked pleased enough. In his eyes she must have seemed soiled – like a leper.

Biting back her resentment, she said enthusiastically, 'No one would ever believe you've been ill, Uncle Mesrop. You look younger than ever.'

A look of delight came over him, although his words were gloomy. 'The ravages of illness are not always apparent. You look well too.'

'Let her be!' said Lucie, tugging him by the sleeve. 'Maro is my sister.' Lucie's words had been spontaneously unreserved and Maro gladly responded with equal openness. They did not say a word for a few moments but both of them felt that their old friendship – forged when Maro had lived in Constantinople – was unchanged.

'Let's leave the men to themselves,' said Lucie, steering her into the kitchen.

Vartan sat down on the divan while Uncle Mesrop, boasting that he had no lack of customers now that the Europeans were here, displayed a bottle of excellent brandy, a present from one of the people in the French Embassy for whom he had done some printing. He filled the snifters and they raised their glasses in a toast. Mesrop sat down in his favourite chair facing Vartan and clicked his tongue approvingly after his first draught.

---

1. Abbreviation for *morakouyr*, a maternal aunt (Armenian).

He sighed, 'Maro seems to be embarrassed.'

The implication was so clear that Vartan replied cuttingly, 'You don't know the terror she has endured. None of us would have come out unscathed from that kind of experience. Hers is the tragedy of all our people. Perhaps it is we who have had it relatively easy who should be embarrassed.'

His uncle understood the message perfectly, but felt uncomfortable. 'I, I only meant . . .'

To change the subject, Vartan remarked, 'This brandy is excellent.'

'I'll try to get some more.'

They discussed the weather for a few minutes; then curiosity got the better of Uncle Mesrop. 'I saw a picture of the governor of Ayntab in the newspaper this evening.'

'The subject is closed!'

'Then he *is* the one!'

'Uncle Mesrop, I don't want the subject ever mentioned again. I don't want anyone to remind Maro of the deportation. Let her forget all the atrocities she unwillingly witnessed if she can! It seems to me to be the least we can do.'

The uncle had to bow to Vartan's assertiveness. The kindness and affection he had always felt for Maro surfaced. 'Poor child,' he said apologetically, 'With our love, we shall help her to forget.'

The kitchen was fragrant with the smell of frying onions and cumin. Maro wanted to help Lucie finish preparing the hors-d'œuvres but Arpiné, who was supervising the food on the stove, stopped her.

'Why don't the two of you go and chat in Lucie's room. I'll take care of everything.'

Maro had been slicing *basderma,* dried garlic-flavoured meat, which always formed part of a meal on festive occasions. 'Please let me do it, Aunt Arpiné. I haven't had my hands in the dough for such a long time.'

'Were there a lot of servants there?'

'Yes.'

'*Mayrig!*' protested Lucie. 'I'm sure that Maro wants to forget everything that happened and start all over again. At least, that's the way I would feel, wouldn't you, mother?'

'You're right, of course. I'm a stupid old goose.'

Maro put her arm around Arpiné. 'Don't say that, auntie. You're an angel and I adore you.'

'Oh, I have my faults just like we all do.' She turned around, looked at Maro tenderly and stroked her cheek. 'I love you, Maro. Remember that! This is your home and I will always be here for you.'

Lucie hated emotional scenes. 'I'm not going to cry again. This is a moment for rejoicing.'

Understanding her daughter only too well, Arpiné excused herself. 'There are such things as tears of joy, you know.'

They finished preparing the meal, talking all the while about everyday things. Arpiné talked about the high cost of food and the swelling in her legs; Lucie talked about the latest Paris fashions on display in the windows of the boutiques on la Grand-rue de Péra and giggled as she added that there were many handsome French naval officers there too. Maro felt she was back in 1908; they were friends again and her aunt and cousin had both completely accepted her. They did not need to know the details of Maro's life these last years. Both of them would have done the same. Their attitude put Maro at ease and she agreed to accompany Lucie to town the day after next.

Despite the efforts of Arpiné and Lucie to keep the same easy-going attitude at the table, there remained a feeling of uneasiness. Maro closed up like a clam, for her uncle kept staring at her curiously. Although he laughed loudly, told anecdotes about the printing shop, said how happy he was that Maro was back, wished for Tomas to be found and avoided any allusion to Maro's recent past, his voice rang false. It was not that he wanted to be like that but old prejudices and narrow concepts of honour were deeply ingrained in him, and he could not help himself. Even if he took into account all the circumstances that absolved Maro from any guilt for what had happened, in his eyes she was a faithless woman. Having never provoked him, Arpiné had never seen Mesrop's jealousy and possessiveness before, but it surfaced now as he put himself in his nephew's place. Everyone at the table felt them. Vartan held Maro's hand under the table, showing her his support. She turned to him, saw his look of love, and felt calmer.

'Aren't Aram and Diran coming to dinner?' asked Vartan.

'They're on one of their mysterious errands, as always,' joked Lucie. She did not take her brother's activities too seriously, thinking he used them to escape from the family's printing shop.

Sighing deeply, Mesrop turned to Vartan and introduced a subject which had been bothering him.

'Did you know they want to leave for the Caucasus in Russian Armenia?' he asked despondently.

'So what?' Vartan shrugged. 'You didn't object when Barkev went to New York.'

Mesrop exploded, 'That has nothing to do with this. New York is New York. They weren't having a war or famine in New York.'

Vartan tried to soothe him. 'Uncle Mesrop, Diran's forty years old – old enough to decide for himself. Remember he has always fought for an Armenia. You should have realized long ago he's not going to follow you in the printing shop.'

'What's going to happen to it?'

'You can sell it when you retire. Then you and Aunt Arpiné can travel.'

The old man looked pitiful. 'I inherited the business from my father. How can I hand it over to a stranger? Never!'

'Didn't you tell me you were thinking about taking Aram in?'

Mesrop shook his head. 'That youngster is never here either. He acts exactly like Diran and he wants to go to Armenia, too.'

Vartan had no more arguments left so he suggested teasingly, 'One day Lucie will find a husband she can love and get married. Your son-in-law . . .'

Lucie did not like this and lashed out, 'When I marry it will be for love and not to find a manager for the printing shop!' She leaned over and, looking directly into her father's eyes, asked coyly, 'And why shouldn't I be the boss? I know all about the trade.'

Mesrop was flabbergasted. 'Mesrop and Daughter. That's a good one!'

'It's not such a bad idea,' interrupted Arpiné. 'I can picture Lucie as a businesswoman.'

Mesrop could not believe his ears and stared at his wife, who looked at him unblinkingly. He shut up and began to eat without lifting his eyes from his plate. Arpiné winked mischievously at the others.

'Anné! Anné!' Nourhan screamed as he ran under the pouring rain behind the car that was taking his mother away.

Maro sat up with the sound of her son's voice still ringing in her ears. This nightmare was like the one she had had in the months after Tomas's disappearance, but Tomas had been carried away by a sandstorm in the desert screaming, '*Mayrig*! *Mayrig*!' And she had been unable to lift a hand to help him.

His wife's sudden movement woke Vartan up. 'What's the matter, Maro?'

'Nothing. Only a bad dream.'

He would have liked her to tell him about it but she turned her back to him, apologized for having woken him and said goodnight. She cried softly, not realizing he could hear her.

He did not dare ask any more questions. As always, she would have answered that she could not put her fears into words – that she was missing Tomas – but Vartan guessed that it was something else, something altogether different. But what? It must be Riza Bey who stood between them, even though he was far away. At first he had been sure that their relationship would be as before, but it had not worked out that way. Maro's restraint had turned into an embarrassed silence – her reserve into frigidity. Every evening when he returned home he found her to be more and more distant. His patience was wearing thin and he had become jealous. On the fourth night, Maro had made it clear she would not repulse his advances and they had made love. At least, Vartan had tried to make love, but he had found a veritable iceberg in his bed, a tense, passive woman without desire, incapable of abandoning herself to pleasure. Vartan was heart-broken! It was so unlike her that he came to the conclusion that she did not love him any more. After that he was politely attentive but he ceased to court her. The wall of silence she had built around her sorrow would have to crumble before he could begin to bridge the distance that four years of separation had created between them. Vartan did not have the least idea of how this was going to happen, so he continued to wait. To avoid looking at her expressionless face, he sat writing at his worktable until it was time to go to bed. Maro's attitude had made him start to think about Aroussiag again. Indeed, she was ever-present in his thoughts. The contrast of her simple, happy love-making made Maro's indifference seem even more cruel.

To escape the stifling atmosphere at home, he began going to meetings of the different Armenian committees in Constantinople. These groups were trying to put together dossiers about the activities of war criminals in the Ittihad in preparation for the peace negotiations that were to be held in

504

Paris. When he returned home late in the evening, the first thing he did was look through the mail. The hope of finding Tomas was the only real link between Maro and himself.

As the weeks went by, they continued to receive letters from orphanages in the immediate region saying that Tomas was not to be found there. They still had not heard from Smyrna, Cilicia, Syria and Cyprus, among other places. To be absolutely sure, they had left nothing to chance and they had also written to Protestant churches in Germany and Switzerland, thinking they might have had missionaries in Anatolia during the war. They had not yet received replies, however, owing to the slowness of the mail.

Vartan had gone back to sleep and Maro lay on her back staring at a ray of light on the ceiling that filtered in above the shade on the window. She was even more upset about the situation than Vartan and his aloofness overwhelmed her. She knew there was still love between them, only waiting to become as strong and vibrant as before, but the words to express it had been lost. It was not only her fault. Their old ritual of love had been interrupted and left without meaning. They could not invent a new one; it would have to spring into being spontaneously. Only at the very beginning of their relationship could a couple create such a ritual out of nothing. Now she and Vartan had to cultivate one that would make peace with the recent past. It had to sink its roots into the marsh left by four years of separation, fear, disappointment and lost hopes – into the earth of passing joys and illusions. And time was against them. They must lance the boil that was poisoning their relationship and neither of them had the strength or courage to do that yet.

Vartan was mistaken if he thought she was grieving for Riza. He was dead as far as she was concerned – even more so than Bedri, who had ended with a bullet through the head. Her wound was the loss of Nourhan and she did not see how it would ever heal. All the children in the orphanages where she worked reminded her of him, and his loss made the finding of his half-brother even more urgent. She still thought, as she had in the first weeks after Tomas's disappearance, that the pain would be more bearable if she were sure he was dead. She also knew she would miss her second child for the rest of her life and every morning she would lose him all over again! Caught in this trap, how could she ever love a man again?

Diran, like the rest of the family, had realized that things were not going well between Maro and Vartan. He cared for them both so much that their malaise made him sad, so he often avoided visiting them. This evening, however, he had an important question to ask Vartan and, in order to ease the tension, he asked Aram to go with him.

Maro had prepared coffee and carried the tray into the living room. She served Diran, who was sitting in the easy-chair, and Aram, who had pulled up the straight-chair next to his mentor; then she sat down next to Vartan on the divan.

'You've been making yourself scarce,' said Vartan to Diran.

'I have my reasons. Aram and I have become detectives as well as spies.'

Aram who had filled out and lost his boyish looks, straightened up proudly. Down had begun to grow on his upper lip and he accentuated it with moustache-wax. Diran drank his coffee, happily keeping his cousin in suspense, but when no one asked any questions, he showed his disappointment.

He explained, 'We're looking for some papers that could change the course of history. Several witnesses at the court martial have said that the minutes of the cabinet meetings, the memorandums from the Ministry of Interior, the telegrams, the letters, in fact all of the papers concerning the deportation have disappeared – many burned by those who would have been incriminated by them and others stolen.'

'I know,' said Vartan.

'Wait. Something new has come to light. We've heard rumours that some of the stolen documents are for sale – for a price, of course.'

'We're on their trail,' added Aram. 'The situation is delicate. A lot of people want to get their hands on them for many reasons and the sellers are wary.'

Vartan thought how well the boy was expressing himself. He had copied Diran's turn of phrase and sometimes even his accent.

'If we have these papers,' insisted Diran, 'we can prove that the government of the Young Turks was using the deportation as a front to exterminate the Armenians.'

'I know. They would strengthen our position with the Allies in the coming negotiations but many people want them to disappear. What you are doing is very dangerous!'

'We're not afraid of anything!' boasted Aram.

However, Diran was more realistic. 'The game is worth the candle. The Ottoman diplomats have been busily casting doubts about the numbers involved in the massacres and, at the same time, trying to put the blame on just a few individuals, not on the entire government of that time. If we don't stop them, one day the world will think these crimes never really took place. That's why we must take risks.'

'As you say, the game is worth the candle!'

'And you, Vartan? What are you working on these days?'

'I have just finished putting together the dossier on Gani Bey.'

'Was that the horrible man who came to Sivas?' asked Maro.

'That's right!'

'Oh! I hope he swings, that filthy swine!'

Diran clicked his tongue repeatedly to show his disgust. 'According to our sources, he left Constantinople for Austria three days ago but he will be condemned *in absentia*.'

Vartan turned towards Maro, who was looking frightened. 'While I was going through his file, I learned something horrifying. Colonel Ibrahim is dead! He died under torture while being questioned.'

'Tortured? Why? He was a Turkish officer.'

'Because he and Halit Pasha helped me escape from prison. Halit Pasha is also dead.'

Maro was deeply affected. So Ibrahim had kept his word! Vartan's escape had been due to him.

'You know he promised me not to abandon you. I hope he went to Allah's Paradise.'

Diran was surprised that Maro did not know how Vartan had escaped from Sivas. It seemed that these two had told each other nothing of their misfortunes and adventures. Their problem must go even deeper than he had thought.

'May I smoke?' asked Aram, taking out a pack of English cigarettes from his coat pocket.

'Of course,' said Maro, pointing at an ashtray sitting on the corner of the worktable.

He struck a match and glanced sideways at Maro. She was prettier than Aroussiag but not as sweet or loving or daring. Vartan was getting soft. This morose, taciturn woman from the city was turning him into a mere scribbler. He would have been happier with Aroussiag, who must have made love with joyous abandon. The evening before, Aram had gone with Diran and Avedis to a brothel where he had lost his virginity; since then he felt capable of judging the sexual potential of any woman at a glance.

507

Diran put his cup down and cleared his throat before broaching the subject of his visit. 'Tell me, Vartan, did Dawson, the American journalist, suggest you go to Washington?'

'Well, he said the best way to serve the Armenian cause was to put pressure on the American Congress, especially on the senators, and the circle around the President.'

'Our committee believes the same.'

'I must say I agree. President Wilson is in favour of the Grand Armenia that we all want and the Americans are the only ones who can make it happen at the peace conference.'

'Exactly! Their goodwill must be fomented during the coming year until the conference is held.'

'It's really a long time to go.'

'Especially as powerful industrial and financial interests are putting pressure on the politicians to be considerate with the Ottoman Empire.'

Vartan made a wry face. 'I know, but our people are also very active, both in Europe and the USA. It seems the Catholicos has personally appealed to President Wilson.'

Diran nodded and took another sip of coffee. Maro had been following the conversation with great interest. She and Vartan knew there was more to come. She knew Diran so well she could tell when he was beating around the bush to gain time. He often did this when he wasn't sure he had made the right decision.

He coughed, 'Things being the way they are, the committee has decided to send you to Washington.'

'Decided!' Vartan jumped. 'Since when do they decide for me?'

Diran backtracked. 'Don't take it like that. The committee wishes . . . would like you to go.'

Maro was worried, as she knew how much the idea of a Greater Armenia meant to Vartan, and she watched his reaction carefully. The idea of his leaving, even if only for a few months, was intolerable.

'No!'

'You can't refuse,' begged Diran.

Vartan said mildly, 'I don't see how I can do more than the Armenians who are working for our cause in Washington are already doing.'

'They haven't lived through the deportation as you have. You are a witness to what happened in Anatolia. Your articles . . .'

'There are many others as qualified as I am who would like nothing better than to cross the Atlantic.'

'The committee believes otherwise.'

Vartan lost his patience. 'Tell your committee to find my son! Then we can talk!'

Embarrassed, Diran blushed and looked at Maro. 'You're right, Vartan. I would feel the same. I was only speaking as the committee's messenger.'

'It's all right. All you have to do is to explain the reasons for my refusal. That should convince them.'

Maro felt great relief. She asked, 'Would you like more coffee?'

Diran excused himself by saying he had a meeting to attend. He did not wish to stay knowing that the conversation would lead to Tomas and he was not as optimistic as they were about the chances of finding him alive.

Aram stood on the landing and shook hands ceremoniously with Maro and Vartan while Vartan and Diran were making an appointment.

He whispered to Maro so the men would not hear him, '*Diguin*, are there cowboys in Wah-shin-tone?'

Maro answered, amused, 'A few, perhaps.'

Aram pretended to be an adult but there was a child still lurking there under the surface.

At the end of February when the first buds were bursting open in the parks of Constantinople, Maro grieved, seeing their life as a couple being reduced to companionship – an association of two people who showed respect for each other, who conversed amiably but were incapable of conveying their innermost thoughts to each other. To think that before, even after eight years of marriage, not one day had passed without their having long hours of discussion. They had confided their worries, their joys and their dreams to each other. Now all that was gone.

Maro could not see how they were going to regain that closeness. There were too many unspoken words that kept them from really communicating. They were condemned to small talk, which did little more than disguise silence. Maro felt guilty. Her secret became heavier every day, but she could not bring it to light. At the same time the image of them as a couple was steadily fading. The demoralizing lack of news about Tomas had also contributed to their drifting apart.

509

She was at the end of her tether, so she decided to visit Aunt Arpiné at a time she knew Lucie would be at the printing shop.

'Excuse me for dropping in like this.'

'Believe it or not, I've been expecting you to come before now.' Her aunt's voice was motherly; her voice was the voice of all women when they comfort, console and forgive – just what Maro needed to hear.

'The water is boiling. You might call it a premonition but I heated enough for two.' Arpiné brewed the tea.

Although Maro was very close to Lucie, it had never occurred to her to confide in her. How could a twenty-nine-year-old woman who was still waiting for the love of her life understand Maro's problems? She needed someone who knew what it was like to live with a man, someone who had nursed a beloved child, someone who loved her children more than herself – a mother!

'Aunt Arpiné . . .'

'Hush,' she said, laying her finger on her lips. 'Not in here, nor in the living-room, nor in the dining-room. The walls have ears. Bring your cup with you.'

They went into her bedroom and closed the door. 'We can talk here. The walls are deaf.'

The curtains were drawn and the room was in shadow. It smelt of roses, shaving soap, sandalwood and mothballs. A commode, a dressing-table and two night stands crowded round the big four-poster bed with its cabled posts. Facing a wall adorned with icons and a cross, they sat on the edge of the mattress, so they could set their teacups on the nightstand.

Maro, who had been ready to tell her everything when she had come into the kitchen, could not remember the phrases she had rehearsed to broach the subject. She kept looking down and wringing her hands nervously.

Arpiné caught them in hers. 'Something is wrong with Vartan? He refuses to accept the situation?'

'He knows nothing about it.'

'It might be better if you told him. He's very intelligent and good.'

Maro kept quiet.

Arpiné took a deep breath and asked quietly, 'Are you in love with that other man?'

'Of course not!'

'Don't you love Vartan anymore?'

'It isn't that at all.'

A sigh of relief escaped Arpiné. Then what else could be bothering Maro?

Since her niece offered no explanation, she tried again. 'Is it something about Tomas that we don't know about?'

'No.'

Arpiné picked up the cups and handed Maro hers. They sipped their tea. Arpiné tried to catch Maro's eye but she evaded her look.

'Then what is wrong between the two of you? Has Vartan changed?'

'It's I who have changed.'

'But Maro, I find you the same as before and Lucie told me she did too.' She took a sip of tea. 'Vartan is also the same but together you seem different. What's driving you apart?'

'The silence, *morak*. The silence!'

'The silence?' Arpiné was astonished. 'Silence by itself is nothing. It can be empty or hide something. Yours seems to be full of sorrow.' She felt she threw out enough lines; now it was up to Maro to cross the bridge.

Maro put down her cup and stared at the wooden cross on the wall. Her eyes brimmed over and she laid her hand on Arpiné's thigh as she burst out, '*Morak*, I had a child by the governor!'

Arpiné's cup rattled on her saucer. She was appalled. 'A child?'

'A boy! Nourhan!' As she pronounced his name, she burst into sobs. She laid her head on Arpiné's round shoulder and Arpiné pulled her close to let her weep her heart out.

Arpiné understood everything now – Maro's vacant look, her absent air, the sadness in her voice. Without anything more being said, she understood the enormity of Maro's tragedy and could feel its cruelty in her own flesh. She caressed Maro's head.

'Poor little thing,' she murmured. 'Poor little thing!'

'I've lost him forever. Why? Why is God hounding me? Why doesn't He pick on someone else?' She gripped Arpiné's arm and wailed.

Arpiné did not react to Maro's blasphemy. God must have heard worse. This was one of the things He would not take into account when He sat in judgement. What greater suffering could a mother endure than to have two children torn from her, one after the other?

Arpiné laid Maro down on the bed and sat close to her, patting her on the back as if she were a sick child. She prayed to the Virgin to give Maro the strength to bear this ordeal and at the same time to intercede with a small miracle and give her oldest son back to this wounded mother – at least that.

Slowly Maro stopped crying. Having shared her secret grief had made it less overwhelming. 'He's an angel, auntie. It's strange but he looks like Tomas – the same smile, the same intelligent eyes.'

'How old is he?'

'Two and a half but he was already drawing better than a six-year-old. He has talent.' With dreamy eyes, Maro continued to describe her son – how advanced he was for his age.

Arpiné was full of questions. Who had stopped Maro from taking him with her? Was there no way she could see him again? But she did not voice them so as not to add to Maro's wretchedness. The tenderness of her description of Nourhan was a sign that Maro was beginning to resign herself and perhaps it was for the best. How could Vartan have accepted this child – the fruit of forced adultery with another man?

'You've been like a mother to me. How can I ever thank you enough?'

'By confiding in me when you need to. If you feel like it, you may call me *mayrig*. I'd like that.

'*Mayrig*,' breathed Maro against her aunt's wrinkled cheeks.

When they went back to the living-room, Maro felt that a weight had been lifted off her shoulders. Should her misery become too great to bear, she would always have a willing ear to lighten her burden.

The conversation became less emotional. 'If I were you, Maro, I would tell Vartan. I think it would simplify things between you.'

Maro looked alarmed. 'I'm afraid it'll hurt him. You know how sensitive men can be where their honour is concerned. I gave a son to another man and lost his!'

'You didn't lose Tomas. You must get that idea out of your mind.'

Maro's face darkened. 'It's not easy.'

Arpiné took her by the shoulders and scolded her gently. 'Nothing is ever easy, my child. Today you can only see the calamities that have befallen you. Tell yourself they are the seed of the good things to come. God knows what He is doing. You must do what He expects you to and endure until He is ready to give you the good things He has in store for you. Your mother lived her life by that faith and I have learned to do the same. It is the only way.'

Maro wished she could have the same blind faith for, in such a philosophy, even death lost its sting. That was how Azniv Hanim had closed her eyes without fear of what lay in store for her. Maro would have to make do with what small faith she possessed while admitting that even God might commit errors; even then, she would call upon her powers of reasoning.

In the Mesropian living-room Noubar was holding forth exuberantly as he generally did when he had a captive audience. He was a born storyteller who knew how to keep people holding on the edge of their seats. The smallest incident was the starting point for a long narrative full of details and digressions. The most run-of-the-mill story became interesting when he told it. He had never left Afyon before except for brief holidays in Constantinople but now, after his exile in Jerusalem, he had enough material for a saga.

They had come together to eat dinner this Easter Sunday and everyone was listening to his tales. His wife, Dirouhi, who was sitting next to him, interrupted from time to time to emphasize a word or insist on the importance of a detail. Noubar would clear his throat to bring her to order and, looking peevish, she would momentarily fall silent but soon the urge became too much for her and again she would add her grain of salt.

Dirouhi had prospered with age and her ample salmon-pink dress did nothing to hide her rounded curves and the short sleeves revealed her plump arms. Her chubby cheeks made her nose look even shorter and rounder. Her portliness cast doubt on her tales of the privations and hardships they had suffered, along with the other Armenians, during their exile in Jerusalem.

Even Noubar had gained a lot of weight. His muscles had turned to fat and he gave the impression of having shrunk. His hair, which had been his pride and joy, was turning grey and thin, and there was a bald spot on the crown of his head. But he still had his expansive gestures, his spellbinding voice and his friendly look.

Vartan marvelled at finding his older brother as full of the same *joie de vivre* as before. It was so much like him. Beset by difficulties and in a situation where others would give up, he still chased after dreams, looking for ways to get out of his predicament and meanwhile throwing his heart and soul into his work.

After her husband had finished his detailed description of the dilapidated

513

room where they had lived in Jerusalem, Dirouhi cut in, 'Not everyone was lucky enough to spend the war in a palace!'

Noubar shot an angry look at his wife. Mesrop said reprovingly, 'Easter is meant to be a celebration of love.'

Everyone looked embarrassed. Arpiné got up and asked Dirouhi to follow her. 'Come and see the eggs I painted on Good Friday.'

Dirouhi realized from her aunt's commanding tone that she had gone too far but to apologize would only compound her blunder. Maro sat unmoved. Her sister-in-law's hostility was nothing new. Ever since Maro had joined the Balian family, Dirouhi had regarded her as a rival. When Tomas had been born she had been positively eaten with envy, as she herself seemed doomed to be sterile.

'Bring the aperitifs,' said Mesrop to Lucie. 'We shall drink to Noubar and Dirouhi's return.' He wanted the incident closed as this Easter was extremely important to him. It was the symbol of the end of the Passion of the Armenian people and the Resurrection of Armenia. The only thing lacking was the presence of his older son and Tomas. Barkev had not been able to get leave from the French Army and there was still no news about Tomas. But this was not going to stop Mesrop from praising the Lord for having preserved those gathered here and from breaking their lenten fast with a grand feast.

Noubar put his arm around Vartan's shoulder and laughed nervously. He had just arrived from Palestine on a French freighter the previous night and was still overwhelmed by the emotion of their reunion on the deserted dock. Although they were tired, the two brothers had talked until dawn. Their love for each other was as strong as ever in spite of the years of separation. They had strengthened the bonds by exchanging mutual memories of the past while putting off decisions about the future.

Dirouhi's outburst had cut the thread of Noubar's story. The conversation had passed to Mesrop, Diran, Aram and Maro. Mesrop was trying to convince the boy to work more regularly in the printing shop, tempting him with the possibility of becoming a partner one day. Aram did not want to disappoint Uncle Mesrop who had welcomed him so warmly, but he did not want to spend the rest of his life shut up within the four walls of the shop. Adventures and nobler tasks lay in store for him in Armenia or so Diran had told him.

Maro was telling Diran about her work in the orphanage and he listened with affection. A fellow countryman who had been on a mission to Ayntab

514

had told him that the governor had had a child by an Armenian woman and he was sure the woman in question was Maro. He had kept it to himself but it explained the rift between Vartan and Maro. It made him feel closer to her, for he guessed how divided she must feel.

Noubar, having lost his audience, leaned towards Vartan, 'A *dervish*!' He was amused. 'That's just like you. I was worried to death about you but a little voice kept telling me they wouldn't get you so easily. You're a man of many resources and I was right.' Still laughing, he frowned as a more serious thought came to him. 'Did you see our plantation?'

Although the question had been muffled by the conversation, everyone heard it and stopped talking. One could have heard a pin drop.

Vartan's answer sounded like a verdict. 'Three-quarters of the field is derelict and the irrigation ditches are full of sand. It would be difficult to get things going again.'

'What do you mean by 'would', Vartan?'

'Well, a certain Ekrem Effendi is occupying the land and I'm not too sure the government will evict him.'

Mesrop saw that Noubar was nodding in agreement and exploded, 'No! That land has been in your family for generations. They can't take it from you!'

'They already have,' said Noubar philosophically. 'Hundreds of thousands of farms, businesses and homes left behind by the Armenians have been taken over by government employees. I agree with Vartan. I can't see the government evicting its own.'

Disappointed by this apparent defeatism, Mesrop looked to Diran for support.

'I think my cousins are right,' he said. 'It would be suicidal for the Sultan's government to anger its supporters.'

Mesrop refused to accept what was evident to the others. 'What about the commission that is studying the problem of the restitution of Armenian property? It does exist, doesn't it?'

'They're dragging their feet.' Diran's grimace was eloquent. 'The most we can expect is some money in compensation for the loss of our lands and buildings.'

Appalled, Mesrop turned to Maro. 'You mean you're just going to stand by and let them confiscate your house in Sivas too?'

'Let them have it!' Her cry came from the heart. 'We're never going back

515

there!' She immediately regretted her bluntness and blushed, but Vartan soothed her with a nod.

'Maro's right.'

Lucie and Dirouhi had started in with two trays but stopped at the door. Encouraged by her brother-in-law's words, Dirouhi added, 'I agree. We don't want to go back to Afyon either, do we, Noubar?'

Vexed that his wife should reveal their intentions so abruptly, Noubar carefully placed a long strand of hair over his bald spot and cleared his throat.

'Is what she says true?' asked Mesrop, who should have already known the answer from Noubar's reaction.

Noubar waved his arms. 'You know me. I'm not one to abandon something at the first obstacle I find, but my father, may he rest in peace, taught me not to pursue a lost cause stubbornly.'

Mesrop had forgotten Noubar's gift for answering without really saying anything. He insisted, 'What are you going to do then?'

'Try to get the most we can in compensation for our plantation. Vartan agrees with me.'

Unsatisfied, Mesrop asked, 'And then?'

Noubar shook his head and said evasively, 'Oh . . .'

Dirouhi, who could not control her tongue, stepped in, 'We're going to emigrate to the United States. We don't want to live here any longer. Violence could break out anytime – like in 1895 – or 1915 – it happens at least once in every generation and that's not counting the random killings. No! Noubar and I want to live out our days in a place where we don't have to worry every evening that the sky is going to fall down on our heads before we wake up in the morning!'

Being a traditionalist, Mesrop hated the way in which women increasingly took the liberty of interrupting men's conversations. He glared at Dirouhi. 'I was speaking to Noubar!'

Dirouhi turned her back on him and began to pass the drinks around. Vartan, who had been as surprised as Mesrop at his brother's plans, stared at him. Noubar coughed. What else could he add to his wife's speech? She had put his thoughts succinctly, using some of his own phrases. Perhaps his uncle would be more receptive to material considerations.

'In America there are many opportunities for an enterprising businessman. I have an import-export business in mind. We did this in Jerusalem with Barkev, so between the two of us . . .'

His uncle interrupted him, 'Why Barkev? What does he have to do with this?'

Noubar had been carried away and said too much. While he was trying to construct a non-committal answer, his uncle continued anxiously, 'Does Barkev intend to return to New York? Did he tell you that?'

Noubar did not divulge they had written each other about that possibility. 'Not exactly. I just assumed that is what he's going to do.'

Mesrop was not fooled and the joy he had been feeling since early morning vanished. He had been hoping with all his heart that Barkev would return to Constantinople to live now that his job as factor for the Balians' opium business in the USA was finished. The thought that both his sons might leave him had stripped this family dinner of meaning for him. How would he respond when his friends and employees came to convey their Easter wishes? He turned towards the door to catch his wife's eye but then realized, from the sound of rattling silverware, that she was in the dining-room. He excused himself and went to seek comfort.

Dirouhi sat down next to her husband. Her uncle's shaking voice had surprised her. 'What's wrong with him? He should be used to Barkev's being in the United States by now.'

Diran sighed, 'He is upset about my plan to go to Armenia and he has been consoling himself that Barkev will be coming home to live.'

Noubar could always find an easy solution for everything. 'Why don't you take your mother and father with you to Armenia?'

'I asked them to come along but father says one cannot transplant an old tree. You must understand. They were born here. For them, Armenia is a mythical country at the end of the world.'

'Let's not talk about departures today. Uncle Mesrop and Aunt Arpiné are celebrating homecomings,' said Vartan. Making sure his uncle had not returned, he asked softly, 'Have you made up your mind, Noubar?'

'Yes.'

'When?'

'First I have to get an indemnity for our plantation. That will probably take a few months, I suppose. What about you, Vartan? You haven't told me anything about your plans.'

Maro and Vartan looked at each other. 'Right now, we have only one thing in mind – to find Tomas. Then . . .' he stopped and shrugged to show his helplessness.

Mesrop came in and said dinner was served. He had recovered his calm and, after saying the usual prayers, he added, 'Lord God Almighty, we, Your children, reunited on this day of Your Son's Resurrection, implore You to bring Tomas Balian, a child brought up in love for You, back to us. Amen.' Everyone made the sign of the cross in silence.

Then Vartan lifted his glass, 'To Aunt Arpiné and Uncle Mesrop, who have such big hearts.'

They raised their glasses and drank. Aram, who was slightly tipsy, said, slurring his words, 'To all of you who have become my family.'

Arpiné touched him on the arm, 'You've become a son to us, too, Aram, so I'll tell you what I've always said to my other sons, "Be careful how much you drink".'

'Today is a holiday. Let him have a little drink.'

Mesrop's good humour was a facade. Still, this was the nicest Easter dinner they had had in this house for a long time.

One evening when Vartan and Maro returned from the orphanage where Vartan had picked her up on his way home from the hospital, they found the lock on the front door broken. Maro turned white. Vartan told her to wait while he went into the apartment to make sure the intruders had left. The wardrobe had been turned over on their bed. The drawers of the dresser had been emptied out and were lying on the floor. The dishes had been strewn all over the kitchen floor. The chairs in the dining room had been broken.

Maro joined Vartan in the living-room where the divan had been gutted with a knife and the curtains had been shredded. She looked around in disbelief and saw that all of Vartan's books and papers were gone from the worktable. Her heart sank and she leaned against the wall. Vartan went over to her.

'It's nothing. I'll put everything back in place again.'

'Nothing!' Maro snapped. 'You think this is nothing? They break down our door, break everything we have, and it's nothing! What if I had been here?'

'But you weren't,' he said coldly.

'And what about the next time?'

He had no answer.

'They'll be back, Vartan,' she said pointing to the table. 'And all because of your articles. They're going to come and take you away in the middle of the night, just like in Sivas!'

He tried to belittle the risks he had been running but before he could open his mouth, Maro started to sob. He took her in his arms and held her close to comfort her. She clung to him and wept. After five minutes, she calmed down.

He murmured, 'You mustn't be afraid. I'm here.'

Still leaning on his shoulder she said between gasps, 'But you often aren't! Meetings here, committees there. Anybody would think you were running away from me.'

'Perhaps I am,' he sighed, 'but when I'm here, you're the one who's absent. You're here but you're not really. Your eyes are empty and your face is haggard with worry. Everyday I see your eyes are red, your lids swollen from crying. We can't go on like this, Maro.' He took a deep breath, 'Tell me the truth. Did I make a mistake bringing you back from Ayntab?'

Astounded, she stepped back and looked him straight in the eyes, 'Vartan, you must know better than that!'

'Then where are you in your daydreams if not in Ayntab?

Unable to deny it, she paled.

'For whom are you crying if not for Riza Bey?'

'You're wrong!' she said vehemently. She looked so sincere that Vartan had to believe her but it only compounded his confusion. When they got a letter saying the search had not been successful and she cried for Tomas, it was in front of him and, each time, he would help her recover her hopes, but what made her continually sad? He waited for her answer.

Maro swallowed hard and kept on looking into Vartan's eyes. At last she had finally overcome her shame and her voice was defiant. Everything would be decided here and now!

'Riza Bey forced me to love him and at moments I thought perhaps I did. I am indebted to him. I owe him Tomas's life and mine too but that isn't it!'

Vartan's heart pounded. This was the first time she had told him anything about this part of her life.

He took her by the hand. 'You don't have to justify yourself to me, Maro. Let's erase the past.'

'First we have to talk. As long as we ignore those years they will be a barrier between us.' She bit her lip tensely. He nodded. 'That man saved my life but I always felt like a prisoner. Then . . .'

'I don't need to know the details.' He was hoping she would go no further.

'No, I have to say it, if only this once. I was his mistress. I lived with him like his other wives did for four years.'

Vartan did not flinch, so she continued. 'But I never stopped loving you. Not one day went by without my thinking of you – without my praying for you – and I never forgot I was your wife.'

Vartan's eyes became moist and his voice shook. 'Your words have given me peace. I want you to know I have never judged you. You did what you needed to do to survive . . . to return to me.' He hesitated, 'I . . . I loved another woman.'

She shrugged, 'I know.'

'You knew?' He sounded astounded. 'Then I must tell you I always cherished you and I left the safety of her house to look for you.'

The shadow of a smile hovered on Maro's lips and they looked at each other tenderly for a long time.

Then Vartan's face darkened. 'Now I understand even less why you are always sad.'

Maro flushed and Vartan, who was holding her hand, felt her palm go clammy.

'What's the matter?' he insisted tenderly.

She beat her breast. 'If only you knew how I suffer! If only you knew how it hurts! Oh, Vartan, it hurts! It hurts!' She took a deep breath and said in a broken voice, 'I had a child by him – Nourhan! Oh, Nourhan!'

The last word was like the whimper of a wounded animal. Vartan pulled her close. She was shivering and vulnerable. His first reaction was one of immense relief. That was all it was! Then it struck him like a bolt of lightning and he was ashamed of the jealousy he had nursed during the past weeks. He had forced Maro to abandon a son whom she must love as much as she did Tomas. She had lost not one but two children. Vartan shared Maro's grief for a child he did not know – another man's child! His pain was almost as great as that he had felt when he had heard of Tomas's disappearance, and he held Maro closer.

'My poor darling! My poor darling!'

His compassion was like a signal that allowed Maro to express her sorrow freely. The feeling of oppression she had had since leaving Ayntab lifted. She would always suffer but at least she would no longer have to carry that suffocating secret that had been keeping her from living fully. She was relieved that Vartan was no longer questioning her and let herself be rocked in his strong arms.

She felt exhausted – emptied – and looked around for a place to sit down. When she saw the state of the room, she came back to reality.

'It can't go on like this, Vartan.'

'What can't go on?'

She waved her arms around. 'All of this! I'm afraid!'

'It's over.'

'It isn't over! Just take a look at the table. They've taken all your papers. They're after you. It's going to be like it was when we were first married.'

Keeping his voice even, he said, 'The situation is different now. The Empire has lost the war. My writing is not a crime any more.'

'But the Sultan's police are still here. If they cannot arrest you legally, they will . . .' She did not have the strength to finish.

'You're worrying about nothing.'

'You don't believe a word you're saying. I can feel the danger around us. These last few days I've had the impression we were being followed. Now I know it wasn't just a feeling.'

He shrugged. 'What do you want me to do?'

'Leave!'

'They'll find us.'

'Stop writing.'

'Maro! You cannot ask that of me!'

'I don't want to lose you for the second time.' She held him by both arms. 'I'm frightened, Vartan.'

Her eyes were pleading. Rather than trying to solve future problems, he concentrated on the immediate one.

'The lock on the door is broken. We can't sleep here.'

Maro had been so upset she had forgotten that small detail. She peered down the hall anxiously.

'Get your things ready. We're going to a hotel.'

'Come into the bedroom with me.' Even though she had been prepared for it, the mess in the room startled her. Vartan pulled the wardrobe upright and pushed it against the wall. Maro picked up the clothes strewn over the bed. Her flannel nightgown had been slashed, so she threw it on the floor in disgust. Luckily they had overlooked the more expensive silk one. Maro packed it with some toilet articles into her tan suitcase, which she had brought with her to Constantinople. At the bottom of the stairs, Vartan stopped to check the pistol that he carried under his jacket.

'You go around armed nowadays?' asked Maro. This was one more reason to be afraid.

'It's just a precaution. Constantinople is a big city.'

They walked through the dark, deserted streets towards the military school where phaetons were always waiting. Maro kept turning her head and listening for footsteps behind them. Several coachmen were playing cards by the light of a lantern placed on the rim of the fountain. One of the group hurried to meet them. They asked him to take them to the Péra Palace.

The moment they stepped into the brightly lit lobby full of foreign military officers Maro relaxed. She caught snatches of French, English and Italian in the general hum of the conversations and they sounded like marvellous music to her ears. It was a different world.

An orchestra was playing in the dining-room but neither of them felt like eating in the crowd, so Vartan asked for a room and bath and requested that dinner be brought to their room.

'The waiter will bring you a menu, sir.'

The bellboy escorted them to their room on the second floor, which overlooked the main street leading to Galata.

A waiter had set up a table by the window and in a few minutes another one arrived wheeling a serving cart. The aroma of the fried fish that Vartan had ordered wafted up. He tipped the waiters.

'You may go. We shall serve ourselves.'

Maro had been in the bathroom changing when she heard the door close. 'Have they gone?'

'Yes. You can come out now.'

She wore a dressing gown over a matching nightgown and her hair lay loose on her shoulders. Because of the way she was dressed and her shyness, Vartan guessed she was in the right mood for his advances. Her eyes were no longer red and her frightened expression was gone. Vartan found it hard to believe that only an hour ago she had been completely despondent.

'You are so beautiful! We could be back in Paris. Do you remember the hotel on the Rue de Rivoli?'

She nodded. Their honeymoon . . . That had been a long time ago but it seemed like yesterday.

They drank a toast to their love and kissed passionately. They ate in

522

silence and spoke only with their eyes. A sudden scream in the street broke the quiet. Vartan opened the curtains. Demonstrators were marching by, shaking their fists and chanting slogans.

'Who are they?' asked Maro.

'Nationalists! They're protesting at the presence of the westerners.'

The police were coming and Vartan closed the curtains. The mob was retreating slowly when a shot rang out. A strange silence reigned, followed by hubbub as the mob dispersed.

Maro was upset and put her fork down. 'This whole thing might explode at any minute, just like Dirouhi said. I can't live in this country anymore. Every night I go through the deportation again.'

'Maro, we cannot leave now!'

'I know that but when we have Tomas back . . .'

Maro's demand brought Vartan up short. The idea of emigrating had occurred to him when Noubar had told him of his decision to leave, but leaving seemed like quitting to him.

'We were born in this part of the world.'

'It isn't our country any more.'

'There is so much we can still do for our people.'

'You have done your part, Vartan. Now we need to think of ourselves. There isn't much time left. We can still remake our lives under another sky. I could never be happy here. This land is soaked in blood – my mother's, Armen's, so many others'. Don't talk to me about Armenia! Our country-men are just starting to build their lives again. I could not bear to see them get blown away again. The idea that you could be torn away from me again is intolerable. You're all I have left. I want us to leave!'

She had spoken calmly but eloquently. Despite her restraint it was evident this was very important to her. Vartan remained sunk in thought.

'You can help our people more from the outside. They have asked you to go to Washington to bear witness to the American government.'

'That's true, but I don't want to think abut it until we know something concrete about Tomas.' He had not used the word 'found' but Maro refused to accept that Vartan had resigned himself to the worst. She rose and went around the table to sit on his lap and put her arms around him.

'Once we have Tomas back, we can go to Washington. That's where you can do the most good. I'm not asking you to leave for good – just for one or two years. Enough time to learn to love again – to forget the horrors – to see how things work out here.'

For the first time since she had arrived in Constantinople, Vartan saw the glow of desire in her eyes, a flame he never wanted to see die out again.

'It's true I could work for the future of Armenia better there.'

Maro beamed and kissed Vartan on the cheek. 'Promise me we'll leave as soon as we find Tomas.'

'Of course, and to have everything ready, I'll start to work on the papers for the American Embassy.'

They had only made love once, a few days after Maro's arrival, he passionately and she dutifully. It had been so routine, so listless, that Vartan had not made any further advances. That evening in bed under the sheets scented with lavender Maro gave herself to her husband totally – ardently and tenderly, at the same time daringly and wantonly. Afterwards they rested on their backs, thighs touching and fingers interlaced, reverently listening to their moans as the last waves of desire died down. It was too soon yet for promises or projects.

Vartan trudged up the steps of his apartment. For weeks there had been no letter from any of the orphanages he had contacted. They were going to have to face it – Tomas had not been taken in by missionaries. If he were still alive, he had to be with the Turks, the Kurds or the Bedouins as an apprentice, a farm boy, a shepherd or a camel driver. In that case the chances of finding him were almost nil. They would have to search each town, each village, each farm in Anatolia, Syria and Arabia. The various aid committees that were working in the area were their last resort but these were snowed under with thousands of cases like theirs and short of help.

It was unusual for Maro not to greet Vartan. He found her pale and speechless slumped in an armchair. An envelope was lying on the floor and she was holding a letter in her hand, which she had read at least ten times.

'What happened?' He did not know whether to laugh or cry. Since Maro was paralyzed, Vartan picked up the envelope. It was addressed to the Committee for Aid to Constantinople and the Near East. Inside was another envelope from Switzerland addressed to a newspaper in Paris for which Vartan sometimes wrote.

'Well!' he said eagerly. Maro handed him the letter and he scanned it, not believing his eyes. At the bottom in Armenian letters was the imprint of a seal with his name in the wax. He read the letter out loud:

'Dear Mr. Balian,

We have recently opened this establishment in Geneva to take in young Armenians, mostly orphans. A German-Swiss missionary brought a young boy to us whom he and his wife had found in Baghdad last year. This child is about ten years old, is called Tomas, and says that his father is Vartan Balian. Since I have read several articles with your byline published in the newspaper, I am taking the liberty of writing you, care of the newspaper. Have you lost a son called Tomas? His hair is black, he has big brown eyes and a beautiful face with regular features. He is slightly taller than most of the boys his age. Since I don't have a photograph of him yet, I am impressing the seal which he says belonged to his father on this letter. I pray to God for Him to return this child to his parents and await your answer impatiently.

Antranig Baghramian'

Maro listened to the words, which she already knew by heart.

'It's my seal! It's really mine!'

'Tomas took it from your desk before we left Sivas.'

Stunned Vartan looked at her and then let out a shout with all the strength of his lungs, as tears ran down his cheeks, 'Tomas! Can you believe it, Maro? Tomas is in Geneva!'

Maro threw herself into Vartan's arms. He was laughing and crying at the same time. He shook her. 'Tomas! Our Tomas!'

Maro could manage no more than a nervous titter. She had been crying all afternoon. Vartan lifted her off her feet, swung her around and kept on repeating Tomas's name.

Suddenly he put her down and asked worriedly, 'Have you answered the letter?'

'I was waiting so we could do it together.'

Vartan looked at his watch. 'The telegraph office is still open. We can make it if we hurry.'

Maro went to her room.

'You don't need a coat.' Vartan was already at the door. 'This is the sweetest April evening in human history.'

When they got to the pavement, he put his arm around Maro's waist and hurried her on. She was out of breath when they arrived at the post office. They were closing the doors ten minutes ahead of time. Vartan knew a protest was useless so he offered some *baksheesh* to the fat employee to keep it open. The clerk looked on impatiently as Maro and Vartan made out a telegram to Antranig Baghramian.

'Please add a few words for Tomas,' said Maro.

'How does this sound? *Indubitably, he is our son STOP Maro and Vartan happy to know he is alive STOP Letter follows STOP Arriving soon STOP.*'

'Loving him above all!' Maro added.

'Do you think that's necessary?'

'Yes, so he'll know we're not angry he ran away.'

They waited while the employee sent the telegram and left the post office with him. As he was locking the door, the clerk, who knew how to transmit the words but did not understand French, asked what they had written.

'We've found our son! He's been missing for years.' Maro was glowing.

'Oh!' said the clerk who was the father of several children. 'I'm so happy for you. Allah is great!'

'May He shower you with blessings,' said Vartan, taking leave of him.

Neither Vartan nor Maro felt like going back to the apartment.

'Let's go to Chez Marquise,' suggested Maro, 'and we can write a letter to Tomas.'

# NINETEEN

On 20 May 1919 Maro and Vartan got off the Orient Express at Cornavin Station in Geneva. Once they had picked up Tomas, they would not be returning to Constantinople. Vartan had accepted the offer made by Diran's friends to work in Washington where he could be of use to his people. It had taken them almost a month to arrange the trip and get the necessary visas. Towards the end of that time, Vartan's patience had worn thin but finally the time had come. Their goodbyes had been very painful. Uncle Mesrop was sure he would never see them again.

They had more than one reason for making this trip. Diran and his friends had discovered that the official documents of the former Ottoman government, for which they had been searching for more than a month, were at present in the hands of a gentleman named Gabriel de Roqueville in Evian, France. Once Tomas was with them again, Vartan would go to Evian before going to Marseilles where they would depart for the United States. Gabriel de Roqueville was a collector and had acquired the documents by way of a French journalist in Constantinople. Being sympathetic to the Armenian cause, he had decided to donate them to anyone who could make good use of them.

Feeling slightly faint, Maro paused at the top of the steps. A porter standing close to the door helped her down.

'Are you all right?' asked Vartan.

Maro nodded. Neither had slept the night before. The excitement they had felt on leaving Vienna had turned into impatience as they approached Switzerland. When the train had begun to run alongside the Alps, they had been beset by misgivings. Both of them had been praying to see Tomas soon and now they were afraid something might happen to prevent their dream from coming true.

While Vartan settled with the porter, Maro gazed absent-mindedly at the other passengers crowding the platform. She tried to see the mountains she knew were near by, but buildings blocked the view. These stone walls that stood between her and the Empire added to the feeling of safety, which had been growing with every turn of the train carrying her away from the Bosphorus. No longer did she have to fear that the police would pick Vartan up. If it were up to her, she would never go back to Anatolia where her mother and father were buried. She wanted freedom for Tomas and the other children she might have in the future – a home country where their rights would not be violated – a place where they could prepare for the future without fear.

'Come.' Vartan's voice startled her. He took her arm. 'You're not too tired?'

'Just nervous.'

He stroked her cheek. 'You'll see. Everything will be all right.'

She knew he was just as excited as she. Pulling a cart loaded with their luggage, the porter followed them to the waiting room, which was buzzing like a beehive. Vartan stopped at the newspaper kiosk, the agreed meeting place with the couple who were supposed to be sent by the Armenian Committee, but they did not see anyone who met the description they had been given.

'We're waiting for some friends,' Vartan told the porter. 'You can leave our baggage here.'

The porter left in search of other customers.

The delay bothered Maro and Vartan suggested they sit down on a bench along the wall near the post office. She refused and distracted herself by reading the headlines in the newspapers displayed outside the kiosk. Vartan kept an eye on the main entrance and the doors that led to the boarding ramps. The waiting room emptied slowly and, just as Vartan was going to say they should take a phaeton and go to the hotel, the couple arrived.

They recognized the man by his mustard-yellow tie and the lady by her tartan suit and the bunch of white carnations she was carrying. Souren Zakarian was in his thirties, had an angular face and radiated strength and calm. Nazenig, his wife, was remarkably beautiful, although her straight black bobbed hair parted severely down the middle gave her a boyish look.

'Souren Zakarian?' asked Vartan.

528

'Please forgive us for being late.' Souren held out his hand. 'They told us the train was arriving late.'

'It really doesn't matter. I'm happy to make your acquaintance, Baron Zakarian.'

'So am I, Monsieur Balian.'

'We've always read your articles with great interest,' added his wife.

Souren introduced her and Vartan introduced Maro. Nazenig handed her the bouquet of carnations. 'I'm so happy for you, *Diguin,* and for your son too.'

Maro glowed, 'Have you seen him?'

'They told us about him at the same time as they told us your husband was coming to pick up some documents that are being kept at Evian. I could not help going to Monsieur Baghramian's orphanage myself and seeing him.'

Maro bombarded her with questions. 'Did you talk to him? How is he? Does he know we're coming today?'

Nazenig's eyes sparkled. She was happy to be the bearer of good news but, before she could answer, Maro asked again, 'Is he all right?'

'He's wonderful, big and strong, over one and a half metres tall already. He's going to be tall like you, Mr Balian. He's bright and intelligent and has the most beautiful eyes. Just like his mother's, I see.'

'Is he all right?' insisted Maro.

'Nobody would ever believe he had lived through all those ordeals. According to the director, he was withdrawn and secretive at first but receiving your letter has changed him. He's much more open and plays games with the other boys now.'

Vartan drank in Nazenig's words just as avidly as Maro. Both of them could have kept on listening forever, but Souren picked up their suitcases and started to leave. Vartan insisted on carrying one of them. They loaded the baggage into a taxi and Souren told the driver to take them to his apartment at 74 rue de l'Athenée, where they could first rest for a while and have a quiet chat.

Desperate, Maro looked at Vartan who picked up his cue. 'That's very nice of you Souren, but we would prefer to go directly to the orphanage.'

'Mr Baghramian is not expecting you until after lunch.'

'Put yourself in their shoes,' said Nazenig sympathetically. 'You'll have plenty of time later to arrange the affairs of the world with Mr Balian.'

Souren smiled. 'All right. We'll drop you off at the orphanage and then leave your baggage at the Belmont Hotel on the way back home. It's very near our place. Driver, please take us to the road to Lausanne.'

'Tomas! Come and be our goalie; otherwise we're going to lose.'

Tomas told Krikor he wasn't interested in playing soccer today. Krikor knew how important today was for his friend and did not insist. Secretly envious, as were all the boys, he went back to play in the game.

Tomas leaned against the corner of the wall surrounding the old school for boys. The wall bordered on the road to Lausanne. From there he could watch the entrance gate and at the same time watch the soccer game in the courtyard. Almost three weeks had gone by, although the days had seemed endless since he had received his parents' letter. Every night all the boys dreamed that they would see their parents again, even those who had watched fathers and mothers die. When Tomas received the telegram informing him his parents were leaving Constantinople, he started tracing the train route on the map in the classroom, moving a thumb-tack every morning, noon and night according to Mr Baghramian's instructions. This morning he had pinpointed the spot which marked Geneva.

He heard uneven footsteps behind him. It was the director, Antranig Baghramian. Bald, portly, and only slightly taller than Tomas, he limped because of an old wound in his leg. He smiled. 'They won't be here until after lunch so you'll have to be patient.'

Be patient! That's what Tomas had been doing forever! Besides, he had the feeling they would come directly to see him. He hesitated, 'Baron Baghramian . . .'

'Yes?'

Looking surprisingly serious for a ten-year-old, Tomas made the speech he had been rehearsing all morning.

'I want to thank you for all your kindness, sir. I was lucky to find you. You found my parents! I'll never forget that.'

The director was touched and patted him on the back. 'The way to thank me, Tomas, is to become an honest, God-fearing man who cares about others and helps them.'

'That's what I plan to do, sir.'

As the director started to walk away, Tomas's voice suddenly became that of a child. 'Do you think my father is going to recognize me?'

'Even though he hasn't seen you in four years, I think he will.'

Baghramian walked back to his office. There he thanked God for this child's happiness and asked Him to work some more miracles like this one. He had studied at the seminary at Etchamiadzin but had left the priesthood to get married and become a teacher. After his arrest, his wife and their four children had perished when a mob set their house ablaze during the deportations of 1915. A Turkish friend had helped him to escape from prison, as Ibrahim had done for Vartan. He had fled the country by way of Persia to Switzerland, where he had lived ever since.

A couple of blackbirds bickering noisily on the lawn had distracted Tomas, so he did not notice the black car until it had entered the gate. His heart leaped! A man and a woman descended from a four-passenger taxi. The first person Tomas saw was his mother and he noticed she had cut her hair. That tall figure . . . that familiar face . . . his father! Tomas opened his mouth to shout but no sound came out. For a second he was afraid this vision might disappear like a mirage but, as Vartan and Maro walked towards the school entrance, he could clearly hear the gravel crunching under their shoes. He could not run to meet them in spite of his overwhelming desire to be hugged. Instead, he backed away and went around the corner so that they would not see him.

His mother might be angry with him for having run away from Riza Bey's mansion. Did she still love him after all these years? He had never doubted his father's love but he did not know how to behave with him. How could he act normally when he knew about his mother's treason with Riza Bey? He did not want to sow discord between his parents. He would have to be especially careful about what he said. But what if his father asked? Hide the truth? Tell a lie? It was all very complicated!

Shouts came from the soccer field. The rival team had just scored a goal. They were tied!

'Tomas! We need you!' His team-mates were shouting for him to come. Suddenly he thought it might be better if his parents found him playing instead of standing in a corner. They would think the game was the reason he had not run to meet them. He ran to the field, took his place as goalie and the game began again. Encouraged by Tomas's presence, the team played harder, trying to score another goal but without success.

Tomas attempted to concentrate on the game but every now and then stole a glance at the pathway where his parents would appear. Finally he saw three figures. Maro, overcome by emotion, stopped by the wall with Baghramian, while Vartan walked on towards the field.

'Watch out!' shouted someone on Tomas's team.

A husky fellow named Toros was dribbling the ball towards the goal. He was the best player on the rival team, fast and cunning, a good strategist.

'Get him, Tomas! Block him!'

Vartan! Tomas had never forgotten the timbre of that voice. His father had recognized him out of twenty-one other boys. Electrified, Tomas ran towards the player who had pierced their defence. Toros was not going to score! He shot at the left corner and Tomas dived and caught the ball. His team cheered. He got up glowing with pride and turned his head towards his father, who was holding his arms wide open, shouting, 'Bravo! Bravo!'

'Papa!'

Tomas dashed towards him. His father had not changed, but somehow he now looked shorter. Tomas's eyes blurred as he searched his father's face. Vartan swept him up as easily as he used to lift him up on a horse and held him tightly.

'Tomas! Tomas, my son!' he choked.

Trembling with happiness, Tomas put his arms around his father's neck. 'I always knew you would come, *hayrig*.'

'I never stopped looking for you.' There were no more words; they just held each other.

Maro was still standing at the wall, as her legs refused to carry her.

'God is great,' murmured Baghramian.

When his father finally put him down, Tomas brought a little silver box out of his pocket. He had polished it that morning. The seal!

'I took it from your desk in Sivas!'

Vartan opened the cover and ran his fingers over the seal with his name engraved on one side in Armenian letters and on the other in Arabic characters. Then he closed the box and gave it back to Tomas. 'It's yours now! Take good care of it.'

'Thank you, Papa,' said Tomas solemnly and slid the box back into the pocket of his short pants.

Vartan could see changes in his son's features that indicated how he would look as an adult. An expression passed over Tomas's face, an indefinable mixture of joy and apprehension. Vartan guessed what his son was thinking and thought he should make it clear that he knew everything about their life in Ayntab. He leaned towards Tomas and said in a confidential tone of voice, 'Riza Bey would not let Nourhan go. You must love your mother twice as much, because you are the only son she has left!'

Now Tomas did not have to carry the burden of knowing he had a half-brother. The gentleness in Vartan's voice told him that he held no grudges against Maro. He had been so afraid his parents might have quarrelled and not love each other any more. He rose on his toes and kissed his father on the cheek thankfully. Then he turned on his heels quickly and ran to Maro, who was still standing beside the director waiting for him.

'Mama!' he screamed.

'Tomas! My Tomas!' she hurried to meet him and put her arms around him.

He rested his cheek on his mother's breast. 'I'll never leave you again, *mayrig*.'

'My darling! At last!' Silent tears ran down her cheeks. She pushed him away and touched his head, his face, his shoulder . . . as if to make sure that he wasn't dreaming. Then she covered him with kisses.

'I prayed to God to bring you back to me!'

'I prayed too, *mayrig*! I prayed to Grandmother Azniv and to Godfather Armen.'

'I'm sure they must have heard you.'

Baghramian, who had been standing aside discreetly, nodded in agreement with Maro. For him the story of this family and those of others who had been reunited after painful separations were eloquent examples of divine mercy.

Maro took Armen's cap from her bag.

'My cap!' He stared at it and then put it on. 'It fits, mama, it fits!'

Actually the cap was still too big but Maro had stuffed paper under the inner leather band. Vartan drew near and put his arms around his wife and son. When he saw the cap, his mind wandered back to Sivas, and he recalled scratching the names of those who had been executed into the walls of the prison and then, in the underground chapel in Cappadocia, chiselling little Anoush's name into the stone. Some day he would have to write all those stories – to raise a monument in words to those who had no inscriptions, so that they would also be remembered. But first he had to ensure the lives of the survivors and help his countrymen to establish a solidly built Republic of Armenia.

'What are you doing, papa?'

Vartan snapped out of his reverie. The others were looking at him in surprise. 'Oh, just thinking about the past and our trip to America.'

'Are we really going by steamship? Can I wear my captain's cap?'

'Of course.' Vartan caressed his neck.

Maro's eyes darted from her husband to her son. She smiled. Her contentment needed no words!

'My heart rejoices to see your happiness.' Antranig Baghramian was deeply touched.

Vartan answered on Maro's behalf, 'We owe most of it to you, Baron Baghramian.'

Thinking about his dead wife and children, Baghramian tried to change the subject. 'Souren mentioned some papers, which Gabriel de Roqueville is to hand over to you. What will you do with them?'

'I'll take them to Washington to strengthen a report, which we hope will enable us to convince the American government to help us during the peace negotiations. If these documents are what I am told they are, they will be incontrovertible proof that the massacres that took place during the deportations were not fortuitous incidents but the result of a coldly calculated policy of extermination.'

His father's eloquence impressed Tomas, who swelled with pride. His father did not have to envy the director, who spoke so well.

'I hope you're successful,' sighed Antranig.

'I'm not alone, you know. Quite a number of our people are dedicating themselves wholeheartedly to seeing that justice is done. By the way, I was told that you know de Roqueville. What kind of a man is he?'

'A most generous one! Our orphans here and in other places have benefited greatly from his generosity. He paid a very high price for the papers you are interested in to keep them from being destroyed. He is an avid collector of rare and ancient documents. Although it will be a great sacrifice for him, he sympathizes with our cause and will turn them over to you.'

'I can't wait to meet him.'

'He won't disappoint you. He admires your writing and has read all your articles. He insisted on handing the papers over to you personally. I'm sure he's impatiently waiting for your call.'

Tomas took his father by the hand. 'I don't want you to leave me anymore.'

'You should take your wife and Tomas with you. Gabrielle de

Roqueville's villa at Amphion-les-Bains is like a museum. The garden extends out into Lake Leman and the view is fantastic.'

These words reassured Tomas. 'I'll go say goodbye to my friends.'

'Don't say goodbye to them yet. We're having a farewell party for you tomorrow.' Turning to Vartan and Maro, he continued, 'Would you like to come and have lunch with us? It would make all my young boarders very happy and give them some hope. Even though I get very attached to them, I try to keep up their hopes that one day their parents will come for them or a family might adopt them.'

Maro turned to Vartan, 'We shall be delighted, Baron Baghramian.'

'I can introduce you to all my friends,' Tomas said. Then he ran towards the soccer field where the game was just ending.

That evening Tomas and his parents dined at the Belmont hotel. He insisted his parents sit side by side across from him where he could see them both. They had not been able to express everything they felt when they had met because their emotions were too strong. They had, however, lived them during the ensuing hours as they strolled around town. Now they were all exhausted but at peace. It was hard to realize the long-awaited moment had arrived.

When he finished eating, Tomas laid down his knife and fork and began to tell his story in a calm, detached voice as if he were reciting the adventures of another.

Night had surprised him in the desert on the rim of Riza Bey's property. In the morning he had tried to find his way back but he was lost. He spotted a caravan of camels in the distance and galloped towards them but the people spoke neither Turkish nor Armenian. They did not, therefore, understand Tomas when he asked them to take him back to Ayntab. Instead, they took his thoroughbred horse. He protested but one of the men hoisted him on to a camel behind him and they travelled for a long time. Tomas and the rest of the servants had to pitch the tents, take care of the animals and serve the men. At last they came to Baghdad where Tomas managed to escape. He went to the police station where he found some English soldiers, but they did not understand a word he said. Trying to explain himself in the little French he knew, he had caught the eye of an officer, who sent for an interpreter.

'Captain McNaught told me I could not return to Ayntab because it was on the other side of the front lines. He was a nice man with a red moustache which curled up on his cheeks and he wore a plaid skirt. He found a room for me below their headquarters. To thank him, I kept his boots polished and his uniforms brushed.'

Maro and Vartan hung on every word of their son's story. He talked in a matter-of-fact tone, omitting the details. Occasionally his emotions showed through but then he would quickly collect himself and calmly carry on. He had survived all this and he had not been more than eight years old!

After a few weeks Captain McNaught turned him over to a couple of Swiss missionaries who were friends of his; they were returning to their country in a few months. Thus, Tomas had arrived in Zurich with Reverend Wartburg and his wife. Although fair, they were strict and never laughed.

'We used to pray for hours every day. I didn't understand a word of what I was repeating but Frau Wartburg made delicious pies.'

Antranig Baghramian had met Tomas at the Wartburgs and easily convinced the pastor that it would be better for Tomas to be brought up with other boys of his age who were being educated in their mother tongue and religion.

'Monsieur Baghramian wrote to Riza Bey but never received an answer. I didn't eat as well at the orphanage as I had at the Wartburgs.' Tomas smiled mischievously.

Now that he was with his parents again, his misadventures seemed distant and insignificant although many were the nights he had cried in despair. They sat in silence while the waiter brought a rack of lamb.

Then Maro declared, 'How lucky you were to find so many charitable people. We must do the same for others to pay back these acts of goodness.'

'You're right,' admitted Vartan, 'but Tomas has been very brave.' He turned to him and said, 'You have done honour to the name of Balian.'

Tomas blushed. No other words could have given him greater pleasure. 'What about you, papa. How did you escape from the prison in Sivas?'

Vartan understood Tomas needed to know his father's story as he already knew his mother's. Otherwise, there would always be a gap in the family's memory. He had always thought it a mistake to dwell on tragic memories. He had seen too many survivors of deportation do that, but now he knew that one must remember. He took a sip of wine and began to tell his story to his son as if he were a friend.

'They arrested me a few hours after dinner on your sixth birthday. Azniv Hanim, Araksi, Armen and your mother and I, were getting ready to leave when . . .'

Maro listened closely, as she knew little about Vartan's life during their separation. She tried to remember what she had been doing at the same time, so their memories would coincide.

The sun had risen in a cloudless sky and the old port of Marseilles was buzzing with activity. The fishing boats drew alongside the shouting fishmongers, who would buy the catch. Heated discussions about prices ensued, at times interrupted by the onlookers.

Wearing his captain's hat, Tomas walked ahead of his parents, who were strolling arm in arm. Vartan had bought him a pair of binoculars for the crossing and Tomas was observing the prison on the Ile d'If, silhouetted against the misty horizon.

'There!' he said pointing to the other end of the port. 'Is that the ship that's going to take us to America?'

'Let me have the binoculars.' Vartan looked at the white prow: *The Star of Peloponnesus*. 'Yes, that's it.'

'Let's hurry!'

Maro smiled at her son's impatience. 'There's no hurry. We still have two hours until boarding time.'

A street photographer, a small man, who carried a tripod and other heavy equipment on his back, approached them an tipped his hat. 'Excuse me, sir, I think you are leaving. Would you like a picture as a souvenir?'

Vartan hesitated. 'It will never be ready in time.'

'My shop is just around the corner from the bistro.' He pointed to the plate-glass window of a café. 'You'll have the proofs in an hour.'

Vartan could see that the idea pleased Maro, so he accepted.

'I'd like a photograph of just the two of you so that I can admire my two men together,' said Maro.

The photographer posed them at the end of the wharf in front of a thick forest of masts. Guy de Roqueville and Vartan had liked each other at first sight and the Frenchman had turned over his precious documents to Vartan. He had put them into a small briefcase, which Vartan now carried in his left hand. He put his right hand on Tomas's shoulder. Tomas was proudly holding up his binoculars.

'They're standing behind us!'

'Who?' Tomas turned around to see who Vartan was talking about. 'There's no one there.'

'Our forefathers, my father, his father. You're the end result of dozens of generations who have created the culture which is your legacy. You must learn about it and enrich it so that it will never die. That way your ancestors can live on.'

Tomas did not quite understand and was going to ask what he meant when the photographer, who was getting impatient, spoke, 'Please stop talking, messieurs, and don't move.'

He took the picture, pulled out the used plate and put in another one. Maro joined them while Vartan set the briefcase down and put his arms around his family.

The photographer beamed. 'What a joy to see a family who has had it easy! The war didn't touch you at all.'

Maro and Vartan could hardly keep from laughing.

'Don't move! Look at me! There!' He was in a hurry. While he was picking up his equipment, Tomas stepped near and the man handed him his card. 'Tell your parents the proofs will be ready in an hour.'

Vartan had turned aside and was gazing at the seagulls screaming and circling over the boats. He looked to the east. There at the other end of the Mediterranean lay Constantinople and, further on still, Anatolia. And beyond that in the shadow of Mount Ararat – Armenia!

Maro knew what Vartan was thinking. She leaned against him and looked in the same direction. She was leaving a son behind, and she would never see him again! She gripped Vartan's arm tightly.

Tomas woke them from their reverie. He pointed to the west. 'You're looking in the wrong direction! America lies that way!

# EPILOGUE

In the months following the Balians' departure, a court in Constantinople found the former leaders of the Ottoman government guilty of the war crime of trying to exterminate the Armenian minority, and condemned them to death. However, most of them had already fled the country. Ministers such as Talaat Pasha and their acolytes were to be assassinated in Europe during the following years by Armenians wanting to avenge their dead.

In the spring of 1920 the Supreme Council of the Allies put President Wilson in charge of determining the territorial rights of Armenia. Even though Mr Wilson attempted to set its borders to include not only old Russian Armenia but also the greater part of the Armenian provinces in Turkey, the terms of the peace treaty signed in Sèvres in August of that year were never enforced. The United States Congress refused the President's plea to accept the mandate of Armenia and no other country was willing to guarantee the integrity of the new state.

For a while there were two heads of government in the Ottoman Empire: the Sublime Porte in Constantinople, which had negotiated the peace treaty with the conquerors, and General Mustapha Kemal in Ankara, who refused to recognize any loss of Turkish territory. In September 1920 Lenin's Red Army attacked Armenia. Bloody battles raged in the Caucasus, but insistent pleas for the League of Nations to come to the aid of Armenia elicited no response. Countries that were just recovering from a world war were unwilling to get involved in another conflict. The following December, the Republic of Armenia was annexed by the Soviet Union but the old dream of an independent homeland, which would take in all the land where Armenians had lived since the dawn of history, refused to die and would haunt Armenia's children forever.

Because of all these events, Vartan decided to stay in the United States. He was disappointed that all his efforts and those of his countrymen had failed. His brother joined Barkev in the import-export business. Like other Armenians who had lost everything, the Balians never received any compensation for their confiscated property in Afyon Karahisar and Sivas.

Vartan never worked as a pharmacist again, having studied the profession only to please his father. Instead, he found employment in an Armenian newspaper, which, with time, became an influential daily. Hundreds of thousands of Armenians were scattered all over the globe and it was important for them to stay in contact with each other across oceans and borders.

Maro managed the newspaper. She also gave Vartan three daughters – Azniv, Araksi and Nayiri – and then a second son, christened Hagop after his maternal grandfather. Tomas, who had an ambition to alleviate human suffering, studied medicine.

Mesrop Mesropian died before Diran could emigrate to Armenia with Aram. As Barkev, the older brother, lived in the United States, Diran felt responsible for his mother and, with his sister Lucie, took over the family printing shop. Following the proclamation of the Republic of Turkey by Mustapha Kemal in 1923, Diran had nothing to worry about anymore. His political enemies were gone forever. He abandoned his subversive activities and became a respected member of the large Armenian community in Constantinople.

Riza Bey manoeuvred adroitly and kept his post as governor when the French replaced the English in that region. As he had secretly helped the people who supported the Kemalists, he had no trouble after the proclamation of the Republic. He quit his job in the government and dedicated himself to managing his property and enjoying his fortune.

Pampered by Riza Bey and Leyla, who had lost her own child immediately after Maro's departure, Nourhan didn't take long to forget his mother. On the day of his circumcision Safiyé wanted to tell him who his mother was, but Leyla stopped her. As Nourhan grew older, he often went through his late grandmother's photo albums, and every time wondered about the group picture taken on the day of Maro's arrival. He admired the face of the woman who had given him life but he never knew she was his mother!

# GLOSSARY OF ARMENIAN AND TURKISH WORDS

*Note: The origins of the words shown in italics are not necessarily etymological.*

| | |
|---|---|
| *agha* | landlord (Turkish) |
| *aghabey* | elder brother (Turkish) |
| *akhparig* | little brother (Armenian) |
| *aleykumselam* | response to the Muslim greeting *selamaleykum* (Turkish) |
| *anasdvadzner* | literally godless people, pagans (Armenian) |
| *anassouns* | animals (Armenian) |
| *anné* | mother (Turkish) |
| *annejiim* | my dear mother (Turkish) |
| *araba* | cart (Turkish) |
| *asma alti* | arbour, literally under the climbing vines (Turkish) |
| *ayp, pen, kim, ta, yetch, za* | the first of the thirty-six letters of the Armenian alphabet |
| *ayran* | whipped liquid yoghurt (Turkish) |
| *bahvdouk* | hide-and-seek (Armenian) |
| *baron* | mister (Armenian) |
| *basderma* | dried meat with garlic and cumin (Turkish) |
| *beli kirik* | split-back (Turkish) |
| *binbashim* | Major, literally my Major (Turkish) |
| *Bolis* | Constantinople (Armenian) |

| | |
|---|---|
| *bulghur* | boiled and pounded wheat (Turkish) |
| *buyuk hanim* | literally great lady, grand lady (Turkish) |
| *Catholicosgatoghigos* | supreme chief of the Armenian Apostolic Church (Armenian) |
| *Chanakkalé* | Strait of the Dardanelles, Battle of Gallipoli (Turkish) |
| *charik* | rustic leather sandal (Turkish) |
| *charshaf* | women's outdoor overgarment; also used as large head scarf by Muslim women (Turkish) |
| *cheté* | band of brigands (Turkish) |
| *cheteji* | member of band of brigands (Turkish) |
| *Chrisdos hariav i merelots* | Christ is risen (Armenian) |
| *der* | particle put in front of surname of married Armenian priest; also master (Armenian) |
| *diguin* | madam (Armenian) |
| *dznount* | Christmas (Armenian) |
| *effendi* | title of Ottoman dignitary, has became a polite form of greeting, mister (Turkish) |
| *effendim* | my master (Turkish) |
| *enguer* | friend (Armenian) |
| *evlatlik* | foster-child placed in a family (Turkish) |
| *eyvallah hemsheri* | greetings, countryman (Turkish) |
| *fedayi* | warrior who sacrifices his life; also *fedai* or *fedayeen* (Turkish) |
| *ferajé* | dust-coat formerly worn by Turkish women when they went out (Turkish) |
| *ferman* | sultan's edict (Turkish) |
| *gaydzag* | lightning, name of Tomas's pony (Armenian) |
| *gazel* | short lyric poem (Turkish) |
| *giaour* | infidel, unbeliever (Turkish) |
| *goebek tashi* | literally navel stone, massage platform placed in centre of Turkish bathhouse (Turkish) |
| *Guiligia* | Cilicia (Armenian) |
| *hafiz* | Someone who has memorized the verses of the Quran (Turkish) |
| *hammam* | public bathhouse in Near East (Turkish) |

| | |
|---|---|
| *han*, also *khan* | warehouse; also caravanserai (Turkish) |
| *hanim* | madam (Turkish) |
| *Hayr mer* | Our Father (Armenian) |
| *hayrig* | father (Armenian) |
| *helva* | sweet made of sesame-seed oil, flour and molasses (Turkish) |
| *hokis* | my soul (Armenian) |
| *hour-grag* | flaming fire, name of Vartan's horse (Armenian) |
| *Insh'Allah* | God willing, if God wills (Turkish) |
| *Iverin yeroussaghem* | chant sung at end of funeral service (Armenian) |
| *jan* | darling, my soul (Armenian) |
| *jezvé* | small copper pot with long handle used to prepare coffee (Turkish) |
| *jirit* | a game in which horsemen charge their adversaries with sticks instead of lances (Turkish) |
| *kabadayi* | tough guy (Turkish) |
| *kahana* | married priest (Armenian) |
| *kalpak*, also *calpac* | Russian-style fur hat (Turkish) |
| *kanoun* | kind of oriental zither with seventy-two strings (Turkish) |
| *karabiyik* | black moustache (Turkish) |
| *kaymakam* | governor, head of a province (Turkish) |
| *kemenché* | small violin with three strings played like a cello (Turkish) |
| *khavourma* | roasted, salted lamb usually eaten cold (Turkish) |
| *kilim* | thin Anatolian rug with geometric designs (Turkish) |
| *konak* | mansion of a rich man or of a governor (Turkish) |
| *krapar* | classical Armenian language (Armenian) |
| *Leyla and Mejnoun* | 1535 love poem, Eastern *Romeo and Juliet* (Turkish) |
| *manché* | it's a boy (Armenian) |
| *mangal* | brazier, usually of copper (Turkish) |
| *mavouna* | motorized fishing boat (Turkish) |
| *mayrig* | mother, mama (Armenian) |
| *medzmayrig* | grandmother (Armenian) |

| | |
|---|---|
| *merhaba* | hello (Turkish) |
| *milli ajans* | literally national agency, daily newspaper (Turkish) |
| *morak* | abbreviation for *morakouyr*, aunt on mother's side (Armenian) |
| *mouhajir* | immigrant (Turkish) |
| *mudur* | director (Turkish) |
| *muezzin* | one who calls Muslims to prayer from a minaret (Turkish) |
| *narghilé* | water pipe (Turish) |
| *oud* | stringed instrument resembling the lute (Turkish) |
| *ourar* | stole put over the shoulder of a deacon (Armenian) |
| *para* | Ottoman coin (Turkish) |
| *parilouis* | hello (Armenian) |
| *pasha* | title given to generals and certain Ottoman dignitaries (Turkish) |
| *patishah* | king, sultan (Turkish) |
| *pilaf* | boiled rice cooked with butter (Turkish) |
| *raki* | grape or plum brandy flavoured with anise (Turkish) |
| *saghavart* | round hat worn by Armenian priests (Armenian) |
| *sarilik* | jaundiced (Turkish) |
| *saz* | oriental musical instrument, the strings of which are plucked (Turkish) |
| *sedir* | divan, sofa (Turkish) |
| *sejjadé* | prayer rug (Turkish) |
| *selamaleykum* | may the peace of God be with you (Turkish) |
| *selamlik* | section of house reserved for men (Turkish) |
| *Sev Dzov* | Black Sea (Armenian) |
| *shahir* | poet (Turkish) |
| *shalvar* | bouffant pants gathered at the ankles (Turkish) |
| *shan zavakner* | sons of bitches (Armenian) |
| *shekerim* | literally my sugar, darling (Turkish) |
| *sherbet* | heavily sweetened fruit juice (Turkish) |
| *shounigs* | my little dog (Armenian) |

| | |
|---|---|
| *soghouklouk* | *tepidarium*, ante-room in a *hammam* where lukewarm temperature is mantained (Turkish) |
| *sourate* | chapter of Quran (Turkish) |
| *Sourp Hagop* | Saint James (Armenian) |
| *Sourp Stepannos* | Saint Stephen (Armenian) |
| *Stamboul* | Constantinople (Turkish) |
| *taksim* | improvisation on musical instrument (Turkish) |
| *tandir* | oven built into earth (Turkish) |
| *tavla* | game like backgammon popular in Middle East (Turkish) |
| *tellak* | employee who bathes and massages clients in *hammam* (Turkish) |
| *temenna* | oriental greeting (Turkish) |
| *tespih* | oriental rosary usually made of amber beads (Turkish) |
| *tezek* | dried dung used as fuel (Turkish) |
| *vali* | mayor of a town, governor of a province (Turkish) |
| *vernadoun* | triforium, gallery above nave of church (Armenian) |
| *vilayet* | province or administrative region (Turkish) |
| *yashmak* | veil covering lower face (Turkish) |
| *yallah* | let's go (Turkish) |
| *yeretsguin* | title given to wife of Armenian priests (Armenian) |
| *yershig* | sausage flavoured with garlic (Armenian) |
| *yildiz* | star, name of Colonel Ibrahim's horse (Turkish) |
| *Young Turks* | also known as Ittihad, group of intellectuals, Ottoman officers, liberals and reformers, who forced Sultan Abdul Hamid II to restore the constitution (1908) then to abdicate (1909). Dominated Ottoman politics until 1918. |
| *zaptiyé* | military policeman (Turkish) |
| *Zeytounites* | natives of Zeytoun, town in Anatolia, who resisted during the massacres of 1895 (Armenian) |
| *zirnik* | depilatory cream used in *hammams* (Turkish) |
| *zourna* | primitive oriental clarinet (Turkish) |

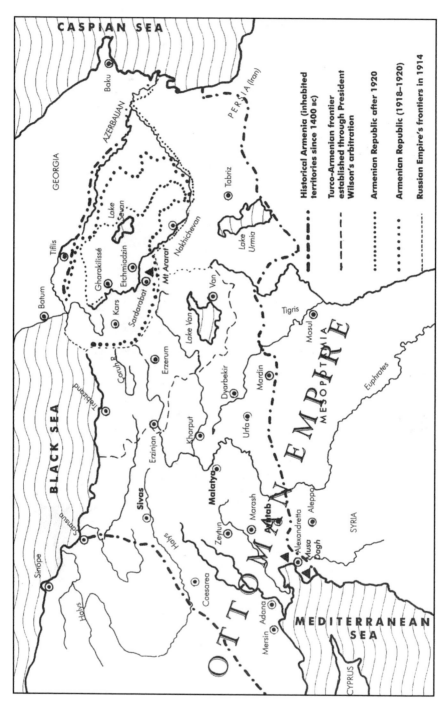

CASPIAN SEA

Baku

PERSIA (Iran)

AZERBAIJAN

GEORGIA

Tabriz

Lake
Umia

Historical Armenia (inhabited
territories since 1400 BC)

Turco-Armenian frontier
established through President
Wilson's arbitration

Armenian Republic after 1920

Armenian Republic (1918–1920)

Russian Empire's frontiers in 1914

Tiflis

Lake
Sevan

Nakhichevan

Batum

Gharakilissé

Etchmiadzin

Mt Ararat

Van

Kars

Sardarabad

Lake Van

Tigris

Çoruh

Erzerum

Mosul

MESOPOTAMIA

Diyarbekir

Euphrates

BLACK SEA

Mardin

OTTOMAN EMPIRE

Trabizond

Erzinjan

Khorput

Ufa

Choroch

Malatya

SYRIA

Sivas

Marash

Aleppo

Halys

Zeytun

Aintab

Alexandretta

Musa
Dagh

Sinope

Caesarea

Halys

Mersin

Adana

MEDITERRANEAN
SEA

CYPRUS

THE EMERGENCE OF MODERN ARMENIA